MALCOLM LOWRY'S
LA MORDIDA

A Scholarly Edition

MALCOLM LOWRY'S
LA MORDIDA

A Scholarly Edition

EDITED BY PATRICK A. MCCARTHY

THE UNIVERSITY OF GEORGIA PRESS
Athens & London

Designed by Walton Harris
Set in 10/13 Sabon by Books International
Printed and bound by McNaughton & Gunn, Inc.

The paper in this book meets the guidelines for permanence
and durability of the Committee on Production Guidelines
for Book Longevity of the Council on Library Resources.

Printed in the United States of America

oo   99   98   97   96   C   5   4   3   2   1

Library of Congress Cataloging in Publication Data

Lowry, Malcolm, 1909–1957.
Malcolm Lowry's "La mordida" / Patrick A. McCarthy, ed.—
Scholarly ed.
p.   cm.
Includes bibliographical references and index.
ISBN 0-8203-1763-2 (alk. paper)
I. McCarthy, Patrick A., 1945–   . II. Title.
III. Title : Mordida
PR6023.096M35   1996
813'.54—dc20   95-12606

British Library Cataloging in Publication Data available

For Anne Yandle

Contents

Acknowledgments

Among the many people who assisted with the annotations I am especially indebted to Chris Ackerley, who read an early draft of the text and annotations and offered extensive suggestions for additions, corrections, and refinements. His impact on this edition goes far beyond what I have been able to acknowledge in the annotations themselves. Jane Connolly, Lydia Herring, and Phillip F. Herring provided invaluable assistance in translating and emending Spanish passages and in identifying Mexican references in the text; without the help they provided, this edition could not have been completed in anything like its present form. I also thank Pierre Schaeffer for corrections of my translations of French passages; Gordon Bowker and Sherrill E. Grace for responses to my requests for biographical information; and Frederick Asals and Paul Tiessen for their reviews of the manuscript and significant recommendations for improvement. I particularly want to thank Mark Pentecost, my copy editor, who caught more errors than I care to admit and made significant suggestions for improvements, both in the text and in the annotations.

I owe special debts of gratitude to R. B. Kershner, who saved me a three-hundred-mile trip in search of one item by locating an article that I could not find through interlibrary loan, and to Laurence Donovan, who unexpectedly provided the book on the history of Burma-Shave signs. Many others also helped with specific items: Anthony Barthelemy with New Orleans, Peter Bellis with Melville, Eustelle France with Lowry's transcription of a dialogue in Creole, Julian Lee with marine biology, Ronald B. Newman with Dostoevsky and William James, Brenda Gayle Plummer with Haitian history, Alfred Reed with Wagner, R. J. Schork with Xenophon, Frank Stringfellow with Goethe and Dostoevsky, Michael Wutz with the order and placement of Lowry's notebooks. For their help I also want to thank Joseph Alkana, John Balaban, Zack Bowen, Robert Casillo, Kathryn Freeman, Barnett Guttenberg, Benjiman D. Webb,

Joseph Youngblood, and my late colleague Bernard Benstock. I am particularly indebted to Mary Dulik for enabling me to continue my research while handling what otherwise would have been very time-consuming administrative responsibilities.

My dedication of this book to Anne Yandle acknowledges not only her importance in connection with the present edition but her pervasive influence on Lowry scholarship during the past two decades. As head of Special Collections at the Main Library, University of British Columbia, until her retirement in 1991, Mrs. Yandle built the Malcolm Lowry Archive into a major scholarly resource. She originally suggested that I undertake this edition, and she provided me with materials that made its completion considerably less difficult.

I am also indebted to George Brandak, curator of manuscripts in Special Collections, for his help in using the materials in the Malcolm Lowry Archive. For their assistance I thank the staffs at the following libraries: the Main Library, University of British Columbia (particularly Special Collections, Fine Arts Reference, and Humanities and Social Sciences Reference); the Otto G. Richter Library, University of Miami (especially Reference and Interlibrary Loan); the Albert Pick Music Library, University of Miami; and the Vancouver Public Library. I am indebted to the staffs of many other institutions, too numerous to mention individually, that provided materials through interlibrary loan. Finally, I would like to thank Elaine Hart, Picture Library Manager for the *Illustrated London News*, Jane Turner, Archivist and Records Manager at the McPherson Library, University of Victoria, and Abe Reddekopp, Director of Publications for the Gospel Missionary Union (Kansas City), for their attempts to locate materials that Lowry used.

My interest in editing *La Mordida* began when I was engaged in writing *Forests of Symbols: World, Text, and Self in Malcolm Lowry's Fiction* (University of Georgia Press, 1994). For financial support for my research on both projects, including summer fellowships and travel grants that enabled me to work with the Lowry manuscripts in Vancouver, I thank the Research Council of the University of Miami.

For permission to publish this edition of *La Mordida* I am grateful to the Estate of Malcolm Lowry and to the University of British Columbia. Published by permission of Sterling Lord Literistic, Inc. Copyright © by the Estate of Malcolm Lowry.

INTRODUCTION

In October 1936, Malcolm Lowry arrived in Mexico for the first time.[1] The trip began hopefully for Lowry and his wife, Jan Gabrial, but ended in disaster: by July 1938, when he left Mexico, Lowry's drinking had worsened, he had had numerous problems with Mexican officials (even spending Christmas 1937 in the Oaxaca jail), and his marriage to Jan was a shambles. He had, however, begun *Under the Volcano*, the novel that would eventually establish his reputation as a writer. Lowry devoted much of the next seven years to writing and revising *Under the Volcano*, staying with the project despite the devastating rejection of a 1940 version, and in June 1945 he finally sent a drastically revised manuscript to his agent. Although the book was not accepted at once, Lowry was sufficiently encouraged to contemplate a return visit to Mexico, accompanied by his second wife, Margerie Bonner. During that trip he intended to recheck local references and Spanish phrases used in *Under the Volcano* as well as to look up a friend, Juan Fernando Márquez, with whom he had lost contact. He also considered using the visit as inspiration for another novel about Mexico.

At the end of November 1945 Lowry left Vancouver to begin his second trip to Mexico. By the time he returned in May, the idea for a new Mexican novel had begun to expand into plans for two books: *Dark as the Grave Wherein My Friend Is Laid*, based on the early stages of his stay in Mexico, and *La Mordida*, derived from the latter half of the trip. As described in *Dark as the Grave*, the first part of the trip culminated in the discovery that Juan Fernando had died in 1939, shot in a barroom brawl that, for Lowry, inevitably recalled the conclusion of *Under the Volcano*. Nor was this the only way in which Lowry's present experiences seemed to resemble the events of his novel: revisiting the sites of his first trip to Mexico meant returning to places and people that he had invested with symbolic importance in

Under the Volcano, and Lowry often felt that he was living within a world created by his own novel—or, worse, that he was no longer in control of his life, which was "being written" by his daemon.[2] During the latter part of the trip, which is described in *La Mordida*, the world turned even more sinister for Lowry, as it does for his auto-biographical protagonist, Sigbjørn Wilderness. Like Sigbjørn, Lowry was arrested in Acapulco for having overstayed his visa during a pre-vious trip to Mexico and for allegedly having failed to pay a fine of fifty pesos (about ten dollars). After weeks of harassment by corrupt officials, the Lowrys were finally scheduled for deportation to the United States, although a sympathetic immigration officer in Nuevo Laredo allowed them to go across the border without being officially deported from Mexico.

Not long after his return to British Columbia, Lowry began making notes for both novels. There is, however, little evidence of real work on *La Mordida* until mid-1947, when he began a pencil draft that relied heavily on his and Margerie's notebooks for descrip-tive details as well as for the outline of the narrative.[3] After complet-ing that draft, Lowry appears generally to have set aside the project until 1952, when Margerie prepared the typescript (here designated Draft B) on which this edition is principally based. By then, Lowry had reconceived *La Mordida* and *Dark as the Grave* as parts of an ambitious series of works entitled *The Voyage That Never Ends*. In his 1951 "Work in Progress" statement, he said that he planned to frame *The Voyage* with a description of an hallucinatory near-death experience, *The Ordeal of Sigbjørn Wilderness*, in which his protag-onist would envision all the other works within the sequence.[4] After 1952, however, Lowry made no more significant progress on either *La Mordida* or the other volumes of *The Voyage That Never Ends*, instead devoting most of his creative energies to two other works: a novel, *October Ferry to Gabriola*, and a collection of stories, *Hear Us O Lord from Heaven Thy Dwelling Place*. When Lowry died in 1957, *La Mordida* was no closer to completion than it had been five years earlier.

Lowry's conception of *La Mordida* was one of the grandest and most ambitious of the many projects he undertook after *Under the Volcano*. On its most immediate level, the title—which means "the little bite," Mexican slang for the small bribe that officials are apt to demand in order to expedite matters—refers simply to Sigbjørn's legal difficulties, but in a larger sense it represents his inability to escape his past or to repay the fine, or debt, that he owes. Since that past is also the basis of the novel he has written, *The Valley of the Shadow of Death* (Sigbjørn's equivalent of *Under the Volcano*), the question is whether his life can be redeemed by its transformation into a work of art. The central narrative of *La Mordida* involves a descent into the abyss of self, complicated by the infernal legal machinery in which Sigbjørn is caught up, but culminating in his reemergence or rebirth at the book's end. As Lowry imagined it, this basic narrative pattern would have been used as the springboard for innumerable questions about art, identity, the nature of existence, political issues, alcoholism, and the like. In particular, it would have been a metafictional work about an author who sees no point in living events if he cannot write them, and who is not only unable to write but strongly suspects that he is just a character in a novel.

The 1952 typescript of *La Mordida*, the basic copy text for this edition, reveals a work in various stages of composition: some early chapters have been reasonably well fleshed out (although all need substantial revision), but the later chapters are mainly transcriptions of notebook entries from the ill-fated trip to Mexico that inspired this narrative. Throughout the typescript are other materials, including notes for future revisions as well as copies of newspaper articles, letters, telegrams, and other writings that Lowry meant to preserve in order to refer to them at a later stage. Given the haphazard state of the typescript, it is easy to see why *La Mordida* has remained unpublished while other unfinished works by Lowry—among them *Hear Us O Lord from Heaven Thy Dwelling Place*, *Dark as the Grave Wherein My Friend Is Laid*, *October Ferry to Gabriola*, Lowry's film script for an adaptation of *Tender Is the Night*, his *Collected Poetry*, and most recently the 1940 draft of *Under the Volcano*—have been published. *La Mordida* is further from completion than any of these works, and many parts are just notes or preliminary sketches for scenes. Even so, it provides us with a fascinating glimpse into Lowry's life and art and demonstrates, perhaps more clearly than any other work, the complex self-involvement of his fiction.

All the materials for *La Mordida* are part of the Malcolm Lowry Archive at the Division of Special Collections, Main Library, University of British Columbia. In this edition, archival documents are designated by the abbreviation UBC, followed by box, folder, and (where appropriate) page number: e.g., UBC 13:18, 35 for box 13, folder 18, page 35. The principal archival materials for *La Mordida* consist of eight notebooks and four manuscripts or typescripts, as well as a few miscellaneous items. For the sake of convenience, I have used numerical or alphabetical designations in the following descriptions of these materials.

Notebook I: This blue "Block Perforado" notebook in UBC 10:11, one of five notebooks in the folder, is written almost entirely in Malcolm's hand. At the top of the first page is the heading *"Further Notes for Dark is [sic] the Grave"*; below that is a second heading, "LA MORDIDA." The notebook contains only a few brief passages that made their way into *La Mordida*.

Notebook II: The blue notebook in UBC 14:18 begins with Margerie's travel notes for 3 March 1946 (shortly before the beginning of the events of *La Mordida*) and continues with other notes on the trip. It also contains the beginning of Margerie's description of her night bus ride to Mexico City, which is continued in Notebook III, and it includes various random notes, mostly in Malcolm's hand.

Notebook III: The larger of two black notebooks in UBC 14:18 contains extensive notes on the stay in Acapulco and is a major source for *La Mordida*. It begins with thirty-nine numbered pages of daily notes, mainly in Margerie's hand, continues with the remainder of Margerie's description of her night bus trip (begun in Notebook II), then picks up the daily entries again through 27 April.

Notebook IV: One of the two blue "Memo Book" notebooks in UBC 7:5, with entries mainly in Margerie's hand, is the principal source of *La Mordida*, chapters XXXIX–XLII, covering the dates 30 April–2 May.

Notebook V: A brown "Golden West" notebook in UBC 7:7, marked "Seattle-New Orleans" and covering the first part of a trip from Vancouver to Haiti that the Lowrys took at the end of 1946, is the source of the description of the trip across the United States in chapter VI of *La Mordida*. The notebook contains entries both in Margerie's and in Malcolm's hand.

Notebook VI: The blue "Herald Square" notebook in UBC 7:8, with "NB HAITI" written on the cover, contains a substantial amount of material that went into the New Orleans to Haiti portion of the trip in chapter VI. The notebook is in Malcolm's hand.

Notebook VII: The brown "Golden West" notebook in UBC 7:8, with "Haiti—Margie" on the cover, is the source of most of Margerie's notes on New Orleans and the trip to Haiti in UBC 7:8 and on the first set of pages 206–19 in Draft C of *La Mordida* (see below). Except for Draft C, however, the materials from this notebook did not go directly into *La Mordida*, and I have not included them in this edition.

Notebook VIII: Along with Notebooks V and VI, this blue notebook in UBC 7:9, written mainly in Malcolm's hand, is a significant source of material for chapter VI. The description of the hospital experience in Haiti derives from this notebook.

Draft A: This is a 268-page pencil draft written in Lowry's hand and located in UBC 13:1–17. In this version of the narrative, which was composed in 1947, the main characters are named Martin and Primrose Trumbaugh. The skeleton of the book is complete in this draft, which includes preliminary versions of all 45 chapters, but it is probably best to regard this manuscript as a set of notes toward what Lowry hoped would evolve into a book.

Draft B: The most nearly complete version of *La Mordida* is the 422–page typescript contained in UBC 13:18–26 and 14:1–9. Because it represents the latest stage in Lowry's composition of *La Mordida*, Draft B has been used as the copy text for the present edition. In this version, which was typed in 1952, Martin Trumbaugh has been changed into Sigbjørn Wilderness, but Primrose retains her first name. Much of Draft B is clearly derived from Draft A, but the description of the Wildernesses' trip across the United States and down to Haiti in chapter VI is apparently transcribed directly from Notebooks V, VI, and VIII, or from a lost intermediate draft which in turn is a transcription of the notebooks. The number of long passages in early chapters that have no counterparts in Draft A suggests that there was an intermediate draft of those chapters. Draft A also lacks the marginalia derived from an Acapulco tourism guidebook, *Acapulco: An Adventure in Living*, as well as various notes and documents that are typed directly into Draft B. In addition, at various points Margerie registered her protest against Malcolm's version of events by typing a rebuttal in the text of Draft B. I have retained all these heterogeneous materials apart from two railroad schedules whose details add nothing to the narrative or to the symbolic dimensions of the work.

Draft C: UBC 14:10–11 contains a partial draft of *La Mordida* that is principally a carbon of Draft B, ending with chapter VIII. The first 34 pages of this typescript, however, are actually the original (ribbon) copy of the "Statement for *La Mordida*" that Lowry apparently intended to use as a preface. This statement is essentially the same as the letter of 15 June 1946 to A. Ronald Button (*Selected Letters* 91–112), but there are some differences between the letter and the statement. There are also oddities in the pagination of this draft, the most obvious of which is that UBC 14:11 has two different sets of pages numbered 206–19. One set of these pages, apparently placed here by mistake, derives ultimately from Notebook VII and belongs with a typed transcription of Margerie's notes on New Orleans that is now in UBC 7:8.

Draft D: This draft, from UBC 14:12–15, is a typescript donated by Margerie Lowry in 1986. It is the latest version of *La Mordida* but for the most part I have not taken it into consideration in the preparation of this edition because it is a substantially revised version composed by Margerie after her husband's death. This version probably dates from the mid-1970s, after the publication of *October Ferry to Gabriola*, and it represents Margerie's attempt to make *La Mordida* into what I believe it never could have been: a straightforward and commercially viable narrative. The title page of this edition reads:

LA MORDIDA
(THE BITE)
a true story
by
MALCOLM and MARGERIE LOWRY

This typescript smooths over much of the roughness of Draft B, eliminates a number of notes and other complexities, and adds some new material derived from the notebooks. It also reduces the number of chapters to thirty-five, changes the protagonists' names back to Malcolm and Margerie Lowry, and transforms the book into a series of first-person narratives by Malcolm and Margerie, one or the other of whom is named as the narrator at the beginning of each chapter. Apart from the biographical details it contains, the main interest of Draft D lies in the fact that Margerie continued to regard this narrative as an autobiographical account and to be more interested in fidelity to her recollection of events than in Lowry's development of his aesthetic and psychological themes.

Miscellaneous items: UBC 14:16 contains two sets of photocopied pages from Draft B, but since the originals of these pages (corresponding to UBC 13:21, 142–44 and 13:23, 162–86) are included in my copy text there is no need to describe the photocopies separately. UBC 14:17, however, has some items that were incorporated into Draft B, including Malcolm's notes on a *TLS* article entitled "The Insufficient Man" and a note from Margerie to Malcolm in which she begs forgiveness for some offense (see pp. 254–55 and 284 of this edition). There are also notes on Hermann Keyserling's *The Recovery of Truth* (mistitled *The Rediscovery of Truth*), to which Lowry refers in *La Mordida* (p. 177). Finally, there are two pages of miscellaneous notes (the words of a song, the text of a telegram, etc.), for the most part in Spanish.

The relationship of the drafts and notebooks to this edition of *La Mordida* is demonstrated by the table of chapters, which indicates the location of the pencil draft and main typescript versions of each chapter as well as the notebooks that correspond to the drafts of the chapters.[5]

CHAPTER	PENCIL DRAFT	TYPESCRIPT	NOTEBOOKS, ETC.
Statement	—	UBC 14:10	Letter in *Selected Letters*, 91–112; three drafts of the letter in UBC 2:4
I	UBC 13:1	UBC 13:18	Notebooks I, II
II	UBC 13:2	UBC 13:19	Notebook III
III	UBC 13:2, 13:3[6]	UBC 13:20	Notebook III
IV	UBC 13:3	UBC 13:21	—
V	UBC 13:4	UBC 13:22	Notebooks I, III
VI	UBC 13:4	UBC 13:23	Notebooks V, VI, VIII
VII	UBC 13:4, 14:11	UBC 13:24	—
VIII	UBC 13:5	UBC 13:24	—
IX	UBC 13:5	UBC 13:24	Notebook III
X	UBC 13:5	UBC 13:25	—
XI	UBC 13:5	UBC 13:25	Notebook III
XII	UBC 13:6	UBC 13:25	Notebook III
XIII	UBC 13:6	UBC 13:26	Notebook III
XIV	UBC 13:7	UBC 13:26	Notebooks II, III
XV	UBC 13:8	UBC 14:1	Notebook II
XVI	UBC 13:9	UBC 14:1	—
XVII	UBC 13:9	UBC 14:1	Notebook III
XVIII	UBC 13:10	UBC 14:2	Notebook III
XIX	UBC 13:10	UBC 14:2	Notebook III

XX	UBC 13:10	UBC 14:3	Notebook III
XXI	UBC 13:11	UBC 14:3	Notebook III
XXII	UBC 13:11	UBC 14:3	Notebook III
XXIII	UBC 13:11	UBC 14:4	Notebook III
XXIV	UBC 13:11	UBC 14:4	Notebook III
XXV	UBC 13:11	UBC 14:4	Notebook III
XXVI	UBC 13:11	UBC 14:4	Notebook III
XXVII	UBC 13:11	UBC 14:4	Notebook III, notes in UBC 14:17
XXVIII	UBC 13:12	UBC 14:4	Notebook III
XXIX	UBC 13:12	UBC 14:5	Notebook III
XXX	UBC 13:12	UBC 14:5	Notebook III
XXXI	UBC 13:12	UBC 14:5	Notebook III
XXXII	UBC 13:12	UBC 14:5	Notebook III
XXXIII	UBC 13:13	UBC 14:5	Notebook III
XXXIV	UBC 13:13	UBC 14:6	Notebook III
XXXV	UBC 13:13	UBC 14:6	Notebook III
XXXVI	UBC 13:13	UBC 14:6	Notebook III
XXXVII	UBC 13:13	UBC 14:6	Notebook III
XXXVIII	UBC 13:14	UBC 14:6	Notebook III
XXXIX	UBC 13:14	UBC 14:7	Notebook III, IV
XL	UBC 13:14	UBC 14:7	Notebooks I, IV
XLI	UBC 13:15	UBC 14:7	Notebook IV, note in UBC 14:17
XLII	UBC 13:15	UBC 14:7	Notebooks II, IV
XLIII	UBC 13:16	UBC 14:8	—
XLIV	UBC 13:16	UBC 14:8	—
XLV	UBC 13:17	UBC 14:9	Notebook II

In editing *La Mordida* I have tried to present Lowry's work-in-progress, as much as possible, just as he left it, apart from textual corruptions that cannot be attributed to Lowry himself. I have kept in mind G. Thomas Tanselle's distinction between editorial practices that are appropriate for editions of private documents and those that apply to works written for publication. Tanselle observes that "just as works not intended for publication should be printed so as to show the roughness characteristic of the original, works intended for publication should be printed so as to reflect their authors' intentions." The editor of an unpublished novel, Tanselle argues, must decide "whether the manuscript . . . is finished enough to serve as the basis for a critical edition or whether it is so rough and fragmentary that it must be regarded as a private paper."[7] The 1952 typescript of *La Mordida* was a repository for materials about a project that was far from concluded, and Lowry never intended that it be published as it stands, so for the most part it fits Tanselle's description of a "document" or "private paper." At the same time, however, it is clear that Lowry would have wanted inadvertent errors in *La Mordida* to be corrected by an editor.

In this edition of *La Mordida* I have corrected all identifiable transmission errors in Draft B that are attributable to Margerie Lowry, whether they involve typing errors, the omission of material due to eyeskip, the misreading of Lowry's handwriting, or other such problems. Whenever possible I have based emendations on Draft A, the notebooks, or a printed source that Margerie was copying, but some emendations are conjectural. I have been far more conservative in my emendation of Lowry's own errors, and any mistake that might conceivably be intentional (e.g., the spelling of "disastar") has been left undisturbed. I have emended obvious punctuation errors that might cloud the sense of a passage but have retained some idiosyncratic practices such as the use of a comma immediately before a parenthesis; likewise, apart from correcting typographical or simple spelling errors, I have not regularized or corrected the titles of works that are typed in Draft B without underlining or quotation marks.

Except for the first instance of the name in the typescript, "Sigbjørn" is typed without a slash through the "o," but I have used the Norwegian "ø" in my text and commentary because it is clear that Lowry meant to include the slash, omitting it at this stage only for the sake of convenience.[8] Likewise, accents in French and Spanish passages, and in the names of governmental agencies, have been restored, but I have not included accents in Spanish personal names (Cárdenas, Alarcón, Pérez) or place names (México, Monte Albán) unless the names occur in Spanish passages or unless the accents may be found in a handwritten note or draft. (An example is José, which is usually accented in Lowry's drafts). The spelling of other names is not regularized when—as with Heywood and Haywood, or Togo and Tojo—the inconsistency is traceable to Lowry.

Draft B has innumerable errors in Spanish and French passages. Some problems involve typographical mistakes, but others may be attributable to Lowry's poor French and even poorer Spanish, or to Margerie's still less secure knowledge of both languages. I have corrected passages, to the extent that it is possible, when Lowry's aim clearly seems to have been to get the passages right, as in the transcription of a document or the extensive quotations from Victor Hugo's poems.[9] I have also assumed that Spanish spoken by Mexicans should be correct, unless the point is that Sigbjørn has misheard something. Apart from correcting obvious typographical errors and adding accents, however, I have not corrected Lowry's (or Sigbjørn's) Spanish and French, since the point sometimes is that his usage and grammar are hilariously bad.

Throughout this edition, I have indicated the relationship of my text to archival typescripts by inserting the location of the corresponding page in Draft B (or in some cases Draft C) at the point where that page ends in Margerie's typescript. These citations, referred to by UBC box, folder, and page number, are set in boldface type and enclosed between fancy brackets. Plain brackets, where they appear in the text, indicate words that I have added for the sake of clarity even though I have no textual authority for the addition. Since there is not always a clear distinction between what Lowry would have considered a draft of a passage and a memorandum or note for revision, I have made no such distinction in this edition. I have also refrained from deleting material that is repeated in Draft B, even when there is substantial overlapping, such as in the repetition of notebook material on the journey to Haiti in chapter VI.

In using Draft B as copy text, I am obviously working from a corrupt text. One alternative solution would have been to adopt the readings in Draft A, or in some cases even notebook readings, whenever a typescript passage might be traced to an earlier draft in Lowry's hand, but this solution in turn would have introduced new problems. For one thing, there are many passages in early chapters, and even some in later chapters, for which we have no text except the typescript. This suggests the possible existence of an intermediate autograph draft of at least some chapters, which means that there are changes that could be attributed to Lowry himself. Moreover, Margerie was not only her husband's typist but also, in a sense, the first editor of this text. As she typed out the manuscript, Malcolm was available to read his handwriting, offer explanations, and perhaps to make changes, all of which means that a later editor of the same text would be well advised to follow the reading in Draft B except when there is strong evidence that the typescript is erroneous. Finally, the title page of Draft D is a clear indication that Margerie regarded herself as coauthor of *La Mordida* (parts of which are, after all, little more than transcriptions of her notebook entries), and her status as a collaborator in the drafting of her husband's books, even if it did not amount to the coauthorship that she later claimed, means that her readings deserve greater credence than those of most typists. Still, there are places where she clearly misread Lowry's handwriting, skipped a line, or put a scribbled marginal note in the middle of an expository passage where it does not fit, and I have not hesitated to emend the typescript in these instances.

The relatively conservative principles of emendation followed here mean that this edition of *La Mordida* differs considerably from the text of *Dark as the Grave* edited by Douglas Day and Margerie Lowry. That book is based on a late typescript of *Dark as the Grave* from which the editors excised a good deal of material, including some long meditative passages, in an attempt to streamline the narrative. In his preface, Day says that they struck a compromise between two extreme solutions: either presenting the manuscript as Lowry left it, "a brilliant but bewildering . . . work in progress," or finishing and revising the novel. Apart from correcting accidentals and adding notes, I have left *La Mordida* essentially as Lowry left it. The result, I hope, is what Day says his edition of *Dark as the Grave* would have been had he chosen the same course: "a book to study, full of anguish, torment, and clumsiness often left uncorrected. There [are] Lowry's occasional pauses to lecture himself on the art of fiction, these lectures occurring in the middle of, say, a piece of dialogue or exposition."[10] Despite its obvious inadequacies as a work of fiction (or metafiction), *La Mordida* demonstrates a good deal about the concepts of life and art, self and reality, that underlay the many projects that Malcolm Lowry undertook in the aftermath of *Under the Volcano*. Inadvertently, this remnant of Lowry's attempt to produce what Sigbjørn ironically calls "a work of art so beyond conception it could not be written" also gives us our clearest evidence of precisely why so many of Lowry's post-*Volcano* projects remained tantalizingly incomplete.

The textual notes and annotations that follow the edited text of *La Mordida* are not intended as a comprehensive commentary either on the editorial decisions made throughout the text or on the significance of Lowry's references. There is not room here for an historical collation of drafts or for an explanation of each emendation, but I have provided notes on decisions that do not involve the routine correction of transmission errors. Likewise, the annotations for the most part are not attempts to interpret passages, just preliminary notes intended to furnish information that will be useful to readers who are trying to follow the basic sense of a passage or to scholars who want to develop an interpretation of the work. Annotations are limited to translations of passages in foreign languages; identification of authors, literary works, films, songs, and paintings referred to in the text; the sources of quotations and passages taken from printed works (ranging from newspaper articles to French poetry); allusions to historical personages and events that might lie outside the range of many readers' knowledge; references to events in Lowry's life, to people he knew, and to his other works; and some random items that seemed likely to require glosses. My basic principle has been to limit annotation to what readers might need, which means (for example) that I have not identified well-known authors (Shakespeare, Goethe, Sherwood Anderson) but have identified references to, or quotations from, their works. Likewise, I have not included translations of Spanish or French passages whose meanings are made clear by the context of the passage or whose translations are provided by the text itself.

In a 1961 interview, Lowry's friend Gerald Noxon said that at their last meeting, in 1947, Lowry told him about his current project, *La Mordida*. Lowry's description of the new book gave Noxon the strong impression that it would be more important than *In Ballast to the White Sea*, the manuscript novel that had been destroyed in a 1944 fire: indeed, to Noxon, *La Mordida* even sounded like a worthy successor to *Under the Volcano*.[11] It is questionable whether *La Mordida* could ever have lived up to such lofty expectations, but this edition at least provides the evidence for scholarly debate over Lowry's aims and methods, as well as the extent of his potential or actual achievement, in this complex and ambitious project.

NOTES

1. Lowry claimed to have entered Mexico on the Day of the Dead (2 November), which would become the date for *Under the Volcano*, but Gordon Bowker says that Lowry's passport shows that he entered on 30 October (*Pursued by Furies: A Life of Malcolm Lowry* [Toronto: Random House of Canada, 1993], 205). In correspondence with me, Bowker has indicated that his source was not the original passport itself but a transcription typed into a draft of *Dark as the Grave* (UBC 9:6, 3–4).

2. For analyses of *Dark as the Grave Wherein My Friend Is Laid* and *La Mordida*, and commentaries on issues raised in this introduction, see my *Forests of Symbols: World, Text, and Self in Malcolm Lowry's Fiction* (Athens: University of Georgia Press, 1994).

3. A preliminary description of the various drafts is provided in my article, "The *La Mordida* Drafts and Notes at UBC," *Malcolm Lowry Review*, no. 28 (spring 1991): 6–12.

4. "Work in Progress: The Voyage That Never Ends," *Malcolm Lowry Review*, no. 21/22 (fall 1987–spring 1988): 72–99.

5. Except for the prefatory statement and the last page of chapter VII, which exist only in Draft C, all references to the typescript are to Draft B. Under "Notebooks" I have listed all notebooks to which I am able to trace specific passages.

6. Although there is a chapter III in Draft A (UBC 13:2), both chapters III and IV of Draft B derive from chapter IV of Draft A (UBC 13:3).

7. G. Thomas Tanselle, "Texts of Documents and Texts of Works," in *Textual Criticism and Scholarly Editing* (Charlottesville: University Press of Virginia, 1990), 15, 17.

8. In unpublished letters of 12 March 1953 to Pamela Hudson of New American Library and 29 May 1953 to Arabel Porter, editor of *New World Writing*, about his story "Strange Comfort Afforded by the Profession," Lowry emphasized the "emotive" importance of the slash through the "o" (UBC 3:5). See also Lowry's letter of 8 January 1953 to Harold Matson (*Selected Letters of Malcolm Lowry*, ed. Harvey Breit and Margerie Bonner Lowry [Philadelphia: J. B. Lippincott, 1965], 327).

9. An example is the typescript reading "Mon ame est in trois mats, cherchait son Icarie" (UBC 13:25, 257), which I have corrected to "Mon âme est un trois mâts, cherchant son Icarie"—and would have done so even if that were not the reading in Draft A (UBC 13:6, ch. XII, 3). Without the authority of Lowry's pencil draft, the primary basis of the emendation would have been that the passage is a garbled version of Charles Baudelaire's phrase "Notre âme est un trois mâts, cherchant son Icarie" ("Our soul is a three-master searching for its Icaria," from "Le Voyage"). I have not, however, emended "mon" to "notre" ("my" to "our"): Lowry's exchange of personal pronouns was probably deliberate, and even if it were not intentional it would be revealing.

10. Preface to *Dark as the Grave Wherein My Friend Is Laid*, ed. Douglas Day and Margerie Lowry (New York: New American Library, 1968), xvi.

11. Gerald Noxon, "In Connection with Malcolm Lowry," *Malcolm Lowry Review*, no. 17/18 (fall 1985–spring 1986): 22.

MALCOLM LOWRY'S
LA MORDIDA

A Scholarly Edition

Statement for La Mordida

Dollarton, B.C.
Canada
June 15, 1946

The following is a statement of what happened to my wife and I in Mexico and wherever possible is verified by dates, names, places.[1]

I am an Englishman, resident in Canada. My wife is American. We left Canada on November 28, 1945, and flew to Los Angeles via United Air Lines, for the purpose of visiting my wife's mother, Mrs. J. S. Bonner, and her sister and brother-in-law, Dr. and Mrs. E. B. Woolfan of 1643 Queens Road, Hollywood, California. From there we proposed to go on to Mexico to spend the winter for purposes of travel and health. At the Mexican consulate in Los Angeles, after making application and waiting the required 24 hours, I obtained a visa on my English passport and we were both given Tourist Cards. These would expire June 10, but we were at that time planning to return to Canada not later than the end of April. I was carrying two passports, my old one, which would expire the end of December but on which I had received my American visa from the American Consulate in Vancouver, B.C., Canada, which was good for one year, and my new one, procured from the British Consulate in Los Angeles, on which I was given the Mexican visa. We also carried my birth certificate, my wife's birth certificate proving her American citizenship, our marriage license, and letters from our bank in Vancouver. At the Mexican Consulate in Los Angeles I produced both my passports and pointed out to them that I had been in Mexico from November 1936 to July 1938. I was not at all sure that I, being English, did not require to go through even further formalities, but I was assured that all regulations had been complied with and that all was satisfactory.

3

After visiting my wife's family we departed by American Airlines and arrived in Mexico City on approximately December 12, 1945. {UBC 14:10, 1} A few days later[2] we left for Cuernavaca, Morelos, where we rented an apartment at 24 Calle de Humboldt, the proprietor of which is Señora Maria Luisa Blanco de Arriola. We lived in this apartment in Cuernavaca with the exception of a few trips to Oaxaca, Pueblo, Tlaxcala, etc.

Certain explanations are necessary at this point. I had written a novel set in Mexico called Under the Volcano and had received a virtual acceptance of it (later verified) by my publishers, Jonathan Cape, in London. A subsidiary reason for voting for the trip was that it would be a possible opportunity to correct, if necessary, some of the idiomatic Spanish and possibly make a few notes for the preface to the book of a friendly nature to Mexico. Not that the book should be construed as unfriendly: to the contrary. On the other hand I felt it might be misunderstood in Mexico, since many shades of opinion are reflected in it, which is not surprising since that country is used as an analogue of the world itself. But there is no political resolution, other, that is to say, than a democratic one: in fact no resolution at all unless it is, perhaps, moral. On our Tourist Cards we gave our occupations as writers (escritores) but we entered as tourists and remained as tourists with no intention of "working" in Mexico, or taking any money from Mexico for any work done while there, and in fact we did not work while there with the exception of a few notes.

On Friday the 8th of March, 1946, after several happy months, we left Cuernavaca for another brief trip, stopping in Taxco and Iguala, and arrived in Acapulco on Sunday the 10th of March, 1946. We stayed at the Hotel Quinta Eugenia at Caleta Beach. On the following Thursday, March 14, two men from the Office of Migración came to the hotel and asked to see our papers. It should be pointed out that Acapulco is a port of entry and as a consequence all {UBC 14:10, 3} names of tourists are sent into this office as a matter of course. My wife had packed our bags while I was attending to reservations, etc., and since we only intended to be away a week at most and she was afraid of theft (we had had many things stolen) she unfortunately left our papers in the apartment in Cuernavaca. Needless to say I knew by experience how important it is to have one's papers with one when travelling in a foreign country. But a new policy of sympathetic attitude toward tourists that pertained in the state of Morelos (superficially at least) did not incline one to take a serious view of our omission. We had never been once asked for our papers since checking in at the airport in Mexico City. I believe it is not, by the way, illegal not to have your papers with you so long as you have them at your place of residence. We therefore explained to the men from the Migración where our papers were and asked them what the trouble was. They announced that we would have to remain in Acapulco, at that hotel, until they checked on our Tourist Cards with Mexico City and said they would send a wire that day regarding this. They also told me that they had an unpaid fine against me to the amount of 50 pesos for having overstayed my leave in 1938 and further, because they had pursued this fine until 1943, apparently not aware I had left the country in July 1938, that they had in their files a letter saying that I was not allowed to enter Mexico without permission of the Chief of Migración. This latter injunction I knew nothing about whatsoever. As to the 50 pesos fine for having overstayed my leave, I must now make a further statement regarding that.

In November 1936³ I had originally entered Mexico through Acapulco, arriving by boat, and had returned to Acapulco again in the early spring of 1938. Since I had then a "rentista's"⁴ status I had had already further extensions on my original visa or card or {UBC 14:10, 4} whatever but at this time I required a further extension and had been wrongly advised, so far as I can recall, that I could get it there in Acapulco, since that had been my original port of entry; and I was also planning to leave from here by the Panama Pacific line. I applied for this extension and was then told, after many delays, that it was necessary to go to Mexico City to procure it. Very possibly there were other factors that I have forgotten, such as the possible defection of the Panama Pacific itself: I have a vague recollection that they suddenly stopped running their ships at a time when I could have left Mexico within the period then allotted me. Either that or my money was delayed in arriving through the American Express in New York. At all events I went to Mexico City, in company with the then Chief of Migración in Acapulco, whose fare I paid to and probably from Mexico City, and also his hotel room at the Biltmore Hotel, and various expenses. I had by now overstayed my leave by, I think, not more than a few days. I cannot, however, swear to this. In Mexico City I went with this Chief of Migración, a man by the name of Guyou (I cannot recall the exact spelling) to the main office of Migración on Bucarelli St. and was given, to the best of my knowledge, a further extension of six months. At any rate I certainly left Mexico well within the new time given me with no further difficulty that I can remember over my papers at any point, though I had other difficulties, chiefly personal. My first wife had returned to America in December 1937 and I had been, and still was, to some extent, very ill, the consequence of dysentery, malaria and rheumatic fever. Also there had been, as I said, some confusion about my income arriving due to my changes of address or other misunderstanding, and as a result I had become somewhat in debt. My parents having become {UBC 14:10, 5} anxious about my health put a lawyer at my disposal and my income was paid through him, and before I left Mexico any and all debts were paid in full. I am certain that if any fine was imposed it was also paid at that time—indeed it *must* have been or I should certainly not have been allowed to leave. I left Mexico in July 1938 and was admitted to America at Nogales. I was not aware, I repeat, of any unpaid fine nor of any such letter from the Chief of Migración. Utterly oblivious that there might be anything held against me I applied for my visa and Tourist Card to enter Mexico in 1946 in good faith, and was given them by the Mexican Consulate in Los Angeles as stated.

To return to Acapulco and my statement of what happened there in March 1946: my wife, who was still not in the best of health, and I, went every day to the office of Migración and waited some hours but no word from Mexico City was forthcoming. Meantime I was racking my brains to discover if anything else could possibly have caused this injunction against me and I remembered this: in 1937 my first wife and I had put up a bond as "rentistas." This had been mainly arranged through her and a friend and when she left in 1937 she took the papers concerning this bond with her. So far as I know I was still within the time limit of this bond when in Acapulco in 1938 and do not believe I could have got an extension if the bond had run out. But late in 1939, or early in 1940, when I was in Canada, I received word through my father's lawyer that the man who had underwritten this bond had been intimidated by the authorities for a whole year on the false grounds that I had not left the country at all. To straighten this matter up I went to the acting Mexican Consul here in Vancouver, produced proof that I had indeed left in July 1938 and this proof was forwarded to the necessary {UBC 14:10, 6} authorities so that they would cease intimidating this man, whose name I cannot now recall. I am certain also that if any compensation was due him it was paid, via funds at my disposal in America, since I believe it was then impossible to send funds out of this country.

Anxious to discover the precise truth with a view to remedying matters I now asked the Sub-Chief of Migración in Acapulco to show my wife and I what was against me in his file and he was generous enough to do this. He only gave us a short while to look and the Spanish was too complicated to take in at a glance. I ascertained however that there was nothing about any bond whatsoever and that the file was mainly concerned with the government's unsuccessful attempt to recover this 50 peso fine. Guyou, however, was mentioned as was my trip to Mexico City with him, and since he was the one directly concerned with my having overstayed my leave, and the intermediary between myself and the Mexican Government, and since, moreover, he would hardly have returned to Acapulco (we were staying at the same hotel in Mexico City) without having seen to it first that the fine was paid, either to the head office or to himself, the obvious implication is that something mysterious happened to this fine, as a consequence of which it was never crossed off the books at Acapulco. I could not help noting that the excuse he had given was that I was too *ebriadad* to do business with. If this were so it seems peculiar that I was not too *ebriadad* to make the trip to Mexico City, not to say to remember over eight years afterwards the hotel I put him up at, or to spend one whole afternoon with him at the head office, and stranger still, perhaps, that I was never arrested for being so *ebriadad,* if it was serious enough to put on a file against me as a matter of character. The fact is I was making many notes at that time in the cantinas or {UBC 14:10, 7} sidewalk taverns I imagined one protagonist of my forthcoming novel to be frequenting and these notes taken at that time make an important part of it. Doubtless this habit counted against me, though no one ever objected to it overtly. I was also, for that matter, making notes for a long dramatic poem entitled The Cantinas.[5]

I ascertained two facts of importance however from this file. First that the edict forbidding me to reenter the country without special permission was filed two months after I had left it, in September 1938, which explained why there was nothing about the bond. For they could scarcely forbid me to reenter the country without having prior knowledge of my having left it, and if they possessed this knowledge, what right had they to persecute the underwriter of my bond for a year on the grounds that I was still in Mexico? The second fact was that my date of entry into Mexico was wrongly given as September 1936. Actually it was November 1936: apparently an innocent mistake, this could nevertheless make it appear that I had overstayed my leave that much longer, for here were two months extra credited to me when I had never been in the country at all. I have gone into all this as fully as possible because this was the only time I was ever allowed a glimpse of what purported to be held against me. When the British Consulate inquired, they were never informed but were merely told somewhat vaguely that "there had been some trouble." Later, when my wife and I were in Mexico City with an interpreter and witness we made every effort, as will be seen, to discover the reason for the treatment we received, but by this time they had emphatically denied that they had anything against me at all.

I now observed something else. The Sub-Chief of Migración showed me the telegram he had sent to Mexico City explaining that we did not have our Tourist Cards with us, etc., and asking for {UBC 14:10, 8} instructions. In this telegram he had given the name of my *first* wife as being here with me in Acapulco, although we had repeatedly explained the situation to him. My wife had given him her name, stated that she was *not* with me in Mexico in 1938, had never been in Mexico at all before, and that she was, as a matter of fact, in Los Angeles in 1938 and completely unaware of my existence. He replied that he had looked in my old file and found out what my wife's name was and we needn't try to tell him it was something else. In the end I believe we convinced him of the truth. He was himself going to Mexico City the following day and he stated that he would go himself and correct this error. I do not know whether this mistake on the part of the Sub-Chief of Migración in Acapulco was ever cleared up or not, despite repeated efforts, for later on, in Mexico City, if not Sr. Corunna, someone in his office still seemed under the impression that my present wife was indeed my first wife who had entered under a false name for some obscure purpose of her own and for all I know nothing ever really convinced them to the contrary.

On Wednesday, March 20, 1946, a man from the Oficina Federal de Hacienda[6] came to our hotel. He refused to come into our room but stood on the porch, having called the manager and several of the employees of the hotel also, he threatened us, using abusive terms in a loud voice, demanding instant payment of the same 50 peso fine. It was very difficult to understand him as he became quite incoherent in the end, but we finally persuaded him to meet us that afternoon at 4 o'clock in the office of the Department of Turista, where there would be a man who would interpret and act as a witness for us. We therefore met at this office, where a man {UBC 14:10, 9} who is second in command of the office, Señor Obregon, interpreted for us and said that unless the fine was paid at once I would be taken to jail. It must be repeated that our papers and money were in Cuernavaca, we had only taken a limited amount with us for the trip and had already paid for telegrams, long distance phone calls, et al to Mexico City in an effort to expedite the matter, our hotel bill was running on in Acapulco and our rent was now due in Cuernavaca, and all this we had explained fully without the slightest sympathy toward our plight being forthcoming. They merely said they would doubtless hear from Mexico City tomorrow, or "Mexico City is very slow." The man from the Hacienda said finally that he would give me until Saturday morning to pay the fine and would take my watch (or something else) as security. Señor Obregon, who was most kind throughout, therefore said that if such procedure was necessary he would himself keep the watch as security and this he did. The Chief of the Department of Turistas had meantime telephoned the Department of Migración and was, at our request, inquiring about a long distance phone call purported to have been put through at our expense that day to Mexico City regarding our case. He reported that they had been told in Mexico City that they had no knowledge of the case at all and knew nothing about me whatsoever, but that still they would not release us. I protested that since there was absolutely nothing against my wife it was wrong to hold her and she went on to add that she should be allowed to go to Cuernavaca and get our papers and money, and that if she was not allowed to go she or I would call the American Consul long distance to Mexico City and apply for aid. This was relayed by phone and the Chief of Turista told us that the Chief of Migración had now said that my wife would be allowed to go to Cuernavaca but that she must leave at once and be back by Saturday. It was impossible at such short {UBC 14:10, 10} notice to get reservations and she was forced to leave on a second class bus to make a night trip alone across Mexico. I will not go into the obvious dangers of such a trip. She arrived in Cuernavaca at 5 A.M., got our papers and money and proceeded to Mexico City where she appealed to the British Consulate. She went to the British Consulate since I am, as stated, an Englishman and it was I and the 50 pesos fine etc. against me that was, or seemed to be, the trouble. Moreover as a British subject herself by marriage she was entitled to his protection. She was unable to see the Consul General but presented our case to Mr. Percival Hughes, the Vice Consul. He looked through our papers carefully, said that they were in perfect order, was most sympathetic, made notes of the numbers of our Tourist Cards, my passport, all dates concerning this matter, etc. etc. She told him of the fine and all that she knew concerning the reason for it and he said that if she would stay over night in Mexico City he would go with her the following morning to the Department of Migración and straighten the whole matter out. The following morning, Friday March 22, he informed her that the Consul General had ordered her to return to Acapulco and pay the fine there. He said that they would go, however, to the Migración office that morning and see that we were released at once. She returned to Acapulco by bus and on Saturday morning we went, together with a Mr. W. Hudson, who acted as interpreter and witness, to the Oficina Federal de Hacienda. There we paid the fine. We saw the man who had come to our hotel to demand payment and the Chief of Hacienda. We asked for the return of my watch and said that we objected to the manner in which this man had acted at our hotel as being totally unnecessary and embarrassing. He then denied threatening me with jail or having taken the watch. We asked that Señor Obregon be sent for which {UBC 14:10, 11} was done. He arrived, very graciously returned my watch, and entirely corroborated our statement as to threats, etc. The Chief of Hacienda then informed us that their man had no right to make threats or take the watch, that all he was empowered to do was quietly to present me with a bill. He further offered an apology, said that the Constitution of Mexico had been breached by this action and that we could make a complaint if we wished and that we had two witnesses. This we declined to do out of a reciprocal courtesy to the courtesy which was being shown to us at this point by the Office of Hacienda. Mr. Hudson, who had also been with us on one occasion to the Oficina of Migración and had seen my file there said that this was a mistake made in their office and not my fault. The Chief of Hacienda, who was very courteous throughout this interview, agreed, while Señor Obregon expressed himself as dubious whether a fine of 50 pesos could be pursued for as long as 8 years anyway and sportingly promised to try and get it back for us if he could.

We then took the receipt for the fine, our papers, and went with Mr. Hudson to the Office of Migración, showed our papers and the receipt and asked if we were now free to leave. They said that we could not leave until they heard from Mexico City. The British Vice Consul had promised to wire us at once if anything was wrong at his end: he did not wire us. He had also instructed us, if we were not immediately released upon my wife's return from Mexico City, to wire him. We did so and received no reply.

They kept us in Acapulco, where we were forced to come every day to the Office of Migración, down into the town of Acapulco where the heat is extreme, and wait for hours, frequently in an empty office. {UBC 14:10, 12}

Meanwhile however the Sub-Chief of Migración had returned from Mexico City and when we saw him delivered himself as follows: that in Mexico City they had, unfortunately, disclaimed any knowledge of receiving his wire, which might account for some of the delay. He said, however, that they had now found my file there, in which was a record of another fine, this time for 100 pesos, which had been paid. He also said that there was a photograph of me there with a beard. This was true, I had grown one for fun in 1937, and it was on the duplicate of my card or whatever as a "rentista." When I asked him if we could go now, he said that he had asked the Secretary of Migración there if he could now let us go and the Secretary had said, "No, don't do that." When I asked him if there was anything further on the file, real or imaginary, which could account for this treatment he said, "I don't know." But he implied that the beard was a bad thing in itself, so bad indeed that my wife, in spite of her papers being in perfect order, in spite of there being nothing whatever against her, and her being an American citizen, could not now go either. So we remained in Acapulco.

A statement of this kind is not the place to describe the feelings with which we received the news that Mexico had disclaimed all knowledge of receiving the wire. But we naturally wondered if it had not been sent very much later than stated, while we were kept waiting in the interim; just as we wondered if a phone call to Mexico that I had suspected the Chief of Turista (suspected because I recognized him as a friend of Guyou's who had formerly been in the Migración) of only pretending was being put through by the Chief of Migración while we waited in the former's office, had ever been put through at all. {UBC 14:10, 13}

So we waited in Acapulco.

About 10 days after my wife's return from Mexico City we received a letter from the British Consul General, Mr. Rodgers, saying that the Mexican authorities had decided to deport me and asking if my papers were in order to return to America, although my wife had shown these papers at the British Consulate to the Vice Consul, Mr. Hughes, who had written all this down, as before stated. We telephoned the Consulate long distance and spoke with Mr. Hughes who could give absolutely no reason for this action by the Mexican authorities and said they did not know why it was being done. He said that he would talk to them further and wire me. This he did not do and I called him again some days later. He then said that I was not to be deported but might be asked to leave the country, but again could not say why as they had given him no reason. Finally, on Thursday, April 4th, the Office of Migración in Acapulco, who themselves disclaimed all knowledge of this deportation order, said they had themselves decided we had been there too long and that they would give us a letter on the following day which would allow us to go, but made it obligatory that we appear at the office of Migración in Mexico City on Monday, April 8th. The following day, 22 days after they first came to the hotel, they gave us this letter permitting us to leave.

We went to our apartment in Cuernavaca (where I promptly received the almost insane news that the book set in Mexico, for which I was proposing to write the friendly preface, had been accepted simultaneously in both England and America) and on Monday morning went to Mexico City with an interpreter, Mr. Eduardo Ford, owner and proprietor of the restaurant "Bahia," 12 Jardín Morelos, Cuernavaca, Mexico. We were kept waiting in the office until it {UBC 14:10, 14} was too late to accomplish anything, and were told to return in a few days.

It should be said that it is about fifty miles from Cuernavaca to Mexico City but this gives no idea of the character of the trip. Though it only takes two to two and a half hours it is necessary to climb to an altitude of over 10,000 feet and one frequently arrives deafened. The climate likewise is completely different: one leaves Cuernavaca in tropical heat and you are likely at this time of year to run into a snow storm in the mountains: beautiful in itself, such a journey repeated under such conditions becomes a nightmare, especially since it is difficult to make reservations either by car or bus, both are prone to break down on the way, and from all this my wife's health especially began to suffer. Despite this we managed to keep every appointment during the following four weeks punctually, yet we never waited less than three hours and usually four or five hours. We are far from wealthy people; had budgeted our vacation very carefully, and we were put to what was for us near fatal expence to make these frequent trips for ourselves and often an interpreter. For though we may specify only what happened during certain visits, it should be borne in mind that there were many more visits when despite promises nothing happened at all and we were kept waiting in a vacuum: we calculated that we travelled well over a thousand miles during those four weeks simply between Cuernavaca and Mexico City and probably it was more like twelve hundred.

To resume: we returned on Friday, April 12, and were informed that our case had been sent to the Office of Inspection. We waited there the usual hours, finally saw an Inspector whose name I do not know but who was in charge of our case and whom I shall have reason {UBC 14:10, 15} to refer to many times more, simply as the Inspector. He took all our papers, (including the receipt for the fine which was incidentally never returned to us) and our identification and consulted with the Chief of the Office of Inspección, one Sr. Corunna. The fine had been paid and our papers were in order. But the Inspector now noted that on our Tourist Cards we had given our occupation as writers. He then said that as writers we should not have been allowed to enter Mexico at all as tourists, and should have had a working permit or some other form of passport and asked if we would like immigration papers. Both we ourselves and our interpreter were astounded at this statement. Our interpreter remarked that there were thousands of writers, singers, and painters, busily painting pictures all over Mexico, and inquired if all of them had entered the country on immigration or working papers, and if it was against the law for any artists to come to Mexico for a vacation. The Inspector was himself somewhat taken aback, but recovering himself stated that while it was true that they did not have immigration or working papers that actually they should have. Since we ourselves personally knew three artists who, on Tourist Cards only, were painting in Mexico and one of whom had been giving lessons to Mexicans and taking money for these lessons, besides writers who had certainly been writing articles for magazines published in Mexico, such as *Modern Mexico*[7] etc., and none of these people had been molested by the Government in any way, we were somewhat puzzled. We protested against what appeared to us to be discrimination, saying that if this were so it was not our fault but that of the Mexican Consulate in Los Angeles, but to no avail. I said that we were not working in Mexico, had taken no money in Mexico for doing any work done in Mexico nor had any intention of doing so; {UBC 14:10, 16} that we had, being writers, naturally taken some notes, mostly in the form simply of a day to day journal, or of the "jot it down" variety, possibly to be transformed later into a short story or some travel articles my wife had thought of writing on our return to Canada, and so on. Whether or not I said anything about having taken notes for my proposed preface I don't remember. The Inspector admitted that the taking of such notes could hardly be called "working" in Mexico. Nevertheless, he insisted that we *were* working, and demanded that we put up a bond of 500 pesos apiece and promise not to do any *more* work while we were in Mexico. We insisted that we had not done any work per se. He said that the bond would be necessary however, and gave us until Monday morning to produce the cash or the bond. This struck me as just possibly poetic justice in my case but our interpreter, Sr. Ford, was highly indignant and said that the Inspector had just remarked to him that actually, of course, this was more or less extra-official, and further that the Inspector said that if I had given the Chief of Migración in Acapulco 50 pesos to put in his pocket that the whole thing would have been settled there and that the head office would never have heard of it. And this I was to hear repeated many times: that the defection was the original defection of my failing to pay the "mordida." The British Vice Consul himself said this to me openly later on in this same office and further advised me that it would be as well to offer the Inspector 100 pesos or so, and in fact it was impossible to sit in that office as long as we did without witnessing with one's own eyes the truth of this.

But somewhere, during the foregoing conversation, we did something in all innocence that doubtless complicated matters still further. In the belief that the Inspector doubted that we were who {UBC 14:10, 17} and what we said we were, or perhaps because by this time we were beginning to doubt our own identity, I showed him a copy of my wife's novel, (The Shapes That Creep,[8] Scribner's, published January 14 of this year) my contract from Jonathan Cape of London, and also the telegram from Reynal and Hitchcock of New York re the acceptance of my book. The book had been finished in 1944 in Canada.

However, on this day, April 12, the Inspector said to our interpreter, Sr. Ford, that if we put up this bond or the same amount in cash by Monday morning that our papers would be returned and that we would be free to stay in Mexico without any further molestation until the expiration of our Tourist Cards which would be on June 10th.

It is, of course, necessary to obtain someone with property to underwrite such a bond and this was difficult to do on such short notice because I knew no one in Mexico City who could do this and furthermore the following week was Holy Week and on Monday all bonding companies would be closed. However, our witness and interpreter, Sr. Ford, was highly indignant at the procedure and offered (in spite of the fact that he was fully informed by myself of my previous error—if error it was—over just such a matter) to underwrite the bond himself, giving as security his own restaurant in Cuernavaca. He managed to obtain this bond for us and on the following Monday morning we presented it and asked for our papers. We were taken in to see the Chief of the department, Sr. Corunna, who was very insulting to my wife, ordered her out of his office, and refused to give us our papers. We had said that we wished to leave Mexico as soon as possible and Corunna, whose technique is to shout, demanded the date of our leaving. I explained that we wished to fly, as I did not feel the long train trip was good for my wife, {UBC 14:10, 18} and since Mexico was the port of exit when flying we could not possibly obtain our tickets without our papers. He then asked for the approximate date of our leaving and I told him as soon as we could possibly get reservations on the return of our papers. Calming down slightly he then told us to return again, as nearly as I can now recall, about a week later when we would be given our papers, which were now in order. He assured us finally that all was well, that there was nothing to be concerned about, that it was a matter of no importance.

It may well be asked at this point why I did not appeal to the British Consulate again for help, or my wife did not go to the American Consul, although she is, as I have said, by virtue of marriage to myself, also a British subject and equally has a right to apply to the British Consulate. She did not go to the American Consul because it was my status that had precipitated the situation and she had only been drawn into it on that account and the American Consul could do nothing for me, and therefore nothing, we thought, would be achieved by this action. I did not appeal again to the British Consulate, save on one more occasion, because by this time I had lost faith in their ability, or willingness, to assist me. And finally, because we were continually assured, by everyone in the Office of Inspección, despite the mental cruelty of this treatment, and right up to the very last moment, that our papers were in order, that they had absolutely nothing against us, and that there was nothing at all to worry about, and the various delays were simply a matter of Governmental red tape and slowness.

The day previous to our next appointment with Sr. Corunna, we had Sr. Ford telephone him long distance from Cuernavaca. Sr. Ford talked with Corunna, who assured him that our papers were there, {UBC 14:10, 19} perfectly in order, and that we could now come and get them any time we wished. Therefore on or about April 23 we went to Mexico City to get our papers, intending immediately upon receipt of them to make application for airplane reservations. Meantime I had wired my bank in Canada to send money to the Banco Nacional de Mexico in Cuernavaca, and also received word that my agent in New York had wired me part of my advance money on my book to Cuernavaca. By this time we were running short of cash, because of all the extra expenses, but it was impossible to obtain either the money from the bank or the money from my agent at the telegraph office, as I was without any identification whatsoever, the Government having it all, so I was therefore also unable to buy tickets to leave the country, although I had several hundred dollars between the bank and the telegraph office. Sr. Corunna once more refused to give us our papers, which, however, he repeated, were now in perfect order, and there was absolutely nothing for us to worry about. At that point, Mr. Hughes, the British Vice Consul, happened to come into the office on some other business and, since he was there, I did appeal to him again to try and get me some part of my papers, some identification I could present in order to get my money, since the telegraph office would send the money back to New York if I did not claim it within a day or two more. Mr. Hughes then spoke to Sr. Corunna on our behalf and Corunna assured him that everything was all right, that the only reason we were not given our papers that day was because they had once more been sent back to the office of Migración where they were on the desk of a man who was not in his office that particular day. He said that if we would return on Friday he would have the papers for us and that there was no further question or delay. We therefore {UBC 14:10, 20} made a definite appointment for Friday morning at 11:30 A.M., at which Mr. Hughes also volunteered to be present. Mr. Hughes further stated to us on that morning that it was he himself who had procured our release from Acapulco on the morning of Friday, April 9, from the office of Migración in Mexico City and had seen the telegram which had been sent. It seemed rather odd to us that it had been on Thursday, April 8th, that the office of Migración in Acapulco had said that they themselves were letting us go, but we made no great issue of this. Mr. Hughes further said that a week after they had first ordered my wife to return to Acapulco (on the promise that he or the Consul General would go that morning to the Migración) they had sent the office boy over who returned with the report that I was to be deported. This trouble shooter, it will be shown, at least told part of the truth.

On Friday, April 26th, therefore, we returned once more to Mexico City to keep our appointment with Mr. Hughes and Sr. Corunna. When we arrived, on time, after a journey of more than usual difficulty during which our transportation twice broke down and which had required four cars to get us there, Mr. Hughes was not there and my wife telephoned him while I sought an opportunity to speak again to Sr. Corunna. Mr. Hughes explained to my wife that he was too busy at the Consulate to keep his appointment with us but said, after my wife once more explained the need for identification so that I could get our money, and asked him for help, that he would telephone Sr. Corunna regarding this matter. He asked her to call him back in ten minutes, which she did. Mr. Hughes then said that he had spoken to Sr. Corunna, who told him that our papers were still on the desk in the department of Migración, and that the man who had them was once more not in his office, or rather {UBC 14:10, 21} was there, but had simply made up his mind not to do any more work that day. Mr. Hughes reiterated our plight, the necessity for some identification, etc., but Sr. Corunna replied that he was unable to give us anything. My wife appealed to Mr. Hughes to make some further effort to help us, or to find out what, if anything, was wrong, but he replied that he could do no more for us at all.

I then spoke to Sr. Corunna myself and was told to return the following morning. We returned once more to Mexico City the following morning and again I spoke to Sr. Corunna. After some long discussion during which he repeatedly shouted at me as usual in an insulting manner—I kept my wife out of the conversations so far as possible because of his savagely hysterical method of conducting them—he went, in the end, to the office of Migración and procured my old, cancelled passport for me. He further told me to come once more to Mexico City on the following Tuesday, April 30th, when the man who had our papers would be there without fail and they would then definitely be returned to us. However he once more demanded when we intended to leave, and I once more explained that we could not make reservations without these papers or buy tickets until I could get my money.

We returned to Cuernavaca and I received the money from the telegraph office that Saturday afternoon, just in time, as they were about to return it to New York. On Monday morning I went to the bank and received the money I had wired for to my Canadian bank.

On Tuesday morning we went once more to Mexico City and to the office of Inspección. The Inspector then informed us that it was necessary for us to come with him and have some photographs taken for our Immigration Papers. I think at this point my wife {UBC 14:10, 22} said, very understandably, that she didn't want Immigration papers but only wanted to leave Mexico, and if I did not say it myself it was only because I was engaged in keeping the temper which I knew it was their prime object for me to lose. I asked to be allowed to speak to Sr. Corunna, saying that he had promised to give us our papers without fail on that morning. This was refused. I then inquired why they suddenly had decided to change our papers and my wife asked to be allowed to go to the department of Turista to

obtain an interpreter who would explain more fully, since the Inspector was difficult to understand, our Spanish not being fluent,
when he became excited. This was also refused and we were taken
across the street where photographs were made under the assurance
that these photographs were for Immigration papers. In them I look
a criminal and my wife, (the Inspector rudely snatched off her hat at
the moment they were taking the photograph and her hair was disar-
ranged) like a mad-woman. Anyone seeing these photographs would
wonder not that we were to be deported but that such people could
be at large at all, which I take it is the impression such pictures are
designed to give. On the other hand, the strain was beginning to tell.
Meantime we had been told that these photographs would be ready
at 2 o'clock and that we must wait in the office of Inspección until
that hour. We were refused permission to go to lunch, or even to go
out for a cup of coffee, though I explained that as usual we had had
to leave Cuernavaca very early in the morning and my wife was fa-
tigued, or, in fact, to leave the office for any reason whatsoever, being
assured, continually, however, that Sr. Corunna would see me in a
moment and that everything was quite in order. At 2 o'clock my wife
went and got the photographs which the Inspector regarded as being
uproariously ridiculous and {UBC 14:10, 23} laughed at loudly and
long. At 2:30 the Inspector suddenly informed us, after Sr. Corunna
had left and the office was just closing for the day, that it would be
necessary for us to be at this office again on the morning of May 2
(May 1 being a holiday) at 12 noon, with all our luggage.

We protested that we could not understand the reason for this.
We wished to remain in Cuernavaca, where we had paid the rent of
our apartment, until leaving Mexico and did not wish to go to the
further expense of living in Mexico City in an hotel. Also we did
not understand why, after being assured, and the Consul likewise
assured, that all our papers were in order, that there was nothing
whatsoever against us, after we had put up the bond, etc. etc., why,
we repeated, we were thus abruptly commanded to bring our luggage to Mexico City. The Inspector became very angry and seized
my arm, said that if I did not understand I should come with him at
once to jail. He further abused us for not living in Mexico City.
When I explained that we loved Cuernavaca and wished to make the
most of living there until our departure, he demanded to know the
name of the hotel we were living at in Mexico City. He further said

that if we were not in the office on May 2, at 12 noon, with our luggage, he would come to Cuernavaca and put us under arrest. The office was then closed, everyone had gone, there was nothing we could do that day. Once more therefore we returned to Cuernavaca. That evening we saw Sr. Ford, who informed us that the bonding company, Central de Fianzas, S.A., Motolinia 20, Mexico City, had telephoned him long distance that afternoon to say that the government had cashed in our bond, and required him, Sr. Ford, to immediately make good the 1000 pesos or be jailed and his business confiscated. They had obviously cashed in this bond while keeping us waiting in the {UBC 14:10, 24} office insisting to us meanwhile that everything was quite all right. The following morning, May 1, Señor Ford received a telegram from the bonding company verifying the fact that the Government had cashed the bond the previous day. We have this telegram in our possession and I now quote it: Hoy hizo efectivas secretarias Gobernación fianzas esposos Lowry. Suplicámosle remitirnos inmediatamente un mil pesos importe garantias objeto no perjudicar intereses. Central de Fianzas, S.A.[9] We therefore paid Sr. Ford the 1000 pesos and we have his receipt for the money.

On the following morning, Thursday, May 2, we left Cuernavaca with our luggage in company with Sr. Ford, who was going to the bonding company to pay them the 1000 pesos, and went to Mexico City. We arrived two hours ahead of time in the hope of finding out what the difficulty was and making some last effort to present our case to the authorities in its proper light. Also another Mexican citizen, sympathetic with our case and a man of some influence, had offered to meet us there at 10 A.M. and act as interpreter and witness for us. We waited for him until 10:45 but he did not arrive. We then went into the Department of Turista, where we had left our luggage for the time being, and saw Sr. Buelna, the chief of that department. The time was short, as we had to appear in the office of Inspección with the luggage at 12 noon, but we explained our case and asked for help. At first he stated that he was unable to do anything at all since it was not in his department. However there were in his office at the time some American tourists who could not help hearing and in the end he kindly telephoned to someone in the office of the Sub-Secretary of the Interior and arranged for us to see the Sub-Secretario, Dr. Perez-Martinez, in a few minutes, when he would be finished with his conference with the {UBC 14:10, 25} Secretario. Dr. Martinez would, he said, at least give us a hearing. We went to the office of the Sub-Secretario, our names were sent in, we said the matter was urgent in the extreme, and waited over three quarters of an hour. By now it was nearly 12 o'clock and the Inspector came into the office and ordered us down to the office of Inspección. We explained that we were waiting to put our case before the Sub-Secretario, since we had been informed that he was the final authority in such matters. The Inspector again ordered us to come at once to the other office but still hoping for a hearing on our case we waited. We were eventually informed that the Sub-Secretario's secretary had refused to allow us to see Dr. Martinez or inform him that we were waiting, on the following peculiar grounds: that since the Americans treated the Mexicans like dogs, in fact worse than dogs since Americans were kind to animals, why should we not be treated like dogs ourselves?

My wife, while I remained there still in hopes of obtaining a hearing at the last moment, then went back to see Sr. Buelna to ask at least that we be given an interpreter and witness. Sr. Buelna at first replied that this was impossible, but in the end was kind enough to provide us with one. In company with this witness we went to the office of Inspección. Here we waited, and asked to see Sr. Corunna. We were informed that Sr. Corunna had his orders from the Sub-Secretario regarding ourselves and that it would be impossible for us to see him. We tried once more to find out why we were being treated in this extraordinary manner and at this time the Inspector became very angry and said that we had "said bad things about Mexico." This we denied—it could be called true only in the sense that we were objecting to this treatment now—stating as we had many times before that we loved Mexico and her people, {UBC 14:10, 26} which was so and still, despite this experience, is so, and that we still wished to discover what was wrong, still wished a fair hearing, as we felt sure that there must be some final misunderstanding worse than all the others, regarding our case. We were then told that we must accompany the Inspector to 113 Bucarelli, where we would be given our papers and allowed to go. Since we knew that this was (as it were) a jail and not a government office we protested. We asked for the British Consul. My wife for the American Consul. This was denied. We were told again that we were merely going to this 113 Bucarelli to get our papers, and were taken, under our protests, to this place. Once inside, we were forced to sign our names in a register.

We once more protested and demanded to see our Consuls, asking what their intentions were regarding ourselves, if they meant to deport us, and if so, why? The Inspector denied emphatically that we were to be deported. We then asked the Interpreter, who was visibly wilting, to please telephone our Consuls immediately and he replied that he would inform Sr. Buelna of the situation.

My wife and I were then taken into a small barred room where there were already two other men in bed and no lavatory facilities for my wife, there being only one inordinately filthy lavatory for all four of us, which had no door and opened directly off the room where we were kept. We were informed that we were being held incommunicado, and locked in. The Chief of this place, however, was extremely courteous and was distressed by the lack of privacy for my wife. He also sent out for some food for us, at our expense naturally, saying that we could not possibly eat the prison food. This was true: there was no prison food. Or if so they were not going to provide us with any free. Everyone here was {UBC 14:10, 27} kind and sympathetic, and the Chief finally opened up another sort of room for us beyond the first one and brought us his own blanket which, he explained, was clean. It should be mentioned however that our luggage had meantime been brought to this place and deposited in an outer room. Later we discovered that our wardrobe trunk had been broken open and half of my wife's clothes were missing and also our camera. This theft can only have taken place at the Turista office, or at 113 Bucarelli as there was no other opportunity. We had had nothing to eat all day and our food did not arrive until late afternoon, simultaneously with the Inspector. He gave us only five minutes to eat and then ordered us into a taxi in which we were taken to the railroad station and immediately put aboard the train. All further protestations or demands to see our Consuls were futile. Escape was impossible: the Inspector was armed.

Our train was a day coach with no berths and my wife and I were forced to sit up all that night and to stay within sight of the Inspector every minute. We both inquired of him several times the reason for this treatment. We asked if we were being deported and he replied definitely, no. He stated that his orders were to take us to Nuevo Laredo and there to give us our papers and allow us to cross the border into America alone and unmolested. We asked him why the bond had been cashed and he insisted that it had not been cashed. We then showed him the telegram proving that it had been cashed and he then said he had no knowledge of it at all. He, of course, had the tickets. He sat where he could watch our every movement, but apart from the sense of shame and embarrassment it caused, he did not actively molest or persecute {UBC 14:10, 28} us and indeed allowed us to eat our meals in the dining car by ourselves. The stewards, conductor and train men were however left in no doubt as to our status and we were by and large made to feel like criminals.

When the train arrived in Nuevo Laredo it was after midnight of the second night: there was a severe thunderstorm and all the lights in the train had gone out. We then asked him for our papers, which he had promised, and with that he began throwing our luggage out of the window of the train and as the train began to pull out (it was a very brief stop) ordered us to get out, and in fact my wife, who had got off on the wrong side of the train had to cross back through the train while it was moving, narrowly escaping a serious accident.

We then all proceeded in a taxi, with our luggage, to the Mexican Immigration Office, situated directly at the edge of the bridge across the Rio Grande River. There we waited again, watching the lights of Laredo on the American side of the bridge, while the Inspector conferred with a clerk whom he had ordered to write something on a typewriter. It was now about 2 o'clock in the morning. Presently this document which the clerk had been typing was presented to my wife to sign. When she read it she discovered it was a deportation order, stating that she admitted she was being deported for having broken the immigration laws of Mexico. Since they had all denied that we were being deported, and had never at any time given any reasons for this action, unless it was the Inspector's remark that we had said "bad things about Mexico," and we had never at any time been given a fair hearing, and it was absolutely untrue in her case that she had broken any immigration laws whatsoever, and moreover I understand that you have to be {UBC 14:10, 29} given 24 hours notice in writing of any such impending deportation, my wife refused to sign. The clerk became very distressed and begged her to sign, implying grave danger to her if she did not. I told her not to sign and stated that I had no intention of signing any such order either. The Inspector became violently angry and incredibly insulting and since he had a gun and she was being threatened in no uncertain terms I finally told her to sign: there was no choice and in order to avoid being separated from her I then likewise signed, but we both stated that we completely repudiated the charge and that we were signing the document under pressure. They then told my wife that since she was an American she was free to go, and could walk across the bridge, but the American Immigration office now being closed for the night I could not go until it opened in the morning. She refused to go without me and they then, curiously enough, urged her to go. I did not, by that time, trust their good will in the matter—if all this, why not ley fuga?[10]—and though I had at first told her to go I now felt it would be safer for her to remain with me. The Inspector then left, having given orders that we were both to be held in the office until the following morning. The clerk however, once the Inspector had left, took pity on my wife, who was utterly exhausted and in a condition of nervous shock, and arranged for us to go to an hotel, under guard, for a short time so that we might at least have a bath and a brief rest. At 5:30 A.M. another man from the Immigration office came to the hotel and took us back to the office.

Once more we waited in the Immigration Office. We had been informed the night before that the American Immigration opened at 7 A.M. and that at that time we would be allowed to go. Therefore, {UBC 14:10, 30} shortly after 7, we asked if we could now leave and cross into America. We were informed that it would be necessary for us to see the Chief of this Immigration Office and that he would be in between eight and nine o'clock. At nine o'clock the second in command of the office arrived and we presented our case to him as well as we could. We assured him that we were positive there had been some serious mistake, that we had been told over and over again that our papers were in order, that we had done nothing to provoke this peculiar treatment, that we had signed the paper the previous night under strong protest, and so on. He was courteous, but said we would have to wait for the Chief. Again we waited; a little later, while I was speaking to someone else in the office, my wife again spoke to the second in command. He informed her that the Inspector had left instructions that we were to be held there until he returned for us that morning. What disposition was then to be made of us we were never quite informed, but it was intimated that my wife was to be taken across the border by the Inspector and deported to America, since she had refused to leave without me the previous night. What they proposed to do with me I cannot make any sworn statement about, but the implication was not pleasant. We now once more briefly placed our case before this Sub-Chief, who took a most charitable and Christian attitude toward the whole thing. He very kindly allowed us to go and have a cup of coffee, saying he would speak to the Chief about us when he came in. These were moments of suspense. When we returned the Sub-Chief had spoken to the Chief and told us that we would be allowed to leave at once, as we requested, before the onset of the Inspector, who was of course by now long overdue, it being after 10 A.M. I believe that we convinced this Sub-Chief at least of our integrity, {UBC 14:10, 31} for he now returned our papers to us and made every effort to help us get away as quickly as possible. He procured a taxi for us, we were rushed through the Mexican customs without their even opening our luggage (while the Sub-Chief, as it were, stood guard outside, watching for the Inspector) and we swiftly crossed the bridge into America.

Our joy and relief at entering the United States were boundless.

While I was waiting in the office of Immigration in Laredo, Texas, as being a British subject my papers had to be inspected of course and my readmission card filled out, we saw the Inspector, who had apparently followed us right across the border, pass by in a towering temper, and that, I am glad to report, was the last we saw of this man. What he did or said I have no way of knowing. My papers being in order I was admitted that morning, Saturday the 4th of May, into the United States.

From Laredo we proceeded to Los Angeles, via Braniff, Continental and American Airlines, where we paid a visit to my wife's family and thence back here to our home in Canada. Immediately upon arriving in Los Angeles we consulted an attorney who advised us to prepare this statement and have it notarized.

To sum up our case my formulation of it would be something like the following:

That against my wife there was nothing whatsoever, that she had contravened no immigration regulations whatsoever, and that she was simply being made to suffer for being my wife. That against myself, setting aside such contributory factors as the 50 peso fine, there was against me fundamentally only the fact that I had entered a country that I was not permitted to enter without special {UBC 14:10, 32} permission of the Secretary of Gobernación, my defence for such action being that I was unaware that any such injunction

25

existed against me, and my proof that I was unaware of this injunction being in their own files, where it was stated that they had pursued an alleged unpaid fine against me until the year 1943 without being able to locate my address. If, since the injunction in question was placed in the files against me in September 1938, two months after I had left the country, they had made any communication at that early date re such an injunction to any second party such as a lawyer acting for my father in Mexico or Los Angeles who might know my address, I had to the very best of my knowledge and belief not been notified of this fact, and the proof that no such communication could have been made without double-dealing somewhere lay in the fact that the only further communication I ever received re my former visit to Mexico was in 1939 or 1940 when I heard something which is incompatible with any edict forbidding me to return: the Authorities claimed to believe I was still in the country. As before stated I then went to the acting Mexican Consul here in Vancouver and established the fact that I had left in July 1938. Furthermore, the Mexican Consulate in Los Angeles granted me my visa and Tourist Card although I told them I had been in Mexico before and waited the 24 hours as previously stated. And finally, if Sr. Corunna did not believe that I had acted in all good faith, why did he profess and reiterate for one month that all was well and my papers were in order and that we could depart unmolested? Why did they tell us the photographs were simply being made for Immigration papers, or insist until the last minute, at 2 o'clock in the morning at the border, that we would be given our papers back and allowed to leave? Why was it made impossible for us to obtain {UBC 14:10, 33} any basis for some proper accounting of what was being done with our 1000 peso bond, by giving us such short notice to leave our apartment in Cuernavaca, and by withholding Consular protection from us at the last moment by holding us incommunicado in 113 Bucarelli? Why, after having told the British Consulate I should be asked to leave the country, did they then require us to put up a bond, giving their solemn promise that if we did so we would be free to stay until the expiration of our Tourist Cards in June? Why, above all, if they sincerely wanted to get rid of us, didn't they simply let us go?

During the entire period of over 7 weeks we made every effort to cooperate with these Authorities in every way, to find out precisely what the difficulty was with a view, if possible, of straightening the matter out. But I was never told the precise reason for this injunction being issued in the first place, or allowed to present my case to anyone in authority who would listen to me. So far as the Gobernación was concerned, we were never given a fair hearing. In fact we were never given a hearing of any sort by them. Whatever their motives in my case for this protracted persecution of the nationals of two friendly countries there seems no excuse nor warrant: and as for my wife, an innocent American citizen, what was done to her amounts to a crime.

I swear this statement is to the best of my knowledge and belief absolutely true. {UBC 14:10, 34}

La Mordida

[I]

On Thursday, the seventh of March, 1946, between the new moon and the first quarter, the Wildernesses set out for Acapulco . . .

"Vámonos!"

Let us go!

Bong-bong-bong; once more the Wildernesses were off,[1] once more the three metallic, familiar, nostalgic taps on the back of the bus, then immediately away from a town he couldn't make out the name of on the sign, the sense of speed; Sigbjørn[2] and Primrose held hands, gay, how good was this sense of holiday again, though the country was rather dull; cactus, heat, mountains; millions of acres covered by dead trees of all kinds, not burned, just dead, the manzanita, in death, like a copper tree, mnemonic of arbutus at home, others seeming to be made of gun-metal: Wilderness can scarcely remember how the old road to Acapulco was, save that it was inconceivably more terrible, but he yet had that feeling that this old road still existed running parallel with the new paved one, and once more the feeling of himself travelling in a contrary direction, in this case with Bousfield and Stuyvesant,[3] was so strong, that it was as if, in every car that passed going toward Taxco and Mexico City, he saw himself sitting, flicking flashing past, sitting there in the careening bumping car, tortured, unable to move, save with the motion, in the inconceivable torture and anguish of that time; how strange it was to pass this way again, actually happy, and Primrose happy too, all that death and sorrow turned into a life of comradeship and laughter—

(Note: the antimonsoon of the past. the Bergson motif again.[4] the antimonsoon—the upper, contrary moving current of the atmosphere over a monsoon;—in this regard, while they are travelling {UBC 13:18, 35} toward Acapulco they are going in the same direction as the monsoon, toward the future; while static in Acapulco, because Sigbjørn instead of going ahead futilely worries about the past, in an attempt to discover its meaning in relation to the present, the monsoon reverses itself, Cuernavaca and Mexico City is now the direction of the monsoon, while Sigbjørn and willy nilly Primrose are

caught in the continually contrary moving current of its upper air in
the lofty Hotel Quinta Eugenia: perhaps this was what Eliot meant
when he said "approach to the meaning restores the experience"[;][5]
be that as it might, Sigbjørn had a sure prescience that for not having
profited by his previous lesson sufficiently he was going to have to
pay a terrible interest in terms of suffering upon its repetition; what
seemed to bear out this strange reasoning was that, oddly enough, in
spite of inflation and the time that had elapsed, and the fact that in
actual value it was a fifth as much, the alleged fine still remained precisely the same—50 pesos, only 10 bucks—a fine moreover that he
must have paid to the dishonest and corrupt—even under the great
Cardenas[6]—Mexican government, but where he made the mistake
doubtless was in thinking that what had been rendered (even if not
entered) to a dishonest Caesar,[7] had been equally rendered to God.)

Though even this trip had not started so well. In the first place
Wilderness had worried about Dr. Amann's advice.[8] The ghost of
Mexico had indeed been laid, poor Fernando[9] might be dead, but the
knowledge of his death had won the peace of his hands. Was it not
indeed time to go, to return and finish the rebuilding of their house
in Canada, the thought of which standing there so forlorn, their pier
threatened by storms and floating logs, with no one to guard it, unless indeed Jimmy[10] would, the thought of their little {UBC 13:18,
36} home and the pull it exercised had almost been too much for
him; but two factors had halted him, the fact that there was still no
news of his book, while it did not hinder him from still working on
his poems, nonetheless acted as an inhibitory factor, both from the
fact of its discouragement, and the fact that should good news
come—which by now he scarcely hoped for—he would undoubtedly
have to concentrate, in one way or another, upon the book again,
when he returned to Dark Rosslyn[11] he wanted a clear field: this was
doubtless an excuse, but stronger than that was again the wish to
make Primrose's holiday still as it were complete, a success: in the in-
terrogative stage they had been drinking too much again, particularly himself, and in Acapulco was the sea, an image of health and
escape. Nonetheless there had once more, just as when they started
for Oaxaca, the same convulsion, the same effort for him to make the
trip, there was the spectre of drinking now as then, but now as then
he was determined Primrose should enjoy herself; and in a sense, just
as with Oaxaca, it was already beginning to represent a triumph;
how different indeed was this from their jittery setting out two days

ago from Cuernavaca, now Sigbjørn's hands trembled scarcely at all,
even though they had been both drinking at Taxco, and last night at
Iguala, at Taxco where Helen and the Italian,[12] whom they had not
been able to find, had thought they were the ideal couple—as indeed
were they not?—and who, as Dr. Amann has pointed out, had such
freedom as they—did they not have everything? But it had been different two days before setting off. (Again there was the problem of
the shaking hands.) Sigbjørn's hand would not tremble all the while,
however: for example he would light a cigarette with ease when they
were once in the bus, actually cupping a match for Primrose: he
thought it was the shaking of the {UBC 13:18, 37} bus itself that
must help in some mysterious way, just as previously he had remarked how its bumping helped the liver: a Mexican bus, like a
horse, or the sea (and they would have plenty of that at Acapulco)
was actually a therapeutic measure. The fresh air flowing in the window, (though it is true now the windows were shut against the
dust)—a psychological point: Sigbjørn likes to sit at the back, Primrose in the front, etc. But no, (harking back to the beginning of their
adventure) when they stopped at Ixtla, he lit a cigarette with ease.

But (two days before, going to Taxco) approaching Taxco itself
he had dreaded, for that reason, the moment he should have to sign
his name at an hotel. He dreaded also—in a manner that recalled a
poem of Wordsworth's[14]—the terrible final moment that the bus
would stop and he would have to get out.

Would he be able to move at all? Or just sit rooted to the spot.
Meantime he was in terror that with the bumping of the bus the
bottle (for they had a half a litre of bulk habanero left from last
night, in the rack) above would break. What could he do in such a
situation? He could do nothing but goggle: he would not be able to
utter a sound (like that man coming back from Yautepec had done
trying to stop the bus)—He was in terror of being laughed at or despised—why? He knew too, but that did not help. That was what
made it impossible sometimes even to go into a cantina, when he
was dying for a drink.

Finally Taxco (or say, any other stop, Cuautla) became to his mind
simply a synonym for another drink.[16] But here again he was afraid.
What would Primrose say or do? Jesus. He was afraid of stopping
but then they had to stop so that he could have a drink so that he was
afraid of not stopping: but then again he was {UBC 13:18, 38} afraid
of having a drink because (although they drank together) he was—at

*From
Cuernavaca, the
road drops
steadily to the
tropical little
village of*[13]

Puente de Ixtla

*and then climbs
upward and
onward*

*through
marvellous
vistas of
mountain
scenery where
the soil changes
in amber hues*[15]
*from delicate
amethyst to rich
copper shades.*

*About two
hours out of
Cuernavaca, the
fabulous*

such junctures at least—afraid of Primrose. He was afraid of stopping and of not stopping, which had become somewhat his feeling, albeit the problem seemed at times solved, by now about drinking.

old mining town[17]

Nevertheless when they had arrived at Taxco (that was already beginning to seem a nostalgic memory), they had walked a mile up a cobbled hill, entered an hotel that was half a cinema (though he remembered it out of the horrid past as a pensione) where he signed his name with a steady hand. Which did not mean that he was not afraid of himself! Nor that he was not, or had not been then, in some mysterious way (he could not explain it to himself) afraid of going to Acapulco. They were stopping in Taxco for the fiesta in Tecalpulco,[18] a native village several miles out, a mile from the main highway, built on top of a mountain. It had been hard getting there and he had found himself often unable to pronounce the word: Tecalpulco, and in fact often got it mixed up with Acapulco. He had so disgraced himself in his own eyes (which was not, however, a hard thing to do) (he did it on an average of about fifty times a day) that he had proposed they turn back without going to Acapulco, turn back to Cuernavaca, without even going to acal-tecal-pulco. But the entreaty and disappointment on Primrose's face decided him. He would go through with it, come what may, and cost him what it might. Though why was he—apart from purely practical considerations of course—always springing to the conclusion that it was going to cost him so much, so transcendentally much? They went to Tecalpulco and toward sunset watched eight people, three of them in masks that must have depicted Spaniards, with long cruel faces, {UBC 13:18, 39} thin lips, black beards of papier mache, and long turned-up round thin noses, bright red and red circles on cheeks, the men with tall headdresses of many-colored fringed paper, with objects like fat horns in peaked caps, all wearing short red cotton pants, and cotton hose imitating tights, and all likewise carrying three feet machetes, and one mounted upon a pink stuffed horse, with which they duelled in pantomime, fight a clashing slashing dance. Spaniards vs. Indians: while Americans, a pretty arrogant-looking girl v. chic, and a man watched from the stone steps, laughing. Even here (though they were beginning to enjoy themselves) in Tecalpulco, there had been the fear that a boy sitting on the ground in front, while they were dancing the Santiago with clashing knives and horned masks and who had turned around suddenly at some sinister equivocal juncture was going to say

34

to Sigbjørn something like: "This means you!" And a little later, with the sun further down, there had been the fear, unspecified, of the devil dancers, the huge dark red face with fangs and tongue hanging out over his chin and his expression of evil lechery and terror, and who made such an impression on Sigbjørn he even wrote him into the Valley of the Shadow of Death.[19] And the child too, with the mask of the skull, and the bones drawn in purple ink on a white cotton jersey. And what, in this dance of the forces of good and evil—for Sigbjørn felt the dance must symbolize something of that sort—was the significance of perhaps the most sinister figure of all, a strange figure who danced round and round and round, not joining the others, dressed in battered clothes, and carrying a small stiff-stuffed animal like a little fox, or ferret, a man like a tramp, all shuffling amicably and secretly however in the dust? But returning to Taxco in the taxi they had held hands, (this part might come later, be actually suggested by their holding hands in {UBC 13:18, 40} the bus) Primrose was enjoying herself again and didn't realise what he was going through (neither did Sigbjørn, for that matter, probably realise it) through the wild twilight, green, clear to the west, but with gigantic black and gold and red clouds coming up from the east. Lluvia.[20] It was not the rainy season but there was a little rain. What a stormy sky! Wild black wind blowing up dust and gravel and a line of fire in the mountains. In the darkness, clouds still dirty white, still illumined by sunlight, so high were they. The city of Taxco was already in darkness and twilight, but that cloud was like a tower that went straight up into the sky above the city, yes, like a great white tower. Then they had climbed the narrow cobbled streets haunted by Alarcon and Hart Crane,[21] and himself, with their soft refrain of silver, and the terrific white cloud above, back up into the room in the Hotel y Cine Casa Grande. One enormous high room in the huge old place had been cut into 6 small ones with walls only 10 ft. high and a ceiling 30 feet above and no windows, even in the rooms on the street. Separated from them by only a partition, it had been difficult to make out if the couple next door were making love or no: laughing and giggling, and a noise as if the man were brushing the sheet with a clothes brush, then more soft laughter. Occasionally glut-glut noises of washing. But no other sounds. It was mysterious. They were very modest. But Sigbjørn and Primrose had been more so. Yet it had been very sweet. They had wandered round the dark bell-haunted cobbled town,

Taxco, the fabulous old mining town, clings, with shining tentacles of silver to the picturesque mountain side. In this colonial village where nothing has changed in the past two hundred years, you will wander through cobbled streets and visit the shops of silversmiths and weavers, admiring and puchasing choice examples of the beautiful Mexican handicrafts. If you have made the side trips to the caverns and the pyramid, you will want to spend the night in one of Taxco's excellent hotels.

(otherwise you will probably continue to Acapulco the same day)

drunk half their litre of habanero, and later slept in each other's arms. A sudden thunderstorm that night had awakened them; rain that poured off the alleys of the roofs like waterfalls and down into the court; how the rain banged and thrummed! The next morning {UBC 13:18, 41} they had come on by a crowded Flecha Roja,[22] the second class, known as the Flecha—and how Sigbjørn loved these buses, just as much as he loathed and feared the trains, though when it came it had been so crowded they couldn't get aboard; the driver kindly made a place for them, by making two peasants stand up—but how gaily and kindly it was done (N.B.)—and a man gave Primrose both his hands around her arms and pulled her up—the bus became less crowded after they had stopped once more below the steep mule path leading to Tecalpulco, where the fiesta was still going on; they came

Iguala, a tropical town, famous for its tamarinds

to Iguala, hot, nondescript, and down in the flat lands. It was in Iguala indeed, the town of tamarinds, that they really had begun to have "fun" (horrible word) and Sigbjørn began to feel justified. Their holiday was in full swing. First of all, there had been again, the question of the hotel, (they tried as usual to put up at a cheap one) which finally bankrupted, if nothing else, all belief. Tremendously long and spacious, and the lantern-jawed man who was always eating but whom one could never be absolutely sure was the manager, or not, the pang of fear—why?—when lantern-jaw had gone out and come back with a man like a policeman, to go on eating—the last they saw of him was cleaning his teeth into the garden. Goats, doves, and ex-cusados.[23] The goat bleating in the evening and Byzantine bells. The bells came from the church opposite, where they went the next day, the previous evening having been spent in their hotel room drinking habanero and making love. It was a huge horrible beautiful church being whitewashed to look like a Christmas cake, a white churrigero-tiose nightmare in the burning sun.[24] And whitewashed with such love too—its beauty of old stones and pure stars on the cupola being whitewashed away. Jesus, however, {UBC 13:18, 42} one reverently felt, would have liked it. The two main doors in the hull of the church were used as a kind of through road to the market. In short this church from port to starboard was like a main thoroughfare. The world rolled south-south-eastward against motionless xopilotes high above a man with ribs showing, dying it seemed in the churchyard, where there was likewise a dying dog. The workers high on the scaf-folding were knocking out all the old stones and somewhere, near at

and citrus fruits

hand, young, going full blast, terrifically loud boogie-woogie.

Inside the church—Sigbjørn and Primrose were always sorry for some reason to leave a Mexican church—a man telling his beads shooed out another dog, while another man, very devout and sweet, was praying—as had not then, as did not for some reason, even at this moment, since there was an image of her in the bus, poor heretical Sigbjørn—to our Señora of the Sacred Heart, patron Saint of Dangerous and Desperate Causes—[25]

"Isn't this fun."

"Isn't this fun."

And now they were going from Iguala to Acapulco. Sigbjørn drew his wife closer, she shivered all over with enjoyment, and they sat holding hands: they were sitting at the back, which was not self-ish of Sigbjørn this time, but simply circumstance. Sigbjørn made a note that if he could possibly bring himself to it they would shift seats to that other front seat not over a wheel. For as a matter of fact, in Iguala, Sigbjørn had made a sacrifice of his love for the back, of sitting where they could not be seen, while Primrose was changing some money, had ensconced himself in the front: but the seat was broken, and so they were now sitting at the back. But Sig-bjørn had at least {UBC 13:18, 43} made the gesture to that end and perhaps this was by no means so insignificant as it sounded.

The fact was, it was Sunday, and there were not, surprisingly, very many people in the bus going to Acapulco, Sunday being the day people mostly came back from that resort to Mexico City. There were some men with rolls of fat behind their collars, wearing that peculiarly funereal black that reminded Sigbjørn of Sunday chapel in England, and an Indian woman, rather fat, but very dignified, with grey hair in two braids, exquisite gold earrings, gold rings on her fat little hands, dressed in a long sleeved high necked long skirt to the ground of dark blue velvet brocade. With her was a thin little Indian woman in clean cotton print and rebozo; these people were both gay and full of conversation. The men in black suits sat silent and upright. A little girl continually changed seats. The driver, like nearly all Mexican drivers, drove swiftly and expertly: the conductor, in the broken seat up front, leaned over his shoulder. Sigbjørn and Primrose sat holding hands, quite private and happy in the back of the bus.

and then winds through wild mountainous country across the Rio Balsas to

"Isn't this fun," she repeated.

Mexcala.

The scenery, however, was not much, though it was growing more mountainous. They had, in fact, already crossed the Balsas river and were entering the Xopilote Canyon. The Vulture Canyon. Three

*After Mexcala,
the highway
enters the
impressive
Xopilote
Canyon where
the road is
flanked by
enormously
high*

brown naked boys were bathing in the lovely river Mexicali, if that indeed was its name. But it was the last of the loveliness, at least for the time being. To say the very least. For it was as if blight, as far as the eye could reach, had smitten this terrible land. It was as if indeed the devil himself, he with the huge tongue, passing {UBC 13:18, 44} through these parts (doubtless also, if one believed the papers that recently had been speaking of Acapulco as the centre of every kind of vice,[26] on the way to Acapulco) had caused it to be shrivelled up and parched, and forever, yet fantastically dead, every green thing, every shoot, every tree, in his infernal path. Only demons could live here surely, though it seemed that people did. There were huts, every now and then, along the way, and people had even climbed high into these lands of the damned to place, upon some high blasted rock, the name *Alemán*. And there it was again, Alemán; moralización.[27] Sigbjørn tried to imagine the expedition, the actual occasion of the inscribing of the name up there, but it was impossible to, as difficult for imagination to give form to as one of those half formed velleities that come to you before you sleep, when you find you have said something, quite nonsensical aloud. Yes, people lived here. Yet only the bus, and the new road, before them, white and sure, winking, on occasion tunneling through all this damnation, seemed alive, possibly because

rocky cliffs.

the latter was new, or newly paved. Then, what appeared the old road would turn up to the left running along the side of a hill to a point where it was washed out by the rains. Sigbjørn, trying to shut out the horrible memories of this old road, pulled a letter from his pocket that he had found in the letter box just before they left their tower in Cuernavaca, and had only glanced at hastily. Sigbjørn was afraid of mail, and rarely read a letter right through, but this letter, which was

*When the
canyon emerges
into*

from Noxon,[28] the people they had stayed with after their fire, seemed to have something nice in it so he read it again. {UBC 13:18, 45}

"Difficult and impossible you have always been . . . But you are one of the few creatures on earth that will grow better, rather than worse, as they grow older." Better rather than worse! Just think of that. Just to think of old Bill actually sitting down to write it. Probably he had been a bit tight. But still, when Wilderness remembered how difficult it was for him to write any letter at all, the fact that Bill had done that seemed like a fabulous tribute. Better rather than worse . . . "You are a good man," he said, too. That was something. That was what Bill thought: or what Bill thought he thought after sinking a pint of bad Scotch. Still, that image of him, as a good man,

who would grow better rather than worse, was at least sufficiently
strong that it quivered somewhere. Good old Bill. Sigbjørn put the
letter, which was rather illegible, back in his pocket. He had remembered that it was Sunday and that they had drunk all their habanero
last night. Thinking of Bill writing the letter had made him thirsty,
and he wondered whether the liquor stores would be open in Acapulco or not. And he was afraid they would not . . .

"My bracelet's so beautiful!"

"Do you like it, darling. I'm so glad you do."

He had bought one that had been stolen to replace one that had
been bought honourably but later stolen—a morality that would
never do—

Follows a conversation about the bracelet,[29] and the scene that led
up to its purchase: a description of the bracelet, either in dialogue,
or interspersed or both—Sigbjørn fears it had been stolen, both fear
this, but Sigbjørn says nothing of the fact that he fears this may
bring bad luck; like Dostoievsky, he was educated enough not to be
superstitious:[30] he was {UBC 13:18, 46} superstitious however.
What was the meaning, for example, he suddenly thought, of seeing
the scrap of newspaper, Tumba No. 7 in the street in Iguala (or perhaps we should put this forward to Chilpancingo)—it had been like
a message, not out of that grave at Monte Alban in Oaxaca, where
they had made some important new discoveries (specify these) but
as if Fernando himself were trying to get in touch with him. Yes, he
was indeed superstitious, so much so that when a fortune teller had
told him the new moon was lucky for him, every time a full moon
approached he expected disastar.[31]

> Notes re Tomb: Keeping one foot on the piece
> Marvellous jewels
> of paper in the gutter he read: Maravillosas Joyas
> found in IInd century tomb.   Objects of
> Halladas en una Tumba del Siglo II. Objetos de
> jade, shell and pearls, in a sepulcre of
> jade, concha y perlas, en un sepulcro de
> adolescents in Monte Alban.
> Adolescentes, en Monte Albán. El Sábado 23 de
> Febrero

(that was, Sigbjørn thought, a fortnight ago, at the last quarter of the
moon, and not so very long after they had left Oaxaca themselves) en

la plaza central de Monte Albán, el ingeniero Jorge R. Acosta, actual director de los trabajos de exploración y reconstrucción de aquella zona arqueológica, realizó el descubrimiento más importante conseguido hasta ahora desde que fué hallada la tumba número 7 en enero de 1932.[32] This was a strange link, he thought,—was Fernando trying to communicate with him? a kind of warning they were to be paid back, rather like the investigation of Tutankhamen's tomb,[33] for investigating it? Exploraba el ingeniero Acosta non túnel[34] . . . It seemed a ridiculous thought, but then why did this have to turn up here? There was a photograph of a jade "pectoral," in the shape of a demon's head with a high patina, a single horn on the top of the head, four ears, with earrings on the lower pair, white eyes with converging irises, and white teeth with tusks at the corner of {UBC 13:18, 47} the mouth, gleamed up at Sigbjørn out of the gutter from the dark frightening mask, and he thought of the dancers at Tecalpulco. This of course was rather the sort of thing that tended to produce itself in Mexico, in one form or another, the moment you made the mistake of thinking yourself at home. "—y hay gasolina en esta capital"—there was gasoline in the capital, the fragment of Excelsior also more comfortably informed him. And as if following his former train of thought it also announced: "Alarma en Chilpancingo por la Meningitis."[35] So Chilpancingo was far from being the peaceful dead place it seemed. Justified alarm existed among the inhabitants, and what was more, at this very moment, for the paper was dated March 4. Yes, the local Coordinated Services of Salubriousness had even dictated the temporary closing of the school of Ayotzinapa. But it was not this that worried him so much and made him look forward to leaving Chilpancingo as soon as possible, as that he had suddenly remembered that he had invested, in the Valley of the Shadow of Death,[36] his character Yvonne's child by a first marriage with "la Terrible Meningitis Cerebrospinal," and that he had caused that child, in a paragraph that made play with the number 7, seven years before the book began, while at the same time he remembered that it was 7 years almost to the day since he had last left Acapulco himself with Bousfield. What a passion for order in all things there seemed to be, down to the minutest detail. No wonder one pined in wars against ignorance and superstition. Nevertheless, if he were to be honest, this was the way he thought. And the way he thought was the way of madness. The thought was almost as relaxing as that of the imminent end of the world. But how many other people really thought like this? And my God, what if it {UBC 13:18, 48} were really true, that is, what if there were "something in it." (this is very important, leads into analysis of superstition) This thought was almost worse in itself than Victor Hugo's[37] "Oh, si la conjecture antique était fondée, si le rêve inquiet des mages de Chaldée, L'hypothèse qu'Hermès et Pythagore font, Si ce songe farouche était le vrai profond." Should the old nightmare be the truth indeed! Terrible creatures that live in the dark, the flattened head of tiger and serpent, the heads on which the divine heel has pressed. Were that to be truth that those are, They whom we call the damned in their torment! Was he, in a sense, like one of those on whom the divine heel has pressed? From which it was but a step to the famous: "Toute faute qu'on fait est un cachot qu'on s'ouvre." The sin committed is a gaol opened . . . The murderer, when death taps on his shoulder, and awakes him, terrified, recognises the prison, built by his crime, crawling after him. Tiberius is a rock, Sejanus a snake. From which it was but a step to his Afrique aux plis infranchissables, O gouffre d'horizons sinistres, mer des sables, Sahara, Dahomey, lac Nagaïn, Darfour . . . Paysages de lune où rôde la chimère,—in those terrible poems where Hugo speaks of nature as having passed beyond reason and man, from which, it having been settled by negro slaves in a familiar jungle atmosphere, it was but a step to Acapulco. WORK THIS OUT.— inadequate because, always changing his mind outside like a professional naturalist who sets off in pursuit of a rare butterfly, only to find several even apparently rarer ones hovering before him and eluding him, and no sooner is he aware of this than he has lost them all by trying to memorize the spot where, upon a hussock over which he has just tripped, a particularly {UBC 13:18, 49} rare gentian was growing, (and all of this rendered even more unsatisfactory and exhausting by the fact that the professor is on a holiday in which he had proposed never to look at a butterfly or a flower save simply exofficio to enjoy his surroundings) doubtless this, in Sigbjørn's case, was a kind of greed—in a word he wanted to eat the scenery, and it was meaner still, for though he did not perhaps want it in the sense that he would actually write about it, he wanted no one else to have it. He was, he felt, a spiritual dog in the manger. However that he felt like this at all was a step forward; perhaps he was not finished and would be able to write again after all.

Short analysis of significance of 13 perhaps in dialogue. The fear
perhaps is not that 13 is, generally speaking, or necessarily, an unlucky number: the fear seems to inhere in the shadowy feeling that
when you see the number 13, that is before the event, or spill the
salt, that some spirit, malevolent, out of spite, or friendly, so that it
may be construed as a warning, has caused you in some inexplicable
fashion, to become aware of it at that particular moment, or to do it:
in this case both were concerned with Judas; but if there were no invisible supernatural agency connected with such superstitions they
would presumably not exist. This of course does not hold so good
when the superstitious one is made aware, after the event, that there
have been 13 at table, or in the plane. At all events, then, the thing
having happened, he would scarcely feel apprehension. But even
then it may seem that it is as if the spirit is merely "signing off" as if
to say, "I tried to point out that there were 13 but you wouldn't listen to me." {UBC 13:18, 50}

N.B. Referring to note p. 48. "It was an order of death, anti-
organic," as Thomas Mann had very properly pointed out,[38] in the
case of his snowflakes, "the living principle shuddered at this
perfect precision." This underlying order of seven was every bit
as god-awful as the order of six in the hexagon of the snowflakes.
Let there be a rebellion, by all means, of snowflakes and Wildernesses

Note: Some notes from the Haitian experience, if not indeed all of
it, might be used (perhaps Sigbjørn attempts suicide again in Acapulco with codeine) but certainly "The Sea rushing through your
soul in great cold waves of anguish" is a wonderful end to a chapter,
and the passages re "Horror" and dreadful importance of sex at
such moments, boiling erections . . . Horror of reading magazines,
particularly with pictures of happy and pretty women, all invested
with this boiling, this cold rushing of disastrous, important, vascular remorse.[39]

> Afrique aux plis infranchissables,
> O gouffre d'horizons sinistres, mer des sables,
> Sahara, Dahomey, lac Nagaïn, Darfour . . .
> Paysages de lune où rôde la chimère,
> Où l'orang-outang marche un bâton à la main
> Où la nature est folle et n'a plus rien d'humain.

Africa with thy unpenetrable folds,
Depth of horizons sinister, sea of sand,
Sahara, Dahomey, Nagain, Darfour . . .
Landscapes in moonlight where fear prowls,
The outang walks erect, holding a club,
Nature has passed beyond reason and man.

Oh! si la conjecture antique était fondée
Si le rêve inquiet des mages de Chaldée
L'hypothèse qu'Hermès et Pythagore font,
Si ce songe farouche était le vrai profond . . .
O ces êtres affreux dont l'ombre [est] le repaire
Ces crânes aplatis de tigre et de vípère
L'ours rêveur noir, le singe, effroyable sylvain,
Ciel bleu! s'il etait vrai que c'est là ce qu'on nomme
Les damnés, expiant d'anciens crimes [chez l'homme].

{UBC 13:18, 51}

Oh, should the ancient guess be then a fact
The awful dream of the Chaldean priest
The thought of Hermes and Pythagoras
Should the old nightmare be the truth indeed [. . .]
Terrible creatures that live on the dark
The flattened head of tiger and serpent
The heads on which the divine heel has pressed
The bear in gloom, the ape, man of the awful forest,
O heavens! Were that to be truth, that those are
They whom we call the damned, in their torment.

Toute faute qu'on fait est un cachot qu'on s'ouvre
Tout bandit, quand la mort vient lui toucher l'épaule
Et l'éveille, hagard, se retrouve en la geôle
Que lui fit son forfait, derrière lui rampant;
Tibère est un rocher, Séjan dans un serpent.

The sin committed is a jail opened
The murderer, when death taps on his shoulder,
And awakes him, terrified, recognizes the prison
Built by his crime, crawling after him,
Tiberius is a rock, Sejanus a snake.[40]

The wolf, he was my father.

To the hunting went
With the youth the man;
From wood and mountain;
Once when they came back
The wolf's lair was empty:
For many years,
Lived the youth
With the wolf in the wild forest
They also
Were much hunted.

Der Jäger viele . . .
Many of the hunters
Fell to the wolf,
In flight through the forest
The wild one drove them;
But I was parted from my father
I lost his tracks
The skin of a wolf,
Only did I find in the forest.

And now the offspring of the she-wolf
Thou bringest to the feet of thy wife.[41]

—WAGNER

{UBC 13:18, 52}

open country
once again at
Chilpancingo
(Ciudad Bravo)

They enter open country.

Then Chilpancingo and the busman says: "En Chilpancingo es nada."

There was, as the bus driver said, nothing in Chilpancingo, even though it was the capital of the state of Guerrero; it was not indeed

the picturesque
state capital of
Guerrero[42]

any longer called Chilpancingo, but Ciudad Bravo. But there were two strong and horrible memories of the place, one while going to Acapulco with Bousfield, and one while going to Acapulco with Wynn and Gilda. On both these occasions he had stayed the night: brief memories of this. The church had been whitewashed and then tinted pink and white, garlands appliqued on like confection. There was a fine old fresno tree by the church. It was very hot. White cathedral, brown policemen, and poor oranges. Though the bus driver had said there would be an hour's stop, Sigbjørn was nervous about leaving the camión too far behind and Primrose set forth into the square for better oranges. (N.B. He is also nervous about the policeman. Also, because the story is at the moment at a standstill this is probably a good opportunity to get in some dramatic exposition re Wynn and Gilda[43]—this leading, via 13 to Riley and Peggy)[44] It was at this point perhaps that Sigbjørn noted, in the gutter, a copy of the paper, Excelsior, or just a fragment of it with the news about Tumba no. 7 and is in an inexplicable way, disturbed. It comes to him suddenly that Fernando is trying to warn him about something. And when he got into the bus he now noticed, for the first time that its number was 13. In spite of Sigbjørn's hanging round the bus like this, they are still in the back seat of the bus when they start and not in the front ones. "Vámonos!" bong-bong-bong; the familiar taps. Sigbjørn, who had however made the {UBC 13:18, 53} great effort of obtaining two bad tangerines for his wife, now wondered if no. 13 *the highway* could be construed as a lucky number. This is a bad number for a sailor: but it is not because of this that he doesn't like it, but because it is Stan's number[45] (mention Stan here) Number of Judas.[46]

"That car's going to Mexico City tomorrow morning."

"Well, I am not taking it."

Recapitulate conversation outside 7 Seas with R. 8 years before,[47] (because the story is, at the moment, at a standstill this is probably a good opportunity to get in some dramatic exposition re Wynn and Gilda—this leading via 13—to Riley and Peggy) also cite incidents leading up to it: at the "Consul's" house, P - R, and also the anguish in that hotel—he could not remember its name[48]—where the bus was now steadily climbing in a tempestuous scenery of wild wet green and full of waterfalls and this scenery, which was something like Oaxaca, he did not remember at all: How could it be? Were they taking another route? But no, they were keeping now much to the old road which had been paved—that's all—in fact, he remembered *continues* the thousands of workers working on it raising their shovels when he had come back with the d.t.'s with Stuyvesant and Bousfield, where the routes were not identical, the old road would turn up to the left running along the side of a hill for a while and then crumbling at some point where it had been washed out by the rains. There was something genuinely upsetting to Sigbjørn about this scenery that now sailed into view, beautiful, tempestuous, wild, green, gorgeous, full of waterfalls, and so in order to forget it he started to whistle.

"It happened in Monterrey . . ." It was not a tune he liked particularly but it had for some reason {UBC 13:18, 54} come into his head. Primrose whistled too, in harmony. How the two of them loved to sing. (elaborate this) He had his guitar with him too—left behind in Cuernavaca, a nostalgia for his evening with Dr. Amann came over him. "We must accept our damnation . . ." "Perhaps your sin is no more than a grey hair in God's eyebrow." It struck them as bad manners to be whistling an American tune so they whistled Las Mañanitas.[49] (Quote this song, for its theme of the little birthdays can relate with rebirth: in fact, even at the end, they might hear,[50] from Laredo, Las Mañanitas being played, from the other side of the Rio Grande) Then it struck that perhaps it would be considered bad manners to be whistling at all, so they stopped, and once more he had to be absorbed in the scenery. While nothing convinced him more certainly that he wasn't anyway, nothing could make him wish more that he was not a writer. His soul would yearn out after it, he could never have too much of it—and it was not easy to see too much of it from the rather low and narrow bus windows—his heart danced to see Primrose's pleasure in it, yet it always left him with a queer feeling of dissatisfaction, and the more "beautiful" it was, the more this mysterious dissatisfaction, as though a word or a clause which was continually escaping from it, the only word that would describe it, was, in spite of being the only one and his futile pursuit of it, he knew, inadequate, and that this breathless mental pursuit impaired the scenery in his eyes, as it might upon paper injure a passage: or the scenery was like a half-finished poem, a sonnet say, of which nature was the octet, but the sestet which he should write and which was his response and comment upon the other, never could be written, or was simply banal. And this {UBC 13:18, 55} happened not once, but hundreds of times, with every new vista, round every new corner, so there were as it were[51] hundreds of these poems clamouring to be finished in his mind, and no sooner would he begin to get hold of one, than another would claim his attention: and what made it worse was that all would be—or seemed to be—lost, for in striving to make the response he would not even have absorbed a modicum of what nature had visually to offer. Finally the pleasure to be obtained was simply vicarious, through Primrose's eyes: so long as she was entranced, so was he. So long as it was she shared his response, or more properly speaking, did not share it, but as it were had it ecstatically *for* him, that his mind could not do much better than "Wild" "Tempestuous" "mountainous" or "it would make a good golf links"—and this had the result that occasionally, as some green tower of dreams rose up in the craggy rainswept distance, he would not look at it at all, "out of spite" as Dostoievsky might have said[52]—did not seem to matter so much. He wondered what Amann would have said to all this. Surely his thought was not without bearing upon the profound wisdom that inheres in the ethic of humbly living for others, as psychiatrists bid us do: unselfishness is a technique to prevent us going mad. (True that was psychologically speaking but a stage in our adjustment to a society that was itself insane and neurotic, but that was another story, especially since its self-destruction now extended to the whole world. There was however something relaxing in imagining the end of the world) From an artistic point of view it might account, on the one hand, for the principle of self-preservation, and the wisdom, in a painter who chooses to be non-objective. Something of the kind might {UBC 13:18, 56} also account for the extreme loathing which certain great novelists are said to entertain for natural scenery. (This needs writing, is merely suggestive of what must be done) And as for his own feelings of inadequacy and frustration, did not that extend, to all nature, all creation, even if there they were only blind impulses, for better or worse, must it not be something akin to that very feeling of frustration and irritation in the face of one's own self expression, and at the same time the need to express, that brings the miracle about, from the flower that rebels against the number of its petals, to the animalcule that divides itself? Yes, yes—for on the other hand Sigbjørn felt that were he alone he would go mad—just as he had been—had he not?—mad before, those eight years ago. But surely all this scenery was new: the old road, the road of the Viceroys, did not go this way. Or could it be that then he had not noticed, had not been—as again he could not now alone—able to bear it? Meantime the earth began to change to a ruddy color, just as in Oaxaca, and the scenery grew more and more like Scotland (Primrose's ancestral home) very high, with on every side great crags of rock going straight up to dizzy peaks and many small green narrow valleys and lush fields, and towns that were all ruddy from the tierra colorada, and a few rush huts: another river: then they began to follow a stream, small, but full of falls and deep pools. Then they began to go down.

"This stream's going the wrong way," Primrose said. (This remark is also "thematic")[53] And indeed it seemed, for some time, to be flowing in a contrary direction to the sea probably it was bound for the Mexicali River. {UBC 13:18, 57}

past

There had been, since Chilpancingo, a drunken Chinaman sitting in the back seat with them. This individual was of no particular account. Doubtless he was a "character." But presumably he would get off somewhere and they would never see him again. Were Chinamen lucky or unlucky? was the question merely that presented itself to Wilderness. A drunken Chinaman, just like a drunken hunchback,[54] (he thought of the sober hunchback Cuzco, at Monte Alban) must surely mean something. This particular Chinaman was perhaps like a character one happens upon by opening a book at random in a public library:[55] there he is, you follow his antics for a page, but what his significance is to the story, since you have already replaced the novel, you will never know. The Chinaman (who was sitting in the corner on their right) was now singing: every few minutes he would jump up as to say something, then sink back. Did he too want to warn Sigbjørn about something? Once he started repeatedly banging his head as hard as he could against the back of the seat, raising one forefinger as though listening. The driver had indeed made his friend, who had also boarded the bus at Chilpancingo, tight as a chaffinch get out from his seat next to Primrose and for this they were grateful to the bus driver. Possibly he had no active intention of annoying Primrose and was just so drunk he could not help leaning over but this was one of the ways trouble starts in Mexico, Sigbjørn thought again, and Sigbjørn was relieved that the bus driver had intervened before it was necessary for him to take action himself. The Chinaman, however, did not at least have to bother with his responses to the scenery. For it he exchanged song and intermittent, blissful, {UBC 13:18, 58} unconsciousness. Probably, as Primrose said, the scenery was familiar to him, so he didn't have to look at it.

the thatched houses of Tierra Colorada

At Tierra Colorada, where their bus was to stop for fifteen minutes, these two friends rallied and walked extremely straight into the nearest cantina.

Sigbjørn watched them—it was so like a scene in the Valley of the Shadow of Death as to be almost eerie,[56] and suddenly a feeling almost of panic again possessed him, inexplicable, and coming from God knows where: occasionally he was allowed such glimpses to remind himself that he had been a creator, but in the larger pattern of their stay in Mexico—though he had never been aware of it till now—it was as if *he* were the character, being moved about for the purposes of some other novelist and by him, in an unimaginable novel, not of this world, that did not, indeed, exist.

(Note: this road was once the China road, for it was the pathway from eastern Asia to western Europe, and Acapulco,—This eastern Asia point v. important when one considers the Chinaman,—as Vancouver is today, the gateway to the Orient, whence unloaded the treasure laden argosies of ivory, sandal wood, jade, jasper, porcelain, tea, and spices from Java and Ceylon, bringing the exoticism and luxury of the east to the primitive little port.)[57]

Into the cantina—where was located also a minor branch of the bus office—it was more properly a cafe, with the bar—where the Chinaman and his friend had already started on their second bottle of beer—to one side now went Sigbjørn and Primrose; Sigbjørn himself wanted a beer badly but his pause, to which was added his natural fear now of doing anything positive, was afraid to go into the {UBC 13:18, 59} cantina; Primrose wouldn't have one for natural reasons: but she fancied a glass of carbonized water. (Describe again what they are wearing) Sigbjørn could not make the decision, or pluck up the courage, however, to fetch one for her from the next room, where other passengers were tipping in from a gigantic glass bottle, anymore than he could, despite Yvonne's "You have one"[58] bring himself to go into the bar, even though it was chilly, for Tierra Colorada was in the mountains. Sigbjørn just stood—as he had so often stood when building the house—uncertain, caught in a fatal inertia, a kind of evil sloth, between the past and the future, while Primrose fetched the glass of water for herself, while she slowly drank it spending the remainder of the quarter-of-an-hour trying to find, or in order to counteract the impression that he was actually doing nothing, pretending to try to find his change in his sticky pockets: the only firm decision he made was at the last minute when Primrose, now it was too late, decided that ice cream could be bought from what looked like a little store at some little distance on the other side of the street. Able at last to exercise his Spanish—for Fabrico de Jello[59] meant, even Sigbjørn could see, Ice Manufacturers, in another sense, yet still too undecided, or frightened—who knows why?—even to relieve himself, he took Primrose's arm firmly and led her back to the bus, almost immediately followed by the China-man and his friend, who climbed aboard the bus at the last moment, where they promptly fell once more into drunken slumbers.

"And the stream's still going the wrong way,"[60] Primrose said happily. It was not, of course, but Sigbjørn, holding Primrose's hand, closed his eyes for a few minutes: perhaps he had really {UBC 13:18, 60} gone to sleep, for so urgently had the past reinvoked itself again, that once more every car passing toward Cuernavaca contained him sitting there in still agony with Bousfield and Stuyvesant, and, when a bus passed them going toward Acapulco once more there, within it, was himself and Wynn and Gilda. (Some mention ought to be made of the trip he had suppressed, the one with Ruth.[61] This sense of the past too should extend to the historical.) The old road? No,—here Sigbjørn could scarcely remember the scenery at all, it was as if for a time now they were covering quite different ground. They crossed the River Papagayo.

and then to the Rio Papagayo which, tumbling over huge, prehistoric boulders, follows the road

Down they go now, out of the cold, the country getting more and more tropical. The bus stops and many boys get on the bus which is soon overcrowded. One man refuses to pay his fare, for some reason, and is holding out for his rights. (This man is rather important, for holding out for his rights) They are getting into Acapulco.

almost to its termination.

It is getting along toward sunset by now and perhaps the palms are bathed in sunset glow, or a red light. There are coconut palms beginning and tall hedges of bananas on either side of the road with glimpses of the sun through them, which though it is low in the sky, is extremely hot. Suddenly:

Then the highway climbs a last height and suddenly

"Πασα θαλασσα θαλασσα"[62] Sigbjørn says, and there, round a hill, there is the sea below them, and suddenly a sense of sheer holiday, of being alive, possessed him, and he hugged Primrose. How beautifully it had all been timed too. What did it matter if by going back to Acapulco he went back to the source, as it were, of his dead youth, the horrors of the past—for it was in Acapulco he had first {UBC 13:18, 61} landed by water, in Acapulco indeed, symbolically he had had, in September 1936, his first mescal—what did all these things matter. Now it was not 1936 but 1946, ten years later, here was Primrose taking such childish delight in all this beside him, there were enough years there to bury the past, so let them enjoy the present. For there, there was the sea, the bay spread out below them, the mountains rising behind and around the incredibly blue water.

in all its beauty, the Port of Acapulco with its smooth harbour

There was a grey American-looking gunboat in the bay, but they *shining boats* could see no other steamers. Now the old fort came in sight, over-looking the harbour, and built in the form of a five pointed star, tangible reminder of the swashbuckling era for it had been built to protect the town, and the galleons' great treasures in 1616, about the time of the death of Shakespeare. What had it not gone through? And Sigbjørn, pointing, and shouting as one does, released, at such moments, told her what he remembered, from the guide book of its history, how it had been captured by Morelos, and held by the Insurgents till 1821, how it had been one of the last strongholds of the Spanish Government, and even after the establishment of Mexican Independence, the fort continued to play an important role in the Republic's Political history, having defended liberals, conservatives, imperialists, and revolutionists, while within its time-stained walls Santa Ana defended his dictatorship[63]—(Mem: the scene in Pie de la Cuesta,[64] just before the catastrophe, should remind one that one is "still on the edge of the jungle" so to say.) Primrose is in wild excitement and Sigbjørn is happy and triumphant all over again, for she is seeing Acapulco for the first time under the best possible conditions, so that Sigbjørn feels {UBC 13:18, 62} as if he were making her a present of it, that is all due to him: it is his strength and generosity that she must thank for these new horizons—And again the sight of the sea thrills them both again, after so long away from it, and arouses mingled feelings of homesickness and adventure, so that one looked upon it, much as one had looked down upon it in youth, with a ship swinging at anchor there, waiting to sail, with him before the mast, for Belawan and Cathay—

They flash past the cemetery, and begin to go down into the town. The way is rather peculiar because they descend almost to the shore and then, passing the airport, begin to skirt, bumping rather, Hornos Beach. (Description.) (Mem: little flavour of Mexico, any seaside places with tourists, curios,—raw, bare, new—no trace of Spanish spirit, jerrybuilt: sleazy shops, sleazy bars: stupid big important hotels up on the hills, miles from the sea, drinks in the German pub, being cheated on the beer, the tankards sweating on the table, and the hatred that had greeted them in the square—)

Advertisements for hotels many of them in English, on hoardings, were everywhere: along the beach, which was disappointing, a bit dirty. Hotel El Mirador, with a picture of a Spanish galleon under full sail, a "different hotel where the service is right, the food famous, and the rooms comfortable," all facing the ocean: La Marina—fishermen's rendezvous facing the sea Acapulco: Los Flamingos—one of the world's most beautifully situated hotels (it was about 7 miles from the beach) with a picture of two flamingoes (which were spoonbills) and Los Pinguinos, Rooms with private bath and the finest meal is $20 and up, with two penguins, on loan doubtless from Melville's Encantadas:[65] they were passing the latter now. {UBC 13:18, 63} Hornos was a rather poor beach, and the Penguins could scarcely have been worse situated, he reflected, for him at least. And the Restaurant America, Specially for the Tourist, imported Liquors and Canned Goods. One or two of these hotels he remembered but now, craning out of the bus, Sigbjørn could see, far beyond, hundreds of new white houses like California on every hill and mostly looking in stupid modern style. None of what were obviously the big new hotels they could make out were on the sea but on inaccessible cliffs miles away. Down here there were not many trees, but to Primrose the sea compensated for all, even if it was crumbling on the dirty interminable Hornos beach. Sigbjørn only hoped for her sake that Caleta[66] beach had not been ruined and built upon or was impossibly expensive for he was counting on finding an hotel there, counting, even, on finding the old Paraiso de Caleta open, for the beach at Caleta was the only thing that to his mind justified Acapulco's existence. But unfortunately it was several miles beyond the town.

They began now to bump through the town which after 8 years seemed so much changed it was as if a gang of bucket cranes had been at work simply plucking up large sections of the town and dumping them down elsewhere. It had always been a horrible town in Sigbjørn's estimation with neither the dignity of a seaport nor the pietistic quality of a Mexican village but now Sigbjørn, as the inevitable wall of solid tropical heat began to wrap up all the passengers in the bus, and he began to sweat, they continued into the circuitous depths. They passed a huge liquor store on a deep high pavement, El Ciclon,[67] which announced that it sold, also, {UBC 13:18, 64} bulk liquors, and Sigbjørn made a note of it, but just as he thought, being Sunday, it was shut, and he wondered miserably what they were going to do for a drink, for if they found themselves stuck in this stoke-hold of a town, they were going to need one.

and red-tiled roofs

is unfurled to the traveller's eye.

The bus was now going slowly and people were running after it and they could see from the window the brown anxious face on a running man man break into a fiendish delighted smile as he recognized the gringoes.[68]

—"Ah taxi! Taxi!"

"Mister O.K. what you want?"

As they stopped, before they had a chance to get out, they were beseiged, swamped with boys trying to grab their shopping bag, which comprised their total luggage, and jabbering, and a hundred taxi drivers shouting: "Hotel!" "You want Hotel!" "Mister O.K. what you want?"

Sigbjørn shook them off somehow and they walked down the street. It was stinking hot. Acapulco, that is the part which was concentrated on the zócalo, and with the exception of the market, which seemed no longer to be there, had always been, to his mind a supremely characterless dull little town, of a quite remarkable ugliness: but not this kind of ugliness. Now its ruination, by virtue of its reconstruction, seemed complete. Hideous white buildings were being rushed up on every side. These buildings looked as though they never could be finished. It was like being lost in a chalk pit or a stone quarry. Huge piles and slabs of white stone had been thrown round in every direction, as if a monumental mason had run wild. A great sign rose up: *Supervulcanization.*[69] They passed a gas station, Sigbjørn thinking of Phaeton. {UBC 13:18, 65}

"I thought at first it said Supervulcanization," Sigbjørn was on the point of remarking, but checked himself, for it might, complicatedly, have hurt Primrose's feelings; Primrose seemed still in a happy daze. "My God, the Bohemia's still there," he said instead. At wicker chairs set along the pavement with the usual high curbstones with steps cut in them, near the zócalo, and hard by a doorless church, in progress of repair, a few Americans in uniform were drinking; it was a cantina named the Bohemia that Sigbjørn recognized from of old; he helped Primrose up the steps, and breaking out into a worse sweat than ever, they sat down.

The beer arrived, they produced their time honoured fruitless spiel "Nosotros no somos Americanos ricos—pobres—Canadianos—" but to no avail. "Cuánto?"[70] and Sigbjørn was disturbed to discover the beer was 60 centavos. (It should be pointed out that the

A town noted by old historians for the courtesy of its natives,

as Acapulco was then, so it is now—a beautiful deep harbour gleaming like liquid lapis-lazuli in a chalice of golden sand,

bordered with palms, thatched houses, and a riotous display

of tropical foliage.

Perfection is the word for Acapulco's climate, where tropic warmth is tempered by ocean breezes that maintain fact that Sigbjørn had not yet got used to the inflation of the peso and regarded it as a personal affront was suggestive of his strange identification with the past.) They drank beer but they were not comfortable. The beer is of poor quality, it gets hotter and hotter, and the small stone tankards sweat, leaving pools on the table. Everything indeed was sweating: the walls, the tankards, themselves. However once Sigbjørn is sitting down he is reluctant to get up again. They are served by a rude boy. Through the door, in the dark interior Sigbjørn sees the proprietor, but is not sure whether he recognizes him as the same man. No—he remembered him as quite a Nazi. He seems to be talking to an American girl—what should they be talking about, there in the dark? Sigbjørn and Primrose discuss in detail their {UBC 13:18, 66} economic situation. Sigbjørn shifts his position—he doesn't quite know why—so that his back is to the street and he cannot be seen either by the proprietor. In doing this he also shifts the shopping bag, and this shopping bag, its theft and adventures down the abyss at the beginning should perhaps be touched on. This of course in dialogue. It should be made plain that they have only two or three hundred pesos with them and another hundred in Cuernavaca, and also make plain the regulations of the Canadian Price Control Board.[71] Absolutely plain too should it be made that they have left their apartment in Cuernavaca "running" on. (And also perhaps the reader should be reminded that Sigbjørn has indeed tried to "show"—and is still trying—Primrose Mexico, her first foreign country.)

Perhaps the general reader's idea of Acapulco is of a place where the sea is easily accessible at all times and from everywhere. Had this been the case the Wildernesses would already have been in swimming. But swimming in the harbour was filthy and unfeasible; Hornos was impossible too at this hour. And the only possibility was Caleta. Sigbjørn glanced at his watch—the one the boy, whom he had saved from the police—had stolen, (a brief history of it should be given for it is important)—it is past eight. Across the street is a sign "Beach Clots" and the question is whether to go to Caleta or not. But one of the insidious things about Acapulco—and Sigbjørn could feel it already—is that it paralyses your will so that you do not want to do anything at all. But Sigbjørn made no move. He even began to forget that he had ever wanted to go to Caleta. It was inconceivable {UBC 13:18, 67} after having been so recently in the Scotch mists

a constantly agreeable and healthful

temperature,

its unique location preventing the heat

from ever becoming oppressive.

Though the ancient galleons no longer call at the port, the harbour waters still reflect the rich shadows of their glamour,

and now as then palms wave gracefully behind white beaches,

and cold of the rainswept highlands, to be in such a place as this. Even more remarkable than the climate was the number of people. How did they get here? To speculate upon this was to understand the term "sink" when applied to some seaports. Without any of the romance of a port Acapulco nonetheless seemed to qualify as a sink (very few freighters ever come there—go into this): and like so much refuse going round and round aimlessly, seeking some vent to be sucked under, seemed the people as they walked round and round the square. But if it was a sink it was a sink with the drain stopped up. There was no outlet. (There is of course the road, but make clear what Sigbjørn means.) A description of the terrific Sunday evening crowd, though not many people in this particular beer parlor. The two American marines sitting near, dressed in some unfamiliar uniform that made them look like out of work English ship's pantry boys, were making—he now became aware—rude remarks about him ". . . god damned Scotchman . . . some cock sucker . . ."

sailors gather in port cabarets

Sigbjørn eyed them with venom and went to the lavatory where there was a sign: Kilroy was here.[72] Who was this goddamned Kilroy? There had been a Kilroy too in San Francisco. Only in Mexico he had a companion. "El Grafe[73] was here too," it said. Though he laughs it increases the inchoate sense of persecution he has been feeling in a strange way. "El Grafe passed a stone here." Who was this man?

They sit watching as the crowd in the square increases. "Shall we go to Caleta?" Primrose asks again, but Sigbjørn hardly heard her. He was thinking indeed of his first {UBC 13:18, 68} arrival in Acapulco,[74] his arrival indeed from Mexico, on the Day of the Dead, 1936, the butterflies coming out to greet the Pennsylvania and then the Pennsylvania which no longer ran, lying out in the bay, and after the customs (the whiskered Immigration man, who looked a little like that film actor, what's his name, had been polite, had not, even though he was English, asked him to put up a bond) coming ashore in the launch, the difficulty of landing, but before that there had been the old man foaming at the mouth in his scending and swaying boat as he corrected his watch, and then his first drink, "where it had all started," though that had been over there by the Turismo, (his first mescal had been the next day, in this very pub, after he had come back from swimming in Hornos—ah, how many memories were there, oscillations, deliriums, disengagements, all the foolishness of his youth and the Miramar—was it the Miramar that Ruth

and there is always an overture of mystery[75]

and he had stayed at that first night, the Miramar in the town too, was that why he was delaying to go to Caleta, and could he anyway, was it honorable to take Primrose to the Miramar, if it was still here, though she knew really how it had been then, she wouldn't care, would even be proud—and he had not discovered Caleta that time, in other words he had not discovered Acapulco till that time with Gilda, with Ruth he had thought "Playa Honda" Beach—a hideous little dark beach on the way with one private bathing hut—must provide the wonderful bathing they'd talked about on the Pennsylvania and now it was getting too late to get to Caleta—and that night too there had been the houses looking as if covered with snow in the moonlight, and the negro sea-cook, who kept {UBC 13:18, 69} the Sandwich y Cigarettes, who had been to Alaska, and whose son— the son of a sea-cook!—kept the coconut stand in the centre of the square and who loved Guadalajara, and who had said of the police-man turned tanner, "He can make 'em pretty l'il," and who had also built a house himself with his own hands, that hadn't fallen down in the earthquake, "I've had my troubles, but not of all that drinking— not like some of these guys—drink, drink, drink, drink,—all that foolishness never got you nowhere," (an unsympathetic character who despised drunks) and now Primrose and he had built a house, and the negro was probably no longer there, it was clear that every-thing had changed, (or had been, as it were, cut out, like he had cut out all the long passages about Acapulco and Yvonne's arrival there, in the Valley of the Shadow of Death, including those concerning the negro)[76] though Sigbjørn was not quite certain in his mind why he wished things were even more changed than they were—"I think it's too late to go to Caleta," he said. "But let's have another beer." But what really related him to this was the fact that his foot, suspi-ciously swollen then so near to the suspicious and horrible cause of this, had given him a twinge again, it was swollen after the bus ride and he put it up on the seat; of course Amann had said he was all right, but would he ever be sure? Perhaps never, and perhaps it was right he never should be, for without it he would never have it use-fully in its place to worry about when the central anxieties of his life threatened insurrection.

It is growing quite dark now and Primrose wants to move {UBC 13:18, 70} off. There is shouting and there seems to be trouble, but Primrose is excited though it looks bad. They have themselves now

and romance of a bygone year

in the crooked streets and barred windows of the village.

gone inside and they gyp the proprietor (it is not deliberate on Sigbjørn's part but explain how this is done) over their beer, and Primrose is pleased about this, though Sigbjørn is disturbed and keeps
looking behind him. They leave, and discover that the last bus for
Caleta has gone. Sigbjørn is looking for the Miramar but they find
the Monterrey (though he recognizes this all right—it is indeed
utterly unchanged—I don't know whether he should realise its significance immediately, perhaps at night, in the next chapter: when
he can remember too, how he owes several pesos there—the same
amount approximately, that he had gypped the Bohemia out of—
he was pleased that it was not the exact amount—and it is the place
where he wrote the sonnet: Love which comes too late is like that
black storm,[77] etc . . .) I think he should recognize it as that and the
fact should give him some pleasure: also directly opposite is the old
Consulate where his book had been saved[78] in one of its earlier versions. The proprietor, however, looks at him too pointedly, he feels.
They begin their spiel—"Nosotros no somos Americanos—" Finally they get a room, (the manager, a German, makes him sign the
register twice). Describe it and the heat, the tear in the mosquito
netting, etc. The proprietor recites the menu. "Tonight we have a
nice chicken, with beans, and a sweet—"

Although it is Sunday, but still a ship stood drawn, like a jewelled
dagger out of the dark scabbard of the town, Sigbjørn goes out
to try and get a bottle. It is a cloudy, suffocating night, with no
moon and no stars; on his way all {UBC 13:18, 71} the lights in
the town go out. In the square is a terrific melee. There are many
white-uniformed American sailors, their uniforms chalk-white in
the gloom, apparently off the gunboat, but they are being jeered at
in the darkness: "Abajos los tyrannicos Norte Americanoes!"[79]
People are throwing eggshells and rice and squirting water at the
sailors, who remarkably kept their temper with an occasional "Hey,
lay off there," it seems to Sigbjørn. But there is a real feeling of hate
abroad and at one point there is a fight going on. It is a nasty nightmarish scene with only the naphtha flares and these picking eggshells out of their shirt collars as the terrific stupid crowd mills
round and round the square. What had they got against them? Still,
what had the sailors got against him, for that matter. It seemed to
Sigbjørn they were behaving extremely well. Sigbjørn tries to buy a
bottle in some old haunts but the prices are impossible. Better to

There is a hotel to suit every taste, and every purse. Accommodations range from modest inexpensive student quarters to luxurious suites.

Comfortable, well decorated rooms are equipped with private baths and Simmons beds.

In this enchanting little port

drink beer at a peso a bottle. The old Seven Seas is now the Siete Mares, and put off by the change and the gloom, and not wanting to find out if the Champ, the ex-champion of California, whom he had once knocked down, and who still owed him 5 pesos, and whom Guyou that day had put in prison, is still there serving as a waiter, he makes to go home. The melee in the darkness and flares is now terrific and symbolises the hatred of the Americans.

time moves slowly and the past colours the present like

Though it was pitch dark in the narrow streets immediately he leaves the zócalo, Sigbjørn, who hoped it will still be dark when he reached the hotel, so that they would dine in candlelight, took a circuitous route home, back to the Hotel {UBC 13:18, 72} Monterrey, avoiding the cantina where they had gypped the proprietor, but first passing the cinema, where he had once been to see We Who Are About to Die, with Peggy Riley, and where now Ricardo Montalban, Virginia Serret, Lilia Michel and Carlos Orellana were playing in The Hour of the Truth.[80] {UBC 13:18, 73}

a lovely golden haze.

II

That night they had dined, as Sigbjørn hoped, in candle-light, while at the next table a young Mexican, who had been divorced from his American wife, told them a story that curiously paralleled Sigbjørn's own, moreover his helpfulness and kindness is important. (This story can be briefly sketched for the Mexican might have been a potential saviour; but the Wildernesses' habit of isolation is such that they don't cultivate his acquaintance. He stands them, however, a bottle or so of beer, and it is important to note that this is the first night for months that they have turned in without drinking at least half a litre of brandy between them.) (N.B. This should all probably be in retrospect, and the chapter open with Caleta! Caleta!) The lights are still out when the Wildernesses turn in, and they take a candle from the dining room with them—the heat is fearful in the room, there is even less privacy than in the Casa Grande, but they are happy, and perhaps make love, and Primrose is happy, saying that "Sigbjørn is wonderful for having found this room, so cheap," etc., and because she is happy, Sigbjørn is, and they go to sleep happily . . . Sigbjørn wakes to find the light on and there is a terrific pounding of a great machine, doubtless the electric light plant. Anxious not to wake Primrose, he turns the light off, but cannot go to sleep again. He remembers how, in the anguish of that morning, after he had been actually thrown out of the old American Consul's house opposite the Monterrey by that drunken bastard of a Hardy who owned the Seven Seas, on which he had once added the word Spray, remembering Potato Jones,[1] the anguish of the Riley incident, and {UBC 13:19, 74} writing that poem here, Love is like that black storm that breaks too late, etc. What a bestial thing that had been of him to do! Drunk or not he could find no forgiveness in his heart for it, even if he never knew precisely—and alas!—what he had done. But to have betrayed someone who had befriended him as unselfishly as had Riley and Peggy, finding him drunk and penniless there writing poems in the Siete Mares, and then buying him clothes, taking him to the Consul's house, succouring him as well as they could for the reason which above all others should have secured his loyalty, that they believed in his talent—at that time rented from the proprietor of the Seven Seas, feeding him, taking him to dine at the Mirador—where someone, also in love with Peggy, had warned them both against him—offering him their car, offering him, even at the very end, their car—the warmhearted, generous kindliness of these two people who could have been friends all his life: and who were indeed as husband and wife so well matched, very like Primrose and he indeed, singing on their guitar together, swimming together, celebrating their anniversary every month: where were they now? Had he done, he wondered, any permanent damage—to say the least—to that relationship? Love is like that black storm that breaks out of its season . . . It slakes no thirst to say what love is like, that comes too late. My God, alas, too late! No indeed it did not, not even with the aid of a half a dozen or so bottles of beer required to write the poem at the end of the little dining room not now fifty feet from him, and which he still owed to the German proprietor, who had looked at him queerly, though without conscious recognition, and made him sign the register twice. And yet certainly he had not been able to help falling in love with Peggy. But perhaps there {UBC 13:19, 75} had not been so much excuse for, when R's back was turned, trying to rape her—though had he? He would never know. The engine pounded on mercilessly, interminably, and taking Primrose in his arms, he dreams he is on board a ship on a long sea voyage—and yet at the same time something within him seemed in-extricably bound, impossible of disengagement from, the machine.

Caleta! Caleta!

They sat, in the square, in the bus, not far from the Departamento de Turismo, right opposite the place where Sigbjørn had had, 8½ years before, his first drink in Mexico, a bottle of Cartablanca, there it all started—in the bus in the square. They had indeed heard the cries of Caleta! Caleta! announcing the bus to Sigbjørn's beach on waking, and the cries had gone on, carrying from the square, inter-mittently during breakfast at the Monterrey. The bus, worse even than the bus to Matamoros, for the benches ran longwise, was so low-roofed that it was impossible to stand, so Sigbjørn was glad when someone got out—though they were still at a standstill—and he could sit. They were carrying their faithful shopping bag. Sig-bjørn had had, for some reason, an uneasy feeling that the man who got out might have been R. He also had an uneasy feeling that he was being watched by the barman, or waiter, of the La Marina Hotel (which had not to his knowledge been built when he was last here) who seemed to him making unnecessary flourishes with his serviette. But that surely could not be the Champ. How could he have survived when the last he knew he had been put in jug? The shopping bag con-tained their swimming suits only and some towels borrowed from the Hotel Monterrey where they had left all their other {UBC 13:19, 76} things, their intention being to find if possible an hotel at Caleta near the beach, but if that proved unfeasible, still to have the Monter-rey to fall back upon. Caleta! Caleta! There was a holiday sound to it, and Sigbjørn smiled, renewed by a night's sleep, and determined all over again to be happy and rejoice in their lives: what had they not got? How lucky they were! What an adventure it was! All these things he told himself even in the face of the demons of persecution and disease and guilt and failure and fear and the past: the only way to deal with them was indeed as familiar spirits (much like the Con-sul's only these were real, not fictitious) whom one could not shake off but to whom one was somewhat amusedly resigned; all right, I know you're there, but I'm going—Primrose is going to—to have a good time nevertheless. Though the better way was, of course, the unselfish way again; he could not succeed in making Primrose happy unless he himself were happy, and if she was happy, why, then so would he be: and by following this policy he saw himself indeed being able to "accept his damnation," accept it, and even, transcend it, perhaps in the end have a kind of affection, a sort of pity, for his poor demons. The driver of the bus, who now started the camión and put it into gear, was an old wizened man who looked rather like some ancient golf-caddy. There was a reproduction of their Señora of Dangerous and Desperate Causes in the bus and also a picture of a pretty girl over the steering wheel, with above it, the contrary of the usual advice to been seen in buses[2] "Molest the Chauffeur!" (Moleste el Chofere.)[3] They start off past the Turismo and begin to bump along a sort of pseudo-esplanade by the shore. They skirted the so-called Manzanillo beach, which was not a beach at all, but a sort of combination {UBC 13:19, 77} city dump and occasional flop house, (and which was later to be immortalized by a Canadian naval mutiny)[4] climbed up past thatched houses where he had gone on his first walk eight years ago, dropped to the Playa Honda beach, where there were now several more bathing huts, but which still looked as ugly as ever, and which he had first thought so wrongly was Caleta itself. The bus was full, but Sigbjørn did not notice the people. (Perhaps he was too busy with the topography of his soul.) Primrose is happy. They were having more than ever a sense of holiday. They passed the Los Cocos Yacht Club—why not los Cacos?[5]—and then another yacht club, they climbed and dropped past the Mar Azul Hotel and there they were at the old Paraiso de Caleta Hotel, which seemed shut. It *was* shut.

They got out into memories already beginning to skim along the sand toward him like machine-gun bullets. There was, now, a road dividing the Paradise of Caleta from the beach, once one had stepped out of the "dining room" on to the sand. They wandered along Caleta beach, which was, it being March, fairly deserted, though there were more people at the far end. Sigbjørn noticed the alterations. They were now walking along a part, or arc, of the beach known as the Caleta, which was divided from a similar arc, Caletilla, beyond, by a sort of causeway that hadn't been there before. Neither had Caletilla been there before, he thought, a decade ago, or rather it had all been one beach, divided only by a sandbank over which you could swim at high tide. Sigbjørn rather resented the whimsy of Caletilla. Little Caleta! So cute. The new causeway led out to an island that had been there before all right but the island had now been entirely converted into the house and grounds of a rather {UBC 13:19, 78} floribund house. But the chairs and the boys with their hair burned white, and the water skis and so forth seemed the same, as did an Indian lad lying absolutely flat on his water ski on the sand in the sun; neither he nor the shadow of his craft might have moved since Sigbjørn had last been there, as if a moment ago it had been midday of March, 1938, and now midday, 1946, (if indeed there would be a shadow at midday). But the surroundings in Sigbjørn's eyes were ruined, at first sight at least, ruined by bad taste and stupidity, and by American bad taste in the bargain. Formerly there had been no hotels at all, merely the Paraiso de Caleta, which had been merely, as it was now, a kind of long shingled hut with a bar at one end and dingy rooms, and a few tumble down annexes of this. Behind a few scraggling coconut palms, which used to provide Sigbjørn with the utensil into which he would pour his 3rd drink of the early morning. In this sense there had been no surroundings to ruin. While the floribund house on the island could not be said to have improved matters, nor the enormous number of hotels like giant ships and warehouses which had gone up on the bluffs all around (while at the end of the beach they were clearing with a bulldozer space for yet another one) and while one could have no reasonable objection in such a place as the inevitable road, lined for all its length with hot dog stands and the like that lent it an air of Coney Island, what rendered it all inexcusable to Sigbjørn was not this but that the Hotel Paraiso de Caleta, with the best location of the lot, was shut, gone indeed to rack and ruin, whereas these other hotels had been built in a position highly inconvenient to bathers; in fact they were placed in such a position that it would cost anyone {UBC 13:19, 79} ten pesos, if he had no car, to get down to the beach at all by taxi, and more than that if he wished not to return in a wet bathing suit. And this, of course, he thought, must be the idea. Acapulco was but another department of the vast dairy farm that Mexico was becoming, for the purpose of milking Americans, as an unconscious revenge for which America was with her money advancing her her bad taste at such a liberal rate of interest that soon Mexico per se was vanishing. Her voice would be deafened by juke boxes, which they fall upon much as a defeated army would fall upon opium. If there had been any valid reason for believing that the sea would still be there when the Mexican and American races were no more Sigbjørn would have felt comforted. (This should be in dialogue—perhaps later in the chapter—it could be made into good bantering dialogue, with some trouble, but it is pretty cheap and unthought through for straight disquisition.)

Sigbjørn at all events takes off his shirt, and paddles a bit in the water, which is beautifully soft and warm, they are walking where Gilda had slapped him down after his suicidal swim, when on top of everything else, way beyond the Governor's house, he had been attacked and fought off a barracuda, the barracuda having in fact saved him, whatever it was had finally pushed him on the rocks, but it was the fight he made against it that had revived his will to live, if only revived it because he wanted a drink: once more he saw the lanterns swinging on the water, saw the people standing on the shore who, having known the corpse, were for a moment, great.[6] Once more Sigbjørn feels like a ghost and reflects upon the sea, so blue, so innocently breaking here on the soft sand though out beyond the island a line of {UBC 13:19, 80} white spray showed where it was roaring against a reef. Just as upon a steamer, so it was here, the water harmlessly pouring past the port is yet the menacing tyrant of old that the drowned know. One would feel so at home here, so safe, on this soft shore, in this harmless surf, nothing could touch you, and it was perhaps like Mexico itself in this respect. But the warmth of the water, (when they are swimming—they are swimming now) annoys him and a sudden yearning for Canada comes over him, since here the sky was stupidly and sullenly blue and unchanging, for the deep deep pure absolute blue of an October sky below the brilliant white drifting clouds, the downswirling dunes and meadows of darker clouds around lakes of cerulean or miles high combed like giant fins, and the continual dark diagonal furrows and flaws sliding every way over the mirror of the inlet, Eridanus, its continual change and movement and flux, and the shock of a swift parabola of a gaggle of geese against it, but above all its stinging bracing cold.

But Primrose is delighted with the sand of Acapulco, and says it is as white as sugar and fine as flower and like velvet to her bare feet and the water is so blue. Sigbjørn tries to conceal his disappointment and they have a council of war. Primrose is practically sold on staying there and they inquire at the Paraiso de Caleta, which after all does seem to be fulfilling some obscure function. And on enquiry, they discovered that it was true. It had not quite fallen: you could obtain cuartos for 9 pesos, but they served no food: and for a small price you could also dress there, in order to swim. But in the strict sense it was no longer a hotel. What used to be the dining room was open once a week on Sunday afternoon for {UBC 13:19, 81} dancing, when the bar was also opened.

"I preferred it before," Sigbjørn said to the man.

"Sí. It was more natur*al*," said the man at the Paraiso.

"Sí, more natural," and Sigbjørn wondered idly, for he was not recognized, where, if not here, Bousfield meant that he and Sigbjørn were still "characters":[7] possibly in the Siete Mares.

Finally they walk in the opposite direction from Caletilla and see a sign Hotel Cordoba,[8] Información en el Bar;—apparently this hotel, which was built in several sections, all of them unfinished, which were scattered about up the cliffside, which was partly a rubbish heap and bore little relation to a building, or even series of logical structures, let alone an hotel, was connected, by an arch to a place named Bar Larqueta next door. This bar was also deserted and seemed in some sense unfinished, if indeed it ever could be said to have been begun; it was a kind of brick ruin over a garage in which, for there was a nice breeze out here, was one lone chair rocking by itself. There were naked electric bulbs in the garage and a motor boat called El Chalaco and above a gasoline motor was chugging endlessly with its belts and pulleys. No one seemed to be about, and looking round, Sigbjørn reflected that the Cordoba and the Larqueta, taken together, resembled what one imagined would be the kind of niche in the next world that someone who had never succeeded in making any positive decisions whatsoever on earth would find himself in. While it was perhaps, taken as a whole, rather in process of slow construction than otherwise, it had an air of impermanence and of not making up its mind to be anything whatsoever, that was almost frightening, and on top of that it had {UBC 13:19, 82} an air too of what one might describe as ruination. (Mem.: perhaps Sigbjørn's recurrent dream of hell where he can recognize the places. Yes.) Finally they saw a fattish old Indian woman standing on a balcony above a garbage dump in the indefinable stone heap known as the Cordoba, and they ascended and were shown, to so speak, around. She was a horrible old woman and flushed the toilet, which was just off the kitchen, to show that it would work, which however it did not. "What goes down must come up," Sigbjørn commented sagely. What went down it, God alone knows—Ah, the old familiar feces—as T. said[9]—but that it worked at all, after Iguala, and indeed almost anywhere in Mexico, was so impressive they almost decided to stay then and there. Finally they got a room, (or asked them to hold it till they made up their minds) abutting on a brick parapet on one side, and with a shower bath on the other and a lavatory. Beyond the lavatory was the ordinary kind of Mexican kitchen and it was necessary to go through this kitchen to reach the dining room. The hotel seemed absolutely deserted of guests and what rudimentary rooms there are seem deserted and open. But their room, though scarcely more than a box, was relatively clean and adequate, the dream like quality of it appealed to them, and since it was, above all, near the beach, they decided, after going through their usual spiel, "Nosotros no somos Americanos ricos," and encountering the manager, a wizened man almost stone blind, and the rather unpleasant manageress, whom they knock down to a not unreasonable price, to take it, or at least give it a trial, but at the same time they say they will give their final word in about an hour, which gives them a chance to see the Quinta Eugenia, a structure up on a hill, which looked like a three-decker steamer that had {UBC 13:19, 83} been stranded there by a tidal wave, which was however in spite of the hill fairly near the beach, and unlike the great expensive American buildings, and which had been recommended to them[10] on account of its cooking, for, run by a Swiss, it was reported to have a French cuisine, it was more of a pensión, in a sense, than a hotel, the prices were reputed to be reasonable, and it would undoubtedly be beautifully cool. They therefore climb up past the sign at the bottom Quinta Eugenia, Pensión Francesca, French, Swiss and American cooking, to the Quinta Eugenia, feeling they may do as well there, terms are quoted by José (and it is important they should be reported exactly) rooms are not all of the same price, some have baths and some not, but José, who looks something like Christ in a cypriot church, and is married to a French woman, explains that there would be no discrimination as to food or privilege to use the high porches and lookouts, or the Venetian gazebos on Benito Cerino's fated craft,[11] that are scattered here and there much again as if it were a ship, that they are all one family here, room 5 is shown them, which has no bath, Señor Mañana de Mañana de Mañana is painting, lying full length down on the floor, stripped to the waist, so ridiculously bronzed that he seems to Sigbjørn to be an Indian, he is painting a seascape of some sort the quality of which is rather difficult to determine, they see the fat pig-eyed proprietor who is playing Chinese checkers with one of the waiters, and the windy, beautifully situated, haphazard hotel is described, Sigbjørn likes the wind that blows through the windowless dining room, high up with a parapet on one side, so that dining there must be like what repeated experience never quite convinces you to the contrary that dining on board ship is like, {UBC 13:19, 84} and at the same time with the sheer drop from the parapet it was something like dining on the edge of a precipice too, Primrose is tickled by the bad classical pictures hanging everywhere, but José is very polite, and patient with their "Nosotros no somos" and is glad to leave the matter open so that they may "se resuelva"[12] in their own time, and for their part, they say they will return at 3 o'clock, but because it is cheaper by the day at least at the Cordoba, and they have not made up their mind to stay as long as a week, which would have recommended the Quinta Eugenia to them, they go down again to the beach, and leaving their things at the Cordoba, and promising to be back in time for supper, hurry off to catch the bus from which they have heard the cry of "Zócalo Zócalo" sounding: this being the opposite and companion cry to Caleta! Caleta! at the other end. They are going down to the town in order to get their things from the Monterrey after having had their commida[13] there, for which they have already paid. This having been done they go down into the town where it is hell all hot and they are glad they have decided to stay up at Caleta. They get a bottle—Sigbjørn cannot find El Ciclon however—or rather 2 bottles (one smashes in the shop—this is unlucky, Sigbjørn reflects, in Africa, for the house would have to be purified afterwards, and Sigbjørn wonders whether or not it really is a bad omen, though in one sense it is not, for the boy who serves them protesting that it is not their fault gives them another bottle without charge) Caleta! Caleta! And they return, in the bus, with their faithful blue shopping bag, to Caleta and this time there is in the bus the same person who had got out this morning and Sigbjørn feels uneasily that it may be R., but if so how much older he looked, how bald, how unhappy—but no, it could not be—and {UBC 13:19, 85} Sigbjørn and Primrose, who are already exhausted by their two crowded bus trips, though the fares are one third as expensive as they had been in 1938, when it had cost 60 centavos to get to Caleta, decide: "when we get there, I recommend we stay up there—if we do stay—and not come down at all. This drive down into town is hell."

"Yes, I'm completely exhausted." "It's only a few miles but it seems like about fifty." "It's the town that's so damned hot," Primrose said. "But how do you like Caleta?" "Oh, yes!" Primrose says, and perhaps here it should be suggested how she too wants Sigbjørn to lay his ghosts. "If I had to come down to town every day I'd go mad," Sigbjørn says. "Yes, Acapulco is hell," they agree. "It's almost worse than Mexico City," he added . . . Back at the Cordoba they get into their swimming clothes and immediately go for a swim, the beach further described, though it is almost quite deserted in this, the siesta hour, and return to the Cordoba where closer investigation discloses that they are right over the garbage dump, the view is blocked by buildings to right below and the abandoned horror of the half-finished Hotel Larqueta, the motor boat garage, where now however a man was sitting quite alone in the huge empty open unfinished lower floor in a rocking chair and the horrible rattling banging gasoline motor that had been silent for a while starts maddeningly rattling and banging again. But they sit on their little porch happily in the cool of evening drinking habanero along with the xopilotes, the sight of which suggests to Sigbjørn what he had been missing from the beach and the sea at Acapulco, though he hadn't been able to put his finger on it till now: it was the flash of white wings that he had missed, for there were no seagulls in Acapulco,—and looking up of course {UBC 13:19, 86} he could see none now—or there were certainly none in March, only thousands of leathery black vultures that here seemed sea-scavengers as well. The pelicans they had seen at Hornos never came up to Caleta and as for the Penguins and the Flamingoes they existed apparently only in the imagination of advertising agents or Hotel managers: when you fixed your mind upon this fact for an instant, the substitution of these odious dirty creatures which in Acapulco for some reason never flew high, their one saving grace being in this beautiful flight, for the brightness and glory in flight and evocation of the white and graceful seagulls in the sunlight, you entered a world of nightmare, for you only had to pretend to recount it to see how true this was: (Most of this in dialogue again, of course) "I dreamt I was in a place by the sea, and though the sea was beautiful, there were instead of seagulls, only vultures, and no trees." And this was a fact: there were no trees at all at Caleta, such as they were, the much vaunted palms, mostly bedraggled and broken, were at Hornos, along with the pelicans. But Sigbjørn did not give voice to this thought, or perhaps he did not, so happy was he that Primrose was happy, think of it altogether: Primrose was wildly happy, and when two people are in love, and moreover can enjoy the grotesqueness of certain situations, such a matter as that of the vultures, far from being a drawback, lent a quality of humour to a situation already being stored up as a precious memory which they were to see later in relation to certain denizens of their bedchamber. It was growing dark, the stars began to come out and along came an hombre with a hissing gasoline lamp and hung it on their porch. Shades of Sam[14]—and how this brings it all back a moment! Comparison between a kerosene and a gasoline lamp {UBC 13:19, 87} here: we may philosophize a bit. Though there is the usual small bulb overhead we find there is no electricity. But they went happily and hungrily to dinner and are given a bowl of soup, then, with creamed sauce, one hard boiled egg. They wait and wait for the next course which never comes and before they have realised the tragedy even their plates of bread had been whisked away, and disappeared. Full of romance they go down for a wonderful moonlight swim and sit boldly in the chairs left there: nobody to say "2 pesos, mistair," one other Mexican couple are laughing and frolicking in the water and one couple necking down the beach in a chair, otherwise they are alone with their habanero, in the faint clear light of a young moon.

Sigbjørn remembers again his suicide attempt (perhaps it hadn't really been suicide any more than his late one, but still) and looking at the shut dour Hotel Paraiso de Caleta, says aloud: "To think I could ever come *here* again and be happy—"

"My darling. And are you happy?"

"Yes, my god I am. And how lucky I am."

"So am I. It's I who am lucky."

Sigbjørn wonders again about Riley, and how they had swum together here. For a swimmer undoubtedly Acapulco beach was one of the finest in the world, that was here at least. Champions liked to come here and swim. And once, in a race round the island Riley had beaten Johnny Weissmuller.[15] But stranger than that, in a similar race, Sigbjørn had beaten Riley,—just; that was how good he was, drunk though he was, he had done it, or done it 8 years ago, and he should be good—his father was good—perhaps because of that, because drink can release tremendous muscular energy in the water. It was a feat, which Peggy had appreciated, {UBC 13:19, 88} the more so since Sigbjørn had adapted to his own use Riley's peculiar crawl, which he had been teaching him. That was nice too, to think of. Was that true of him as a writer too, that he adopted technique so easily, and as it were, or in order to humiliate, humiliated the creator by beating him at his own game, which had been the point, technique, and speed, virtuosity only, like a hot trumpeter but who at the same time gives one the mind and heart of Sir Philip Gibbs?[16] Poor Sir Philip. And yet, all his strength and virtuosity had not prevented him being knocked flat by Gilda. "Whatever a woman play, whether she know, or whether she don' know, she beat you at it," he thought . . . a negro had once said that to him.

"A centavo for them," said Primrose.

"I was thinking of the British Weekly the mater sends me,"[17] Sigbjørn said, remembering Miss Gleason,[18] he divided a centavo by five to see how much his thought was worth in American money. "Perhaps we're like the Children of Israel. Full of advertisements for Welgar shredded wheat, Dr. Bardardo's homes, and Embassy cigarettes, the cigarette of destruction in advertisements, showing carefully *empty* wine glasses—since it is a temperance paper—(They'd drunk it all up) and constipation makes him liverish, and rheumatism do not despair (I did) and Lingford's famous mother series (Cornelia Gracchus)[19]—being an advertisement for Lungford's famous Baking Powder Famous in the Homes of England for more than 80 years (she had no interest in an idle life of pleasure and luxury, my sons are my jewels. Cornelia was greatly loved by the Romans who at her death erected a statue to her memory.) Langford's Baking Powder—the British Weekly says . . ."{UBC 13:19, 89}

"Yes, dear, but I didn't quite follow . . ."

"No. I thought we were maybe like the Children of Israel. Life was stagnant, but reasonably secure, Moses arrived, and led them into the desert. Hunger and thirst assailed them. And they were puzzled and frustrated. They wore themselves out, like sailors, as Erikson put it, like sailors chipping rust, wearing themselves out behind a barrier of time.[20] But maybe it was God that did it. They absolutely had to have that experience, to be thrown out of their nest, to have, as it were, their house burned down. 'As an eagle stirreth up her next, fluttereth over her young, spreadeth abroad her wings'—

the poor bugger, the mother eagle having smashed up the next first[21]—'so the Lord alone did lead them'—never mind me, I'm slightly drunk, though in a new way—"

A car shot past along the new road past the Paraiso de Caleta and looking round Sigbjørn thought he recognized one of the stool pigeon cops of old from the Turismo in it: he froze. It gave him a bad moment. He heard the car going right on and on past Caletilla and it would therefore have to go back to the town that way for in Acapulco the channels of choice, as of escape, were few. (Mem: Juarez had landed on this beach.[22] relation of Juarez to New Orleans too. FROM PASSION TO ASSASSIN)

(Margienote: we swam in silky warm water, floated on our backs we looked at the stars and noted again how high Orion was in the sky, the north star gone, and the dipper, and saw Achanar and Canopus, I remember this best of all)

—Back in their room the Wildernesses undress and put out the gasoline lamp, with how much calculation and courage! (Remembering still the fear of fire) which they had left on the ground {UBC 13:19, 90} as it were, outside on their porch, they sink sleepily into their hard twin beds, they make love—and how beautiful it is even after six years!—and then it started: the chinches, and the thin angry whine of mosquitoes. (Note: but there is a terrific artistic necessity to give the fulness of his transference of PASSION from Ruth to Peggy of which Primrose is the super—for he really loves her—coefficient) Great God, what a night! They scratch and slap and turn and range from fury to near hysteria. There seemed millions of mosquitoes. Primrose even takes a cold shower. Then she wraps herself in her sheet and paces the porch, tries to sleep on the floor: no use: finally she remembers seeing a coal-oil lamp, a friend, in another room, and gets it, they light that and they go round and round the walls killing mosquitoes and leaving drops of their blood on the walls. This helps some: but now, suddenly, the cocks begin to crow: they are stupid fowl in Acapulco—mem: Peggy's anguished, from the Consul's house: "I never heard a night so noisy and full of anguish." (ref: also beginning of letter in the Valley)[23] Mem: eating the mosquitoes. It was dawn before they sank into an uneasy sleep.

They decided at that point that cost what it might to move to The Quinta Eugenia, and the next morning, after a swim, and a meagre breakfast of insipid papaya, where they encountered another American woman, lonely, middle aged, squat, nice, a crashing bore, and recently—as what American woman is not?—divorced, as if indeed the object of marriage on the part of American women was not marriage happiness or children or even companionship, but simply alimony, a nervous breakdown, and a lonely and frustrated life on the edge of existence in some dump like Acapulco: she had had a bad night too and didn't know how to turn out her lamp so {UBC 13:19, 91} had to leave it on: just about midnight the lamp burned out, and then on came the electric light and no wall switch and she had to "climb up on a chair and table and turn bulb and get it out" etc. etc. etc. and "I came down here"—and here it came, it was inevitable, Sigbjørn had known it before she said it, "because I had a nervous breakdown." "We too," Sigbjørn was on the point of saying, but feeling sorry for her. Alas what tenderness and self abnegation had gone astray here, and he made up his mind to endure her as much as he could, if that would help her loneliness at the same time feeling rather ashamed of this emotion, as if it were something Sir Philip Gibbs might have devised too or which related to a boy scout mentality, (Sigbjørn had once been a Lion)[24] Sigbjørn tries to pay the bill in the Cordoba to the one-eyed, blind, and indeed deaf, as he now proves to be, ancient landlord, with only two teeth too who spits as he talks unintelligibly, Sigbjørn attempts to pay the bill, but has only a fifty peso note, manager has no change, and Sigbjørn with many misgivings goes to seek change from the Administración of the Beach, in the person of a fat man who always sits right down below on a chair outside the Hotel del Pacifico, no luck, and after another encounter with the manager, whom he suspects of not having change because he wants to keep them there—my god, will I ever be like that? why sure, I was like that, in my twenties, but now I am nearing 40, time to grow young; he, anyhow, will charge 5 pesos for supper, because he has sometime yesterday dispatched the cook for supplies—had the cook been on the bus? was the cook a spy? 1 peso for an egg, we presume, another five pesos for keeping the lamp burning all night.

"Nosotros no somos ricos Americanos," said Sigbjørn severely. {UBC 13:19, 92}

"Americanos! Sí!"

"No. No Americanos. Nosotros no somos Americanos ricos. Canadianos. No," Primrose pleaded, "hombres ricos, Hombres pobres, pobres."

"Sí . . . Sí, . . . You har much money."

Irresolute again they go for another swim, a motorboat is down there, José is getting on it, the boat is going to Pied de la Cuesta, and Sigbjørn avoids José's eyes because he has promised to meet him at 3 o'clock the previous day—how difficult and tiresome were the most simple human relationships to Sigbjørn but the fleas have decided them almost so they climb up to the Eugenia again: the Swiss of course, José is not there, only the dark-haired Mexican with a sour expression who somehow chills Sigbjørn, they park their shopping bag in room 5 however and descend to the Cordoba again to settle up.

This time Sigbjørn is triumphant, and they don't pay extra. Sigbjørn has discovered some rules, they are torn (on the wall, and half hidden) but they mention the clause about payment for dinner Cordoba has invoked. Sigbjørn says "hotel rules demand strict moral and hygienic conditions and the damn lamp is dangerous and moreover the mosquitoes are not hygienic. No." In the night Sigbjørn has been so hungry that, wondering if it might taste like locust (i.e. bacon) he has suggested wistfully that they might even kill a mosquito and eat it. There is much to do but in the end all is well, and when Sigbjørn goes with his 50 peso note to pay the bill the poor little man, who was asleep, got out all his money (having earlier said there was no change) out of his pockets, and began to throw bills around on the bed—he couldn't see and Sigbjørn had to make the change for him. {UBC 13:19, 93} He could have easily pinched 100 pesos but draws the line at a blind man and has even a sense of triumph he hasn't done it, hopes it will compensate for La Bohemia especially as it would have been so easy, he being blind—(ref. here right back to Bonn-Doumerghue business, where he stole the money because P. said he had from his mother, and to his own childhood and blindness the death of P.)[25]

To get from the Wildernesses' room to the dining porch you went through the excusado, shower and laundry, all one big room, up steps through a very long door, through another room of no apparent purpose full of junk, and finally on to a porch. Or you went down a flight of stairs—"es mejor"[26]—the old man said, to come again by means of a sort of sinister alley-way resembling a chute-the-chute. The place was confusing, the one white building, the "heap" seemed to have only 4 rooms, 2 above (one occupied by the squat

American woman), and two below, one by us; what seemed to be another little building belonging to it, turned out to be the office of the
huge Hotel del Pacifico next door, which was shaped rather like
shelves in a pantry. Another building 100 yards away and up a hill
behind the dining porch was part of the Cordoba too, further from
the beach, so, illogically, more expensive, though seemingly unoccupied. Now and then there is an explosion and a few rocks bounce
off the roofs—they are blasting the hillside just above to build yet
another hotel. Sigbjørn had just made this journey down the chute-
the-chute twice, for the old man had at last got up and insisted he
sign the register before leaving, the hotel pen wouldn't write, so he'd
gone to try and borrow one from the American woman, she hadn't
one either, so he'd gone to get a pencil from Primrose, but the manager wouldn't {UBC 13:19, 94} have it in pencil, and meantime had
come out with another pen: Sigbjørn, at the last moment, has another moment's irresolution, not to say fear: though he had no hangover, the swim having dissipated it, his hand was by no means steady
and anyway he hated signing registers—why should he sign it?—but
it was not this reluctance, for having to sign a register was a subtle
imposition on your freedom, like being fingerprinted—he remembered how he'd hated that—as a sudden temptation that had come
over him to sign it with a false name. Why was this so difficult? It
went strongly against the grain. Even escaping criminals must find it
difficult, so strong is the ethical impulse not to deny your own identity. But perhaps there was something even stranger than this. Something seemed to tell him that they should not, in spite of the fleas,
and at this very last moment, move. Sigbjørn had remembered,
partly with pleasure, for as he was by no means alone in thinking it
seemed to him one of the finest stories in any language, but partly
with a kind of frustration, for this particular setting of Acapulco
was one of a kind for which Thomas Mann had a peculiar affection,
and one which he did supremely well, the story of Mario and the
Magician[27]—a story about a popular summer resort on the Tyrrhenian Sea (Mem: as an adjective for blue—Tyrrhenian, or Tyrolian
blue) and also, if he remembered rightly, not quite in season, or just
after it had ended. Yes, the same atmosphere of flat bottomed boats,
sun bathers, inviting sandy beaches, oyster sellers, swimmers and
motorbuses as at Acapulco. Only it happened to be in Italy. Yes,
Portoclemente—or was it Torre di Venere (that was it, for there was

73

a tak in it) might indeed have been Acapulco, save that Acapulco happened to be in Mexico, and not the Tyrrhenian Sea. (This remembrance of {UBC 13:19, 95} Mario and the Magician may well have to come later: N.B. avoid overpraise of the story, as well, if possible, same quotations as Fadiman made from it.) However this did not seem to be the point so much as that the protagonists, or rather the observer, the we of the story had been compelled to change hotels, and then "it" had happened. They had put up first of all at the Grand Hotel where there was unfortunately also a Principe and a Principessa staying, the latter of whom had raised Cain because one of the "we's" children had whooping cough, or rather had not whooping cough having just recovered, but still alas, whooped, as a consequence of which they had had to move to another hotel called the Casa Eleonora. This embarrassment was the first in a series of unpleasant incidents—for instance they had next been fined for allowing their little child to run naked on the beach—which had its culmination in the shooting of a magician—not, like Mussolini, the hanging upside down, unless it amounted esoterically to the same thing, (and what a compliment, when one thought of St. Peter!)[28] at a performance they had taken the children to, by a subject he had hypnotised. It was not these two first incidents, the moving from one hotel to another and the unpleasantness with the management, the absurd and unjust fine, were precisely connected with the third, though the misuse of power was in a different measure common to all three, it was that in the first there was contained an invisible warning, which, if acted upon, would have avoided the second, which contained an even stronger warning of the same kind, namely of the advisability of leaving altogether, which if acted upon, would have prevented the third, not indeed the tragedy itself, but themselves being a witness to it, which had to say least, put the finishing touch to {UBC 13:19, 96} spoiling their holiday. What had held the narrator there in Torre di Venere was precisely the integrity of the artist in the face of experience, "Our stay," Mann wrote, "had by now become remarkable in our own eyes." "Shall we strike sail, avoid a certain experience as soon as it seems not expressly calculated to increase our enjoyment and self esteem? Shall we go away whenever life looks like turning in the slightest uncanny, or not quite normal, or even rather painful and mortifying? No, surely not. Rather stay and look matters in the face, brave them out, perhaps precisely in so doing lies a lesson for us to learn." Sigbjørn had later far more occasion than now to reflect upon this. In fact he did not know he thought of it at all. Had anything happened to spoil their holiday, any unpleasantness at all? No, nothing, save perhaps the matter of his having gypped the Bohemia, but still that might be considered almost permissible under the circumstances, considering how much they had been robbed already in Mexico, nothing indeed, unless it was the fleas, but the fleas, like the vultures, were the kind of thing that Sigbjørn and Primrose would be able to relish and laugh over in memory, so that he could almost be grateful for them. There remained, therefore, merely the matter of changing hotels, and the fact that Casa Eleonora was perhaps as a mere name not so remote from the Quinta Eugenia as it should be. How absurd he was being! Their holiday in fact was turning into an immense success. Well, it wasn't turning, it *was*. All these thoughts had gone through his mind in a flash as he hesitated with the pen and now as he realised that he could scarcely avoid signing the hotel register now, after such a fuss had been made, even if he did stay, he smiled and signed, signed rather too elaborately, with a kind of {UBC 13:19, 97} deliberation combined with his slight shakiness, to show, so to speak, that he could do it: Sr. and Sra. Sigbjørn and Primrose Wilderness, Eridanus Inlet, Vancouver, Columbia Brittannica, Canada—Inglese y Americano.

Now everything is arranged so they start to go back up to the Eugenia. They pause at the bottom of the hill, not without a look of wistful sentimental regret at the preposterous Cordoba, at that moment a shower of pebbles falls on a nearby roof as the blasting behind the hotel recommences, and this has the effect of startling a nearby flight of vultures into turning round: one of them zoomed right into the telegraph wires in doing this, losing in doing so a batch of black feathers that came flapping down through the air, while the vulture flapped off sheepishly.

In a lot to their left, where Stuyvesant, an ugsome friend of Bousfield, had once shot an iguana, a kind of lizard, or gila monster eyed them: they had seen it yesterday, just over the top of the rocks, a snake, a monster, or lizard, and it seemed indeed part of the rock, it never moved save to vanish utterly, and this was purely hypothetical for they had never seen it happen: it was an uncomfortable feeling to walk past this sinister stoat-like creature, just sitting motionless on the hot barren rock, as if silently expressing a will outside its own nature, perhaps even that of the baking rock itself. Sigbjørn shied a stone at it, not to hit it, but to disturb it, but it did not move at all, did not even blink its reptilian eye. "Tiberius is a rock, Sejanus is a snake."[29]

Exhausted from the sleepless night they plodded up the hill to the Eugenia where no one was about at all so they took possession of the new room number 5 and sat happily drinking habanero {UBC 13:19, 98} with their feet on the parapet, meantime watching Señor Mañana Mañana y Mañana[30] and José return in a motor boat from Pied de la Cuesta. (This—the observation from a distance, and from a height might if carefully done be an excellent opportunity for character drawing, for they are all slightly tight, perhaps drinking out of a wineskin.)

José is glad to see them, in an expansive mood, and insists that they be shifted to another room on the top floor, and won't hear of any payment in advance, or signings of names; Sigbjørn being rather anxious to get the business of name signing over, now the habanero has corrected his tremor slightly. But he is, just the same, relieved that he doesn't have to. This room has two beds and a shower bath and another bed outside on the balcony. The only thing wrong with it is that its number is 13; here, in fact they have shifted from the perfectly good Emersonian number of 5[31] to 13. Primrose is delighted because they are being offered this much better room at the same price as 5, Sigbjørn tries not to let his face fall, but can't help it. (Mem: the Phillipson incident and the gratitude he got.)[32]

(If the life at the Quinta Eugenia were to be made into a movie, Sigbjørn would have beer at breakfast, with a shaking hand rather a fat and pudgy hand is all you see; the camera goes from table to table; still nothing but hands, all shaking; a hand tries to pick up a coffee cup, shaking, the coffee is spilled; difficulties with napkins are then broken into by scene in kitchen; different hands, but all of them are shaking.)

"Oh I know what's worrying you, you dear silly. Now I know, it's because the number's 13. Oh what a ridiculous one you are, Etc." {UBC 13:19, 99} "Yes, I know I am a ridiculous. On the other hand I am a sensible too, for we have another garbage heap." Sigbjørn agrees that it was ridiculous, but now he notices that they are over yet another garbage dump on the right, and moreover there are little cylinders overhead on the porch that suggest fluorescent lighting which Sigbjørn and Primrose abominate; nonetheless there they are, they can have it for whatever it is they've settled on, perhaps 13 pesos a day each or at all events the same as room 5 (what precisely, and what money they have is enormously important) they drink more habanero in the fourth room they have had since reaching Acapulco, and then at twilight go down for their evening swim. Primrose is very happy, and Sigbjørn takes her out into deep water; coming back he sees, half concealed by the Hotel Mar Azul and the Case Verde the round window of Mr. Baldwin and just the corner of the house his old rentier at Cuernavaca, the rentier indeed of the Consul. This is the window of the house he never lived in, but which he might have lived in with Ruth, at that moment of crisis at the end of 1937. This he had most completely forgotten until this very moment. They could have had it at a small rent too, but they had refused it because there were only oil lamps, and instead of living there, they had separated and he had never seen Ruth again. Ah, yes, he thought, as he stood on this shore where Juarez had once landed, bedraggled and drenched, from New Orleans, another fellow doubtless—and a Zapotecan to boot who gave one the mind and heart of Sir Philip Gibbs—had he not too, like Juarez, looked, if not for the salvation of Mexico, to Acapulco for his moral rescue? But he had tragically declined the gambit. It was strange to think that in that house might have lain his salvation. (Or even worse destruction that had occurred.) {UBC 13:19, 100} It was strange and tragic to think of it too, for if it had, in either event, he might never have met Primrose . . . It was a lovely evening with beyond Caletilla a windmill pump whizzing in the setting sun, and, revived, they ran up past the snake or monster still sitting there on the rock performing its motionless will, to dinner, at which they ate enormously and well.

After dinner, because it was their first night here, and also because José and Señor de Mañana had invited themselves up to see them, because in short it was an occasion for celebration, they broke a rule and went on drinking habanero, and even after the others had gone they sat there, under the glare of the fluorescent light with their feet on the parapet, holding hands and looking out to sea, crashing eternally against the reef, where the surf showed its teeth in the moon. Sigbjørn remembered too on the innocent shore, that evening, the barbed shadow of the surf at evening.

(Note: Induction into dream of Haiti should be easily managed: the upheaval in Haiti was what at first had threatened. Now Spain: Acapulco was associated with Juarez, and Juarez in turn with New Orleans: Amann had mentioned Baron Samedi[33] etc. Acapulco also has negro villages.) {UBC 13:19, 101}

III

Life at the Quinta Eugenia, Pensión Francesca, Spanish and French Cooking, Sigbjørn remarked to Primrose one fine morning after breakfast, could best be interpreted by a film director, with intentions comic rather than otherwise: it would begin, at breakfast itself, with a shot simply of a human hand trembling upon a tablecloth, this was the manager's hand, rather fat and pudgy: from this the camera might pass to other tablecloths, other tables, and other hands, of all shapes and sizes, from the sensitive and refined like the Wilderness[es'], in different degrees, and the darker hands of José, and of course the blacker and even more beautiful and Indian hands of Señor de Mañana y Mañana Y Mañana, to more spatulate and workmanlike hands in the kitchen, male and female, all of which, however, would have this one thing in common, that they trembled; in the morning, yes, it is regrettable to say, the whole Quinta Eugenia from top to bottom had the shakes, and there might even have [been] a hand, either Sigbjørn's or the manager's, that would make a sudden futile assault on a coffee pot, the coffee would be spilt, the tablecloth ruined. (Much of this that deals with the routine of the Quinta Eulalia[1] would undoubtedly be more effective in a later chapter, to give the effect of monotony, and at the same time to counteract it; at present I am toying with the idea of V in this chapter too, but may abandon it.) And the cause of this was by no means mysterious: for everyone in the Quinta Eugenia, from the manager to the newest guest, got tight as a bird every night. While the atmosphere of Acapulco is decidedly conducive to this ancient and admirable pastime on the part of its visitors it was the only hotel Sigbjørn had ever lived in which the habit {UBC 13:20, 102} extended to the staff too. For this also there was a reason; the majority of the staff, like its guests, were European. And any European who has been to Acapulco, if he is honest, will understand better than anyone else how it is almost impossible to live within a few miles of the town of Acapulco itself, as was the Quinta Eugenia, without feeling in it an atmosphere from which you very signally wish to escape in some form or another, and for this reason, (since the historical interest of Acapulco has to be taken on faith—it is present doubtless, but the fort alone gives evidence of it, the whole town has such an air of the jerrybuilt, the transient, and has been said, the impermanent, that even when one student is informed by Roeder that as short a while back as the days of Maximilian, as history goes, Ignacio Altamirano,[2] say, was to be found reading Tasso there, one tends to be somewhat skeptical about this—where? For it is impossible to imagine a single dwelling in Acapulco in which Ignacio Altamirano was reading Tasso or anything else, and one cannot believe that this has anything to do with the earthquakes to which the town has been subject—witness Oaxaca—) It is for this reason, among others, say, that the sea is so indispensable. But for the reason that I speak of, I mean the aforesaid habit, it was perhaps by no means so remarkable that the place should be run in a haphazard fashion. The Wildernesses were given a better room for less money, certainly, but such articles as towels and soap, for example, were forgotten, and when asked for, put off till tomorrow, when, not arriving, would be promised once more for mañana. But let us be fair. The Quinta Eugenia in many ways was one of the most admirable places to spend a holiday that one could well conceive of, and the Wildernesses' judgement in this {UBC 13:20, 103} regard is to be commended. There it was, as has been said, sitting on a cliff over the sea, with the Wildernesses' own room on the top of three stories on the right as you faced the sea, as indeed all the other rooms indeed, looking hopefully in the opposite direction from Acapulco itself, which just over the shoulder of the hill to the hotel's left one could not quite see, had you wanted to, which you did not: the view from the Wildernesses' end commanded the beaches of Caleta and Caletilla, the Governor's brother's house on the island with the causeway dividing the beach leading to it, the windmill pump whizzing on the bluff, and the mountains, such as they were, not much: the other end, that is the dining room, ceilinged and pilastered but windowless, and on the edge of the precipitous parapet commanded the sweep of sea running round from the bay, and the great rock island out to which Sigbjørn had once in his twenties, in fact on that near fatal occasion, god knows how, swum: outside the bay the sea combed the rocks in a constant moving white line along the base of various little islands . . . But perhaps, to get a more complete picture of life in this windy beautiful hotel on the top of a crag, which from a distance with its name in huge letters along the side QUINTA EULALIA, looked like an ancient trampsteamer, washed up there high and dry by a tidal wave, it would be better to go back to ten o'clock at night. At this point, the machine having wound down with a sickening final thudding, while the Wildernesses would be sitting out on their porch, perhaps casting now and then a look of nostalgia at the Cordoba, already in the past, the floodlight along the balconies and the single bulbs having therefore been extinguished, and the place in darkness.³ At the crack of dawn over (place where dawn is) the proprietor, {UBC 13:20, 104} a short many chinned paunchy hard-drinking Swiss, would rise with a monumental hangover and sink half a basket of Vino de Mision San Tomas,⁴ and go down, with a basket, in shorts on bare fat padding feet to the beach. He was a seemingly kindly careless man with small eyes and a mean aspect. Here a fishing boat would be awaiting him, manned by natives with their trousers rolled up to their knees: he would wade out fatly, clamber aboard, and go and fish for the hotel's breakfast. Shortly after this the other servants would be busy in the kitchen. José, the manager, would also arise, with a slightly less but still formidable hangover, (a word that will be found, alas, to occur in our narrative almost as often as the word know-how in Toynbee's recent history)⁵ and go about his business. Almost a pure Indian, José looked like a Greek, or a Cypriot, with a dark and tragic face like a Christ on a Greek Catholic Church in Cyprus, but he was the best of fellows. He had black lustrous hair, wide compassionate eyes, and an almost Christlike face, a swarthy complexion, he was of middle height, if tall for a Mexican, and when he had a hangover, which was ⁹⁄₁₀ths of the time, he slumped his shoulders, and prowled, stooping, rather than walked about. "Horreebly," he would say, though it was rarely that he allowed himself to be inhibited from doing his duty, which he did with seriousness, though he had an enormous sense of humour. He did not however often go fishing with Schwartz. He was married to a Frenchwoman, plump, pregnant, with a sharp nose and a face like a watch, who sailed rather than walked, who was perhaps flirtatious, drifting round to the tables, but was essentially silent and perplexing, and, even to Sigbjørn, somewhat terrifying. "She is my lady-me," José would say of her—he was very good to her, and they seemed much in love, when they {UBC 13:20, 105} had a spare moment toward evening walking down to a rock together and gazing out to sea. They had lived in the United States. There was also José's rather sinister henchman, the assistant manager. His business seemed to be looking after the accounts, seeing to the soft drinks and bottles of Cartablanca Dos Equis and Noche Buena and Saturno beer kept in the inevitable "Bebe Coca Cola bien fría"[6] icebox in one corner of the high dining room, keep an eye on the guests, and other duties that for the moment, (for I have anticipated) were obscure to Sigbjørn, at all events he seemed to go to town almost every day on business that seemed to have to do with the vast number of papers he carried under his arm—and of course, as we shall know later, this business was taking down the names of every new arrival to the Immigration, for Acapulco being a port of entry, such was, at any rate in 1946, the custom. Breakfast, the time for which depended upon Schwartz' return from fishing, which was sometimes mysteriously delayed, also upon the arrival of papayas and other fruits from the town, was from seven to ten, and consisted of so and so. Most of the guests would get up early and swim before breakfast. These guests were so and so, and in this regard the Hotel Quinta Eulalia would have been a good place to set a novel of "character" or even a murder mystery, for it was a very obvious unity, but this book, the possibilities of which were immediately perceived by Sigbjørn—a book that might be called anything from Acapulco, an adventure in living,[7] to Murder in the Quinta Maria, a Crime at Caleta,—must be forever unwritten, interesting though it might be, and this for the simple and unhappy reason that Sigbjørn, while a writer, was so far from having any interest in "character" as such that he might be said not to be interested in people for {UBC 13:20, 106} what they *were* as characters: or at all events it was against this that he sportingly fought, but the inhibition, flaw, was rooted in his best instincts. But perhaps there was something deeper than "lack of curiosity" in this, and an artistic principle at work that made his rejection of this kind of interest valid on artistic grounds themselves. It had always seemed to him that nobody is more disastrously ill-equipped than precisely the kind of novelist who does it to observe character. The so-called average person who doesn't feel he has to write about it can often do it better. So-called, I say, because the average person, being bound up, like Sigbjørn, and rightly, with his own problems, does not, perhaps, do it at all: the sizing up of character is largely a matter of self-defence, an instinctual habit perhaps of protection, so that other people, while they appear to possess characteristics that would be useful to the novelist too, doubtless seem more as forces, for good or evil, menaces, and warnings of good or ill, emblems of the financial or spiritual bettering of one's own lot, investments against a time of need, or unselfishly, on the other hand, as creatures requiring one's assistance, which assistance if it is not to be to their great detriment of the subject involved, is perhaps most usefully expressed by liquor or hard cash or even sometimes simply a smile, and a kind look—or they are, and this is by far the most common, simply presages of endless waste of time, or crashing boredom. All this being so (in Sigbjørn's estimation at least) among the most unnatural devices, that is of devices removed from nature of all the unnatural ones, which a novelist employs in the attempt to be naturalistic is the one most taken for granted, the means by which character—and even the radical departures from {UBC 13:20, 107} the norm on the part of genius such as Lawrence amount to the same thing—is developed and portrayed. And least of all are to be trusted those novelists guilty of that inverted narcissism which takes the form of saying how much they love their characters; and how indeed too they love them, love them, even as the Oxford Grouper[8] or the social reformer loves a potential convert, very often, that is to say, unto death, at least in the memory of their readers. For the man who truly loves his fellow man is extremely rare. And with very few exceptions the novelist who is anxious to show how much he loves his characters loves only himself, just in fact like dear old Sigbjørn, alarming, even terrifying, though that thought may be, with the evidence at our disposal. The narcissism is indeed necessary—but the great characters, (or at least I, who am no novelist, would think so) in Shakespeare, Romains, Tolstoy, etc. and Dostoievsky—they seem to come about by a gigantic projection, or in the case of peopled novels—a breaking down of the central atom of the author's central personality: with exceptions, of course: but this certainly did not apply to the majority. And strangely enough, even in the most admirable cases, how much do we remember? how much do we retain of Quinette? or Jerphanion?[9] This of course does not alter the fact that those two extremest examples of the Paul Pry, Proust and Dickens,[10] were among the most successful creators of character, even though their approach was diametrically opposite. But some of these reasons mentioned here the school teacher who hummed, the two homosexual but well-meaning artists who sat down on the beach all day, like idols, baking, like unspecified works of art, or sculpturings that had been left there in the sun to set, the Christ-like José, and {UBC 13:20, 108} his watch-like lady-me, must, though bound beautifully in the unity of the Quinta Eugenia, remain forever unwritten about, characters who might have been, voices overheard sometimes, but whose owners do not come very close to us. And this must be true, alas, also of Herr Schwab, who must have seemed to any other writer but Sigbjørn the most interesting character of all, the Swiss whose presence at all in Mexico might have been such an invitation, and in whose manner of eating breakfast at this time Sigbjørn might have been more interested than he was, for in it was to be seen not only the image of the results of the indulgence and to some extent the fight against its tyranny, which Sigbjørn himself was, so to say, putting him up, but, in little, the pattern of what may more nearly concern us, namely that of breakdown, and had Sigbjørn watched more closely than he did, or not been so identified with it himself, he might also have seen some of the causes for it. (But if Sigbjørn cannot see them I can have a shot at describing them myself???) In his youth, Sigbjørn, a golfer, had judged people by their golf swing, and the way they putted, and played approach and chip shots etc; and probably he had never deviated from this . . . It has been said that Sigbjørn, despite the good habit of his morning swim; had difficulty with his coffee cup. This however—a fact which subtly mitigated in Sigbjørn's eyes the disgrace—was nothing to the difficulty which Señor Schwab had, who was be it said unable, or unwilling (as had been the case with Sigbjørn in his extreme youth) because of his bulk to swim: but with Herr Schwartz, neither his morning potations of Vino de Mision San Tomas, nor what oxidation of alcohol that matutinal fishing trip afforded him, seemed of much avail: if Sigbjørn had moments of extreme {UBC 13:20, 109} discomfort at breakfast time Herr Schwab's breakfasts were patent crucifixions: he was driven indeed to eating in remoter and remoter places in the dining room, and at the most unpopular hours, and finally even took to eating it on the porch, opposite the kitchen, or the lavatory, near Sigbjørn and Primrose's room, in the remotest corner of all, together with yet another bottle of red wine—I say bottle, though it sometimes contained a lighter and browner liquid not altogether consonant with what should have been its contents, and sometimes the bottle would not be in evidence at all: he would use a bottle of cocacola or some soft drink as a cover, meantime devoting himself—for it did not seem that his health was in any way affected, albeit with none too great, if any, success, to some succulent looking red sausages that, however, never found its way on to the table of his guests, and rarely into his mouth, even there. And in regard to this matter of health a further word. It is very doubtful if in a place like Acapulco the health of a person who combats it with any energy at all, especially by means of the sea, will be seriously affected: we say nothing of mental health. But Sigbjørn and Primrose would get up early and take their swim, (the artists would be already bathing, and the monster whose eye never moved upon its rock) and any slight hangover which they did have would be immediately dispersed, and in this connection it should perhaps be pointed out that Acapulco is a place where a man might get as tight as Titus Oates[11] four or five times a day so long as he takes as many swims, with little effect. This is not true of tequila: but it is of the brandy, especially Berreteaga, and it is even true of the bulk habanero procured by Primrose and Sigbjørn, whose palatableness depended rather {UBC 13:20, 110} upon how near it was to the bottom of the barrelhead, from the Ciclon. It is, however, possible to get an erroneous picture: though this routine did not entirely do away with the shakes, Primrose and Sigbjørn now only drank in the evenings and very cheery evenings they were: Sigbjørn did not even allow himself a bottle of beer at midday. But I have anticipated again. I had left Sigbjørn and Primrose in the evening of their arrival and of their transference to the new and better room, the number of which to our hero's primitive soul had been the only drawback.

(N.B. Anatomy at one point of the time elapsed, i.e., between 1938–1946, no longer than between 1926 (when he'd first gone to Paris) and 1932 (yet what a lifetime) and how much had happened. The whole face of the world had been altered beyond recognition, cathedrals, and whole cathedral cities ruined, whole populations imprisoned, dispossessed, departed—what heroism had he not achieved since then, obstacles overcome—and yet all this while, as if it were indeed, on another plane, a candle someone had kept alight, this little fine stood there against, seemingly immortal, a fine it is important to remember that was in part at least the result of his goodheartedness, and yet he knew that this was not the most terrifying aspect of it, for what made his hair almost stand on end was: (Wynn, etc.) if this could be remembered, had been preserved, intact, what else that he thought had been so triumphantly transcended and expiated, might not be forgotten?)

But prior to that, in fact during dinner that night, they had already made up their mind to stay. A fresh sea-breeze—in this sense it was a place that fulfilled the most roseate view of the advertisements—blew through the dining room with its gaps in the parapet for windows. There was a glorious view and, {UBC 13:20, 111} reasonably cheap, as even the Wildernesses were convinced, had all the advantages of the great hotels, and few of the disadvantages. For example, in the great hotels, it was necessary, as has been said, to take a taxi for ten pesos every time you went down on to the beach: then, if you did not hire somewhere to change, that anyway was inconvenient, you would have to return to your hotel in a wet bathing suit; and soon; true, none of the toilets in the Quinta Eugenia worked and you had to throw the used toilet paper on the floor: it was a vicious circle, because you revolted at doing this, and put it in the bowl, as a consequence of which all the toilets in the Quinta Eugenia were stopped up, a phenomenon that could scarcely even be traced to the mysterious Kilroy, (who caused Sigbjørn later to make his sole contribution to the literature of the toilet, in a manner that had it been observed, might have resulted in his arrest by the F.B.I., at all events caused him to be misunderstood, for to the rhetorical question Who is Kilroy? he had replied, in a moment of anger with it, American Civilization, something he was very far from agreeing with on a somewhat later occasion, on another occasion he was to write, in a toilet, Read The Valley of the Shadow of Death)[12] since all the toilets in Mexico were, in one way or the other, save that strange one at the Hotel Cordoba, stopped up: and anyhow it might have been described as a step forward for them, for in Canada the Wildernesses had no toilet at all to speak of. The food was good, and Herr Schwartz, sitting there as always in white, with his great belly, and little hands and feet, and small eyes behind spectacles, and small mouth, and who, after his retreat of the morning, had become progressively more friendly during the day, and at the same time as if {UBC 13:20, 112} he had been approaching closer and closer to the dining room, and who was even sitting at the next table but one to the door, as if he, on the rebound of his withdrawal of the morning, had made a slight spiritual advance, promised both to be a genial host and provide a good table. It was after midnight when the Wildernesses finally turned in, once more in candlelight, but before going to sleep, Sigbjørn made a resolution. He had nearly, by his absurd superstition, managed to spoil Primrose's day, both as a penance for doing this, and as a proof that it was of no significance, and he decided to make amends; he would rise earlier—he would rise indeed—and get Primrose up at 6—so that she could see the morning star, as she loved to do: and later he would hire a "vizor" or even a flat-bottomed boat, from which they could see the famous tropical fish of Acapulco, an enchanting experience that would delight Primrose: he would sacrifice having beer at lunch time and there would be no bones about this, else he would be sleepy and unable to be the magician of a delicious afternoon for her, as he wanted to, which he proposed to do by hiring a couple of floats—or waterskis—all of these things being the kind of efforts of the will that Sigbjørn found peculiarly difficult; meantime without consulting Primrose or putting her to any trouble at all he would pay the bill in advance and sign their names and so forth and arrange for a week's stay, calculating it himself, so that they wouldn't be gypped; the next night, if Primrose wanted a drink, she should have one, of course, but he would refrain altogether, for it seemed to him he was beginning to drink a little too much again, it was, as they used to say, creeping up on him slightly; and then the next day he would take her off early to Pied de la Cuesta which was the only place near Acapulco he had {UBC 13:20, 113} visited with Ruth, and that on the very first day he had been in Mexico, with its atmosphere of the Belgian Congo,[13] and its jungle, and its roaring beach. And in keeping these resolutions Sigbjørn succeeded remarkably well; rising at six, even before Herr Schwab and standing with Primrose on the uppermost balcony while she watched with delight the fading of the morning star, though they still couldn't find the Southern Cross; and though they were not able to procure vizors in the morning, and flat bottomed boats not at all, they amused themselves all morning trying to balance themselves on floats, and how Primrose delighted in the tiny silver fish in schools that jumped out of the water, in the early morning, leaped out, under, out, under, so swiftly in formation, and, Sigbjørn having refrained from any beer before dinner, they were successful in procuring vizors in the afternoon.

With the vizors, binoculars which, despite the slight inconvenience of feeling that you were drowning when you put them on, you were able to peer straight, as it were, into the sea's unconscious, they entered into a kind of submarine world of honeymoon; their souls mingled, and became one in the blue tropical water; they drew the Pacific sky over them like the sea and disported themselves below.

(N.B. According to Ellsworth Huntington,[14] as civilization develops, it moves towards colder regions. Though there might seem at first sight to be on every hand proof to the precise contrary, no one who has lived in Acapulco for very long could doubt that this is true. And was the converse of this true. When it becomes over-developed it seeks—or seeks symbolically—hotter ones again, where, overripe, it falls to pieces.) {UBC 13:20, 114}

And with the vizor they saw royal purple fish with gold bellies and slender silver ones with a pale gold stripe from head to tail, and a pale gold tail; looking under water with goggles was, to Primrose, a new fluid world of shifting light in a transparent blue-green medium; the vela, the seaweed, and the coral. Even Sigbjørn was impressed. In the morning there had been delicate clauses of silver fish leaping out of the water: now there were whole purple passages[15] of these little fish:—he could not feel, thinking this, even as he had about the sunset—semicolon technique of fish: and others, good only for the goldsmith's art. And so happy were they indeed that when they came back to the hotel they forgot to look to see if the unwinking monster was still sitting on its rock but noticed instead, for the first time, a great purple-blue convolvulus 6 inches across growing at the edge of the lot, by the beach road, so that looking at them, it was difficult to be certain one was not still beneath the sea.

Sigbjørn had not failed either to remember to settle the matter of the bill and so forth, and these he did, having waited until Herr Schwab had become genial towards evening, and though José had insisted that it was perfectly unnecessary for him to trouble about signing the register, insisted on doing this too, resisting the temptation to have a drink also before doing it; even though it was not so terrible signing in front of the afflicted Herr Schwab himself, Sigbjørn had overlooked the fact that since he was not to have a drink that night, it might have been wiser to waive the fact of Herr Schwab's lack of geniality in the morning, and take account of the more important fact that Herr Schwab would then be shaking worse than he: as it was, he managed it, even though shaking himself, more with fear that he {UBC 13:20, 115} would shake than anything else, and even adding some more extra flourishes to those with which he had adorned their registration at the Cordoba: Sr. y Sra. Sigbjørn and Primrose Wilderness, c/o Eridanus Post Office, Columbia Britannica, Canada—Inglese y Canadianos y Americanos. El Mundo. El Universal.[16] And this completed to his rather idiotic satisfaction, and Primrose delighted by the issue, and scarcely missing his self-bereavement, from habanero before dinner, in which abnegation Primrose had joined him, they went to supper. Just before this, while Sigbjørn had been registering, two old American ladies who spoke no Spanish had arrived and to her great amusement had mistaken Primrose for the hired help. At dinner these ladies were conversing with the two artists, Lewis and Post, at the next table: "We wish we could paint too—" "What a nice view!" "I suppose you've made some pretty pictures." They rattled on. "Do you do character studies?" (Lewis was an abstractionist) "What's your name, young man. We'll go and see your pictures and shine in reflected glory." (giggles.) "How exciting to meet an artist! Mmmmm." (the subterranean humming.) Oh Jesus! Lewis flashed a friendly S.O.S. but now they had descended upon Primrose and Sigbjørn. (N.B. Somewhere describe what is, for Sigbjørn the complete agony of dining, save severely alone, or at least in semi-darkness, or in an enclosed booth.)

"Do you like this place? Is it safe here?" the schoolteacher asked, with a complete disregard of anyone's feelings that might be hurt, including, conceivably, Primrose's own, whom they had presumably not recognized as the "hired help"—"Perfectly," Sigbjørn replied, with his weather eye out to see that no one's feelings were being hurt. {UBC 13:20, 116}

"Our room had no lock and we pushed all our furniture and bags against the door and took turns sitting up all night—we heard strange noises and laughter—" she hummed—"the room wasn't clean: I told the tourist bureau, I said, I don't demand luxury but I *do* demand it be clean! Hmmmmmm. But our young friends told us it was safe—Hmmmmmmm—" This school teacher, who was seeing the world on her pension, interpolated all her remarks with this kind of humming, or singing, that was utterly maddening, though doubtless she was the best of persons, far better indeed than either of the artists, Sigbjørn thought, replying in a quiet voice: "Actually the doors have padlocks but can't, as usual, be locked from inside. On the other hand I'd say *you* were as safe as houses in Mexico—a great deal safer in fact than most houses in Canada."

(Later, one should say, on seeing her outside the Immigration in Mexico City: Mrs. Oxborough looked as though she had hummed for the last time.)

(N.B. Perhaps later, in Mexico City: an image for gloom and sorrow: some song, like I'm Dreaming of a White Christmas,[17] being played by a juke-box, for about the 3rd time in succession, in a nearly empty diner, or bar, a cold slushy night: or worst of all, perhaps, on a Xmas Day that you are spending alone, and that a Christmas that is really white: there is not merely a sadness but a gruesomeness, as of the wailing of the lost, that coalesces with some quality of utter desolation in the dreamy place itself and the dreariness and wailing of the night, and your own lack of anything like warmth or comfort, or your hangover, and perhaps even old lost memories of being in such places with someone loved, but which inheres doubtless in its very mechanicalness, that seems expressive of everything that is most utterly hopeless in our civilization, yet this is what every night is like in Mexico) {UBC 13:20, 116}[18]

After dinner Primrose felt sleepy and Sigbjørn was restless and had been asked down to the artists' room to see their pictures and he had a strange desire simply to talk with strangers so Primrose giving her sleepy assent to this Sigbjørn went down: the artists' room was almost next door to the room the Wildernesses had had previously. They offered him some beer and Sigbjørn accepted it and when the artists' beer was finished he went up to the dining room where Schwab and Madam and Juan the assistant patron and some other hombres who seemed to be employees but did nothing and José, who was tight, were playing cards and Chinese chequers and Sigbjørn bought some more beer. Sigbjørn felt that this was wrong: still, he wanted to return the beer: he didn't want to look at the pictures either—which barely interested him—and without beer doubtless he felt he couldn't look at the pictures for the length of time that politeness would demand before he would decently have an opportunity to talk: what was peculiar also was that his own interest in these two people was of the very faintest, and perhaps the truest thing to say would be that what he wanted in spite of his resolutions to the contrary was a reasonable excuse to have a few drinks without feeling any remorse for it. (In spite of this, as the narrator of this story,[19] I feel that I should mention here especially in the light of later events, the extraordinary affection with which the Wildernesses seemed to be regarded and remembered, even by those who had never met them, and to have inspired even in those whose object to put it mildly would have seemed to be rid of them.) He had an opportunity to talk sooner than he expected however for some of the pictures, non-abstractionist, those of the sunburned man he'd seen sprawled on the porch on that first day, happened to be of Oaxaca, and soon he had launched into an {UBC 13:20, 117} account of the fire, the events and circumstances that succeeded it, everything indeed that he had told to myself, the identity between Vigil and Fernando, how Fernando had called him "The maker of tragedies"[20]—and after yet some more beer, how was it that there was a kind of gruesome pleasure in that?—and ending up with the discovery of Fernando's death, and the coincidences that there seemed to be to him anyway, both numerically and otherwise, in their being in the tower and how now they'd been changed to room 13: "It is as if, at every turn, I keep running into the past, just as indeed my characters did in the book."

Post said with a queer look: "I suppose you haven't overlooked that today is the 13th."

"Yes, by god I had," Sigbjørn thought in bed, lying snugly by Primrose who had scarcely stirred, and where he was immediately suffering the most horrible remorse in spite of all for drinking the beer, not so much on account of having broken his word to himself, as for the fact that out of the six pesos he'd spent he might have bought poor Primrose something pretty for herself, that is precisely what I have overlooked. Today is the 13th, or rather it was, for it is now just after midnight, no my watch—my faithful watch that is always a mnemonic of my generosity—is a little fast: so it is still the 13th. But what unlucky thing have I done on the 13th? Was there anything else that would more overwhelmingly prove the madness of this ridiculous obsession with coincidences and the tyranny of numbers (still, was not Newton also obsessed by the tyranny of numbers,[21] and was not Newton a genius—passion for order[22] at the base of all things. He should remember what dear old Hippolyte,[23] I refer to myself, said) as this fact, that today has been one of the happiest days since our fire, a day when we have {UBC 13:20, 118} struck a chord for our future, a day of complete freedom and joy? True I have spoilt it a little at the end by drinking beer: just as last night was spoilt a little at the end by the discovery that the room was number 13: but as a matter of fact not only is today March 13th, but our first night last night, for we turned in after midnight, was spent in our room 13, and on the 13th, and still nothing but what was absolutely joyful has happened. It was hard sometimes for an intelligent fellow like Sigbjørn, who had lent more than moral support to a war against ignorance and superstition really to admit to himself that he reasoned like this: for while some of the undeniable and strange coincidences that coloured his existence had a strange and even sombre quality, these obsessions with numbers doubtless seemed to him a petty tyranny that one couldn't even make a good story out of: but in this case it seemed to have a happy outcome, for reasoning that he might as well have been bothered about yesterday's having some significance because it was the 12th, and there were twelve chapters in The Valley of the Shadow of Death, or any other day (and this way madness lay) and that he had already laid the "jinx" if any by turning this into one of the best of their days he went to sleep more fully resolved to make tomorrow, when he would take Primrose to Pied de la Cuesta—and Ah, today, he thought, with blessed relief, the 14th, even more successful than was yesterday, even if it was the day before the Ides of March.

(End here, if chapter to be broken.) {UBC 13:20, 119}

IV

And in the morning all these superstitious vapours had indeed vanished, they rose early, they swam, they breakfasted heartily, and went down past the rock temporarily vacated by Sejanus (Shakespeare it is said performed in Marlowe's play of this name,[1] Sigbjørn might say—this leading to the discussion of the Elizabethans) and the huge convolvulus, and taking up their stand by a favorite old log they had nigh on the beach, on which, when they went swimming they put their towels and their dark spectacles, and under which their cigarettes, which was opposite the Paradise of Caleta, waited for the bus to the Zócalo. A man who seemed faintly familiar drove by in a car from town, and threw them a look, or Sigbjørn a look, frowning with a little grimace: he drove a little way in the direction of Caletilla and then turned the car round, and drove back past them casting another glance it seemed at Sigbjørn, and drove to a little distance and came to a stop at a low building that had once been an annex of the Paraiso de Caleta,—it was indeed the precise spot where he had [lived,] just up [from] Gilda and Wynn—but was now conjoined with another small hotel on the slope called the Mar Azul, the Ocean Blue, which was shut, but which had, in front of it, a public telephone booth, where this man, a Mexican quite tall and slender, who had a handsome but weak face, and was dressed in yellow seersucker, with what might have been either a yachting cap or an official cap, put in a call, then drove away. "That's bad," said Sigbjørn. "Why bad?" "I think that bastard recognized me." "Well, why shouldn't he? Wouldn't it be remarkable if nobody recognized you especially after what Bousfield said." "Nobody has yet. And you forget Bousfield said I looked 100% better than I had and was scarcely recognizable." "Is there any reason why the poor man should not recognize you? Is there a law {UBC 13:21, 120} against it?" "No," laughed Sigbjørn, "It's just my persecution mania, that's all." "Who did you think he was?" "I thought he was a fellow named Guyou—an old bloodsucker and bummer of drinks from Americans at the Siete Mares, a dung cart, except for the straw, and that's in his feet."[2] "Do you have to recognize him?" "I suppose I don't. Anyway he's gone." "Persecution mania" it certainly was, and it was something he must get rid of: here he was giving in to it already, and in a moment they would have a quarrel, and the day would be spoilt. He wouldn't do it, damn it. "Zócalo! Zócalo!" The little bus came along, quite empty, with the boy hanging out on the step, shouting, they climbed in and went off to the square. "It's going to be a glorious day, and we're going to have a wonderful time," Sigbjørn said, and it certainly was glorious, with a fair fine breeze blowing through the windows of the bus, till they sank into the stokehold of Acapulco. It was an hour before the bus left for Pied de la Cuesta so they set off through the town, and past the Banco Nacional de Mexico, past the abarrotes where that first day the bottle had broken, past the garage, with its sign Supervulcanizacion, and the white church being built, where dust motes swam in a ray of sunlight at the entrance, and avoiding the Bohemia, went into the "Beach Clots" where Sigbjørn bought Primrose a new pair of sandals—symbolic too—to make up for himself, having been selfish about the beer the previous night, and after this since they had brought their shopping bag and a couple of empty bottles, they went into The Cyclone, where they could also buy American cigarettes, at wholesale price, for it was kept by a buxom woman who prided herself on giving good service to foreigners, and to whom courtesy seemed no empty form: Sigbjørn loved the atmosphere of {UBC 13:21, 121} El Ciclon with its great green barrels and bustle and funnels and strange smells but their object had been not so much to get any habanero to drink that night but to have some on hand, should they want it, or their artist friends drop in, which would make it unnecessary to make this godawful sweltering trip into Acapulco. It turned out that El Ciclon would be shut just for an hour about the time they would return from Pied de la Cuesta so the buxom lady, very kindly offered to have their shopping bag left with the bottles filled in the house next door where they could call for it. "Acapulco ees a Paradise, no?" the lady said, and Sigbjørn, feeling like saying "No!" was reminded of his old servants at home in England, always rejoicing in another's account that it was a nice day, while they were condemned to slave in servitude inside. On the way back to the square they caught the bus returning from Pied de la Cuesta but they still had a long wait at the bus stop outside the Departamento de Turismo. From where they sat in the bus Sigbjørn could see the Seven Seas and suddenly remembered that he had indeed, as several times before, and always as a drunk, figured as a character, but this time actually in a book about Acapulco, a murder mystery of the cheapest sort, by a person by the name of Walt Ferries, known to his friends as Pisspot,[3] which while in Canada he had picked up running serially in a cheap magazine of the blood and thunder type, which was alone procurable in Canada during the war, all American intellectual magazines being banned. It certainly seemed for better or worse that he impressed himself on people, but was it any wonder, when he had figured so many times as a character that his fictitious characters had perhaps been stronger than his real one. But what was worse to think of. Sigbjørn wondered about the {UBC 13:21, 122} generosity of authors. Truly, what is above is like what is below.[4] And what was below was certainly Pisspot, who, on the only occasion he had met him had been, owing to certain marital difficulties, combined with other difficulties with his agent, drunk in a manner in which scarcely even Sigbjørn himself, who had been quietly writing The Valley of the Shadow of Death at the next table, was ever seen, rolling about on the table, sobbing, vomiting, and even, a phenomenon Sigbjørn had never before witnessed, and which shocked him more than anything else especially in an author, tearing up five peso bills into little pieces and stamping upon them, and all this in the presence of a woman who if not his wife certainly had not improved matters by making an imperial and public scene: Sigbjørn had pacified the lady, who then abandoned him, paid for Pisspot's drinks, and the lady's (Pisspot having torn up all his money when refusing to pay for hers) restored him the keys of his car, which he had thrown in the gutter, helped him into and paid for a taxi, taken him to his hotel, the same hotel where Bousfield was staying, and put him to bed, as a consequence of which Sigbjørn had appeared in Pisspot's book as a drunken cameraman named Pulley,—poor Gilda had not been spared either—given to tearing up dollar bills, and howling and spewing in front of the Seven Seas, and of whom his readers had one splendid generous glimpse of lying outside the Seven Seas, at that time a completely phoney tavern established by an American who had seen no ocean greater than the Salton Sea,[5] but now with its name changed, having even an air of the "real thing," of being autochthonous, which, indeed, in a place like Acapulco, it was—in the very spot where in real life R. had said,[6] "This car's going to Mexico City tomorrow" and he "I'm not {UBC 13:21, 123} taking it," and where a moment or two later Peggy herself has waved; yes she had,[7] yes waved him goodbye forever, but waved—drunk, shot by a thing, and being comforted by a bawling Mexican prostitute. Sigbjørn could not help laughing, looking round as he did so, at the huge white stone buildings that housed the Immigration and the Fish Office. It seemed to him that a Wells Fargo office used to be situated there in the old days when Acapulco had been more humble and underpopulated, but nonetheless had boasted a Consul, and a Wells Fargo, but this was not the memory that stirred so much as an historic incident that had occurred there. Having [been] told by a mutual friend back in 1938, that he had told Sherwood Anderson, whom Sigbjørn tremendously admired, to look him, Sigbjørn, up in Acapulco, Sigbjørn had proceeded to the Wells

Fargo here to discover his address where upon he was informed that Sherwood Anderson had moved, leaving no forwarding address, albeit a number of unclaimed letters had arrived for him since his departure: Sigbjørn had caused these letters to be forwarded to the mutual friend in the U.S. with instructions to forward them but the next he heard was that Sherwood Anderson—though that may have been some years later—was dead, as if in a sense he, Sigbjørn, had been death who had forwarded the letters, he had thought, from Wells Fargo. (Describe the square a bit again, the coconut place, now refurbished, a bit, in the middle, the cigarette booths, the boys selling chiclets, Excelsior—and on the way back Tremendo Siniestro Tremendo Choque[8] in the dull foetid little town graced here by a few coconut palms.) But what is below is like that which was above: and Sigbjørn was not to escape even from Sherwood Anderson, for many years later, had he not read a posthumous story by Anderson,[9] reputed almost the best thing he had written, in which the principal character also was a drunkard, a suicidal swimmer. Sigbjørn felt a twinge in his foot. {UBC 13:21, 124} Worse than that, this drunkard and suicidal swimmer, who was in the habit of swimming far out to sea to look at freighters, and had been once a writer, had started to go crazy, and taken to shooting canaries in cages, because he, Sherwood Anderson, had invested him with the very disease, the rumour of which as attaching to himself could only have reached him through that very mutual friend, to Anderson going to Acapulco, because the mutual friend was the only person with whom Sigbjørn had shared his suspicions, and who knew he was a swimmer, and suicidal, now proved groundless. Or were they? Would one ever be sure? Was not the very pattern of his worries symptomatic of an advanced stage of the disease, Or had it only been varicose veins? And what might not these fictitious projections of one's self—For Anderson's character had undoubtedly been based partly on him too—into space capable of causing? (N.B. Would the fact that he [was] actually wearing the clothes of a man who died of G.P.I.[10] be a good point.) But the bus had started, and as it turned, Sigbjørn watched a figure going into the Departamento de Turismo—when the door opened he could see right into it, see the calendar with March 14 on it—he was almost sure it was Guyou, or whatever his name was, the man who had frowned at him this morning from his car and phoned at the Ocean Blue. And had he now, cast yet another glance at him?

Excursions to nearby tropic Paradises

Acapulco is the golden gateway to a rich and unexplored jungle country

The bus went round the square past the booths where they sold coconuts and threaded through the boys selling Chiclets and newspapers that made him, even though Primrose was not wearing her white fur coat, look straight ahead for they announced a Canadian spy scare,[11] Communists had given away secrets to the Russians, and they were away to Pied de la Cuesta, which brought Sigbjørn right back to the very first day he had ever spent in Mexico in his life. {UBC 13:21, 125}

which, because until recently inaccessible, preserves a wild primitive beauty and atmosphere.

"Are you happy?"

"So happy!"

The road was very bumpy and the bus crowded, and became more so, the service inefficient and did not moreover run on time; it was so far as the bus was concerned, rather more like, say, so he had heard, a Haitian bus—and how would they be enjoying themselves had they gone there?—it ran on no schedule, picked up anyone, stopped anywhere, and Sigbjørn reflected that just as he was going back to a source of sorts, so indeed was the bus, it was going toward the primitive, in fact it went twice a day, for African slaves had settled in these remote regions, albeit Sigbjørn had searched in vain for any of the good nature and sweetness one found in Haiti in Acapulco, and doubtless it would be a little difficult to explore: on that first day, Ruth and he travelled some way, in a rickety bus over grass fields beyond the lagoon, or between it and the sea, in a bus nearly tumbling over as it changed from furrow to furrow, and loaded symbolically with clanging cans of raw alcohol, while Wynn himself, whom he had left in Acapulco with the remainder of his money the day after G. had knocked him down, had joined a hunting expedition there, he had heard been lost perhaps for a while, in the regions of the Balsas, you can have my passport if you need it "Thank you for the lift—" he had written—All Sigbjørn could remember of Pied de la Cuesta was a violent sandy sea with terrific surf, a little hotel kept by an American, many fishing nets, perhaps there were hammocks by the sea, a boy from whom he would have been delighted to buy, but for Ruth, (it had been the Day of the Dead, too) a bottle of mescal, and the lagoon, of course, on which they had sailed coldly, and quarreled, and where, upon a {UBC 13:21, 126} two-decked motor boat perhaps, he had had his photograph taken. It ought, Sigbjørn thought, to enchant Primrose, its tropical atmosphere, the palms, the curious sense of the Congo. It would be a

A half hour's drive from Acapulco brings you to Pied de la Cuesta as isolated from the modern world as a seaside settlement in Central Africa.

compensation too for not having gone to Haiti. It was only in fact a short distance, but it seemed to be taking a hell of a long time: The road was better, but it was still rugged. Sigbjørn missed a rustic bridge, and the old road, in memory, seemed a good deal higher than this one. And now there seemed more trees. But Primrose did not mind the bumpy road or the crowd nor the lack of air and they were happy. Soon a cemetery of crooked crosses came in sight and they heard the long roar and sigh of the surf.

(Mem: when they start taking the bus from the other end of the beach, the view of Pied de la Cuesta, from high up, and five miles away, just a few inches long, of the roaring surf and spray that you couldn't hear.)

Pied de la Cuesta, such as it was, was built on a narrow sand dune between the sea and the lagoon: there was indeed a South Sea atmosphere, or a Belgian Congo atmosphere, grass thatched huts, coconut palms, the head, people sleeping in hammocks, pigs, dogs, etc., even a pet tapir, one new empty looking hotel, and a thatched covered restaurant with long rustic tables covered with pop-eye type murals.[12]

They went down through sand, immensely hot, and very difficult to walk through—not at all unlike one's pilgrimage on earth, this difficult tramping through red-hot sand—to the beach, and there, facing the sea, was a pavilion made of poles and roofed with palm-thatch, and in fact hundreds of hammocks—perhaps Sigbjørn's fishing nets of memory—and on the hammocks, people were lying in the shade, watching the surf and drinking green coconut-milk. {UBC 13:21, 127}

(Mem: In the meaning of Existentialism, discussing Heidegger, Barrett says:[13] everyday existence, no matter how public and banal, is always permeated by some feeling, some affective state: (Befindlichkeit) FEAR ANXIETY TRANQUILITY JOY—I think this book should too, vacillate between these states, Primrose's consciousness being used to express joy, or sometimes tranquillity, THEY when they feel a combination of both the last or WE: Sigbjørn for the most part should express FEAR ANXIETY motifs)

As soon as they saw the sea they regretted not bringing their bathing suits, but in a moment Sigbjørn realised that his memory had not deceived him: there were numerous sharks close inshore. Nevertheless people were sitting on the very edge of the surf. And Primrose saw, just in time, a giant ray of some sort there (or perhaps

The breakers at Pied de la Cuesta are a challenge to the best swimmer...

97

this should be the other way round and Sigbjørn should in some sense save Primrose from the ray) a thing as big as a house, or at least as long as theirs, would be fairly accurate and sliding stealthily along close inshore; they gazed at the horrible thing for a while with its flat body, and eyes on the upper surface, and rather small whip-like tail; this like the barbed shadow, already deprived the surf of some of its cosiness: it was indeed, literally, as big as a house, or their house, that is in length, and it gave the effect indeed of a huge mobile floor. "Sahara, Dahomey, lac Nagaïn, Darfour—Paysages de lune où rôde la chimère . . ."[14] Sigbjørn said.

"It's a horror."

"No, it actually is a chimera, I believe. A giant chimera. I meant that was the name for it."

"I thought it was a she-monster that vomited flames. And I don't see its lion's head and goat's body and dragon's tail. Or is it a serpent's tail?" {UBC 13:21, 128}

"It's an imaginary monster. A frightful, vain or foolish fancy."

"It looks like all three."

"Actually, I think it's a devilfish and the chimera's a shark. I think they weigh up to half a ton and the natives harpoon them. See. It's like a devil—with its tail and wings. A bit like a devil and a bit like a gigantic bat."

"It *is* the devil," Primrose said.

"I notice it's going in the opposite direction from Acapulco" Sigbjørn said.

(N.B. This dialogue can be broken between here, and with the couple. Or perhaps it would be far more dramatic to have them not see it, but to have the couple, who are later murdered, discuss it and later hear it discussed at lunch at the Eugenia. This would explain "bat boats" in Haitian section.)[15]

They were actually following the beastly thing along the shore. The beach is miles and miles long—a great windswept blaze of thundering surf.

This sheer noise and blaze and thunder silences the voices of care and anxiety within them and, forgetting about the chimera, they have a sense of tranquillity in spite of all the mighty uproar, walking along on their bare feet in the glittering and much firmer sand, gazing up together at the high mountains rising up behind, and the jungle, a rich green of palms, thick beyond the beach, they felt as free as two little negroes in Liberia or Haiti itself, as though the spirit, not of their own childhood, but of the childhood of the race, had come to greet them and beckon them on, beyond the Americans, and the other Mexicans in hammocks, sipping coconut milk or eating dried fish. {UBC 13:21, 129}

On the way back, however, with the thundering blaze now cut off by the view of the village and the people in hammocks, though he was not conscious of feeling a sharp reversal of this feeling, and sidestepping and stumbling in the slant of the beach, Sigbjørn finds himself declaiming from Tourneur's Atheist's Tragedy, his words (somewhat like those of Mynheer Peeperkorn,[16] he thought, at an obscure but not insignificant tangent, half blown away by the spray and roar)

> "Walking next day upon the fatal shore,
>   It was my unhappy chance to light,
> Upon a face . . ."[17]

he said, and then, since Primrose doubtless hadn't heard him, added:

> "He lay in's armour, as if that had been
> His coffin; and the weeping sea, like one
> Whose milder temper doth lament the death
> Of him whom in his rage he slew, runs up
> The shore, embraces him, kisses his cheek,
> Goes back again and forces up the sands
> To bury him, and every time it parts
> Sheds tears upon him, till at last (as if
> It could no longer endure to see the man
> Whom it had slain, yet loath to leave him) with
> A kind of unresolved unwinding pace
> Winding her waves one in another, like
> A man that folds his arms or wrings his hands
> For grief, ebbed from the body, and descends
> As if it would sink down into the earth
> And hide itself for shame at such a deed."

(Mem: see also Richard III, 709–710, Act V Sc 1., Buckingham on All Soul's Day—ref. Consul—also mem: Hastings on uncertainty of man's lot: see Richard III.)[18]

(Mem: the reflections below might better come while Sigbjørn is drinking the Saturno; or perhaps better while Primrose is praising Sigbjørn in the car going back. It comes too close here)

There was, he thought, as back at the thatched huts, but still watching the surf, they drank warm green but delicious coconut milk, while the others went on eating the little fried {UBC 13:21, 130} fishes, absolutely no reason why he should have thought of that melancholy passage, when they were enjoying themselves, save that the passage itself, suggested by the seashore, and perhaps by its threat and menace of the ray or the sharks or the chimera of death, was beautiful: but was there not? Not even Tourneur, any more than Pisspot's or Sherwood Anderson's, an idle quotation, had spared him or more particularly it was the anthologist who had selected the passage in the volume from which he had learned it by heart had not spared him: for the anthologist had been none other than A.,[19] the individual who, like Pisspot and Sherwood Anderson, had written a story about him, the individual of whom he had told himself, whom he was reluctant on some occasion to meet, and who had lent yet another reality to the story which Sigbjørn had written himself, but which had been burned, about the death of P.[20] only with the difference that this story was true: was this far fetched? It was. But it was the human consciousness that, tireless seemed always capable of such far fetching, to the remote corners of the earth, and to the remotest recesses of memory, and back again, it travels, all day & all night at every moment, to bring us fresh forms and food with which he may torture himself, even if while it is going on, we are as seemingly carefree, and may even feel such, as little negro boys on a beach in Haiti or Liberia: not even a pack of sharks, or chimeras, are as avid, as bestially greedy, as these scavengers of the sea of the unconscious of remorse, for which reason it is perhaps duty, as sailors cruelly do to sharks, to split, or split and maingaff them, trysail them, should we be capable of ever catching one, with a stake pierced through its jaws wedged forever open, and send it back again into the deep {UBC 13:21, 131} to go hungry forever; all the while this cheerful little thought had been going on in his mind, Sigbjørn had been smiling and laughing with Primrose and drinking his coconut milk, and now they strolled back through the deep sand to the town. (over the billows of inexhaustible anguish, hunted by the insatiable albatross of self.[21] sprit-trysail is, I think, the phrase. The publication of Primrose's bird-book glowed between them.)

They took a look at the hotel—"Nosotros no somos—" but it was empty and expensive and they strolled down to the lagoon. It was calm and mysterious looking, and of a dark green colour, and its contrast with the tremendous surf on the other side was astounding. (What we are anxious about in such states—i.e. when it is about nothing—is our very Being-in-the-world as such, Heidegger tells me. Care is the being of man.)[22] There was a quaint old double-decked launch if you wanted to hunt ducks, something for which the Wildernesses, although both crack shots had such a distaste, contempt, for that it amounted to a dislike of everyone that did, a distaste that even found its way into his literary appreciation, for his reading of even Hudson was always disturbed by a vision of the saturnine Hemingway-like honeymoons of slaughter[23] he would occasionally treat himself to: perhaps it was an unconscious method of getting rid of aggressions which might prove even more socially damaging if given in to, but Sigbjørn, like Hitler, was not tempted in that direction[24] and felt proud of himself for it. And it would have seemed criminal to kill any of these beautiful white ducks, or doubtless the very flamingoes (actually perhaps roseate spoonbills, said Primrose) from which the hotel ten miles away where a flamingo however had never been seen, took its name, or the egrets, if they were {UBC 13:21, 132} egrets, that stood majestically by the edge of the water by the jungle, and the many other birds flitting about near the water and jungle beyond. So having nothing to do, they drifted back to the smaller hotel with the murals and since this is what Primrose wanted they ordered two beers, and since Saturno, though more expensive, was the only make they had, and since this was, anyway, the best brand, being of a deep dark rich colour, two Saturnos, which was doubtless a better name than Capricornos. They sat watching the rings round the planet Saturn on the bottle and with their cigarettes dangling, for they didn't have any matches, nor Sigbjørn having conquered his inhibition to ask, did the waitress. In this sort of stockade an American, with wavy platinum hair, by the unusual pop-eyed murals, was sitting so absolutely motionless that Sigbjørn had a sudden idea that he was some kind of dummy American, put there to attract other Americans. But at the sound, in the distance, of what sounded like two muffled explosions, (as though someone had turned an invisible key in the sky: two locks; perhaps better when they are lying on the shore: the two shots have significance for these are the two people who are later murdered) almost to Sigbjørn's horror, this American moved, gave them a match, offered them another beer, which they refused, and the next moment, hospitably, a lift. This they were glad to accept for the bus did not return till two-o'clock which would have made them too late, since they were proposing to call for their bottle at the house next El Ciclon, and the American and his wife drove them slowly back. (Believe it would be better if the American spoke about the manta ray.) These two Americans, rich, well-dressed, from Ohio, who had driven down via Tamazunchale, had stayed at the best hotels, seen little of the {UBC 13:21, 133} country, and were amazed, both at the high prices, and at the hostility with which they had been received, the more especially since the husband, having been locked out of their hotel in Taxco, had climbed up to their balcony from outside, a romanticism frowned upon by such classic races as the Mexicans.

"But can you blame them hating us?" Primrose said and, having met a fellow countryman, launched into her favourite discourse, much to the delight and pride of Sigbjørn, for her thesis was that "though they had been warned they would," they had never "had any trouble," for Sigbjørn had taken her everywhere on second class buses, or they had walked to remote Indian villages, where they had always been received by the natives with the utmost courtesy, they had seen all of the out-of-the-way fiestas, she spoke even about Tlaxcala, becoming in fact quite ecstatic, and what delighted Sigbjørn so, hugging himself with pride, was that Primrose herself was obviously and extremely very proud of Sigbjørn himself for the manner in which he'd showed her the country, any "trouble" in which she attributed to the habits of loud-mouthed Americans in boasting how much money they had, (which is far from being the truth, for it would be more true to say that in the case of the Mexicans with whom they were dealing the amount of money a gringo has is perhaps the sole criterion of his merit, without it, he has none at all) so that Sigbjørn began to warm even towards the Americans themselves (who were staying at the Americas Hotel) even though they were going hunting in the Balsas region: "We don't tell many people this," they said, telling that also their name was Heywood, "But we're on our honeymoon." Which necessarily elicits from the Wildernesses the gleeful response that so are they, {UBC 13:21, 134} even after five years, and with many protestations of friendship, and hopes of meeting again, (the flaxen-haired American and his wife—describe—he is ex-service man) again when they have come back from their hunting trip (even though afterwards the Wildernesses knew they were going to decide that they didn't want them in their hair) (but this is important, for like the Mexican the first day at the Monterrey, they might have been later potential saviours) that they part at the Ciclon; they obtain their bottles faithfully waiting next door in their faithful shopping bag, and wander toward the square discussing their conversation with the Haywoods, how they had spoken of getting plastered in Taxco and nearly being arrested, some of Rendon's Vanishing Enchantment from Modern Mexico[25] might be worked in, though that part is mostly for Hudson's office later, the Heywoods have told too how the money has mounted up for them "I don't like to think of the number of pesos"—and Primrose and Sigbjørn hug themselves again with having had no trouble even though they have gone into the remotest places, and how even they haven't spent much money and how nice they are to them in the Ciclon, and how generally clever Sigbjørn is, and they are, and how queer it is they knew Bousfield (a link again) then he thinks it's a bit queer their name is Heywood, just when he'd been thinking of Tourneur,[26] and the usual gossipy things husband and wife say to each other, even when they pride themselves on not gossiping, invariably gossip about. Caleta! Caleta! and they approach the bus waiting outside the Turismo. In addition to the usual "Tremendo Siniestro" and the Canadian spy story there is now an extra in the streets, it seems that the explosions that they heard when the American turned round were at Icacos, at the naval base, where many people had been killed: since Sigbjørn in his mind immediately imagines {UBC 13:21, 135} that people will somehow if they know he is Canadian [link him] also with the explosion at Icacos he tries his best not to look Canadian but, as it were, American, looking straight before him with a conquistadorial yet childishly fascinated expression, pretending to be concentrating upon some toys and rattles in a shop opposite, at the same time laughing at himself for it, and so happy and so used to the torments of his persecution that he is not really startled when somebody (Margie will describe) sitting opposite says: "You are Wilderness."

Sigbjørn, whose first instinct is to admit that he is, this instinct being related also to the instinct to sign your right name, which we have discussed, so long as nobody hears him, instead pretends to be deaf for a while, and looks round the bus—Herr Schwab the fat manager is sitting in it which makes it rather difficult since he has only yesterday signed his register to say that he isn't, and doubly difficult indeed, now, since having given the impression that he was deaf, the question was repeated in a louder tone: "You are Señor Wilderness. You not remember me?"

Since this was now a direct appeal to his courtesy Sigbjørn tried to throw a politely ambiguous look of remote recollection in his face, avoiding directly answering the question, but at the same time advancing his hand, and saying in a low tone:

"Yes, it is many years ago. What passes, man?"

"How do you do?"

"All right."

"Are you Wilderness?"

"Permiso?"

"Is your name Wilderness?"

"Sí. Qué pasa?"[27] {UBC 13:21, 136}

"I remember you," the man said, smiling with bad teeth, who now struck Sigbjørn as so odious that he was not sure whether to introduce him to Primrose or not, "You do not remember me, waiter at Caleta Hotel. You and Mistair Bousfield."

"Sí."

"I read your play. I see your film."

There had been no play, and no film, as Primrose well knew, but the calibre of his recognition on the grounds of fame, even if based in this case upon a complete lie, compensated for the shock of recognition at all, at least to the extent that (for they had gone round by a longer route, and alighted at Caletilla, with a "see you again" to the waiter) Sigbjørn now felt as they walked home behind the little fat legs of Herr Schwab, which walked fast, however, that the explanation which he had, doubtless quite erroneously (he knew himself) been feeling was owed to him (Schwab) could now be made gaily and upon a basis which should cause Schwab himself to feel proud to have such a well known person in the hotel at all: they caught up with him just by the Cordoba, at the sight of which both Sigbjørn and Primrose felt a pang, where Sigbjørn began hastily to say something that he could scarcely follow himself, about how small the world was, which was scarcely the point, and about how cornish it was at all events that the man in the bus had recognized him after ochos annos and that he was delighted about it because he had "my película gesehen"[28]—to the polite bafflement of Primrose: in all of which Schwab however did not seem very interested, turning off, it seemed to Sigbjørn, abruptly even rudely to go and speak with the Administración of the Beach, fellow, from whom Sigbjørn had failed to get change for 50 pesos, and who was sitting outside the Hotel del Pacifico on his {UBC 13:21, 137} chair, a fact for which Sigbjørn disliked and distrusted Herr Schwab forever after.

But their monster was on the rock, their giant convulvulus was singing, the blasting began again behind the Cordoba, it was just like the first day they had gone up to the Quinta Eulalia,[29] and they ascended to the hotel happily with their faithful shopping bag, they just had time for a quick swim which Sigbjørn decided they could now take, since Herr Schwab had now arrived too after his conversation with the Administración, so they wouldn't have to speak to him, they did this, returned, and ate with giant appetites in the dining room, an appetite not quickened by more beer, which he resisted, and that was scarcely abated by the fact that everyone in the dining room was talking about the explosion at Icacos, an incident which Sigbjørn put down to a certain safety belt that he drew round himself from his touselled appearance, for Communists—mem Mensch[30]—were undoubtedly were not supposed in the popular mind to go swimming or do healthy things; they went to take a short siesta and suddenly Sigbjørn said:

"They were ungallant."

"Who?"

"The bloody Elizabethans." Sigbjørn himself, at this moment, could see no connection. "It is their bankrupt attitude towards death that bothers me. And Shakespeare, with whom immortality was simply so many noisome children. If I were an Elizabethan and you had died I wouldn't mourn about the horrors of your skull.[31] I should try to write some poem, like: 'I swore to love thee, dear, beyond the grave,' but I should end, 'And send my prayers through the earth, to comfort and bless.'—Or, 'to gather up and caress / thy poor sweet darling lonely skeleton.'" {UBC 13:21, 138}

They laughed and kissed and Primrose said: "Oh, why that's the only poem you've ever written to me, and there it's to my skeleton."

But Sigbjørn had written, for that matter, a song to Primrose. "Don't you remember, 'And Fair as Herself is She?'"[32]

"To my Skeleton!" Primrose pretended to mourn.

"Or, 'Thy little lonely darling skeleton.'"

"Or, 'Thy poor bereft sweet lonely skeleton. Thy strange sweet cold, thy own darling skeleton.'"

"But my own darling . . . My own cargo of ducklings and cheese bound for Rotterdam—"

Sigbjørn began to worry that perhaps the poem was not original anyway.

They were ecstatically happy. {UBC 13:21, 139}[33]

From the Vancouver Sun—column: Along the Waterfront, Jim Smith.[34]

Seven N's Mystery Name Puzzles Seaman

"Cap't Seven N's" is a veteran Norwegian skipper with a name full of N's" and a strange affinity for the figure seven.

His real name is Capt. Normann Nymann, but around the coast-lines of both South and North America he has acquired the nick-name of "Seven N's" (the seventh N is in his title Captain.)

For many years with Westfal-Larsen Line, in their South America U.S. B.C. trade, he now plies the same areas for Panamanian Independence Line, as master of their trim MS. Don Aurelio, which took on cargo at Pier A yesterday.

"That number seven—it crops up everywhere in my life," laughs the captain. His first name has seven letters; so has that of his only son, Sigvald, who is chief officer in the Aurelio which name is also seven-lettered.

"I was one of seven children; so was my wife," says Capt. Nymann. Mrs. Nymann travels with him on the ship.

Note:
—A minor character knocked at the door. Already Wilderness had decided what significance it had before Primrose had half-opened the door and Sigbjørn himself had hidden the bottles and the glass. Could it help? It was saying. Those others were bad characters. It had been in trouble in the United States and would be only too glad to help. Did they want any money? It would be only too pleased to lend them some. The beautiful dialogue blew into the room over

Primrose's shoulder but Sigbjørn's hand hunting for a pencil only found a glass. A trapped clause sprang out of it {UBC 13:21, 140} but Sigbjørn could not catch it. All he swallowed was the habanero.

"What did that man say?"—

Primrose tries to explain.

"What did he look like?"

Primrose tries to explain.

"No, I've forgotten that already. Say it again."

"But what's the use, you'll forget it unless you write it down."

"Wasn't I writing it down?" Sigbjørn said, shaking all over and now finding the bottle of habanero.

"Sigbjørn, listen to me. We're living this. You're not writing it."

"But my god, what earthly point would there be in living it if I didn't write it?"

"You'll never write again," Primrose said cruelly, "If you go on as you are doing."

"But what good would there be in living it if I can't even write down why it is that I can't write it," Sigbjørn said.

Primrose began to walk up and down the room:

"Oh, Sigbjørn, sometimes I think you're not sane."

"That sometimes is funny."

"We're in terrible trouble. Can't you see that?"

There was silence between them. Then Sigbjørn, being some eighteen hours from remorse, even permitted himself to laugh, almost dreamily listening to the measureless sea beating its great unconscious metres on the shore . . . or beating its secret terrible meters on the shore. {UBC 13:21, 141}

"It's quite easy to get a drink," he said, "You only have to hop across the border."

Gesture of putting your fingers in the corner of your mouth and stretching it gives look of all Mexicans like Fatty.

They danced the raspa in the bathroom. They made love until they were exhausted and then danced again. They drank half a bottle of claret but their hangovers had already been swept away from them. Then they stood by the window looking out into Nuevo Laredo. Sigbjørn turned her suddenly toward him and their lips met in a long kiss. "We will cling together." Carta Blanca, winked the lights over beyond the Rio Grande in old Mexico.

"But Fatty's still here," Primrose said.

"What makes you say that?"

"I just saw him, down in the street."

"So did I, but I wasn't going to say anything about it. Anyhow he can't hurt us now."

"Why can't he?"

"Because," Sigbjørn said, "He is not the—Fatty is not the—the instrument of . . . my . . . he isn't the instrument of our . . ." And even as he took her in his arms again it was as if he heard a voice behind him saying: "I can see you . . . I'm watching you. You won't escape me."

Sigbjørn was as staggered as once when he had stepped out on deck into a hurricane of young owls being blown into the rigging. {UBC 13:21, 142}

It was as if they were wrestling with an invisible enemy. Or like Hudson's fabled fox biting the air, struggling, yet becoming more and more exhausted, he were being sucked from a distance into the maw of a lampalagua, that serpent which so resembled the Mexican immigration in that also while extremely sluggish in its motions, yet captures its victims by following them into their burrows. See The Purple Land, p. 233.[35]

Should this be as far as I get before I said; I need—Carlotta on hell—mem protraction of Maximilian's execution[36]—and as much Haiti as possible—for Eridanus,[37] as much of In Ballast[38] as possible, some Norwegian quotations, Santayana in Fadiman,[39] what is above is like what is below from Hootnanny,[40] and poems "Light in the Sky" "The Beagles" Salmon, My God why have you given this to me—[41]

The Wildernesses, like Monsignor Meglia,[42] to talk to whom gave poor Carlotta her truest picture of hell up to that point, had arrived in Mexico City in time to officiate at the celebration of the great religious holiday of the year, the feast day of the Virgin of Guadalupe.[43]

Carlotta wrote to Eugenie (see Roeder)[44] Nothing has given me a truer idea of Hell than that conversation, *for Hell is nothing but an impasse without issue.* To try to convince someone and to know that it is sheer waste, that it is like talking Greek to him because he sees black and you see white, is a task fit for a reprobate. Everything slipped over the Nuncio like polished marble.

But Carlotta was in the right place to practise patience. What a farce is the vaunted courtesy of the Mexicans! The philosophy of mañana betrays that it is a mere empty form. The Mexicans {UBC 13:21, 143} have a fundamental lack of respect for man's true nature, fundamentally a complete reversal of Juarez' words, a fundamental lack of respect for the rights of others, without which according to him, was no peace—I have always thought (since reading Roeder) that the ultima thule of lack of courtesy (p. 668 Roeder) and the philosophy of mañana was when after poor Maximilian even after having heard that Carlotta was dead[45]—a false report for which one could almost be sure that a Mexican was responsible—after he had made all his preparations, dictated his last letters, communed, given a physician a letter to his mother, thought he met his hour punctually, and graciously, even that hour, of all hours, had to pass, no wonder the poor man did not delight in his reprieve. {UBC 13:21, 144}

V

(N.B. If this really is a separate chapter, there must be more of a sense of attenuation—the sense, at the beginning, of this endless long day.)

The mood of dreaminess, of satisfied love, of ecstasy, persisting beyond the communion of their bodies, and the common sense of their bodies, as it were into the communion of their souls, and of triumph, so that they felt, even without an habanero, like angels that were soaring, skimming down to the Caleta beach—there they were, though they were walking in bare feet, first down rough steps, then over rough ground, without seeming to have touched that ground— where the two artists, who now resembled creatures stuck in a quicksand, and with their faces plastered with some sort of disgusting clay, were preparing to return, and the American lady from the Cordoba (it should be pointed out, either here or elsewhere, before or after, in dialogue, that she knows Eddie)[1] having been waiting for a glimpse of them all afternoon, was already, in a wide hat, making her way down to begin a querulous conversation—

It is really their first honeymoon, the day has been so successful (it had been, like the Consul's, the longest day in Sigbjørn's experience)—and they are looking forward to a swim, and a drink, and a discussion, and afterwards Wilderness has even planned to take his wife dancing at Las Americas. (where they possibly might dance.)

—Primrose is afraid to swim, however, alone, into the very deep water, owing to a diving accident as a child, and they have an arrangement—Camiónes a Hartebeestepec y Anexas,[2] whereby she lays her hands on Sigbjørn's shoulder, and he swims, carrying her along as if on his back: they have, this way, a wonderful feeling {UBC 13:22, 145} of warmth and comradeship, and when they return (though there can be, after the foregoing omens, a suspense about this swim, is something going to happen?) their log, with its cigarettes and dark glasses, beneath it, seems to welcome them, (as Sigbjørn was not sure that he'd read in some book of someone doing) seems to welcome them with a joyous shout. The artists have gone, (it was sad to see these sensitive, perceptive, selfish, kindly fairy souls go) Miss America (they should call her) gone rather gloomily over to some rocks, Primrose is a bit chilly and perhaps feels she ought to say something to Miss America; Sigbjørn feels like a long swim.

(N.B. A hangover like an iron vise: beyond remorse—waking with your face as if glued to the stovepipe; your lone shoe containing your amputated foot, should you think at all, which you almost succeed in not doing in this state, a slight pain in your knee, for example, produces at once all the possibilities of everything that can happen to your knee, including the clear vision of it lying, under the electric light, hard on the floor, gashed open to the bone: surely this is the secret of the impact of man's dream upon reality.)

In a moment he has gone. He swims the way he had swum on his suicide attempt. To swim! It was one of the most unalloyed pleasures of his life. He was perhaps not so good a swimmer as he thought he was, but his father had been a champion—he thinks of his 2 medals from the Humane Society—Ally Sloper![3]—and his father's 4 or 5—the time he had saved the Swede from committing suicide and the Swede had knocked him flat, and he was almost first-rate. He was both extremely fast, or had become, of later years, extremely fast, when put to it, and he had an extraordinary endurance. He thinks while swimming of their lovely day and their {UBC 13:22, 146} lovely afternoon. In swimming the crawl the best thing is the sensation of your own speed, the water tearing through your mouth and nostrils, the very taste of the water, the sensation of *cleaving* straightly and powerfully, the swift glimpses or glances of the landscape or the mountains, especially when, as in Canada, there is snow; and yet with all that a feeling almost of *rest* in motion, or in swiftness, it is at best quite effortless, you could go on forever, and not get tired (it is perhaps related to infancy, this ecstasy of crawling on your elbows, and perhaps to the primordial beginnings of man himself) unless your breathing, as often happens, gets irregular. But the disadvantage is that though you may set yourself a dim choking and blind goal, or in a race follow the lines at the bottom of the pool, you cannot see really. In one sense, if you wanted the enjoyment of swimming, of the sea, as opposed simply to the exercise, or to what Sigbjørn had, a delight simply in this swiftness and oceanic light with which you were involved, it would be better to swim a sort of sedate side-stroke simply, like the President of the United States,[4] or, like our grandmother, just lie on our back staring at the sky, or like old Hootnanny, not swim at all, but simply stand, or wade, like a flamingo, or a heron, massaging yourself, but at the same time as it were becoming involved with all the ancient elements, the earth, the shore beneath your feet, fire, the sun, the air, and (though it had indeed salt in it) the water. The way Sigbjørn was swimming (running) swiftly, effortlessly, and with the current, it was like a dream; a dream of swimming, and dreams of swimming are said to be related to dreams of love, and this was like a continuation of their idyllic afternoon. Sigbjørn was heading, so he thought, past the left (the south?—try and get points of Acapulco clear in mind—) {UBC 13:22, 147} of the governor's island, president's brother's island, but he had not aimed to get much past it and in fact was aiming simply to swim round it, land at Caletilla, and walk and swim home, as he loved to do also, along the margin of the beach: the sea seemed to have been running more and more swiftly and roughly lately and when he came to himself it seemed to him that he must be half way to Larquete Island. (Griffin Island?) Stopping and looking round he saw that this really was so. The Quinta Eugenia (is this possible?) was almost out of sight. (N.B. We can

have suspense here, quite considerable suspense indeed) He has indeed some considerable difficulty in getting back, but what a sensation it is when he gets toward shore again, and he sees Primrose
waving at him from the high balcony, what a feeling of joy and relief
(mem the feeling of "safe" this gives him) ah, the love of it—all the
pain of the last years seemed swept away, all the pain of the old Acapulco, he passes the parked car, which was unfamiliar (with Migración on it, this is dubious) then begins to climb the steps: he
meets Mrs. José, José's "Lady-me," who seems to be sailing down,
because of her wide skirt, but actually has come down about two
steps: she seems rather worried about something, which was
nothing unusual, for she was, in fact, pregnant.

"There are some people to see you," she said.

"People? Where?"

"Outside your room . . . Your friends are waiting."

"What kind of people?" Sigbjørn asked again, half frightened but
again, half flattered or excited. Perhaps it was the artists come to return the bottle of beer.

"Up there." {UBC 13:22, 148}

Though it seemed to Sigbjørn, who had however thought immediately of the Haywoods, that she had turned away rather sharply, it
did not occur to him to be unduly worried about this because she
was always rather sharp and dumb and in effect somewhat rude,
and besides Sigbjørn was too happy, and he even arranged his towel
in a ridiculous turban effect on his head in order to amuse Primrose
as he came on the lower verandah, where the school teacher was sitting in the deck chair outside room 5, and began to climb up toward
the kitchen and past the dining room to his own room.

As he went up he heard voices, Primrose's voice, and it seemed it
was raised in anger:

"But that is absurd . . ." and then, the inevitable, "Nosotros no
somos Americanos."

"We want to see your papers."

"But they're in Cuernavaca."

"Where is Meestair Wilderness?"

"On the beach. I just left him. I think he's just coming up. He'll
be along in a minute. What's the matter?"

"We want to see Mr. Wilderness—who are you?"[5]

"Señora Wilderness."

"He was here in trente ocho—verdad?"

"In 1938. Yes, but—"

"You were with him."

"No. I've never been in Mexico before."

Sigbjørn runs up on to the porch, still with his turban on, and Primrose, who had obviously just showered and got into shorts, with her hair wet, and still with the look of bliss and happiness not quite departed from her face, was talking to two men: describe them, the degenerate Warner Baxter[6]—actually he has a rather {UBC 13:22, 149} fine face, and the other.

"Qué pasa?" Sigbjørn said.

These men have, with them, a file, which they laid on the table where Herr Schwab was wont to eat his more lonely breakfasts.

"We have ah a fine against you here for 50 pesos."

"Yes?"

"For overstaying your leave."

"And it say here you not to be allowed in Mexico again."

Sigbjørn stood there a moment, like a man struck by lightning, he had the sort of feeling one might imagine a sleepy happy turtle paddling through the Gulf of Tehuantepec might have when suddenly he sees the huge bow of a freighter bearing down upon him, and it is too late to change his course. Also give other analogies for the sinking feeling that must be his, even taking some Baja California imagery into account. This must be a terrific moment.

"We have orders ah to put you in prison, but we're not going to do that." He paused. "But you ah stay here. In this hotel. You not leave Acapulco."

Primrose is very angry.

Sigbjørn says: "Let me get this clear," his voice remote and faint like a schoolboy who has been caught cheating. "We must stay in the hotel. But we have no money to stay in the hotel. Our apartment is running on in Cuernavaca. Why don't you let me get our papers."

"You stay here. You not move from here."

"No move! Comprendo?"

"You mean we can't even go swimming?" Sigbjørn said.

"Yes. You can do that," the man said after some hesitation. "But do not leave from Acapulco." {UBC 13:22, 150}

"But then we can't pay the hotel bill," Sigbjørn said.

"Sí. We wire Mexico."

"We will sended a telegramme to Mexico City."

"But—"

Sigbjørn shook hands with these people in the despairing hope that this gesture would soften them.

"It say here you have fine of 50 pesos."

They went, taking the day with them, their back appearing for a moment below, going toward the windmill, which, a mere carefree object, seemed for a moment happy too for not knowing that that day, together with being the day before the Ides of March, was likewise the seventh of their trip—whizzing in the setting sun . . .

N.B. It should be made very plain about the 50 pesos so that you feel all might be solved by simply giving him 50 pesos. And the dialogue must be done much better—dialogue that, while largely in English, must convey the almost deliberate quality of their misunderstanding. {UBC 13:22, 151}

VI

Sigbjørn was like a man struck by lightning. In a situation such as the Wildernesses now found themselves in, there were a number of reasonable things to do. These might be listed as follows: to get a Consul, to get a lawyer, to find an interpreter of influence etc. Now Primrose and Sigbjørn both had, strictly speaking, different Consuls. Nosotros no somos Americanos—was not quite a statement of fact. Primrose still had preserved her American citizenship and so hence could call upon an American Consul. But Sigbjørn was British, even if he could, when he wished, become Canadian. There was, for that matter, a new trade agreement with Canada: there was a Canadian ambassador. Whether there was a Consul or not Sigbjørn didn't know, but there was certainly a British Consul in Mexico City. Sigbjørn had his reasons (as will have been shown) for wincing at the word. But there were no Consuls at all in Acapulco; he had seen advertised in the local paper an attorney-at-law (quote) but something warned him away from following this up. The Consulates would be shut in Mexico by this time, in fact long before this time. By the time he had drunk 3 double habaneros Sigbjørn realised he

had failed to do the only thing that would have prevented disastar—
as he phrased it to himself. And by the time he had begun on his
fourth, Sigbjørn had more objectively and certainly at least a dreadful and full[1] percipient prescience of the anguish and catastrophe all
this would cause: again, he had his reasons. It was as yet, of course,
ostensibly only a small shadow: but still—

(N.B. while the obscene world rolled on to ever bigger and better
explosions, into the era of the stool-pigeon.) {UBC 13:23, 152}

(The feeling that you are in a country where you have no right to
be—relate this to Wilderness' dream—persisted in these days in almost any country, including your own: the feeling that you have no
right to be in Mexico, is there anyway, to some extent, from the
start, but it is because of the churches, the faith, particularly poignant:[2] but the feeling that you have legally no right to be where you
are is awful in the extreme, it takes some time to sink in. Point out it
is the week-end; everything will be shut tomorrow night.)

(N.B. While the dance is going on, Sigbjørn and Primrose look at
each other, and then away from each other, with a long look, a look
so agonized that perhaps each seemed to see in the other, that it
seemed to embrace the immedicable past and future, its inescapable
horrors, its boundless possibilities, of sorrow, and yet so long and
intense was that look that both could not but think it contained
some resolution of happiness and adventure, and suddenly Sigbjørn
realised that it was the same look which, standing above on their
steps from which they could see both, they had taken in with one
gaze the anguish of their burned house, and the hope that was lent
them from the frame that had gone up of the new, while between the
two, braving the waves, stood their steadfast little pier in the sea,
one post alone of which had been charred.)

"Well," he said, "I must get down town."

"Why? The Immigration will be shut."

"If I give that bastardo his 50 pesos, all will be well. But he must
at all costs be prevented from wiring Mexico City."

"But it will be perfectly O.K." Primrose said. "Our tourist cards
are in perfect order. And surely they'll have copies of our cards in
Mexico." {UBC 13:23, 153}

"Yes, they take them in triplicate," Sigbjørn said. "That's true.
But, damn it, if I could be sure it *was* only the pesos—"

"Well, that's absolutely all it is."

"La Mordida. Well, we must pay."

"But we haven't got 50 pesos."

"On the other hand—yes, let them wire to Mexico City—our papers are in order—what I'm more afraid of is that they *won't* wire to Mexico City.

"I'm buggered if I'm going to pay it anyhow . . . Well, we could wire the Bank for some more."

"We can't . . . We did, before we left, and it'll be in Cuernavaca."

"Well, we can wire the Banco Nacional de Mexico in Cuernavaca."

"Yes, we could do that."

"But no we couldn't," Sigbjørn said immediately, "They wouldn't send it, I don't think. They don't always have the signature. Besides, I don't know what kind of a cheque they'll have sent."

"Anyway the telegraph offices will be shut."

"Besides, the War Prices and Control Board will forbid it—we can't get any more for a month."

"And anyhow, not in time."

(N.B. Margie note: Malc darling, the *whole* point of this was that we had 500 bucks, or some such sum, in the bank in Cuernavaca but since we hadn't our papers with us, we could not identify ourselves in Acapulco bank, and we'd only brought enough cash for a week's vacation.)

Primrose tries to cheer him up, saying that all it is is the fifty pesos, but Sigbjørn becomes more and more morose. The theme of La Mordida is stated: but La Mordida is also involved {UBC 13:23, 154} etymologically with remorse:[3] Sigbjørn imagines he sees the shadow of God's punishment, and the shape of a frightful ordeal: Primrose remonstrates with him not to go to pieces: Sigbjørn says that it will result in what he most dreads—deportation—and if that happens, how is he going to get back into America, let alone to Canada—he will perhaps be sent to England in some kind of disgrace and they will be separated, the loyalist-communist angle, the spy scare and so on—and long before that happened, worse would happen—Sigbjørn hates himself for it, but he piles it on, better get it all over with at once, though he is drinking habanero like water, and only stops when Primrose bursts into tears.

"Well, supposing even what you say is true. What is important is not what has happened, or what may happen, but how we meet it."

"How true," sneered Sigbjørn. "How one meets an octopus is—Christ how stupid!—of not much importance to anyone, I should have thought."[4] (Mem: later, the lampalagua)[5]

"There was an octopus too. There is. He's still there—" Sigbjørn said, remembering now that only yesterday there had actually been an octopus, stranded in the tunnel under the Governor's brother's causeway between Caleta and Caletilla, stranded, yet dangerous, blocking the way between the past and the future; an omen; Sigbjørn also recalls now his conversation the other night with Lewis and Post—he had gone down and told them about the past and how it was always catching up with him, and also paid for all the beer—6 or 7 pesos—which still hurt him, because he could have bought Primrose something with it—though he has now bought her some shoes—and in fact, above everything, it is the thought of poor Primrose's spoiled holiday that anguishes him and breaks him to pieces. Primrose now has a large drink. {UBC 13:23, 155}

"Well," Sigbjørn said, "Suppose we proceed on the basis that you're right, that the whole thing turns on the matter of my overstaying my leave. There is, in the first place, no fine. Or rather, the fine was paid. I paid the Mordida then. And since I am, in a sense, in the right, that is sufficient to put us forever criminally in the wrong." (Mem: see note on back page re rendering to Caesar,[6] rendering to God, etc.)

He tells her the story of Guyou, whose name he can't, however, remember, a story he had told her often before.

"And even supposing that they have this against me—how did they find out I was here?"

They cast their minds back; they have signed their names in 3 hotels: there is the stool-pigeon: they suspect the Monterrey, Cordoba, Schwab (Sigbjørn does not know yet that all names have to be sent in as a matter of course) the man whom that very morning he has seen in the car on the promenade. This is all in dialogue—perhaps it is slightly stylized—the gist of it, the progression, must be worked out in prose first, for it is the *sense* that matters, though there is opportunity here for character drawing.

(They quarrel over Primrose's having left the papers, make up poignantly, sit on the porch, night covers Mexico, they are called to dinner again and again, can't bear to go in—*this ties up with a scene later in the dream of the ship where they are called again and again by the steward to come to dinner*—their poor lamp comes on in the Cordoba—if only they were there now, the machine winds down.)

This dialogue between them which rockets between the past and the future, between exposition and drama, and every {UBC 13:23, 156} possible cause and effect, ends up with a terrific quarrel over Primrose having left the papers.

"Then why didn't you see to it yourself?" Primrose asked him, "If you'd only take the responsibilities of a man!"

"You know bloody well—"

"*I do not!* If you—"

This should lead straight back to the fire, and the conflict during that show, when Sigbjørn had told her to do something and she hadn't.

(N.B. for the dream, the two *alternatives* of going to Haiti, or to England on a freighter—though this second dream is related to his first trip to Acapulco—are more important: i.e. they should be mentioned objectively.)

"You know bloody well I was seeing about the bus to Acapulco. You know damn well I never wanted to come to Acapulco. You know god damned well I never wanted to come to Mexico either—"

"Ah—there's always something: you remember Bousfield, in Oaxaca."

"I only came here for your sake," Sigbjørn yelled and whined. "You had no consideration of the shattering things that I've been going through. And now you see the result. It'll be the end of me. It'll be the end of us, you'll see. It'll drive me mad."

"You always were mad. You were mad when I married you."

"And drive you too, before they're through," Sigbjørn thundered. It leads however to a reconciliation, a touching one:

"I'm being more than unusually bloody craven I know," Sigbjørn said. "Forgive me. You're right. It isn't really so bad. It's really funny, when you look at it one way." {UBC 13:23, 157}

"Yes," Primrose said. "Ha ha." Laughing and embracing they went out on the porch.

"It's even a sort of adventure, if you look at it one way."

"Though nothing has happened yet."

"It's probably just a matter of waiting."

"After all, our papers are in perfect order. And they can't do anything to you, you're an American citizen."

"Nosotros no somos Americanos ricos—" This now struck them as very funny.

"And probably the whole damn thing will be cleared up in a day or two."

They go out on the porch, where someone has been listening and now moves away. They put their drinks on the parapet and sit holding hands. The complexion of things, however, certainly had changed. There was a certain final dark look to everything, or it was as if everything were ending, or lost. The view from the tumbril, the last view from the hangman's hill, of Cambridge—the happiness it represented was spurious: the convicted thief thinks back to before the crime—if only—the day before the fire, and the day after. The sun that set behind the low rocky hills was not the sun setting the night before; to think even of the sun setting the night before was poignant and sad; just as the sun that set the day after their fire was not the sun that set the day before it, and to think of it was agonizing.

The sea turned from cobalt to sapphire to purple and then to silvery green: it did these effective tasteless honeymoon things (in useless gradations, for in Sigbjørn's heart it was already night) but it, the sea, was also more menacing than {UBC 13:23, 158} ever before. Ah, what it was to lose that precious freedom Amann had been talking about, and of which they'd often been so sceptical. Swim! Yes—you can do that. But not to leave Acapulco. The sea harmlessly pouring past the scuttle is yet the menacing tyrant of old that the drowned know, Sigbjørn thought again. This was an oblique thought, it was a kind of attempt at some verse form, yet it was the same thing: for once there was a certain comfort in its menace, in its titanic roar. Objectively the tide was rising, ever higher and higher. Nevertheless that had not disturbed the people down on the beach with surfboards. Ah—*they* still had their holiday,[7] those lucky people, to the poor Wildernesses they were now but people seen through a prison window. One couple were having a bad time and had fallen in 6 or 7 times. But what a gay time they were having! The girl had a red bathing suit on, that was vivid in the twilight. A beach boy, slim and graceful, ran along the surf with a board, and jumped on it, riding it standing up, balanced, a slender dark figure gliding against the water.

A man doing exercises—a child watching him was trying to imitate him—another group of evening bathers arrive—a girl in a blue cloak that billowed out behind her in the wind. All the umbrellas had been folded up and put away. That was another point of empathy, which afforded Sigbjørn a tiny spark of curious comfort (or that was a tiny comfort): the holiday for the umbrellas was over for the day, and at least no one could be happy under these umbrellas any more to mock them. True, they would be brought out again early tomorrow, but Sigbjørn did not want to think about tomorrow. Most of the surfboards were in and the beach was emptying, and that was a vague comfort too. A tiny lizard—the "weehaus" clattered along the wall—"Zócalo! Zócalo!"—and the last bus snorted along the road down; and like a {UBC 13:23, 159} huge star, like indeed the light of the prison watchtower in Cuernavaca—and how their poor little apartment in the tower called to them now, how they wished now they had never left that!—"their" lantern came on in the Hotel Cordoba on the porch—how they could wish they were there now, for if they were, their destiny would perhaps be different—the few trees looked green in the evening light.

Now the sea was silver grey and the little boats riding at anchor nodded and turned and dipped and scended. They hurt. Sigbjørn had not yet taken Primrose out in one of these boats. The hard white lights of the Hotel del Pacifico flashed on: the sea was dull silver now, but the wet beach where the waves recede is bright and smooth. Sigbjørn remembered the shadow of the surf seen on the beach that evening, every bubble in fact casting its small lucid shadow, elongated and moving—(some relation here with things casting their shadows before)

Now one hombre with a lantern goes up (the causeway?) and walks toward the house of the President's brother on the island, swinging his light.

"We have orders to put you in prison . . . But we're not going to do that."

"We're not going to—"

Yet, in fact, that was precisely what, without having done it, they had done. Ah yes, it was true, only too true, only too obviously true, that Sigbjørn had been in a kind of prison all the time, that of his emotions, that of his fate, that of his conscience, but this other was a prison where Sigbjørn was, if not quite by choice, at least the warden, it was a prison of which, even if he had not yet discovered where the key lay, whatever faction of himself had lost it, if he had ever possessed it, the key at least {UBC 13:23, 160} belonged to him: and it was indeed his prison, his own beautiful prison, in which he and all his faculties and their minions lay incarcerated; but this—Sigbjørn thought, as they called him in vain yet a third time for dinner—was different, was very different.

And a sudden awful vision of the jail in Oaxaca opened for his mind, at Christmas Eve, the bells—dolente, dolore!—and the night came into Sigbjørn's mind with the policeman's lantern—the policeman who would however yet bring him mescal—the policeman's lantern swinging against the wall, and the policeman's shadow swinging against the wall . . .[8]

(After this should come the "recognition" etc, which may precipitate the dream, which certainly should not be before this chapter.)

(See also end to Chap XI—it might be better to end Chap XI thus.) {UBC 13:23, 161}

The Dream—From Haitian Notes.[9]

For a dream—induction is "We'll have a plate of beans in New Orleans."[10] Perhaps not mention Louisiana—just "somewhere down south" though this is very good. Hangover on Christmas morning, sense of slowness, the pleasure in other people's hangovers—the negro waitress standing outside the kitchen chewing gum, who seems to be "talking," though in fact she is saying nothing; passing the church, the essence, sunny, of Oaxaca, and the sense of personal filthiness. Tombeau de Rosémonde Bertonnière . . . décedé le 12 Novembre 1838 à l'âge de 57 ans . . .[11]

Sigbjørn and Primrose were going down Basin Street to the New Orleans cemetery, with the western sun in their eyes, drifting through the evening sunlight past voodoo square, where a policeman, with a wheel on his arm, evidently from St. Catherine's College, Cambridge,[12] was standing, chatting under the magnolias, and a man was selling hot roasted peanuts, and then they were in the cemetery, kneeling images against a rose sky, a little plane above, bowed little images, and a bearded man with keys, the sexton. There were strange names on graves: Eulalie Aarang. Ici repose Antoine A. Piccaluga: Ci Git Faustin Joe de Gruy Décédée 3 Juin 1846:[13] For a time they were shut up in the cemetery: then they climbed over the wall, and saw, at the end of Dauphine Street, against the sunset, Christ received them with his spreading arms.[14] They went to the Haitian Consul, who was surrounded by doves, they received a visa: they had a drink where there was a man, groaning on a manhole, the word Oh, but whinneying it like a horse, the secret manhole underneath the bar, and they were on a ship, totally unlike any other ship he had been on, with what looked like a great iron perpendicular centipede on top of the foremast, the mainmast looked {UBC 13:23, 162} like a telegraph post, and what seemed to be motorcar headlamps dangled from the mainmast, like the vizored helmeted heads of mediaeval warriors: there were things like macintoshed tennis rackets squatting on the bridge, on which the captain never came at all, spending all his time below decks in an inferno learning how to typewrite, and the crew apparently never did any work at all, signboards appeared suspended by hooks to the taffrails abaft the bridge and running from fore to aft with the name of the ship on it, gave the whole the appearance of a railway station, than which it seemed rather more noisy: the lost first night of sailing and the hallucinatory mountain of the sunset, changing into ladders of gold chiffon: the sun, a pendulous vermilion drop: sun sinking behind a cloud that looked like a horse riding across it; then becoming just a tiny little scalloped rim of vermilion against slaty clouds: chamois clouds: going on the bridge deck at 8 p.m. the Donald Wright sailing smack at Orion: the brilliant first crescent moon following us, flat on its back, slicing through some moon clouds, like a bright silver machete.

An unyielding iron ship, infernally hot and ugly, difficult to walk on. Such a sea too on the moon. Caribbean means sea of the winds. The stars of the Caribees. Though a small sea, it seems bigger than the Pacific. Few flying fish—and where are the porpoises in this sea. It seemed inhumanly broad and long and blue and monotonous. And the nearness of the stars and their wild brilliance made it all the more inhuman and unearthly. No wonder Hart Crane committed suicide here[15]—in any other ocean there would be a hope—but in this moonlit empty maniacal immensity none: that is, of being picked up. Sigbjørn seemed now to hear a voice as if dictating to him: With a bad hangover your thoughts are {UBC 13:23, 163} often incredibly brilliant but you can't put them down because you cannot believe yourself capable in such a state of doing a single constructive thing, least of all what your higher self wants to do. One of the fatal deceptions of drinking: if you took a drink then you would want to put your thoughts down again—but the last state of that man would be worse than the first. When you start putting your thoughts down again, that means you are getting over your hangover. But by this time the thoughts are no good. The brilliant wild thoughts and inspirations have gone. I think that is another deception. The sea rushing through your soul in great cold waves of anguish. Muttering words: any words, bits of phrases—why? Psychology of remorse. The horror and dreadful importance of sex at such moments: boiling erections. Horror of reading magazines, particularly with pictures of happy and pretty women, all invested with this boiling, this cold rushing of disastrous, important, vascular oceanic remorse.[16] Hallucinations in regard to words: the mistaken words sometimes make strangely good sense such as moonaridity for moribundity—the curtains craning forward, for the curious craning forward out of a bus window when there is a smash-up. A vast hangover of sea. Mer de mort. Hallucination: someone coming up the companion-ladder in the darkness in the half moonlight. Repeated several times with a twitch. The psychology and horror of the shakes. The real horror is in the hands. All the poison—mental and physical—seems to go down into the hands. Burning hot, there seems almost a buzzing *inside* your hands. Fear of going into dining room with shakes, especially with captain present. Why are shakes sometimes controlled when no one is present? Beer hangovers. Enjoyable hangovers. Other hangovers. Anatomy of the sense of shame—of persecution in relation to the shakes. {UBC 13:23, 164} But why should one be afraid even of going to the lavatory, even of cleaning one's teeth. Question: Can a writer write anything really great, finally, without a home, or having had his house where he once wrote a great work burn down, in a house he is continually in fear of burning down? Fear of going upstairs. Conversely, fear of going downstairs. Psychology of sadness. The face of yourself as you were in the past, hovering in the room, your passport picture.

Going up on bridge-deck later with Margie on same night, at 4 bells, Eridanus[17] spread down all the sky on the starboard side to

Archanar, always due south, on the starboard horizon, Orion way up there too, Regulus was rising just on the port bow, and then below, the V of Virgo with The Retreat of the Howling Dog—way on the port side the Great Dipper was raised from the sea as if clutched by some hand below the horizon about to crown some celestial second cook, the Pleiades straight overhead, the moon now sinking fast in Aquarius astern but a little to starboard, like a Persian melon, a hanging basket. Strange behaviour of Sirius, framed by a gadget on top of the funnel, and blurred by its steam: it was not twinkling and seemed about to explode.

Drama of mate who left the bridge completely to show us the chartroom: and when skipper objected "We've got a million dollars worth of cargo and we're on one of the most crowded sea lanes in the world" (though Sigbjørn had not seen a ship for hours): "Some of these old skippers think their chartroom's their cathedral."

Death of a sense of fun, ditto humour, ditto of sense. Death. How do you recover from this? If what you fear is being found out why do you always give yourself away? If you really want to hide why do you always go out and make an exhibition of yourself? {UBC 13:23, 165} How to conquer the death of the rebellion against this cowardice? And if it is oblivion that you seek, why do you drink in such a way as will inevitably cause the most agonized kind of remembrance in such a way in short as you will ever have to stop. The Donald S. Wright sounds astern like a very very slow freight train, chuffing . . . Justification of fear of what other people think. Remembrance of the awful Spanish moss on the poor trees, millions of acres of death under the moon of Louisiana . . . I, too, have the Spanish moss upon my soul. (Mildew)[18] Why did you take books like Julian Green's Dark Journey on a trip like this? Leviathan.[19] But the terror of reading sad tragic books. Bloat. A man so superstitious that when a fortune teller had told him the new moon was lucky for him, every time the full moon approached he expected disastar. Ah, but we are having a rebirth! We have rounded the Cape of the cross, and we land in Haiti on New Years Day. (This is the engine at the Quinta Eugenia) New Years Eve. Ship. Still crashing into the seas at 4 A.M.: the Southern Cross appeared tilted in the sky, as if an invisible priest were holding it up, to ward off evil: up at 7 into a blue sea-drenched morning: rounding the Cape of Our Lady: Haiti right in the sun, mysterious, folds of hills, gigantic shadows on wave, like shadows of rain, and sheets of silver, and blue, blue . . . The American flag flying (bravely) why do all flags fly bravely?—(as we approach Haiti) against white clouds; its blue scarcely more dark than the sea, its stars scarcely less bright than the stars last night.

Rolling into Port-au-Prince, the mountains of Haiti in sunlight, the bowwave leewarding into silver as far as the land, opposite Jéremie. The Île de la Gonâve to port, Haiti to starboard: woke to a vast flat blue broiling misty calm, as if sailing into {UBC 13:23, 166} the widespread jaws of some sea animal (Conradian)[20] The crew busying themselves, though not seriously, on the derricks, playing about somewhat foolishly on the yardarms of the mizzen. Île de la Gonâve, weird desert, Haiti like an abstract Scotland, the sense of sailing on and on and in and into some strange vague mystery: and now mysterious almost motionless black sailed boats put out—barren mysterious hills seemingly endless, easy to believe anything may go on there. The steward's "You won't like it there. All them niggers and half breeds running around. I was there 37 months. General Smedley Butler,[21] under his command . . . They got a dictator there. Steal Christ off the cross." Arrival New Years Eve at Port-au-Prince: apparently a town of the dead: a few feeble lights gleaming. Something that might be a train, then stops. Something that might be half an hotel. Lanterns hoisted, our riding light. Blow whistle to no avail. Drop gangway. In the gloom, on the fore deck, sailors tell stories of drunks and fights, hopefully. The skipper went up topside to fish with little pieces of salami. And then they came, silently, the boats: a native fishing smack comes by without any lights at all, slipping by slowly, noiselessly, with a sinister black sail. A few Roman candles half explode feebly and soundlessly in one corner of the dark abysm of the town and people look at them with yearning. A strange New Years Eve but what a feeling of good resolutions and a sense of rebirth on the morrow. Contrast of the veiled mystery of approach and this darkness. The noise of waiting at night for customs officers that never come aboard is the noise of an electric fan in a hot ship's cabin. Nobody comes: Not even ship's agent. The captain takes off his shirt and puts on a singlet and retires to cabin with a cup of tea and a cheese sandwich. And we prepare to celebrate New Years Eve {UBC 13:23, 167} reading O. Henry Memorial Prize Stories of 1919[22] from the American Merchant Marine Library Association, eating nuts and drinking icewater. Then on deck with the captain's binoculars and now without having another drink they have the most miraculous N.Y.E. of their married lives. Previously there had been the strange little sailboats passing, so silently, without lights, from which emanated a curious gnat-like singing, or wailing, very few notes, repeated again and again, various voices, one high and always cracking on same note, tune like part of an ill-remembered Guadalajara.[23] Boats like wings, boats like bats, stealthily, silent, lightless, from which this singing and again—could it be?—or was that from afar or rowlocks, came for the first time the sound of drums. The terrible sound of drums. Battement de tambours![24] Now they saw the boats, in the moonlight, through the binoculars. A boat with a little jib made a sound of snoring as though the boat itself were asleep.

Sea near at hand, through powerful binoculars wrinkled like the moon, with millions of little moons reflected on it, but on this surface, in motion, to the horizon, to the rim of the world. A bat boat, imprisoned in an icefield. The great frozen lake of the moonlight on the sea. The binoculars gathered light so even otherwise invisible boats would take shape. Under the huge silver slice of the wrinkled moon itself. Port-au-Prince through the binoculars seems [to have] no sky signs, a square building picked out in colored lights, other odd lights that may be ships, away to the right an hotel—shadowy something behind square building which may be a church. Someone in Port-au-Prince singing Tipperary very loudly at one point: but that was the only noise. It's a long long way to Guinea, and death will take you there.[25] First mate and Sparks[26] sit glumly in his room. Third mate says he's going to blow all the {UBC 13:23, 168} sirens, ring all the bells, and even send up a spare rocket he has. At midnight no sirens blow, no bells ring, not a sound, but one soft rocket finally does whoosh off the stern past our open porthole, the torch of the third mate, Bergson,[27] staggering back, the quiet and beautiful and strange end to the year, I thank God and the Blessed Virgin and pray to her that the next year may be a real New Year of goodness love and happiness for Margie and myself and acting as a man and bring a real change of character for the better.

Next morning—New Years Day, I get up bright and early, on bridge look at first disappointedly at a few things like factory chimneys and oil refineries from the porthole.

Port-au-Prince is smack in the sun in the morning from the sea consequently difficult to make out: strangely beautiful houses of

pointed roofs and of seemingly Norwegian design, church spires
here and there rise vaguely in the sun giving it a look of Tewkesbury,
while to the right mist lay in pockets of rolling mysterious mountains like Oaxaca, this truly resembling Mexico, for in Mexico too is
that sense of infinite mystery as to who lives up in the mountains—
who can possibly live there?—what voodoo, what mysterious rites,
which does not pertain. Futile invitation to see non-existent shark
playing about the bows. After breakfast, in the mid-morning, a boat
puts out from shore. They came aboard, "What are they like?" All
black as coal. After ordeal of medical inspection, nice doctor with
open coat, pale blue and white tie, and stethoscope—he feels our
pulse, someone hands a letter. It was from his English publishers,
saying that his book will come out the next month, and everyone be-
lieves in it as a book of importance. Ordeal then in skipper's cabin—
by that time, strange, Sigbjørn {UBC 13:23, 169} can scarcely sign
his name, police etc: "You're free" finally, he says: I manage anyway
and get back with feeling of relief. But no sooner have I got back to
the cabin than the fellow appears again. I have not signed my name
hard enough to make any impression on the carbon. I do it this time
on the bunk very steadily by pressing the pencil hard against the
yielding surface: the yielding surface is an excuse for any illegi-
bility—the ruse works. They go: we warp in. Approaching it looks
more like Tewkesbury than ever but also something like Africa and
we try to recognize some of the landmarks of the night before. As
they approached the wharf they saw bales and sheds, negroes smoking
pipes, or resting on their oars below, and a mangrove swamp to the
left what looked like a Mexican freighter went on ahead. A gangway
at a fantastic angle, impossible to go down, yet it is done, and a fantastic beautiful city of mangroves and tin roofs. Here nightmarish
architecture has been turned into bizarrerie and good taste—a credit
to the mores. An hotel—Dominicans with Goering trousers, ambas-
sadors from a neighbouring state, and medals like the inside of fantastic watches.

"You like egg?"
"Oui. Sí."
"What egg?"
Loathsome American playing dice—for whose dead bodies: yet
it is Acapulco in reverse. A fairy in a blue seersucker suit, blue
shoes with bulging eyes, like one always suspects the original of

the cover of Esquire, turns out to be a Protestant Bishop. The honor of "Esquire." Making love in a mosquito net is like making love in a gossamer handsome cab. Mosquito net, casket, coffin-shaped. Think of the handsome cat, says Lewis. Out to the top of the hill with Lewis, a strange language spoken, "Coté route ça aller?" "Route ça rivé la kay de Senator Erikson." "Est-ce-que {UBC 13:23, 170} même route ça rivé la key de Senator Erikson?" "No." "Est-ce-que on connais route laqui aller la kay de Monsieur Erikson?" "No."[28]

Morning I[29]   "You like egg?" "Sí. Oui." "Whose egg will you have?"
Morning II   "You like egg?" "Sí. Oui." "What egg will you have?"
Morning III   "You like egg?" "Sí. Oui." "Which egg will you have?"

—I recognized, behind green curtains, her sniff.

What about an author, who after, like Milton, having finished his masterpiece, threw his inkpot at the wall,[30] threw the author after it.

Woman in a poinsettia dress against green palms.

A man with a face like a boot.

Windy privacy—breezy pioneer!

A rainbow that lasts for ten minutes, blowing colour, still high, multicolored comet, in the red sunset, they say it swallows the rain—arc du ciel.[31]

—hot tambours—

cocks that bark and dogs that crow, *all night*.

the abyss behind the eyes, and the hand that forgets to shake, on the glass

—trumpet trees—

beautiful women with black hair, Cuban: why cannot I look at same: but I *know*—

losing my dangerous cigarette: out for 2 minutes. But what if it were not out? and where?—horror of people talking about you in hotel, everyone talks about one. Fear, therefore, of getting even a drink—(is this a help?) One at last with the great lunge and perfect final equilibrium of the perfectly possessed. Battement de tambours! {UBC 13:23, 171}

The fear beyond the fear of the fact that your cigarette has not gone out, but still is somewhere: the fear that you think yourself damned clever for this, but what is worse, the fear that you do not finally fear anything of the sort, and even that that fear is dishonest, which it is, finally the acknowledged comment that this comprises no fear at all: and no hope either (O Primrose)

Palms like women with multitudinous fans, in the wind.

the blind staggers: unique hangovers.

The sea rushing through your soul in great cold waves of anguish.[32]

The effort—is it really being made, or is it itself the result of fear, fear of going out, fear of staying in, fear of the servants, the dining room, of the look of shame?

wild tragic beautiful and somehow boiling importance of sex in such states of mind—

the eyes

the shakes

—This is a story without any characters

doves with ruby eyes

doves with only eyes

—toy cemetery with cages and open graves (and the shadow-filled green hills behind with an iceberg sitting on top)

(When self-sacrifice becomes absurd it is at about three o'clock in the morning, when, after a late night and just upon the point of discovering the riddle of the universe, cowardly, you begin to fear reproach less, unfortunately, for not being in bed, than for drinking all the rum, and possibly beyond that, simply for staying up beyond dinner time)

Panpan, on a grave and a hansom cab (real) behind distant {UBC 13:23, 172} trees, slowly moving, tottering in the hot afternoon . . .

—a pregnant negro woman in sky blue, with a scarlet sash, sauntering through the cemetery.

—a handsome cat

—What about waking up in the morning and just *thinking* you have no hangover for nearly two hours, and still the hand does not shake (the shrunk trousers, the disastrous laundry in the mind) when will it hit you?

Ma femme desire la toilette: c'est une complication universelle.[33]

—Take ½ an inch as truth (ref. drink low) moral for drunkards and prostitutes.

Sigbjørn hears whispering

—This man, friends of friends of mine, coincidence piled on coincidence, rationalizes it all: a moral forest: stamps past door with
whittled stick, shouting Men of Harlech[34]—Cricket bat out of hell.

—all the lads that come from Norway
sticking peas up a nanny goat's doorway

—The horse, loaded with great stones, panting and sobbing,
through the awful sun, its poor legs giving: hauled up by a black
fury. He whipped it, too. Self-pity.

toy tin houses, with peaked roofs.[35] A house like a child's toy,
made of lace paper, beaming flamboyant trees, leaning flamboyant
trees, made of ferns, made of fears.

—the dark man that follows us behind graves—

—cure hangover with Enos Fruit Salts.

—leaning flamboyant trees—trees that will never be written: dt's
ditto . . . leaving flamboyant trees

Paracelsus?[36] {UBC 13:23, 173}

—the tragic swim at dawn

the awful awful American whose house had also first burned
down and who played Cricket. Would you like to wear my cricket
cap? Broke.

Tragedy of money gone in the real lost weekend[37]—but the humour of it.

—I won't let Primrose take photo in cemetery—tragedy of this

—an invisible whispering voice from behind a wall: Gimme five
cents please. It is a boy, up a trumpet tree.

—healthy and swimming at midday, normal, wondering how soon
crisis was going to hit again, servants chuckling: "Fou" "Bouveur"[38]

a thunderous cat
being constructive
being conclusive

—the tumultuous sobbing behind the eyes—watching yourself
shake;

the progression again into the cold still sad misery
the terrible passion in the midst of the misery
but in spite of the resolution, all over again;

Rhum Barbancourt. Distillé et mis en bouteille par Sucrs. de Paul
Gardère and Co. Port-au-Prince

clouds like pink ice cream Hills like Zapotecan gods, filled with shadow, purple.

—terrible scarf of black smoke, from factory chimney, across purple hills at evening.

Tragedy of Oaxaca, repeating itself. People going to the sweet little church with candles at twilight—of the dead? but no, it is the feast of—(St. Peter?)

negroes playing ping pong before front doors in houses like England. {UBC 13:23, 174}

scarlet runner beans like England . . . horror of cleaning one's teeth (Dentiste)—food like England, roast beef and Yorkshire—the whole thing like England, can I make it? Oh Jesus, can I make it? Can I make her happy and still make it? And still drink?

The little boats—the pathos of the little boats—nostalgia for little silver sober moment.

Oh Jesus Christ and Baron S.[39] deliver me from this torment for it is all about nothing.

But this, of course, you knew. At night, just a little bit of lighted streets, hooded street lamps like bended women.

The horrible bright line of the streets, in the night, silent, and the dogs crowing.

Marcellin[40] and I shouting at each other across an abyss, under the stars. A desire to die for Haiti overcome in an ecstasy. A feeling of never having loved anything so much overwhelms, not even his father or brothers (I never had any) It will beach me to leeward. But it won't kill me just the same. It will beach me to love and work and help. M. did that. He is my father and brother. That is why we cannot comprehend each other. But there is something even greater in man than what I have conveyed, and this greatness alone can save the world from when he is living too close, I mean the devil.

Put your back into it, old fellow. Fight the bastard down. All right, dark, houses just sitting there curved, like assorted sweets.

. . . searchlights on the pool . . .

Behind my elbow, at night, the street we should have taken . . . Bending elbow. Insects, the sound of them—onomatopoeia for insects: klang-maleri.[41] Quatamapoeia for noises of cocks that begin {UBC 13:23, 175} to crow at midnight. Clip-clop-te-whit-Ic-whoooo! It'sjusthurra! Eeeeee! Booooot! Wooowowwoowowwoooo!

Amesalfabor! Oh Oh Oh Oh Yapyaydedyup! Cockkkor! (Excrucior!) Yapayapadooo! Oooo! Ahahahahaha! Bab bah!

A man who tried to combine in himself all the good and bad qualities of all men. A psychoanalyst who put God into a lunatic asylum. Missing numbers of the pages, waiting for the page to turn over. "Desperate dooms of down valley," says the man, whose house burned down.

"Where's Mummy in the shower?" The day in the cemetery . . . Dove with vermilion eyes. Cloud like iceberg. House like toys, woven out of lace. Woven out of love. Houses like tin toys . . . 105 du code penal, staring at him from pack of Chesterfield . . . Sinking feeling when he saw it was six o'clock; only an hour till dinner—Or had he again turned his watch on . . . turning the watch toward five, the hour of drink. Avance ses montres[42]—the hour of—? Man singing Rock of Ages,[43] cleft for me, and the water and the blood, passing one on the porch . . . Turns out his house has burned down. "I'm going to write a story about that, feller," he says, meaning me . . .

Significance of soldier—bought—Kansas City watch.

Bousfield again! I would meet you here. Moves into same hotel . . . Has handkerchief embroidered with Spanish obscenities . . . He moves into our hotel. This is the end. (This Bousfield theme is most important in relation to Dark as the Grave)

Voodoo—the club?

In the streets, the devil, with a tail, huge,[44] smeared with axle grease and waving a long wand—putting out his tongue. "H'mmm— a wild man." (says our wild driver, who is mad as a hatter himself.) {UBC 13:23, 176}

The awakening, the 5 giant Haitians with the stretcher . . . Hospital Notre Dame . . . The clinic: a long corridor of tall grey blue doors with a lattice work at the top . . . Jesus being crucified high up at one end of corridor by my room, a little virgin below, crowned and porcelain . . . At the other end: light, a kind of porter's lodge on a slope, and a telephone . . . Usual history of the hangover . . . only this time it was a cough. Outside my mosquito window carmine poinsettia and a leaning forest of small green nameless trees: crowned by a very little sweet tree, blowing. A mocking bird, a bird that pipes . . . A bird that makes a noise like a soft kiss . . . A high room with a high bed and high grey open windows. On the wall, set on a climbing incline, three small pictures:[45] (a) a reproduction of

Andrea del Sarto's La Charité from the Louvre. (b) Une robe longue, by Albert Guillaume, Paris, Salon 1929, I won't describe this, cut out of a mag, I think. (c) Lady Hamilton, by George Romney.

The man next door who has been castrated (?) *moos* with pain.[46] Bloodstained cloths or bedclothes piled in bathroom, something like part of something human, peeping from among them, gives me a bit of a shock. I say to Phito he has been deraciné. Phito is shocked. Phito (Phaeton) who stays with me all day on first day "The suffering will pass," and on the fourth day, sure enough, the little pink grasses waving in the wind and bending so shyly cause me no pain . . .

Onomatopoeia for poor man moaning next door: Ezshy! Avor! gesahund! uueieeeee! ooooooasigesiahinnashee! Aaaaaaahmooosha-naahmoooo!—

man who comes one day, brother of doctor proprietor, advises me to live in Haiti, buy a bee farm—"You will have 1500 little {UBC 13:23, 177} employees out working for you (while you do your work) Honey fetches high price now. Life in the United States is horrrible."[47] I agree.

Emanuel comes to talk about Malraux.

Phito comes bringing younger brother, a handsome hypnologist, who once, on finding he had syph, shot himself right through the body, just missing his heart, and felt fine ever after . . .

Primrose comes to talk about a new life: perhaps this time we will win through.

When I look out of my window in the hospital into the garden, there are the sweet trees and bending grasses before me, to the left, between bougainvillea and a house, the mountains with their tilted trees on top, to the right, beyond the poinsettia bush that grows outside the patio—and why am I always looking out of hospitals, out of windows, but more especially out of hospital windows?— stretches upwards a kind of wasteland of grey purple and white stones, and rubbish heaps, with a lone coconut palm waving like a God half way up; beyond the garden a trail follows the gradient of the slope, with glimpses of thatched huts climbing, and sounds of voodoo drums.

"It only looks like spring, that's all."

swifts that dart, little goats that bleat, pigs that crow, and play the sousaphone. The swifts that dipped their wings into the Hotel Olaff-son swimming pool.

When I asked for more macaroni and a little butter to help down the bread, why did I not have the courage to ask for more soup too?

The creole lessons—un—deux—trois—in creole, lampe etc (goes on half the night, shouting, good for the nerves) the negroes {UBC 13:23, 178} that sleep beside me in long chairs—afraid of the dark? Amelie brings me more soup anyhow . . . Amelia, (I am Amelia) who offers me more and more in honour of the Virgin of Guadalupe when I say: "But I shall become an elefant." "Ah no, no, charmant."

I get to like my room in the clinic: I can stand about on one foot, dream, work, have a shower—I almost said swim—and look out of the window, and I don't give a thought for a drink, except when I think of coming out: reason is partly due to fire: old house was Paradise but also monastic death surrogate (Huxley)[48]—I needed such to do my work then, and seeking it in vain elsewhere, see death itself instead: idea, go and work in monastery. Impulse doubtless due to pictures of monks getting gloriously plastered. Fear of fire in monasteries? Suddenly I have a conception for a great novel: can I get away with it. Why does not Primrose come? Am lonely. Desolation without Primrose.

Food in hospital; a kind of tasteless gruel for a sweet always dry bread: cold soup: and then sometimes in the middle of that, a really good steak. No salt. A couple of things that might have been bantam eggs for breakfast once.

Damn it, they have forgotten all about me. Am I dead? Is no one here? This is an observation ward: where I observe myself.

Man next door is dying, I think family gathers round: ah, mon famille! Tragedy of little words, little things.

A small spider, seen close to, though supposedly distorted vision, in a Haitian lavatory, that seemed like a ballet dancer, a negro cricketer, a Will Rogers ropetrickster,[49] a boxer, doing all these things furiously and *clicking*. (Delirium when sober—without hangover—and quite happy) {UBC 13:23, 179}

—fear of seeming to stay too long in lavatory is doubtless fear of being thought masturbating: but why should a pretty nurse think that W. was masturbating, especially when that was precisely what he was doing?

Everyone has forgotten about me in the whole clinic: I ring my bell in vain, thinking I should drink more liquids. But nobody comes. Dying of t.b.

At night, lying down, the little trees make a citadel with horns and God's bowing, or a kind of Olympus.

A tree with horns—clock strikes twelve, like our old clock at home—pretty girl gives me tea—goat bleats—man suddenly howls—I cannot even say Vous etes belle[50] to pretty girl.

Surprised to find the notebook in right place, like Consul's whisky bottle:[51] eyes? I am full of hallucinations and the crickets are singing—I write this in the dark.[52]

Next morning I seem to have been alone for an age: five days in the tomb seems a bit much, but I'm beginning to like this little room. How I see why! Like Philoctetes,[53] I shall be sorry to leave it. Tell Phaeto this. Good title: Batterie de tambours.[54]

Frankly I think I have no gift for writing. I started by being a plagiarist. Then I became a hard worker, as one might say, a novelist. Now I am a drunkard again. But what I always wanted to be was a poet. (one ending) (This relates too to his being sorry to leave the ship in Ultramarine, the ward in Lunar Caustic,[55] and the Chief Gunner's cabin in the dream . . .)

A bottle blue fly, basking in the air, motionless . . .

A deracinated matchbox, sitting on a palm frond

A soft voice at the gateway: five cents please.

The five funerals.   Battement de Tambours. {UBC 13:23, 180}

Another ending to this dream section might be, most effectively, the Spanish moss. The Spanish moss might represent, in one sense, American civilization, in another, the madness that threatens Wilderness;—"I have become a tree, dying, and already hung with the mourning of Spanish moss, in a Louisiana bayou, under the terrible moon." (Mem: the Louisiana bayous might also suggest Edgar Allen Poe . . . This certainly was where Poe had put his terrible House of Usher[56] . . . The slow accretion of Spanish moss upon the trees, is like the slow giving in to drink, once more, the stealthy inroads of madness.)

On that last morning they had been passing through strange scenery in Mississippi, slightly rolling, not flat. They wake up feeling they are in Dollarton. Red line of dawn on left, it seems beyond swamps. Pine, pine, pine, sometimes tall and lone, others just Christmas trees, an earthly sense. A pine suddenly seems growing taller and taller in the dawn. Tierra Colorada too. And some of the houses seemed snow-covered, tin roofs—this was the first chord of Haiti—

unearthly scenery. Red grass, red earth, and a deceptive sense of being high up. Yellow roads leading through the forest and grass roads. "He married one of these gypsy yallers, one of them over there somewheres." Golf course, green against red grass. Frazier's Grocery. Magnolia, a beautiful town, just over the line in Louisiana. Some even quite respectable houses have tin roofs. Superb trees. Scenery supernatural, but as it were, kindly. A sense of autumn. Bayous. Swamps, and swamp things growing in them along the road. The first sight of Spanish moss. Makes a tree look like old Chinese. Autumn landscape through Louisiana. But mixed with other exotic trees that have kept their leaves, so that they are glossy and {UBC 13:23, 181} green, and it's like autumn and spring at the same time. Pines, pines, pines, but with a faery land of delicate copper-leaved bushes beneath them. But not too much undergrowth. A sense as of the heavenly enchanted forest, such as you get in England. Land of Christmas trees and swamp adders! But instead of feeling at low level, you feel again as if on a plateau, with all these pines. Some little pines stand up very queer and abstract, with twigs and needles like rudimentary hands, like a contraption of Calder's, or a figure of Paul Valdes.[57] Dapple shadowed gold of the forest, red berries, swamp full, almost to top of low wire fence below road. It was here that one first encountered the Spanish moss. At first this Spanish moss gives trees a waggish rather than a sinister air, contrary to everything one has heard, as if someone had hung them with false beards, or as if nature had playfully added to them some arboreal equivalent of the beards children add to pictures of people: if they are sad, you think, they are sad in the way of last year's Christmas decorations, or to be more precise old decorations that are left up after Christmas, and now are to be taken down, for never is there Spanish moss that has the air of recent growth. On the contrary, in spite of its vitality, it seems grey and moribund. Luziane coffee. Street scene through windows (in pantomime) Smartly dressed negro and his gal standing on pavement. Double breasted suit in good taste, dark brown shirt, and spanking bright tie. They are laughing and talking, she jerking her knee out rhythmically from time to time. He is anxious to know if he is well shaved and dressed well, strokes his cheek: she looks. She is satisfied, he evidently not, for he goes on stroking his cheek and yawning. She makes gestures and movements with the lapel of {UBC 13:23, 182} her own garments so that you know she is praising his suit. He makes several attempts to button his double breasted coat on the inside button; gives up, yawns. Formerly she had leaned a moment, affectionately against him, even done a little dance about him. He smiles and yawns and finally yawns cavernously. Previously to this nice looking negro, shortish, in green neatish suit, with briefcase, possibly a lawyer, had left these two, who were possibly waiting there for our bus to draw away, for he was about to board it. He continued to smile to himself after leaving them for many paces—the universal free-wheeling of the smile—until he reaches the small line up before the bus door, then two enormous frowns appear, his face becomes serious and studied, half contemptuous and yet wary of possible insults, but at the same time as wary of giving cause for them. All gestures in former scene are dramatic and significant: you know what they are saying: in similar scene in Canada, none of the gestures would have been significant, if you had known what they were saying it probably wouldn't have been worth hearing, and the gestures, if any, would have been unnecessary, and signified nothing, or little: to the negro, life is a dance, slow or fast, sad or tragic, or despairing, it never seems to be without rhythm.[58] Going into New Orleans, glorious morning, green swamp followed the road full of water hyacinths; but here the Spanish moss really began to show its sinister quality. It is as ubiquitous as cactus and ten times more sinister. In one place a whole tragic forest of pines is killed off by it. The trees stand tragic, desolated, ravaged, shrouded—beyond imagination. In other places it is as if, again, they had been hung with the moss, as if decorated for Xmas in some ghastly black magical celebration of it. Strange shapes appear {UBC 13:23, 183} in the moss draped, moss-shrouded pines in eternal mourning. Strangely mostly that of a ghostly Christ crucified. But elsewhere a whole tree will be reduced to nothing but a pillar of Spanish moss, resembling a thin abstraction of a negro, with a death's head, holding a ghostly headdress, or bouquet. Twisted horrible woman of a tree with hair blowing back. Draped skeletons in every attitude of supplication. A tragic slow shrouded delirium of trees. Black water in the swamp now following us, with gold leaves reflected in it: pampas grass. When the moss has killed the tree, the needles remain, but burn red, look as though they are burning. The tragedy of the trees gets worse as you approach New Orleans. Ah, it looks so delicate, this moss, as it starts. It gets worse, so much worse, becomes heartbreaking, unimaginable, terribly beyond belief. Spanish moss has done to the trees what a blitz would do to a city and with the same beauty, (this is dubious, now I have seen bombed cities. St. Malo, perhaps)[59] Occasionally a not yet killed tree holds up despairing arms, as yet some of its limbs unkilled, it seems to be crying. The Heart is filled with pity at the sight. The beautiful trees finally reduced to attenuated delirious shapes of cactus. Even the young beautiful healthy trees growing along the creek by the roadside live in this continual shadow of death—proof that while man might not be able to prevent death, he could certainly make anything he wished out of it—Death that now takes these shapes: Bats, old men creeping. Beaked shapes of the damned. The Virgin Mary appears too again from time to time, seeming to be lost forgotten gods and stricken spirits of the forest who have died with them but yet preserve their shape. Mississippi appears a moment widening on the horizon. Dead trees now right to the horizon, trees with no {UBC 13:23, 184} hope of life. Worse than a forest fire. Ah, now to think of the naked and clean and living trees some way back. The tragedy of the trees began physically to upset him. Think of these shrouded figures for hundreds and hundreds of miles, it seems to the horizon, as far as the eye can search. Think of them under the moon. It is a country far stranger than Africa. The bayou full of water hyacinths. Thirdly, didn't someone do something at the very beginning about the Spanish moss. Never were the vital powers of life and death so contiguously violently exampled. Cabins along the bayous, path cleared in the water hyacinths. Sunlight on the water hyacinths. The final lap through the forest is so absolutely different from anything one ever saw that it is difficult to believe our bus has penetrated it. But even New Orleans could not escape the suburban horror. Burma Shave comes on scene again. Doctor said, It was a boy. The whole durned factory jumped for joy.[60] Burma shave. Trees leaning back in supplication. Others resembling Druids pointing: knights of the Orders that even Alexander Nevsky[61] never saw. Horrid festoons. Some trees seem to have emerged, dripping from the weeds, or actually trying to extricate themselves. Hollywood Tourist Cabins. Royal Tower Cola. For a good nite rest. Metry Tourist Court. Reasonable rates. But strangely enough the suburbs seem to fade out and the Spanish moss begins again. Gigantic tortured snails and giraffes made by moss. This is the Garden of Memories Cemetery. Individual never disturbed resting places . . . Drink Dr. Nut. It's delicious. Royal Crown Cola (the cola that now defaced the Western Hemisphere) Scoffy Auto Store. Drink Jax. Bottled Beer. Fresh up with 7 Up. 7! Kilroy was here. We waited for a long train of oiltanks at a level crossing rolling by like great plump boloneys,[62] rattling {UBC 13:23, 185} and chinking past, at first with a sound as of castanets, then with a clashing dancing noise like the sound of the feet and swords in a Mexican fiesta when the music has ceased. Louisiana Hatcheries. Pelican Football Stadium. Welcome to New Orleans. The Air Hub of the Americas. An interesting point: would jazz rhythm at its best be inconceivable at least before the days of trains. The washboard beater's slashing chuffing rhythm of a train at night. Sigbjørn was haunted by the conviction that there was a hidden meaning in all this. American civilization itself, might be a sort of Spanish moss . . .

Credit Dentist—Gas Given. Think! When working in the square or on the apron, watch the hook, it can't watch you![63] S.S. Aristotelis, bound for Buenaventura, Colombia.

But it was into this realm that Sigbjørn's soul now seemed to go. Why not, had not Juan Fernando Marques said that he would meet him there . . . {UBC 13:23, 186}

SEATTLE TO NEW ORLEANS / Margie Notes & Malc Notes

Sat. Nov. 30 we leave Vancouver—plane late, have a few beers— wait as usual in airport, but uneventful trip, munching sandwiches. Arrive in Seattle, decide to take midnight bus to Portland, drink sherry in nice pub—1911 Tavern—dinner in strange cafeteria where we are floored by prices but food is superb. Frightful night on bus due to getting back seat, very bad, draughty, uncomfortable and no sleep. We wrap ourselves in my coat and curl up together and night passes somehow with great feelings of adventure and love. The skiers standing in formation in the bus line-up, going to ski in the Government Camp.

Breakfast in Portland and off at 7. A cool, cloudy morning with very grey dawn just breaking as we leave but this time good seats and full of love and joy despite exhaustion. Leaving P. the usual shambles of suburbs but suddenly without warning between the dreary houses I see a great cold white and grey remote peak that vanishes behind rows of flats and stores so I can hardly believe I've really seen it. Presently Malc sees it also and there we are, out of the city, on a long straight highway running between neat farms and there it is: Mt. Hood, so like Popo we are both aghast, even with the jagged bit on one side that saves it from complete perfection. Now on the other side Rainier,[64] pure, pure, dim, white in the far distance, pure and perfect. The sky was clotted silver, the two volcanoes were whitely silver, Hood splashed and gashed with leaden grey—all the landscape colors muted and with winter and the grey cloudy morning—save in the east where there was a long gash of saffron and gold. As sometimes happens on grey days the visibility was excellent. Rainier wheeled and sank away till it became a white muffin behind a hill and was gone. Hood grew nearer and clearer, then was lost as we {UBC 13:23, 187} entered the Columbia River Gorge. This is magnificent, with waterfalls dropping from sheer cliffs around every curve. One fall so delicate, so fine, drops from 600 feet and is swept away by the wind, transformed into a spray a cloud of mist half way down the sheer face of the black cliff and drifts away in dissolving puffs and wisps—vanishes!

Multnomah Falls at about 10 A.M. for 10 m. stop. Grey skies still and tearing wind. The falls crashing 620 ft. and we stand, shouting and exultant at the foot for a moment, then run back to the bus. No one else on bus goes up path—all are drinking coffee in station or huddled against the wind. There is a trail to the top and Malc says it would be like climbing Tepoztlan. The picnic tables there below, and we think of people there in summer.

(Malc note: From Portland to Salt Lake strange noises on board bus: I actually thought the brakes were equipped with some kind of musical instrument: they blew little trumpets and horns of their own every time we rounded a corner: whatever it was blew actual notes and kept up a continual whining but not altogether unpleasant musical accompaniment: though sometimes they wailed and even screamed.)

Then on, on up the Gorge, cliffs, mountains, and always waterfalls—then the long unexpected stretch of desert. Cliffs as flat as houses, and walls, sagebrush, mesquite, and tumbleweed then a whole valley of black broken stones like a stormy sea, no soil, no anything, a few leafless willows along the river but nowhere else—a monotone of grey and sand-color and black rock. Lunch at Arlington and foul it was and expensive and hurried—Umpatilla was cold and windy but dry frosty mountain air. Pick me up cocktail guaranteed advertised in stupid little station but {UBC 13:23, 188} no cocktail since Oregon only sells beer and wine at bar. (only beer)

But now we really begin to climb; as we climb frost grows thicker until all is covered with delicate feathery crystals, the bushes of mesquite and mountain laurel are lilac colored, the sage white, the grass whiter still. Now we plunge into a misty fog and all is ghostly with wispy streamers flowing and drifting down the canyons. Then the mist begins to thin out somewhat and through it is a smoky rose sunset, more like the smoke of a distant fire at twilight. In a slanting field a few patient ponies stood hunched with cold against the sunset, the mist puffing round them. Then suddenly the mist is gone, it is below us, and we look down on lakes, flowing rivers and a vast sea of clouds, sometimes calm and flowing, in other places storm swept, dashing against cliffs and throwing up spume and wisps like cotton. Behind this the sunset, a strip of the strange burning orange only seen from a plane or very high altitude, with distant peaks and piled clouds of violet and royal purple—that which below is gold and blue, here is intensified to orange and purple. It was like being on top of the world, vast sense of seeing the curve of the earth. Wasatch—name of the range.

The wonderful driver—"O.K. folks, tighten up your cinches and put on your spurs and get out your cigarettes, we're in Wyoming." But Cheyenne!

Malc notes: Tremendous Oaxaquenian sense of rolling distance unwinding and unravelling upon distance; not so much space, but just pure distance—lone tumbleweed at Multnomah falls, sagebrush like flocks of sheep. Sagebrush grazing among the rocks—rock falls look man-made: dead country, treeless to the east, save an occasional line of birches in an oasis at the mountain's foot, their filigree sliding across white Mount Rainier. {UBC 13:23, 189}

Between La Grande and Union, the bus rises above the clouds in a manner suggesting E. M. Forster's Celestial Omnibus:[65] clouds like lakes in the valley below, very much as from plane entering Mexico City: beyond insane tremendous sense of distance, hills meadows farms rays of light, endless Oregon: a red sunset crumbling and blazing away almost behind: ponies standing in a field of crystal frost, mist swirling around them, against the silver sky with blowing rose in it and the sunset behind them: lilac colored bushes . . . snowy mesa, high up in Wyoming. White sun and white sky mesa, nothing but mesa, giving the effect of prairie, but without either the yearning boundless quality or that of infinite boredom of Saskatchewan or Kansas: high ranges way over on the right don't look high because we are so far up ourselves; a cheery driver makes the whole trip delightful. Soon as we are in Wyoming every one lights up their cigarettes. Fort Bridget and Church Butte and a cowboy in a horse and buggy: exciting ranges very far away to left beyond ranges. Diesel engined monsters puff past: a few sheep, no cowboys, nothing just moribundity, though Wyoming is somehow impressive: difficult to (Wyoming—moon-aridity) understand how anyone wrote anything so social as a waltz about it: but leaving Salt Lake City the mormon table like the Teeters.[66] Wonderful beginning: Folks, you've had your town, now it's mine. The state law of Utah prohibits smoking in the coach, but in about 2 hrs we'll be across the border in Wyoming, then you folks can smoke all you want. I'd just like to ask you one thing. There is no law prohibiting it, but please, no pipes and cigars. If you want a sick driver, just light a cigar and I'll have to get out and walk. There'll be a rest stop of 10 minutes at Evanston and we stop for half an hour for lunch at Rock Spring. Be careful stepping {UBC 13:23, 190} from your seats into the aisle because you can twist your ankle mighty easy and there's just one thing more. If anybody's got a bottle keep it in your case—or keep it out of sight. I don't even want to see it.

Each state has its own characteristic: customs men and gloom of Seattle: drunken GI's and tarts—even a drunken colored tart: fantastic necking of a sergeant and a Waac[67] in the 1911 bar: the mild mannered barkeeper who'd locked his help in the privy: the long lines outside the garish movie on the slope, waiting to see The Killers.[68] Tense and terrific: Beer and Wine: the endlessness of Oregon, sadness of its wilderness, surprise of its waterfalls: on and on: Beer only in Oregon, and your last chance for Strong Beer at Shell station, just before Snowfields. Note: I forgot Idaho.

Leaving Salt Lake—cold nole me tangere[69] of Utah—a sense that everything important is enclosed, insulated: beauty of farms, houses seen sunk in the ground: but fine Tlaxcala feeling is Hotel Marion; chill of Mormon religion but moving story about the sea gulls: beer only—and liquor stores few and far between sordidity of beer joints

and contrast between this and Moroni on the dome:[70] few people
smoke and you're told not to in restaurants this undoubted survival
of tenet in Mormon religion. Going out of Salt Lake City great
factory chimneys twinkling, look like obsolete steamers or Mississippi river boats lying alongside wharf. Sudden Oaxaquenian clarity
on mountain tops, clear and near: then lost in haze. Venus swimming among pink clouds. White frosty salty look of ground, white
light in salt white house, salty snow on top of salty mountains. a
frosty dawn. a frosty little cemetery with frost all over the grave-
stones, {UBC 13:23, 191} closely cropped grass, neatly tended. A
canyon. Weeper Canyon. Devil's Gate. Frosty seats under the grey-
white willows—the High Sierras (?) huge oblique breakers of rock
over to right. Sunrise on a corner of rock, sudden vermilion hymn
of praise way off there. The sun rises again. Devil's slide: going
down to Echo City. 290,000,000 years old. Wasatch range of the
Rockies. Willow and osier and birch along frozen stream. After
Echo City Elephant Rock—

Between the frost-painted hills to the right, young birches marching down a defile, from a platinum sun. Birches seem like a kind of
blooming sagebrush. White maned train, the Challenger, advancing
behind one platinum eye:

In Wyoming we see what looks like a forest fire, a gigantic pillar
of smoke: we approach it with evil feelings of excitement but it is a
train with a terrific head of steam, smoke seems issuing straight out
of a hole in the boiler: soon we see more of these gigantic pillars
of smoke, very exciting—in this desolate rocky landscape; then we
see what looks like a huge black bar of iron with a white wake of
smoke above it. This too is a train: Little America, which has been
pursuing us, since Oregon, turns out to be a roadhouse with a bar,
rooms in the middle of frozen waste, with penguins bought from
Byrd's Expedition,[71] Wyoming begins to be a disappointment at
Rock Springs, a horrible soulless bituminous mining town, where
we have a grim class-conscious lunch. Free Souvenir Penguins. Little
America. STOP: live penguins from the frozen south. Post Cards.
Little America. Idaho: wildly hot music coming out of a nightclub
on the first floor at 1 A.M. {UBC 13:23, 192}

Margie notes: Dinner in Union was hurried but delicious and we
slept most of the way to Boise. 40 min stop. It is now midnight and
then our wedding anniversary. Meet strange man in tan overcoat

who invites us to his club and buys drink of fine Scotch. Club was like speakeasy, little orchestra, small bar and few people gambling. Back aboard bus and finally settle down and sleep right through to Burley, where breakfast at 5:40 and then off the last lap to Salt Lake City.

As we leave Burley the first faint green light in the sky to the east where Venus, the morning star, shines, between Antares and Jupiter. A clear cold exquisite dawn with splashes of salmon-colored light on the high peaks all around us. Mist is rising from the icy ground as the sun rises 3 times, distorted into a vermillion egg, swallowed by mist, rising again. Then we are all swallowed by fog or a cloud, nearly into Tremonton and now we have crossed from Idaho into Utah and soon are in Ogden, and then S.L. City.

Malc notes: Thence (after Rock Springs) into primeval country at Medicine Bow a pub called Old Diplodocus. Telegraph poles combing the crests of the plains, literally like combs. And further on, a dinosauria. The swinging red-lighted signals, pendulums, at level crossings. Another tremendous sunset—red astern. Black swordfish like clouds, very pale primrose sky to the right, in the south, with the Dali cliffs along the horizon. The south-eastern horizon, on our right front, powdered with mauve or magenta, like a fire running down its length. The silhouette of an irregular ridge near at hand was that of an embankment, which sneaked and writhed along against the further horizon. The funnels of two freight trains appeared from time to time just above this {UBC 13:23, 193} embankment as they raced along in a sunken track. Grimness of Laramie, but once houses on outskirts; old frontier town. Christmas trees between Laramie and Cheyenne. Cheyenne itself appeared as lights racing and twinkling disappearing and commingling on the far horizon of yet another plateau. It rather resembled Hoylake as seen from Moreton in Cheshire—and we passed Moreton-like towns. The lights of Cheyenne would drop out of sight for a time in the road then jump up again like a jack in the box. Chill, drear, inhospitable feeling of Cheyenne: worse than Huehuepan de Leon. The Albany Hotel and Richelieu Burgundy. Such American capitals are so soulless one thinks of them in terms of their individual liquor laws. Here they have packaged liquors i.e. a combination liquor store and bar, every one a Farolito.[72] Meet man coming out carrying glass of beer on to the street. Is this against the rules? Margie sick. A horrible night and a bad drop in the holiday. Up betimes and set off for Denver—bad news of coal strike. Fields the color of rye crunch. Endless potato fields. Ranges follow on right like Wales. Snow turns fields into fens and inlets of snow. But I am thoroughly tired and abysmally depressed. Margie admires the red barns. Birches and locusts. Suburban horror—the eternal suburban horror of the motel horror, the tur-o-tel horror, the Bar B.Q. horror, the liquor store Plates put up horror, and again, the motel, the Texaco, the horror of a soulless nothing ness. Ridiculous system of numbers delays us for Kansas bus. Denver is entirely, is almost entirely, a suburban horror—but some of its Kansas side out-skirts are pretty: houses of sandstone. The suburban houses of chiro-practors horror. The mountains all round the horizon must give you (I even half recall it) a feeling {UBC 13:23, 194} of hope when you're approaching it, We are leaving them behind. A holy atmosphere in the bus: the reluctance to get out once you're in—though why ever get in? Movement of trees when bus is going is interesting, their dif-fering motions rather. The further world of fields moves round in a circle but a tree stands still. Trees that seem to be sliding across you as if in grooves. The curious craning forward and eagerness when there is a smash up. I look round in time to see the result of a villain-ous collision of two cars, smashed windshield, and an old lady, evi-dently seriously injured, being helped up a bank, among numerous hens: were the hens in the car?

The horrors of:

U-Smile—Steam Heated Cottages

Mobilgas

Ace of the Hi-way

Wimpy's Modern Garage

Burma Shave: Big mistake, use your horn and not your brake.[73]

Well-come Cottages

Coca-cola

Hardware Auto Store

Wizard Furniture Company.

Wonderful breakfast in Kansas. Leaving Kansas, Missouri, sweet little valley with a stream going through it: dawn again, and Venus swimming in rose. Tires and Accessories: Old Friends are the best—Falstaff: Budweiser: Pete's Cafe: New and Used Pipes: Jack's Lan-tern: Dine and Dance: maples, oak willow; sage-green grass by the roadside, the filigree of apple trees against a blue-shafted grey-white

sky: little maples behind a cottage against a cream sky. All States
Village Mizzu Motel {UBC 13:23, 195}

> When the stork
> Delivers a boy
> Our whole darn factory
> Jumps for joy
>> Burma Shave

> Car in ditch
> Driver in tree
> Moon was full
> So was he
>> Burma Shave

> I use it too
> The bald man said
> It makes my chin
> Feel like my head
>> Burma Shave

Boonville Flying Service. Crossroads Missouri. Phillips 66. Removes
the goo. Improves the go. Literature at roadside never lets you alone.

> That she could cook
> He had no doubt
> Until she creamed
> His brussel sprout
>> with Burma Shave

Auto-Lite Spark-Plug. Leaning telegraph poles and corn shocks of
Missouri. King Edward Cigars. The Tetrach Coca Cola and Kozy
Kottages. Need seat covers? Balz label. Hotel Tiger, Air Cooled, $1.75
and Up. Columbia—operator in charge. Max Crawley safe, reliable,
courteous: he had all his virtues down. The difference in, importance
of—even the metaphysical importance of—ever changing driver.

A store station, like a bridewell in Columbia, with, hewn into its
facade, the one dignified word: Wabash.

Margie Notes: In Kansas City at 5 A.M. weary and excited we
don't make the most of our time there but Malc has wonderful huge
breakfast of hash, egg, potatoes, toast, jelly and coffee for 40¢ and
we are happy and prices are coming down.

There is a fine sunrise, Venus wrapped in a rosy veil and {UBC 13:23, 195A}[74] now, in Missouri, there are trees again and how they delight the mind and senses after the endless white Siberia-like plateau of eastern Colorado and Kansas—or worse, without snow, in some places, due to the strange warm spell which the Kansas City Morning Star claims is God's answer to Lewis' coal strike,[75] the plains this time of year are the color of death and are as endless and boring. So that the lovely rolling landscape of Missouri with fat farmland and everywhere brooks and streams bordered by birch and willows and charming old brick farmhouses surrounded by elms and locusts and great oaks are like a bath to the spirit, however badly the body needs one. The corn shocks are fine and here and there gold spills of corn lie in the fields or pass by in open trucks (much nicer than the trucks and fields of turnips in Wy. and Colo). In the meadows is a kind of copper-colored grass blowing in the breeze and some fields are emerald green (winter wheat?). One thinks how marvellous this country is in other seasons when it is so beautiful in bare winter.

Well, in St. Louis we pass Mound City Dye Works and enter the city over a long, rolling road of old red brick with the afternoon sun intensifying the color so that this street (actually rather sordid and the usual stupidity of suburbs of large cities) shines ahead like a road of glory.[76]

The bus station is crowded and foul but we walk through a market to get out of it that is stupefying to anyone who has coped with Canadian shortages. What, we think, are these stories about shortages in the States? My God! Cheese! Wonderful cheeses of all kinds (we buy Liederkranz) tinned and bottled delicacies we've forgotten ever existed. The delicatessens crammed with mouth-watering sausages and meats and the fruit and vegetable {UBC 13:23, 196} counters overflowing with avocadoes and pineapples and grapefruit, besides all the green fresh vegetables.

Malc goes to find hotel while I send wire and see to tickets and meets me looking alarmed, saying the only hotel for blocks around is foul and I better come and see it. Up 2 dingy flights in a filthy little lobby an old Jew tries to make us register before we see the room. But we see! The stench nearly knocks me over and I open the window, only to find the smell comes largely from the stinking court just below about 2 feet where everybody has been throwing garbage and general refuse for a century. The bathroom—why a bathroom in a place like this?—is filthy! painted dark red over plaster slapped on anyhow, with floor, walls and ceiling all one swab and a tub that looks like a child's—about 3 ft. long. We left and walked down the street where, in the next block, we passed a large department store, obviously one of the best in the city, with such clothes in the windows as I haven't seen since New York. Then Malc sees a small sign over a dark doorway in the block beyond (we are walking round the block so are near the station again) and goes up to inquire while I wait below in case it is just too fuerte.[77] We are here in a very old section of town with ancient brick buildings walling a narrow street, I wait, watching people pass: negroes, tarts, clerks from dept. store, clerks from office buildings, tramps, people—I look through dirty glass door and see M. coming downstairs looking joyful. The room, 3 floors upstairs, is ancient, high ceilinged, somehow reminiscent of Mexico and fantastically, sordidly, romantic. Peeling wallpaper, narrow windows to the high ceiling with shrunken lace curtains are on 2 sides, bed with only one sheet, large electric fan (not working) closet door firmly {UBC 13:23, 197} locked, mirror so old and clouded you can't see at all, but all this somehow romantic instead of hideous. We are delighted and get bags from station, then buy cheese, burgundy and sausage and repair to room to luxuriate and ah! bathe. But there is no hot water.

To Your Health!

Our bathrooms are sanitized daily with Bac-Trol . . . This process, insuring freedom from bacteria, is another feature of our efforts to provide you with immaculate surroundings.

The Management—Delmar Hotel.

MALC NOTES: Entering St. Louis, on a bright winter afternoon warm as summer, down a stone pavement of gold. Mound City China Co. Gast Beer. Stag Beer. Stemerick Supply Co. Leaving St. Louis on a glorious day, past the glass foundry and the advertisements: Smooth as silk but not high hat, and the Russ Barber Shop, Baders Ford Inc. past the S.S. Peter and Paul Catholic Church, going down 7th, crossing Russel Blvd, past Allis Chalmers, Cooke Tractor Co., Syers Truck-Lettering. The leafless sycamores. Slow. Approaching Fire Lane my Thirst mate, Dr. Pepper. Phillips 66—whole town built of red bricks, past Pestalozzi street, the whole town glowing, roseate, past Mobilgas, Groceries and Meats, brick pavements, we give eagle stamps. Star Athletic Club. Puzzel Inn Down Missouri, U.S. 67, past the Western Last Company, rosy pavement, beautiful herring-bone sidewalk, Fine Wines since 1873, BELZ, lovely lovely red brick alleys, red in middle of streets, asphalt on either side, ruby red, soft Indian red, queerly beautiful old city. Goffs Confectionery. High adventure at going off to Memphis. Caution, Slow Down. Topmost American Lady Prune Juice down the wine-colored streets, streets of claret, my ancestors {UBC 13:23, 198} were stuffed with Taystee Bread, past Peopping Street, rose-red factory chimney. Voochook Company Inc, entering St. Louis County, past the Heine Meine Liquor Store, Lemay Grill, Plate Lunch, W. C. Sullentrop, Home Appliances Store, past the Ideal Roller Rink, and now the physicians and surgeons again, the Shell, the stop, the Sinclair H.C. Gasoline, Shellubrication. Tell him O.K. he's got a new Nash, the Nic-Nac Tavern. Beautiful Mount Hope Cemetery Valley of Peace, past beautiful cemeteries, and a lone thick ochre factory chimneys belching cream fur against a vague turquoise sky, by Melville,[78] the way the St. Louis man went when he done left this town, Tampa Nugget Good as Gold, Campho-Phenique, Join our Brushless happy throng,[79] 100,000 Users can't be Wrong, a pretty red Lutheran church with a bow-backed fence, paradisal rolling country of Missouri, like Devonshire near Hartland, Your Operator G. C. Chroeister. Safe—Reliable—Courteous. Strong copper leaves on the oak trees, some amethyst and garnet, and copper-colored grass, the rosy theme of St. Louis repeating itself in the country. Imperial City, of Imperial, says the operator, when we stop at a little village where soldier, going home from the war, gets out, carrying blue suit, freshly-pressed in St. Louis, on a hanger.

"Thanks a lot."

"Thank you," says Mr. Chroeister.

—Safe reliable courteous—(all the bus drivers were; that was on the plate, it was only the name that changed.)

Cinnamon-brown cat tails (bulrushes) growing along the streams, the creeks tumbling down—did we cross the Mississippi?

Peaceful country that demands little of you. {UBC 13:23, 199}

Landing in St. Louis. Go to Bus Tavern to decide plans: Tavern is sensible kind of place, something like a cafe, with red tables, and booths, and wonderful meals at cheap prices, braised sweetbreads only 40¢ for example: I have seen a hotel opposite advertising rooms for $1 Up: annex of St. Francis Hotel: go through brothel-like entrance, climb bleak stone stairs like 113 Bucarelli to first floor, where find a scene at first somewhat resembling Gorki's Lower Depths.[80] Beaky Jew bawling man out, gives me, suspiciously, key to look at room—"just as I'll know you're satisfied." Horrible sordidity of room 109. Smell as of sulphur and smoke. Heat is working. Stinking bathroom, window upon garbage heap. Presence of dark filthy bathroom, even though there is hot water, yet it seems to make it more sordid. He wants $2.80 for room, obviously can't ask Margie to face it, but it seems the only one. Margie can't: so we look for another. Find the Delmar and spend a glorious evening drinking claret and eating liederkranz and looking out over gloomy St. Louis. In top room across the street opposite doves are living. Though our own hotel room is unbelievably filthy and the hot water utopian,—none the less it occurred to me what a good thing one had done in having had the strength of will to *search* still further (after 48 hours in the bus) for it brought such happiness;—however, here is the beautifully deceptive card of the New Delmar, complete with an embossed stencil of a negro carrying three bags, two as black as he SPECIAL RATES BY WEEK   REASONABLE PRICES   PHONE GARFIELD 9651. NEW DELMAR HOTEL 712 North 7th St. (at Delmar) In the Heart of the Business, Shopping and Theatre District. Running Hot and Cold Water in every Room. For Good Eats visit Brussel's Restaurant 608 Delmar Blvd.[81] St. Louis. Mo. {UBC 13:23, 200}

Three beautiful names—also for hot tunes—of towns: Herculaneum Junction, Golden Rule Tavern, Festus Crystal City Junction.

Trunks of jet, and leaves of copper, copper and bronze trees, and copper grass. Muted color of autumn. A jade creek with white reflections—copper corn and pale gold corn.

Gravel being spewed out the maw of a dilapidated but Wagnerian looking machine. Innumerable streams and creeks of every kind. Going further south: Oshkosh B'Gosh, World's Best Overalls.

A scene, as follows: something like a screen, with so and so in so and so advertised (Gary Cooper) therein, in front, a notice Rummage Sale Saturday, a white dovecot rising behind the screen, and an iron swing—a white dismal house, a weeping willow. Opposite a car, resting on its axles, smashed to hell in garage, result of frightful accident, rusted, peeled, a horror, but with the numberplates quite clear and bright and new.

Our lunch stop: a town with vast heaps, resembling sand.

Last morning, strange scenery in Mississippi. Slightly rolling not flat. But wake up feeling we are in Dollarton. Red line of dawn on left, it seems beyond swamps. Pine, pine, pine, some tall and lone, others just Christmas trees—an unearthly sense, etc. See page 181 to 186.

GOING DOWN THE MISSISSIPPI—Afternoon trip.

—Los Angeles, with steam up.—Cape Archway; Brazilian ship, the Comte Ligra, flying its green Brazilian flag; a ship like a great black long shoe s.s. Lucano N. Barrios: Iriona—Tela (this ship from Honduras); Snakehead—Savannah, little funnel, it seemed, set slightly to starboard, red stripes and blue stars on funnel; William B. Travis (Am) grey, black, squat funnel, {UBC 13:23, 201} red lead; Platano—Panama, white and buff—black top funnel—yacht-like, "the banana": bananas conveyors, all kinds of American landing war vessels L.C.Y. Grande Victory, black ochre funnel, bring tobacco and sisal; Chinese characters of Plimsoll line;—the load line; ships in salt water, which has greater buoyancy, would ride higher; S.S. Oregon Fir—yellow, queer funnel, with black twisted tip like a shoe horn.

The President goes first upstream past the steamship docks, the Porto Rican docks, Banana docks, Army Store Houses, Industrial Canal, levee, Jackson Barracks, Sugar Refineries where about opposite the Chalmette Battlefield it turns and proceeds back down the other bank, past the truck gardens, U.S. Immigrant Station, U.S. Naval Station, and the dry docks (where it blows its whistle) crosses to other side of river again past the place where she docked, ocean vessels, cotton docks, and grain elevators, round again and home via the other bank again, truck farms, molasses plant, oil docks, cottonseed oilmills, Gretna, Sulphur Docks, salt docks, crossing over again here back to foot of Canal St. Later, lock gates rise, from one angle, look like fallen factory chimneys; describe sunlight; other ships—mostly coming back—Austrangen—Oslo, L.S.T. boats, our boat—the President—remember the Arcturian—300 ft steel built 3146 passengers, who'd turned by separate engines, independent; later, a tiny Peruvian ship, the S.S. Wanks, red and white Peruvian flag, looked as though they were black circus tents erected on the deck, so small and wee. Gigantic coal tipple. S.S. Sea Scorpion, an almost eyeless coast of bridge, enormous, white Murnauesque facade,[82] football boat; S.S. Cearaloide, this white and black funnel, list to starboard, against wharf; tiny little Honduran {UBC 13:23, 202} freighter (probably from Tela) with what looks—when we return—like a candle burning in its bow scarcely larger than a yacht: so small she could be carried on the back of the other, or, like an embryo, in her womb. The very word yacht was obscene to use of a deep water boat; tremendous ship, raised by floating dry dock, S.S. Noonday; get Margie descriptions of sun, describe the various attitudes of crew at rest on Sunday, first at 4, then later, at teatime: The English second mate on the bridge and the purser on the saloon deck, Brazilian likewise and so on, S.S. Georgianna—Tela, Honduras, multiochre ventilatored and ochre funneled with black top, wide ladders to climb rigging: ratguards; Mississippi sunset, wild dark blue cloud shadows cast upwards raying on the blue sky by silverlined black clouds above orange setting sun; Merchant Prince, London, bound for Dublin, the various crowd at rest—later they've gone below for tea; low black ship, yellow funnel with D. in a white square or yellow and black top to funnel white line along the black at deck line, British ensign, Merchant Prince, London, S.S. Ocean Vanity, Glasgow, lumber, cottonseed, petroleum products, carbon black, a green ship with a checkerboard on her funnel and barrels on the foredeck—bound for Dublin; bales of cotton on the wharves, standard bales and higher densely bales for compression into the cargo. Mahogany stacked for loading; marine legs, for grain; level covered with asphalt pavement, crude cottonseed oil refinery, cloud like a hugh mountain peak, Tio Corrientes, Buenos Aires, with tall towering old fashioned masts, and a nondescript flag, colors fading one into another like a dishtowel; a green ship with a checkerboard on her funnel and barrels on the foredeck bound, again, for Dublin, most American ships recognizable by funnels which are small and {UBC 13:23, 203} squat, as if wearing a beret; copper and jade powder room, the golden Petal Powder Room, the Plaid Powder Room, etc.

At the Ursuline convent hundreds of smashed glass sacramental candle vases in a corner, among dwarf palms, and the debris behind of pruned bushes.

The end: Kilroy had been there even on the convent wall.

Copper model of the noble Robert E. Lee

Grand Moonlight Excursion on the steamboat Robert E. Lee from foot of Canal Street Mon May 29, 1882, 6:30 P.M. Benefit of Church Mission School. Admit one adult. Price one dollar.

Extra: Lee arrived at St. Louis at 11:20, Time out from New Orleans, 3 days, 18 hours, and 19 minutes. Natchez not in sight. Natchez old time—3 days, 21 hours 58 minutes.

Newspaper extra: Issued in New Orleans when result of race was known.

Through the bayou by torchlight, wonderful blazing picture of steamboat among the Spanish moss. The double funnel and noble pennants of Robert E. Lee. European better didn't agree race with Natchez was fair. Tennessee Belle. Blazing night passage of U.S. gunboats down the Mississippi River April 16, 1865.

The cemetery, western sun in one's eyes going down Basin St. drifting through the evening sunlight past voodoo square, where a policeman with wheel on his arm (looking as if he'd been at St. Cats Cambridge) is chatting under the magnolias, and a man is selling hot roasted peanuts, and there is a palace—Arts, Dancing, Architecture—Poetry—Music—facing it, the trams running down the middle, and the lone railway carriages; the cemetery, kneeling images against a rose sky, a little plane above, bowed little images, and a bearded man with keys: the sexton . . . Names on graves: Eulalie Aarang and, on in front of one of the tombs {UBC 13:23, 204} in the wall, an open bottle of Spanish Grandee Giant Olives . . .

We nearly get shut in . . .

The grotto, the peace: and Christ, with his spreading arms at the end of Dauphine (?) St.—or is it St. Peter?[83]

The crew drunk our ship won't sail till Boxing Day.[84]

Mem: The Haitian Consul with doves, and before going to the bank, in the pub, the man with d.t.'s, saying unearthly the word "Oh" but whinneying it, like a horse; the secret manhole underneath the bar.

Hangover on Christmas morning: the sense of *slowness*: pleasure in other people's hangovers, the negro waitress standing outside the kitchen chewing gum, who seems to be talking, though in fact she is saying nothing; passing the church the essence, sunny, remote, of Oaxaca; the sense too of personal filthiness; in love with my wife but she doesn't realise it—I shall go to church, and hope we don't get lost in the cemetery—

N. O. Ameta Famille C. O. Lafferranderie
Louis Antoine Peychard

Adeline Cossé, Epouse D'Abraham Brown, décédée le 11 Septembre, 1866, a l'age de 43 ans[85]

Elenora Brown. Romaguera etc. see page 162 passim {UBC 13:23, 205}[86]

S.S. Donald S. Wright.—what looked like a great "iron perpendicular centipede" on the foremast was "a telescope mast" for raising the antennae (that did not telescope) named after collapsible masts on English ships going up Manchester Ship Canal: jumbo booms—booms for carrying greater weights than the others—booms are derricks, jumbo booms with their tops encased in mackintoshes standing upright parallel with the mainmasts; gadget looking like a berreted funnel on foremast was crow's nest: the motor lamps were just floodlights—don't have clusters down hold: things like mackintoshed tennis rackets on bridge were blinker-lights; lamp in metal case on foremast yard-arm blinker: berret on funnel, through which we saw Orion, was not berret, but some kind of dismantled contraption to put over the funnel when they were loading ammunition: supernumerary mast head and funnel, mate didn't know name of—called antennae mast, when he wanted bosun to do anything to it; this mast was something special to get the antennae out of the way of the high bauxite shoots.

Dec. 30, sighted C. Cruz in Cuba in afternoon, believed I could see some of the Caymans over to starboard. Second mate very important with binoculars. Later Jamaica could not be far to starboard—

Chief steward tells us very good sailors and captains come from the Caymans, most of them Banks: they steer by the stars and one of them nearly rammed a submarine.

Sinking sun gliding along horizon.

The moon: lovely leewardings of Melville; her undinal vast belly moonward bends of Crane.[87]

We round the Cape of the Cross and head toward the Windward Passage. {UBC 13:23, 206}

It was as if we are having a real rebirth this time.

We stand in the wind on the bridge and watch Cuba and the moon, relishing everything.

Towns in Jamaica: Savanna la Mar—Falmouth—St. Ann's Bay.

Blue Mountain Peak 7,388 ft.—could I have seen this? In Jamaica. Utterly impossible I think.

Towns in Cuba: Sancti Spiritus—Santa Clara—Holguín—Guantánamo

After dinner we go up on deck again—First mate says:

"You people love the wind."

My God, it is at last true again, too!

He shows us into the wheelhouse: smallish wheel, a finger touch
does the trick, controlled hydraulically—it's too damn complicated:
Mate gets himself into trouble by taking us down to chartroom, in
short leaving the bridge with no officer in one of the thickest sea-
lanes in the world—and we are a slow ship who has to give way to
others and the skipper has 200,000 cargo on board. I suppose he
wanted to show off, but I should have known better too. Margie
goes to apologise to skipper, I wait for Mister Mate to come off
watch to apologise to him. I have not heart to apologise for I feel
partly responsible; explain psychology of this. Margie after apolo-
gising to skipper comes back with his German binoculars, and we
go up on bridge, ship is pitching like hell, and we stagger around,
watching the stars, afraid to break the binoculars: the wonder of the
Pleiades—now about fifty of them as big as Sirius: the great moon:
stars changing color—wonderful, wonderful night. We turn in at
12, planning to rise at 4, wake up at 2, again at 3, but get up at 4,
see ship is still crashing into the seas, see the Southern Cross—the
other had {UBC 13:23, 207} been merely The False Cross—the
Southern Cross appeared tilted in the sky, as if an invisible priest
were holding it to ward off evil: to bed again at 5 but up at 7 into
blue sea-drenched morning.

We approach Hispaniola. Exciting names in Haiti: Mirebalais,[88]
Léogane, Miragoâne, Petit Goave, Ile a Vache (Island of the Cow),
C. Tiburon (Cape of the Shark) Jacmel.

Wireless operator has written down radio symbols of weird
places, viz: Port-au-Prince: H H H, Guantánamo: N A W, Baran-
quilla: H K A. Some place between Martinique and Castries, St.
Lucia, it seems, S U F, Port of Spain, Z B D, Maracaibo: Y V J, etc.
and weirdest of all Y N E against a port strangely called Bragman's
Bluff in Nicaragua.

The Donald S. Wright is bound for Puerto Cabello in Venezuela
after taking Bauxite in British Guiana.

But her way getting there is curious. After Port-au-Prince she goes
through Jamaica Channel round to Ciudad Trujillo, thence to La
Ceiba in the Lake of Maracaibo, thence to British Guiana (skipping
Morawhanna) down The River Essequibo (can it be?) to get her
bauxite—she is only allowed a partial draft in this river, so then she
goes back with about 1200 tons of cargo or so to Trinidad, Port of
Spain, to which the rest of the cargo of her bauxite has already been
transported on a barge or barges from which it is loaded on board
by people with shovels: then the whole amidships has to be battened
down and with the heat fearful and maddening she proceeds to Pto.
Cabello and hence home to Mobile. This so far as I can gather.

The wicked steward says enigmatically at breakfast, re Haiti,
"You'll get no protection there. General Smedley Butler's dead."[89]
{UBC 13:23, 208}

"You been there."

"Been every country in the world—been at sea 27 years."

Another glorious morning; Haiti sighted on the morning of New
Years Eve. Rounding the Cape of Our Lady.

Haiti right in the sun, mysterious, folds of hills, gigantic shadows
on waves, like shadows of rain, and sheets of silver, and blue, blue.

Man at the wheel going off duty—little mate in shorts says:

"Lee, what's your course?"

"Huh?"

Has to be asked this twice, then: "100"

"Lee, will you bring me a cup of coffee?"

Has to be asked this twice: shuffles off

Get what first mate says about winds.

Sailing between two coasts—Cuba and Jamaica, wind doesn't get
a chance to grip on the sea, there is one long lovely lilting swell.
Heat rises, etc.—low pressure areas—reason for storms. Don't
understand it myself.

The American flag bravely flying at stern as we approach Haiti:
against white clouds its blue is scarcely more dark than the sea, its
stars scarcely less bright than the stars last night.

Rolling into Port au Prince—the mountains, Haiti in sunlight—
the bow wave leewarding into silver as far as the land—opposite
Jéremie.

3rd mate at 11:30 phones down to get engineers to turn water on, "The engineers are rather inefficient."

Cheery 3rd mate in shorts waxes poetical. {UBC 13:23, 209}

—at lunch, am unable to ask steward to put our iced tea in icebox—why? Fear of being ridiculous.

Île de la Gonâve to port, Haiti to starboard: woke to a vast flat blue broiling misty calm, as if sailing into the widespread jaws of some sea-animal, Conradian.

the crew busy themselves on the derricks, playing about somewhat foolishly on the yard arms of the mizzen.

Île de Gonâve, weird desert, Haiti like an abstract Scotland, sense of sailing on and on and in and into some strange infinite vague mystery.

mysterious almost motionless black sailed boats put out—barren mysterious hills and mountains, seemingly endless, easy to believe anything may go on there.

English 1 bell at quarter to is 2 bells at ten to.

Apologise to first mate: tension while he goes down again to chart room: "Some old skippers think their chartroom's their cathedral."

Have not heard word "bloody" once.

More accurate account of Donald S. Wright itinerary: Ciudad Trujillo, Puerto Cabello (Venezuela) then north to Curaçao, then to Aruba, Maracaibo, Lagunillas, in the Lake itself, then right over to Dutch Guiana, Surinam, to Paramaribo. The other ships are not barges but smaller ships that shuttle between Paramaribo and Trinidad and have to be backed down jungle overhung river, another river that empties in Paramaribo. They take a limited amount of bauxite back to Trinidad and get the remainder from one large barge, an empty husk of a ship large as the Donald S., into which the smaller ships have put the bauxite. Two sort of railway lines and contraptions with shovels go up and down either side of this {UBC 13:23, 210} barge and unload into chutes and hence into the hold of the Donald S. and hence home.

Further encouraging remarks on last night re Haiti.

—What are your impressions of Haiti, steward?

—No good. Have you ever been there before?

—No.

—Agh! No good. You won't like it there. You'll get out quick. Won't be long before United States will have to take it over again—too much trouble.

—Why, what's wrong?

—Ah, all them niggers and halfbreeds running round. I was there with General Smedley Butler, under his command, 37 months. They got a dictator there.

—Isn't that in San Domingo?[90]

—Same thing here. Nothing but a voodoo, that fellow . . . We're the first ship there since October. We boycotted them.[91] Too much trouble.

Other opinions:

Nothing fit to eat there. They got a funny way of cookin'. Don't know what it is at all.

Can't swim out above your waist. Place is full of sharks. Barracudas too.

Main engine room emergency stop (on our door).

In Officer's lavatory: Emergency Crash Panel. Kick Out.

New Years Eve. Arrival at Port au Prince. Apparently a town of the dead. A few feeble lights gleaming. Something that might be a tram, then stops. Something that might be half a hotel. We drop anchor. Lanterns hoisted, our riding lights. Blow whistle {UBC 13:23, 211} to no avail. Drop gangway. In the gloom, on the foredeck, sailors tell stories of drunks and fights, hopefully. Skipper goes up topside to fish, with little pieces of salami. "I love to catch fish, dogfish, catfish, anything." A native sailing smack comes by without any lights at all, slipping by, slowly, noiselessly, with a sinister black sail. A few roman candles half explode feebly and soundlessly in one corner of the dark abysm of the town and people look at them with yearning. A strange New Years Eve but I am full of good resolutions and we of dear duckery. "A black republic."

Contrast of the veiled mystery of approach and this darkness.

The noise of waiting at night for custom's officer to come aboard is the noise of an electric fan in a hot ship's cabin . . .

Customs officer does not come. Nobody comes. Not even ship agent.

The poor purser, all slicked up.

The Captain takes off his shirt and puts on a singlet and retires to cabin with a cup of tea and a cheese sandwich.

And we prepare to celebrate New Years Eve reading O Henry Memorial Prize stories of 1919 from the American Merchant Marine Library association, eating nuts and drinking icewater.

The third mate is only one not frustrated, since he and the gangway watch would have been only people on board; consequently, he has a bottle. Save where I go down to borrow binoculars. First mate is jealous that skipper has other binoculars.

Previously there had been rather awful scene where I was hesitant to get coffee from crew's quarters—I felt they were frowning at me—even after 20 years.

Odd scene where 3rd mate offers me drink, after getting {UBC 13:23, 212} binoculars. Don't want to take it without taking Margie one. He pours from Regal bottle into minute tankards. I propose dividing mine up but get one and drink it and take Margie one in larger glass and binoculars. Difficulty of pouring from minute tankard even after 4 days abstemiousness, yet I have no hangover.

We go on deck with binoculars and now, without having another drink, have most miraculous n.y. eve of our married lives.

Previously there had been these strange little sailboats passing, so silently without lights, from which emanated a curious gnat like singing or wailing, very few notes repeated again, various voices, one high and always cracking on same note, tune like part of an ill-remembered Guadalajara.

Boats like wings, boats like bats, stealthily silent, lightless from this singing, and again could it be—or was that from afar on rowlocks—the sound of drums.

Now we saw the bat boats in the moonlight, through the binoculars.

A boat with a little jib made a sound of snoring as though the boat itself were asleep.

Sea near at hand through powerful binoculars wrinkled like the moon, with millions of little moons reflected on it, but this surface in motion, to the horizon, to the rim of the world.

A bat boat, imprisoned in an ice field—the great frozen lake of the moonlight on the sea—the binoculars gathered light so even otherwise *invisible* silent boats would take shape. Under the huge silver slice of the wrinkled moon itself.

Port au Prince through binoculars: seems no sky signs, a square building picked out in colored lights, other odd lights {UBC 13:23, 213} that may be ships, away to the right an hotel—shadow of something behind square building which may be a church.

Someone in Port au Prince was singing Tipperary very loudly at one point: but that was the only noise.

Psychology of Margie returning binoculars and glass to 3rd mate, who says he's going to blow all the sirens, ring all the bells, and even send up a few spare rockets he has; first mate and Sparks sit glumly in his office. We go to bed, and make resolutions. At midnight no sirens blow—no bells ring, not a sound—but one soft rocket finally does whoosh off our stern, past our open porthole, the 3rd mate's torch dragging back, the quiet and beautiful and strange end to this year. (compare end of 1946) I thank God and the Blessed Virgin and pray to her that the next year may be a real new year of goodness love and happiness for Margie and myself, I acting as a man and bring a real change of *character* for the better.

Next morning, New Years Day, I get up bright and early (in spite of little sleep), go on bridge—after first disappointed look at a few things like factory chimneys, oil refineries from port hole. Port au Prince is smack in the sun in the morning from the sea so difficult to make out. Strange beautiful houses with pointed roofs of seemingly Norwegian design, church spires here and there, rose vaguely into the sun giving it look of Tewkesbury, while to the right mist lay in pockets of rolling mysterious mountains like Oaxaca, this truly resembling Mexico for in Mexico too is that sense of infinite mystery as to who lived up these mountains, what voodoo, what mysterious rites, which does not pertain in Canada, where what goes on is simply {UBC 13:23, 214} nature and scenery.

Note: one of the subtle beauties of life on a freighter: these early mornings in a new strange port—the stillness, the heat, the silence, the oil smells of old winches and fragments of hot ship.

—Futile invitation to see non-existent shark playing about the bow.

After breakfast, in the mid-morning, a boat puts out from shore. They come aboard: "What do they look like?" "As black as coal." After a long while, ordeal of medical inspection, nice doctor with open coat, pale blue and white tie and stethoscope, he feels our pulse—mine must still be pretty bad.

Man from Alcoa comes with letter from Cape—

Ordeal then re skippers cabin—by that time—stranger I can scarcely sign my name—police etc. "You're free" finally he says, I manage anyway, and get back with feelings of relief—

But no sooner have I got back to the cabin than the fellow appears again: I haven't signed my name hard enough to make any impression on the carbon—I do it this time on the bed very steadily by pressing the pencil hard against the yielding surface. They go: we wait, and finally we begin to go in.

As we approach it begins to look more like Tewkesbury than ever but also something like Africa—we try to recognize some of the landmarks of the night before.

A good scene as we approach P. au P. wharf: bales and sheds, negroes smoking pipes, resting on their oars below, black policemen, mangrove swamp to the left; Panamanian freighter ahead: a French freighter—also lend-lease-liberty ship built on our pattern is anchored in the roadstead; waiting; and heat; a fabulous gangway {UBC 13:23, 215} put down for us, too steep for anything.

We go down—Mr. Kane—through customs—Port au Prince fantastically beautiful city of mangroves and tin roofs and they have turned nightmarish architecture into bizarre and somehow good taste—a credit to the mores—Hotel Olaffson—drinks with Georges at bar (mem, write up the Dominicans with their wide trousers, medals like the inside of fantastic watches, etc.)

"You like egg?"

"Oui. Sí."

"What egg?"

The loathsome Americans playing dice—get this dialogue.

Characters in the hotel: Georges (teaches me Creole, French) a man who likes the odious cover[92] to Esquire, dressed in a blue seersucker suit, blue shoes, bulging eyes, white hair: a fairy, like I always suspected the man on the cover of Esq. was—turns out to be a bishop.

Haïti Journal. Edition Spéciale de Noël 1943. Lago-Lago. Poèmes de Philippe Thoby-Marcelin. Précédés d'une lettre de Valery Larbaud.

On next page we find: La Distillerie de Prince, Alfred Vieux Propriétaire, adresse à tous ses clients et amis qui ont su apprécier la qualité de ses produits particulièrement à la Rhumerie Barbancourt et à la maison américaine Krauss avec ses remerciements, ses souhaits de Joyeux Noël et de Bonne Année. Then follows an announcement from the Haiti Journal (Pour Nos Abonnés et Lecteurs etc)

Nous avons la certitude de plaire à tous nos abonnés et lecteurs, en présentant un cahier de poèmes inédits de Philippe Thoby-Marcelin qui vient d'ajouter tant de gloire au nom haïtien—[93] {UBC 13:23, 216}

(G.M.U. No. 544)
Is There a Hell?[94]
Rev. J. C. Ryle

Reader, when a house is on fire, what ought to be done first? We ought to give the alarm, and wake the inmates. This is true love to our neighbor. This is true charity.

Reader, I love your soul, and want it to be saved. I am therefore going to speak to you about hell. Do not throw down this tract when you see that word, but read on.

There is such a place as hell. Let no one deceive you with vain words. What men do not like they try hard not to believe. There is such a place as hell.

When the Lord Jesus Christ comes to judge the world, He will punish all who are not His disciples with fearful punishment. All who are found impenitent and unbelieving—all who have clung to sin, stuck to the world, and set their affections on things below, all such shall come to an awful end. Whosoever is not written in the book of life shall be "Cast into the lake of fire" (Rev. 20:15) This will be hell.

Do you believe the Bible? Then depend upon it hell is real and true. It is as true as heaven, as true as the fact that Christ died upon the cross. There is not a fact or doctrine which you may not lawfully doubt if you doubt hell. Disbelieve in hell, and you unscrew, unsettle, and unpin everything in Scripture. You may as well throw your Bible aside at once. From "no hell" to "no God" is but a series of steps.

Do you believe the Bible? Then depend upon it hell will have inhabitants. The wicked shall certainly be turned into hell, and all the nations that forget God. The same blessed {UBC 13:23, 217} Savior Who now sits on a throne of Grace will one day sit on a throne of Judgement, and men will see there is such a thing as "The wrath of the Lamb." The same lips which now say, "Come unto Me," will one day say, "Depart, ye cursed!" Alas! how awful the thought of being condemned by Christ Himself, judged by the Savior, sentenced to misery by the Lamb!

Do you believe the Bible? Then depend upon it hell will be intense and unutterable woe. It is vain to talk of all the expressions about it being figures of speech. The pit, the prison, the worm, the fire, the thirst, the blackness, the darkness, the weeping, the gnashing of teeth, the second death,—all these may be figures of speech if you please. But Bible figures mean something beyond all question, and here they mean something which man's mind can never fully conceive. Oh! reader, the miseries of mind and conscience are far worse than those of the body. The whole extent of hell, the present suffering, the bitter recollection of the past, the hopeless prospect of the future, will never be fully known except by those who go there.

Do you believe the Bible? Then depend upon it hell is eternal. It must be eternal, or words have no meaning at all. "Forever and ever,"—"Everlasting"—"Unquenchable,"—"Never-dying"—all these are expressions used about hell, and expressions that cannot be explained away. It must be eternal, or the very foundations of heaven are cast down. If hell has an end, heaven has an end too. They both stand or fall together. It must be eternal, or every doc-trine of the Gospel is undermined. If a man may escape hell at length without faith in Christ, or sanctification of the Spirit, sin is no longer an infinite evil, and there was no great need for Christ making an atonement. And where is the {UBC 13:23, 218} warrant for saying that hell can ever change a heart, or make it fit for heaven? It must be eternal, or hell would cease to be hell altogether. Give a man hope, and he will bear anything. Ah! reader, these are solemn things. Well said Caryl, "Forever is the most solemn saying in the Bible."

Reader, I beseech you, in all tender affection, beware of false views of the subject on which I have been dwelling. Beware of new and strange doctrines about hell and the eternity of punishment. Beware of manufacturing a god of your own—a god who is all mercy, but not just—a god who is all love, but not holy—a god who has a heaven for everybody, but a hell for none—a god who can allow good and bad to be side by side in time, but will make no distinction between good and bad in eternity. Such a god is an idol of your own, as true an idol as was ever molded out of brass and clay. The hands of your own fancy and sentimentality have made him. He is not the God of the Bible; and beside the God of the Bible there is no God at all. Your heaven would be no heaven at all. A heaven containing all sorts of characters indiscriminately would be miserable discord indeed. Alas! for the eternity of such a heaven. There would be little difference between it and hell. Ah! reader, there is a hell. Take heed, lest you find it out to your cost too late.

Beware of being wise above that which is written. Beware of forming fanciful theories of your own, and then trying to make the Bible square in with them. Beware of making selections from your Bible to suit your taste—refusing like a spoiled child, whatever you think bitter, seizing, like a spoiled child, whatever you think sweet. What does all this amount to but telling God that you, a poor short-lived worm, know what is good for you better {UBC 13:23, 219} than He? It will not do. You must take the Bible as it is. You must read it all, and believe it all. You must read it with the spirit of a little child. Dare not to say, "I believe this verse, for I like it. I reject that, for I do not like it. I receive this, for I can understand it. I refuse that, for I cannot reconcile it with my views." Nay! but, O man, who art thou that repliest against God? By what right do you talk in this way? Surely it were better to say over every chapter in the Word, "Speak, Lord, for Thy servant heareth." Ah, reader, if men would do this, they would never deny hell.

Please save the life of this Silent Messenger by passing it on.

Further articles pertaining to Correct Doctrine and Right Living, Missionary News and Bible Lessons, The Glorious Gospel and The Drift of the Times, will be found in "THE GOSPEL MESSAGE"—published monthly at 60¢ per year; and communications concerning the work of the Gospel Missionary Union may be addressed to the office, 1841 East 7th St., Kansas City 1, Missouri, U.S.A.

As God supplies our need, we publish our tracts and send them out to those who will prayerfully and carefully distribute them. Friends who are able should send postage for mailing.

Gospel Missionary Union
1841 East 7th St., Kansas City 1, Mo.
{UBC 13:23, 220}

Lost Logger's Body Found Upcoast[95]

The icy, impersonal waters of Queen Charlotte Strait cast up the body of a logger on a lonely stretch of island beach Sunday and in the swirling eddies vanished the future hopes of his wife and their seven children.

For Valerie MacDonald it was the end of a 12-year idyll, much of it spent in waiting for the return of the husband who loved the sea and lived by its bounty.

Her husband George, whose body was washed ashore at lonely Donegal Head, Malcolm Island, near Alert Bay, left no insurance to make a fresh start for his tiny, 31-year-old wife and their family, the eldest of which is an 11-year-old girl.

Today, she sat dry-eyed with grief in the kitchen of their tiny rented cottage at 1229 Mitchell Island, and stared out the wind-swept window into an empty future.

MacDonald, 34, went out with his partner Harry Belveal on their small gillnetter November 15, bound for the lush islands of the northern inland waters.

They planned to comb the shores for logs, and hand-log on unrestricted tracts of forest.

MacDonald found his island forest Sunday.

An RCMP search continues for his 50-year-old partner Belveal, still listed as missing, but also feared dead. {UBC 13:23, 221}

Trio Fight Off Sharks to Save Man

Brisbane, Australia, Nov. 27—(Reuters)—Three men battled for three hours through shark-infested seas holding above their heads a stretcher on which an injured man lay helpless.

As their strength ebbed, the stretcher and the patient slipped slowly from their numbed hands and sank.

The story was told today after the survivors of an air ambulance crash staggered ashore.

The story began when John Albert O'Loughlin, 30, was seriously injured in a circular saw accident in a remote cattle station in the Gulf of Carpentaria. The air ambulance set out to bring the man to hospital in Cairns, Queensland.

The plane ran into a thick smoke from bushfires raging inland. Soon afterwards it crash-landed in the sea and the struggle to save the injured man began.

The three survivors were met by a land-search party. {UBC 13:23, 222}

Noted Empress Hotel Lobby "Fixture" Dies

Victoria, Nov. 27.—The chair beside the grandfather clock in the Empress Hotel lounge is empty today.

John Rowland, the shabby but courtly gentlemen who became a beloved fixture at the Empress by plumping himself into the chair each evening, is dead.

He died at Royal Jubilee Hospital Friday night after a few day's illness.

John Rowland was a Welshman, 73 to 74, who lived in a room with a gas plate and a naked light. When he entered the Empress lounge, he bowed to acquaintances, took his familiar chair, folded his threadbare coat on the floor, graciously passed the time of day with newsmen and politicians.

Mr. Rowland fancied himself as a composer and last month, Billy Tickle, paid his devoted fan—Mr. Rowland, you see, loved music—a rare compliment.

He placed one of Mr. Rowland's compositions—"The B.C. Marching Song"—at the top of the musical program for the government luncheon for Princess Elizabeth and the Duke of Edinburgh.

Said Empress manager J. K. Hodges, "A lot of our guests will miss him." {UBC 13:23, 223}

Lightning Reduces Home to Shambles

Family of Five Has Narrow Escape

New Westminster, Nov. 27—A Surrey family of five escaped death by a miracle when a lightning bolt reduced their home to a shambles during the weekend storm.

"It is nothing short of a miracle that we are alive today," said Peter Heppner, 50-year-old miller, as he surveyed the wreckage of his four-room house.

With him in the house at the time were his wife and three sons, Elmer, 20, Alvin, 17, and Ronnie, 3.

This is what the lightning did to the Heppner farm:

Split a huge 40-foot cedar tree alongside the woodshed to shreds, and hurtled huge chunks of the tree on top of the roof.

The bolt killed the family Labrador dog which was lying beneath the tree, blew out the electric fuse box and tossed it 12 feet across the room, embedding it in a plaster wall.

Lifted the Roof

An internal explosion pried the roof from the wall studdings by a height of one foot.

Knocked down the ceilings, ripped the furniture apart and shattered every window in the house.

Mr. Heppner was sitting in a chesterfield in the room a few feet away from where the fuse box exploded.

"There was a deafening explosion and seconds later I was struck by the falling ceiling," he related.

Hit by Cage

"I was also hit by a cage with two love birds hanging from the ceiling. The birds escaped uninjured." {UBC 13:23, 224}

Mrs. Heppner, holding her youngest son, was standing near the kitchen sink.

She was thrown backwards by the force of the explosion but was uninjured.

"I hung on to my baby boy and tried to protect him from the falling sheets of wallboard ripped off the ceiling," she said.

"Like an Earthquake"

"It was just like an earthquake."

Alvin was standing beside his mother and although rocked also escaped.

Elmer was standing in the front room near the radio when the fuse box just whizzed by his head.

The fact that the explosion blew upwards and outwards saved the family. All the broken glass was blown out.

The lightning missed three-quarters of a case of stumping powder in the woodshed and a 30–gallon steel barrel of gasoline just outside the house.

The family are being looked after by neighbours pending rebuilding of their home which is covered by insurance. {UBC 14:11, 225}[96]

VII

Thursday March 14–Friday March 15. The Ides of March.

The Quinta Eulalia had indeed become a kind of prison—Sigbjørn thought late that night. Like Ahab, they were imprisoned in Paradise.[1] That night they had been called ten times for dinner and only gone in at the last moment, and with that reluctantly, though Primrose held her head high, and they ate, or Sigbjørn ate, like a criminal. José, and his Lady Me, Pedro, Schwab and the rest, regarded them curiously. There was something hostile in the air. There was a loop of rope dangling below the parapet (describe) and Sigbjørn felt that it had been put there purposely, that everyone had immediately sprung to the conclusion that he was a spy or whatever, and would be hung, and perhaps he would be hung. Just the same, they put on a bold face at dinner, laughing and drinking and talking; they drank beer and immediately after dinner went to sleep. There is, in sleep, or the unconscious, a certain kind of stern yet half merciful mechanism that does not allow the sleeper to forget for a moment the disaster of the previous night so that in the morning the poor devil will not wake from dreams of trefoil and campion to that most dreadful of all tortures, that of slow disillusionment, or for that matter instantaneous, though this is said sometimes to happen where one wakes on the floor in a cold prison cell, having dreamt one was comfortably in bed in one's childhood home:[2] thus the poor devil who is to be hanged next morning, in a disused elevator shaft, like that other Wilderness, say, for lack of a decent scaffold,[3] if he sleeps, which he probably does, due to other more humanitarian causes, has the whole thing present in his mind, including the disused elevator shaft and he may even repeat to himself over and over again {UBC 13:24, 226} "disused elevator shaft and not a scaffold" and so on: if he is sensible the thought of death will be like thoughts of Costa Rica or Mexico, he rises, says This week is beginning well, or whatever, and drops into the abyss, to meet, in the comparative convalescence of death, his victim, who he hopes by that time—if the trial has been long—will be somehow mellowed or tempered to mercy: doubtless he does not precisely, as Dostoievsky's characters have a habit of doing, wake up and remember everything immediately (a phrase Sigbjørn himself had also used) or he has remembered it the whole night through, every nerve and muscle of his body in fact has been concentrating, like a fisherman upon fishing, upon remembering it, in order precisely to avoid that horrible, all-dreaded disenchantment; moreover by not sparing himself, by dying every minute, by being hanged every single minute, all during the night—as the airman flies the Atlantic a thousand times before actually flying it—he has subtly inoculated himself against the reality, which when it comes will be a sort of anticlimax; he has at least the comfort of not having anything more horrible to look forward to than less than a minute of his sleep and beyond that is a sort of surprise. Now Sigbjørn was not indeed going to be hanged or shot in the morning, or at least not tomorrow morning, he was merely going to be tortured, and at that more by himself than any other outside agency. A peculiar loathsome memory kept returning to him during the night. It was of seeing a news film in a news theatre on Broadway, New York. This film dealt with a subject very common, an inventor had invented and contrived with soap boxes, a kind of flying machine: actually it was, so far as Sigbjørn's memory went, one of the first helicopters. You saw the inventor sitting smiling in his {UBC 13:24, 227} cockpit, before taking off, laughing indeed, apparently fearless, his friends shaking his hand, the photographers took photographs. The man even "mugged"; it was funny and there was laughter in the audience. Then you saw the take off itself, a bit wobbly, but he made it, the spectators were shading their eyes. The contraption rose powerfully enough, (rather to one's surprise, for one had expected the resolution to be comic, that the thing would not rise at all, which would be the point, and the next thing you saw would be Lew Lehr)[4] to about five hundred feet. But then you saw, because it was a newsreel theatre doubtless, something that one devoutly hoped had been cut out of any other version which most other people would see. The invention met with some kind of disaster, came apart in mid-air, fell to pieces. You saw this, and this was bad enough, but not yet terrible. You did not quite believe it: and anyway it was only a machine, so that it was almost abstract. What was dreadful was not that but what followed almost immediately after. You saw the inventor falling feet first from his contraption, frantically kicking his legs, as if trying to run on the air, falling falling all the way to the ground, kicking his helpless legs, over which the individuals who had been playing such a good humored part only a moment before were now frantically running. It was not only that these moments, before the man hit the ground, while he was still alive—what was he thinking?—was he thinking?—were so horrible: it was that the whole thing was in such dreadful, as it were, taste, as if in a two reel Laurel and Hardy comedy Laurel, say, would actually be killed. Moreover one had identity with the live man for those few moments, now he was alive, and now, in the space of your crossing your legs, or a man passing you to get another seat, dead. (Well, it was too late to {UBC 13:24, 228} head off the telegram now, but the point is Sigbjørn doesn't want to for their papers are in order, what then is troubling him?) There was that point, which to Sigbjørn's mind related it to life. That indeed was what life was like. It was bad art, bad taste, mostly. What was happening to Sigbjørn, on the contrary, was good art, unless it was for his number 13: the daemon was writing a book in real life with Sigbjørn as the character. But the joke was that Sigbjørn himself would never be able to write it. That, however, was totally irrelevant. What was more to the point was that, over and over again during the night Sigbjørn seemed to be identified with that poor inventor. Sigbjørn yesterday was the man in the plane smiling: Sigbjørn now was the man falling, and nothing—he felt—could save him. Of this, even though the thing was but a shadow, he hadn't even fallen out of the plane, he had an extraordinary prescience, and the worst part of this falling was that it was going, inevitably, to be incredibly protracted. (Then they had done something worse: the man was falling in slow motion. No—they had not done that, but just for a moment Sigbjørn could not be sure that they had not: this was in his mind) There was now also another film or newsreel that came to his mind. This was of the man who is left behind by the Zeppelin. Describe this too. What on earth would be the thoughts of such a man? What would he, Sigbjørn, do, say? All right, you buggers, don't stand there looking as though you'd swallowed Pat Murphy's goat and the horns were sticking out of your arse.⁵ I'm going to drop. Watch out! In ten seconds I'll know what it's all about, which is more than most of you will, alive or dead. Fine. {UBC 13:24, 229}

N.B. Don't forget the rats—real rats—the illusion is real—also relates to La Mordida.

Primrose was asleep:⁶ Sigbjørn took several pulls at the habanero. It had a fine burned taste and though pretty intoxicating never seemed to make you really stinko: and so long as you stuck to it, it didn't give you any too terrible hangover. Discuss the art of drinking at night. And also discuss the art of drinking in the morning. He has as yet to be pretty careful about Primrose who might blow up. Why had he thought "as yet": was he indeed looking upon this as an excuse to drink? At one point Sigbjørn should enumerate the perfectly good reasons he has for going mad: 1.2.3.4.5.6.7.—N.B.—I never think of an immedicable grief—this poem.⁷

The beauty of drinking in the morning is something few women would understand. Sigbjørn staggers up on the tower in his bare feet. It is not yet light. Lanterns on the sea and a man spearing fish in the dawn. Sigbjørn hunts for the Southern Cross—he has an idea if he can find it he will go back and get Primrose out of bed and this will make her happy. Describe the dawn and the silent beach, a few people sleeping on it get up, soon there will be the umbrellas, he remembered how the boys used to be blowing on their conch shells— no more: that seems out-dated. The terrible Paraiso de Caleta sleeps. In the dawn and the sea he makes a resolution that he is going to face everything bravely and that Primrose is going to have her holiday after all. He cannot find the Southern Cross however: the kitchen is shut. He feels a mood of well-being. What after all am I bothering about. He returns to his room, hovers like a ghost over the habanero, takes a drink: it was "working" constructively now, he was {UBC 13:24, 230} using it, he knew precisely what to do, what to call on, how to go about it, etc: a wild idea strikes him, he will even find the Migración man himself and get to him before he rises, and make an impassioned appeal. But this energy is wasted: it is too early: Primrose still sleeps, once she groans—Sigbjørn pauses with his habanero bottle in hand, cautiously, Primrose's eyes are open:

"Oh," she said, and turned over.

"Yes. Oh," Sigbjørn said savagely. He sleeps. When he wakes Primrose is not there. His first feeling is relief, for he can have a habanero: "I am drinking rather a lot for a fellow who wrote a book about drinking, but after all I know when to stop. Besides why fight against a drink that does you no harm." Actually the habanero makes him feel much better and after a shower he feels better still. Primrose comes in from a swim and the pathos of her having gone down for the first time to swim alone is swallowed up by the fact that he has now a constructive plan; the habanero is out of sight but she is looking at him in a manner which from time immemorial[8] has, he thought, driven man into a drunkard's grave.

"If I were you I'd have a swim," she said unsmilingly.

"I had a plan."

"Oh—" she says, taking no notice.

"I did have a plan, but now I think I'll take one of my rare drinks," said Sigbjørn touchily.

She shrugs her shoulders indifferently but the next moment Sigbjørn is sorry for her and wants to buy her shoes of emerald, shoes of saffron, shoes of cerise and cobalt and gold and vermillion suede soft as silk, in town today, only then he remembers the financial situation. {UBC 13:24, 231}

"I shall not be in very good shape," he decided at length.

"I'd take that swim if I were you," Primrose said very quietly not looking at him, and going to the mirror.

"This morning," continued Sigbjørn, "to go to the Migración. But I have a plan."

"That *I* go," Primrose said, doing her hair.

"No. I have a plan," Sigbjørn repeated, leaning back and placing his hand. "We will save the day."

"Oh yeah—"

"You should go to town this morning but not see the Migración, but go to the Department for the Protection of Turismo. The whole point is that there is, according to Eddy, this new policy toward tourists. True, it isn't always pursued. But they have nothing against you, you're an American citizen and I think it might be better, would undoubtedly be better, if you went alone to the Turismo, and I keep out of it."

"I agree there."

"This morning. It is true I am shirking my responsibilities but courage is relative. And you can find out about an American Consul."

"And you can stay here and drink."

"No, I will stay here and plan what we have to do."

"Is there anything else you'd like me to do?"

"Yes," Sigbjørn said. "Get a bottle of habanero from Madame Cyclone."

"Oh Sigbjørn—"

"No, get two litres from Madame Cyclone."

Primrose turned round dramatically but said nothing. {UBC 13:24, 232}

"You'll need them—we'll both need them, before we're through."

"All right, I'll get two litres," Primrose said quietly as before.

"And now I'm going to have that swim."

"But first you're going to have that drink, aren't you. First you're going to have that drink, aren't you," Primrose said, beginning to be deliberately hysterical. "First you're going to have that—"

"Yes, first I might allow myself one of my rare snorts," said Sigbjørn, suiting the action to the word.

"You're not sober enough to get down to the beach," Primrose said after a minute.

"Then I shall take a shower," Sigbjørn said.

"You've already had a shower," Primrose said.

"Then I shall take two showers," Sigbjørn said, feeling at the same time that this scene, while all too original, was on the other hand spoiled by being slightly derivative.

"And two drinks."

"And two drinks." {UBC 13:24, 233}

VIII

Friday March 15.

It should be made clear in this chapter that word from Mexico City cannot be expected till Monday.

On that Ides of March, 1946, it was in Sigbjørn's mind, as they set off down to the town that afternoon, in a not too crowded bus, with the wind blowing through it, that to anyone hearing their conversation of that morning before breakfast, their present state of mind and harmony would have been absolutely inconceivable: and he knew this time that this was not self-deception: their present state of mind was happy, the harmony existed. It should not have been, but there it was. Sigbjørn had had his second shower: he had descended soberly to the beach, he had swum a mile, he had exercised, had returned, eaten, with Primrose, a hearty breakfast, and had dispatched her to town. He had slept during the morning and when Primrose had actually returned to the Quinta Eulalia, and moreover returned with two litres of habanero, they had had several drinks themselves, early as it was (this was a matter of some humour to Sigbjørn), descended to the beach, to their old log, and swum once more and exercised. What Sigbjørn was doing was a difficult thing which can only be attempted by the hardy: he was pitting, like Paracelsus, the effects of alcohol against the effects of increased physical exercise[1] and it was no use saying that the result would have been better if he had taken no alcohol at all, which was possibly true, although too late to say, for what Sigbjørn was doing, had indeed to do—he had seen this morning—was to drink through and out the other side of a nervous breakdown, or worse. (Mem: squat woman at Cordoba.) {UBC 13:24, 234} The symptoms had been arriving for some time. Alcohol was partly the cause of it: but alcohol was also the cure. It was a circle, the dependence on alcohol was there: but the circle was not necessarily vicious. It was damned dangerous: it was perhaps unmoral, and all wrong, but there it was. He had had at one time to have the courage to give up alcohol. Now he had to have the courage to be cowardly enough to give in to it. For a brave man such as Sigbjørn was this was asking a good deal. It is a fact that this looks as though someone were deceiving himself . . .

It should be brought out in dialogue that during the morning Primrose had visited the Turismo, and she had told the story. She reports that the man there is very nice, but has told her that the American consulate is closed in the sense of there not being one. Primrose asks about ship and leaves.

Now they go to the Turismo again and Sigbjørn recognized the shifty-eyed effeminate man, as a hanger on of Americans and bummer of drinks, a stool pigeon, and also the man they had seen driving his car before they went to Pied de la Cuesta, and he knows no help is to be got from him. He has been chewing chiclets and is trying to dissemble his breath. He is not tight but he knows how important it is not to be showing any effects.

At this point it should be mentioned that Mexico is not only a land of stool pigeons but in the main a bad place, very often. The temptation is great because the drinks are wonderful and cheap. But to get a man on a drunk charge is the ambition of every petty official. It should be stressed that a man does not have to be drunk. He can be writing at a pub and merely having a few beers but the stool pigeons will carry that report round and some {UBC 13:24, 235} people also vaguely connected with the police will be drinking with him and it will not be very long before that person is robbed or put in gaol or if he is an extreme case even murdered. Every other man in Acapulco for instance is a stool pigeon. The State of Morelos is good in this respect and in the State of Tlaxcala are neither stool pigeons or thieves and it is an insult to lock your door, where live the so-called traitors of Mexico and where the gospel was first preached, but the Tlaxcaltecans were even traitors to the Mexican tradition.[2] Consequently Sigbjørn knew by experience that even if he showed the slightest signs of a hangover, of being tight, the word would doubtless get back to the Migración: at least that is what he told himself.

Turismo has a shifty look, and a hangover himself; S. remembers his delight in tripping up foreigners and cannot help looking at him with contempt, a contempt which is returned although a third observer might only have seen a twinkle in his eye.

He phones the Migración, who say they must wait till they check on our tourist cards.

"I should have thought you would have many friends in Acapulco," he says rather sarcastically.

He refers them to an unofficial acting consul, a Mr. Hudson who has a dozen Mexican sons. They tell their story—this should be in dialogue—They are stupid at first, but at last understanding and helpful and they offer to go to the Migración with us the next A.M.

—Beach Clots— {UBC 13:24, 236}

"Come een, mees, w'at you want? You want nice dress—muy bonita, 50 pesos, come een, mees . . ."

Though it is reckless he buys her a pair of emerald shoes, a crazy thought coming through his mind that should he be seen doing this, that this would also get back to the Migración, just as he had been seen, as he had a littler earlier, having his sandals mended, that by doing an innocent thing like that, by not, for example, been seen "drinking," by the Migración, they might decide not to send the report to Mexico City after all. Shades of the Prison House[3] are growing upon him but his will is paralysed so far as the Migración is concerned.

A notice: Abajo los tyrannicos Americanos.

They return a good deal happier. They cling together, swim, and are happy.

Strange attitude of the staff at Quinta Eulalia. "All is settled with the Gobierno." They tell a little of the story to Americans at dinner, one of whom says:

"If I were you I'd look out for your life."

"Isn't that a little extreme," said Sigbjørn, taking a draught of Saturno.

"You heard that two Americans were robbed and murdered on the Chilpancingo road yesterday."

"Good God no! When? Who were they?"

"They managed to keep it quiet. They were a couple staying at the Americas. By name Haywood."[4]

"What were their names?"

"Some name like Hayward—"

"Not Haywood!—"

"Yes, that's it. Haywood." {UBC 13:24, 237}

N.B. Perhaps put a scene of looking at Post's and Lewis' pictures in this chapter prior to going to the Turismo, describe the pictures, these lazy people's happiness, no one molests them and the contrast. {UBC 13:24, 238}

IX

Saturday March 16.

(N.B. Life, tragic in its very essence, has a happy beginning beyond the border. That is, it was a rebirth, hence an assent to the realization of his true purpose, which was to write it. And Wilderness took the pencil the sea had sent him out of his pocket and began, while meantime, like the souls of the dead in flux, a constant procession went back and forth across the border, for Cinco de Mayo.)[1]

In A.M. Sat to Acapulco: scene of waiting in Hudson's; describe Hudson's; Hudson has forgotten appointment: they sit and wait in the stifling heat, though there are fans, Wilderness almost doesn't mind, sitting in a kind of stupefied trance, he knows perfectly well he will have a lot of waiting to do before he is through, but he also knows perfectly well that this kind of inertia is evil, or a sin, that only action will obtain him his freedom, but does he really want freedom? What is his unconscious up to—apart from that, the keynote of this weekend should be the strain of waiting for the verdict from Mexico City—I do not believe Wilderness should arrive at any philosophical conclusion until the end, à la Keyserling (from whom take notes)[2]—as a matter of fact the construction, though it ties up with "The Maker of Tragedies"[3]—that he has done or is doing all this himself is too hard for him to take, and possibly not wholly true (The Daemon)—there is a sense of something *outside* him—but always remember that what is happening to Wilderness will lose its dramatic effect unless we continually harp on his sense of persecution—remember the faithful bag which links up with Dark as the Grave— {UBC 13:24, 239} the bag should be described, faithful silent poor bag—Wilderness remembers in Hudson's how it had been stolen by the boy, hark back to the Carlins,[4] "I don't want to leave hating Mexico"—how they had their last 500 pesos pinched on the tram to Xolchimilco, and all this brings him back to the all-important point, which should have been stressed before, that he is damned if he will pay the mordida, and bribe his way out of this— (he thinks of the boy he's saved from the police, the wristwatch incident, but had that Christian action on his part been merely a saving of himself, did his unconscious have pre-knowledge of all this— which led to yet another question: was there anything against him, from 8 years back, in Cuernavaca, where he had lived?—where, if anything, there *would* be)

Meantime he reads Rendon's Vanishing Enchantment[5]—Vanishing Enchantment was right—in Modern Mexico: and becomes extremely interested in this. (See précis of this at end of this chapter: I should use more [illegible] perhaps)

Relate this article to the general erloff.[6] Meantime, hours pass, hours that would never come off, hours when Primrose might have been happy, dancing on the beach, and looking at her precious tropical fish, dear dear Primrose—the vanishing enchantment, the vanishing vacation—Strike a chord here of under the sea—Illustrated London News.[7]

When Wilderness was young he too had loved to hunt along the shore in their holidays on the South West coasts, for sponges and tunicates and the like. The Golden Stars, the carweeds, and the sea-firs and sea-mosses, *Clava squamata*. And the gooseberry sea-squirt, in early life a free-living tadpole, having in its tail a rod of gristle—the notochord—the forerunner of the {UBC 13:24, 240} backbone in higher animals, and which notochord vanishes during metamorphosis of larva into adult—sacrificed in favour of a sedentary existence—was this what had happened to Wilderness?

Eventually, after waiting hours—they are informed that Hudson is in the fish-office: there is the fear, approaching these white buildings again—for the Fish Office is in the Immigration Building—that he will run into Soto:[8] describe the building, the pseudo white brick arcade, the armed men outside, so sleepy—how they could have discovered something like this about Wilderness? but they run slap into Tojo,[9] and a strange scene transpires, half in, half out of the office: the files are arranged, 1934, 35, 36 and so on, and Tojo brings out the 1938 file, with Wilderness' name on it. (Mem: again Chambers and the gratitude he got)[10]

This scene must be dramatised in dialogue: with description of Tojo, and the dead colorless foetid waterfront outside—Wilderness is petrified—his attempts at Spanish must be dramatised.

"And we pick you up here." (Wilderness winces.)

"Borracho—borracho—borracho—Here is your life."

"But what have I done?"

There are pages and pages in this file: Wilderness is aghast. Here, perhaps, should be analysis of[11] the status of a drunk in Mexico.

"And we pick you up here."

"Siempre ebriedad."

"It say you are always too drunk to do business."

He catches sight of Guyou's name, however, makes a note of that, for it is to him he has paid the fine: Prim. expostulates, but he won't listen.

"I send a wire to Mexico City. Here is your name. You are Janine."[12] {UBC 13:24, 241}

"No—No!" Primrose is angry and exasperated because Tojo won't listen.

"But it say here you are Janine. You are rentista. You come on such and such a date. You overstay your leave."

They are aghast—the name of Sigbjørn's first wife has been sent in and he has sent a wire calling her Janine: refer to statement for this chapter, for there are such points as the other mistake that he has entered the country in Sept 1936—not November—thus making his overstaying his leave more serious. And all the while he is in a terrible state of tension re his book.

In the end Tojo sees the point.

"I correct this mistake. I send another wire."

"But when? Today? Saturday and they'll be shut. And by the time they receive your wire they'll already have made up their mind that she is Janine—"

The spectre of the endless difficulties that this mistake may cause rise before Wilderness.

"And so all this is a surprise to her." Tojo indicated.

"No—we have no secrets from each other."

"But what did I do?"

"Borracho—borracho." He shakes his head. "There is your life."

The temptation to give in and pay the mordida has to be suppressed because Sigbjørn hasn't got the money—he is again afraid of the trembling hand.

"But I was writing a book."

Tojo shrugs one shoulder, pursing his lips.

Sigbjørn tries another tack.

"We've had a lot of trouble. For God's sake tell them in {UBC 13:24, 242} Mexico City . . . etc. We haven't much money . . . Here's our apartment rent running on. My money is in Cuernavaca."

"Ah—sí—it says here in the file, Cuernavaca." He begins to look suspicious again. "You not leave the country? When did you leave the country?"

Wilderness tells him.

"And your wife?"

Wilderness tells him.

"You live in Cuernavaca. You no leave the country. It says a here. You no leave a the country."

"But if I didn't leave the country," Sigbjørn said almost as much triumph as despair, "how the hell could there be an edict forbidding me to come back."

This is a wonderful opportunity for a sort of good soldier Schweik scene.[13] In the end, for Primrose's sake, he appeals to his humanidad, to put the thing to Mexico in as fair a light as possible.

He says he is going to Mexico on Monday or Tuesday. There are two other people in trouble. Again Wilderness appeals to his humanity. At least let me go and get my papers and prove her identity.

"Humanidad—humanidad—" he says. "Many would be in prison but for my humanidad," he says. (So you shot them instead, Sigbjørn thought) not failing to shake hands, however, and going off, shrugging his shoulders, into the fish office opposite, where however Mr. Hudson was not, and in fact Mr. Hudson had not, that morning, been. {UBC 13:24, 243}

Let there still be a niche with a saint in it at every street corner, brought into mysterious relief through the night by an archaic lamp. This is worlds of beauty ahead of the bronze-cast statue of some liberator or the mighty advertisement of a commercial enterprise.

Point of this article, by Eduardo Rendon, was that Prosperity and Inflation were changing beautiful Mexico into Ugly Mexico—two necessary pages are missing in the magazine. That its mystic beauty—its half Franciscan, half Indian quality—was being lost. There should be more of this. It was a brilliant article, written by a Mexican architect from Vera Cruz. That the object of society was an increasing enchantment.

"Here amidst the patter patter of little donkeys, long come down from those sierras of lapis lazuli into this cobbled street, it has received that half Franciscan, half Indian quality that so spellbinds"

In the U.S. man is no longer part of the myth. "Listen to this, Primrose . . ." The world of supreme and archaic illusion, which man built to be the foundation of his consciousness as history in a mythical sense is dispelled, and poetry disappears from the world.[14] How true—he must be a good man! {UBC 13:24, 244}

X

Sunday March 17.
    (Agony in Acapulco—alternative title)
    Saturday afternoon, Sunday, Monday, Tuesday—
    They return to hotel, not quite so happy, but O.K. Sat. P.M. buy Post some drinks and discuss—they are leaving at 5:30 A.M. and we hate to see them go—now a flood of stupid Mexicans descend on

Quinta Eulalia, not interesting or polite, as other guests, but noisy, like monkeys, they chatter and clatter into the dining porch. Sunday is a trying day: to Hornos in the A.M., Sigbjørn is making a noble effort, analysis of the black dog on the back, how the day is different: this the way he had gone—was it unconscious on his very first day in Mexico, mistaking Hornos for the beach—the day he had his first mescal. The walk from the Zócalo in Acapulco had no character: there seemed no real race in the people: everyone was such a mixture—all some negro.

Perhaps begin this chapter here:

Hornos beach was very large: miles of beach in great lonely curve, deserted since it is A.M. and Hornos is "afternoon beach."[1] There seemed nowhere to change, but they are courteously permitted, after walking endlessly along this second rate California scene, carrying their faithful bag, to change in a tent behind a sort of bar, etc: no change. There is mescal and tequila and habanero—Sigbjørn restrains temptation. Lovely tall tall slim coconut palms leaning into the seawind, not too much surf, but water very dirty. But at Hornitos, the end near town, the great fishing nets are spread to dry in the sun, hung on poles and the pelicans. They are big clumsy birds but impressive. They hunt in a group, {UBC 13:25, 245} flying round and round, then, suddenly, with a clumsy narrowing of leathery wings and webbed feet, hanging absurdly, they dive like kingfishers straight into the water in a spin-like nose dive. With the ravening pelicans were xopilotes and a kind of small grey and white gull all wheeling round together—the native children, their wet brown skins shining in the sun, the boy standing motionless poised on a rock of shore with his harpoon raised and birds flying round him. The trailer camp: cows, burros and goats. A boy flying a kite, standing in a tree.

Sigbjørn's heart goes out to the boy, soars with the kite: that was what their own heart was like, they flew it like a kite, like children standing in a tree: then he remembers.

Analysis of this remembrance. The feeling is, momentarily, like a feeling of dizziness, of the worst kind of tightness when the room goes round and round, but you feel you are going to be sick, absolutely have to be, or to lie on something hard, lie on the floor, tie yourself with ropes to stop it: something like this, but brief, followed by a cold contraction of the stomach. Although perhaps not in essence different from the feeling that succeeds any feeling of happiness, or indeed permeates it, or that the feeling of happiness always has to strive against, that hits you in a cinema, swimming, everywhere, that can never wholly be conquered, and perhaps never should be, though one must always strive by making oneself better to annul it, annul it, accept it, the sense of one's conscience, the unforgivable sin, the moment of dishonour, the time one betrayed oneself, or hurt a friend's feelings, think again of Riley—he had been with him and Peggy here in Hornos, although in fact the same thing, the particularization of one's sense of sin, of one's homelessness on this poor {UBC 13:25, 246} planet, and one's imprisonment upon it, it nonetheless is intolerable and becomes like a sorrow that only alcohol or something that will dislocate and wool time can help: it is like the feeling, and perhaps not unrelated to sometimes even the thought, that besets men before going into battle, or before going aloft on a ship, or even—and Sigbjørn had (or had not) experienced both these latter—going below, in a storm. Bravery inheres in the transmutation of fear into energy. Bravery is thus not something that belongs to hot blood but to cold. The man who is physically shattered by fear, as one can be, say in mountain climbing, beset by uncontrollable tremors—we should never brand offhand as a coward: we should wait to see what he does, not in that situation, with his life after, the worst of all things to bear, a public exhibition of his cowardice. Probably he has been ill brought up in this respect and has no example to fall back upon and it is a truism that it is a fear of precisely this kind of behaviour, this kind of exhibition, that brings on his apparent abjectness—and it is the wild reaction from such fear that subconsciously is responsible for extraordinary acts of courage, which is simply constructive action in the face of what seems to be fatal such for instance with some people as getting up in the morning. (N.B. But it should be pointed out that Sigbjørn's life had largely consisted of this kind of unbearable tension) Bravery is a technique that can be learned: yet courage and fortitude, like sacrifice, bring their own rewards. But here this feeling could only be forgotten, for a time, else it resolved into unbearable tension. Still they had not heard from Mexico City. What kind of {UBC 13:25, 247} courage could the inventor falling from the plane call on—nobody could see it, except God, anyhow. That was a fact. And any kind of courage that Sigbjørn showed would be such a pose. But it would be a pose that demanded a sacrifice, for Primrose, and hence it was worth making. To have given in would have been an immense relief but Sigbjørn conquered himself at this point. "When ye pray say 'our father'"[2] Sigbjørn said. It was true, of course, that Sigbjørn did not wholly know what he was afraid of: it was in fact the suspicion that one faction of his soul knew perfectly well and would not let on that made his predicament so terrifying. As a consequence Sigbjørn proposed a drink but not now—that would have been cowardice—but when they got back to the Quinta Eulalia: if he got back to the Eulalia, Sigbjørn reasoned, without allowing either of them to fall into abjectness this drink would be as deserved as to the man who climbs Snowden.

When they got back (they avert their face from the Immigration) to Caleta there is a dreadful din in the Paraiso that in fact goes on all day: they are dancing, a dance called The Raspa, a sort of explosive demented noisy and incredibly monotonous Mexican version of the English Sir Roger de Coverley, is played over and over again—it was as if the past were gloating over its victory—and Sigbjørn remembers that only a few days before he had thought "That ever I could come back *here* and be happy!—"

Again the temptation to give in (which was not however the same as the temptation to take a drink) assails him but he doesn't.

Their afternoon is saved by the Goggle. (Dramatise this—they want them to leave 50 pesos deposit—50 pesos!)

But the experience is so filled with enchantment they return to their room happy. {UBC 13:25, 248}

"You don't like to dance?"

But later they dance around the room.

While the birthday festivity goes on, the mariachis, from the Paraiso, this empty dead noisy imitation of American music clacking . . . {UBC 13:25, 249}

XI

Monday March 18

Still by Monday morning this tension could best be expressed by a bell that would not stop ringing or an electric horn that will not stop blowing. (Or a guitar string?)

But the ocean wind blowing cleanly through the dining room helps them. There is always a tempest, a full sea gale blowing on the top floors of the Quinta Eulalia, which gave it much the quality of the top deck of a ship, across which storm-tossed stewards struggle with the morning beef tea.

Describe the glorious view from the dining room, the glorious blue morning, all the invitation to happiness, and their morning swim.

Sigbjørn's courage of the previous day had taken effect: he was ready, after this morning ecstasy, to take a drop into the abyss: but Primrose, thanks to him, has taken new courage, and she has a plan that defeats despair. Even the old Paraiso de Caleta seems beaten, its boast of the triumph of the past empty, and forlorn. It lies moribund in the morning, the chairs piled in a corner, or on top of the tables, the bar at one end, battened shut and dead.

In brief, however, the psychological set-up is something like this: both feel that the "verdict" from Mexico City is imminent, either today or the next day and they passionately desire this verdict one way or the other and cannot bear the waiting for it; on the other hand if it is "unfavourable,"—imagination boggled at precisely what form such an unfavourable verdict would take—it would mean, anyhow, the end of their stay in Acapulco: for at best, Sigbjørn presumed, it would {UBC 13:25, 250} involve a trip to Mexico City. Point out that Sigbjørn is terrified of traffic, having lived for so long in the wilderness. He feared Mexico City like the plague. At worst: but Sigbjørn did not think it wise to dwell upon what it would involve at worst, for if Acapulco was any criterion, there was no knowing what they might have trumped up against him in the files at Mexico City. Because of this, while desiring it, they fear equally also the arrival of any word from Mexico City. After all, there were, other things equal (which economically they were not) worse places to be incarcerated in. Like Ahab, damnation in the midst of Paradise.[1] Sigbjørn's fear of telephoning the Consul etc. should be analysed: this is difficult for here, and later in the story, his fear of taking action is his fear of becoming involved with authorities that would take away his freedom: sure enough, that was what the authorities were doing anyway, but if it was psychically or psychologically his fault, this fault was nebulous and still unconscious. Mention fear of lawyers, his father—also his character, the Consul, and his fear of going broke, and her fear of going broke, and their worst fear of all, of being separated. (But point should be made that they are legally in the country, so why stir up trouble.)

So, in the midst of these antinomies, these ambivalences, they go to town, avoiding ambulacrum which led to the Immigration—where they half hoped news hadn't arrived (they see Immigration man too—actually have an appointment for Tuesday—white flannel drinking beer with a friend) buy a couple of litres of bulk habanero from Madame Cyclone.

Note: Words which have bearing on this situation:

Antinomy (anti-nomos: law)—1. Opposition of one law or {UBC 13:25, 251} rule to another. (In this usage, Sigbjørn and Primrose are caught in an antinomy, because there is the law itself that is changing: also the business of civil rights. They are both in the right and the wrong. 2. Metaphysical. A contradiction between two principles each taken to be true, or between inferences correctly drawn from such principles.

They are caught up, work this out, in a kind of quadruple antinomy.

(2) Ambivalence—simultaneous attraction towards and repulsion from an object. (This is useful in describing Sigbjørn and Primrose's feeling about the news at this time coming from Mexico City.)

(3) epiphenomenon—an attendant phenomenon appearing with something else and referred to that as its cause. (The man from the Hacienda was an epiphenomenon.)

They return and raise the pulse of the cosmic heart by having a giggle, a goggle, and a gurgle—as they call it. Actually meantime there is no possible answer to their situation other than courage, of the old fashioned sort, and old fashioned faith. Both of them have a sort of consummate charm that should make them extremely likeable.

So they return and have a drink, a swim, rent a pair of goggles, and behold—a fish—the vela, long slim and pointed at both ends, pale green, it slides along the bottom. They are happy, in an old fashioned and peculiar way, it is fine—they have another snort, and with good appetite they eat a fine dinner of veal seasoned with saffron. Then after a slight rest they go down and rent a surfboard. They paddle out beyond the island and it is quite rough but they do very well with our little craft and there see, in the evening, an ancient freighter puffing into {UBC 13:25, 252} port—the lofty masts, ancient derricks, high superstructure, tall funnel, with dense black smoke, is marvellously exciting, and arouses in Sigbjørn all his old intense longing for the sea: (longing for escape, above all)—could they escape? and then he remembers, the shadow falls again with the remembrance, as if a cold hand were clutching his stomach: they hear the clatter of the motorbike with its cutout and near shore a man on a motorbike goes up the hill to the Quinta Eulalia: "this is it" they think—the police or the Migración—or both . . . But it is not, and that is both bad and good.

Note: see p. 31 in Margie's black notebook,[2] also end of VI

(See present end of Chap VI—we might use some of this, or use it wholly, or use simply the end of it, the man with the lantern on the island, and the vision of Oaxaca—or repeat it here—and end:

"Death," suddenly said Sigbjørn Wilderness, for no reason.

"What was that, darling?"

"Nothing."[3] {UBC 13:25, 253}

XII

Tuesday March 19.

(Perhaps they discuss, on these day, the events leading to their marriage: "Do you remember?" etc. etc.)

Tuesday, they've had a bad night, and arise full of cheer and swim.

Then they go to town—they are going to the Migración but Sigbjørn wants to take Primrose to the mercado.

But first they walk out down past the façade of the Immigration along the new wharf they are building. There are American gunboats, grey and ugly, Margie says black, tied up near at hand: the boats roll at the moorings, ropes groan and strain at the bollards, and rise to trip you up just at the moment you are going to step over them. A bearded bosun and wolf-cries at Primrose. Where has courtesy gone?[1] Courtesy, that greatest of all qualities and reverence and chivalry toward women. An American world would be a nightmare. Mexicans had courtesy: an empty form at best with them, if you took that away from them they would have nothing. There are horrible tough ugly bleached grasping old children diving for coins; their hair seemed grey, rather than bleached, with avariciousness, and one especially had the face of an old man far gone in vice, in spite of all the energy. "Hey Mistair! Hey lady!" There was a school of lovely black-green fish jumping from the water and people fishing all along the breakwater, a queer one-sided wharf. (2 black American warships of some nature, sailors (one bearded) who whistle at me—Margie's note) Their lofty-derricked freighter was at the far end and such a ship Sigbjørn had never seen in his life. Margie's description, see p. 34, Margie's notebook)[2]—a converted old {UBC 13:25, 254} windjammer, so old she is wood, stinking, coal-burning, (this is doubtful, she was not even a coal burner) too much even for Sigbjørn, flying a strange flag with stars (see p. 35—Panama?) with a crew part American, Chinese, Mexican, Filipino, God knows. She was immensely lofty—enormous tall derricks—this must have been, Sigbjørn said, the original ship that was reputed after having rolled all the way from Vladivostock to have rolled into Archangel and, continuing to roll at the wharf, rolled all the sticks out of her. Roll—she certainly did— "She certainly is rolling." "She certainly is."—through an arc of 54 degrees. Extreme heat—no breeze this A.M.—(the pelicans seen close are hideous and ragged, thin ugly dark brown rough leathery birds.) Tar all over its sides, they are trying to load a truck and some kind of machine like a cream separator with much difficulty. He reflects upon the ship, the engineer smoking his pipe so high up amidships, the bulwarks so wide that a man was actually running along them, tar all over its sides: if the galley were amidships Wilderness tries to compute the difficulties of running the chow down to the fo'c'sle, either forward or amidships he can't make out which: they seem insuperable, these difficulties: the so-called companion ladder, for example, that normally would connect amidships with the well deck was at least thirty feet high and what was worse, perpendicular: there would be more freedom of movement in a windjammer with a deck cargo of lumber than on board this ship. He contemplates the vast closed-in stinking hot prison of the shut-in-amidships part of the vessel and concludes that he is afraid of it. The ship is a nightmare certainly—if this were a symbol of freedom! His division from the modern world is shown by the fact that he cannot gauge whether she is {UBC 13:25, 255} an oil or a coal burner: her equipment, winch machinery, life rafts, tilted gadgets for launching lifeboats, seem super-modern, so he assumes that she is some moribund old craft that has been exhumed for war. The wonderful soaring feeling of escape that she has given him a moment fades and he concludes he is afraid of her. God, had life dealt with him so that there was nothing he was not afraid of, that in order to take *any* action whatsoever he had to screw himself up to a pitch of extraordinary courage. Remember Wilderness and Primrose have more freedom than most people and this whole thing must be given a philosophical basis: I must learn, but God will help me if I am *good*. And *try*. And conquer *sloth*. Analyse his attitude of *separation*, caused by non-participation in the war. Sigbjørn thinks of his grandfather: every life has its Cape Horn.

(a dream of escape on the West Coast, only this ship is called the Narcissus[3]—Henley, in which the captain crew etc, are various factions of his soul,[4] the Quinta Eulalia burning behind, the firemen are the unconscious, ending up with an encounter with a man who says: "I am the fireman of my fate. The chief steward of my soul."—or the fireman of my life, the chief steward of my soul, he said, as Wilderness, waking, winced and cried aloud.—perhaps in this dream some dim ancestor is the skipper, his grandfather the first mate, his father the chief engineer—while Sigbjørn plays some weird half-feral role, as if he were his own mother.)

Wilderness continues to watch the West Coast—ridiculous, unimaginative name, although it would be beautiful if encountered, say, in the Indian Ocean—or would be beautiful in French Côte Aouest— which makes him reflect about the prophet being without {UBC 13:25, 256} honour—unimaginative, but as it were eponymous, and certainly not so unimaginative as the beautiful horrible romantic old freighter he'd seen in the Indian Ocean, the British Motorist—the ship has a cargo of rolls of rusty barbed wire. Possibly she'd done yeoman service in the war. Ugly ships. Had oil-tankers got souls? Could their captain love these diesel-engined monstrosities to the extent, like his grandfather, of going down with them?[5] Probably. Even if cargoed with obscenities toward death. Mon âme est un trois mâts, cherchant son Icarie. That was where old Henley must have got it.[6] The liar. Never winced, or cried aloud indeed. But of course, psychologically, the ship personifies the dreaded spectre of authority: and it also again brings up the question of freedom. How free were sailors?

They pass the outside of the Immigration again—was the news here? Their appointment is that afternoon. They resist the temptation to go in and find out because it may be an end to their freedom one way or the other and Sigbjørn wants to take her to the market that had delighted Post and Lewis but which in Sigbjørn's memory had been shifted.

They go past the back of the Marine, where again a waiter stares at them, past the Migración, avoiding the ambulacrum, past the bank from which Sigbjørn averted his eyes—he hated banks which were connected in his mind with paralysis agitans and the next moment forgot it was ever there—to the market.

Primrose, he was glad to see, was enjoying herself. The mercado had a good fine hot primitive quality that is unexpected in this town but sleasy goods outside of many bright baskets, etc. Outside are hundreds of xopilotes, a few pigs and pariah dogs {UBC 13:25, 257} fighting over the garbage. There ought to be a related and extremely powerful passage about the xopilotes: they arrive at a sort of meeting place, a parliament, convocation, the palace of vultures. They are doing a kind of dance among the loathsome offal, half flying, half fighting, half jumping. The tension returns in the market, the strain.

Describe the low-roofed solid houses, something like Oaxaca, earthquake resistant, and the high curbstones. They return to Caleta and get goggles, but it is too dirty and rough to see. They are disappointed but still cling together. If there is any *meaning* in their not being able to see beneath the water at this juncture it should be pointed out. The full moon tide is in (remember this is the afternoon).

At the hotel a marimba band is trying to get the marimba past place where they are building a new pergola. That was before they went to swim. When they come back into their room, from the dining room, the marimba suddenly bursts out, sounding as though they'd taken it to pieces, Sigbjørn says, and can't get it together again. Anyhow, now starts the wonderful irony of the music and a terrific fiesta: we go out and are given wine and a wonderful dinner, habanero—we can't drink much because of appointment with Migración but it is the Saint Day of José[7]—"My Man"—and his Lady Me is sailing round—and My God, the gaiety!—You no like dancing?

Primrose and Sigbjørn don't want to come out, partly because they are still embarrassed by their position, partly because they don't want to get tight. So they dance in their room, dance ironically as at Tepotzlan (this scene might be repeated at the very end in Laredo, Tex.). The agony of listening to the Raspa. {UBC 13:25, 258} But when you start to dance it you may have to go on until you are exhausted.

Later, "their loins," as Margie says, "suitably girded with chiclets," they go downtown again to the Migración to keep appointment. The office is closed. The knock. Inside is a boy, asleep, who opens windows. The papers blow all over the room—for there was sometimes a breeze at this time of the afternoon—and the boy then goes through a terrific time finding paper weights for each individual paper, the dust, a rocking chair, the boy pretends to put letter in huge old typewriter, upside down, he has big bare negroid feet, continues to pretend to write on typewriter, then in some American digest begins to read a story by James Thurber: the heat, the breeze, the waiting, the dust—Sigbjørn could have stolen his file—could an office so carelessly arranged, so devoid of any kind of order or authority—be a scene of so much tension, despair, the seat of judgment,[8] of perhaps life and death . . . Note: Tojo is not there, but in Mexico City.

"A qué hora regresa el señor?"

"Quién sabe?"[9]

Describe again, through the windows of the Migración, the S.S. West Coast, unloading, and still rolling.

In despair, Primrose goes—while Sigbjørn remains—to Turismo who says man is busy with ships in port and won't be back today. (Mem: find out from Margie if this is day when they put through the phoney phone call from Turismo—what day does Hacienda man come? Thurs., Fri.)

According to Primrose, however, the Turismo man got in touch with one of the Migración people who had said that tomorrow morning he would phone Mexico again, please to come at 12 next day. {UBC 13:25, 259}

(Actually the fat immigration man is busy holding up the Americans on the yacht, which we should place earlier if we mean to use it)

Mañana, mañana, mañana—

They return to Quinta Eulalia—fiesta is going strong, the irony is repeated—

The weehaus

Towards midnight they go for a swim—a flattened yellow moon is rising behind the hill through long misty clouds, Orion declining, Canopus bright above the lighthouse. (Margienote: you said earlier it was full moon tides, but a flat moon rising at midnight is at least two days or three waning from full) What a sense of cleanliness and

of being cleansed, of renewed strength and the coolness and courage. There was phosphorous in the sea and the tides are running
strong and high, even in this protected bay.

And all night they seemed to be swimming against the tide, Sigbjørn
supporting Primrose when she became weary. {UBC 13:25, 259}

XIII

Wednesday March 20.

The next day the tides were running still higher: they have now
been held six days: down town to keep appointment with Migración
at noon. This time the fat fellow is there. So are two empty bottles of
pargas. Describe him, so far as possible. He is not uncheery: is somewhat obsequious. Primrose fears him. He has expected Tojo back—
but he is not yet back. Sigbjørn offers to pay for a phone call if he,
Fatty, will put it through: he agrees, but says phone call will take an
hour or two to put through. His gestures can be described. Will they
come back at 4:30. Sigbjørn agrees, but asks again if he can go, explains once more about apartment (their poor lonely apartment
there—they think—Nosotros no somos ricos Americanos, etc. . . .)

—Trouble is, not that Sigbjørn cannot understand Fatty, but that
Fatty keeps interrupting, as it were getting the idea over that he
couldn't understand Sigbjørn. "No spikka the Eenglish." But of
course these people's delight is to trip up and to interrupt.

Meantime they have been kept waiting agonizingly: and either here,
or in chapter before, should be a description of the pictures in the
Migración: or perhaps these should be described some time before.

1. The Mexican eagle tearing to pieces the Nazi flag, with a wild
cloudy sky behind in colours of Mexican flag underneath the legend: México por la libertad.[1]

2. Poster put out by the Tourist department: large and innocent—
Indian girl in native dress they no longer wear, leaning by doorway
of clean adobe house covered with flowers, eyes coyly downcast and
caballero by her side complete with sombrero, scarlet {UBC 13:26,
261} neckerchief and broad belt leaning over her in sweet amour
and fondling the head of a donkey—Visit Mexico!

3. The sweetest little abode Indian house so clean! Indian family grouped tastefully around in clean brightly colored clothes with Ixta and Popo[2] in background. Visit Mexico!

4. Calendar advertising some kind of tirez called General Popo, very Hollywood in style, voluptuous amber miss naked except for 3 golden blobs is being chained hand and foot by 2 fierce looking hombres in bright feather headdresses—pyramid in background.

Sigbjørn and Primrose go back via the Turismo where bad Turismo promises to go over with them and interpret, that is, later when the phone call arrives: they say they'll be there about 4, but not before they have disappointing talk with Turismo fellow and try to state their case again. "Your husband, he is bad, bad."

In fact Sigbjørn and Primrose go back—and how much was contained in this going back!—to the Quinta Eulalia in a state of melancholy and frustration: it is impossible not to feel something malefic in what is happening to them, a sense of something sneering, effeminate and at once of active ill-will in the Turismo guy whom Sigbjørn now remembers very well as a bummer of drinks, a hanger on, an aper of everything American, the lowest kind of human being, in fact almost unimaginable, unless it was the stool pigeon whom they had met again,[3] that day, outside the Immigración with a sheaf of papers who had said:

"Hullo, Wilderness."

"Hello, Judas." Sigbjørn had said. "You going to work now. *In the theatre.*"[4] {UBC 13:26, 262} Of course there was no theatre in Acapulco—or in Mexico for that matter. Again Sigbjørn reflects upon the psychology of Mexican stool pigeons, the system, the machinery, of the mordida. It was a dance of stool pigeons, in fact. Nothing sporting about arrests in Mexico. A man is sitting on a park bench (this is what Sigbjørn had been doing) at midnight. A policeman arrests him, blows his whistle, other policemen come up from other street corners, whistles are blown: it is an arithmetical progression. Every blower of the whistle gets his rake-off right up to the commandante. The same thing in the Immigration.

Kilroy had been in the toilet there too, when he found it. He had passed a stone there. But much impression he seemed to have made. Abajo los tyrannicos Norteamericanos, it said, next to this.[5]

Somewhere a Mexican should say, or shout:

"Look out . . . Corazón . . . You know what we say. All the time you hear it. We are a poor people, we have little money but much corazón. With Mexico it is always corazón. Verdad. Look out— Mexico is a country, verdad, with an octopus instead of a heart." The way he said it contained unbelievable venom, because it has rhymed with Bass in bottle. These *bas*tards, he went on. Good people, going all time for charity. Good works. But these donkey, these man. These *bas*tards. They give you corazón. Palpa—sí— palpa en su tinta. Muy sabroso[6] . . .

One morning, a blue dawn, turquoise and gold: cool absolute stillness. Their great machine shop window giving on the sound. In calm you could almost see the branches on the trees reflected {UBC 13:26, 264}[7] 2 miles away. The fathomless depths of this mirror: white shiny sea. And the scarf of smoke from the quiet muted factories in the southeast, factories, beautiful, shot through with lilac, also reflected. Seabirds drift downstream, a seal—the one they had befriended— seemed to answer their call, appeared and went. Sigbjørn wouldn't have noticed it, he had to pick Primrose's brains to get it—his mind was moved too swiftly from one enjoyment to another to catch on.

(This is flashback to home): The curious thing was a double shadow of the window on the wall, one cast by the sunlight, one cast by the reflection of the sun in the water which was so strong it too cast a shadow. The shadow cast by the reflection, being of the water, was waving; the other was apparently motionless, only moving as the sun moved down the wall. You actually could see the *shadow* of the heat from the stove on the wall (though you could not see the heat itself) fading as we discussed it and the sun went under a cloud: and the shadow of imperfections and flaws in the glass of the window which they had never seen with the naked eye, were plainly seen, some vertically, some horizontally, striped, on the wall. (A sudden vision or memory of home from which is deduced the following)[8]

What could one deduce from this?

(labile—horrible word—labilely profound—*blubbery*—characterised by adaptability to change or modification: plastic: unstable: Sigbjørn less than Primrose.)

(a) of the two shadows that cast by the reflection was the more mobile and exciting. So it was with Sigbjørn now. He seemed to see at this moment, with his eyes, the shadow of something that they were as yet sitting a fairly respectful distance from and could not as yet feel—even this felt anguish and suspense and {UBC 13:26,265} discomfort and even fear—at all. And this shadow differed from other shadows in that, terrifying as it was, he knew it was less terrifying and evil than that which cast it.

(b) you saw the shadow of a reality (and hence could deduce this reality from the visible shadow) i.e. the heat, or is the heat a reality?—which otherwise you could only have perceived[9] with another sense, or senses, a reality in short that normally speaking, though its *impact* might have been greater, you could only have deduced from something invisible. In short, you could, under certain circumstances, *see* the shadow of energy, without being able to see energy itself.

Primrose and Sigbjørn are thus chewing the rag of frustration in their room when there is a knock at the door, it is Lady Me—and a servant—and the pimply pocked man from the Hacienda. Sigbjørn hides their glasses of habanero, there is a frightful embarrassing scene—the pimply man (for complete draft of the letter, which Sigbjørn might snatch, see end of this chapter) will not listen, he should be described, and his attitude: he demands the same 50 pesos again and again, in a speech which is based on the actual document in our possession; the dialogue here should be taken from it.

When he has gone, after having explained again and again that they cannot pay the 50 pesos because they are not allowed to go to Cuernavaca, and there is a frightful scene, which should, however, be extremely funny at the same time—and they have persuaded him to meet them at 4 at the Turismo—the good Mexican, stripped to the waist, with the cross round his neck, comes to try and help them. He should be most sympathetically described—he offers to lend them 50 pesos. "I have 50 pesos just now . . . I know what it was {UBC 13:26, 266} like . . . I overstay my leave in U.S. . . . It was as a matter of fact because someone was ill . . ." He has had harsh treatment in the U.S. but he, in the book, together with his friend, represents the true Christian charity which is at the basis of the adjustment of the Mexican people to life, just as Eddie, represents the chivalrous, pearl handled pistoled, courteous, false, empty—but not altogether—*form* of chivalry and courtesy, without love, as it were, and which is powerless to move anything save by force. Perhaps to give this man some verisimilitude he may show a startling knowledge of English cars, he has been in England too—he is an engineer, he knows all the English cars and motorbikes and Sigbjørn and he can have a wonderful time later in a kind of Isle of Man conversation.

—Sí, el A.J.S.[10] Muy bonito.

—Y el Sunbeam.

—Sí, el Sunbeam.

—Y Harley-Davidson.

—Esta es Norteamericano . . .

—Y el Bat—he says.

Sigbjørn thinks, and then says, "Sí, El Bat."

Then the schoolteacher comes humming to their aid: everybody knows about it, and it is all more embarrassing than ever.

At 4 o'clock, after having swum, and trying to keep up their spirits, (note—something might be written about the increasing difficulty Sigbjørn is having in coping with reality at all, for instance) they go into the Turismo: they wait, and wait, and wait—there is a Mexican girl there with a charming smile. Terror Sigbjørn feels at the sight of the word: Deportivos,[11] which means, after all, only sportsmen. The feeling that he is legally in {UBC 13:26, 267} Mexico, but by mistake, related to the feeling that is one's lot, also in the world. The homelessness of it, and a sudden vision of the burned house waiting to be rebuilt. The homelessness of man's lot. The dying and being reborn. One would wish for death—surely one would not find stool pigeons there too, more indeed than here.

The Hacienda man comes in, then the good Turismo.

There now should follow a terrific scene with the Hacienda man restating all his nonsense, and saying that Sigbørn will be put in prison if he doesn't pay immediately and Sigbjørn saying that how can he pay unless he can go to Cuernavaca and get the money for the money is in his name. The good Turismo saves him: he puts up the security of his watch (religious significance of the watch, which has stopped, should be placed before, how it had been stolen and he'd saved the boy from prison). Sigbjørn is not altogether a fool: he is putting up for security something that was essentially valueless, although it has a sentimental value, Primrose has given it to him: the psychology of presents—why under certain circumstances is it almost impossible to buy presents for the one one loves?—remember too, it had been this knowledge that the watch had meant something sentimental, that had caused the boy to be moved, this scene should flash through his mind as he leaves the watch—meantime, there are other Americans in there, and the good Turismo is looking more and more concerned: finally Sigbjørn and Primrose explain the situation to him angrily—for Sigbjørn is now overcome with rage at the idea of putting up this watch at all: but the situation is now this: unless the fine is paid in 3 days Sigbjørn will be put in prison, but how can this fine—even though of 50 pesos—be paid unless they can go to Cuernavaca and get the {UBC 13:26, 268} money and still they have not heard from Mexico City:

"Whatever you may imagine you have against me, you have nothing whatsoever against my wife and you are committing a crime by holding her. That of course means nothing to you."

"If you don't let her go I'll get in touch with the American Consul in Mexico and get you put in jail," Sigbjørn said.

And Primrose rages, "I certainly will get in touch with my American Consul. You can't do this to us, etc."

"We have a public."

This remark causes the bad Turismo positively to blench with fear: and either at this point, or earlier, he will have phoned up the Migración and—and it is this that causes the storm—given them the information that still they haven't heard.

"He say they don't know anything about you in Mexico City," he said shortly, hanging up.

Now they persuade him to phone again. "He say he will get touch with Mexico City if you pay for the phone call."

"He say he is getting in touch with Mexico City again." While this latter conversation is going on, a series of mute exchanges goes on also between the good Turismo and Sigbjørn: the telephone conversation should be dramatized entirely with the gestures of the bad Turismo, the twitches, the shrugs, the down-drawn lips: the mute exchanges bespeak volumes, the half-shaken head, the girl begins to blush with shame: they know that he cannot get in touch with Mexico City in that short time. I will have to ask Margie for the more exact sequence. Finally to Primrose:

"He say you can go. But you must go immediately. Today, right off. And be back in 3 days."

"But how can I go today? The planes will be all booked up." {UBC 13:26, 269}

"You go by bus."

"But the first class bus will be all booked up."

The bad Turismo shrugs.

"Quién sabe . . ." and is about to do something else. Sigbjørn shouts at him:

"Isn't it your business to see that tourists get a fair deal?"

"It is not my department."

"If not, what is your department then?"

"Well, we work with the Immigration."

"He means by that that should we have been so foolish as to have borrowed 50 pesos and paid it to the Migración he would have got a rake off," Sigbjørn explained to Primrose. "Come on, let's go."

Bad Turismo is already doing something else: arms around good Turismo. Judas outside, going toward Migración.

"Hullo, Judas," Sigbjørn said, "You going to work again?" They are turned down at the Estrella d'Oro. They can only get tickets for the Flecha.[12] Sigbjørn thinks of getting a ticket, but they have been followed. Armed policemen are standing around.

When one spoke glibly about simply going from Caleta to Acapulco, it was sufficient of an understatement. The torture of standing under the cramped roof. But to speak glibly of going to Mexico City was quite another thing again. Mexico itself, a night mare of klaxons, the most unspeakably noisy and unattractive city in the world, the very thought of which struck Sigbjørn with terror. But the journey, the night journey, on a second class bus. True, it would not be so bad as eight years ago. But it is awful and Sigbjørn says on the way back: {UBC 13:26, 270}

"I can't let you go. Or I'm coming with you."

"Well—there's only that one seat. You're in trouble. You'll go to the jug if I don't go."

"I'd do something else—I'll bum a ride somehow, I'll get there."

"But I'm only going to Cuernavaca—"

"Only—" Sigbjørn exploded as they prayed to the Saint of Desperate and Dangerous Causes.

Back at the hotel they have a drink and explain the matter to José, who is bowed down with a hangover. "Horreebly."

José has a face like a Greek Christ, or a Cypriot. He is very sympathetic, offers even to perjure himself for them, to say to the Hacienda man that he has gone—(but then would not the Hacienda man go to the Migración, and then where would José be—so Sigbjørn doesn't take advantage of this) he makes a little parcel of food

for poor Primrose while she is dressing, and Sigbjørn sits in the bleak
dining room, the roar of the sea outside, writing a letter as follows:

Quinta Eulalia, Acapulco.

Banco Nacional de México,
Gentlemen:

Two weeks ago I wrote to my bank in Canada, Bank of Montreal,
500 Granville St, Vancouver, B.C., to send me $300 Canadian—ap-
proximately 1500 pesos—to the Banco Nacional de Mexico in Cuernavaca, this being the amount permitted under the War Prices and
Trades Board Regulations.

In the meantime I have gone to Acapulco and will be very grateful if
you will wire this money to me here in Acapulco at the above address
as this is extremely urgent.

This letter will introduce my wife who will, I hope, produce the
{UBC 13:26, 271} necessary identifications.

Thanking you in advance for this service, I remain, yours sincerely,

Sigbjørn Wilderness.

To this Sigbjørn added a postscript, that did not occur to him till
later that it certainly was a symptom that his mind was already
going—

—if the money has not arrived will you please consider this letter
as providing my wife with power of attorney and yourselves send a
wire immediately to the Bank of Montreal to wire the funds in question to me here in Acapulco.

This odd epistle presented to Primrose, who does not seem to
think it peculiar, they have a final snort: the last indeterminate buses
to the Zócalo were already going—they take the parcel of food[13] and
go off down into the town again—the setting off from Acapulco has a
kind of grandeur and a horror: the bus waiting there like a plane or a
ship. There was a certain dignity attaching to the Flecha Roja at night
that did not pertain in the day. Next to her was a fat half negro with
long nails and a scar as if made by these nails and the driver had a
rather effeminate face, though Sigbjørn could not be sure he noticed
these things. One felt much as one might feel seeing off the dead, on
Charon's boat. Sigbjørn again things of going, but police are standing
round: names have to be written meticulously. Three taps. "Vámonos!" The bus roars off into the night. The anguish of nostalgia.
Primrose's holiday! the rage. Sigbjørn has little habanero left at home

and is half crazy with anxiety and fear: he goes into the cantina opposite in which he is too afraid to take a drink: "Yo no estoy un Americano . . ."[14] and buys three bottles of tequila. {UBC 13:26, 272}

"Es mucho."

"Sí, es mucho."

Then he walks back in the dark. The half recognized waiter in the
Marina who seems to be waving at him with his dishcloth. "Champ."
Avoiding the Monterrey and the first pub they'd been in. Resisting
the temptation to drink. It is not hard for in any place where your
throat will not be cut you have to wait so long for anyone to take any
notice of you that the waiting is worse than the going without—almost. Describe this walk back. There is a waning moon which is not
going to use for home—possibly Primrose would see it over the
Tierra Colorada—and it is horribly dark. You can even get suspense
that he is going to be run over or arrested. Even Mexicans do not
walk along this road at night. He remembers the past—again in this
darkness. Out of the darkness a man calls "Burro" at him, very
briefly, much as, in the French film of Crime et Chatiment,[15] a man
remarks quite mildly to Raskolnikov one night:

"Assassin."

Out of the darkenss, from the other side of the street, a man said
to him simply:

"Burro." {UBC 13:26, 273}[16]

This document ran something as follows.[17]

Hotel Quinta Eulalia (this much written)

    Están muy Lejos Geográficamente   this printed
    neustros territorios, acérquemoslos   very tiny
    económica y espiritualmente

    There are many places
    geographically our territory,
    encircled economically and spiritually.

    In a circle: Poder ejecutivo Federal
    Estados Unidos Mejicanos   México D.F.
    This around an eagle swallowing a snake.[18]

    Secretaría de Hacienda y Crédito Público.

    Dependencia Número Expediente.
    Direc. Gra. de Población

Dept. de Migración
de Estudios y promociones
inversionistas y rentistas
4/351.0"37"/4001

(Which so far Sigbjørn and Primrose can have some fun as translating. Grand Direction of Pubkeepers, Department of Migración, of students and promoters, inverts and rentiers.)

> Asunto: Se impone multa de 350.00 Al Señor—
> Sigbørn Wilderness, súbdito inglés.

1 señor
Sigbjørn Wilderness
c/o Oficina de Población
Acapulco, Gro.

Hago de su conocimiento que esta Secretaría en oficio 9781 de 29 de marzo último, que se le dirigió a Humboldt #621, Cuernavaca, Mor., impuso a usted multa de $50.00 en virtud de que su documentación migratoria venció el 17 del mes citado y tanto usted como su esposa no han hecho gestiones sobre (?) el referente de su documentación.

Se le concede un plazo de quince días, a partir de la fecha de salida de este oficina, para que cubra la multa de referencia en la oficina Federal de Hacienda de ese Lugar y al mismo tiempo {UBC 13:26, 274} remita documentos bancarios para comprobar que subsisten sus características de rentista, apercivido de que en caso de no (?) den cumplimiento a lo exigido se procederá como legalmente corresponda

> Atentamente. Sufragio Efectivo. No Reelección.
> Mexico, D.F., a 11 de Mayo de 1938
> EL JEFE DEL DEPARTAMENTO
>
> Andrés Landa y Pina (Rubrica)

Point about this document is the incredible overproportion of bureaucratic signatures etc in contradistinction to the content—former goes on next page.

Un sello que dice; Secretaría de Gobernación Dirección de Población May 12 1939 Despechado Mesa de Correspondencia y Control. Otro sello que dice Oficina Federal de Hacienda Mayo 16 1939 Acapulco. Gro.
. . . c.c.p. la Oficina de Población en Acapulco, Gro., Contestando

su telegrama de 7 del actual.

c.c.p. la Oficina Federal de Hacienda, Acapulco, Gro., Para su conocimiento y fines.

c.c.p. Control de Vencimientos.

R G/ctm.—4129—es copia del Original que certificó Acapulco, Gro. 21 de Agosto de 1941.

Jefe de la Oficina

Ismael Pozos Alcántara—P—O—159

(signed in green ink.) {UBC 13:26, 275}

XIV

Night of Wednesday the 20th, Thurs, 21st, Fri 22nd.

Now where was he?

—Sigbjørn tries to plot his position. Dinner had not been quite over when he entered the dining room; his friend with the cross was still there and they have a desultory conversation; he says he has been in trouble in the States trying to help someone and Sigbjørn says that he too had been helping someone here and perhaps that was the trouble. But he thinks over these things in bed. The floodlights are still on outside his room, the weehaus has started; the engine is going here and in the Cordoba; his tequila is unopened. He is drinking habanero, he is still half crazy with suspense, thinking, following her in his mind—ah, their honeymoon. What would it be like on that second class bus? What had it been like in 1936, and indeed in 1937 etc. What was going to happen? Why was he in this position?

Sigbjørn takes it for granted that by himself he will go to pieces and reasons like a child: he has resisted temptation etc. so far—he has not drunk the tequila.

Again the problem of freedom comes up. He has freedom and he has not got freedom. He has freedom to act, but what is he doing with it? He admits to himself his inability to think through the situation, his feeling that he is being *used* as a protagonist in a novel written by daemon. The room described: the feeling of night. He follows Primrose in his mind—the heat—she must be thinking she will die. God that long trip in the darkness (their honeymoon) and her seat had no back, there would be the horrible noise of the cut-out, and the smell of gasoline, and the fat half-negro with the long nails and the scar on his face {UBC 13:26, 276} (as from finger-nails—place him in previous chapter) but perhaps he would be decent, and offer her his coat as a pillow or even a shoulder to rest on, and she would be watching the effeminate profile of the driver, and the bus full of strange dark people and the dark hills and trees and the long hours ahead and the moon would not have risen yet.

Sigbjørn rises on his elbow; yes perhaps it would be about rising now—it would rise, he calculated, some time after reaching Tierra Colorado—or there would be a forest fire to look at in those dead trees and then back of the road near some nameless village, an Indian fire round which in silhouette dark figures were dancing—Indians, all night long, dancing, in their white clothes, or walking, or riding burros—where?—and animals: burros, cattle are resting or apparently browsing on gravel by the roadside, do they never sleep these beasts?—they wait and rest and wait, some Indians are lying on the road itself, moving out of the way of the bus now: suddenly a village of flaring torches: then nothing for miles: darkness, only the sense of moonrise now, a faint yellow hint behind mountains; people in the bus snore and spit and cough and sprawl in the aisles: perhaps the man behind her, damn him, would offer his knee as a head rest, and the bus roaring on through dark great Catholic evil compassionate cruel indifferent Mexico—and the poor darling torn with sleepiness and unable to find any possible position; just as, likewise in life, eating a dry torta and banana: thirst, sleepiness, discomfort, war with feeling of fear and lostness and also some objection, feeling she should note all this, but too sleepy to care—and in fact, one should "note all this" whether one is a writer or not,[1] {UBC 13:26, 277} if it is meaning, or faith you are after. The Indians, the villages, asleep or awake, going by, always the animals who seem never to sleep and she will be dying of sleepiness and cannot find any way to sleep, even on the knee or the shoulder, and finally, beyond Tierra Colorada, the flattened late moon rising—she would see the same moon, a contact—rises and she would be in that beautiful maniacal country of gorges and steep dark of cliffs whose touring towering shape she could now see but whose maniacal beauty she will not be able to feel because she will be lost without me. What questions will she ask herself now, too tortured, for sleep? Why did she marry me? Looking for peace she found a sword.[2] And what of the pathos of her own destiny? Perhaps I shall make her a music critic, and all her troubles with publishers are anatomised. The agony of unreceived letters: but then the confusion! Had he begot this confusion. What was the meaning? Cause and effect he could dimly see. He begins to put questions to the darkness, the darkness seems to take the form of Fernando. Why is she suffering this and not him?

Because you have to be brought somehow to an abject sense of your refusal of responsibility. It is this which brings objective disastar[3] on others.

"How?"

You know.

Is this an objective disastar? It depends on how you look at it.

Don't say that it is a disastar I am bringing upon Primrose. I said nothing.

Is death involved? How should death not be involved?

I mean is the death of one of us involved, in the physical {UBC 13:26, 278} ordinary sense. Perhaps.

But nothing has happened yet! Oh yes it has: it depends on your viewpoint. From mine, more than enough is happening.

Why should you care? The dead care. Sometimes it is their job to care. Love is not the only thing that survives you know. Chivalry and compassion do too.

It is as well there should be some chivalry where you are. Because there's damn little here. It is as you arouse it.

Tell me—are you a dead, a ghost, as it were—are you really talking to me. Fernando. Or are you partly just a figment of my imagination? Not always.

Tell me why then, have I run into the past like this? Because the past is not dead.

Can I not annihilate it—have I not expiated it? Yes—you have, in part. But then you brought it to life again.

How? In your work.

But my work was burned. You have that to thank for the fact that not more of the past was exhumed. (etc.)

An imaginary conversation on these lines, interpolated with as much of the past as is relevant or feasible and punctuated also by

Sigbjørn's action or inaction, the sense of the dark Mexican night, the pounding of the tide, the sense of love, anxiety.

"I sent you a warning."

"How?"

"Tomb number 7!"

Sigbjørn remembers how a newspaper article in dealing with (and showing a picture of) the excavations in Tomb 7 at Oaxaca had been open in Iguala: had this been a warning? {UBC 13:26, 279}

Sleepless, he drinks some tequila, and is then relatively calmer, but still sleepless, continues to follow Primrose in his mind to Cuernavaca, back in reverse over the mountains that had seemed damned, and where he'd thought of his frightful trip with Bousfield, he'd been wearing Fernando's clothes—another fire burning far away—centuries later Tierra Colorada going by in a burst of naphtha flares and she is trying to remember how many hours to Chilpancingo where they will surely stop; landmarks remembered looking so different—go by the river—at Chilpancingo they don't stop—and then the agony of the long long hours to Iguala—Then Iguala—dies minutos, señores—and the chap who's offered his knee now offers coffee. Ah, Iguala! Would she go into that hideous little bedraggled gas station with a few trucks there—the trucks, the night trucks all along the road—Primrose—drinking coffee, Primrose refusing sandwiches, Primrose, looking for the damas—Alas, she may have trouble, it will be closed; a tired woman in red sleazy coat and frowzy hair (but not so frowzy as she feels) looking like American housewife, is kind—un otro ahí—dónde[4]—she gestures me to follow and leads back of station where a few women are peeing on ground to half-seen building—aquí?—no luz?—sí, no luz—she enters, gasping—es muy sucio, sí, es muy sucio:[5] she does the best she can while woman guards door that won't close—back on bus, driver offers her chiclets—very grateful, for she is dying of thirst but from here on she is awake, and no longer tortured by sleep, only fear, and longing, further and further away, watching the white signposts K325—K324—K323—seeming further and further apart—what if she should never see him again? And what if they should never see each other again? Trouble with the immigration had been the keynote of their {UBC 13:26, 280} life: flash back to Blaine perhaps;[6] then back to the bus: the fat Mexican that kept falling against her, leaning against her in his sleep, a woman vomiting, the noise, and then the smell, the terrible terrible cut-out roar of motor—at Taxco we change drivers and the new one is large and fat and drunk—where is your husband?—he tries to take her hand and feel her knee while changing gears—he and the conductor talk about her—Iguala amor Americano[7]—she is silent when she realises what is up and presently they are hostile—when I see the lights of Cuernavaca[8]—the triple-barreled *meaning* of Cuernavaca—it is wonderful, they drop her down literally at the Cathedral. Would she enter and pray? It is still dark but the moon gives some fading light. A man is following her. She has some idea she'll look less like a prospective victim if she eats so she struggles with a dry torta and nearly chokes—the familiar streets, the Palace, the building operations, the new road, the little street, our tower, and finally the door and safety. The spiders. Oh god there would be spiders—and the long long dawn—la madrugada; before Eddie would awake . . .

But it was la madrugada here in the Quinta Eulalia and Sigbjørn can't stand it. He puts on his bathing trunks goes up to try and find the Southern Cross, the boys sleeping, the fishermen, he is nearer to her doing that, returns to his room, he has been meaning to swim, but the sea looks rather dark and dirty and rough for once, he drinks himself into a kind of thick despair in which the shadow of prison seems to be enclosing him.

When he wakes the Zapotecan is standing by his bed with a telegram:

"Muchas gracias."

"Un poco crudo,"[9] said the Zapotecan. {UBC 13:26, 281}

"Sí—un poco."

Sigbjørn reads the telegram, can't believe his eyes, and reads again: it is from Primrose but from Mexico City—to the effect:

Am in Mexico City trying to fix things this end with British Consul will wire again—Primrose.

Describe the telegram.

Sigbjørn drank nearly a glass of tequila in one gulp in anger. What in the name of God was she seeing the British Consul for! But the first thought is: Primrose is in Mexico City. How would she be able to stand it: the noise, the chaos, the wrong directions, the overcharging, the utter lack of communication. Then he takes comfort from the fact: "trying to arrange things at this end." Then, the endless connotations of "British Consul" rise up to worry him. He drinks some habanero: comfort comes from this all right, the connotations of British Consul, Primrose's discomfort in Mexico City, fade into the background; now the salient point is, "things are being taken care of . . . And not by him." These thoughts are unworthy, but cannot be helped. Schwab is sitting outside—

"Todos es reglado con la goberno,"[10] Sigbjørn tries to explain.

"Buen . . . buen . . ."

Sigbjørn goes down to the beach to swim. He swims a long way. Having returned he lies on the beach by their log, their bereaved log. Other thoughts now torment him. Why hadn't Primrose got hold of Eddy? Had the money arrived in Cuernavaca? If not, how was she to get on? Why had she left Cuernavaca? Would she go to the Migración herself in Mexico City? And if so, would she ever get out again! Were the British Consuls any longer powerful, {UBC 13:26, 282} honorable men? Was she in touch with a Consul who remembered him, before Mexico broke off relations? What was the meaning of a Consul anyway? He lies rotting on the beach, sleeps, burns in the sun, does not wake till nightfall (or perhaps the Zapotecan comes all the way down to call him for dinner)

Now the worry as to what they had against him. The papers were full of "Communist Plot Sweeps Canada!"[11] But they had nothing against him. And then the 50 pesos. 50 pesos! He could borrow it in a moment from the good man, what was he afraid of? He would be in jail tomorrow if he didn't bring it. Fear of the half-known. Memories of Oaxaca. He cannot face the dining room. Zapotecan brings him his food in his room. He gives people drinks. Tries to sleep. Cannot. From every direction forces seem to be moving against him from which there is no escape—unless he escapes on the West Coast.

Sleeps. Dreams of West Coast freighter in half delirium. Very realistic dream for which use real experience. Possibly the one where his father is waiting on the dock for him. See notes: I am the Chief Steward of my soul.[12]

Wakes in fear and with terrible shakes—cold too. Takes a codeine of Primrose's washed down somehow by habanero, though he chokes, given her by humming school teacher. Is calmed in a while but wakes shortly feeling much worse. He remembered a scene in Simenon.[13] A cold draughty café with a greenish light falling through the windows, a cold southeasterly gale outside in the small French town blowing spray over the square and people sitting round a table in this sordid café drinking pernod, in which someone had put strychnine. That was how he felt or his consciousness felt, not like any of the individuals but as it were like the scene it{UBC 13:26, 283}self. Or in some cinemas the men's toilet is on the top floor. The projection room is there, but it is cold, a window gives on a narrow alley. There are comfortable, but meaningless, couches, where no one sits. It is a sort of image of hell, the hell of suicides perhaps, the lonely niche reserved for them. They are aware of the spirits downstairs watching their lives on the screen but cannot get in touch with them. There is no meaning, nor reality. Even the sound of the infernal machine[14] cannot remind one distinctly, or call one back to one's existence. There is a terrible nostalgia, an agony, a longing for familiar comfortable things of which there is the barest suggestion here but in fact one's consciousness is so fully identified with the pain of remorse that there is no room for anything else.

But remorse for what? Sigbjørn sat up, shaking worse than ever. Was his lot really so bad? He prays for Primrose to the Saint of Dangerous and Desperate Causes. Our Señora of the Sacred Heart, divine patroness of difficult and desperate causes, help me. Help us . . . Though I prayed to Thee on a bus . . . Oh help me (he managed) though my soul be not yet ready. For that final cross where all man's hands are steady[15] (He is beginning to be afraid he may have to sign something at the Hacienda) He also writes, or thinks—for he is now hot, now cold—Sweat on the hands, the burning hands, aching to betray us, is not this, Judas and Christ at once. Horripilation[16] of sweat on hands, the burning hands. In an agony, half praying, he writes:

I am now going to sleep, please, sweet mother of Jesus guard Primrose on her night trip; help me to want to help myself so that in her return she may have joy. You have already given her faith, I pray thee to abate the forces {UBC 13:26, 284} that are destroying me, but abate them with wisdom, plenitude, and some result of joy: for if I am dead—should I even sacrifice my life—how should she live? (It was perhaps significant that he began every time with a capital letter as though he half imagined he were writing a poem.)

Then he fell to thinking of the habanero problem and wrote:
I intend to pay José $48 pesos
   help   go myself
     of 58 I have.
Then, almost as an after thought, he set down these words:
Good end for a chapter.
Is my brain going.

But do I care![17]

Even in unconsciousness, Sigbjørn still seemed to be moving like a composite nightmare through this world of his own injured creation.

(the end of chapter)

He wonders too either here or in the next chapter: was death like this? the slow and sodden vigil of the night.

Is death like this, this Manchester October Moribund, half tight, half sober, the slow and sodden vigil of the night. {UBC 13:26, 285}

XV

Night of Friday 22 — Saturday 23.

"Get up—"

"—"

"Get up, you drunken bastard."

Primrose was shaking him and Sigbjørn half rose and took in everything immediately. The candle was guttering. His dinner half eaten, half over the place was lying here and there. The Zapotecan had failed to wake him and he had fallen asleep and had failed to meet Primrose. He'd had another wire sent from the Vice Consul himself saying she was leaving though he hadn't said by what bus. He has even been down town[1] to meet the only bus he had been told she would come on but he has been misinformed. The pathos of this situation had hardly time to grip him because Primrose was in an hysterical rage.

"I get in—at 2 o'clock in the morning . . ."

"You've got to pull yourself together, and no, you will not have another drink. Listen. Do you hear me . . . You drunken . . . you've got to pull yourself together . . . or you'll be put in prison . . ."

Sigbjørn half turns over and remains in an attitude on the edge of the bed where he could be pushed off with a little finger.

"I'm terribly glad to see you," he said. "It must have been dreadful."[2]

For this chapter believe it necessary to consult statement. Primrose won't let Sigbjørn drink but relents on a codeine: this, again, has a bad effect. Sigbjørn notes that Primrose has brought a bottle of habanero herself: all tenderness seems to have gone between them, and now Sigbjørn is more afraid of Primrose than of the immediate situation of which he is not even at once particularly curious. He even forgot to ask her if she had their papers. {UBC 14:1, 286}

"I didn't get to see the Consul. I just saw the Vice Consul. Eddie was in Taxco."

"Did you get the money from the bank?"

"The cheque was in the post then."[3]

"Yes."

"Why didn't you come straight back from Cuernavaca?"

"Abbarrotes advised me to go to the Consul."

"Did you go to the Immigration in Mex. City?"

"No."

"So you wouldn't have seen Tojo."

"I suppose we must have crossed."

"So you've really done nothing."

Another awful scene: heartbreaking and frightening.

"But you've got to pull yourself together. We've got to go and cash that cheque and pay the Hacienda."

"But I shall have to have a few judicious drinks first or I won't be able to sign my name."

"No you don't . . . Wait till afterwards."

"What'll be the good afterward?"

"You know, you promised never to let me down."

"And have I?"

"I don't know whether I'll ever get over this, whether I'll ever ever trust you again."

"But what have I done? I meant to meet you. But the Zapotecan didn't call me."

"The Zapotecan didn't call you because you were too stinking drunk to move!"

"I'll do my best," Sigbjørn said wearily. {UBC 14:1,287}

"Do your best! How I hate that phrase!"

"I'll even do my best to eat breakfast. I want you to be happy," Sigbjørn said hopelessly. "No one saw me drunk. Ah—women!"

Breakfast is a ghastly meal. Primrose is adamant about his not taking a drink after and her face closes even at the suggestion they get some more habanero.

"Haven't you got enough?"

"I've only got tequila. You don't want me to drink tequila," Sigbjørn said, who was beginning to feel like Dostoievsky's Marmeladov—and how he envied him his fate—if only a carriage would come out of nowhere and drive over him⁴—and yet what was he afraid of—signing a cheque, that was all.

"The Consul congratulates us on our papers," Primrose said.

"Oh, you got the papers," Sigbjørn said.

"The Consul said he'd never seen papers in better order."

"What about the Consul's own papers—did you see his ex equatur?"

"He was a tower of strength—" Primrose was saying, meaning "compared with you"—"I don't know what I'd have done without him."

"Never mind about the tower of strength, are you sure he wasn't simply a trouble shooter."

"He was the Vice-Consul."

"I thought as much. Then you didn't see the Consul at all?"

"The Consul was busy."

"Then you haven't gone to the Immigration. In fact, you haven't fixed anything."

The actual condition of things should here be stated—beginning with the fact that of course Sigbjørn has received the {UBC 14:1, 288} telegram from the Consul himself stating when Primrose would leave; that the Vice-Consul had transcribed every detail of the papers: previous to which it should be as well to follow events up to that time, after she has got back to the apartment:

—the bus ticket—Eddie in Taxco, she finds out at 1 P.M. after looking all morning trying to buy M. a ring but her poor market seems hard and foreboding and menacing—all these strange dark people and her Spanish fails her: talk with Chandler⁵—can't get money back on ticket—dash to house—to Turismo (all this Primrose is telling on the way down to the bus) the trip to Mexico—our old stone road the Tres Cumbres—In Mexico still can't get money back on bus ticket—trying to find Consulate in telephone book with radio blaring—find and hand shaking—

"You too," Sigbjørn observed.

"So much I couldn't write the address."

"Then why don't you relent?"

(They have gone down into Acapulco with the shopping bag by this time.)

"Perhaps you need one too."

"After."

She is telling him, but almost as if he wasn't there, about the taxi, to Consulate: wait in office: snippy clerk: but then Mr. Hughes: God bless him! the Hotel Canada:[6] walk back to get money on ticket— knees giving from fatigue . . .

"I can't bear it. Let's stop and have a beer."

"But don't you realise the spot we're in? You'll go to Prison unless we pay this fine. Just this once—just this once please, you've got to pull yourself together and not leave everything to me." {UBC 14:1, 289}

Sigbjørn has interrupted this by saying: "That's nothing to the spot we'll be in if I actually can't sign the cheque. I've never been in that position before I may say not even in the past. But this is more than a mere hangover I have. I simply wouldn't be able to sign my name."

"But you'll go to prison!"

"Let me go to prison. Maybe I'll have a little peace."

They go past the Beach Clots once more, averting their eyes from the Immigration, that also housed the Hacienda, and past the bank: it seemed a policeman was watching by the bank and followed them along the high sidewalk as far as El Ciclon. They got 2 litres of haba- nero: Sigbjørn was trembling and sweating and Madame Ciclon looks at him curiously. "Acapulco is a Paradise," said Madame Cic- lon. Primrose and Madame Cyclone have a ridiculous conversation about Acapulco being a paradise.

Then they go to look for the bank. Sigbjørn knows perfectly well where it is, but Primrose never notices such things, so he pilots her toward another darker bank where he felt he might just survive (perhaps because he knew he couldn't cash the cheque there and so wouldn't have to write anything) the ordeal, called the Commerce Bank, in an arcade that also sheltered the front of the wine shop where he'd broken the bottle that morning. In this place they pre- sent the cheque but are referred to the other bank.

Sigbjørn again suggests they have a beer; he knows he cannot sign his name: Primrose is adamant. Sigbjørn scarcely hears the rest of her story. The long long night in the room in the Hotel Canada— just like "our" room (first night in Mexico) but on the second floor and window giving on stone wall opposite alley like a sense of prison— {UBC 14:1, 290}

"Go on—or stop."

"Well, I read Time and there was this terrible noise. And the crowds in Mexico!—and all night the roar of accelerating motors down the Cinco de Mayo, which at dawn became increased till they overlapped and reverberated in the alley—"

They go into the bank, outside which Sigbjørn now notices the bad Turismo, he crosses the street and looks into the Beach Clots. There is a terrible scene in the bank. Describe Sigbjørn's absolute inability to make the pen move, even to make anything that even looks like a M,[7] let alone endorse the cheque.

Primrose stands by and simply curses him.

"My God, can't you even do this one little thing—" practically in hysterics, while sweat and tears roll down Sigbjørn's face in agony and the man stands by absolutely (?) quiet,[8] making a queer shining on one side.

"Sorry. Yo—ich—bin—estoy muy enfermo," Sigbjørn said. "Vamos por un médico y redonde."

The shrug.

"Paralysis agitans," Sigbjørn explained.

"Come on," hissed Primrose, "Come on and have your drink."

"Yo avait un poco paludismo,"[9] Sigbjørn stuttered to the man, completely broken.

They go out in silence.

"Well, that is the end," Sigbjørn said finally, looking round him and now remarking that the bad Turismo was going into the bank.

"Yes, that is the end."

"Now see what you've done," Sigbjørn said. "I told you. Now we'll never be able to get out of Mexico—even supposing they gave us permission. And even if we get out of Mexico I'll never {UBC 14:1, 291} be able to get into America."

"Well—why didn't you give me a joint bank account."

"I had to hang on to a little authority, old pal."

"You infantile pimp," Primrose said.

"Thank you. I think I will have that drink."

They go and have a beer at the place they'd been to when they first entered Acapulco. The floors are all wet. It is early, too early. A hell of a long time before the beer arrives. There is not much in the tankard and Sigbjørn spills most of it even with both hands. Primrose just sits and watches him in naked contempt, without having a drink.

Sigbjørn has several.

"Well, it's twelve o'clock and the bank will be shut. We won't be able to pay the 50 peso fine now so what are we going to do?"

"I thought I was going to prison. I'm rather looking forward to it. Anything would be preferable to this."

"Well—I've got 50 pesos, if you want to know, without cashing the cheque."

"How did you get it?"

"I borrowed it from Chandler. Or rather he offered it to me. It was he who had advised me to go to the Consul."

"Well, we don't need to cash the cheque then. All the same—I'll endorse it. I doubt whether I'll even be able to endorse it. I doubt whether I'll ever be able to go into a bank again. Or sign my name. Or do anything again."

"Except drink."

"It doesn't look to me I shall even be able to do that," said Sigbjørn, spilling more beer, even though he was using both hands {UBC 14:1, 292} still. "I doubt even if I shall be able to endorse this check back in no. 13."

"You said that before."

"Did I?"

There was, in Acapulco at this time, a beggar suffering from some kind of dreadful ague. He was dumb, stooped, and black. Describe him. He would go round all the bars in the morning picking up what he could get and then in the afternoon and so on. He shakes dreadfully all over. The man now appeared on the scene and stood shaking dreadfully by the table where Sigbjørn and Primrose were sitting, his shaking hand extended, waving, trembling.

"I'm going," Sigbjørn said.

"Where are you going? Are you going to abandon me again. Let me down again?"

"No, I'll meet you here in half an hour. I can't stand it. I've got to be alone. For God's sake, don't make a scene . . . There's the Turismo man watching. He's been watching all the time."

"Well, you've only got yourself to blame if you've given everyone the impression you've forged a cheque."

"Quite so—I'll see you in half an hour."

—It had been in Sigbjørn's mind to go to a cantina beyond the church, up a hill as it were—he would not quite be sure—it was up a hill, but on an eminence at any rate, and not far away, it was at the beginning of the road to Hornos, and was the first place where, eight years ago, he'd drunk his first mezcal. Instead of that, however, he went into the church.

The church, which had a huge white dome, was all smashed and broken or was being rebuilt. Stringers and uprooted planks lay all over the floor. Ladders, dust floating in rays of sunlight, {UBC 14:1, 293} wheelbarrows. People were praying, however, while Christ was being repaired. The Saint of Desperate and Dangerous Causes was there.

A pig went in with him and when he came out, the shaking man[10] was waiting for him.

Note for bank scene. When Dante speaks of the artist who "has the habit of art and a hand that trembles,"[11]

"C'ha l'abito dell'arte e man che trema," he makes it clear that art is less in the hand than in the head, less in execution than in intuition. Sigbjørn bitterly says this to the man in the bank when he can't sign the cheque.

The habit of art and a hand that trembles.

Mem also the Consul's That's the bit I like . . .[12]

Trembling man waiting outside perhaps.

From the Jesuit writer Gerald Walsh's book on Dante Alighieri {UBC 14:1, 294}

XVI

Saturday March 23 Cont'd

—Should be a description—a most accurate transcription of Sigbjørn's papers here—and if possible Primrose's too. It is conceivable this should have been done before: in fact, it would be very good if the whole book opened with it.

Scene opens with Primrose and Sigbjørn, on way to Hacienda, meeting Hudson to whom he hands papers: Sigbjørn, who after these few beers is in complete control, has meantime been wondering how it is, that the first day he has some proof of his identity, is the one when he can't sign his name: this incident has hurt him deeply, it is as if he had been saying to himself: "This is not me. It is they who have forced this on me." Sigbjørn knew that it was on the contrary God, and hence had to lay the blame on himself.

Hudson is coming out of the Fish Office and they go into the Immigration opposite: the eagle tearing the Nazi flag is still there, and the girl doing so and so—but it is quite empty.

Primrose says that she has seen the Consul—that they have the 50 pesos fine, and that the Consul has told them to get in touch with him if they are still held . . .

Hudson is considerably angry on their behalf, on the way to the Hacienda, down those undulating heartless hot white arcades, they encounter the pimply one who had threatened them with prison.

"Well, we have to pay this fine by 4 or my husband'll be put in prison."

"Let's take him along then."

"You can't be imprisoned for debt under the Mexican constitution. Or threatened with it." {UBC 14:1, 295}

"*He* certainly threatened. He raised a row at the hotel."

"And anyhow, the fine has already been paid once."

"How long ago?"

"Eight years."

Hudson explodes.

Meantime the pimply one is making his spiel and they go on into the Hacienda—it seems that their freedom is at least in sight and Primrose and Sigbjørn exchange a look of pure love and forgiveness: the incident is now taken up with the Chief of Hacienda, who stands up and is immensely courteous, in spite of the fact that he also has had smallpox.

Hudson now presents their case:

They have been held up for this fine, and what is more, their wristwatch has been taken as a pledge. The pimply man has no right to do this.

The Hacienda man, perplexed, and continually moving the position of a pencil on his papers, asks the pimply man if he has done this: the pimply man denies it.

"All right. Send for the good Turismo."

Hudson himself goes for the good Turismo: Sigbjørn waits: the pimply man waits: Tojo puts in an appearance behind, but Sigbjørn is so busy controlling himself he doesn't realise the significance of this, that Tojo has come back from Mexico City.

The good Turismo is simply good, corroborates everything that is said, and brings out the wristwatch. It was good to feel the wristwatch—symbol of pure love and charity—even though it had stopped. The latter was of little importance in Acapulco.

—A timeless heaven—they call it Paradise, but its name is Acapulco.[1] {UBC 14:1, 296}

Mention the number of counts on which the Mexican constitution has already been violated. At end of this, the Hacienda man says:

"Do you want to make a written complaint?"

The idea of making a written complaint—for the shakes would come back at any time—seemed such a final irony that Sigbjørn laughed as Primrose said:

"No—we just want to get out . . . We're writers (?) etc."[2]

Sigbjørn notices Tojo in the door: he is horrified at the idea of making a written complaint because he is afraid of breaking down again and not being able to write.

"No."

"Who went with you to Mexico City before?" asks the good Turismo.

"Guyou."

(Possibly a whole chapter every now and then should be given to the past, including one devoted to the trip with Guyou, Richard Rowe, Bousfield, the Biltmore.)

"Do you remember what hotel you stayed at?"

"The Biltmore."

"Even if you had not paid the fine—" the good Turismo, "it's doubtful if it's payable after eight years."

"Anyhow it's been paid now all over again. Because it is quite impossible that I should have left Mexico in 1938 if it had not.—Or been allowed to stay on longer then."

They go, after shaking hands with the Hacienda man—both Hudson and the good Turismo are now thoroughly on their side: Sigbjørn sees the bad Turismo standing near, and also a moment later catches sight of Judas. {UBC 14:1, 297}

"We'll go to the telegraph office and send a telegram now. Perhaps we can get your 50 pesos back too."

"You are a good man."

Hudson, still with the Wildernesses' papers, now goes into the adjoining Immigration, and explains how Primrose has gone to Mexico City, seen the Consul and returned, how the Consul had told them to wire him if they are still being held—can they go now? Tojo is not there, but the fat man says "No. We have to wait for our orders from Mexico City. They know nothing about you in Mexico City," he added.

(Margie must be consulted as to precisely how the land lies at this point.)

"Do you mean you haven't heard yet?"

He shrugs. "They are very slow."

"Well—we better wire the Consul immediately."

"You should wire the Consul. But it is no good now. Every thing will be shut. Come back mañana."

It was true, another Saturday had come round. Sigbjørn and Primrose again exchange a look of love, even though Judas is hanging about in the corridor, and even Raul from the Quinta Eulalia has just come in with a sheepish expression.

"Mañana is Sunday. You will be shut then. I thought you were shut on Saturday afternoon. Last Saturday afternoon they said you were always shut then."

"We are shut now," said the fat man. {UBC 14:1, 298}

XVII

Sunday March 24.

There should be, at this point, a subtle change in Primrose and in Sigbjørn: during the first week of their incarceration, before she went to Mexico City, they drank together companionably and without excess, but from the time she came back something seemed to have happened to Sigbjørn and from that time on until the very end when they were thrown in jail he was to her a stranger: then he became Sigbjørn again. Before she leaves for Mexico City there is a passionate warmth and love for Sigbjørn, between the time she comes back until they are in jail it is as if there is a glass wall,

Primrose feels, between them: and until then, it was as though Sig-bjørn had gone through a door and shut it. They didn't drink to-gether. Sigbjørn drank alone. Sometimes she drank too, but from that time on Sigbjørn drank alone.

The Wilderness now had 1500 pesos and their papers: if they were imprisoned in a sense, as has been said before, it was in Para-dise. You would have though they'd be happy, in a way.

Of course they were not, but they were endeavoring to be gallant.

Study how Ouspensky's remarks 196–197 Tertium Organum[1] have bearing on the situation.

"We do not know the world of causes, we are confined in the jail of the phenomenal world because we do not know how to discern where one ends and where the other begins.

We are in constant touch with the world of causes, we live in it, because our psyche and our incomprehensible function in the world are part of it or a reflection of it. But we do not {UBC 14:1, 299} see or know it because we either deny it—consider that *everything existing* is phenomenal and that nothing exists except the phenome-nal—or we recognize it, but try to comprehend it in the forms of the three-dimensional phenomenal world; or lastly, we search for it and find it not, because we lost our way amid the deceits and illusions of the *reflected* phenomenal world which we mistakenly accept for the noumenal world.

In this dwells the tragedy of our spiritual questing: *we do not know what we are searching for.* And the only method by which we can escape this tragedy consists in a preliminary *intellectual* defini-tion of the properties *of that for which we are in search.* Without such definitions, going merely by indefinite feelings, we shall not ap-proach the world of causes or else *we shall get lost on its border-land.*"

At all events, it is Sunday, and Sigbjørn has been possibly telling her the story of "Westward Ho!"[2] as before he has told her—up to the point where the Immigration officials arrive—the story of Tonio Kröger.[3]

We might plot the alcoholic situation here to some extent: the Wildernesses have as good as decided to go on a prolonged but con-trolled debauch (or Sigbjørn has)[4] punctuated with much exercise: they are going to stick to habanero however. One reason for this is that it is only under the influence of alcohol that the situation seems at all normal. Confronted coldly it seems like a dream. Since the latter they are more frozen from taking action—or Sigbjørn is—than in the former, they choose the former.

The problem of the shakes remains: and the problem of persecution, but Sigbjørn is curiously unbeset by any feeling of impending disaster. The impendingness of the disastar[5] had indeed {UBC 14:1, 300} reached such a pitch already that they live in it: they are wrapped in its sable cloak and so do not notice it. So familiar is it to them by now that it is scarcely more than the inevitability of death itself. It is the element in which they move. (N.B. This may be right for Sigbjørn but it is totally wrong for Primrose, who feels quite different about the whole thing.) Whether these contradictions be mentioned or no the scene in question involves Sigbjørn and Primrose lying on the beach—Primrose going on with her story—Sigbjørn listening—lying on his back with his eyes closed—

—She'd had breakfast at the little place near the Canada—dressing to go to the Consulate—and the walk through morning sunshine—looking at medals S. wanted in window—praying all the way—the Consulate—another wait—I (she)[6] read, or tried to some article on Gibraltar in some magazine I'll never know what it was and a review of a child's book. Then Mr. Hughes again and a dash to the bus station. I get my ticket and walk round the block distractedly waiting the half hour till 12—the bus is late and leaves at 12:30 but I'm on my way back to Sigbjørn—then outside Mexico the bus falters on a hill—parallel with the Appointment in Samarra breakdown[7]—we turn round and head back—wait at gas station until 3 o'clock—no phone—oh yes, but it is decompuesto[8]—driver uses phone—O.K. I call—Consulate closed—now we hail bus headed for Mexico, change and all get aboard again—Nobody seems particularly upset about delay—loathsome patience of Mexicans—but I am wild. Back over the Tres Cumbres and down to Cuernavaca, media hora for commida[9]—shall I forget commida which I don't want and dash for apartment for a toothbrush etc.—suppose I miss bus—finally eat a ham sandwich {UBC 14:1, 301} and drink limonada and then off again. Heat from here to Taxco is frightful. In seat beside chauffeur is Mexican army officer, very correct in tie and buttoned coat and cap. The sun pours in on him, he has shut the windshield and his window and there he sits and sleeps in the heat and roar and clattering and jouncing and jerking of the old bus. The fat man who is eating and drinking refrescoes all the way. The little dark Mexican and his American floozy. He has tried to help me at Mexico bus station and I am a bit snappy because I am so tired. At Iguala I apologise to him and the girl asks me to recommend a hotel in Acapulco. I am trying to think of a cheap one for them but it turns out they want an expensive one! At Chilpancingo they buy me beer. The damas—muy oscuro.[10] Sí, muy oscuro. No hay luz? Si, hay luz. Dónde? Ah, quién sabe.

(All this business of Primrose in Mexico might be presented objectively, in third person, then after a long while we would simply realise that Wilderness is listening to it, and unconsciously putting it into novelistic form.)

"Much dark," Primrose said.

"Yes, much dark."

"There's no light?"

"Yes, there is light."

"Where?"

"Ah—who knows?"

Since someone has said that genius lies in the power of analogies—might we not see many analogies here?

Does this not correspond horribly to the waiting for the gestation of a disease, years ago, and could he be *sure* even now? Had not that a further correspondence in his osteomyelitis? The {UBC 14:1, 302} Lost Week End?[11] for waiting for the money that never arrived here 8 years ago? for waiting—as both of them are—for news of their books? But did it not somehow recapitulate, especially on her side, all the errors and delays in relation to her work? Surely there were correspondences here—and these correspondences can likewise be tremendously dramatic.

Sigbjørn knows that, if he has shown seeming and even real cowardice, that he has real courage: for there is far more than enough to drive an even better than average man insane or to suicide. If he transcended—if he only lived to tell of it—might that not help some other trembling at the brink of some similar abyss. If he could do it another could—and if he could do it he would be furthering the cause of man himself, for few possessed such a mingling of stupidity and foresight, of genius, desperation, weakness and strength as Sigbjørn Wilderness. Mention the contradictions in his character. There can be marvellous counterpoint in this chapter, between the green Acapulco-Mexico guide book and the persecution scene . . .

(Use of green guide book[12] should provide separate problem, particularly titles Down to the Sea in Ships, Galleons, Pirates and Buccaneers, magic casements opening on the foam of fairy seas) Perhaps we will have a running commentary à la Ancient Mariner on the margin,[13] with the last chapter accompanied on the margin Here time stands still, and beauty marches on, while the traveller lingers reluctant to break the spell of so much loveliness. It sounds like heaven, but they call it Acapulco.)

Notes for persecution scene follow:

Malcolm notes: go to beach to swim after breakfast, feeling terrible, but bearing up after night of horror, feeling everyone {UBC 14:1, 303} is looking at us; ordeal of breakfast, the crisis of coffee— shall we speak to friend who offered us lift or not?—the feeling everyone in Acapulco is stool pigeon—after pre-breakfast swim, hurt because Host Schwab, also with usual morning shakes, doesn't return our good morning, note his breakfast was a piece of salami, papaya and 2 tumblers of wine taken in an alley, down to beach and sit on familiar log, Sunday morning crowd beginning to arrive suddenly—who should appear but our W. Baxter[14] and amigo bastardo of the Migración, so innocent with family, that at first I think he is going up to hotel to ask more questions presumably about whether I have been plasterando or not. But no, it turns out he is with his family of all things, leading little children by the hand like sentimentality and brutality coalescing reasonably enough by the Sunday morning sunlight, he has even brought chair for old man who may be his father but who is the sort of commissioner as it were of the beach with whom I have tried to change 50 pesos when (this 50 pesos now seemed to have an added significance) we were at Cordoba and who sits all day below Cordoba—if Baxter is in cahoots with him perhaps Cordoba is villain. Anyhow we prepare to have swim. I cannot take my eyes off Migración man (quite forgetting in a way it is Tojo who has now returned from Mexico—ev. of their minds wandering from situation) and in order to impress him swim several times out to sea to show him that anyone who swam so boldly could not be having the shakes under water which indeed, for inexplicable reasons, one was not. Return swimming inland to see Tojo, he sees me—cruelly imitates—or does he not?—drunken man stumbling on shore. Next time I look he is dandling child on knee and next time we look he is making sand castles for child. I met him swimming in water and he gave {UBC 14:1, 304} me a cheery smile. Meantime commissioner sits on a chair in the shade, other children are dandled and Tojo gets down to business of sandcastles and pies in earnest while we have many sweet Hartebeeste[15] swims. But I cannot keep eyes off him and he is too near the hotel already and I wish somehow to freeze him from getting any nearer. Sitting on log I see him in earnest conversation with another man to whom he seems to be describing our case. He ends up with many gestures ending up with a gesture as of throwing something out (deportation—mention terror at only too common word deportivos.)[16] Whole thing strikes us as wonderfully amusing, we feel sure Dostoievsky would have been delighted and actually have a very good time but even when I am swimming Margie out to sea to give her "feeling of safe" I cannot take my eyes off him. He has incidentally undressed publicly on the shore with his wife (she is fat) thus disobeying regulations. Having previously seen him talking and gesturing to a man in car I think I have seen in Immigration office, I have a sense of relief when I get to room and see from balcony that he is gone. We pass on balcony Schwab fast asleep. I look down and see he is gone, then it declines into amusement when we see him coming down from Pacifico loaded down with bottles of beer. We have wonderful afternoon on beach and see a bird called a digarilla, very beautiful and rare and large, tail like a swallow, black bat wings, long bill, white belly. Frigate bird. (end chapter on digarilla.)

Last night and this a.m. we see migrating birds heading north. Even birds have something to do with Migración.

Further note re wild geese.

Wild geese going north, against a tilted half-moon in the morning sky, manoeuvering for position, avoiding the governor's brother's house . . . {UBC 14:1, 305}

Margie notes re this day.

The ocean going jeep, the picnic party of gay Mexicans in launches, with much chatterings and laughing, arrive with lunch baskets and bags of bottles and set off. Return later—4 women very fat in scarlet bathing suits: much ugsome horseplay with coconut in water and snapshots. Earlier a man squirting wine into his mouth, head tilted back, from wineskin. They set off for Larqueta. Something noisy and at the same time as it were formal and also *Americanized* in these Mexican enjoyments made them seem indefinably offensive. On the other hand, the people seem carefree (They seemed also to be mocking at Wilderness: you see we can enjoy ourselves too, and without drinking like pigs, and all be back fresh at our beastly little desks tomorrow, to our beastly little duties, they seemed to be saying to him.)

Last night the flock of great proud wild geese flew low over the Quinta Eugenia, heading north. Today a smaller flock of smaller geese. They circle and circle our bay, gaining altitude changing formation and apparently getting their bearings. Then the leader (frightened by a plane, so that they fly back)

Held 10 days in Acapulco.

Give in this chapter various reasons for not confronting Baxter. {UBC 14:1, 306}

XVIII

Monday March 25–Monday April 1
(Mem: Monday: terrific difficulty of Sigbjørn trying to endorse cheque and Primrose cashing it. Even after he prays to Virgin cannot. Now he has had medal from Primrose)[1]

This week of agony is largely unrecorded, but it is punctuated by fantasies such as the following, the discovery of missing hairbrushes, and dark glasses, and Sigbjørn's attempts to put this tactfully for Primrose:

"J'ai perdu," Sigbjørn was rehearsing over the habanero, "un cepillo para la cabeza—une brosse (with gesture) de cheveux de ma chambre il y a quatre jours quand j'étais en Mexico—c'est une brosse irreplaceable—et j'en parle avec les femmes de chambre et elles disaient qu'elles connaissent rien: alors, un jour après mon retour je perdu mes spectacles noirs—c'est possible que je les ai oubliés sur la plage mais je pense que non. Les spectacles noirs sont bien et difficile a replacer. Après votre génerosité et la génerosité de tous en la Quinta Eulalia nous voulons à dire rien mais si c'est possible pour vous à parler avec les femmes de chambre avec discrétion j'en serais—" he added almost hysterically—"très obligé pour possiblement c'était une tentation insuperable. Je veux seulement leur retour. Les objets ne sont pas très valables mais sont seulement très utiles et avaient aussi une signigicance sentimentale—"[2]

The brushes and the glasses meantime turn up: but this kind of futile thing can be a counterpoint to their conversation which deals with their attempt again and again to cope with the situation—they must not give up—and this is resolved by their sending out a note to Madame José—Lady Me. {UBC 14:2, 307}

—C'est difficile à dire en français. Alors—Mais nous serions bien heureux si vous auriez—si vous voulez un cognac avec nous. Pardonnez-moi, le cognac n'est pas cognac, c'est habanero. Je pense aussi que c'est possible que le habanero n'est pas habanero. Malheureusement. Pero así es la vida. C'est la vie,"[3] said Sigbjørn.

Plan for day (this note possibly pertains here) After breakfast you go to town with money I shall draw from José, I meantime stay here having asked for bill; will await news from Consul either here or on the beach, taking the judicious snort. In town you will buy yourself whatever you want out of 45 pesos (this being what Sigbjørn has left on her return from Mexico) the other 5 being for supplies. Drop in at the Migración and that will head them off from coming here: but meanwhile I shall have got wire saying all is well as can be expected, on your return, failing the goggle, we will take a rowboat out to Larqueta, possibly taking gurgle with us. Complete solidarity between dear ducks. (I think the trip to Larqueta, on the cumbersome waterskis should be dramatised as still an attempt to make something out of their holiday, the difficulty of landing at Larqueta equal difficulty at getting away.)

Mon. Mar 26. Nothing. After cheque has been cashed usual trip to migración. This time see Togo.[4]

"Were those your children on the beach?" (attempting to be very matey and placate him.)[5]

"Yes, I had 3 but I lost one."

Sigbjørn, loathing him, was nonetheless moved: he too, this bloody swine, has had heartbreaking vigils, sorrows, deliriums. "And in Mexico you saw my case," he said. {UBC 14:2, 308}

Togo has seen another photograph of Sigbjørn: "with a beard."

"Yes, I had a beard. I was young and thought it funny to grow one."

Togo implies there is nothing to do but wait, also that the beard itself was serious. (My Consul also had a beard.)

"They said that they did not get my telegram," he said.

"Do you mean to tell me that when you got there they knew nothing at all about us?"

"Nada!"

"Well, can we go now?"

"I told the doctor that you had been here long enough and that you should go now because you hadn't very much money," he looked at Sigbjørn meaningly, "but he said No-don't-do-that." He shrugged. (shrug described.)

"What doctor?"

"Doctor Martinez."

"Is he head of the Immigration?" etc.

Sigbjørn said to himself that perhaps it would not be necessary to be deported in order to meet the extramundane demands of his punishment. (This phrasing is derived from Flaubert, Salammbô)[6] Like Flaubert's Matho, fearing, when tempted by Spendius, to steal the sacred veil of Tanit in Carthage, he did not go to the bottom of his thought, but stopped at the boundary, where it terrified him. More than that, he was afraid that if he dared to descend to the bottom of his thought, it would set the mechanism in motion that would bring the disastar then about.

They go home and have a goggle, but the water is clouded, and they can't see a thing. They go dismally to their room and drink habanero. {UBC 14:2, 309}

"The first week was brave and fine and full of courage but now we bicker and heckle constantly. You're fine. I'm foul," says Primrose.

"I'm bloody," says Sigbjørn.

But this leads to a quarrel, in which Sigbjørn blames her for bringing them to Mexico in the first place, reminds her of all the evil omens, the date they got the American passport, missing the plane, and so on: blames her whole impulse and reminds her that he has known it was a fatal thing all along to go back to Mexico.

"But you said you wanted to get those things right for your book."

"Said. I only came for your sake. And nobody'll take the book. Look what they said about it."

"Oh Sigbjørn—"

This leads to a gigantic quarrel, but they make up, decide to do something else about the matter: to meet it squarely, Sigbjørn knows that Primrose will think of human resource, but knowing that the situation is infernal, and himself only partly human, he has to resort either to divine providence or the dead.

(Note: it should be said somewhere in this book, perhaps at the beginning: Sigbjørn had been on this planet for so long that he had almost tricked himself into believing he was a human being. But this he felt with his deeper self not to be so or only partly so. He could not find his vision of the world in any books. He had never succeeded in discovering more than a superficial aspect of his sufferings or his aspirations. And though he had got into the habit of pretending that he thought like other people, this was far from being the case. It is thought that we made a great {UBC 14:2, 310} advance when we discovered that the world was round and not flat. But to Sigbjørn it was flat all right, but only a little bit of it, the arena of his own sufferings, would appear at a time. Nor could he visualize the thing going round, moving from west to east. He would view the great dipper as one might view an illuminated advertisement, as something fixed, although with childish wonder, and with thoughts in mind of his mother's diamonds. But he could not make anything move at that instant. The world would not be wheeling, nor the stars in their courses. Or when the sun came up over the hill in the morning, that was precisely what it did. He was non-human, subservient to different laws, even if upon the surface he was at best a good looking normal young man with rather formal manners.[7] How else explain moreover the continual painful conflict that went on between him and reality, even him and his clothes? Like a man who has been brought up by apes, or with gazelles, or among cannibals, he had acquired certain of their habits; he looked like a man, but there the resemblance ended. And if he shared some of their passions, he shared these equally with the animals. Describe The Getting Up of Sigbjørn Wilderness, in the complications, futility, complications with clothes, reality, etc. And yet, also, in his deepest self, he possessed aspirations that were neither animal, or, alas, any too commonly human. He wished to be physically strong, but not, strangely enough, in order to defeat people, but in order to be more practically compassionate. Compassion he valued above all things even though he saw the weakness in that desire. In fact anybody that said anything like this would immediately seem to be condemned for some sort of hypocrisy in his eyes just as he felt himself condemned at that moment. That weakness of self-pity {UBC 14:2, 311} he wished to correct too. He valued courtesy, tact, humour. But he wanted to find out how these could be put into practise in an uncorrupted form. But above all he valued loyalty—or something like loyalty, though in an extreme form—loyalty to oneself of course, not false loyalty of the patriotic nature, but loyalty to those one loved. And again he wanted true loyalty. Above all things perhaps he wanted to be loyal to Primrose in life. But the loyalty went much beyond that. He wanted to be loyal to her beyond life, and in whatever life there might be beyond. He wanted to be loyal to her beyond death too. In short, at the bottom of his chaos of a nature, he worshipped the virtues that the world seems long since to have dismissed as dull or simply good business or as not pertaining to reality at all. So that, as in his lower, so in his higher nature, he felt himself to be non-human too. And he was in general so tripped up by the complexities of his own nature that too often he exhibited no virtues whatsoever and all the vices, once glaring but now obscure, sins, that for all her victory, Prostestantism is responsible for rendering less deadly than they in fact are. And he had good cause—(cite some of the causes) Sigbjørn would also cite the good reasons he has for going mad here: (a) (b) (c) just like that. Some of this in dialogue and not necessarily in this chapter.)

They quarrel, but they decide that the next morning, they won't go to the Immigration at all, but just pretend they are on holiday, (meantime they are helpless, waiting for word from the Consul whom they have wired on Saturday, no reply) But next morning Primrose has a cold or a cough, and the morning passes miserably: but you feel they are making an effort still. {UBC 14:2, 312}

Miss Mandy, nice old lady who had previously given Primrose codeine for her cough, and told them about how bad all consulates are: "Why don't you write a story about a Consul."

"Ha ha," said Sigbjørn.

Miss Hill, the retired schoolteacher.

Wed:—to the Immigration again—no one is there or can be found. They have not had a drink up to this point to clear their heads perhaps, but they break down and go to El Ciclon.

Thurs: In magnificent scene of irony, punctuated with La Libertad advertisement Tojo phones Mexico City (on condition we will pay) are told that they know nothing of the case.

Fri Mar 29—a nightmarish day—Miss Hill has recommended Mr. Stallings—we go to Aca: to meet and talk to Miss Hill's friend Mr. Stallings. But just the agony of the great fish. Black dead and cancelled like dried fish. Great sail fish strung up on the wharf. Then Hotel La Marina porch. The appalling conversation with this American who is not interested, and the almost equally appalling avidity and morbid curiosity of Miss Hills. Sigbjørn here states the theme i.e. what has happened in the past re first wife etc. but Stallings interrupts him all the time, goes off at some idiotic tangent, this conversation should be dramatised. N.B. Champ in dialogue. The good Turista. The American who is being held—Baxter—who keeps talking about Champ (another note of past) and these robbers who take 1% of his import business and how he outsmarted them and giving us conspiratorial winks—they kill a guy here for 25 pesos and I ain't fooling—they're all crooks and thieves—that fat man, he held up a guy on that there yacht for near $500 the other night

—Baxter proves a friend of Stallings

a degenerate "Warner Baxter." {UBC 14:2, 313}

Sat. Mar 30—Pay telephone co for Baxter's call. Morning: phoning, drinking Saturno—the British Consul in Hotel Colonial, an ordeal, the whole thing dramatised. A great empty echoing place and phone on desk; no privacy. Immigration again and Tojo sends wire in A.M. (Chapter ends with scene on next page Lost Week End—so this latter part in the fair might be another chapter—we will call it tentatively XVIII A.)

That night, Saturday, we see 20 or 30 baby sharks all about a foot long dead or dying on the surf and beach. "Pobres."[8]

Sun. Mar 31. Usual Sunday inferno in the Paraiso. In late afternoon go with José and Lady Me to Acapulco, walk along wharf, memories of that day seems years before now when they saw the West Coast, walk along wharf, see Champ in La Marina, then drink beer and eat almegas. Again, the shaking man. Very good, then to mercado for more. Dark by now, flares burning and all the tiny shops and fondas with flares and candles and lamps. Mariachis singing on both sides and one in our tiny fonda—the night is warm with soft cool sea breeze—Primrose, Sigbjørn, José, and Lady me all talk in bad French. Feeling and fear the whole thing is going to burst out with a chaos of barbarous African revelry and cruelty like Salammbô. N.B. this is too close analogue to end of Chap I expressing the hatred of the Mexicans for Americans? The mercado is full of smells and darkness and flares and music and noises and color. Leaving, we meet an hombre who wants to make trouble but José says we speak no Inglese only French and Spanish—we are still and presently we leave, arm in arm, through dark streets back to bus.

"Es Peligroso—comprende?—peligroso," said José.

"Sí, es peligroso,"[9] Sigbjørn said. {UBC 14:2, 314}
Substance of telephone conversation in Hotel Colonial over the Saturno.

"Bueno . . . Bueno." Telephone handed to Sigbjørn.

"Bueno—" Begins from Sigbjørn's end, these are the points recorded in notebook, but intersperse the conversation with utter sense of dislocation he has talking with a Consul, when a Consul is his character, when a Consul is himself (also the telephone no. involved with the Consul's fate—Erikson)—[10]

(a) Thank you deeply for your sympathy and generous treatment to my wife. (Use Warren's technique of replies not in inverted commas)[11]

(b) Thanks also for not at all wiring me when my wife was in Mexico.

(c) I understood from her you would wire if anything went wrong.

(d) We have wired you twice but fear you have not received our wires, or if you have that something serious has happened at your end.

(e) Meantime we are still held.

Should be pointed out rent in apartment in Cuernavaca is still running on: anguish of this, they almost weep when they think of it.

"I said, we were still held."

"*What?*"

"H for hell. E for Elysium. L for Latrine. D for damnation."

—Have you been to the Migración? Have you seen them since Thursday?

. . . My wife understood you to say that if all was not well here we should wire you. We have wired you twice and received no reply.

. . . Last Thursday we persuaded the Immigration here to telephone {UBC 14:2, 315} the Immigration in Mexico City, where they said they knew nothing at all about the case and it seemed had never heard of us. They found the file and promised to look at it and wire. Still no word. We wired you, and no answer. I said, no answer.

"Well, do your best."

"We will" came, very faintly, the Lord Nelson England expects every man to do his duty voice.[12]

"We are going mad" Wilderness said.

"Going?" he heard Yvonne's[13] voice say.

"Muchas gracias, señor."

"De Nada."

They went out in the square where was both the shaking man and Judas. "Wilderness," he began.

"What's the matter with you. You look as though you swallowed Pat Murphy's goat[14] and the horns were sticking out of your arse," Sigbjørn said savagely.

This restores their sense of humour and Sigbjørn tells Primrose the actual story.

They went past the cinema toward the Cerveceria Bavaria. At the cinema however they were not still playing The Hour of the Truth. They were playing The Lost Week End.[15] {UBC 14:2, 316}

XIX

Monday April 1.

A.M. trip to Migración. Nada. Return to Quinta E. Disputable whether or no this trip should be made by Primrose or by them both together. Possibly by Primrose alone, to show Sigbjørn is beginning to crack. State of their health should be mentioned. Tension re letter from Consul. Wait. We have a goggle.

Tuesday April 2.

A.M. Trip to Migración. Nada. Return to Quinta E. Same problems re disposition of characters as on Monday. The sea was queer in A.M. We wondered why they had cleaned beach day before if expecting high tide for water has been right up to first low stone wall. (Tension increases in Sigbjørn's mind for the papers are full of communist scare in Canada, as well as the usual Tremendo Choque, Tremendo Siniestro. He is sure that if deported he will never get home. This is another important point.) On porch about 1 P.M. Sig-

bjørn suddenly shouts.[1] I run (these are Margie's notes). A long
wave has slid right up beach, washing over wall and nearly to road
at our end, sweeping away chairs, boats, surfboards, umbrellas. It
sweeps back, sucked out 30–40 feet behind low tide line, tearing
down beach with great speed until great rocks are exposed that
were always before 5 ft under water. A current like river in freshet
sweeps and boils around rocks beneath Quinta E in and out—
our log is gone (the poor log, last love symbol of their holiday)
people are chasing chairs in raging sea. Water is boiling and lines
of foam and sand make swirling patterns clearly seen from high
above. Boats and floats race past. A man standing on a board
seemed to be travelling about 30 m.p.h.: motorboats swung wildly
and swiftly at anchor or simply were being swept right out to sea.
{UBC 14:2, 317}

Everyone in Quinta E. is on balcony, jabbering excitedly.

Primrose: "Con frequencia?"

José: "No! No!"

Primrose: "You have seen this before?"

José: "Never!"

The sea again curls its lip right back and then overwhelming
crunches the beach with its sinisterly elongated jaws. All are excited
and gather on porch, looking at this wild scene far below, laughing
and as it were happy, though some cross themselves. At the height
of this phenomenon Raoul[2] delivers letter. But it is not from the
Consul but from his uncle Hootnanny[3] and reads as follows:

Dear Sigbjørn (Primrose reads)

This morning I was impressed to look up record of your I Ching
Divination[4] of September 1943, incorporated into Magical Record in
form of letter to you dated Sept. 26, 1943. Since this seems as if it
may have a bearing on your *further action* in a certain matter against
which I advised, I will therefore give you details and you must of
course use your judgement—

"What in the name of all that's wonderful is this?"

They remember and the letter is proceeded with. (Hootnanny's
relation to book)

I first quote from page 2 of my letter to you of Sept 26, 1943.

"Now the *second vision was obtained* by Sigbjørn from figure
XXIV the Fu Hexagram. This indicates that there will be free course
and progress. The subject finds "no one to distress him in his exits

and entrances, friends come to him, and no error is committed. He will *return* and repeat his (proper) course.

(When you were not satisfied and tried again you got your vision to do with Eagle, etc. and that *"repetition is blasphemous"* {UBC 14:2, 318}

(Now I will give you XXIV The Fu Hexagram, in detail. There is no telling how long a period is indicated following one of these divinations, they may work out in various ways for a long time.

"Fu indicates that there will be free course and progress (in what it denotes). (The subject of it) finds no one to distress him in his exits and entrances, friends come to him, and no error is committed. He will return and repeat his (proper) course. In seven days comes his return. There will be advantage in whatever direction movement is made."

That is the *general meaning of the full figure* and it is good and has worked out for your life ever since. At the very time of vision you kept trying and returning: then you went to Toronto and returned all right. Also in regard to rebuilding you returned to your job, and also, literally you did rebuild, if you did not finish your home. (Rewrite this bit) But the I Ching then goes on to show the meaning of each line making up the Hexagram, from bottom up, and the last section contains a warning. It may have been bad to repeat (or revisit) the scene of your book. I therefore quote:

(1) The first line, undivided, shows its subject returning (from an error) of no great extent, which would not proceed to anything requiring repentance. There will be great good fortune.

(2) The second line, divided, shows the admirable return (of its subject). There will be good fortune.

(3) The third line, divided, shows one who has made repeated returns. The position is perilous, but there will be no error.

(4) The fourth line, divided, shows its subject moving right in the centre (amongst those represented by the other divided lines) and yet returning alone (to his proper path). {UBC 14:2, 319}

(5) The fifth line, divided, shows the noble return of its subject. Three will be no ground for repentance.

(6) The topmost line, divided, shows its subject *all astray on the subject of returning*. There will be evil. There will be calamities and errors. If with *his views he puts the hosts in motion*, the end will be

a great defeat, whose *issues will extend to the ruler of the state. Even in ten years he will not be able to repair the disastar.*

This is a grave warning, I think, but it comes in time, and as the general meaning of the Hexagram is so good, and indicates that "no serious error is committed, from all this going and returning," I feel assured all will now be well, only I would not forget the implied error for trying to *repeat* experiences (actual words, perhaps better, if they can be made to make sense) and we may all have learned something of the error etc. I shall add this to the Magical Record. Yours with sincere affection, etc.[5] P.S. Let's not brood over ills of the past but go ON to a free and glorious future.

"April Fool," they both had the gallantry to say.

This reminds them of happy days, and it should be pointed out that, while this may seem hocus pocus to the ordinary person, it bears in part upon the most remarkable book in all the world's literature: perhaps they go outside: the tidal wave is rising higher and higher, the boats swinging wildly at their anchors, tide racing out beyond the rocks, describe and Raoul brings them yet another letter he'd forgotten to deliver or as Sigbjørn immediately suspects he had opened. It is marked O.H.M.S.[6] and reads as follows, the embossed lion and unicorn disputed for the crown over the following: {UBC 14:2, 320}

Consulado General

Airmail:
Britannica
26/52/15
Dear Sir:

In find on enquiry at the Secretaría de Gobernación that the Mexican authorities have decided to deport you. I therefore beg to enquire whether you have a reentry permit for the United States and tickets for your transportation.

Failing such permit or visa for the United States, it would be necessary to consider a destination in British territory.

Yours faithfully,
So and so.

H.B.M.—Consul-General.

As Sigbjørn stood there leaning over the parapet high above the ever rising lengthening wild reaches of the dark tides the only thing greater than his terror was his admiration for that daemon, who seeming to be standing higher still on yet some loftier point of vantage in a different dimension, seemed to be looking down on him as he had used the other Consul, a breathing figure of supernal prose, for some dark purpose of his own. (end of chapter.)

Note re sender for letter.

Not the least remarkable thing about Uncle Gwynn,[7] apart from his being his uncle, was that he had been a Brigadier General in the British Army. Retired after the first world war he had lived ever since in a place called East Sark, on Vancouver Island, a wild place, with extremely "poor communications," as he said, with the capital, Victoria, and even Sark itself, whither he was obliged to ride horse for supplies. But for such things as chicken wire—for he had a small farm at one time—he was dependent upon the game warden who owned a car. Badly wounded in the war. Lost his wife. {UBC 14:2, 321} Whenever he came over to the mainland, thought Sigbjørn and Primrose, it was as if he had hit town. They would row out to an island and discuss the cosmography of the world. He did not like most Brigadier Generals hold himself erect, but, tall, and incredibly well preserved, walking with a perpetual stoop, as if trying to avoid bumping his head on the roof of some raftered Welsh pub. For he was, like Henry V, a Welshman. The same could not be said so strictly of Sigbjørn and Sigbjørn's father both of whom had been born in England on the Welsh border. But Uncle Gwynn, his father's youngest brother, had in turn been brought up by his father's uncle in Anglesea and in fact, until he was fifteen, when he had gone to Uppingham, could not speak a word of English. His interest in retirement reflected the dark druidical traditions of his race but to Sigbjørn and Primrose they were a matter of amusement and the letter brought back happy days on the Inlet of sunbright and blue water and wine. The vision he referred to could not properly be called a vision at all but his remarks pertaining to an (in Sigbjørn's eyes, psychological, though so superstitious was he that at once began to believe in it) experiment, less childish than it first appeared, which they had all made after tea after such a picnic, the experiment being moreover, not at Uncle Gwynn's instigation, who was afraid of it, but at Primrose's. Sigbjørn's chief objection to such goings on was that in no respect could it be reconciled with the aesthetic. While willing to accept the fact that a mystic might be a higher type than a genius he nonetheless considered the two things irreconcilable and moreover in his opinion the one fatal to the other. The poetic diction of occultism was ruinous to the common usage timbre of prose. Simply as {UBC 14:2, 322} images they were, beyond a fatal point, fatal to poetry. In his estimation William Blake had been crushed in its giant machinery. And more pertinent than commonsense it seemed irreconcilable with intelligence itself and Uncle Gwynn, although a first rate mathematician and even military tactician, could not be said to be intelligent. It seemed impossible that he could not be, but there it was. Every time he came down from the heights his tastes were those of the vulgarest of the vulgar. But he was a very lovable gay fellow and a mnemonic of happy days for them both.[8] {UBC 14:2, 323}

XX

The only thing greater than his terror and misery was, as he looked down at the wildly racing ever rising tide, Sigbjørn's indecent admiration for the daemon, who from an even greater height, seemed to be looking down upon him, and, as if he were some unearthly novelist in some other dimension, somehow mercilessly causing all these dispositions of which he and Primrose, like characters in *his* book, were the victims. It was not so simple as that even. For it looked much as though Primrose were his, Sigbjørn's, victim. Psychologically he knew he might be causing the whole business himself: or if he were not—and Sigbjørn had a horrible suspicion that actually he was not—the psychological basis was the only safe one, it was as far as human knowledge had got anyway, from which to stem one's future course of action; the other way madness lay. For that matter petrified with fear though he was his mind had gone so far the other way that he might be said to be involved with madness. What significance did Consul have, qua Consul, for example? Imagination did not boggle, reason did not stand still, at the thought: they fled into holes in the ground, they abandoned the field altogether, and left it to the devil. To make matters worse Sigbjørn, while not understanding Uncle Gwynn's letter, was convinced in a flash it was probably the truth. It had indeed to him more significance than the Consul's letter. What were all those choices? What did it say about free will? Dark things may happen to those in the Lion,[1] on the other hand they can, with will, triumph. But what was will? Any fool knew—even if every philosopher from Pica de Mirandola to Keyserling had not so—or ought to know that it was involved with desire. But Swedenborg's dictum was enough. When a man is in evils {UBC 14:3, 324} he is in the love of them.[2] Was Sigbjørn in evils? Was he in the love of them? To some extent, to the extent of drink at any rate he was, they both were. Or was that itself common sense? Goethe himself could have advised no better course [than] that they numb their minds to some extent, go on a prolonged debauch.[3] That they were both on one gave it an extra Jamesian turn of the screw.[4] That his whole life work had been involved with the problem gave it another. What had happened? Perhaps the answer was to be found in Yeats' Vision but then he could not in spite of repeated attempts in the past, understand Yeats' Vision. And Uncle Gwynn had refused to interpret it for him—not wishing to involve himself with another system.[5] Cones vaguely interpenetrated, tumescent like colored expanding concentric circles in a drug store, destiny came and went, and a man bounced out of one phase into another, and the moon solemnly circled after the whole bolus. Perhaps Sigbjørn was in the phase of the hunchback.[6] Or one more terrible still. Far, far more terrible. But Sigbjørn had forgotten God. He had forgotten the Virgin Mary, the Mother of Mexico. He had even forgotten the dead, Juan Fernando. To Sigbjørn's mind the most terrible remark ever made in history had been made by one of his country's own kings: God has deprived me of what I most love; I will deprive him of what he most loves in me![7]

Since Sigbjørn had not, to any observer, lost anything whatever he did not understand quite why he said this aloud: and as for his being deprived of what he most loved, or at least at that moment, he went back into room 13, drank 4 double brandies in as many minutes and had as many showers, one after another, before speaking a single word. {UBC 14:3, 325}

"What shall we do?"

"Drink!" Sigbjørn said.

"I am."

"We'll have to stand fast."

"Oh yes."

"What's going to come out of it all?"

Since it seemed to Sigbjørn at that moment that the only thing that could come out of it was his own death, either by murder or suicide, or by some other unique distortion in the general pattern, he said nothing for a minute: then still towelling himself vigorously he remarked:

"The Consul's letter is illogical."

"Quite!" said Primrose.

"Or at least it is on the basis of what you told me. You said that the Vice-Consul had transcribed all our papers, taken them down in detail, and that he had never seen papers in better order. Since it is abundantly clear in those papers that I have a reentry permit for the United States, and a visa, how could the Consul-General possibly ask such a question, if he had seen the Vice-Consul's transcription in the first place?"

"Then the answer is that he hasn't seen them."

"And the answer is that we've been let down."

"Quite," Primrose said again.

"By me?" Sigbjørn said. "For if I had seen the Consul personally perhaps none of this would have happened."

"Have you the nerve to tell *me* I didn't do everything possible?"

"At least you should not have left Mexico City until the whole thing was settled." {UBC 14:3, 326}

"But it couldn't be settled without money, without paying the mordida, and I didn't have money, I couldn't cash your check."

"You could have seen to it that the Consul or the Vice Consul fixed it up. And you could have got the Consul to lend you money on the strength of the cheque. It was his duty not to let you down."

"Then why didn't you go and see him yourself. I'm not English."

"They would have imprisoned you here. And if I'd left it would have incriminated José here. It would have been a breach of faith with them."

"You mean you thought more of their feelings than of mine. It's always that way."

"In a case like this it's a private matter of honour."

"Honour. Honour! If you'd have had any honour you'd have escaped to Mexico City, fixed it up yourself and been back before anyone was the wiser. To let me make that trip by myself, and then talk of *honour*—"

"It's a port of entry. They keep a check up at the bus station."

"What would you care if you'd been a man. You could have given a false name."

"They were on the lookout for precisely that. Probably they would have shot me out of hand. And you would not have liked that."

Primrose began to cry.[8] "Well then, why didn't you phone?"

"But I did, I did phone. Yesterday. The day before yesterday. In the Colonial. Can you have forgotten?"

"But before."

Sigbjørn poured another habanero for them both.

"Primrose," he said. "Darling. My God, this is complicated. Do you understand fear? Not the normal kind of fear, not fear of death, not terror such as you might feel rock climbing, when you {UBC 14:3, 327} lose your handhold, not even like the terror you feel in nightmares, or in war, or of drowning, or even of being tortured, or of anything else at all, which is bad enough: I mean something infinitely worse than that."

"What do you mean? Are you afraid of a British Consul who probably means well just because you once wrote a book about one?"

"No, I mean something like fear of myself. Terror of myself."

"That's still fear. It still means you're just afraid."

"I mean fear of any *action* I may take. I believe that that's why so much has been left to you."

"How do you mean why?"

"Some spirit of preservation of your and ourselves and our love dictates it because I find myself in a position where something seems to be telling me any positive action I may take whatsoever, especially if it has to do with British Consuls, may prove fatal. But if it comes to that the situation is already fatal. Even you can't make it any worse. And even I cannot."

"That's very courageous of you to say *that* to me."

"Isn't it. Don't think I don't despise myself for saying it."

"You might tell me what you consider so absolutely fatal—while I grant that it's highly unpleasant—" said Primrose "about being deported. Especially from Mexico, which is widely known as the most corrupt country in the world."

"Not so widely known as it should be," Sigbjørn said, "though by now we're almost willing to be parties to its corruption."

"Are you?"

"If you mean am I going to pay a bloody cent to these swine after all they've already done, no."

"I like to hear you talk like that rather better." {UBC 14:3, 328}

"Though you may say it's my Scotch soul."

"I thought you were Welsh," Primrose said. "But you still haven't answered my question."

"What question?"

"What is so finally and dreadfully horrible—fatal as you say—about being deported?"

"Well, it's a disgrace."

"Pardon me if I laugh."

"It's a dishonour."

"—!"

"It makes me feel as though I were being excommunicated."

"That's not it."

"No."

"No."

"But you know."

"Do I? Then what is it?"

"I don't know."

"Yes you do. Though I admire you for not saying it," Primrose said. "But my father was an American Consul and I do know. You cannot be deported to American territory. It's a contradiction in terms, whatever they say. They won't even give you a transit visa back to Canada, especially since you have that "public charge" business against you, when you were trying to get to see me at the beginning of the war. Consequently they'll send you back to England[9] wherever they deport you from, which will probably be a place without a British Consul, and in the interim we'll be separated. And that's what you fear."

"Too true. But the excommunication feeling is still true, even though I'm not a Catholic. It would be like being deported {UBC 14:3, 329} from God, even if for God's ends."

"And especially since they suspect that you're a communist because of that other business. That makes it worse for you in America than here."

"And worse still in Canada. At the moment. With this spy scare."

"By the way, you were not a communist, were you?"

"No. And the atom bomb. And all this is the atom bomb."

"What?"

"All this outside etc."

"Consequently we have a tough time ahead of us. But what matters is not what we do, but our attitude toward it."

"So we better hit on another plan of campaign. We can try. We could drink less—and think more."

"That won't do any good at all for once. For once we seem to be thriving on it."

"But the problem will raise its ugly head again, sooner or later, from your point of view."

"I promise not to be a bitch. We have to be careful not to go mad too."

"I promise to try. In all senses of the word. We'll pull through. We better take stock though. Swear fealty."

"I swear."

"Well, for one thing they'll let us go home *here* at least."[10]

From here on notes:

After Consul's letter. Madness! S. takes showers, one after the other. We decide to phone but Erikson is closed[11] until 4 P.M. We rally and eat dinner—how? At dinner people are talking about the atom bomb. Somehow experiments with that, they say, are {UBC 14:3, 330} causing the strange disturbances: this connects up with the Canadian spy business and adds to Sigbjørn's torment: but they draw on their sense of humour.

The day is ghastly hot, and for the first time no breeze. Brassy sun and glassy sky, palm trees beyond porch are as though carved from stone: earthquake weather: keeping up a gay front: Hill and Moody: after comida to Aca. and phone: this should be a terrifically dramatic scene, the telephone hombre is one of Baxters' best friends, Primrose phones first, and does not improve matters by bawling the Consul out; Rogers is not there—Hughes does not remember Primrose telling him about Guyou; appalling hot in the phone booth and Sigbjørn is drenched with sweat: he goes on and on about Oaxaca, and so on: why hasn't he wired. He'll try again and wire. Will he? We will, the Nelson voice. But surely the Migración has already informed you! No. (This should be dramatised like the other conversation and balance it.)

We go to Migración, to Baxter, Sigbjørn turns thumbs down as soon as he sees him but Baxter shakes his head.

"You mean you haven't heard?" (about deportation.)

"Nada. Possibly mañana."

"But at any rate we can go now to Cuernavaca."

"No—he say don't do that."

"But he said they knew nothing about our case." Baxter shrugs his shoulders (it is too late to pay him mordida now) and on the wall the Mexican eagle goes on eating the Nazi flag. {UBC 14:3, 331}

XXI

Wednesday April 3

Yet for all that these two people had the guts to get up before breakfast and go for a swim.

The sea hedgehog on the beach: as well as the hosts of baby sharks. It (the former) seems still alive, Sigbjørn does not want it to drown, so he takes it into deep water.

Still no breeze and very hot: tide wild: this time Primrose goes into town alone. Maddeningly, Togo says to her:

"Why don't *you* go to Mexico and see the Consul."

"But I did," almost shrieks, but quietly, Primrose.

"Oh, you *saw* the Consul."

He fusses around with papers: "I had a message, I thought saying you could go. But it is another fellow. You are Clarence," he said to Sigbjørn.

"Yes."

Sigbjørn again wonders if he is going mad: mention the diabolical coincidence of Clarence Hoover. Anatomise this: his own first name, Mary Hoover's last, best man, etc.[1]

They return: But in spite of the coincidence maybe they can go to Mexico City with Togo and Clarence Hoover: but why oh why hadn't they thought of paying Togo before and going with him?

To go or not Togo:[2] but the apartment, the rent running on and on: Primrose must go to Cuernavaca.

The sea is still wild and strange, but they pull themselves together yet once again: Sigbjørn asserts himself with some of his old determination that she will get something out of her holiday: they get the floating ski—than which nothing could have been more inaccurately named—and with enormous difficulty {UBC 14:3, 332} in getting off row to Larqueta: difficulty in landing: here the difficulty is in getting off again, with every wash the heavy iron contraption is swept further up the shore, but is so heavy it takes two men to lift it. Primrose could not help because of her insides, and Sigbjørn, strong as he was, could not shift the unwieldy thing, which could not be in any sense pushed, but weighing several hundred pounds, had to be lifted bodily, lifted. The lighthouse is up there beyond a cliff of nondescript bushes. Sigbjørn remembers going there before with Bousfield and also Wynn, whom he had helped. And yet that generosity, it seemed, was not going to pay off. (This wretched contraption, the water ski, seemed somehow odiously symbolical too: for it was as if indeed they were adrift on a rough unreal sea in some craft that was, like the giant waterski, without precedent, neither one thing nor the other, yet which was half awash, and from which it was impossible to land, or if, having landed, impossible to refloat again.)

They talk on the way, they have a lemonade bottle full of watered habanero, it is quite like old times: every now and then the spectre falls on their spirits but they are quite happy.

The power plant motor that starts up each evening like a ship's engine.

The negro boy who sleeps and sits outside our door with eternal comic magazine which he can't read.

The mysterious flares of fishing boats in the water before dawn seen from tower or porch. Scorpio and the milky way. Still can't find the Southern Cross. {UBC 14:3, 333}

Sigbjørn lies awake, feeling he is someone whose life obeys different diabolical laws to others. The sea is wildly rough, and the moon, which is still in its first quarter (last) had not yet risen.

That night Sigbjørn made his will and went down on a sudden impulse to drown himself. {UBC 14:3, 334}

XXII

Yet in spite of this they went down for their morning swim as usual.

Sigbjørn has gone for his old 1938[1] swim and as soon as he had begun to swim, his courage reasserted itself: it is terribly difficult for a strong swimmer to drown himself, but the sea was so rough and the currents so strong, even after he had made his mind not to, he almost did: but it was not the desire to live for himself that reasserted itself. (This is not quite believable or honest.) When he landed way round on the Caletilla side he wanted to drown himself as much as ever. And though he was now sober and chilly, his feeling had not changed. But courage of another sort had sprung out of his skill and his battle with the elements. Perhaps he decided to live simply because he could not leave Primrose here simply because it was a dirty trick. The pathos of her situation was one he could not stand. But as he battled for shore a terrific desire for mere revenge came over him. And how better can you avenge yourself than writing about it, a voice kept saying in his ear. It was the voice of the daemon, who also seemed to be saying: and besides, I can't kill you off old boy, because I half like you by now, I thought you would have gone off your head by now, but you've fooled me by your endurance, such as it is—and endurance is certainly how it appears to me—and I've half a mind to make you both triumphant after all. Go back upstairs and have a drink, as if nothing had happened. He stubbed his toe on something on the beach: it was a pencil and he took it up with him.

Sigbjørn had done this: Primrose, who had been rather tight the previous night, did not wake. Sigbjørn did not have a good {UBC 14:3, 335} night. Quietly but steadily and in the dark he drank nearly the whole night through. But not even in his book about alcohol had Sigbjørn imagined anything like this. His feelings were not in the book. In one way he seemed utterly and completely to be mastered by alcohol. He was drinking not two quarts but nearly two litres[2] a day. Deliriums gnattered continually, waking or sleeping, only just below the surface of his mind. Everywhere were half formed visions, hallucinations, voices. And yet here he was (it was true because he was still tight) shaving without a tremor, here he was going down for a swim—and somebody even had greeted him:

"Hullo there—Wilderness. God, you're looking well. I guess you're laying off that old habanero."

And even Primrose, who was herself in bad shape, took courage from his appearance and they breakfasted heartily.

So in another it appeared to him that he had mastered alcohol too: it was equally subservient to him. King Alcohol and he shared the throne that looked, like King Stephen's, down on this rabbit warren of the past.[3] He knew it was all wrong: but that was how he felt. The morning after he had tried to commit suicide he felt better than [he] ever had in his life. But after breakfast he was so sleepy he could not get to town. He lay flat on the bed, saying:

"You go to town, once more, Primrose—but this time for God's sake buy yourself something. If you have to see the Immigration tell them I don't think they—or Tojo is not—(whatever I really think) we have to be hypocritical—is at fault. But somebody clearly is. A situation has been evolved by the Government in Mexico City whereby by force majeure we are in default in {UBC 14:3, 336} in Cuernavaca. A man has a right to object to his wife travelling alone in Mexico—"

"But I've *been* to Cuernavaca—"[4]

"—and this is one source of my argument: it should be taken up, together with other injustices, with the Turismo, later in Mexico City. You anyhow must go to Cuernavaca, so get hold of the Champ at the Marina—bring him here, if necessary."

"The situation at Migración re American or whoever going to Mexico may let you down."

"The British consulate already has done that, so far as I can see; since the Vice-Consul has contradicted the consul General, we'll take this up later in detail."

Sigbjørn was rambling: his words did not make sense: this was delirium itself, he was almost asleep.

"Meantime," he heard himself say, "they are morally involving ley fuga,[5] or something—hell, the whole thing is an international abrogation of human rights, but what is more important, another violation of the Mexican constitution—What am I saying? Violation of constitution that's right. But who gave a damn whether the constitution was violated or not." Sigbjørn sat up: "Another potent point: The Consul General implies in his letter that we have no home to return to—"

"That's true too" sobbed Primrose. "Our poor little home."

"It isn't true—there's not a word of truth in it. He should have taken all these matters into account with Hughes, for it puts us into the false position of having come to Mexico with the idea of making *it* our home . . . Doesn't it, Primrose?"

He had not seen her go. {UBC 14:3, 337}[6]

XXIII

Thursday April 4

"Well, we'll start all over again," said Sigbjørn. "We'll try a different plan of attack."

It was the next day, and the sun was rising, neither of them had slept.

"We'll go back to our old discipline. I haven't had a drink in 20 hours. And even if it's torture I guess I can stand it another 20. Twenty minutes anyway."

"But I can't, Sigbjørn. I'm cracking up." Primrose sobbed. "Maybe I need a drink myself."

"All right. You shall have one. But I won't. How's that? We'll reverse the process. *You* have a drink and *I'll* suffer. Then we'll go down—and have—ha ha—"

"Ha ha."

"Our morning swim. And then we'll go down to the Immigration again. Or if you like, I'll go."

"No, I'll come with you. I'm loyal."

"Is that a dirty crack?"

"No."

"God, how utterly good you are."

They feel low, but cling together. The bus waits and waits at Caletilla till they think they are going mad. To make matters worse they cannot stand up properly. They are bent together under the roof in the sweltering heat. The extremity of this physical and mental torture makes them laugh. On the way they pray to the Saint of Dangerous and Desperate Causes. Will you help me, a descendant of the burner of Catholics and Huguenots. Please include us in your infinite mercy since we cannot change our religion of {UBC 14:4, 338} our fathers without spiritual treason, without disobeying your laws.

Why didn't more people think of this, too? Was not this equally true for communists, for most denominations indeed that were not based upon a fundamental abrogation of those laws of humanity to which man knew somehow in his higher self God gave his assent.[1]

Point is Togo now lets them go: they go and have a beer at the pub where they had their first beer in Aca. etc.

The heat in town is worse than usual. To Migración. Togo and fat fellow are talking, there are bottles of parras or something on the table. They pay no attention while they stand there. (In notes it is Margie who went alone, so we should play with the idea of having Primrose go alone, while Sigbjørn is doing something else, possibly going to the Ciclon.)

They go on and on talking, then say they have no news yet, but will they come back in an hour: perhaps we will let you go but they must see.

So they go out, with a kind of renewed hope, and drink beer at Bohemia, in spite of Sigbjørn's resolution, still, it is only beer.

At one point Sigbjørn should suddenly see their life like a battle: a kind of Agincourt, or another battle of Britain—perhaps the strongest point in their favour is that the enemy is so heavily armored, and their forces are so pathetically few, and yet if they won Sigbjørn cannot help feeling that it would be likewise a victory for God.

"What's wrong with us?" they ask each other. They decide it is the burned house: they have never accepted it, they have never got over it, perhaps there was something neither had forgiven the other, but it was after that their love had taken a wrong turning. After their conversation each feels a need to be alone: or it is decided between them that it is senseless for both of them {UBC 14:4, 339} to go to Migración. Primrose has some shopping to do so she stays and Sigbjørn goes back to the hotel.

Togo and Fat Fellow are still talking when she goes back and pay no attention to her while she stands there.

Then Togo says they can go tomorrow—he has had no word but will give them paper allowing them 2 or 3 days to go to Mexico.

—Why not 2 weeks ago? I cannot make reservations at Estrella d'Oro because they won't refund 30 pesos and I don't trust Migración. S. is miles out at sea when I return but finally sees me and waves. I go to room—maid is cleaning and we sit on porch while I tell news. We dance in room. Swim. Miss Monta says: "Why don't you write a story about a British Consul?" Perhaps the Virgin whose medal I bought for S. has helped.

Note: Technique of this chapter is still very uncertain. Perhaps it should definitely be through Primrose's eyes, i.e. Sig. has stayed behind. In which case it should be altered considerably, their conversation in the cantina would have to be omitted, though the matter is elsewhere fairly much the same.

But Sigbjørn was pleased with his medal for other reasons too. Perhaps people would think it some kind of military identification disk. Or even a medal for valor. {UBC 14:4, 340}

XXIV

Friday April 5

They go to Migración again, keeping their appointment, and God help Mexico, they again tell them to come back in the afternoon, however it is with a virtual promise that they will be given the paper. (Occasional characters like the good Turismo should flicker by with shocked cries of: Still here! etc.)

This fact is very interesting and should be stressed as having direct bearing on the pattern and *attenuation* of the situation as also of the whole book, for when the scene shifts to Cuernavaca, there are the same shiftings back and forth between the former and Mexico City: absolutely no consideration is given to the inconvenience the two must suffer and it is difficult not to believe it is not deliberate, or caused by the assumption, well, they must have a car, being Americans, it won't hurt them: but if this deliberate torture is interesting as being a condemnation of Mexico it is even more so in its bearing on the working out of a destiny or punishment: (considerable reading and thought will have to be indulged in before this becomes clear) the oscillations, the swingings of the pendulum grow longer and wilder, the suspense more awful, as whoever guides the destiny of these two protagonists, waits for the act of will, or desire, that can alone get the mechanism working in a constructive way of them: perhaps it is also something like the distance between subject and object getting wider and wider: and again it is like the repetitions and repetitions and repetitions of experience in theosophy that have to be endured, and which become more and more bitter each succeeding time that the lesson is not learnt. In fact, the distance is *much greater* from Cuernavaca to Mex. City: {UBC 14:4, 341} but there is a very analogous difficulty in the shift: the climate is different in each, and each time they move down from the sea air of the Quinta Eulalia into the sweltering town they feel it is going to be their last.

This time it is almost ultimate in its horror: Togo is round the corner or somewhere:[1] Primrose stays behind in the office while Sigbjørn goes to look for him; a scene of delirious horror, which is crowned by their (and they know it is their last day in Aca) meeting again the black shaking man, the bad turismo, and, above all, on the bus, the evil looking Judas whom they think betrayed them: Judas—who is very drunk—hails Sigbjørn.

"Hullo, Wilderness"—then "Riley is here."

"Oh? How is he?"

Judas' friend says: "Riley is dead."

Judas: "No, that's a joke."

Sigbjørn: "Is Mrs. Riley here?"

Judas: "Peggy. No—not here." He makes a gesture as of cutting with 2 fingers, grinning maliciously. "Divorce."

Sigbjørn suffers: has he been responsible? Is he being punished for this? To make matters more diabolical, the bus stops, for five minutes, for some reason in front of a house (place where, on the map).

Sig: "Riley is living here, in Acapulco?"

Judas: "Yes."

Sig: "Where?"

Judas: "In this house. (House is described) You want to go and see him now?"

Sig: (shattered) "No. (though undoubtedly Riley would be able to help) But remember me to him kindly should you ever see him. {UBC 14:4, 342} He was very good to me." (S's remark here might be better)

Judas grins cynically.

Going up the hill—they get out of the back of the bus, leaving Judas in it—Sigbjørn says:

"Oh god of battles! steel my soldiers' hearts!" said Sigbjørn.

(Possess them not with fear; take from them now

The sense of reckoning, if the opposed numbers
Pluck their hearts from them) Not today, Oh Lord,
Oh, not today, think not upon the fault
My father made in compassing the crown . . ."[2]
"Why not today?" Primrose asks.
"Tomorrow then," Sigbjørn said. "It seems that we didn't speak to God early enough about today."
They had been held 22 days in Acapulco. {UBC 14:4, 343}

XXV

Friday April 5–Saturday April 6

That night Sigbjørn and Primrose Wilderness left Acapulco by bus for Cuernavaca. They had with them their papers and a letter from the Migración in Acapulco to the Department of Migración in Mexico City, to be presented in the capital within 3 days.

The parting described—going by El Ciclon. Something tremendous about these departures at night. Everything goes on schedule. Everyone is honest. The drivers are marvellous. But there is a sense of drama that pertains nowhere else in the world. Each of these departures at night is as solemn as a send off to the North Pole. The huge bus looks sealed, dignified, mighty. It sets off and soon, the Star of Gold[1] is travelling at an enormous speed.

How different to all previous trips back to Cuernavaca. He thinks of those others 8 years ago, and the relationship of this to the past: there are silly American girls (perhaps use some of the dialogue Margie had on Canadian buses?) on the bus, Sigbjørn gives one his coat. Primrose is v unhappy. Sigbjørn has a lemonade bottle full of habanero and sleeps the whole way, save for five minutes almost sleepwalking in Iguala, looking for a lavatory. He is as if sealed, waxed, encased, within the horror of the situation: he is enclosed in it as if in a coffin that was flying through the night; and flying they seemed to be.

He opened one eye and yet indeed they did seem to be flying: they were whizzing, flying through Taxco, actually bypassing it altogether: the shape of the cathedral where Hart Crane rang the {UBC 14:4, 344} sad church bells[2] could barely be made out, and memories of

Tecalpulco and the devil and the poor hopes of their trip vanished astern forever in their wake.

Catastrophes crashed past, threats glimmered in the hills,[3] madness rose over the mountains of damnation and fled with them.

The great bus thundered on through the night.

They reach Cuernavaca at 5 A.M. and get out by the cathedral.

Very dark walk home. They could not see each other's faces. Dark, dark walls. Like two little pilgrims, hand in hand,[4] with such feelings of pathos and terror and remorse and half stifled hope, they crept back into the dark tower of Sigbjørn's dream. {UBC 14:4, 345}

XXVI

Saturday April 6

When Sigbjørn wakes one of Cuernavaca's most bloody minded heartbreaking sunsets is in full swing across the horizon: enfilades of intolerable purple passages were strung together across the sky: a sadistic sunset, suggesting feasts, and royal gowns and blood and burning elephants, exactly like 3 pages of Salammbo read on an empty stomach.[1]

But the cathedral was etched, sad, against the sky: and the arcade of Cortez' palace, with a few figures, looked soft and beautiful, the figures on the mural almost indistinguishable from the real human beings.

In one of the rooms of the tower, of which he had written, the one that now had the chevron shaped windows, though these had been taken out, the room of Chapter VII,[2] Sigbjørn stood a moment. Where was Primrose? There is a crimson stained glass window that takes the upper half of both windows in this room and seen through these the sunset had a lurid quality beyond all description, that is to say beyond Sigbjørn's ambition to describe.

Suddenly Primrose comes in and tells him of the news from Cape.

Sigbjørn can't take that—he looks down and sees the little postman of his chap VI[3] (who had brought the news too late, leaving).

"But I see the postman's late. He's only just been. Did it come by this post?"

"No, it must have come by the early one. It was in the box when I went down."

"Aren't you happy?"

"No . . . I haven't assimilated it." {UBC 14:4, 346}

"Look, I've got an idea, let's go to Eddie's, but first let's have a drink."

"You've got a drink!"

She had been to the market and got a drink.

According to way I'm thinking at this moment: Primrose and Sigbjørn should then go out, and superstitiously avoid going down to the postbox again, and then walk up to Eddie's and tell him the news: they decide to drink, go down to his house, and get the news of the acceptance in America, but I think the way suggested by the notes is better: i.e.:

Sigbjørn wakes at midday, Primrose is not there, he hears the chumbling and commotion of the termites, outside is the old bougainvillea, with the old man beneath it, and the boy chasing the dashund—"Siggie, Siggie—"

A slight description of the room, still in the disorder they'd left it before going to Acapulco—before, as once it had been "before the fire," now it was "before Acapulco."

Suddenly Primrose bursts in: "Cape's taken your book!—" There is the contract, incomprehensible. Get passages from Innes Rose.[4] Sigbjørn's reaction is as on p. 1:[5] he can't assimilate it.

They go to Bahia to find Eddie—tell all—"Let's swim." They come back with Eddie here to drink and celebrate. "Just forget. Just take it easy." They drink, they swim in the pool: the mailbox, the only thing light in the garden:[6] the mail comes again while they are drinking—"Sigbjørn! Sigbjørn! America's taken it too!" She is ecstatic.

Query: whether this letter should be, as it was originally, uncertain, which would attenuate things still more. {UBC 14:4, 347}

They are now standing on the porch where they had been at the beginning of Dark as the Grave[7] and on New Year's Eve, when they got Cape's virtual refusal.[8] People gather round to congratulate him and he and Maria Luisa[9] even discuss Yogi, but he has to be alone.

He goes back to the tower and now there are the reflections suggested on p. 1 of this chapter, to which we will add this:

The little postman, late, is going down the Calle Frey de las Casas (Calle Tierra del Fuego) and through the lurid window it was a Street of the Land of Fire indeed: he reflects about the letter that is too late: thinks of the dreadful coincidences surrounding Erikson—[10]

And the theme of that "should you travel to the scene that has informed the work of some great artist you would be nearer truth (get this) and all it implies—"[11]   (get the sunset)

The little red postman through the scarlet window was now passing El Vacilon. A red drunk reeled out at that moment and sat down on the curb.

"You are Clarence?" a voice seemed to whisper in the room, though Sigbjørn was not sure of this.

Suddenly, even at the moment that he realised that this was precisely what Raskolnikov had done in a French film of Crime and Punishment[12] he had seen, Sigbjørn fell face downwards as if he had been shot, across the bed.[13] {UBC 14:4, 348}

XXVII

Sunday April 7

Day of suspense and tension—get every kind of image for suspense, as he sleeps in the afternoon, the man waiting to be hanged, in New Westminster and what is so awful is that it's a disused elevator shaft he's going to be hanged in, so that every now and then he hears himself whispering "disused elevator shaft and not a scaffold"; waiting for a disease to develop: the deserter found in a refrigerator car in Empress:[1] his father came from Coquitlam to see. The murderer escaping in his canoe: skilled in woodcraft, the sleepless policeman who watched for signs of smoke in the mountains: cold and sleet coming on and even his mother had said: "Perhaps it will be better if they find me dead." Shall I ride the rails to Medicine Hat? I cannot escape. I might as well die. And yet I feel no remorse. I'd kill him again if I had the opportunity. When he wakes he hears music for the bullfight, he knows it: five o'clock in the afternoon, Sunday: the brutalities of this bullfight in the sticks mingle with fear of the Immigration, rows and rows of officers, behind high desks, enfilading, browbeating,— and what, precisely, was he afraid of?—and this fear mingles with the fear of having to sign things and that his hand will shake: through all this he remembers the news of his book's acceptance after so long failure, it warms him for a moment, and then, as he rises, and as the dreadful condition he is in overwhelms him, he wonders, what shall it profit a man if he gain the whole world and lose his own soul?[2]

For that was what mysteriously Sigbjørn conceived he had done, on waking and seeing Primrose's poor hairbrush and rings—and ah, the poor stolen bracelet!—and Primrose is not there {UBC 14:4, 349} and Sigbjørn gibbers about the apartment, saying where is my soul? Then he finds the medal of the Virgin and has another idea: "Perhaps I haven't got a soul! How can I lose my soul if I never had one in the first place." He prays to the Virgin mother, and crosses himself, and then wonders if he has not crossed himself the wrong way, so that he will bring further curses down on his head. This gives him an opportunity to have a drink of tequila, and he begins to laugh. Surely the situation is richly humorous.

Another point:[3] the stern blue purity of Canada is essentially puritanical, Protestant, clean, bare, cold. The churrigueresque tropical complex beauty of Mexico essentially Catholic—And yet the beauty and passion of that faith haunted him in the mystery. Perhaps it was its naivete that appealed to him, as one uninstructed. Think of the calculation of the Protestants! It was as if they did not share the same God, let alone the same Church. And yet perhaps there is one God. Sigbjørn sometimes longed for some image of worship in his mind, in which the two principles were combined, as passionate, yet as tragic and lone, as Christ of the Andes.

Primrose comes in and they go to Bahia—we drink too much, but good God, tomorrow in A.M. must see Immigration.

See Eddie and wife at Bahia, and learn they can't get tickets on early turismo. Another turn of screw is given by fact that Eddie and wife are going to be divorced. Eddie's wife says "I know someone who could fix it for you but it will cost you a lot of money" and Sigbjørn is just exasperated enough he won't pay the mordida.

Eddie restates the theme of La Mordida. The lieutenant pays the captain etc. (perhaps when his wife has gone out, being drunk he tells them a perfectly false story of how he'd taken a plane up without permission.) {UBC 14:4, 350}

"No—nobody's going to push me around. Only if Uncle Sam's in trouble."

"Uncle Sam's in plenty trouble now," said Sigbjørn, "And so is John Bull."

But Eddie is going to come with them. "I've never failed yet." The noise, the juke boxes, the draughty Aeolian horror of Cuernavaca at night against which Sigbjørn suddenly sees the sparkling blue glorious tide of home, and the little house, unfinished.

We arrange to meet at 10 A.M. at Bahia, he will have some arrangements for transportation. Sigbjørn tries to be business like but writes down, by mistake, arrangements for horripilation.

That night was worse than the last for Sigbjørn, though Primrose was in tears at his gloom: in his dreams Sigbjørn was hanged and goes down the elevator shaft but that was the least of his troubles, at the bottom of the elevator shaft the immigration men were waiting for him. And so was the Shaking Man.

Notes: see The Insufficient Man artic. Times Lit Sup.[4]

The Historical element is brought out by the significance of the songs . . . Après la Guerre, etc. The Houngan.[5]

Note: Wilderness wanders down Calle Tierra del Fuego, drunk, crying "I am a murderer . . ." Because Sonya had told him that if he did God would give him peace again. (This is from article on other side of my review) "You can love nothing but your shame too"—had not someone said, and had it not been, "Undergraduate Suicide of Shame—"[6]

One could see too how it could be dramatic in Dostoievsky, but how, when the apron advancing down Bridge Street, past Supply Searles, past Johns, in the rain, unmistakably said, to oneself, {UBC 14:4, 351} the murderer: "Undergraduate Suicide of Shame." Christ, what a horror of self-congratulation? For this murder was, as the saying is, perfect. He, cleverer than Raskolnikov, had not evaded detection by accident, but by design. He too had made the same kind of half-confessions that had (according to some inspired reviewer of Dostoievsky) failed either to create suspicion or to relieve his conscience, but what was the terrible thing was that, with him, for once, and for once only, apparently in his life, there had been no blunder. Nothing indeed could catch up with him, unless it was Nemesis etc.—How much more terrible then was it for him to accept payment indeed from the bitch-goddess, success. He sees the whole horror of it in advance—for a moment in its overwhelmingness it seems like the fire, with its sounds of ruination (and better to have been left in the dark forever to blunder and fail)—a betrayal—the infinite betrayal indeed ("It's your luxurious life," said Alyosha softly, "It is better then to be poor." "Yes, it is better.") I sing the good of poverty not such etc.

Life is a kind of trial—it is (according to the article) unimportant to banish suffering from the world: it was certainly impossible, but (D. again) it was antisocial. {UBC 14:4, 352}

XXVIII

Monday April 8

But in spite of that Sigbjørn wakes early, staggers out, and on the little encrusted electric stove—how brave Primrose had been coping with the charcoal one!—and brave as herself is she—makes coffee.

He prays to the Virgin for strength. Am I afraid that I lose you? He even composes a love-song—Fair as herself is she.[1] He has the most appalling shakes, and curses himself for drinking over the weekend, when today they have to go to the Migración.

He leaves coffee to boil (give some acct of chores, here and how water has to be boiled etc). It is real heroism to manage it: he doesn't touch the tequila until he even goes back to bed for a while with Primrose. The pure dawn. Popo and Ixta.

Notes: Awake frenzied but with early love. All will be over one way or other today (and this is the theme of their breakfast conversation—all will be over today, today we'll know the worst, let us cling together, and anyhow there's your book, and your book)—but prior to that Maria Luisa's little muchacha bangs on door—we drink black coffee and dress and go to Eddie's. There he has tickets for 11. 2 more habaneros and we leave.

Terrible anguishing journey described: agony at Tres Marias—hark back to the old women and again the day at Huitzilac . . .

Gobernación at 1—wait, dying,—clerk finally gets chap who says file has been sent to dept now closed but he has received notice we paid fine and wired Aca to let us go 5 days ago (this belies Tojo)[2] Eddie says things like: "Triumph of mind over matter—" Sigbjørn with hands in pockets. "Come back Wednesday." We go to restaurant, have drinks and dinner, Eddie tells story about {UBC 14:4, 353} crazy man, who wants to hide in rumble seat, all arose out of a promise of man and wife not to drink any more, this man was on a construction project with Eddie, Eddie finally gets man over border but is mistaken for crazy man himself—they go to Wimpy's, and this daemonic scene in a sunset like the lurid one with the red windows in Cuernavaca, but with all the devils on the wall, and devils in stained glass on the windows—though Eddie thinks it cute— "You're *ner*vous, don't *wor*ry!"—and dancing to some awful tune on the jukebox, and the place perfectly empty, hellish (the news from the Consul untold to Sigbjørn) should be one of the most terrific scenes in book.

Notes end: back to C. Eddie stands drinks: we eat hamburgers and so to bed—but scene should end at Wimpy's.

Appendage to XXVIII   Important note[3] to be made into dialogue:
I had originally meant in XII, the sentinel to be something like sentinel that Schopenhauer somewhere imagines,[4] who, representing the terrors of death, stands like a sentinel at the gate leading out of this world—

A passage of coincidences:

(1) the torture in the immigration—when we think of going to Haiti—where things have gone wrong—absence of Gibson—(our immigration fellow)

(2) back to the Consul (American) where it does not seem they are going to go right—

(3) I leave and go to bus stop, rain, rain—and previously the sailor with crabs—are crabs black or white? waving his tool—thinking of word Bond (relating to La Mordida) I see opposite me immediately BOND bookshop,[5] and enter, ask the old sloping man can I browse: I do: enter a printer (I hadn't known there were such {UBC 14:4, 354} things in Vancouver) who says: Have you a copy of a book called "You'll hate me for saying that! . . . poems."[6] "No, there's a limited market for poems." "Well," he says, "We're just printing it, I guess it's a second edition, we've just got to the second part and I was kind a curious." "Well, what's the author?" "Name of Gibson." (*I* think Gibson!) Printer exits, saying: "Must be pretty good—Longmans and

Green putting it out—" I ask, still browsing and thinking of the galleys *we* have, "I didn't know there were any printers in Vancouver—are there publishers too?" "No—no publishers—only printers—I guess they do it here for the wholesalers out east." I—who want to buy Schopenhauer—look over National Geographics: practically first thing I turn to is picture of Haiti—or rather picture of a ruined castle in mist, "From here Black Majesty reigned over Haiti"[7] etc.—i.e., Emperor Christophe's Castle—but then, two pages beyond this, this article (from a Nat. Geo of 1931) being called Skypaths through Latin America—a picture—see p. 30 Nat. Geo in question—An Antiguan's Unique Memorial to his beloved wife—an entablature, in short, portraying the drama and climax of the XII chap of Volcano[8]—the man bending over his wife—and the horse flying away in the distance—and the subscription—An Antiguan's unique memorial to his beloved wife—Long ago a horse ran away and killed the wife of a resident of St. John, Antigua, in B.W.I. Set in the cathedral there, the sculptured tablet portrays cause of her death. Then I leave: in bus read Schopenhauer passage—absolutely necessary to find—because it exactly parallels the end of Chap IX[9]—the young man carrying his father—but FROM A VOLCANO—and Naples—etc—[10] return to Dollarton and turning at random in Nat. Geo. find p 43—description of Gorget in {UBC 14:4, 355} Demarara—(still skypaths Nat. Geo) "This is the only place in the world where pigs have learned to swim without cutting their own throats with their front feet," said a Vice-consul after we had landed in the reddish Demarara, swift with a seven knot current. "They have to swim or drown in the wet season."

Coincidence here is I'd been thinking of making pig analogue of drunkard after, only two nights before Sam had told precisely same story about pigs (the only thing we couldn't remember afterwards, and the first time I've ever heard of that in my life—for I cited pigs at Bikini, pig swimming races, etc—)

Margie also remembers that Sam said, of monkey that cut its throat: "This monkey had been brought to his mother and sister by his father who had been far away and they loved it very much. But Sam's uncle didn't like monkey because it was mischievous and he was always threatening it. So one day Sam's Uncle went into bathroom, took razor (st razor), turned it round, and drew the back of it across his throat. And sure enough, a few minutes later, the monkey did likewise but cut its throat. Sam's final remark: His mother cried for 3 days. My uncle knew, monkey see, monkey do!"

All this brought in in a kind of insane dialogue.

Now, supposing this kind of thing happened to you—what dimension do you suppose I was in touch with. Cite also In Ballast. Have Sig. tell Prim. *real* story of In Ballast.[11] {UBC 14:4, 356}

XXIX

Tuesday April 9

(Technique here in abeyance, but tentative plan is this chapter should comprise quite a few days.)

We are dying but try to hold selves together saying all will be over one way or other tomorrow. About twilight we meet Eddie on Calle Tierra del Fuego who says he can't go to Mexico tomorrow but has phoned and Thursday is O.K. "But they say it was a feather in your cap you went on Monday because you didn't have to go until Tuesday." Sigbjørn contemplates this adornment dubiously. At Eddie's, drink and discuss possible plane trip—dine at Mexican place near oficina of Flecha very late—Sigbjørn is pretty drunk—three mariachis try to gyp them, later down at Bus Terminal, a sense of foreboding and evil.

Wednesday April 10

We pull self together and endure somehow—bad thunderstorm at night: describe. The thunderstorm seems out of its season—but the weather is breaking up, becoming turbulent, windy, dusty, cold: Cuernavaca darker and more forbidding than ever: the cantinas are unbelievably sinister: Sigbjørn realises that he is in the grip of something evil, he prays to God and the Virgin, and also to Fernando Marquez: perhaps this is a kind of experiment, and if we win through, we will have pleased God: we will have made the path easier for others. In the heart of the panic there is a sort of still place: the thunder gives him some relief and he remembers the story of his brother's about the suspense, the torture of waiting for the bombardment, which was related also to the feeling of Christ on the cross waiting for the thunder— {UBC 14:5, 257}[1]

That night they remember that it is a month since they left for Taxco: and 4 weeks ago they were held: they cling to each other in the thunderstorm like two little creatures in a forest.

Suddenly Sigbjørn thinks how cold the poor Christ of the Andes must be and cries himself to sleep in Primrose's arms. {UBC 14:5, 258}

XXX

Thursday April 11.

The Immigration is housed in a series of buildings, around a stone courtyard, beyond an iron gate, that reminded Sigbjørn rather of St. Catherine's College, Cambridge. Some fun might be had with this analogy.

Notes are: Go to Mexico—describe trip—on 9 A.M. bus, dying, Eddie is late: then the Migración sends us to Department of Inspección—a horrible cold office with pictures of deportadoes on wall: describe these murderous unhappy faces, so and so of Guatemala: etc. Describe also the office: 6 desks for inspectors, 2 female typists, lady in red with baby—we wait for three hours in foul red leather chairs, but inspector of our case doesn't come.

Sigbjørn here shows at his best: though insanity seems to be staring him in the eyes and he has the most horrible shakes which he does his best to mitigate with bits of pheno. that Primrose feeds him, he comforts her and even has to comfort Eddie, who is in bad shape and shaking slightly and continuously as inspectors come in and out. Eddie is very funny again with his "Triumph of mind over matter." "Drink isn't the only thing that gives you the shakes," Eddie said brilliantly.

At the end is the office into which various people go and the curious thing is that in the three hours they are there he has seen many women go in there and they all come out weeping.

Once Sigbjørn sees a rather good looking Spaniard go in there: this is Corunna: give him fabulous name from Westward Ho!—but whether he had been there before, he can't know: everything is being loyally left to Eddie, but Eddie does nothing at all, {UBC 14:5, 259} occasionally speaks to an inspector in an obsequious manner: in spite of being the Chief of Judicial Police it is apparent that Eddie, for some reason, has the wind-up. Primrose is in a *state!*

The Inspectors are: 1 fat inspector, 1 lean grey one, 1 young, smartly dressed, tall, but sneaky one, 1 fat and nasty, 1 very sinister: describe how they are dressed, some with green glasses, others with vizored eyeshades, most rather shabby. There are phones and files on the desk and one old fellow seems to do nothing but copy.

It becomes apparent too that Eddie is not going to do anything ever finally: all three sink into a sort of shaking stupor.

Sigbjørn says once: "I'm sure if we were to speak to that decent looking cove over there we might get somewhere."

This is considerably more than ironic, for this decent looking cove he is speaking of is Corunna.

People drift past on the balcony outside eating ice cream cones: a shoe shine vendor actually comes in. Sigbjørn expects at any moment perhaps someone will come in selling pulque. From this point they can see right over the quadrangle to the other building with a similar balcony and S. sees Miss Hill at one point looking very worried. She it is whom Primrose and Sigbjørn have saved from trouble about her tourist card: but so as it were petrified and stupefied are they it does not occur to them to go over and see her: had one done so, however, it did not seem that anyone would raise an objection. But actually all this aspect of carelessness is a little bit deceitful: Sigbjørn notices two or three people standing about who seemed to have little function but to pretend they are not listening, but one {UBC 14:5, 260} of them utters a word of English and Eddie says: "Be careful." Moreover when Sigbjørn goes into the lavatory at the end of the balcony to eat a phenobarbital, he is almost immediately followed by one of these men: afraid, lest he be mistaken for a drug-fiend, to swallow it in the mignitorio, he therefore goes into the latrine (he has to suck it) to be immediately handed a roll of paper over the wall by this man.

Sigbjørn returns laughing: Eddie and Primrose are both sitting shaking, shouts and vilifications come from the further office, and another woman comes out crying and two Americans a moment later saying "son of a bitch!"

At last our inspector comes over to us, carrying our file: he is fat, sinister, nasty, beady-eyed, and smug with fat loud shrill voice: Eddie gets up rather obsequiously: so do we, and we are told to sit down. There is much conversation: we must *both* put up a bond of 500 pesos or be deported in 2 days. Impossible to get anyone to underwrite bonds and Sigbjørn has now to be frank over this business of the bond re Vallejo:[2] and Sigbjørn thinks too, that this has been foreshadowed, for the Unitarian minister that had married them,[3] had done so in the Vallejo apartments. (also the apartment where we were married)[4]

But he says we are working in the country, therefore must have a special permit or immigration—which they offer us—it's quite easy to get—come and get it now—but both Sigbjørn and Primrose smell a rat (perhaps wrongly) moreover Sigbjørn is outraged: he tries to explain that they are earning no money in the country—no good—they plead—still no good—they try to hang on to their papers till the last moment, when they go, and {UBC 14:5, 261} the Tourist Card, it is dreadful as Acapulco again—(Mem: also they think they have to go smack off to New York)[5] they have taken all our papers, even the Form H thing, of which Eddy says: "I shouldn't have given them that"—and perhaps there was no need to have done so but Sigbjørn was trying to be too honest—final result is we must have bond by Monday 1 p.m. or be deported (In dialogue Sigbjørn points out to Eddy that this deportation will be fatal, with the charge against him there) and promise not to write another word until we leave.

"Not a word," says S. "But we are writers. In one sense we can't help writing. (N.B. they have brought Primrose's books and also the contracts to intimidate these people with their effect but it is quite futile and in fact has the contrary effect.) How can you stop us?"

"But suppose we set a trap and walk in and *find* you writing!"

"Presumably we can write letters to our mothers?" says S.

"Posseebly es posseebly escribir en el escusado"[6] and so on.

They go out and have dinner at half past at the Chanticleer: there is even a diabolic chord of the Volcano in this—half past tree by the cock.[7]

All the bonding companies are now shut but Eddy nobly offers to put up his little business as security, Eddy, who looks like a croupier, and whose hobby was drinking, and raising carnations.

"Don't *worry*. Don't be *ner*vous."

"In my defense I must say that you were rather more nervous than I, Eddy," Sigbjørn says good naturedly.

"You were wonderful, Sigbjørn," says Primrose. {UBC 14:5, 262}

Eddie is in jovial mood and says that they have, far from deporting them, offered them the "gates of the country," and there is a note of pride in his voice.

(Some of this dialogue should not be here, see chap XXXI Fri Apr 12 e.g. Inspector has said no bonding company in Cuernavaca and Eddie has demurred?)

"And shut them behind us," Primrose says, and Sigbjørn pats her hand.

"No—the only snag is they've asked us to put up their damn bond in Holy Week, when all the bonding companies are shut."

"So to that extent they may be said to have set their trap already," Primrose said.

"Not necessarily," said Sigbjørn. "But what was in the file against me?"

"I don't know," said Eddy.

"But the worst snag is now they've got our papers how the hell are we going to get our money?"

"Well, we'll have to wire the agent. Not much good wiring to England."

"Or appealing further to the Consul."

(It is an important point that Primrose is concealing the second letter of Hughes to Sigbjørn and Eddy boasts that he is doing what the Consul can't and Sigbjørn thinks this naively too.)

Outside the noise, the horror, the klaxons, cut-outs, thunder and rain: suddenly the sense of having no freedom, of no papers, and finally not being allowed in this moment of triumph to write seems something of a unique and insuperable horror in itself. Elaborate all these feelings. {UBC 14:5, 263}

Eddie was going to buy some earrings shaped like a lantern (describe) for 2 Russian girls and Sigbjørn and Primrose went to the Plaza Netzalcuahuatyl (describe) and until it was time for the bus to leave for Cuernavaca drank Saturno in thunder.

Or end like this:

But they met Eddie again in the Plaza N.

"I hope you're not superstitious."

"Oh no," said Sigbjørn.

For the bus that took them home was number 13, and, in the Calle Tierra del Fuego, where Sigbjørn had in the Volcano seen a coffin and had later seen the wedding, a hearse was drawn up.[8] Then the three of them sat in the square and drank Saturno in Thunder. {UBC 14:5, 264}

XXXI

Friday April 12.

Margienotes: meet Eddie while going for morning buns at La Minima (pathos of this). Discussion of bonds—arrange to meet later at Bahia—try to write telegram to Hal[1]—meet Eddie at Bahia who has been trying all morning to get bond—

Primrose has a few habaneros at Bahia, describe its awkwardness, the chill, the bad service. Eddie has been trying all morning to get bond—no bonding company in Cuernavaca as Inspector had said—Holy Week—vacations—bond is impossible, but Eddy finally arranged that friend who is representative should go to Mexico Saturday and return with papers Eddie will countersign: we are to pick up papers Sunday, go to bonding co Monday A.M. and thence to Inspection—3 more days of suspense—suppose something goes wrong with the bond—

But we pull ourselves together and send wire—Christ, that red ink—and go to market and Eddie and ourselves make reservations on Turismo for Monday A.M. to Mexico . . .

Saturday April 13.

Margie records this simply: This is a bad day.

Actually day is compounded somewhat as follows: Sigbjørn wants drink and Primrose goes into hysterics, yells, lying down on the floor, where's Sigbjørn gone? Where's Sigbjørn? Sigbjørn, who goes to pieces at hysterics, goes up on the roof where he can't hear and prays no one else can hear either: he bakes on roof, sweating and loathing the sun with its overtones and memories of health: this is where the Consul made his decision not to drink for fully 5 minutes, the damned fool, where he has {UBC 14:5, 265} written his long letter in defence of the Volcano itself:[2] fortunately the Volcanoes were hidden: a hazy hot day and it would be vile again tonight: occasionally he goes down to visit Primrose, she is still in hysterics, shouting "Where's Sigbjørn—Sigbjørn!" Sigbjørn returns to roof and tries to meditate about the significance of the tower etc: he is making a battle again about drink himself but it is all confused with fear—finally he goes down, worried by Primrose—there is about to be a dreadful scene between them—she is in hysterics again, and clearly half out of her mind, when steps are heard outside: Sigbjørn for some reason runs into the shower but the knocking goes on—is the Immigration—the police—then dodges to a place where he can see without being seen—is this the trap? just in time to see an extremely pretty head and a pretty girl go down the steps. Primrose decides it must be Janice (the name like his wife's)[3]—why didn't you ask her in?

"How could I ask her in when she'd only say why haven't you got a doctor—and I'd have to say I haven't got enough money for a doctor and then she'd have to say well here you've got enough money for habanero but no doctor and so on—"

They make up however: it rains: the vigil: the lights fail as in book,[4] they have a frightful tremendous quarrel in which Primrose rips the Virgin off Sigbjørn's neck. Rainy season begins two months early. Thunderstorms. {UBC 14:5, 266}

XXXII

Sunday April 14.[1]

(Get phrase somewhere: you might end chapter: all night long he was attacked by swarms of clichés. Not here.)

Find Janice at Bellavista at evening and spend night with her and Rhea Deverly,[2] drinking. Janice sings Butterfly and Ave Maria like an angel and offers to help.

She also sings of things that seem to have ironic significance re Chief of Police, etc in opera and offers to help them the next day.

Sigbjørn has his drinking boots on.

Janice: "Corunna!—If you're mixed up with Corunna you'll end up in 113 Bucarelli." She also warns against Eddie, saying he's well known as a crook and cheap gambler etc.

This should be one of the most terrific scenes in the book.

And when he slept this singing did not cease for an instant.

The beastly character of Rhea Deverly.

Describe the soaring celestial glory of that voice, of how it told of everything that was beautiful in life, of the untold potentialities of the human soul: this beauty was in Primrose's cousin's face too—describe how it clashes with her childish personality and the things she said: she was the voice: somehow or other this gets Sigbjørn into thinking of the power of the word: and again, he feels himself enclosed by a work of art—was it his work of art?—an opera: what she is singing seems touched with the intensest tragic significance: she was singing for *them*, and at the same time that he felt himself drawn upwards, as by the singing of angels,[3] by this, it was as though {UBC 14:5, 267} the voice *itself* knew, if not Janice,[4] the tragic significance of what she was singing. Images of love pass in his mind: cornfields, windjammers, freighters on the horizon, lovers on a lonely beach, in the rain, wrapped in each other's arms; the ballet mécanique of the raindrops[5] on Great Howe Sound, the intersecting circles, spreading to infinity, like the pulsations of this angelic voice.

Sigbjørn's Dostoievskian trust, or pseudo-trust, of Eddie.

Stories of the absolute corruption of Mexico, also Ron's story of the police and the forged cheque: and the diabolical character of Corunna. Bousfield's man who wore the bloodstained ring.

Point here is: we imagine that now we are getting bond, all will be O.K., and my trust of Eddie.

Chapter should end with the description of the dawn and on a great note of Hope. {UBC 14:5, 268}

XXXIII

Monday April 15

Notes: Maria Luisa's muchacha calls us after one hour's sleep and we go to Mexico, nearly missing Turismo: bond is O.K. (see end) but don't get papers returned—

Try and cast mind back as to what happened precisely on this day—First: the long long trip, that seems to get longer and longer, unlike the trip to the spring at the Martins,[1] bring in this little story. There is the going to the Bonding Company with hangovers, or perhaps still half tight, dazed: description of bonding company: will hand falter, is always the question, and overtones of Vallejo.

Then to Immigration again. I tangle with Corunna? They'd promised to give us papers. Yes, bond is O.K.

But you promised to give us our papers as soon as we had the bond. And now no papers.

People walking about as before . . . Sit down . . . Picture of Camacho[2] on the wall. Margie is furious. I deal with Corunna alone.

"Well, the papers aren't finished. They had to fix them up. Come back in a few days and you can pick them up."

"Look here, Sr. Corunna, have you any idea how long you've been persecuting us, me and my wife?"

"Speak French!" suddenly shouted Corunna. "Entrez—" he says to someone else.

"But—"

"No spikka the Eengleesh."

Corunna makes gestures before he speaks, so that it is more or less possible to understand what he says: describe the gestures: {UBC 14:5, 269} gesture of reaping, of cutting throats with the thumb, of gripping them, of cramming gunpowder in people's ears, of pulling teeth, and a magician-like gesture as of one about to cause everything to disappear, of pulling triggers, of drinking, and of ejection, and a curious gesture with his fore finger, as though, Sigbjørn thought, which was the most probable, he were putting the finger up someone's rectum, probably, in this case, that of Dr. Martinez: it was clear, Sigbjørn said to himself, uneasily, to him that he was dealing with that rarest of all people, an absolute devil and a devil, moreover, who was in some sort—as perhaps indeed, when you thought of his prime historic almost philanthropic interest in men, was the Devil himself—a pansy: This rarity as of a man given over entirely to evil was expressed in its face, as it were, by its absence: his face, which was by no means bad, was in fact purely a mask and reflected nothing at all of his soul: there was not even any particular cunning in it, just a fixed, almost a benignant or amiable cruelty.

Sigbjørn is his match.

Also a picture of Mexico, por la Libertad: indeed the inside of the undersecretary's office is a kind of replica of the one in Acapulco.

Sigbjørn realises that the discipline and technique is something like that imposed by the sea: never be frightened, have patience, be simple. He waits for the raving to cease (possibly Primrose will already have been thrown out).

"Why do you hate us so much? Don't you think it'll prove dangerous to you in the end to show this attitude towards members of a friendly country?" Sigbjørn was thinking how odd it was, for he could still hear Janice's singing, this evil shouting could coexist in the same universe: he wondered if Janice would be at her apartment. And yet how well Janice had appraised Corunna's {UBC 14:5, 270} true character.

"When you are in a foreign country you must obey the laws of that country," Corunna said.

"Come now. You speak English fine," Sigbjørn said in French.

Corunna begins to rave again.

"So far as you are concerned," Sigbjørn says, "I am perfectly innocent. I've made a mistake. I'm here, as the saying is, legally but by mistake. It would seem to me I've paid for more than the penalty already. Would you mind telling me precisely what you have on the file against me? I wouldn't mind betting it isn't serious."

"No es serio—no es serio" shouted Corunna. "Just come back in few days—etc."

"Then why don't you give us our papers?"

"When are you leaving? I want a date. Dr. Martinez wants a date."

"How can I give you a date when I can't make a reservation without my papers?"

"I have to have a date. You got money!"

"How can I get any money unless I have the papers to identify myself with?"

"Ah, you have plenty money." Sigbjørn realises this is unpleasantly like a novel.

This scene should be balanced with great cunning and be perfectly realistic: meantime Primrose, who has gone out to meet Janice at 11 (having previously been thrown out by Corunna) comes back and says no Janice.

They walk dejectedly out into the street. {UBC 14:5, 271}

"Well, he won't give us our papers yet, and Janice has failed us."

"Why wouldn't he give us our papers!"

"It would appear that, by some categorical imperative,[3] Sr. Corunna has to have the mordida. But the problem is who to pay it to. For Sr. Corunna is so placed that he can't receive it himself directly from the injured party."

"But that is precisely where Janice comes in. She said she had the only person that could fix it."

"Then we better phone her up. Obviously she couldn't make it with a hangover like she must have had."

"What about us?"

"Well—we're used to it," Sigbjørn said grimly. "We can take it."

"You may be able to take it," Primrose began hysterically, "but I can't."

Primrose phones, first in a sort of sidewalk stall that sells tobacco and sea-food, and is attached to a cantina: then in a huge garage-like half empty echoing shop of electric accessories and appurtenances etc.

Terrific noise, klaxons, prevents hearing anything: and Janice is not in. The noon in Mexico City, the danger of the traffic, the strangeness, the loneliness, the awfulness, the effect of it on these two people who had lived in the wilderness was so great that they could make no further effort: to go to the Consulate to find nobody but a trouble-shooter there, all this seemed too too much, worse even at last than going back to Cuernavaca, into the darkness and cacophony of Juke boxes, and rain and thunder, and the inevitable bender with Eddie. {UBC 14:5, 272}

They take each other's hands tenderly though, like brother and sister, and go have a fine meal with plenty of wine, at the Chanticleer: the hunchback proprietor ceaselessly prowls up and down through the alleyway made by the booths into the dining room and back again to the kitchen. People seem to be watching them but Sigbjørn doesn't care. They are close to one another again and talk of the goggle and the tropical fish at Acapulco. Sigbjørn makes a point of touching the hunchback as they go out. (That reminds him of Gugno and Oaxaca.)

Primrose has felt objective clouds lifting but subjective ones closing in but Sigbjørn has said: anyhow we have each other.

Once more they went to the Plaza N., and once more go home to Cuernavaca. Alemán—Moralización.[4] "I hope he means it." Alemán

on the trees, everywhere, even on the volcanoes. But how pathetically different it was to their first trip to Cuernavaca. At evening a
bus thundering past like a shower of sparks, in the turismo, the car,
Sigbjørn was suddenly unable to believe in the reality of the ashtray,
sitting on the left, a sudden vision of another bus ahead, as the lights
came on, hurtling over the barranca in flames with people scream-
ing, the fear of the trembling hands, the multilighted trucks thundering to Acapulco . . . {UBC 14:5, 273}

This should be used on first page of this chapter.

> *Central de Fianzas S.A.*
> *Edificio Banco Mexicano*
> *Motolinia 20*
> *Mexico D.F.*
>
> Serie A No 5062
>
> Recibimos de Clarence Malcolm Lowry
> Premio $20—
> 5% Adl 1—
> Total $21—Veinte y un pesos 00/100
> Correspondiente a la Fianza no III 16090 por el período de
> 4/15/46 al 4/14/47
> Abril 15 de 1946
>
> Ramírez
> Cajero.[5] {UBC 14:5, 274}

XXXIV

Tuesday April 16

"This is the end . . . How can I live in such dirt and degeneration?
I am losing, have lost my love of life, even can't start to organize the
household again, which is a *mess*, no clean linen, bugs in kitchen,
floors filthy with cigarette stubs and dirty clothes covering all chairs.
I feel my own moral fibre and grip slipping," thought or said Primrose, who half imagined perhaps as she lay on the bed she was talking to Janice, but talking in the dark of the tower that looked as

though a hurricane had struck it. "I am so tired, so tired, tired, tired, I don't care except for a dull anger that flames and rages now and then against Sigbjørn."

"And hatred, and disgust that I'm dragged down myself with trying to drink with him and a hatred of bottles and exhaustion and a sense of my soul slipping away and my whole grip on life. I feel at once that I will *not* be brought to this bestial state, that I will regain my decency and cleanliness and love and at the same time a despair so utter and weariness so that all I want is death. Why don't I kill myself? Is it some vague lingering loyalty to Sigbjørn whom I must still love but now only hate and despise and fear—above all *fear*—" she said aloud. "Do you hear?"

"Too well," said Sigbjørn.

"And that these days of his triumph which I have prayed for, offered to God my soul in payment for—"

"No one would sympathise with you for doing that."

"And how many times have I said in passionate prayer, and meaning it, oh God, give Sigbjørn his success, let his Volcano be recognized for the great thing it is." {UBC 14:6, 275}

"I think it's lousy," said Sigbjørn, looking round the scene of chapter VII, the tower,[1] as he had described it, built against the second floor, where the Consul had so signally failed to withstand temptation.

"I will die or be damned in payment—so perhaps this is what happens—"

"Liar," said Sigbjørn gently.

"But Sigbjørn without me will have no joy of his success, and must it be bought at that price? And why do I care, why am I in such agony about him if I despise him? How can you love a man with all your being and be willing to be damned that he may have what he wants the most of all, and still feel as I do, that he has outraged and insulted our marriage and himself so that I could kill him? And the stabbing burning unendurable agony of seeing the one you love reduced to a shambling idiotic dirty animal—"

"That's good," said Sigbjørn, thinking he was pouring some habanero, though he found he had a bottle of vinegar, the habanero was on the floor—it was so dark, and though they were in the tower, he had the feeling neither of them knew what room they were in, "all save the reduced to. But shambling. Yes, I am. Idiotic, yes. Dirty, unquestionably. And animal, yes. So, indeed, are we all."

"I can't even pray any more . . . I have searched and searched for the medal, the virgin I tore off his neck," Primrose sobbed, "but she has gone and we are damned in Sigbjørn's hour of triumph."

"Doubly," Sigbjørn said. {UBC 14:6, 276}

XXXV

April 19 — Good Friday
(Notes—what with one thing and another this has been quite a week but we are reborn!)

It was Good Friday. Holy Week here is one long fiesta—stores closed, merry-go-rounds and sideshows and fortune-tellers in square, crowds and crowds and noise and a frightful din of gaiety.

Later, send wire to Hal and go to cathedral. Outside is crowd of every kind of Mexican from top to bottom and people selling medals, tortas, tacos, peanuts, rattles, balloons, toys—a goose very peaceful and sweet with feet tucked in resting amid the clamour under the row of cypress trees. At first crowd in church seemed too great to get in but edged in and found place in rear. Today huge cathedral is bare—no decorations or flowers and every statue except one of Christ kneeling in stiff gold robes and one of carving of Christ in Mary's arms as taken from cross (the one painted by Mary Hoover—refer back to Clarence Hoover—you are Clarence)[1] is covered with great cloths of deep purple. The usually garish altar is covered by huge purple cloth extending from ceiling to floor and only one rude wooden cross—empty—and two statues, one of the Mary Mother, and the other of Magdala kneeling before it and a few huge candles burning. There is a priest on a little balcony on right telling of the death of Christ as we enter and somehow I (we) understand him—perhaps we ought to get the right words from Maria Luisa—now He is dying—there is a great groan of sorrow from the people with tears streaming down their cheeks—their music of lament, priest chanting, people answering. At the altar appears {UBC 14:6, 277} man robed in white who drapes a small white cloth over the cross as the candles are quenched. People weep and groan. Then silence, except for few babies crying and people weeping and praying—Now we see approaching through the crowd candles, great silver cross, and something, can't see what, but excitement grows among people who fall back to allow passage—suddenly it is directly before us—a procession of: first, three men, one in middle with cross, other two, with candles; following are choir boys with candles and then great casket containing image of dead Christ carried by pall bearers casket draped in black gauze. Followed by statues of 2 Marys and the procession of weeping people carrying candles. The intense absorbed passionate sorrow and belief on people's faces. The procession goes round the church and back to altar. While it is going by a tiny Indian woman longing to see, edges in beside me and closes hand over my (Primrose's) arm. Primrose takes her hand and moves to allow her to see. She looks up at me (her) with beautiful dark lined agonized face.

Outside in the sun and heat the noise and glare is astonishing. All week there has been storm after storm with thunder and lightning and thunderous downpours and tonight there is another; lights go out—they watch lightning from tower window, the lurid red window, thunder and wind shake the house, lightning crashing down on Tres Cumbres on Popo, then the storm sweeps round and they see a great jagged fork of light hit the dome of the cathedral, lighting the whole town.

Query: Easter Sunday—or have it in memory in XXXVI[2] {UBC 14:6, 278}

XXXVI

Tuesday April 23.

Eddie phones Jefe says all is O.K. and we can come in any time for papers.

The Mexican General in Bahia gives us his card, says he will fix all: you are a very calm man.

Neither of us quite believe in this deliverance—

We have drinks: scene of the buying of the obsidian bracelet.

(Mem: how much money have we got at this point)

(Mem Easter Sunday. Hands of the Daemon.)

Swim at Marik. Richard Knight. Fake Barrymore. acting kind of man. Sigbjørn plunges entire length of Marik pool, watched by Mrs. Gooch . . .[1]

R.K. can be worked up in New Orleans.

That night Primrose shows Sigbjørn second letter from Consul, and Sigbjørn thanks Eddie over again. Letter from Consul follows:[2]

> British Consulate General
> Apartado 90—Bis
> Mexico D.F.
> 5th April, 1946[3]

Sir:

I am informed by the Ministerio de Gobernación that they are willing that you should return to the United States (instead of, as they first required, to British territory) and they will give facilities for your collecting your belongings at Cuernavaca. The first thing necessary is that I should be able to produce to the Ministry your reservations for the journey and show them that your passports are in order for admission to the United States. If you have not sufficient funds for this purpose, I recommend that you obtain them immediately and let me know the result as soon as possible.

> Yours faithfully,
> A Rodgers   H.B.M. Consul-General

Sigbjørn Wilderness
Quinta Eulalia
Playa Caleta
Acapulco Gro. {UBC 14:6, 279}

XXXVII

Friday April 26.

Off to Mexico again on 9 A.M. Turismo hopeful but not too sanguine. In office we see Jefe who says no papers. By now money has arrived from Hal, only to be held 10 days and we must get it as cash is nearly gone and can't without identification. (Margie's notes) I am angry and Jefe throws me out of the office, very insulting; nearly slapping me across desk with gestures: S. is magnificent![1] Puts arm around me and says so tenderly and sweetly, will I please wait outside. I wait, praying. Hear voices, the Jefe yelling hysterically, M. calm and dignified. Meanwhile a little English sailor is there who will translate but speaks horrible Spanish and is getting everything wrong. M. finally persuades Jefe of urgency and we are told to return at 1:30, the papers, it seems, having been sent back to Migración. But the Jefe has asked M. for his passport, yelled that he was breaking the law by having no identification and refused to believe that they had taken *all* our papers. He then asks what hotel we're staying at in Mexico City. My God!

The sailor comes out with M. and says: "I'm a Britisher too, and a *good* Britisher—wife and three kids in England, I've been through the *mill*, mate, 5 months in the jug and now I'm being deported to Cuba!" Meantime other chap, obviously American born of Mexican parents, says he's from N.Y. and says look, this is how it's done, bud—I've overstayed my leave 2 months, but I'll be fixed up in half an hour. These chaps all have to take La Mordida and pay off the Chief every week or lose their jobs. This is how it's done. I see he's given 50 peso note to Inspector who is immediately very friendly and while other things go in in about half an hour his papers are {UBC 14:6, 281}[2] fixed and he is all set. Meantime I see Mr. Hughes and we enlist his aid. He congratulates Sigbjørn on success. He talks to Jefe and reports that papers are now all in order and O.K. but are in desk of other Jefe in Migración who just hasn't showed up today to keep appointment with him but says he'll be there mañana 11:30 A.M. Papers will be procured at that time and we make definite appointment with Mr. Hughes for 12 tomorrow. He also tells us they have sent pro consul over to Migración on our case (presumably at least one week after I saw them since letter arrived 10 days later) who is a stinker, and says he himself personally saved us from deportation though there is a 24 hour discrepancy in his story (see previous note) and there has been no question of deportation in all our talks with Jefe. Hughes also tells us when he was a lad in S. Africa the sailor's uncle ran a very famous circus: "They've got him in a kind of boarding house now."

"Where is that?"

"113 Bucarelli."

(I might build up this character of the sailor a little from Ultramarine,[3] etc.)

The point should be made here that this appointment for 11 is quite ultimate and final: and a feeling of all or nothing.

Return to C. through thunder rain snow and hail (Memory of Tres Marias, the road covered with broken glass, and the second half of glorious day) But we have had cheery dinner at Chanticleer the name of which has hope. (Every night the forty horrible miles back to Cuernavaca) Either at the end of this chapter or another there should be a terrific scene of the Plaza N. in a whirlwind of dust and sleet, the ruined church among the rubble, appearing and disappearing through the murk. {UBC 14:6, 282}

XXXVIII

Saturday April 27.

(One of the main motivations—if not the main—is that they are down to their last 50 pesos, i.e. 10,000 pesos between bank and telegraph office, 50 pesos in our pockets.)

—Not trusting the girl to call us we awake—or Margie does all night—frequently, thinking it's time to get breakfast and catch the bus: this is der Tag, and mention of this will heighten it. The little trip to get the morning rolls, as if all were well.

Margie gets up and fixes breakfast and once more to turismo at 9:30. Car doesn't start till nearly 10 because of lack of passengers. We have to get, moreover, at the last minute, another turismo. But this breaks down with ominous gasps and sputters long before Tres Cumbres. We see driver and smelly lad tinkering; they say better return to Cuernavaca—we get out and hail car. Meantime very swell Mexican who speaks perfect English takes us in, it is now after 10 and we are frantic; now our friend's car breaks down—we stop for pail of water—from soldier's camp—pump is broken—and we go on, limping agonizingly up to Tres Cumbres. It is almost too much. There more water and he puts soaked hanky on carburetor which is overheating. We limp on, gasping not only now on every hill, but even on every slope. He is reading Appt in Samarra.[1] We have a good laugh and Margie says: "They've got into the machinery." Sigbjørn tries to remember the story of Appt in S. but can't quite, yet the coincidence seems a fateful one. Mexican likes Hemingway: we discuss American literature (might get some of Sigbjørn's ideas on literature in here), El Indio etc. while car limps on. Mexican has {UBC 14:6, 283} had trouble before also taking child down to Vera Cruz. We stop yet again at La Cina (La Ana) for water and our Turismo whizzes by! But we now have loyalty to him and can't leave him: theme of whole book is restated by Sigbjørn and Primrose by their telling him their story, he is shattered by it and "Malos hombres" is all he can say. "These *bas*tards." He is obviously ashamed but he is the best kind of man.

"There is something rotten in my country." The car won't seem to go, I even get out and push. Sigbjørn is eating fragments of pheno out of his ticket pocket like acidrops.

Then recovery and we pass turismo and struggle up grade—the car really goes blooey and we coast downhill and pray uphill but turismo must have broken down again because it doesn't pass us and we are crawling. We pass overturned jeep in a field and further on two absolutely plastered Mexican soldiers staggering toward it: the nature spiritual significance of the whole thing, the feeling that everything was artifact, and yet perfect, a work of art, even if he were only a character and wouldn't write it, is so overwhelming that Sigbjørn again loses his fear and sense of horror in admiration of the daemon who would go to these lengths . . .

Tension is terrific. We pray. Finally after agonising gasps and efforts car stops dead and we have to abandon friend, though we hate to, in a desert road: we hail another car, with two aristocratic Spanish ladies in back seat, Mexican driver and calla lilies in front and red sweet williams: the whole car is full of flowers and they might be either going to a wedding or a funeral. We explain the urgency of our appointment and ask them to drop us somewhere where we can get taxi for Bucarelli. They move lilies and we get in front and drive down Insurgentes, past the airport {UBC 14:6, 284} where we'd landed but which is a new way to approach Mexico City from Cuernavaca and we seem to be miles out of our way. Most lovely and gracious tree-lined and beautiful avenue and they take us miles out of their way straight to the Gobernación. Farewell and adieu, my good Spanish ladies.[2] (They dispute what is the exact wording of the song.) We dash in just on time and of course nobody is there at all: no Consul.

(And yet, so far as the daemon was concerned, it was so far from being finished it was as if he had approached him, even today, as might someone imagine that the boat builder had finished his boat, just the planks up and ready for bending the ribs in it, and they come and say, "Oh, you've got it nearly finished.")

M. has another session with Jefe while Primrose telephoned Hughes, who is suddenly very offhand and says, oh yes, but I've been very busy here this morning. Primrose insists—the consul says he will phone Jefe. Back in office M. has situation in control although other translator's English is hopeless, M. is better in Spanish, who is this man by the way? A stool pigeon?

There is also an absolutely frightful ravaged German who tries to interpret: "But—bitte schön—vestehen sie?—the Herr Doktor is busy etc. etc."[3]

I (Sigbjørn) persuaded Jefe actually to go and get passport so we can get money (motive for this is not at first apparent) but it is the old cancelled passport. But even that is something and battle tide has turned for us thanks to M. (says Margie—the last quarter of an hour.) Down to their last 30 pesos.

Primrose calls Hughes again who [says] Jefe has refused to do anything and is quite snippy. {UBC 14:6, 285}

"Everything has been done that can be done under Mexican law."

"And under human—" Primrose said.

"And under English—" she yelled into emptiness. (I didn't say anything of the sort, ducky, I pointed out to the fool that they'd already broken their Mexican law with us, and repudiated the Mexican constitution, etc.)

"We're driven back on American perhaps," Sigbjørn said, who couldn't help enjoying this scene. (actually you weren't there, you were talking to Corunna while I phoned Hughes.)

"For Christ sake no," Primrose said. "Then, what with your having been turned down and so forth, that would be the end." (actually, I said that since you were English and had your own consul the American Consul couldn't help you—and what was the use of his helping me?)

"Well, I guess it's still the last quarter of an hour," Sigbjørn said. "But I've got my cancelled passport, which is something."

Back in Cuernavaca, in a thunderstorm, in the rain, I go to telegraph office, with cancelled passport, hoping they won't notice and they don't, sign things with frightful trembling hand (for he has been again trying to stop drinking)—but manages it, explain, on way back to abarrotes:[4]

"These swine are really evil."

His Catholic wife.

(Margienote: Great sheafs of pesos—60 in 1 peso notes—I am prostrate with admiration.)

He says: "Well, they'll be a revolution, not now—oh no, it will be quiet this time. And then all these people will be blown up into the air and then they'll come down and make a mess of a lot of people's good roofs . . ." {UBC 14:6, 286} He goes on to say he was in Morro Castle[5]—remembers days of coaches, leather braces, the old road.

"And do you see who that is, up there, against the sky?"

"Where?"

"On the tower."

"The tower. Which tower. Whose? Where?" said Sigbjørn.

"Your wife," said Abarrotes.

(Sigbjørn heroically cashes check because they haven't got enough to get a bottle: Margie note: you *couldn't* cash cheque at bank, *or* get money from telegraph office without identification. That was a Saturday night, we were down to something like 5 pesos, and would be stuck over week end if you hadn't got to telegraph office, alas, they would have sent the money back, that was the last day they would hold it. And you got there *just* under the gun.) {UBC 14:6, 287}

XXXIX

Tuesday April 30.

On Sat, April 27, we have had to make a definite appointment at Immigration at 11 A.M. Tuesday 30th because there is a holiday on Monday of some nature . . . So once more, wearily, over the Sierra Madre to Mexico to have papers turned over to us on promise to B. Consul. Arrive promptly at Dept of Insp. and shortly, for them, that is to say in about half an hour, Inspector comes with seedy man (obv. interpreter cum stool pigeon) who says in broken English "You must go with him and have your pictures taken for Immigration visa—"

We repeat: "But we don't want an Immigration visa. We just want to leave!"

"Well, you gotta go with him."

Insp. v. tough, grabs M's arm and we start protesting.

Primrose wants to go to Turismo but we are more or less dragged across the street.

Primrose is very angry and at last suspects the worst.

Photographer's shop like a brothel: and full of shambling thugs, obviously potential deportees. Pics taken—Primrose's hat swept off: no chance to comb hair: in moment of indignation pic is snapped:[1] she looks like a madwoman. We are dragged back to Insp. office— Primrose goes to Turismo but de Lima and Buelna are out. Back to Inspección we are told to wait ahorita, momentito. "Your case is being decided."

I tell Margie to go and get photographs at 2 else the Inspector will overcharge us for them and get his mordida that way. While he is out I get hold of a fellow who had interpreted before: {UBC 14:7, 288}

"You are going to Laredo with that man. He say—"

Then later I say, "I guess he was only joking."

"Yes, he was only joking."

Primrose returns with photos—18 pesos for them—Inspector is angry and he and another woman are laughing at Primrose's pic. Sigbjørn laughs still louder.

"Que pasa?" says Fatty.

"That little business of my wife's hat is going to cost you and your subhuman colleagues your life one of these days, you terrible little pimp," Sigbjørn said calmly.

But Fatty just laughs and taps his head: "Must be loco."

We wait until 2:30, office is closing for the day, and Insp. comes with interpreter who speaks 5 words of Spanish and one of English—we must be at office May 2 at 12 noon with all our luggage. Why—are we being deported? Oh No! Why? Well, you must be. You must move to Mexico City. You must leave the country. Why? You don't understand. Oh, you don't understand? I take you to jail now then. Then you understand. We appeal, argue, find other interpreter,

no use, not deportation—what hotel you staying at in Mexico City?—
but they must be there with luggage or police will come to C. and
they *will* be deported. Fatty definitely turns wicked: takes Sigbjørn
by arm, and starts to drag him off.

Unable to go to Chanticleer and eat we drink some beer and eat
oysters and try to plan: Sigbjørn then takes Primrose to cathedral
before they catch bus. (cathedral scene follows this) But the weariness of the eternal journeys back and forth between Cuernavaca and
Mex City are symbolised by these sort of signs, in whatever order,
coming or going, is convenient: {UBC 14:7, 289}

El Puente del Chavacano—mi Pueblito—El Everest—Pemex—La
Esperanza—La Providencia—La Flor de las Américas—Se Vende
esta casa—No se permite fijar anuncios—666 gotas nasales—El Farolito—Supervulcanización—Llantas—Whiskey Bellows—Pulquería La
Judía—Hay un Ford en su futuro.[2]

With the dark mountains rising on either side, and Tres Marias in
the middle—like some sort of lesson that has to be learnt over and
over and over again.

Cathedral scene placed tentatively here.

Cathedral in Mexico City. We hire cab—Cathedral is closed and
driver says it won't be open for 2 hours, driver tries to cheat us.
Why not Guadalupe? this is a ten peso trip at least, as we know, but
he doesn't know we know—no. We discover that cathedral will be
open in 35 minutes. We walk around the block. I think it is really an
ugly building only imposing from across zócalo in romantic mood:
we try and remember, somehow, holiday again, opposite I bought
bracelet—and there was the Canada—[3]

Building covers square block but is muddled: part of dark grey
stone, part sort of red brick, and churrigueresque, but fine old carved
doors. At one side hombres are working on repairs: in the very doorway sits somebody else who promptly goes after us for a mordida:
(elsewhere—mem Notre Dame—someone is selling dirty pictures).
Queer little book stores and catholic shops, stifling, thundery heat
with sudden gusts of cold breeze that stop suddenly.

Back in front again, great doors are now open—is very large but
loses effect of size, like the one in Oaxaca, by being broken up, into
many compartments. There is, inside, mingled sound of hammers on
stone from workers, Latin service and chanting with priests in {UBC
14:7, 290} cerise robes and hats they keep taking off and putting on

again in central large cubicle, guides constantly importuning one to come and see relics and murmur of prayers. Double doors to right are wide open: workers working with trowels and slicks: barrows being wheeled in and out, the old floor like waves in ice, danced on by boys in Denmark, shafts of late sunlight and the dust dancing, searchlights of dust. There is at once a feeling of passionate devotion and holiness and a casual market-place atmosphere: an Indian woman places candle before shrine for virgin patron of difficult and dangerous causes as we pray there.[4] A middle class woman with purplish jacket over head goes on knees all the way from door (as in Oaxaca, before Soledad)[5] to other shrine of marvellous life-size ebony Christ—so good aesthetically there is no feeling to me of the usual dislike of usual horrors. Before this shrine a middle aged fattish man in grey suit kneels with arms outstretched like the Christ for such a long time I am sick with fatigue watching: I think this image of the supplicating man should recur at the end—possibly identify him with Fatty—but he is in a state of ecstatic prayer. Some boys are giggling and chatting and pinching each other in a side pew—a family, man and wife and little girl about 4—come in very gay and kneel and pray and go out laughing—the guide hooks some tourists—but despite the guards and the hammering there is a sense of peace and faith of eternity. The priest in black robes telling beads—later was seen in penetenaria (spelling Margie's) a wooden carved seat with high side and back walls and open front {UBC 14:7, 291}—the profound separation between kneeling figures and tourists: and the profound identity two of the kneeling figures and two kneeling tourists.

Sigbjørn found that he was staring toward an angel—though later he could not be sure it was not a daemon or a gargoyle—he was staring toward this, while to his right, in a little enclosure, as it were a Shakespearean scene was going on in a little conclave in full panoply, a conference of cardinals—he expected that at any moment they would turn out to be wax figures—a wooden angel numbered thirteen.

At bus station medal of Virgin falls out of Sigbjørn's pocket. and the man crossed himself (here or elsewhere) It's a little difficult to decide how to end this chapter.

(The priest in black robes telling rosary who made graceful, habitual, almost unconscious bows before shrines as he paced up and down old bumpy wooden floor telling beads. M.) {UBC 14:7, 292}

XL

I think the last ride back should be dramatised with Sigbjørn cursing Mexico[1]

April 30th.

At Cuernavaca to Charlie Pickard's. Describe ancient house. Pickard, Eddie, a woman named Sylvia Godwin[2] are playing poker. The valet. Orendain.[3]

"I am just a common citizen." But he says he can fix everything, just sit and wait and he'll call us Thursday morning at 10—it is today Tuesday, though Sigbjørn keeps thinking it's Sunday, so gloomy, but all are drinking. Primrose is panic-stricken: none are trustworthy.

Eddie says: "The Government have cashed in your bond. So if you'll just get someone else to underwrite your bond" (see telegram)[4] He fears we are being deported.

We drink: all say not to worry.

"Well, you know perfectly well we won't let you down. I can give you the thousand pesos now."

Sigbjørn is absolutely collected (but gets v. drunk) but Primrose is almost hysterical: everyone offers to help (except Pickard—who really could) in one way or the other: Eddy quarrels with Pickard.

Sylvia Godwin keeps saying of Eddie "He's a crook. I'm going to get him run out of town" and Sigbjørn defends him.

"I can't forget that he put up his cafe as security. He had no security from us that we wouldn't let him down."

"You won't be deported."

They are now with really influential people and Sigbjørn feels that all can be fixed, but one after the other things happen to interfere: either it is Sylvia Godwin, who wants to play poker with Pickard, just as Pickard is willing to consider what may be {UBC 14:7, 293} done, or something else. Pickard wants to stop playing poker and has deliberately allowed Sylvia to win: then she refuses to quit while a winner, so he wins back: then she insists on chance to recoup. Pickard becomes drunk and exasperated with everything.

Eddie and Pickard quarrel and Eddie leaves.

"No, I'd rather not come to your house if that's what you think of me." Eddie is v. drunk.

Sigbjørn would love to write down this terrific scene with the dialogue but he is too upset to: this is the writer's ultimate tragedy: far worse than anything else, was the feeling that he would never be able to recall this adequately—compare with similar feeling re sunsets etc.

Sigbjørn goes out to buy some Berreteaga and says his farewell to Cuernavaca, though perhaps this scene would have been better on Easter Monday, where the notes were taken. Here is the scene:

In Cuernavaca on Easter Monday, coming down at nightfall from the market with habanero and roses, stopping outside the little half-burned chapel, its bell ringing bong-bong-bong-bong in the wind, the dark green cypresses blowing against a dark twilight sky, a parrot slyly negotiating its way across the side of the electric wire strung from somewhere in the market to the side of the little church, the electric bulb, shaded, no 786, burning against the side of the half-burned chapel. And next door, the butcher shop La Lucha Eterna (the eternal light) shut. And the heart shut. Not then, when you were feeling just right. And the names of butcher shops in the market: La Sin Rival (The Without Rival) La Maravilla (The Marvel) La Luz del Dia (The Light of Day) La Tentacion (The Temptation) La Reina (The Queen)[5] and the market itself where the music of the radios was playing {UBC 14:7, 294} so portentously it made you think you were the protagonist great, which indeed he was, of something never dreamed of before, a work of art so beyond conception it could not be written.

Primrose and Sylvia are deep in discussion in his return—she says she'll go to the Governor of Morelos.

To Pickard's "Why has it all happened?" Sigbjørn's answer:

"Perhaps I was sympathetic to the Loyalists during the war," to which Pickard replies surprisingly:

"You shouldn't tell me these things. I have connections with the F.B.I."

"But good god," said Sigbjørn, "Weren't you sympathetic?"

"Christ no," says Pickard.

Again Sigbjørn fears what will happen getting back into America.

Sylvia inveigles Pickard into playing poker again: he doesn't want to, she loses, Pickard refuses to accept payment.

The horrible character of the Godwin woman. This poker scene should be one of the high spots in the whole book. (Margienote: what was worst was the feeling of *actual danger* for us, while all these *safe* people got drunk and made idiot remarks and promises they would never keep, one knew, yet Pickard could have fixed everything by one phone call.)

Sigbjørn plays piano: his piano playing is a history of his whole life and it seems to him that he comes near expressing it in music but he has such a frightful prescience of disastar that he is virtually on the point of losing touch with the situation per se.

Frightful scene going home outside El Universal (The Farolito). Primrose here betrays Sigbjørn to the cop—and La Mordida is paid by both. This is most dreadful thing that could happen: it {UBC 14:7, 295} seems now the end between them. Now he tears off the virgin and throws it at her.

(Perhaps he thinks he has murdered her.) Then he goes down to Eddie's and gets him up and tells him the story and drinks himself to sleep. Worse could scarcely come: and yet he knew perfectly well that worse, inevitably, would.[6]

Secretaría de Gobernación:

Recibí las fianzas Nos. 16090 y 16091—que por las cantidades de $500 Canadá unas expidió la cía, Central de Fianzas, S.A., para garantizar la repatriación del Sr. Clarence Malcolm Lowry y esposa Sra. Margerie Lowry.

México D.F. Abril 15 de 1946
El Jefe de Contratos y Fianzas
Angelica Machiavelo[7] {UBC 14:7, 296}

XLI

May 1

My own darling—Please with all my heart I ask you to love me we will die without each other—I have forgiven you perhaps this is your turn. In the name of the blessed virgin I gave you please love me—

I have gone to Charlie Pickard's to ask for help because I have talked to Eddie and am sure we're going to be deported otherwise. Key is under can. Love—Margie P.T.O. Eddie has just showed me wire government has cashed our bond and will deport us. Christ. Pray for help.—[1]

Dies irae for Primrose and Sigbjørn. Primrose up at 5 A.M. and starts to pack. Eddie at 9 with wire from Firenza. Quote this.

Primrose goes down to Eddie's where she and Sigbjørn have originally lived; finds Sigbjørn tight on couch. There is a dramatic and terrible scene between them. She takes one of the bottles of habanero.

Poor Primrose goes to Pickard's: he won't help, and is asleep and has a hangover. She goes from person to person seeking help: she lunches with odious Sylvia at Salon Ofelia—Rodriguez, who says if deportadoes according to law we should have been notified in writing. He will go with us in A.M. to Mexico and see cousin in Migración. Eddie says Rodriguez hasn't the pull he used to have. Sylvia has now changed mind about going to Governor and says she'd let them do their worst and write it up as an exposé. Finally pay Eddie the 1000 pesos and Pickard gives Primrose name and private phone of Sanchez who can fix at once. He will do no more though she begs and begs him for help. {UBC 14:7, 297}

Sigbjørn meantimes takes a reckoning with himself: things are now so bad that as an Englishman he feels can put up some fight. But he does precisely nothing, because there is no one to be trusted—the situation seems beyond explanation—save that he meets Primrose and Sylvia uptown with Eddie: Sylvia says to Primrose: "How can you stand him?"[2]

Sigbjørn disappears: actually he has gone next door to the Farolito (El Universal) memories of chap XII and the end,[3] but instead of getting tight, seeing someone else asleep, he goes to sleep too, is discovered by Eddie after many hours of everybody searching all Cuernavaca and Primrose running home every half hour to see if he's there etc. etc. there is great to-do about his being tight, but he has actually been drinking comparatively lightly during the day.

Primrose finishes her packing and gets taxi for A.M. and goes to bed but not to sleep: Sigbjørn has terrible night, as if the night had somehow turned into a cold damp sheet that was wound round and round him. Up before dawn, light charcoal fire, coffee and turkey eggs, but can't eat: drink coffee somehow, try to clean apartment finally and are ready.

M. to see Dr. Amann who gives us prescriptions for pheno.[4] Tries to explain to the Viennese why they are invoking Clause 66 but he doesn't understand. "Mexico was against Franco," he says. He says goodbye to Maria Luisa: the agony in the garden.[5] He does not tell her he is being deported: but she says that the story, as relayed by her, to a friend who had been dying in the hospital has excited her so much she is getting better and Sigbjørn wonders if this is not the true meaning of what is happening, that it is all for this one person's benefit. Sigbjørn thinks in that {UBC 14:7, 298} case their story better have a happy ending: but then remembers that Mexicans like all their stories to end unhappily, no matter how bad they are: but just for a second, daemon and protagonist are one.

Terrible moment of goodbye to apt. but won't be pathetic. Volcanoes still hidden: day stifling, sultry. Discuss with Eddie all way in but Sigbjørn's mind as if wrapped in cotton wool. Primrose's, on contrary, sharpened to supernatural degree of perception and feeling. The Tres Marias seem to be weeping. He prays. They stop while Sigbjørn has two brandies. He tries to suppress, above everything else, his terrible fear of trains. Eddy gets out and goes to straighten things out with bonding company. Psychology of this. "Oh I am not coming."

Arrive with bags at Gobernación but instead of taking bags into Immigration Sigbjørn carts them into Turismo. Then they wait in the sun for Rodriguez. He doesn't show. Primrose phones Orendain. He is out: Phone Sanchez—he is with Alemán in Mérida, Yucatan. While Primrose is doing this Sigbjørn is feeling faint and walks up and down street, he feels he is being watched too—he goes into cantina that is not open, the iron shutter half down and floor wet: a boy barman, perhaps sensing the desperation on Sigbjørn's face, gives him two Pantagruelian shots of rum[6] for only 30 centavos and Sigbjørn feels better:[7] he sucks a pheno. and he feels ready to meet the world.

Nobody has turned up—it is getting toward 12 the Immigration man Fatty turns up but Sigbjørn says their appointment is not until 12.

—and your equipajes.

—Aquí.

—Pera dónde.[8] What is your hotel in Mexico City. {UBC 14:7, 299}

Apparently Fatty hasn't got it through his head that they were staying in Cuernavaca.

They go to Turismo and appeal to Buelna, who is cold and not very nice, says talk to Corunna, who is a very nice chap. But he has to be fairly nice because there are other American tourists present. We plead for help or at least interpreter. No. Finally Buelna, who senses something is wrong, calls office of sub-secretario of Dept. of Interior and makes appointment for us to see him at once and state our case. "You can be sure you will get a fair hearing."

So upstairs to his office and wait with some hope and feeling it is at any rate a sanctuary. It is now nearly 12 and we wait and wait and wait. Finally told we can't see him: we appeal.

Description of the office: the nonchalant boys with papers they hand you—the paperweights.

Woman comes in who speaks very good English offers to translate—she is Cuban—goes in to see Sub-Secretary, saying she'll tell him about us. Wait. Meantime Fatty has come in very angrily and nearly dragged us out but I refuse to be dragged and he apparently realises we're in as it were a court of higher appeal.

Woman comes out of office and says secretary says Mexicans are treated like dogs in America and come here and expect everyone to bow. (She says that's true, worse than dogs, for Americans are kind to animals—I know, they were terrible to me, asked me if I was a murderess.) Why shouldn't we treat them the same here.

"I am not American and I'm gratified to know that you appreciate that Mexicans are not kind to dogs," Sigbjørn said. He hates us and has seen to it that we *can't* see sub-secretary, in short. Primrose leaves M. still trying and runs to Buelna to try and get {UBC 17:7, 300} him to call American Consul (for various reasons, their last resort) B. will do nothing, but is finally persuaded to give us interpreter. Meet Insp. get M and to Inspección office where try to see Corunna but are refused. Insp. yells and is foul. "You say bad things about Mexico!" (to Primrose) "I say it's not so! I love Mexico and don't understand. (to Sigbjørn) You said bad things about Mexico and wrote—we know—we have it all." Turismo interpreter is nice but weak and helpless and out of his depth. You must go to 113 Bucarelli to get your papers. I say no—they're taking us to jail! No, just to get your papers but Interpreter from Turismo turns pale. Help! Call the American Consul—Embassy—British Consul—Orendain— we are taken to jail and held incommunicado, in short in the "sort of boarding house" that contained his ex-shipmate.

(note: this 113 Bucarelli was most feared of prisons: it was said once in there you were never heard of again. We recognize it when walking down street.) {UBC 14:7, 301}

XLII

May 2

Details not in Margie's notes here are too unforgettable to forget. Upstairs in an old grimy building are taken into big empty room above street. There, must sign names. I am talking fast to Turismo—call Consulate, quick! etc—then through another dark dirty room with narrow tumbled cot to room about 15 ft. sq. with barred windows giving on small airshaft and one electric light burning through it is about one o'clock or one thirty and a hot sunny day, which makes it even weirder in one way. But we are together.

The place is old and dirty and with rough board floors, mustard-dirty walls with messages written: samples.

"That man who don't believe it's a good friend are no man."

Also John Powell "Two Times" 1944–1945.

Like Borda Gardens, why are you my sweetheart, why, whom?

Recuerdo José Martinez,[1] and names and dates. (contemplate putting Juan Fernando here—this would link it with Dark as the Grave)—also Kilroy? On the back wall is a huge airplane drawing: Rose Marie, Virginia on its wings—and smaller ones going away in formation. There is also a Nazi plane there, the huge swastika. Conspicuous by its absence, however, was any sign saying Mexico por la Libertad.

They have clanged shut double doors, locked them. In the room are simply 3 cots with bumpy mattresses and dirty quilts or blankets beside the window, a door opens to a large dirty filthy bathroom with horrible toilet, used toilet paper piled high, encrusted washbasin with no running water—main point is there is {UBC 14:7, 302} no door—all in full view of all inmates of this cell—Primrose says—but Sigbjørn says what in Christ name do you expect?—Sig. is in good form, and in fact shows his true colors here—and a large tub half full of dirty cold water. On bed beneath drawing of Nazi plane is a young chap 22 or 23, black hair, blue eyes, handsome, wrapped in a dirty sheet.

(Kilroy p-d here today. El Pollo was here too. El Grafe did his c-sking here today. Kilroy was looking. Kilroy was here today too)[2]

"I am a German boy," he says. "I had no papers, and you see?" He makes gesture of resignation. He explains that his clothes are being washed. We sit gingerly on cot expecting bugs. Door opens and in comes small dark narrow-faced merry chap who sits on other bed and removes shoes. He has three pairs of old shoes under bed and keeps changing from one to the other and going barefoot. Pedro. He is from Ecuador and has sailed round the Gulf of Mexico—he can't understand why anyone who can live in the States wants to leave. He speaks broken English. "Ecuador is a poor country. I enter as a student." Because he has not been able to show enough money he has had nothing but trouble. German also speaks some English but no Spanish, both have been there a month or so—German had been there two years. Pedro has apparently jumped ship? (Mem: We see Circus man briefly in outside room.) Pedro who sweeps from time to time—says we are incommunicado but grinning negro who appears at door will, for a price, so he says, go to our consulate with messages. We produce habanero—order agua de selis from the negro who brings orange crush and we offer everyone a drink: German takes one, Pedro refuses and drinks something—wine?—from large bottle under his bed. Presently Chief comes in: well-dressed, {UBC 14:7, 303} and dapper and even handsome except for gold teeth. He is very cheery and most polite and with great trouble to get doors open brings in large office chair for me and other for M. Negro will go for food or anything we wish. (He has no English.) We are silent, but cheerful, afraid to talk. Pedro, who is a privileged character or stool pigeon, and chief decide it is wrong for la señora to be in room with men while German says: "We are all men here," and they open adjoining room and clean it out and set up 2 cots amid refuse of broken chairs—Chief gives me his blanket—es mío (contrast of all this is ironically refreshing after treatment by Migración) muy limpio[3]—señora—and even 2 clean sheets. We move to other room and order ham and eggs.

"It's the ideal life," says Sigbjørn.

They are enchanted as children by my coat. While Pedro and German go out to eat prison stew we hold swift conference and swear fealty. This is almost fine and somehow funny and everyone is so gay and polite and kind.

But presently comes Inspector and we must go. Negro arrives with eggs—we eat saltless and with fingers and we are hurried out. Goodbye to sailor. Good luck—see you in Liverpool—everybody is so happy we're going and kind and helpful with luggage.

Taxis (2) and to station "No Pullman" and aboard day coach.

"But I want to fill a prescription."

"What prescription?" Sigbjørn has forgotten the pheno.

The nice guys or somebody stole our camera and all Margie's clothes, and there is the nightmare of Fatty being generous with our 1000 pesos. {UBC 14:7, 304}

Train starts—there is drunk in front, shaken by guard—people go up and down selling beer etc. So there we are with Fatty with 2 guns watching us every minute, we have bottle of Berreteaga, thanks to Primrose, the one Sigbjørn had thought (ungenerously) purloined by her, in their bag. Primrose produces it and we buy cococola and drink out of paper cups—we even offer Fatty one, behind, with the Literary Digest. (Ties up with Acapulco, boy reading Digest upside down.)

And though going to certain death, they sleep, contrary to everything they might have expected, like children. {UBC 14:7, 305}

XLIII

(First started late afternoon, passed through several pretty little towns.

This chapter is of course liable to revision. (Time table)

Guard brings Saturno.

Pheno—Saturno—habanero.

The icewater, the toilet, the day coach is not too uncomfortable. There is an unused seat for Primrose at night.

Anything to Sigbjørn is better than a Pullman: he is thankful at least for that grace and he remembers going on the West Coast Route with the d.t.'s, the heat, the woman yelling at him, the lost manuscripts (In Ballast, Men at Mazatlan),[1] the endless desert, the cats at Guadalajara, falling rather than stepping out, and then imagining one had perhaps not after all stepped out: unable to dress in the Pullman, the lack of privacy, the terrible net in which one's clothes were caught, and everything falling out of one's pockets, being locked in the toilet: here at least there was not that, one was delivered of the tyranny of the conventional attitude for sleep, and could be almost grateful, after several habaneroes that Fatty had the tickets . . . and the passports . . .

Loathsome suburbs of Mexico City—get Margie to describe—Alemán, Moralización[2]—memories of their first day in Mexico—Virgin of Guadalupe, the fair, the Saint of Dangerous and Desperate causes—man eaten by rats. Dreadful difficulty of *opening* the Berreteaga.

At first the attempt to keep alive, or revive even a feeling of holiday, and this succeeded by a sense of sorrow, of failure, of having given in, of cowardice, and self-betrayal and horror that is unbearable: but above all of sorrow— {UBC 14:8, 306}

During the night they recall starting off to Acapulco with such high hopes . . .

The great train grinding through the night.

The mood of sorrow is intensified when they crash through Guanajuato in the dark—or what they think is Guanajuato—just a few scattered lights and gone—the mood of lost opportunity, might have been, and shattered honeymoon—mem Vigil and Juan Fernando—

After Primrose is asleep (Margienote: I never slept a goddamn bit on that horrible train, I can't sleep sitting up anyhow) Sigbjørn sinks into this cold sphere of his own horror and agony: relate his reflections perhaps to Schopenhauer on the will:[3] he is gripped again by the awful cold that strikes up from the abyss, conscious of Fatty sitting behind all the time, and yet he is conscious of weariness, and rest: (must not lose sight either of Sigbjørn as a writer: *I shall never write this: I shall never write this: I shall never write this*: fumed the train. Memories of other trains: Hotel Room in Chartres, Metal, perhaps) he sinks into this and feels he is truly dying—mem—dreams of trains are death dreams[4]—going, yet also he feels during the night as if a new consciousness is replacing the old: but early in the morning as dawn creeps it is the sense of danger, of tension soon to be at an end, almost of exhilaration that comes over him and he wonders how long it will last and when the hangover will strike, or the hangover of death.

And yet he waits, and it does not hit him.

Fatty again in the morning, and the strange breakfast in the Pullman (the dining car) the Americans, but the sense of persecution grows, even the stewards know and are rude, Primrose says {UBC 14:8, 307} afterwards she wanted to cry out for help—

But Primrose is very brave: they sit and look out of the window: the same landscapes, same kind of stations, get the names of the stations: every time Sigbjørn thinks of what is going to happen at Nuevo Laredo his mind comes up against a brick wall: for remember he is as terrified of America as of Mexico: what if his hands should tremble—he cannot get in—

And they are running out of pheno, in spite of the prescription and also out of habanero; at eleven or twelve again the technique with the habanero and the ice water—

Lunch again and Primrose wants to cry out among the Americans or with a kind of last gesture they buy tortillas—

Primrose continues to be brave but what Sigbjørn was most surprised at was his own grip of this situation—after they eat, a nap, another nip, Fatty watching them all the time, then Sigbjørn actually tries sarcastically the mordida on Fatty, who laughs and shakes his head, having their money: "No, I have mi ordenes. Son todos."

"Have you got enough to eat?" Fatty says.

"Are we going to be deported?" Sigbjørn asks again and Fatty says, "Oh no. Not deported."

"You'll give us our passports at the border then?"

"Sí."

"Then finito?"

"Then finito."

All this in a kind of pigeon Spanish[5] etc.: there should be the punctum indifferens[6] of the stations going by wherever they are on the timetable: Sigbjørn returns, half elated, or pretending {UBC 14:8, 308} to be, to Primrose, with the news that Fatty has refused the mordida of 50 pesos and they laugh and also that they're not going to be deported: but Primrose a little while after seems sad, and casts a sad look around at their luggage, the shopping bag . . .

"What is it?"

"Nothing."

"But I thought that news would make you happy."

"Do you believe it?"

"As much as I could believe anything in Mexico . . ."

Again the stations, the landscape, they don't look at it—"Why—don't you." Advertisements, take them out of the time table, they will give the *feel* of the landscape, or of an approaching town, viz: (p 11—timetable)

!Salud! Coma Usted
en el
Restaurant
de los
Ferrocarriles
San Luis Potosi

Hotel Ambos Mundos
Visítelo y Quedará Satisfecho (is a good one too)

Hotel Progreso
El Mejor y más céntrico de la ciudad
Gerente: R. F. Diaz Infante
San Luis Potosi[7]

—or En Monterrey—Hotel Bermuda—Plaza Zaragaza

"No," Primrose says, "My father was a consul and I know. What he means is that *you* can't be deported."

"Why should you be deported and not me. That's the last straw."

"The last straw is just what I fear. They can't deport an Englishman to the United States . . ." {UBC 14:8, 309}

"Well, I'd thought of that. But what's the good of thinking of it. We are together."

"Are we?"

"And are we?"

"Are we."

"We'll win through."

"I'm so—so—frightened."

"Don't be."

Another dinner, another night: the next day—the Canadian and his stuttering dialogue:

"Whhhy are there six gg-guards on this train?"

"Wh-h-hy have they st-tolen my c-camera. I just took a p-picture of a c-c-c-cactus and the mm-man said you can't do that. Since when was a c-c-cactus a m-military objective!"

Guerra a la Ignorancia. !Enseñe a leer![8]

"I g-gave him t-t-ten pesos."

"C-Canadian t-trains are much b-b-better than this."

"I think they're much worse," Sigbjørn said. "Much worse," knowing that Fatty was listening to every word.

They prescribe Castamargina for the kids—

Guerra a la IGNORANCIA! En analfebetismo es dolor y lastre de los pueblos. !Enseñe a leer y escribir! Disponible para Anuncio—[9]

—a plane even passes going the other way.

Primrose dreaded going up into Nuevo Leon—memories of plane trip—flat irrigated country baked reddish country Monterrey looked like Birmingham Ala, flat plains, brick buildings with advertising signs—lines take a big turn to the left, mountains appear beyond flat plains, sky begins to reflect the color of soil, Monterrey is approached obliquely, in fact you seem to be almost going in the {UBC 14:8, 310} other direction, stormy grey wet reddish sky—

(City of Monterrey—memories of landing in plane—how different—it seemed rather Hoylake England, that kind of flatness but with the Welsh hills moved nearer)

Factory chimneys in the murk, not yet rain, but sense of storm, and also terrible sense of "drop," as if, on the way back to school one had reached Rugby or Crewe.

A corpse will be transported by express—*deported*.[10]

Clipperty *one*—and the pheno.

The great scene on Monterrey platform when before Sigbjørn realises what has happened Primrose is magnificently off beyond the barrier to get the pheno: Sigbjørn engages Fatty in conversation, though Fatty is continually nervous, casting jittery glances toward the barrier. Conversation between Fatty and Sigbjørn on platform in the fresh sweet air, by the grunting hissing engine.

S: Monterrey es muy hermosa.

F: Sí. Sí. Muy hermosa.

S: Pero es muy industrial.

F: Sí. Es muy industrial.

S: Muchas fábricas aquí.

F: Sí. Muchas fábricas.[11]

Sigbjørn sees himself looking with anguish straight at an advertisement for the Hotel Papagayo situado en la Playa de Hornos a la Orilla del Mar. Gerente Isauro Flores Acapulco, Gro. and tries another tack.

S: Nosotros habemos arriberado par avion, etc. Las montanas son tres hermosa[12]—he produced. "We have seen many mountain goats from the plane," he almost squalled, and restraining himself with {UBC 14:8, 311} an effort from catching Fatty's sleeve. "Muchos automobiles here," he says. "Cadillac. Chevrolet—" then he sees with relief that Primrose is coming back.

They get back on the train that has been changing engines and behaving much like a train on the Great Northern or London to Scotland.

"My God how did you do that," Sigbjørn asked. But Fatty does not seem too annoyed, engaged with the Literary Digest behind, in fact he seems enormously relieved, and Sigbjørn approaches him again as they pull out.

"You will give us our passports when we get to Nuevo Laredo," he said, of course not believing it.

"Sí."

"What about our money?"

"Perhaps that has gone on a multa."[13]

"A quel heure do we arriberamos a Nuevo Laredo?"

"No se . . . Mañana. Temprano. Midnight."

. . . . .

"They would only give me twenty."

"I hope that will be more than enough."

They go on into the evening, the dark, Sigbjørn resists the impulse to garrotte Fatty, they are entering the desert, the stations flash past in the dusk, Topa, Leal, Morales, Mamulique, El Jardin, El Puerto, Alamo, etc. etc.

(Calculate where desert is) Sigbjørn gets into tweed coat for dinner but regrets it when he goes into dining car: it is boiling hot: the Americans sitting there: sunset in the desert of Nuevo Leon: they have two engines now and the reverberation is suddenly terrific, smiting, hitting, like a loud motorboat engine or {UBC 14:8, 312} tugboat heard in the fjord against the mountains at home when the fjord is empty, it is hard to see out of the windows: they are dirty, glimpses of agonizingly beautiful sunset seen through sweat and embarrassment: the faces bent on eating American food now, American soup, chicken a la king, whatever they eat. The stewards ruder than usual: Sigbjørn only does not appeal for help because he feels it may make matters worse, precipitate, that is, immediately, a disastrous situation, and explanations he will not be able to make explicit or in time, he feels a certain security as of a somnambulist, but he knows he has to go through whatever it is he has to go through: thunder claps in the desert, the awful effect of thunder claps banging against the mountains in the desert against the sudden accelerated accumulated mighty thrusting and smiting and hitting of the two engines in this awful heat of the dining car with its windows clamped shut: clap-crash clap clap crash smite boooom smite booom (yet this noise is *outside*, insulated from them) they go back to their car without leaving a tip: darkness falls and the thunder really begins to break, shattering and sliding along the hastening and moaning train with its two engines that[14] seems now doing its utmost while the lightning throws the whole train into darkness: the lights come on dimly, then go off, then come on, it is pouring with rain outside too: Sigbjørn and Primrose have a couple of difficult habaneros and half a pheno: the train hissed to a stop as Bustamente—"Bustamente!"[15] HISTORICAL PLACES (see Life, Mem American war)[16] when he remembered his cinema manager and the lights going out in the cinema—at Bustamente, the baritoned terrifying official tough gets on with files and so on and everybody is told to get {UBC 14:8, 313} their tourist cards ready etc. They seem to take too long at Bustamente, *Here Comes Everybody*[17] i.e. the tourist card inspector and Fatty have an enormously long and loud conversation—it seems to Sigbjørn—entirely about them while Primrose and Sigbjørn sit drinking habanero—occasionally HCE turns round, watching them but never once stops talking: the train whizzes, sways, moans, and the thunder and lightning crackle after them like a force: the light goes off and on in the train, and then seems permanently dim: Primrose with tactless yet obvious secrecy, betraying to Sigbjørn's mind that it isn't a sweet or an aspirin, offers Sigbjørn a pheno which he takes, looking round, with tactless secrecy again straight into the face of HCE and Fatty: he swallows it but thereafter in the swaying train the following conversation for a while seems to be going on, though he cannot be actually sure that it is:

—They're spies.

—Clearly, we've known they were spies all along. But we were too clever for them and picked them up in Acapulco.

—Yes man—so it was Corunna gave you your orders. They are to be deported.

—Naturally.

—Naturally.

Fatty—Naturally not. We cannot deport the Englishman. We will (making a gesture) shoot him.

—Sí. Naturalmente.

Primrose offers another pheno to Sigbjørn and this time Sigbjørn sees that Fatty has seen it and has imitated the gesture of his eating it to HCE while the train whizzes and moans and the thunder crashes and HCE also seems to be eating something {UBC 14:8, 314} slyly out of his briefcase.

—They are not only spies, they are drugfiends.

—Estupifaciontes.

—Sí. Estupifaciontes. They har escaped through many states. We have founded out they har the head of a drug ring.

—They are drunkards too, are they not?

—Drunkards, drug fiends, and spies. And writers.

—So they will be shot.

—Clearly.

—But you say they are writers.

—No, they are not writers, they are espiders and we shoota the espiders in Mexico.[18]

—You mean they are drug fiends and will be held.

—Yes. When it comes to that (Fatty imitates or seems to imitate in the dusk the trembling hand and the taking of the pheno, and then imitates it again) it is time for the law to step in.

—Besides which they are borrachos.

—Always, said Fatty.

HCE stands up with a gesture of contempt: Time to take the Tourist Cards, though meantime somebody has been down the cars saying this to everybody but Primrose and Sigbjørn.

La Lagunilla, Palma, Golondrinas, (p. 12 guide) Candela, Brasil, Lampazos, Naranjo, Mojina, Mesa, Rodriguez—Ah, Rodriguez who never turned up at 10—here there is a longer stop still and when they start, HCE being away, Sigbjørn approaches Fatty again:

"How long before we get to Nuevo Laredo?"

Fatty shrugs. "Una hora." (or whatever.)

"What about our passports?"

"No passeporte." Fatty is insolent again. {UBC 14:8, 315}

Sigbjørn does not convey this news to Primrose nor how near they are, merely suggests that they have a habanero or two but conserve it also: he goes to try and have a shave but cannot see in the dark: in the *open* lavatory suggesting to Primrose she does the same: he says before, "Possibly it's of the utmost importance that we look like something at the American border." "If we ever get there," says Primrose. When he comes out again Fatty says, insolently but not unkindly, queries: "Lista?"[19] Thunder and rain are now seething along with the train: Sigbjørn gets the icewater and oh—those paper cups—and they discuss discreetly another habanero with irony: a station called Anahuac—Quauhnahuac—waves, sways, gleams, crashes wetly past: Camarón (cabrones!)[20] Huizachito (see p. 12 timetable) Altos, Jarita—at Sanchez, as both the thunder and the lightning, the train and the rain seem to make a sudden thundering sprinting spurt together all the lights go out, though one remains very dim—goes on for a while long enough to reveal and outside too (though the lights are dim there) advertisements: Hotel Rendon Cada Cuarto con Baño—Hotel oficial de la Ama Nuevo Laredo Tamps swayed away into Hotel Continental Albos Edificio Escamilla[21] 25 cuartos 25 baños, Nuevo Laredo Tamps, this into Se Marga Vd Cuando Pesca.[22] Mothersills, and this into Four Roses Fine American Whiskey and this into darkness of rain and thunder: then suddenly—too soon—they were in Nuevo Laredo. Everybody save ourselves and Fatty had left their dark coach.

"Give us our papers!"

A certain feeling of hope—we'll get rid of Fatty—we rush across the aisle—he gets out of train—lights go out— {UBC 14:8, 316}

Then the luggage, in the dark, is thrown out of the window, Sigbjørn again asks for the passports, Primrose protests the luggage being thrown out, they are ordered out of the train—Primrose gets out the wrong side—(point out of course that Nuevo Laredo is on the Mexican side of border)—"look out for the shopping bag, the habanero's in it!" sticking out, no platform, Margie nearly killed, yanked back and across between cars as train starts, they get out somehow into the drenching rain and the pools of blackness.

While the train for America went on through the thunder without them.

Or:

And the train for America had gone on through the thunder without them. {UBC 14:8, 317}[23]

XLIV

(Good names for towns also: Alacranes (Scorpions), Dr. Coss, Sinai, Timones—These are all on the way between Monterrey and Matamoros but might be worked in on our route.)

They get—or Fatty gets—a taxi in Nuevo Laredo, Tamps, it is after midnight and pouring, they think they are going to an hotel, but Fatty (who has by the way helped with the luggage) says simply: "No hotel—"

They speed through the town in the rain, there is a nice square, there are some horse cabs, their wheels revolving in the rain, it seems a nice old town in the wet light, a town to explore, Sigbjørn and Primrose still half think they care or are going to an hotel, more wet lights spring ahead of them, and a high sky-sign Cartablanca Exquisita, there is a bridge, a brilliance of light on both sides of the road and windy voices, sentry boxes: it is the bridge over the Rio Grande, the border—

On one side now is Nuevo Laredo in the state of Tamaulipas, and on the other Laredo in Texas: one side is Mexico, on the other, America.

In a sense it is difficult not to breathe more easily: in another—

They unload into the Immigration office on the left, and from now on we must have some at least recourse to our statement; they are garish lights,[1] naked bulbs overhead, a man with a vizor is banging on a typewriter, a contraption for measuring people, a weighing machine, a picture of Camacho, there is somebody else there also whom Fatty greets as a long lost friend—

The Mexican eagle is also, as at Acapulco, tearing the Nazi flag, there is an advertisement for the Fiorenzas—and also—who knows?—for Acapulco. {UBC 14:8, 318}

Fatty's air of pseudo-helpfulness has dropped as soon as they get in and Sigbjørn sees he is showing their passports and Primrose's paper.

They have brought in their bags and their poor shopping bag from which the bottle of habanero is protruding: Fatty now hands the passport to one of these night clerks.

Fundamental difference between these night working clerks and the day working ones: one is definitely good-looking and seems a good egg.

Then the cross-examination begins, typing, much of this should be done in dialogue—after a lot of typing they are handed a paper saying they are going to be deported and they refuse to sign. This scene should be very dramatic though I shall have to have recourse to Margie. Fatty becomes petrified with rage, the kind man pales, Sigbjørn says to Fatty:

"But you have told us all along we were not to be deported."

"It is not I who am deporting you," says Fatty (Catholic).

"You have deceived us deliberately all along."

"I said it was not myself who was deporting you. It is Corunna. See here—Corunna. I have my ordenes."

"Never mind about your ordenes and never mind me for the moment. You can't deport my wife. You're committing a crime against an American citizen—Where is our money?"

"Perhaps it has gone on a multa," Fatty says vaguely.

"I advise you to sign," says the kind man eyeing Fatty's revolvers.

"This stooge told us that when we reached Nuevo Laredo we'd be given our papers and we could go." {UBC 14:8, 319}

"If your wife should sign, then she can go."

"Shall I sign, Sigbjørn?" said Primrose.

"No," said Sigbjørn.

Again the revolvers: and Fatty starts raging again.

"All right then, Primrose, you sign. But remember, and you witness it," Sigbjørn says, looking at the kind man, "that we're signing under protest."

(Margienote: you've missed the drama here old boy: what we were signing was an admission that we had broken the laws of Mexico, and this we strenuously denied as being a lie. Also, we finally signed because the kind man got so frightened he began to shake all over and said to me please, Señora, please, I dare not talk, but please, Señora, it is dangerous, etc. etc.)

"It's a mere formality," said the kind man.

"Sign and then go—make the most of it and go," Sigbjørn says to Primrose, "and leave me to deal with them."

(I absolutely refuse to be made out such a fool: this is not true: why not tell the truth? If you'd said any such thing I would never have signed at all! Truth is we both signed, finally, because we had to. Then they said I could go and I flatly refused to leave you. You said I should go, I said NO. You said I might get help across the border and return for you. I said no.—well, could I? I felt strongly that I would not leave you)

Primrose signs and is told: "Now you can go." And then there is the dramatic moment of ley fuga.² Sigbjørn tells her to go:

How innocent it looked too, the bridge over the Rio Grande into America, the tall lamps with bulbs, the gleaming pavements, no more fearsome than the toll-gate at the second narrows bridge {UBC 14:8, 320} at home,³ yet perhaps dividing life and death.

"No. I won't leave you."

"Why not? I'll get through in the morning."

(Point was, old boy, when they said I could go, we said why then couldn't you, they said American Immigration was closed until 7 in the morning, I could enter my country because it was my country, but you'd have to wait for immigration to open.)

"I've told you why not."

"That's right. You go," said Fatty, looking nasty:—the upshot is Primrose doesn't go, then Sigbjørn signs, not before saying, "I sign under protest."

Now he almost wishes his hand would fail him, but he signs: there is a lot more formality to go through with him: the humiliation of the measuring machine—

"Only 165."

"I told you it was only 165" says Fatty—(though for God's sake get away from Hemingway.)⁴

He is still in a rage and Sigbjørn asks him can they now go to an hotel, knowing that looking like this (he has not been able to bathe or shave on the train) if they ever get to the American border, and the deportation is reported, it will be a bad business.

"No hotel. You stay here."

"But my wife has nowhere to sleep."

"You ah sleep here."

"While you go to an hotel on our money, you bugger," says Sigbjørn.

Fatty leaves orders for them to remain "till I come for you in the morning." (This is a mistake, darling, for you were told you could go at 7, as soon as Immigration opens—more dramatic) {UBC 14:6, 321}

The light is on, the typewriter is going, the Mexican eagle is eating the Nazi flag. Sigbjørn and Primrose sit on the sofa just staring blankly for a while at the wall: the vizored man types on. The nerve-wracking horror of the noise, the naked electric light.

—Sigbjørn talks to him from time to time and from time to time asks him if at least his wife can go to an hotel. "For one thing if we can't get washed up a bit they won't let us over the American border and you don't want that"—this argument carries some weight, though this manner has humanity. They also try to find out if the case is closed so far as Fatty is concerned.

The handsome vizored man keeps asking them to wait, in the end is broken down, goes to a phone perhaps, phones.

Apparently he is phoning some hotels, but each time he fails to find any room. Finally he is saying:

"Bueno . . . The Hotel Ambos Mundos" (I think is the best name but it should be one of the names of the hotel seen from the train in XLIII[5] in which case we must transfer Hotel Ambos Mundos there)

"But you must promise to stay in hotel. You must be back here at quarter to six, before the shift changes and I will send someone for you."

Finally the kind vizored man is ready. Taking the faithful shopping bag, they go out into the wet night, though it has stopped raining. "Would you like to have a coffee?"

(Margienote: please please don't forget he had two guards with him every minute whom he left to guard us.)

It begins to rain and they get a taxi: they draw up at the Hotel Ambos Mundos—Sigbjørn pays, but almost gives the taxi driver the little Virgin of Guadalupe by mistake. Sigbjørn and {UBC 14:8, 322} the taxi driver cross themselves, slush through the lobby of the hotel—"Nosotros no somos Americanos ricos—" even to the last—give the kind man some money to pay the bill in advance—he pays, but has not failed to keep some mordida for himself.

The room is as it were outside, flush with the ground floor, with the garden indeed, or a kind of green lawn (a garden). But it has a hot shower. (It was the best room we were ever in in all of Mexico, dearduck, and the cleanest.) Sigbjørn showers and shaves: they finish the brandy, or leave a bit for the morning, calculate the right amount of pheno to take, warm and luxurious, they are too tired to be frightened and they sleep like the dead. They had three hours. {UBC 14:8, 323}

XLV

Once more they sit in the Immigration office, 5:45, already light. Another negative nice chap, whom vizored man had persuaded to let them go, is departing. The Wildernesses had been called at the Ambos Mundos at half-past five, been up and dressed in a minute, found the taxi outside with someone quite polite with the taximan, and driven to the Immigration—though the taximan even under these circumstances is unsatisfied with his tip, even though they are prisoners.

It is now quite light. The Rio Grande could be seen through the window, a muddy sluggish little river with goats tethered down the bank on the Mexican side. It looked easy to cross for all the splendid lamped bridge vaulted it: the lamps were still on even in daylight, but now they twitched off. A different man was now sitting at the typewriter and they felt lost without the kind vizored man. There was a great difference between the scene at night and now in the hard light of day. They sit and sit.

Six o'clock and the dayshift comes on, first a few clerks straggling in with khaki uniforms, pretty quiet clerks opening up the office, who take absolutely no notice of them. The Wildernesses sit and sit: the clock ticks on and every now and then Sigbjørn wonders why they are sitting. Only the picture of Camacho and the tireless Mexican eagle seemed familiar, staunchly eating the flag, and their bags with their uke in the corner. After a while Primrose gets up and angrily copies down the address of the Fiorenzas on the wall in a notebook she has taken from her bag . . .

Mexico por la libertad! {UBC 14:9, 324}

It was six-fifteen, it was six twenty, it was half past six, and they would presumably have to wait till—(remember, they had told us absolutely we could go at 7, when American Immigration opened) Sigbjørn's mind shied away from any brute facts, but they had at least the confidence of three hours sleep, and Sigbjørn has that of a shave, of having exactly calculated the amount of drinks and pheno: he feels indeed a sense of queer elation, that is sharpened by the terrible sense of danger.

Twenty to seven, and the Wildernesses sit on the couch facing the empty desk of the Chief, on the couch where last night they had sat under the glaring intolerable light (and now the light was soft and sweet with morning) though then there had been the vizored man.

But Sigbjørn forced himself not to think about the chief, nor speculate upon what kind of man he would be. At quarter to 7 Sigbjørn realises that they have both fallen into a kind of stupor, perhaps they had forgotten why they were there, or what they were doing, as so often had happened in the Immigration Offices at Acapulco and Mexico City. But this feeling was accompanied also by that prescience felt by the captain of the rugby team on the losing side when he realises that there ought to be only a quarter of an hour to go. While their conversation resembled less that between vital human beings than the patter between weary tap dancers, or even marathon dancers.

"Only a quarter of an hour."

"Only a quarter of an hour till what, Sigbjørn."

"Only a quarter of an hour till the American Immigration opens."

"*So* what?"

"Then you can go." {UBC 14:9, 325}

"Yes, then *I* can go. Or can I? Perhaps there isn't anybody here who knows our case."

"But that was the understanding, Primrose, that we could go at seven, and that the matter's out of Fatty's hands."

"What if Fatty has our papers?"

"He hasn't"

"How do you know?"

"I saw him give them to our vizored friend. Apparently he had orders to hand them over."

"Oh yeah?" said Primrose.

"Why do you say oh yeah?"

"It seems as good a thing to say as anything else."

Like a cinema clock, the clock ticks toward seven. Ah, the fatal seven—the seven of the tower.[1] And the Wildernesses sat, waiting for seven, half thinking or pretending to think that at that time some khaki-figured angel of deliverance would come up to them and say: "Now you can go."

But it was now five past seven and Sigbjørn was almost relieved to think that no one had come up to them; and now half-past seven, and still no one had come up to them. Primrose rose wearily and spoke to a clerk:

"We are just simply waiting—" she began.

"Por favor—"

"We are just simply waiting," Primrose pronounced every word with icy annunciation "until the American Immigration opens at seven—and surely we can now go—"

"It is just half past seven" said the man, correcting his watch by the clock on the wall. {UBC 14:9, 326}

"And surely we can now go, for it is now 7:30 and the *American Immigration is certainly open*," Primrose said.

At this point (or it is Sigbjørn who has asked the above questions) they get the first real objective notice that they are not free to go: everyone looks at them in a very hostile manner and the clerk said:

"No. You cannot go until the chief comes, he has to sign your release." And then returned to a paper he was reading.

They fretted on the couch: Primrose (or Sigbjørn) asks somebody else and gets the same reply, and Sigbjørn walks over to the desk where the vizored man had been sitting and asks (avoid chords of Kafka):[2]

"Then when will the chief be in?"

"The chief?" snapped the man.

"Sí. El Jefe."

"Oh, he's due here at 8 o'clock," said the man rudely without looking up. "He'll be along."

It now gets hotter and hotter: (perhaps this is the point too to describe the *reflection* of the heat on the stove mentioned earlier) and the strange thing about this heat it had the sort of quality that pertained at home on the inlet on a summer Sunday morning, a dead calm, a thick haze bisecting the spiked mountain from its ragged shadow the reflected sun burning and expanding through the water, the strangely idle fleet of ducks and gulls motionless on the water, near shore the barnacled rocks raising their heads like volcanic Azores from a visible Atlantis,[3] flashes of sparkle and quicksilver in the water and through the haze, the flowing reflection of the cross-traces of the pier—the little pier—their little pier—and such a promise of picnic and islands where in the afternoon pennyroyals would be blowing on the rocks—more clerks arrive: describe the Wildernesses' {UBC 14:9, 327} seething state of mind, for they are sitting in the very front of the office with the backs to the road and they feel uncomfortably this activity going on behind them without quite knowing what it is.

It was past eight o'clock and the chief had not arrived: 8:15 and the Wildernesses became aware that there is enormous activity now, noise, many typewriters are in full operation and desks near the road, turnstiles are swinging, and cars are continually drawing to a stop outside: it is a continuous stream of American tourists in their cars flowing across the border from Laredo, Texas for their holidays in Mexico and they sit, and though it is hard to turn round, watch them, or listen: (the horns of elfland are blowing across the magic border to magic Mexico)[4] get point: and yet were separated from them as surely as if a dungeon gate of the Chateau d'If,[5] and not simply a turnstile, stood between them.

Get dialogue from Margie, particularly that relating to Junior (here dialogue of tourists). What is your name? Gleason. And this is Junior.

"Don't go—don't go!" the Wildernesses screamed in their hearts.

"Don't go—or if you do don't get in trouble," Once it seemed almost a wise thing to shout: "Help, you civilized people—look at us—"

"Don't go, don't go," said the Wildernesses.

It was now eight thirty and now all their senses were alert for the arrival of the Chief. Eight forty five, and Sigbjørn recalled that he was suppressing the most important query of all: what time would Fatty arrive? The same question was voiced by Primrose and again their slow patter with long intervals between {UBC 14:9, 328} question and answer began. Only now they whispered.

(Margienote: listen: we didn't know Fatty was coming back at all until that man who freed us told me—you *still* didn't know, you were in the john—and I didn't tell you)

"It doesn't matter," Sigbjørn said.

"Why doesn't it matter? We'll be ditched if he arrives before the chief." (this doesn't make any sense—M.)

"Why should we, the case is out of his hands. Anyway, maybe the chief will be worse than Fatty."

"How cheerful you are!"

"Well, it wasn't I that was worrying. And don't you either."

"I'm not worrying about myself."

"I know you're not. You're marvellous."

"So are you."

"But I'll tell you one thing hopeful," Sigbjørn said. "I've had a long time to study Fatty's habits and he won't get here before eleven if he can help it."

"That's very cheerful."

"Well, perhaps something else will turn up before eleven," Sigbjørn said, "And here's the chief."

He came in very slowly stopping to talk on the way to a few clerks, a rather good looking man, in khaki shirt and khaki trousers with ribbons, with grey hair and a grey moustache, with dark eyes and dark skin. He looked part American and part Mexican, a little like Eddie, Sigbjørn thought with a shudder, but at least more intelligent and kind than most of them: he hadn't at all events the hard cruel stupid look the rest of them had, but Sigbjørn remembered the mistake he'd made with Corunna as he watched him with his eyes take his place at a desk behind them on their left next to the mignitorio. {UBC 14:9, 329}

"I don't think he's the Chief. I've got the impression in my mind that that's the Chief's desk in front of us."

But he was obviously of more importance than the clerks so the Wildernesses rose and went together over to him and the man, who had sat down, politely stood up. Sigbjørn could not at first find words so Primrose began, the words seeming merely a dull repetition of a boring record, the repetition of the words spoken and spoken and spoken and spoken and reiterated and spoken again so wearily during the everlasting weeks:

"What we want to know is why we are being held beyond 7, when we were told last night we could go at 7 when the American Immigration office opened—"

The man pulled at his moustache. When he spoke it was kindly. He was very polite and very pleasant and he looked disturbed: it seemed to Sigbjørn that he did not become non-committal without first making an effort.

"I'm afraid you will have to wait for the Chief," he said finally.

"Are you not the Chief?"

"I? . . . No . . . I'm afraid not." He was looking down intently at some papers on the desk and suddenly and with absolute terror the Wildernesses saw that it is the terrible pictures that had been taken in Mexico City and which had been pasted on to the forms they had to sign the night before:

"Hold on," Sigbjørn said to Primrose. "I see you have our photographs there." Sigbjørn addressed the kind man, who said nothing, looking down musingly at the photographs, but who, a clerk approaching at this moment, excused himself with a distracted expression: {UBC 14:9, 330}

"Will you sit down a moment if you please?"

"A moment," thought Sigbjørn, "Will we sit down a moment!"

(Perhaps in this book, so far as *consciousness* is used at all there should be in addition to Primrose's and Sigbjørn's their *collective* consciousness, although there can be (a) Primrose's selfish thought, her unselfish ones, (b) Sigbjørn's ditto, (c) their collective self-preserving consciousness, (d) Sigbjørn's consciousness of injustice, (e) Primrose's ditto.)[6]

Sigbjørn and Primrose sit down on the couch, their hearts sinking: behind them on their left was their sheet-anchor, the sub-chief, before them the empty desk of the unknown, the Chief, and even hurrying along the streets now, his mind full of wickedness and paltry revenge, would be Fatty. The clock with a final jerk quickened to nine.

"Hold on," Sigbjørn said, reassuringly taking Primrose's hand. "It's just occurred to me. Don't—don't go lose your head, that's just what they want you to do, no, sit down, Primrose."

"No, let me go, he hasn't got anybody talking to him now—"

Sigbjørn lit a cigarette and out of the corner of his eye saw that Primrose was speaking to the sub-chief, who had again courteously risen, and again he heard the familiar words, though it was as if Primrose this time were making a last impassioned plea: "Some ghastly thing has happened . . . of course not the fault of the government . . . just one of those tragic things . . . we have been falsely accused . . . we're not to blame . . ."

"Didn't you know you were being deported?" the sub-chief answered after quite a while. "I can't let you go."

Primrose then tells him that Fatty has tried to get her to go alone across the border saying she was free to go and why then {UBC 14:9, 331} if that was so was she being held here this morning?

The sub-chief looks very distressed at this, and thinking so deeply before answering that when he speaks Sigbjørn has come up beside Primrose again:

"I believe you," the sub-chief was saying. "That there has been some wrong done somewhere. But what," he added, "can I do? I

have orders from headquarters . . . See?" And he then shows Primrose or them a letter on the desk, which says that they are to be deported for violation of the Immigration regulations and this is
signed by Corunna.

(Intellectually speaking there can be resemblances between this
and Measure for Measure.)[7]

"But my husband is English," Primrose expostulated, "And you
can *not* deport an Englishman into America. And they will throw
him right back here on your hands."

"Wait a minute," smiled Sigbjørn. "Nobody is going to throw
anybody anywhere. But—"

"And I know what I'm talking about. Because my father was once
an American Consul!"

"But I can't do anything," said the sub-chief at length, looking
even more distressed. "The Inspector has left explicit orders that
you are to be held here under guard until he returns and he himself
is going to take you across the border. And I dare not let you
go. He is from Headquarters, from Mexico City. I am only a little
man, at the border. And he will be back soon. In fact," he looked at
his watch, it was 9:15,[8] or round at the wall, "He will be here any
minute."

"Let him take us across the border then," Sigbjørn said desper-
ately, not indeed knowing what he was saying. "If the {UBC 14:9,
332} Texans have had any experience of him or Corunna before
they must know what a bloody swine he is and won't listen to him."

"No . . . No," Primrose says. "He won't, that's the whole point . . .
it's only *me* he'll take across—"

"Let him. While he's away, I'll be in good hands here at least."

"But you won't be here," Primrose said. "You'll be . . ."

"Yes, but what about you? Still he doesn't have more than a few
feet to misbehave himself in."

"That's enough."

Primrose now makes an impassioned speech—get details from
Margie later (Note, order of this is slightly different in Margie's
notes)—(what I said here, old boy, was about the bond, and how
they'd cashed that in, and then he *knew* we were in a fix, because
that was illegal and they'd stolen it.)

Sigbjørn now makes an even more impassioned speech in which
possibly he sums up all persecutions they have suffered and lays on

the fact that whatever he may have done in the past certainly Prim-rose is not to blame while the plea is addressed more to the man's Christianity than perhaps to law, at the end of which the sub-chief says:

"I will do what I can . . . But they are those papers you must sign first—" he pushes over Corunna's deportation orders with the photographs.

It seemed futile to refuse to sign again but Sigbjørn resisted it for a moment. "This is a lie. Do you advise me to sign?"

"Yes."

"Last night we both said we were signing under compulsion," Sigbjørn says. "If we sign this time, if not under compulsion it is still under protest that a wicked injustice has been done." {UBC 14:9, 333}

"Your signing means nothing."

Primrose signs and Sigbjørn wonders why now his hand would not tremble and make it impossible to sign but they sign in tripli-cate, in quadruplicate.

"You will witness that we are signing under protest," Sigbjørn re-peated.

"It is a mere formality. Yes."

They finished, and pushed back the papers.

"I don't suppose you've had any breakfast," said the second-in-command gathering up the papers. "Would you like a cup of coffee? I can let you go to a little restaurant around the corner, though I'll have to send one of my men with you. I'll tell him not to come in," he added. "He can wait outside."

Our breakfast: dramatise this. The brilliant sunlight outside, the bridge, the dirty straggling little street, the men in khaki by the turn-stiles, the American signs mingled with Mexican, the American tour-ists going into town in their Cadillacs bound for Temazunchale,[9] the hotel catercorner, and their two cafés con leche, sitting at a dirty little table, and getting coffee from man standing behind a bar, the sense of people *pottering*, or asleep, who have your destiny at stake, Primrose seems as if frozen in amber, they even forgot to wonder whether they are being cheated or no, but they were; their futile con-versation, like conversation in dreams or nightmares:

"They can't do this . . ."

"But what are they doing?"

"I don't know, but hold on."

"I never felt more like giving up."

"I feel fine," Sigbjørn said. {UBC 14:9, 334}

"But why are we going out to breakfast . . . What if Fatty comes back. We're playing into their hands . . . I don't want this coffee. We're wasting time." (Margienote: truth is, the sub-chief had told me Fatty *was* coming for us, but that he'd try and get us out before he came: this coffee moment was the moment of my greatest *fear* in the whole experience: I didn't tell you about Fatty because I saw no reason to worry you since you had done all you could. But I had horrid visions of being separated, and of what they were fixing to do to you—)

"Don't worry, Fatty won't come till eleven or so—you'll see. And I have a kind of confidence in the second-in-command."

Both of them realise that what has happened has mercifully driven them temporarily out of their minds. (Margienote: my mind was never so clear, sharp, alert as at this moment) After they come out from their coffee the man who has been standing across the street falls in behind them and walks back to the office with them, past the turnstiles, the desk, the clatter of typewriters into what is now a terrific hustle and also terror: for someone who could only be the Chief is now sitting at the desk in front of their couch: he alone of everyone there is wearing khaki coat covered with medals and sambrowne, he is packing pistols and has hard little cruel eyes: no mercy could be expected from that quarter (the Chief savagely tearing at, almost seeming to be *eating* papers); obviously he is a terrible man, Corunna, Fatty, Huerta, and General Goering[10] all combined into one chill revolver-bound menace and the threat of ultimate confusion; Sigbjørn feels he has to pull himself together to face come what may so he goes into the mignitorio to do his do, throw some water on his face and comb his hair: he can see out of the window down the bank of {UBC 14:9, 335} the Rio Grande and he wonders if he can be seen: he takes about a tenth of pheno, throws water on his face, and prays to the Saint of Dangerous and Desperate Causes. While this is going on the second-in-command comes up to Margie and says: (how this next scene should be done technically, since it is through Primrose's mind, is still in doubt)

"Just wait a minute or two, I think I can do something."

(Fatty had been due since 8 o'clock!)

Nice man went over to Chief who was 2 hours late: desk piled with stacks of work and 4 or 5 clerks standing around his desk subserviently but anxiously handing him papers to sign trying to get his attention urgently, so the nice man went over to him and got his attention over the clerks and speaks almost casually but swiftly (with an undercurrent of anxiety) both pointed toward Primrose, a moment when Chief's hard little cruel eyes looked at Primrose, nice man spoke smoothly and casually, another clerk presses with papers trying to hurry him, and the Chief flung up his hand like this, like a waving fan, in an impatient gesture: all right, all right—whereupon nice man came over to Primrose in a terrific but controlled flap and frantic hurry and said:

"All right, you can go. But you must go *quick*. At once. Where is your husband? I have a taxi outside. The Inspector will come at any moment. I cannot help you after he comes. Be quick."

Primrose says Sigbjørn is in the mignitorio. "He'll be out any moment."

The second-in-command repeated: "Quick. You must go, at once. Rapido! I will call a taxi for you. You must stop at customs across the road. I have one of my men watching for the Inspector. But you must go before he gets here." {UBC 14:9, 336}

Margie thanked him with gratitude and deep sincerity: he rushed out in front onto the portico in front of the bridge, came back, sweating: "Where is your husband?"

Taxi was waiting at the door. All their bags were put into taxi. Taxi was parked where it was not supposed to be parked, in front of Immigration. Man who'd guarded us at breakfast stood holding door open, another man at corner watching anxiously for Fatty. Nice man stood by Margie and got so wrought up he clutched her by the arm. "You must get your husband. You must go!"

Taxi door open, nice man clutching Margie's arm and sweating: moments seem to stretch and stretch and stretch: Margie thinks:

"What would anyone think if I were to start pounding on the door of the mignitorio, but I mustn't do that, for if the Chief ever realises what's up we're sunk."

Door to mignitorio is directly beside the Chief's desk. No one dares to go and knock, to call Sigbjørn, for fear of attracting Chief's attention, who is now busy and has forgotten it, but at any moment, if his attention is called, or he calls for his sub-chief, or Fatty comes . . .

Still Sigbjørn does not come . . .

Finally the door opened, and he came sauntering out, slowly, smiling, perfectly calm, and came sauntering over, smoking a cigarette. We whisked him out of the door and into the taxi. With a squeal of tires and brakes pull around corner and into customs office, Mexican Customs: Without a word they are already slapping stickers on luggage and hurling it back into taxi:

"You have anything?"

"Anything . . .? No, that is—"

"No. You don't. No. No. O.K. You can go. You go." {UBC 14:9, 337}

They were through in 30 seconds: men very courteous, but quick: not a bag was opened, just yanked out, stickers stuck on, hurled back in, we get out of taxi and are all but pushed back in, Customs man ran out of his office at end and came back to window of taxi just as we started and said:

"You have your visa for America, haven't you?"

"Yes, why yes, I have."

"Good luck. And you'd better hurry." Then to the driver: "Rapido!"

The taxi pulled out and flew across that bridge.

It seemed too easy, there they were flying over the Rio Grande, the lampposts of the night before seemed like standards, a guard of honour: they were half way across, they were, by god, in America: the taxi had stopped.

"You didn't get any illness down there or anything, did you?" a tall Texan was saying through the taxi-window, smiling.

"No. Nothing."

"O.K. Thanks."

A rope was looped outside the American Immigration: another polite Texan directed the taxi to the customs. (Note: Primrose is panting with relief and joy: Sigbjørn, still calm, does not know what it is all about yet, or why he was practically *swept* out and across the border in such a hurry. In the taxi he turned to Primrose questioningly and said—"What's up—" Sssh" . . .)

They got out onto American soil: their bags were taken in, they went through the Customs. They were through the Customs. Their hearts danced. Everything about them was dancing and flying around the room. {UBC 14:9, 338}

"All right, you're clear."

But this was a mistake: Sigbjørn's heart sank a little, he could have gone now, Primrose was clear, but he had to go through the American Immigration.

There was an enormous crowd beyond the ropes waiting to go into America, mostly, almost entirely Mexicans: all of them were given numbers and were awaiting their turn. There is among them a very unshaven Englishman: "Since getting to Mexico we've had nothing but trouble." "No!" said Sigbjørn.

"Didn't you know it was Cinco de Mayo tomorrow?" Sigbjørn hardly heard a Texan say to him, and Sigbjørn wondered if that was why Fatty had come all this way on their money, to celebrate Cinco de Mayo in America . . .

Re Mexican Independence Day, or whatever Cinco de Mayo represents, get this in, very tiny, in this place.

Holding Primrose's Arctic skunk fur coat (which he had always felt made them look like Russian spies) because Primrose has gone to look for a hotel (on the advice of a nice Texan who says if we don't get a room they'll all be gone in another hour) Sigbjørn wanders restlessly round the sheep pen. The bronzed tall Texans, with papers, shambled and shouldered in and out. In spite of the inordinate amount of work they have to do they are always courteous.

"They are my brothers," Sigbjørn almost purred, for the situation was causing him the most benign joy he had ever experienced. The sensation was like roast beef, like claret, like the wonderful sensation after a swim in cold salt water, like a good drive at golf, it was all he could do to stop from singing and dancing in the crowded pen. He was so relieved, playful indeed that he quite {UBC 14:9, 339} forgot that he had not the slightest grasp of the reality of the situation, that word would certainly be relayed from the other side that the Texans had two deportees on their hands, and that moreover Fatty, if other Mexicans had got this far, could certainly get through, and that, although on American soil, he had not yet been given permission to stay in America.

Suddenly he became aware that a Texan was standing before him slowly, courteously studying him:

Sigbjørn felt that it behooved him to look him calmly in the eyes, not to smell of last night's habanero, and he also profoundly hoped that the phenobarbital—Enobarbus[11]—had not in any way dilated his pupils.

As if he were satisfied finally the Texan said, softly and courteously, with a smile:

"I think your wife's outside and would like to talk to you a moment. But you can't go beyond the barrier."

Sigbjørn goes, carrying the fur coat, as far as the rope barrier:

"Oh Sigbjørn, I've found a lovely cheap hotel," she began, "and—"

But that moment Sigbjørn saw Fatty over Primrose's shoulder. Livid with rage he was stalking past, shrugging each shoulder with agitation.

"Did you see who I see," Sigbjørn said calmly.

"No . . . who . . . where?"

"Fatty," Sigbjørn said in a voice adjuring caution.

"What!"

"Naturally," Sigbjørn could not see if he had turned into the {UBC 14:9, 340} baggage room or not. Nearby the Texan stood smiling. "What did you expect? He's probably making for the nearest pub . . . See you later," Sigbjørn added softly, and carrying the fur coat, he sauntered back into the pen.

In spite of the fact that all at this moment threatened to be lost, Sigbjørn could still not help purring to himself. At worst Fatty could have told everything to the baggage man, or demanded entrance through the baggage room into the Immigration Department: a door opening now, Sigbjørn sees through into the baggage room and for a moment thinks he sees Fatty there. On the other hand could the courteous Texan have been sizing him up and been satisfied. Some minutes later his number was called and Sigbjørn went into the Immigration. It occurred to him that he was not afraid and moreover he was not going to lie. If there were an investigation, let there be. The relief was so great to be among these Texans that it no longer seemed to matter.

Sigbjørn is now asked about his passport, etc.—and perhaps his passport is quoted again in full.

The paper with his fingerprints and the account of his having been turned back at the border. The slow Texan is almost incredible in his politeness.

"I see, that's just where you-all went there and decided to come back again . . . That's O.K. Fine . . ." He stamped the passport till July.

Sigbjørn has one moment's fear that his hand may tremble when he has to sign but it does not. He is free.

He goes out and embraces Primrose. It is a wonderful moment.

The other Texan is standing near:

"Did you find a hotel?" he asks. {UBC 14:9, 341}

"Oh yes—we did—thank you *so* much."

"Are you all set, young fellow?"

"Yes sir, thank you for your courtesy," Sigbjørn says.

"Well, no sense in spending all your money on an expensive hotel. Spend it on something sensible, like a beer," the Texan added.

Then the other Texan comes out: Sigbjørn had left his paper with his reentrance to Canada behind.

They wave hands to the Texans and with their faithful shopping bag and luggage and their poor uke they drive to the cheap hotel Primrose has found.

"If the Texans like to think they are the best people in the world," Sigbjørn said, "so far as I'm concerned they may."

"They are."

"You're darn right they are."

Perhaps this hotel is also called the Ambos Mundos and at any rate it is kept by a Mexican and again they produce their spiel: "Nosotros no somos ricos Americanos—" etc, but they don't really care.

They danced the raspa in the bathroom. They made love until they were exhausted and then danced again. It grew late. They drank half a bottle of California claret but their hangovers had already been swept away from them. Then they stood by the window looking out into Nuevo Laredo. Sigbjørn turned her to him suddenly and their lips would have met in a long kiss but it was as if the situation were suddenly too much even for that. Sigbjørn remembered the film Warning Shadows[12] where the lovers stood at the end and watched the Stealer of Shadows ride away on a pig.

"We will cling together."

"But Fatty's still here," Primrose was saying, her hand on the curtain. {UBC 14:9, 342}

"What makes you say that?"

"I just saw him, down in the street."

"So did I . . . But I wasn't going to say anything about it. Anyhow he can't hurt us now."

"Why can't he?"

"Because," Sigbjørn said, "He is not the—Fatty is not—the instrument of . . . my . . . he isn't the instrument of our . . ."

And even as if as he took her in his arms again it was as if he heard a voice behind him saying: "I can see you . . . I'm watching you . . . You won't escape me . . ."

But all at once the voice didn't seem to matter: it was as if also it were proud and pleased. The Daemon! What a mistake he had nearly made. He had arranged such a good tragic work of art and then at last moment woken up to a startling fact: My God, it was as if he had suddenly realised, I can't kill these people. Or I can't kill him. Else who is going to write it! Sigbjørn laughed, and gave himself up to the rejoicing of the moment. And yet they still did not kiss. The moment was too strong for comment or action. It was like that time at the very beginning in Mexico when suddenly they had come out of a cantina to see the full moon rising over Ixta, seen over the junkyard of an orange garage full of broken rusted tin cans, and then suddenly realised as they walked home that the moon was in eclipse, that was becoming total, the strange glimpses of the eclipsed moon down the narrow Mexican streets, and then suddenly realised that the eclipse was over and there were the stars again winking like jewels (stars don't go *out* during an eclipse, they become stronger as the moon's light grows less,)[13] out of the white fleecy clouds, and the brilliant full moon again sliding down a sapphire sky, silver clouds and a {UBC 14:9, 343} white ocean of fleece, and the Mexican, as if rejoicing, singing at the other end of their balcony . . .

"I was just thinking of the man who said, when I went out to get the claret, It's quite easy to get a drink. You only have to hop across the border . . ."

"Yes. Only."

Night drew on. The lights came out. Over beyond the Rio Grande in old Mexico the lights on the advertisement winked: Cartablanca, Cerveza Exquisita. And the lights on the bridge came on. They slept: woke up: Hallucinations of fatigue and strain flickered in the room: Lovers must notify clerk at Hotel office by 12 noon became Guests must notify clerk at 12 o'clock on the guilty line.[14] Cartablanca Exquisita! And there, separated from them by the Rio

Grande, by centuries, by eternity, was ancient Mexico, great dark Catholic mysterious Mexico, to which perhaps they could never return. What was Mexico? What did Mexico mean? Why was the thought that one could not return so terrible?

Sigbjørn had no particular religion, yet called himself a Protestant: but what could a Protestant pray for, of Mexico. It was not forbidden him, even here, to pray to the Virgin of Guadalupe, the Virgin for those who have nobody with,[15] nor to thank her for his salvation. It was not forbidden to him to pray for nor to thank Fernando. It was not forbidden him, any more than had he been a Catholic, to pray even that the Mother Church might become more Catholic still and embrace such poor heretics as he and she. Nor to pray to become a better, a wiser, a more courageous, a worthier, a more decent, a compassionate and understanding man. And a better writer, nay, a writer at all. Primrose had come to look at her first foreign land, had come for a honeymoon, it was {UBC 14:9, 344} not forbidden him to hope she had found some greater faith in the meaning of life, in its depth, its terror. Nor to hope that what had died was himself, and what came about through these confusions, these oscillations, these misunderstandings and lies and disastars, these weavings to and fro, these last minute dashes to no end, this horror, this treachery, these projections of the past upon the present, of the imagination upon reality, that out of these dislocations of time, these configurations of unreality, and the collapse of will, out of these all but incommunicable agonies, as of the mind and heart stretched and attenuated beyond endurance on an eternal rack, out of arrant cowardice before little danger, and bravery in the face of what seemed slight to overcome, and heartbreak, and longing, had been born, darkly and tremulous, a soul.

Suddenly a vision of absolute joy seized him or them. They would return and finish the house: perhaps they would return by bus: how strange it would be to see hayfields made up in Spring and the wild mustard powdered over the hills and the monkey flowers and Indian paintbrush, white roses and dark pines at Santa Barbara, and then their proud beautiful pier, and their little house, their hammers raised, the blue sea, the star flowers and spring beauties, and again the hammering . . .

(reborn into a spring sense of *creation* too, as an artist or poet. Also get the flowers that have sprung up in their garden in their absence: Parsifal.[16] The glory of a blue morning in Canada at home, with the sea gulls floating white against the pines in motion and the breath of cherry blossom, the white horses running swiftly down the inlet, and by the little lighthouse on the shore, and dogwood, thimbleberry and wild rose in one swathe blowing— {UBC 14:9, 345} Get notes from Haiti here: it should be pointed out that Primrose is disappointed she never saw the Southern Cross.)

But a dark ocean swell seemed to overwhelm this dream, it was the tide rising in Acapulco, it rose ever higher and higher, engulfing the beach, the dark flood rising and rising: and yet, locked in each other's arms it was as if their souls were being borne or lulled like children over this flood into an ocean peace; a limitless peaceful moonlit swell running to the horizon, behind which rose slowly, tilted, as though held up by an invisible acolyte's or priest's arm, to ward off evil, the silver, the cross. {UBC 14:9, 346}

ADDITIONAL NOTES TO XLV

Once more they sat in the Immigration office, six o'clock, already light. They had been called at half past five, been up and dressed in a minute, found the taxi outside with someone quite polite with him, driven to the immigration, and there they were. Now light. The Rio Grande could be seen through the window, a muddy little river, with goats tethered on the Mexican side. The bridge, splendidly lamped, vaulted it. A different man was now sitting at the typewriter and they feel lost without the kind vizored man. There is an incredible difference between the scene at night and now in the hard light of day. They sit and sit: the clock ticks on and every now and then Sigbjørn wonders why they are sitting. Only the tireless Mexican eagle seems familiar, staunchly eating the Mexican flag. After a while Primrose gets up angrily and copies down the address of the Fioranzas on the wall . . .

It was six, it was six-five, it was twenty past six, it was seven, and they would presumably have to sit there till—his mind shied away from any brute facts: but they have the confidence of three hours sleep, and Sigbjørn has that of a shave, of having exactly calculated the amount of drinks or pheno: he feels indeed a sense of queer elation, that is sharpened by the sense of danger.

Margie notes: Got back there about a quarter of 6—the nice vizored chap, who had persuaded them to let us go, departs as soon as
or shortly after we arrive—day shift comes on at 6—first a few clerks
straggling in with khaki uniforms—and from 6 to 8 pretty quiet
clerks opening up the office—people began to arrive about 7:30—
meantime we sat on couch facing the empty chief's desk where we sat
night before under glaring light—but we didn't think about Chief,
because we'd been told that when the American {UBC 14:9, 347}
Immigration opened at 7 A.M., we could go (why we should have believed this after their record of lies and subterfuges I don't know, but
we did or tried to, or half did) so we just waited for seven, and we
thought, or half thought, or pretended to think to each other someone would come up and say "Now you can go"—But at 7 A.M. nobody came up to us, we began to get a little nervous, by 7:30 we
were beginning to get really apprehensive, and I went and asked one
of the clerks about it saying we were just simply waiting till American Immigration opened at 7 and surely we could go now, for it was
7:30 and it was already open—at this point the first real objective notice that we were not free to go that morning—they looked at me in a
very hostile manner and said, No, you can not go until the Chief
comes, he has to sign your release—we fretted then I went and asked
somebody else and got the same reply and I asked again, saying:
"Then when will the Chief be in?"
"Oh—he's due here at 8 o'clock. He'll be along."
So by 8:30 or 8:45 we were in quite a state, though it was at
8 o'clock that the American tourists began to stream in from across
the border and we sat and watched them.
(Get dialogue from Margie when I want it. "And that is Junior,"
etc.)[17]
"Don't go—don't go!" they screamed in their hearts.
About 9 o'clock nice fellow came in—grey hair, looked partly
Mexican, partly American, dark eyes, dark skin, looked at least
more intelligent and kind than most of them, not the hard cruel stupid look the rest of them had—wearing khaki shirt and trousers for
it was getting hot—
Nice man came in with ribbons on his chest, we spoke him as
having nicer face and saw also he was sub-chief and more important[18] than clerks so we went together and spoke to him and asked
why we were being held beyond 7, we had been told we could go

at 7, so he was very kind, very {UBC 14:9, 348} polite, and very pleasant and looked disturbed, but he was noncommittal and said we'd have to wait for chief and while we were talking I saw on his desk our terrible pictures that had been taken pasted on to the forms we'd had to sign the night before with that hearts sank and we went back and sat down on couch, then I Malcolm went to talk to another man with desk in centre who seemed another kind of sub-chief, not a nice fellow: meantime Margie went back to nice fellow and this is where Margie hit her low ebb, Margie knew we were for it, and spoke to this nice man and tried to tell him that some ghastly thing had happened, of course not the fault of the government, that it was some mistake, that we had been falsely accused, that we were not to blame, he then said:

"Didn't you know—but you're being deported. I can't let you go!"

Margie told him they had insisted we were *not* being deported, etc. etc. that Fatty had tried to get her to go alone over the border at 2 A.M., saying she was free and to go, and that if that was so, why was she being held there in the morning. He looked distressed at that, thought deeply before answering, then said:

"I believe you, that there has been some wrong done somewhere. But," he said, "what can I do? I have orders from headquarters. See?" and he then showed Margie the letter on the desk signed by Corunna.

Margie said: "But my husband is English and you can't deport him into America. And they will chuck him right back here on your hands. And I know what I'm talking about, because my father was once an American Consul."

Margie then made a terrific, passionate speech, get details later, just finishing {UBC 14:9, 349} telling him how they made us put up bond, then cashed it, we are innocent, we will be separated, etc. etc. when I came over from other table and joined her, then I made impassioned plea.

Before I joined Margie at desk Nice man had said to Margie: "But I cannot do anything. The Inspector has left implicit orders that you are to be held here under guard until he returns and he himself is going to take you across the border. And I dare not let you go. He is from headquarters—from Mexico. I am only a little man, at the border. And he will be back soon. In fact," looks at his watch, "He will be here any minute."

Margie's impassioned plea follows this, at this point I join Margie, and my impassioned speech clinched it. When I finished he said: "I will do what I can . . . I don't suppose you've had any breakfast. Would you like a cup of coffee. I can let you go to a little restaurant around the corner, though I'll have to send one of my men with you. I'll tell him not to come in . . ." He added "He can wait outside."

Some rough notes for end: Hallucinations in Hotel in Laredo: Lovers must nattily look at clerk at 12 o'clock on the guilty line was actually: Guests must notify clerk at Hotel office by 12 noon.

Perhaps end with a vision of building the house: it would be strange to see hay made up in the fields in May, and the dark cypresses in Santa Barbara.

Cartablanca exquisita! And there, separated from them by the Rio Grande, by centuries, by eternity, was ancient Mexico, great dark Catholic mysterious Mexico to which they could perhaps never return. What was Mexico? What did Mexico mean? Why was the thought that they could not return so terrible?

Sigbjørn had no religion yet he was a Protestant: and there seemed a moral law against changing your religion; but what could a Protestant pray for, of Mexico. It was not forbidden him, even {UBC 14:9, 350} here, to pray to the Virgin of Guadalupe, the Virgin for those who have nobody them with. It was not forbidden him any more than had he been a Catholic, to pray that the mother church might become more catholic still, to embrace even those who perhaps only protest against the guardian of the very mysteries that upon which their faith rested, and whose power to protest was exhausted. It was not forbidden him to pray to become a better, a wiser, a more courageous, a more compassionate man. Primrose had come to look at her first foreign land, had come for a honeymoon, and found a faith. Nor to think that what had died was himself, and what had come about, through these confusions, these oscillation, these misunderstandings, lies, disastars, these weavings to and fro, these last minute dashes to no end, this horror, this treachery, the projections of the past upon the present, of the imagination upon reality, out of these dislocations of time, these configurations of unreality and the collapse of will, out of this all but incommunicable agony, out of arrant cowardice before little danger and bravery in the face of what seemed slight to overcome and heartbreak and longing, out of excess and abstinence, as of the mind and heart stretched and attenuated beyond endurance on an eternal rack, had been born, darkly and tremulously, a soul.[19] Nor to think that what had died was himself, and what had come about what had been born, or was it being tremulously born, was in one of faith—and as the dark tide rose ever higher and higher on the shores of the world as she now entered the Great Era of the Stool Pigeon—and in himself, a soul. {UBC 14:9, 351}

Just a few notes for end, which may be useful in the 2nd draft:

In hotel in Laredo hallucinations such as the following: Lovers must nattily look at clerk at 12 o'clock on the guilty line. (actually)

—Guests must notify clerk at Hotel office by 12 noon.[20]

Kilroy turns up here: Kilroy passed a stone here. Kilroy is dead. Who is Kilroy?

The Manhattan in Laredo: No swearing or vulgar language allowed—please respect the ladies. Favor de no usar lenguage profano—Respete las damas.

the nostalgia for the vanishing myth, the beauty—memory of the man with his arms spread out, the tide rising in Acapulco, the virgin for those who have nobody with, end with vision of their little house, the hammering, in spring. {UBC 14:9, 352}

Note: for the very end: In the dining car, the heat, with the closed windows, became suddenly insufferable, and the noise of the train suddenly twenty times more urgent and working and powerful, like the combined noises indeed of a powerful motor-tugboat heard at a little distance, and a freight train over a narrow stretch of water. In Laredo a vision of Chartres Cathedral—mem—of arrival in Acapulco—end must be musically chiasmic—some substance perhaps of Mouris letters etc.[21]

For Later: Lower California—the stinking hot ship sailing down—beyond hangover, utter exhaustion and forgetfulness, Yet sad as the coast of Lower California, Mexico itself began to show its sinister and strange islands as barren as icebergs, and nearly as white, formations through piles of sombre violet grey clouds. Then, at sunset, a leaden ship with a lone line of burning vermillion like a forest fire 3000 miles lone and far away over a leaden sea, only between dark sea and sky is this line of cliffs of red fire, going down past third coast, past even more gorgeous and terrifying coastline in utterly barren mountains, sharp formed, peaked like cones or icebergs in their pale desolations and barren and desperate as my heart. Peaks like machetes, pointing down. Volcanoes at dawn and a clear glowing sky and then again there is an indigo sea, and the black tortured barren shape, sharp, pointed islands, a nightmare against a gold sky. {UBC 14:9, 353}

Annotations and Textual Notes

In these annotations I have used the following abbreviations and short titles for Lowry's works and for other sources cited more than once. References to notebooks and drafts for *La Mordida* use the designations set forth in the Introduction. All other sources are cited in the notes themselves.

Acapulco: *Acapulco: An Adventure in Living.* N. P.: Departamento de Turismo de la Secretaria de Gobernación, Asociación Mexicana de Turismo, n.d. [Lowry's copy in UBC 32:11.]

Ackerley and Clipper: Chris Ackerley and Lawrence J. Clipper, *A Companion to "Under the Volcano."* Vancouver: University of British Columbia Press, 1984.

Barrett: William Barrett, *What Is Existentialism? Partisan Review*, PR Series no. 2, 1947.

Bergson: Henri Bergson, *Creative Evolution*, trans. Arthur Mitchell. New York: Modern Library, 1944.

Bowker: Gordon Bowker, *Pursued by Furies: A Life of Malcolm Lowry.* Toronto: Random House of Canada, 1993.

Bradbrook: M. C. Bradbrook, *Malcolm Lowry: His Art and Early Life—A Study in Transformation.* Cambridge: Cambridge University Press, 1974.

CML: *The Cinema of Malcolm Lowry: A Scholarly Edition of Malcolm Lowry's "Tender Is the Night."* Edited by Miguel Mota and Paul Tiessen. Vancouver: University of British Columbia Press, 1990.

CP: *The Collected Poetry of Malcolm Lowry.* Edited by Kathleen Scherf, with explanatory annotation by Chris Ackerley. Vancouver: UBC Press, 1992.

CSHM: *The Complete Stories of Herman Melville.* Edited by Jay Leyda. New York: Random House, 1949.

Day: Douglas Day, *Malcolm Lowry: A Biography.* New York: Oxford University Press, 1973.

DG: Malcolm Lowry, *Dark as the Grave Wherein My Friend Is Laid.* Edited by Douglas Day and Margerie Bonner Lowry. New York: New American Library, 1968.

Halliwell: Leslie Halliwell, *Halliwell's Filmgoer's Companion.* 7th ed. New York: Charles Scribner's Sons, 1980.

HL: Malcolm Lowry, *Hear Us O Lord from Heaven Thy Dwelling Place.* Philadelphia: J. B. Lippincott, 1961.

MPG: Jay Robert Nash and Stanley Ralph Ross, *The Motion Picture Guide.* 12 vols. Chicago: Cinebooks, 1985.

NS: Malcolm Lowry, with Margerie Bonner Lowry, *Notes on a Screenplay for F. Scott Fitzgerald's "Tender Is the Night."* Bloomfield Hills, Mich.: Bruccoli Clark, 1976.

OF: Malcolm Lowry, *October Ferry to Gabriola.* Edited by Margerie Lowry. New York: World, 1970.

PS: *Malcolm Lowry: Psalms and Songs.* Edited by Margerie Lowry. New York: New American Library, 1975.

Roeder: Ralph Roeder, *Juarez and His Mexico: A Biographical History.* 2 vols. New York: Viking Press, 1947.

SL: *Selected Letters of Malcolm Lowry.* Edited by Harvey Breit and Margerie Bonner Lowry. Philadelphia: J. B. Lippincott, 1965.

Sugars: *The Letters of Conrad Aiken and Malcolm Lowry 1929–1954.* Edited by Cynthia Sugars. Toronto: ECW Press, 1992.

U: Malcolm Lowry, *Ultramarine.* Philadelphia: J. B. Lippincott, 1962.

UBC: Unpublished materials in the Malcolm Lowry Archive, Special Collections, Main Library, University of British Columbia. Citations by box, file, and page number.

UV: Malcolm Lowry, *Under the Volcano.* New York: Reynal and Hitchcock, 1947. Reprint, New York: New American Library, 1971.

UV [1940]: Malcolm Lowry, *The 1940 Under the Volcano.* Edited by Paul Tiessen and Miguel Mota, introduction by Frederick Asals. Waterloo, Ontario: MLR Editions Canada [*The Malcolm Lowry Review*], 1994.

Cross-references to other annotations include the chapter number (or the letter S for the preliminary statement), and then the note number, e.g., II.3 for note 3 in chapter II. The same system is used in the index.

STATEMENT FOR LA MORDIDA

1. *The following is a statement . . . dates, names, places* [p. 3]: This prefatory statement is the original (ribbon) copy, and therefore should have been part of Draft B, but at some point it became separated from the re-

mainder of the text and attached to the carbon (Draft C). It is a later version of the letter to A. Ronald Button published in *Selected Letters* (*SL* 91–112).

2. *A few days later* [p. 4]: At some point—probably in 1952, when Margerie typed *La Mordida*—page 2 of a set of her Cuernavaca notes was inserted into this statement, which would otherwise have no page 2. In May 1992, that page was moved to UBC 7:6, where the remaining pages of Margerie's notes are located; a photocopy of the recto remains in 14:10.

3. *November 1936* [p. 5]: Actually, 30 October 1936 (Bowker 205; see my introduction, n. 1).

4. *rentista* [p. 5]: Spanish, "property owner," "person of independent means" (hence a tourist who is unlikely to become a public charge).

5. *The Cantinas* [p. 7]: For the text of "The Cantinas"—part 3 of Lowry's *The Lighthouse Invites the Storm*—see *CP* 57–64.

6. *Oficina Federal de Hacienda* [p. 8]: The Mexican internal revenue service.

7. *Modern Mexico* [p. 14]: A monthly magazine published by the Mexican Chamber of Commerce of the United States from 1930 through 1950. See also note IV.25.

8. *The Shapes That Creep* [p. 15]: A murder mystery by Margerie Bonner Lowry. See Sherrill Grace, "Margerie Bonner's Three Forgotten Novels," *Journal of Modern Literature* 6 (April 1977): 321–24.

9. *Hoy hizo efectivas . . . Central de Fianzas, S.A.* [p. 20]: "Today the Interior Ministry has cashed in the Lowry couple's bond. We ask that you remit to us immediately 1,000 pesos, the value of the bond, to avoid paying interest charges. Central de Fianzas [private bail bond company], S.A." There is a pencil draft of this telegram in UBC 13:14, ch. XL, 5 (see note XL.6).

10. *ley fuga* [p. 24]: "Law of flight," a policeman's right to shoot a fleeing suspect. The implication is that the police might claim that Margerie was trying to escape and shoot her in the back. See also pp. 244, 301.

CHAPTER I

1. *once more the Wildernesses were off* [p. 31]: Lowry uses the same phrasing near the end of *Dark as the Grave* (*DG* 254).

2. *Sigbjørn* [p. 31]: This is the only place in the typescript where Sigbjørn is spelled with a slash through the o.

3. *Bousfield and Stuyvesant* [p. 31]: On John Bousfield (or "Bonsfield," according to Bowker), who appears in *Dark as the Grave* as John Stanford (*DG* 218 ff.), see Day 246, 351–53, and Bowker 238, 240–41, 356–58. On Stuyvesant see Bowker 238, 240.

4. *the antimonsoon of the past. the Bergson motif again* [p. 31]: I have not located this specific image in Henri Bergson's work, but there is a con-

nection between Lowry's emphasis on the forces that propel Sigbjørn's life and Bergson's ideas in *Creative Evolution*, a copy of which Lowry owned. See, e.g., Bergson's description of life and consciousness as "an immense wave" that stops everywhere except with man (Bergson 290–95). See also note VI.27.

5. *"approach to the meaning restores the experience"* [p. 32]: From Part 2 of T. S. Eliot's "The Dry Salvages," the third of his *Four Quartets*:

> We had the experience but missed the meaning,
> And approach to the meaning restores the experience
> In a different form, beyond any meaning
> We can assign to happiness.

This part of Eliot's poem is related to *La Mordida* through its meditation on attempts to come to terms with the past.

6. *the great Cardenas* [p. 32]: Lázaro Cárdenas, reform-minded president of Mexico (1934–40).

7. *what had been rendered . . . to a dishonest Caesar* [p. 32]: See Matthew 22:21 and p. 117.

8. *Dr. Amann's advice* [p. 32]: Dr. Amann was the real name of the person who is called Dr. Hippolyte in *Dark as the Grave*. The identification is confirmed in Draft D, where this passage reads "Dr. Hyppolite's [*sic*] advice" (UBC 14:12, 3). See also notes II.33, III.19, and XLI.4.

9. *poor Fernando* [p. 32]: Juan Fernando Márquez, who befriended Lowry during his 1936–38 stay in Mexico and served as the model both for Dr. Vigil and for Juan Cerillo in *Under the Volcano*; Lowry calls him Juan Fernando Martinez in *Dark as the Grave* and Fernando Atonalzin in his 1950 essay "Garden of Etla." Lowry hoped to see him during the 1945–46 trip but was shocked to learn that his friend had been murdered in a barroom brawl in December 1939 (see Day 240–44, 353–54, 361; Bowker 235–37, 357–59; and *DG* 237–41). See also note III.20.

10. *Jimmy* [p. 32]: James Craige, a Dollarton neighbor who "was taking care of the shack in Dollarton" during the events described in *La Mordida* (Day 366).

11. *Dark Rosslyn* [p. 32]: A housing development in "Gin and Goldenrod."

12. *Helen and the Italian* [p. 33]: Helen and the Italian (who is called Guido in UBC 9:5, 307) are also mentioned in the notebooks and in drafts of *Dark as the Grave*.

13. *From Cuernavaca, the road drops steadily to the tropical little village of* [p. 33]: This is the first of a series of marginal notes taken from a travel booklet, *Acapulco: An Adventure in Living* (hereafter *Acapulco*), which Lowry picked up during this trip. The copy in the Malcolm Lowry Archive (UBC 32:11) bears several annotations in Lowry's hand. The title of

the guidebook is referred to below, p. 81. In addition to supplying the marginalia for chapters I and IV, the pamphlet is quoted or mentioned in the text in several places (see notes I.57, I.63, III.7, III.13, XVI.1, and XVII.12). In the typescript all of the marginalia are typed single-spaced in the left margin.

14. *a poem of Wordsworth's* [p. 33]: If this refers to a specific poem, I have not located it. In a note to me, Kathryn Freeman has suggested that Lowry might be alluding to Wordsworth's frequently expressed fear of losing poetic inspiration, a recurrent concern in *The Prelude* and elsewhere. For a related reference to Wordsworth, see note VIII.3.

15. *amber hues* [p. 33]: *Acapulco* (22) has "rainbow hues." The typescript diverges from the guidebook at some points, but in no case do the changes affect the basic sense of the passage. I have not made any emendations in the marginal notes except to correct obvious typographical errors and supply initial capital letters and terminal punctuation where their absence might make the passage confusing.

16. *Finally Taxco (or say, any other stop, Cuautla) became to his mind simply a synonym for another drink* [p. 33]: As Chris Ackerley suggested to me, Cuautla probably appears here as an allusion to Lowry's poem "Thirty-Five Mescals in Cuautla" (*CP* 60).

17. *About two hours out of Cuernavaca, the fabulous old mining town* [pp. 33–34]: This is not in *Acapulco*, but is apparently derived from a passage on p. 22 and one on p. 23 (incorporated into the typescript below, p. 35).

18. *Tecalpulco* [p. 34]: Both Draft A and the typescript have "Tecelpulco" at this point. I have emended the spelling because it is spelled correctly elsewhere in both drafts and in Notebook II, from which this passage is derived.

19. *he even wrote [the devil dancer] into the Valley of the Shadow of Death* [p. 35]: See *UV* 232–33. In the post-*Volcano* fiction, *The Valley of the Shadow of Death* is *Under the Volcano*. See also the devil dancer in the Haitian sequence (below, p. 132).

20. *Lluvia* [p. 35]: Spanish, "rain."

21. *Alarcon and Hart Crane* [p. 35]: Juan Ruiz de Alarcón (c. 1581–1639), Golden Age Spanish dramatist, was born and raised in Mexico City, but his parents had previously lived in Taxco, and there is a portrait of him in the cathedral there (Walter Poesse, *Juan Ruiz de Alarcón* [New York: Twayne, 1972], 17–18, 145). The American poet Hart Crane (1899–1932) was in Mexico in 1931–32 and made several trips to Taxco. For other references to Crane, see notes VI.15, VI.87, and XXV.2. See also "Elsinore was the battlements of Oaxaca," an unfinished poem in which Lowry mentions, inter alia, Crane, Alarcón, and Taxco (*CP* 358).

22. *Flecha Roja* [p. 36]: "Red Arrow," a bus line.

23. *excusados* [p. 36]: "Toilets" (see note XXX.6).

24. *a white churrigerotiose nightmare in the burning sun* [p. 36]: A combination of one of Lowry's favorite words, "churrigueresque"—referring to a baroque architectural style named after the Spanish architect José Churriguera (1650–1723)—and "otiose" (lazy, ineffective). For uses of "churrigueresque," see below, pp. 253, 280; *Under the Volcano* (UV 298); and Lowry's letter to Jonathan Cape, in which he compared *Under the Volcano* to a "churrigueresque Mexican cathedral" (SL 85).

25. *our Señora of the Sacred Heart, patron Saint of Dangerous and Desperate Causes* [p. 37]: This passage, along with those on pp. 61 and 207 and one in *Dark as the Grave* (DG 241–42), appears to identify the Virgin Mary with the Saint of Dangerous and Desperate Causes. Lowry's knowledge of Catholicism was shaky, however, which might account for the fact that the Virgin seems to be mixed in with St. Margaret Mary Alacoque (1647–90), whose claim to have had a number of visions of Jesus led to the Sacred Heart devotions. To further confuse matters, Margerie Lowry said that her husband's "patron saint was St Jude, the saint of hopeless and desperate causes" (interview in *Malcolm Lowry Remembered*, ed. Gordon Bowker [London: Ariel Books, 1985], 137), and Bowker identifies the Saint of Dangerous and Desperate Causes as Isabel la Católica (Bowker 346, 609–10). See also below, pp. 245, 291, and 311.

26. *Acapulco as the centre of every kind of vice* [p. 38]: For a similar view of Acapulco, see Lowry's poem "Shakespeare should have come to Acapulco" (CP 58).

27. *upon some high blasted rock, the name Alemán. . . . Alemán; moralización* [p. 38]: Draft A has "upon some high blasted rock the name Aleman, the apostle of Moralazacion." This political advertisement for Miguel Alemán Valdes, successful candidate in the 1946 Mexican presidential election, indicates that Alemán ran on a platform promising moral reform. The "dogmatizing" sign also appears in *Dark as the Grave* (DG 95).

28. *Noxon* [p. 38]: After a fire destroyed their shack in June 1944, the Lowrys went to stay in Oakville, Ontario, with Malcolm's college friend Gerald Noxon (here called "Bill") and his wife Betty. For the full text of the following letter, see *The Letters of Malcolm Lowry and Gerald Noxon, 1940–1952*, ed. Paul Tiessen (Vancouver: University of British Columbia Press, 1988), 118–20. On the Lowrys' stay with the Noxons see Bowker 325–30.

29. *Follows a conversation about the bracelet* [p. 39]: At this point in Draft A (UBC 13:1, 10), a note in the right margin reads, "Perhaps more description, here, of the Xopilote Canyon. Vulture Canyon[.] Canyon of Death[.]"

30. *like Dostoievsky, he was educated enough not to be superstitious* [p. 39]: A reference to the opening of *Notes from Underground*; see note I.52.

31. *disastar* [p. 39]: Lowry frequently (but not invariably) used this spelling, presumably to call attention to the impact of astral influences on our lives, as Chris Ackerley suggests in his annotation on Lowry's poem "Success is like some horrible disastar" (*CP* 310).

32. *en la plaza . . . enero de 1932* [pp. 39–40]: "In the central plaza of Monte Albán, the engineer Jorge R. Acosta, present director of exploration and reconstruction of that archaeological zone, realized the most important discovery achieved up to now, since tomb no. 7 was found in January 1932."

33. *rather like the investigation of Tutankhamen's tomb* [p. 40]: The 1923 opening of the tomb of Tutankhamen (1343–1325 B.C.), a pharaoh of the 18th Dynasty, was followed two months later by the death of Lord Carnarvon, who along with Howard Carter was in charge of the expedition. This and other deaths among people associated with the tomb and its contents led to the popular belief that there was a curse on the tomb.

34. *Exploraba . . . non túnel* [p. 40]: The construction here is unclear. It could mean "Engineer Acosta explored the odd tunnel" or, if Lowry has miscopied the phrase, the sense could be that the tunnel is unparalleled (*de non*, "without equal").

35. *y hay gasolina . . . Excelsior . . . Alarma . . . Meningitis* [p. 40]: Newspaper headlines in *Excelsior*, the leading newspaper of Mexico City (also referred to on pp. 45 and 95): "There is gasoline in the capital"; "Warning in Chilpancingo about meningitis."

36. *he had invested, in the Valley of the Shadow of Death* [p. 40]: The details that follow are confusing since in *Under the Volcano* Yvonne's child Geoffrey died six (not seven) years before the book began, at the age of six months (*UV* 72). Moreover, Lowry had last seen Bousfield (or Bonsfield) in 1938, *eight* years before the events of *La Mordida*.

37. *Victor Hugo's [poems]* [p. 41]: See pp. 42–43 and note I.40.

38. *"It was an order of death, anti-organic," as Thomas Mann had very properly pointed out* [p. 42]: See Thomas Mann, *The Magic Mountain*, trans. H. T. Lowe-Porter (translated 1927; reprint, New York: Modern Library, 1955): "Yet each [snowflake], in itself—this was the uncanny, the anti-organic, the life-denying character of them all—each of them was absolutely symmetrical, icily regular in form. They were too regular, as substance adapted to life never was to this degree—the living principle shuddered at this perfect precision, found it deathly, the very marrow of death—" (480). The "Snow" chapter is also excerpted in Clifton Fadiman's *Reading I've Liked*; see note IV.39. On "passion for order," see pp. 40 and 90. For other references to Mann, see notes II.27, IV.16, and XVII.3.

39. *"The Sea rushing through your soul in great cold waves of anguish"... vascular remorse* [p. 42]: See below, pp. 123, 129. An early set of Lowry's notes has the passage "My soul is breaking in anguish with the sea" (UBC 1:75).

40. *Afrique aux plis infranchissables ... Tiberius is a rock, Sejanus a snake* [pp. 42–43]: *Afrique aux plis infranchissables* is from Victor Hugo's "Tous les bas âges sont épars," part 7 of *L'Art d'être grand-père* (*Oeuvres poétiques complètes* [Montréal: Éditions Bernard Valiquette, 1944], 789). *Oh! si la conjecture antique était fondée* is from "Toutes sortes d'enfants," part 10 of *L'Art d'être grand-père* (*Oeuvres poétiques complètes*, 791). *Toute faute qu'on fait est un cachot qu'on s'ouvre* is from "Ce que dit la bouche d'ombre," book 6, poem 26, in *Les Contemplations* (*Oeuvres poétiques complètes*, 409–10). I have corrected some obvious errors in the French and, in brackets, I have restored some missing words. Each of the selections omits several lines from the original. The translation, which I assume is Lowry's, is rather loose, but it follows the general sense of Hugo's lines. See also notes I.37, II.29, IV.14.

41. *The wolf, he was my father ... the feet of thy wife* [pp. 43–44]: From act 1, scene 2 of Richard Wagner's *The Valkyrie* (*Die Walküre*, 1870). Siegmund, the son of Wolfe (actually Wotan in the guise of a wolf), is relating his history to Sieglinde (who will turn out to be his long-lost twin sister) and to her husband, Hunding. For another Wagnerian reference see note XLV.16.

42. *the picturesque state capital of Guerrero* [p. 44]: The typescript omits the remainder of the sentence from the guidebook: "the landscape becomes increasingly tropical" (*Acapulco* 24).

43. *Wynn and Gilda* [p. 45]: On Lowry's relationship to Teddy Wynn and Gilda Gray, see Bowker 209, 238–39. The suicide attempt from which Gilda allegedly rescued Lowry is mentioned below: "they are walking where Gilda had slapped him down after his suicidal swim" (p. 63). "Gilda Gray" was the Hollywood name of the Polish dancer Marianna Michalska (1901–59), who appeared in films in the 1920s and 1930s and "is credited with inventing the shimmy" (Halliwell 282). For other references to Wynn and to Gilda, see pp. 50, 56, 69, 85, 92, 94, 96, and 242. They are also mentioned in drafts of *Dark as the Grave*.

44. *Riley and Peggy* [p. 45]: These are the names of people Lowry knew during his stay in Mexico in 1936–38; they are referred to under the same names in the notebooks and in drafts of *Dark as the Grave*. Other references to Riley and Peggy are on pp. 58, 59, 60, 66, 68–69, 70, 94, 182, and 248. See also Bowker 239–40.

45. *Stan's number* [p. 45]: Stan is presumably Charles Stansfeld-Jones, alias "Frater Achad" (see Day and Bowker), but it is unclear why his num-

ber is 13 or why Sigbjørn should dislike the number for that reason. At this point in Draft A, the number 13 is said to be "Hoot-nannie's number" (UBC 13:1, 10). Hoot-nannie or Hootnanny, a nickname for Stansfield-Jones, is also mentioned on pp. 108 (see note IV.40), 111, 231 ff.

46. *Number of Judas* [p. 45]: Thirteen is often said to be unlucky because it is the number of people at the Last Supper, one of whom—Judas—would betray Jesus (see p. 42).

47. *conversation . . . with R. 8 years before* [p. 45]: As the snatch of dialogue just recalled indicates, R. was Ruth, Sigbjørn's first wife, who left him eight years earlier. The scene is recalled again on p. 94. On Ruth, see note I.61.

48. *the anguish in that hotel—he could not remember its name* [p. 45]: In Draft A, the hotel is identified as "the Monterrey,—where he had written the poem and still owed 4 or 5 pesos for beer" (UBC 13:1, 11). Presumably this is why Sigbjørn soon begins to whistle "It happened in Monterrey." On the Monterrey, see p. 57, where the poem referred to in Draft A is identified as "Love which comes too late" (*CP* 73–74).

49. *Las Mañanitas* [p. 46]: For "Las Mañanitas," a Mexican birthday song, see *A World in Tune: Folksongs of Mexico*, collected by Amalia Millán (Park Ridge, Ill.: Neil A. Kjos Music Co., 1948), 46–48. The song "was originally addressed to the Virgin of Guadalupe," and the second stanza is a birthday greeting to the Virgin.

50. *they might hear* [p. 46]: The typescript has "they might here."

51. *as it were* [p. 46]: In the typescript, this phrase is crossed out in pencil.

52. *"out of spite" as Dostoievsky might have said* [p. 47]: Here and on p. 39 above, Lowry refers to the opening of *Notes from Underground*: "I am a sick man . . . I am a spiteful man. I am an unpleasant man. I think my liver is diseased. However, I don't know beans about my disease, and I am not sure what is bothering me. I don't treat it and never have, though I respect medicine and doctors. Besides, I am extremely superstitious, let's say sufficiently so to respect medicine. (I am educated enough not to be superstitious, but I am.) No, I refuse to treat it out of spite" (Fyodor Dostoevsky, *"Notes from Underground" and "The Grand Inquisitor,"* ed. and trans. Ralph E. Matlaw [New York: E. P. Dutton, 1960], 3). For other references to Dostoievsky (Lowry's characteristic spelling), see pp. 82, 169, 199 (note XIII.15), 209–10 (note XV.4), 252, and 254–55 (note XXVII.4); see also note IV.12.

53. *"This stream's going the wrong way," Primrose said. (This remark is also "thematic")* [p. 48]: A marginal note at an earlier point in Draft A reads "his mind like Robert Frost's backward runnin[g] stream" (UBC 13:1, 11). See p. 50 below and Frost's 1928 poem "West-Running Brook."

54. *A drunken Chinaman, just like a drunken hunchback* [p. 48]: This might allude to the Chinese hunchback who collects the fares for the Infernal Machine in *Under the Volcano* (*UV* 221).

55. *like a character one happens upon by opening a book at random in a public library* [p. 48]: This is a variation on the technique of *sortes Shakespeareanae* that Lowry derived from Conrad Aiken (who uses the phrase in his *Blue Voyage*) and passed along to the Consul and Jacques Laruelle in *Under the Volcano*. See *UV* 34, 209, and Ackerley and Clipper 59.

56. *it was so like a scene in the Valley of the Shadow of Death as to be almost eerie* [p. 48]: The scene resembles the bus ride in chapter 8 of *Under the Volcano*, which concludes with the bus driver and his friend entering a pulquería.

57. *(Note: this road was once the China road . . . the primitive little port.)* [p. 49]: From the Acapulco guidebook (see note I.13):

> Through [the ships], the Port of Acapulco became the gateway to the Orient, and the Mexico City-Acapulco road, the "China Road", for it was the pathway from Eastern Asia to Western Europe.
>
> The treasure-laden argosies of ivory, sandal-wood, jade, jasper, porcelain, tea and spices from Java and Ceylon, brought the exoticism and luxury of the East to the primitive little port. (*Acapulco* 5)

58. *Yvonne's "You have one"* [p. 49]: Either Lowry is confusing Yvonne, the Consul's ex-wife in *Under the Volcano*, with Primrose (as on p. 230; see note XVIII.13) or—more likely—he is alluding to Yvonne's statement in the earlier novel, "You have one and I'll cheer" (*UV* 48), which Primrose echoes in *Dark as the Grave* (*DG* 172).

59. *Fabrico de Jello meant . . . Ice Manufacturers* [p. 49]: Lowry is poking fun at Sigbjørn's misplaced faith in his Spanish, unless he has miscopied the sign himself. Jello is an American brand of gelatin; ice factory is *fábrica de hielo*.

60. *"And the stream's still going the wrong way,"* [p. 50]: See note I.53.

61. *Ruth* [p. 50]: Lowry's first wife, Janine Vanderheim, who adopted the name Jan Gabrial. She is called Ruth here and on pp. 55–56, 70, 77, 86, and 96. On p. 178 she is called Janine, and on p. 264 her name is recalled by the name Janice. See also notes I.47 and IV.6.

62. Πασα θαλασσα θαλασσα [p. 50]: The immediate source of this quotation is a passage in chapter 6 of Conrad Aiken's *Blue Voyage*: "For everywhere the sea is the sea. . . . It was Silberstein who added this last phrase: Silberstein of Sidon, Antipater of Harlem. Yes! It was Silberstein, and Smith repeated the Greek after him, taking the cigar out of his mouth to do so: Πασα θαλασσα θαλασσα" (*Collected Novels of Conrad Aiken* [New York: Holt, Rinehart and Winston, 1964], 132). The Greek phrase reappears later in the same chapter (138). Lowry used the passage in a 1945 letter to

Aiken (Sugars 192). As Sugars notes in her edition of the Aiken-Lowry letters, the ultimate source is Xenophon's *Anabasis* 4.7, where the Greeks cry
"θαλαττα! θαλαττα!": "The Sea! The Sea!" In a letter to me, R. J. Schork
observes that Aiken (and thus Lowry) "uses an alternate (and equally correct, but not the spelling used by Xenophon) spelling: sigmas for taus, σσ for
ττ ('ss' for 'tt')," and he translates the passage as meaning roughly "Everywhere, the sea, the sea."

63. *what he remembered, from the guide book . . . Santa Ana defended
his dictatorship* [p. 51]: This passage is not recited from memory, as Lowry
implies, but adapted from the Acapulco guidebook (see note I.13):

> In 1813 [the Fortress of San Diego] was captured by Morelos, and
> held by the insurgents until the early part of 1821 when it was re-
> linquished to the royalists. It remained one of the last strong-holds
> of the Spanish government, which held the fort until the fifteenth
> of October, 1821. Even after the establishment of Mexican inde-
> pendence, the fort continued to play an important role in the Re-
> public's political history. Within its time-stained walls Santa Ana
> planned and initiated his dictatorship, and on various occasions
> the fort defended liberals, conservatives, imperialists and revolu-
> tionists. (*Acapulco* 6)

On Antonio López de Santa Anna (1795–1876), a soldier, revolutionary,
and politician who served first as president and then as dictator of Mexico,
see also note II.22.

64. *Pie de la Cuesta* [p. 51]: This is the correct spelling, but Lowry more
often changes it to Pied de la Cuesta, probably confusing Spanish *pie* (foot)
with its French cognate, *pied*.

65. *two penguins, on loan doubtless from Melville's Encantadas* [p. 52]:
Sketch Third of Melville's "The Encantadas, or Enchanted Isles" includes
a paragraph on penguins, describing them as "outlandish beings" whose
"bodies are grotesquely misshapen" (*CSHM* 62–63). For other Melvillean
references see notes II.11, VI.87, and XI.1.

66. *Caleta* [p. 52]: The typescript reading of this passage (which has no
corresponding passage in Draft A) has "Calete," but the correct spelling is
"Caleta." Both spellings occur in the typescript and in the pencil draft, but
I have regularized the spelling because it appears that Lowry meant to get it
right.

67. *El Ciclon* [p. 52]: Properly, this should be "El Ciclón," "The Cyclone"; but the "o" is consistently unaccented in Lowry's notes and Draft A,
and might well have been so on the bar itself.

68. *he recognized the gringoes* [p. 53]: At this point in the typescript
a note in the left margin, in Margerie's hand, reads, "mem: shaking man of
p. 294" (see pp. 213–14).

69. *Supervulcanization* [p. 53]: A variation on the common sign "Vulca-nizadora," tire repair. (If there really were such a sign, it would more likely read "Supervulcanización"; cf. p. 92.) Phillip Herring has suggested to me that Lowry may be passing a sign advertising Mobil oil, whose logo—a fly-ing horse—would remind him of the horses that pulled the chariot of He-lios in the myth of Phaeton (unless Lowry is simply confusing Phaeton with Pegasus). The next paragraph, with its reference to what Sigbjørn initially thought the sign said and his fear of hurting Primrose's feelings, makes no sense, and I suspect that the second reference to "Supervulcanization" is a mistake for another word—perhaps one that plays more obviously on "volcano" and refers to *Under the Volcano*. See also chapter 5 of *Dark as the Grave*, where Sigbjørn passes "the familiar sign, Euzkadi, another Vulcanización" (*DG* 96; see also *UV* 324). There is another curious refer-ence to Phaeton on p. 133.

70. *Nosotros no somos . . . Cuánto?* [p. 53]: A variation on the phrase "Nosotros no somos americanos ricos, nosotros somos canadianos pobres" ("We are not rich Americans, we are poor Canadians")—a refrain through-out *Dark as the Grave* and *La Mordida*—followed by the question "How much?" (*¿Cuánto?*). Lowry's "Canadianos" is an error for "canadienses."

71. *Canadian Price Control Board* [p. 54]: Established September 1939, the Wartime Prices and Trade Board introduced wage and price controls and currency regulations that largely remained in effect until 1947. See also pp. 116 and 198; in the last occurrence, Sigbjørn almost gets the name right.

72. *Kilroy was here* [p. 55]: An American contribution to the art of graf-fiti, found often in *La Mordida* and in *Dark as the Grave*.

73. *El Grafe* [p. 55]: The word has no meaning in Spanish; perhaps it is a coinage for a graffiti artist. See also note XLII.2.

74. *his first arrival in Acapulco* [p. 55]: On p. 50 Sigbjørn remembered having had "his first mescal" in Acapulco in September 1936—a date that also appears in *Dark as the Grave* (*DG* 139); now he says he says that he first arrived in Acapulco "from Mexico, on the Day of the Dead [2 Novem-ber], 1936." In fact, however, he arrived on 30 October 1936 (see note S.3). The arrival is also commemorated in *Under the Volcano*, where Yvonne ar-rives in Acapulco on the *Pennsylvania* amidst "a hurricane of immense and gorgeous butterflies" (*UV* 44).

75. *overture of mystery* [p. 55]: This might be a transcription error; the guidebook has "overtone of mystery" (*Acapulco* 6).

76. *he had cut out all the long passages . . . concerning the negro* [p. 56]: In the 1940 version of *Under the Volcano*, chapter 2—which takes place in Acapulco—begins with Yvonne's recollection of her arrival on the *Pennsyl-vania* and her impressions of Acapulco, including the square where a Negro owns a "Sandwich y Cigarettes" stall (*UV* [1940] 44–46).

77. *Love which comes too late is like that black storm* [p. 57]: The opening of an untitled poem from part 5 of Lowry's *The Lighthouse Invites the Storm*; see *CP* 73–74 and Chris Ackerley's annotation, *CP* 254. Lowry alludes to a later line in the poem in chapter 1 of *Under the Volcano*: "It slaked no thirst to say what love was like which came too late" (*UV* 10). There are two more references on p. 59 below. See also note I.48.

78. *the old Consulate where his book had been saved* [p. 57]: On this incident, see Day 246, Bowker 239–40, and *DG* 220.

79. *Abajos . . . Americanoes!* [p. 57]: This should read *Abajo los tiránicos norteamericanos!* ("Down with the tyrannical North Americans!") Although *norteamericanos* might appear to include Canadians, the word normally refers to people from the United States.

80. *We Who Are About to Die . . . The Hour of the Truth* [p. 58]: *We Who Are About to Die* (1937), starring Preston Foster, Ann Dvorak, and John Beal, is a prison film "based on the true life story of a prisoner who spent 13 months [on Death Row] in San Quentin before winning a reprieve" (*MPG* 9:3757). *The Hour of the Truth* is *La hora de la verdad*, starring Ricardo Montalbán, Virginia Serret, Lilia Michel, and Carlos Orellana, which opened on 15 November 1945. The plot concerns the tragic life and loves of a bullfighter (Montalbán). See Emilio Garcia Riera, *Historia Documental del Cine Mexicano* (Mexico City: Ediciones Era, 1970), 2:241–45. On *The Hour of the Truth*, see also p. 230 below.

CHAPTER II

1. *the Seven Seas . . . Spray, remembering Potato Jones* [p. 59]: "Potato" Jones, the captain of the *Marie Llewellyn*, attempted (but failed) to run guns to the Republicans during the Spanish Civil War, with the weapons hidden by a cargo of potatoes. In *Under the Volcano*, Hugh imagines himself as "Potato Firmin" (*UV* 103; see Ackerley and Clipper 160). Lowry mentions Potato Jones in his poems "Peter Gaunt and the Canals," line 139 (*CP* 53), and "Lying awake beside a sleeping girl," line 15 (*CP* 93). In the latter poem, Lowry makes the same mistake that he makes in *La Mordida*: assuming that Potato Jones was the captain of the *Seven Seas Spray*, which successfully ran the blockade (see Chris Ackerley's annotation, *CP* 266).

2. *the usual advice to been seen in buses* [p. 61]: Obviously there is something wrong with this typescript reading, but the phrase does not appear in Draft A, and there is no basis on which to choose between "to be seen" and "to have been seen."

3. *Moleste el Chofere* [p. 61]: Someone has obliterated the initial word on a sign reading *No Moleste al Chófer* ("Don't Bother the Driver"). It is

more likely that the sign would read *No Distraiga al Chófer* ("Don't Distract the Driver"): cf. *DG* 167, 179.

4. *Canadian naval mutiny* [p. 61]: I have found no evidence that there ever was a Canadian naval mutiny in Acapulco.

5. *Los Cocos . . . los Cacos* [p. 61]: "The Coconuts . . . the Thieves."

6. *the people standing on the shore who, having known the corpse, were for a moment, great* [p. 63]: See the final line of Lowry's poem "Thoughts while Drowning, But Try to Eliminate the Argument" (*CP* 109–10).

7. *still "characters"* [p. 64]: See *DG* 233.

8. *Hotel Cordoba* [p. 64]: This is the correct spelling, which is normally used in *La Mordida*, but at this and a few other points Draft A and the typescript both have "Cordova."

9. *Ah, the old familiar feces—as T. said* [p. 64]: In part because of the tone of undergraduate scatological wit in this pun, Sherrill Grace has suggested to me that T. may be Tom Forman, a Cambridge friend of Lowry's.

10. *which had been recommended to them* [p. 65]: The typescript reading is "which they had been recommended to them." The passage does not appear in Draft A, and I have made what seems the most likely emendation.

11. *the Venetian gazebos on Benito Cerino's fated craft* [p. 65]: From the description of the ship in Melville's "Benito Cereno": "Toward the stern, two high-raised quarter galleries—the balustrades here and there covered with dry, tindery sea-moss—opening out from the unoccupied state-cabin, whose dead-lights, for all the mild weather, were hermetically closed and caulked—these tenantless balconies hung over the sea as if it were the grand Venetian canal" (*CSHM* 258).

12. *se resuelva* [p. 66]: Lowry's attempt to fit a Spanish verb into an English sentence runs into trouble: "they" is inconsistent with the reflexive pronoun *se* (himself, itself), and "may" is redundant because *se resuelva* is in the subjunctive. The sentence could be recast as "so that it *se resuelva* [may be resolved] in its own time" or as "so that they *lo resuelva* in their own time."

13. *commida* [p. 66]: Lowry's almost inevitable misspelling of *comida*, "dinner."

14. *Sam* [p. 68]: Sam Miller, a fisherman, was one of the Lowrys' neighbors in Dollarton, British Columbia.

15. *Johnny Weissmuller* [p. 68]: Johnny Weissmuller (spelled "Weismuller" in the typescript), 1904–84, was a champion swimmer who became famous playing Tarzan in the movies.

16. *at the same time gives one the mind and heart of Sir Philip Gibbs* [p. 69]: Sir Philip Gibbs (1877–1962) was a minor literary figure. In his review of *Under the Volcano*, Jacques Barzun wrote that "while imitating the tricks of Joyce, Dos Passos and Sterne, [Lowry] gives us the mind and heart

of Sir Philip Gibbs" ("New Books," *Harper's Magazine* [May 1947]: un-numbered back pages; the paragraph on Lowry is excerpted in *Malcolm Lowry, "Under the Volcano": A Casebook*, ed. Gordon Bowker [Basingstoke, Eng.: Macmillan Education, 1987], 69–70). Lowry refers to the same review below, pp. 71 and 77, and in *Dark as the Grave*, where it is treated as part of the publisher's reader's report on *The Valley of the Shadow of Death* (*DG* 142, 249), and he responded to Barzun in a long letter that specifically mentions this line (*SL* 143–48; see also Barzun's reply, *SL* 440). On the reader's report see note XXVI.8.

17. *the British Weekly the mater sends me* [p. 69]: The *British Weekly: A Journal of Social and Christian Progress* (founded 1886) was a Christian newspaper that, as a result of a sequence of mergers, later became *British Weekly and Christian World* and then *British Weekly and Christian Record*. In 1991 it was merged into the *Church of England Newspaper*. In an August 1947 letter to Albert Erskine, Lowry said, "my mother sends me the *British Weekly* and the *Illustrated London*—or someone sends it for my mother" (*SL* 151–52). On the *Illustrated London News* see note IX.7.

18. *Miss Gleason* [p. 69]: Perhaps the airline stewardess in chapter 2 of *Dark as the Grave*.

19. *Cornelia Gracchus* [p. 69]: Mother of the Roman tribunes Tiberius and Gaius Gracchus and ten other children, nine of whom did not live to maturity (second century B.C.).

20. *as Erikson put it, like sailors chipping rust, wearing themselves out behind a barrier of time* [p. 69]: Erikson is Nordahl Grieg, a Norwegian novelist whose *The Ship Sails On*, translated by A. G. Chater (New York: Alfred A. Knopf, 1927), influenced Lowry's *Ultramarine*. In chapter 7, Grieg's protagonist, Benjamin Hall, compares the tedium of chipping rust on the ship to the Israelites' wanderings in the desert, when "the Lord made them wander for forty years and wear themselves old and grey behind a barrier of nonsensical time" (Grieg 169–70). On Erikson, see also notes VI.28 and XVIII.10.

21. *'As an eagle stirreth up her next . . . smashed up the next first'* [pp. 69–70]: I have not identified the allusion.

22. *Mem: Juarez had landed on this beach* [p. 70]: Benito Pablo Juárez was arrested in 1853 after General Antonio López de Santa Anna seized control of the Mexican government. He escaped to New Orleans but returned in July 1855, landing in Acapulco, to overthrow Santa Anna (Roeder 1:103–15). On Santa Anna see also note I.63.

23. *beginning of letter in the Valley* [p. 70]: This refers to the beginning of the Consul's unposted letter to Yvonne in *Under the Volcano*: "Night: and once again, the nightly grapple with death, the room shaking with daemonic orchestras, the snatches of fearful sleep, the voices outside the window" (*UV* 35).

24. *boy scout mentality, (Sigbjørn had once been a Lion)* [p. 71]: Lion is a rank in Cub Scouts, a Boy Scout organization for younger boys, rather than in the Boy Scouts proper.

25. *Bonn-Doumerghue business . . . the death of P.* [p. 72]: The reference here is murky, but it appears to suggest that Paul Fitte, whom Lowry met in Bonn, tried to get him to steal money. On Fitte see notes IV.20 and XXVII.6.

26. *es mejor* [p. 72]: "It is better."

27. *Mario and the Magician* [p. 73]: Thomas Mann's novella "Mario and the Magician" was first published in 1930 and translated into English in 1931 by H. T. Lowe-Porter. In the discussion that follows, Lowry refers both to the English translation and to an early review by Clifton P. Fadiman, "Thomas Mann's Obsession," *Nation* 132 (11 February 1931): 156. Despite his hope of avoiding the "same quotations as Fadiman made from it," Lowry quotes (at greater length) a passage cited by Fadiman: see pp. 74–75 below and Mann, *"Death in Venice" and Seven Other Stories*, trans. H. T. Lowe-Porter (New York: Vintage International, 1989), 143. Fadiman also reprinted "Mario and the Magician" in his *Reading I've Liked*; see note IV.39. See also Dieter Saalmann, "The Role of Determinism in Malcolm Lowry's Response to Thomas Mann's *Mario and the Magician*," *Malcolm Lowry Review*, no. 25 (Fall 1989): 42–54.

28. *not, like Mussolini, the hanging upside down . . . St. Peter* [p. 74]: The former Italian dictator Benito Mussolini, captured by Italian partisans on 28 April 1945, was shot to death and his body left hanging upside down in a final act of humiliation. According to legend, St. Peter was martyred by being crucified upside down, a position he chose to avoid comparison with Jesus.

29. *"Tiberius is a rock, Sejanus is a snake"* [p. 76]: From Hugo's "Ce que dit la bouche d'ombre"; see note I.40.

30. *Señor Mañana Mañana y Mañana* [p. 76]: In the next chapter this name is given as Señor Mañana y Mañana y Mañana—Mr. Tomorrow and Tomorrow and Tomorrow—which makes it even clearer that Lowry is combining a standard joke about Mexicans' preference for putting things off until *mañana* with an allusion to Macbeth's "Tomorrow, and tomorrow, and tomorrow" speech.

31. *the perfectly good Emersonian number of 5* [p. 76]: I do not know why five is an Emersonian number.

32. *the Phillipson incident* [p. 76]: In *Under the Volcano*, Hugh Firmin recalls that an artist named Phillipson drew a cartoon of him "as an immense guitar, inside which an oddly familiar infant was hiding, curled up, as in a womb" (*UV* 177). For a possible source of this Phillipson incident, see Bradbrook 7.

33. *Baron Samedi* [p. 78]: In voodoo, "chief god of the Petro clan, the evil gods of the voodoo hierarchy. Also known as Lord of the Cemetery. If

one wishes to put a hex on anyone he is the god to pray to" (Philippe Thoby-Marcelin and Pierre Marcelin, glossary to *The Pencil of God*, trans. Leonard Thomas [Cambridge, Mass.: Riverside Press, 1951], 203). According to Day, Lowry's "conversations became full of references to Baron Samedi, Papa Legba, and Damballah the Snake God" during his 1947 trip to Haiti (Day 375). In *Dark as the Grave*, Dr. Hippolyte (here called Dr. Amann: see notes I.8 and III.19) says that Sigbjørn is possessed by himself, "not by Baron Samedi nor yet by Papa Legba" (*DG* 152).

CHAPTER III

1. *Quinta Eulalia* [p. 78]: Lowry's notes in Draft A indicate that he planned to change the name of the Quinta Eugenia to Quinta Eulalia, but the changes are not made quite consistently in the typescript, whose readings I have generally followed in this regard.

2. *Ignacio Altamirano* [p. 79]: Mexican poet, novelist, and political figure (1834–93). Referring to the disarray of Juarez's Liberal allies in 1864, when Maximilian and Carlotta were installed on the throne of Mexico, Roeder says that "Ignacio Altamirano was in Acapulco, reading Tasso" (Roeder 2:577).

3. *and the place in darkness* [p. 80]: A handwritten marginal note next to this sentence in Draft B reads "mem: candle in bedroom—sometimes."

4. *Vino de Mision San Tomas* [p. 80]: More correctly, *vino Misión de Santo Tomás*.

5. *Toynbee's recent history* [p. 80]: Probably Arnold Toynbee's *Civilization on Trial* (London: Oxford University Press, 1948); for "know-how," see 22, 23, 25, 27, 85, 144, 146, 167, 181, 262.

6. *Cartablanca . . . Bebe Coca Cola bien fría* [p. 81]: Four brands of Mexican beer, the first of which should read "Carta Blanca," followed by the familiar American advertisement: "Drink ice-cold Coca Cola" (for which see also *DG* 73, 170).

7. *Acapulco, an adventure in living* [p. 81]: See note I.13.

8. *Oxford Grouper* [p. 82]: "The Oxford Group [founded 1908], which was a campaign for the truths of Christianity within all Christian sects, is distinct from the [nineteenth-century] Oxford Movement . . . within the Church of England" (Sugars 58 n. 1). Lowry's letters contain many complaints about the "notoriously prohibitionist" Oxford Group (Sugars 79). See also Lowry's poem "Hypocrite! Oxford Grouper! Yahoo!" and Chris Ackerley's commentary on the poem (*CP* 181–82, 296), as well as the poem "When I was young I broke all drinking records," which advises the reader to "Distrust the sober, the columnist, the Oxford Grouper" (*CP* 223). On Lowry's strained relationship with the Oxford Grouper A. B. Carey, see Bowker.

9. *Quinette? or Jerphanion?* [p. 82]: I have not identified either figure.

10. *those two extremest examples of the Paul Pry, Proust and Dickens* [p. 83]: Paul Pry was "a very inquisitive character in a comedy of the same name by John Poole, 1825"; the name may be used as a noun, referring to a snoopy person, or as a verb ("to Paul-Pry") meaning to be snoopy (*OED*). Proust and Dickens are apparently linked by the detailed ways in which they present their characters.

11. *as tight as Titus Oates* [p. 84]: In English history, Titus Oates (spelled "Tightus Oates" in Draft A, "Titus Oats" in the typescript), 1649–1705, was an anti-Catholic conspirator who gave false information about the "Popish Plot" of 1678. The phrase used here is probably an undergraduate witticism on the order of "Ah, the old familiar feces" (see note II.9).

12. *Who is Kilroy? . . . Read The Valley of the Shadow of Death* [p. 85]: On Kilroy see note I.72. In *Dark as the Grave*, Sigbjørn imagines an alternative: "Suppose that, instead of Kilroy, you had, Forgive Your Enemies. Or say, Read *The Valley of the Shadow of Death*" (*DG* 31).

13. *atmosphere of the Belgian Congo* [p. 86]: Chris Ackerley has suggested to me that the comparisons of Acapulco to the Belgian Congo here and on pp. 96 and 97 might imply that Lowry was considering developing a parallel between *La Mordida* and Joseph Conrad's *Heart of Darkness*. The comparison was probably suggested by the Acapulco guidebook (see note I.13), which compares the countryside surrounding Acapulco to "the deep jungle of Congo Africa" (*Acapulco* 13).

14. *According to Ellsworth Huntington* [p. 87]: The idea that "as civilization develops it moves towards colder regions" appears frequently in studies of the development of cultures by the American geographer Ellsworth Huntington. See, e.g., *The Human Habitat* (New York: Van Nostrand, 1927), 161.

15. *purple passages* [p. 87]: This is a common phrase (repeated, p. 250), but one that might recall Conrad Aiken's witticism that Lowry should name his first book *Purple Passage* rather than *Ultramarine*, in recognition of its debt to Aiken's *Blue Voyage*.

16. *El Universal* [p. 88]: In Spanish, "the universe" is "el universo." *El Universal* is, however, the name of a Mexico City newspaper that is mentioned several times in *Under the Volcano* (UV 87, 90, 137, 180, 181); more ominously, on pp. 284 and 285, El Universal is given as the name of the cantina which in *Under the Volcano* is called the Farolito (on which see note VI.72). Both the newspaper and the cantina are mentioned in a draft of *Dark as the Grave*, where Sigbjørn comments that the cantina "is still called *La* Universal for some reason I can't quite fathom" (UBC 9:5, 339; see also *DG* 85, 105 ff.).

17. *I'm Dreaming of a White Christmas* [p. 89]: The opening line of Irving Berlin's "White Christmas," first sung by Bing Crosby in the 1942 film *Holiday Inn*. The scene has parallels in *Dark as the Grave* (*DG* 82, 101) and in *October Ferry to Gabriola* (*OF* 90).

18. *UBC 13:20, 116* [p. 89]: In the typescript, this page and the previous one are both numbered 116.

19. *the narrator of this story* [p. 90]: This passage and one further down the page, where the narrator identifies himself as Hippolyte, are the only points in the typescript that indicate that Lowry intended to narrate the novel from the perspective of Dr. Hippolyte, identified in *Dark as the Grave* as "a Haitian [who] had been the Haitian chargé d'affaires in Mexico at one time, but for some reason had not returned and still lived in Cuernavaca, a gigantic Negro, clad all in classical white, and with a black tie" (*DG* 147). Lowry also toyed with idea of making Hippolyte the narrator of *Dark as the Grave* (UBC 9:5, 361–62). He is the same character as Dr. Amann (see notes I.8 and II.33).

20. *the identity between Vigil and Fernando, how Fernando had called him "The maker of tragedies"* [p. 90]: On Fernando (Juan Fernando Márquez), see note I.9. For Fernando's phrase "maker of tragedies," see *DG* 22, 24, 26, 32, 46, 64, 65, 127, 150, 191, 197, 230, 240, and below, p. 177.

21. *Newton ... obsessed by the tyranny of numbers* [p. 90]: This might refer to Isaac Newton's fascination with alchemy, in which number symbolism plays a prominent role. See Betty Jo Teeter Dobbs, *The Janus Faces of Genius: The Role of Alchemy in Newton's Thought* (Cambridge: Cambridge University Press, 1991).

22. *passion for order* [p. 90]: See note I.38.

23. *dear old Hippolyte* [p. 90]: See note III.19.

CHAPTER IV

1. *Sejanus (Shakespeare it is said performed in Marlowe's play of this name)* [p. 91]: Shakespeare did act in *Sejanus his Fall* (first performed in 1603), but the play was written by Ben Jonson rather than Christopher Marlowe.

2. *except for the straw, and that's in his feet* [p. 92]: This might recall Hugh Firmin's reflection, "eyes in my feet, I must have, as well as straw" (*UV* 94).

3. *Walt Ferries, known to his friends as Pisspot* [p. 93]: Not identified.

4. *what is above is like what is below* [p. 93]: A central doctrine of alchemy and other mystical systems is the correspondence between spiritual and physical planes of reality. The phrase "as above, so below" is popularly

said to derive from the legendary figure Hermes Trismegistus; hence the phrase "Hermetic correspondences." Ackerley and Clipper (30–31, 59) suggest that Lowry's interest in correspondences might be traceable to his reading of Swedenborg; Bowker (322) credits the influence of Charles Stansfeld-Jones, who is referred to in *La Mordida* as "Stan" or "Hootnanny," a suggestion that seems borne out by the reference on p. 108 (see note IV.40). Lowry might also have encountered the phrase used here in any number of occult sources. See, e.g., S. L. MacGregor Mathers, *The Kabbalah Unveiled*, (1887; new edition, 1926; reprint York Beach, Me.: Samuel Weiser, 1983), 96, 155 n, 243–44 n, who says that the inscription on the Smaragdine tablet of Hermes Trismegistus includes this precept: "That which is below is like that which is above, and that which is above is like that which is below, for the performance of the miracles of the one substance." See also note IV.40 and Lowry's notes on *Tender Is the Night* (NS 34).

5. *the Salton Sea* [p. 94]: Not a sea at all but a shallow salt lake in southeastern California.

6. *in real life R. had said* [p. 94]: Margerie typed "in real life Pisspot had said," then crossed out "Pisspot" and wrote "R" (i.e., Ruth).

7. *waved; yes she had* [p. 94]: This is my emendation of a passage, not in Draft A, which in the typescript reads, "waved yet; she had."

8. *Excelsior . . . Tremendo Siniestro Tremendo Choque* [p. 95]: On *Excelsior*, see note I.35. The headline "Terrible Disaster, Terrible Collision" apparently refers to an automobile accident.

9. *a posthumous story by Anderson* [p. 95]: I have found no evidence that Sherwood Anderson ever met Lowry, much less that he wrote a story about him.

10. *wearing the clothes of a man who died of G.P.I.* [p. 95]: According to *Dark as the Grave* (DG 39), Sigbjørn's clothing belonged to "a Christian Science practitioner who had died of general paralysis of the insane"—i.e., general paresis, a deteriorating mental and physical condition caused by syphilis.

11. *Canadian spy scare* [p. 96]: On 5 February 1946, the Royal Commission on Espionage issued its final report on an investigation into a Communist spy ring that, it charged, had been operating in Canada since 1924, passing Canadian and American military secrets on to the Soviet Union. The spy scare is referred to in *Dark as the Grave* and "Strange Comfort Afforded by the Profession" as well as on pp. 103, 116, 206, 230, and 240 below.

12. *pop-eye type murals* [p. 97]: In Draft A, this paragraph continues: "Martin noticed absolutely nothing about those murals save that they were unusual, for except in certain matters, M. was as unobservant as Raskolnikov" (UBC 13:3, 8). On Raskolnikov, the protagonist of Dostoevsky's *Crime and Punishment*, see also notes XIII.15, XV.4, and XXVII.4.

13. *In the meaning of Existentialism, discussing Heidegger, Barrett says* [p. 97]: Lowry goes on to refer to ideas set forth by the German philosopher Martin Heidegger (1889–1976), in particular ideas from his influential *Being and Time* (1927), as explained by William Barrett (misspelled "Barret" in the typescript) in *What Is Existentialism?* "What are the full characteristics of this fallen state of everyday existence [as described by Heidegger]? They have to be seen from another point of view: everyday existence— no matter how public and banal—is always pierced and permeated by some feeling, some affective state (*Befindlichkeit*). To exist is to be in some mood or other: fear, anxiety, tranquillity, or joy. Feeling is a fundamental mode of existence. The world is given to us in feeling" (Barrett 29). See also note IV.22.

14. *Sahara, Dahomey, lac Nagaïn, Darfour—Paysages de lune où rôde la chimère* [p. 98]: From Victor Hugo's "Tous les bas âges sont épars"; see note I.40.

15. *"bat boats" in Haitian section* [p. 98]: See below, pp. 126, 159.

16. *Mynheer Peeperkorn* [p. 99]: A wealthy Dutch colonial who commits suicide in Thomas Mann's *The Magic Mountain*. See also "Through the Panama," where three Dutch engineers who are passengers on the ship are all dubbed Mynheer von Peeperhorn (*HL* 71–72, 96) and *Dark as the Grave*, where a bishop is compared to "Mynheer Peeperkorn prior to his suicide making his final speech before the clamour of the waterfall in *The Magic Mountain*" (*DG* 101).

17. *"Walking next day upon the fatal shore . . .* [p. 99]: These passages come from Borachio's false report of Charlemont's death in Cyril Tourneur's *The Atheist's Tragedy* (1611), 2.1.72 ff. In Draft A (UBC 13:3, 11), the speech is introduced by the note, "(p 273—Aldington)," which—along with the reference on p. 100, below, to the editor of the anthology as "A." (see note IV.19)—makes it clear that Lowry derived the passage from *The Viking Book of Poetry of the English-Speaking World*, ed. Richard Aldington (New York: Viking Press: 1941). Lowry owned a copy of this book, on pp. 273–74 of which appears the passage from *The Atheist's Tragedy*. The following passages in the same book (pp. 274–76), selections from Tourneur's *The Revenger's Tragedy* in which Vendice addresses his mistress's skull, are the source of Sigbjørn's complaint about Elizabethan writers who mourn their lovers' skulls (see note IV.31). On Tourneur, see also note IV.26.

Although it does not survive into the typescript, it is worth noting that in Draft A, immediately after the quotation from *The Atheist's Tragedy*, Lowry wrote, "or Brooke's:—/ the little dulling edge of foam / That browns & dwindles as the wave goes home." These lines are from Rupert Brooke's poem "The Great Lover."

18. *see Richard III* [p. 99]: For Buckingham's references to All Soul's Day (2 November, the Day of the Dead in Mexico), which Lowry associates with the Consul in *Under the Volcano*, see Shakespeare's *Richard III*, 5.1. For "Hastings on uncertainty of man's lot," see *Richard III*, 3.4.95–100:

> O momentary grace of mortal men,
> Which we more hunt for than the grace of God!
> Who builds his hope in air of your good looks
> Lives like a drunken sailor on a mast,
> Ready with every nod to tumble down
> Into the fatal bowels of the deep.

I assume that 709–710 refers to the page numbers in an anthology (not yet identified) in which Lowry found these passages.

19. *the anthologist had been none other than A.* [p. 100]: A. was Richard Aldington (see note IV.17), but I have found no evidence that he wrote a story about Lowry. There *was*, however, a novel by Charlotte Haldane, *I Bring Not Peace* (1932), in which James Dowd is based on Lowry and Dennis Carling on Paul Fitte (see note IV.20).

20. *the death of P.* [p. 100]: The suicide of Lowry's Cambridge friend Paul Fitte underlies this passage; see the annotations on other references to Fitte's death (notes II.25 and XXVII.6). Sigbjørn's story, "which had been burned, about the death of P.," was Lowry's novel *In Ballast to the White Sea*, which he wrote in the 1930s, based on his concern about the influence of Nordahl Grieg's *The Ship Sails On* on *Ultramarine*. The manuscript was almost totally destroyed in a fire in June 1944. One of the novel's major themes was the protagonist's guilt over a suicide. On *In Ballast*, see also notes IV.38, XXVIII.11, and XLIII.1.

21. *over the billows of inexhaustible anguish, hunted by the insatiable albatross of self* [p. 100]: In "Through the Panama," Sigbjørn thinks about "the inenarrable inconceivably desolate sense of having no right to be where you are; the billows of inexhaustible anguish haunted [sic] by the insatiable albatross of self" (*HL* 31).

22. *What we are anxious about in such states . . . Care is the being of man* [p. 101]: See Barrett's discussion of anxiety:

> [In describing anxiety, Heidegger] is concerned not with the genesis but the content of the state: namely, in what manner we are existing when we exist in that state. What we are anxious about in such states, Heidegger tells us, is our very Being-in-the-world as such. That is why anxiety is more fundamental to human existence than fear. Fear is always definite; about this or that object in the world; but anxiety is directed toward our Being-in-the-world itself, with which every definite object, or thing, within the world is involved. (Barrett 30)

The next section (31–32) deals with Heidegger's belief that care is the "unifying concept for the human condition" and concludes, "Care is the being of man."

23. *Hudson . . . Hemingway-like honeymoons of slaughter* [p. 101]: W. H. Hudson (1841–1922) was an Argentine-born English novelist; his novel *The Purple Land* is referred to on p. 108 (see note IV.35). Chris Ackerley suggests that this passage might refer to the descriptions of hunting in Hudson's books, including *Idle Days in Patagonia*, which contrast strangely with the "passionate interest in birds" that led Hudson to establish a bird sanctuary in London. For evidence of Hudson's passion for, and knowledge about, birds see such books of his as *Birds in a Village*, *Birds and Man*, *Adventures among Birds*, *Birds of La Plata*, and his posthumously published *Letters on the Ornithology of Buenos Ayres*. A possible source for the Hudson-Hemingway connection is the fact that in chapter 2 of *The Sun Also Rises*, Robert Cohn is said to have been obsessed with *The Purple Land*.

24. *Sigbjørn, like Hitler, was not tempted in that direction* [p. 101]: Adolf Hitler, ironically, was a vegetarian and non-hunter. If the comparison seems strange, it is only a little more so than Hugh Firmin's comparisons of himself to Hitler, first as a "frustrated artist" and then, more briefly, as an anti-Semite (*UV* 156, 171).

25. *Rendon's Vanishing Enchantment from Modern Mexico* [p. 103]: See Eduardo Bolio Rendon, "Vanishing Enchantment?" *Modern Mexico* 18, no. 9 (February 1946): 14–16, 27–28. Lowry refers again to this article on pp. 177 and 180 below; for *Modern Mexico*, see also note S.7. The Malcolm Lowry Archive contains a set of typed quotations from the article, headed "From the magazine MODERN MEXICO / VANISHING ENCHANTMENT?—by Eduardo Bolio Rendon" (UBC 7:4). The name Rendon is consistently misspelled "Redon" in the *La Mordida* typescript but is given correctly in Lowry's notes.

26. *Heywood, just when he'd been thinking of Tourneur* [p. 103]: Sigbjørn is thinking of Thomas Heywood (c. 1574–1641), a dramatist of the same period as Cyril Tourneur (c. 1575–1626). In Draft A, when the couple is introduced, Lowry's note reads, "the man has a name you can't forget—Tourneur—or perhaps, Tom Haywood" (UBC 13:3, 12). See also note VIII.4. On Tourneur, see notes IV.17 and IV.31.

27. *Permiso? . . . Sí. Qué pasa?* [p. 104]: "Pardon me?" (i.e., "Are you talking to me?"). "Yes. What's happening?" The question "Is your name Wilderness?" does not appear in the typescript, but a parallel line—"'Is your name Trumbaugh'"—appears in Draft A, so obviously a line has been dropped.

28. *my película gesehen* [p. 105]: An English-Spanish-German composite for "seen my film."

29. *Quinta Eulalia* [p. 105]: The typescript reading here and at one other place is "Quinta Aulalia," but both are apparently errors for "Quinta Eulalia."

30. *Mensch* [p. 105]: On Harry Mensch, see Bowker 228, 229, 232, 233, 356; Sugars 97; and Day 237. Mensch was the man for whom Lowry claimed to have played Sydney Carton (see *SL* 11). In *Dark as the Grave*, Mensch is called Hölscher (Bowker 630 n. 1; *DG* 87, 124, 208, 215, 219, 223).

31. *the horrors of your skull* [p. 105]: The reference is to Vendice's speech to his mistress's skull in Tourneur's *The Revenger's Tragedy*, which appears in the same anthology as the passage cited above from Tourneur's *The Atheist's Tragedy* (see note IV.17).

32. *"Don't you remember, 'And Fair as Herself is She?'"* [p. 105]: See Lowry's poem "Song for My Wife," *CP* 212–13. The poem is referred to again below, p. 255 (see note XXVIII.1). In Draft A, it is written in the margin of chapter XXVIII, p. 1.

33. *UBC 13:21, 139* [p. 106]: This concludes the draft of chapter IV. The following pages in the typescript consist of a series of notes and sketches, beginning with the newspaper article copied from the *Vancouver Sun*.

34. *Along the Waterfront, Jim Smith* [p. 106]: The text that follows is taken from the first part of a column by Jim Smith that appeared in the *Vancouver Sun* on Wednesday, 29 October 1947, p. 33.

35. *Hudson's fabled fox . . . See The Purple Land, p. 233* [p. 108]: See chapter 19, "Tales of the Purple Land," in W. H. Hudson's *The Purple Land*. (In the copy owned by Lowry [New York: Modern Library, n.d.], the episode is on pages 233–36, so I have emended the typescript reading, "133," as a transmission error.) This paragraph is virtually identical with one in *Dark as the Grave* (*DG* 217). Lowry refers again to the lampalagua on p. 117. On Hudson, see also note IV.23.

36. *Carlotta on hell—mem protraction of Maximilian's execution* [p. 108]: See notes IV.44–45.

37. *Eridanus* [p. 108]: In "The Forest Path to the Spring," Lowry identifies "the starry constellation Eridanus" with the mythical Rivers of Life and of Death (which in turn are generally identified with the River Po), and he retells the legend that Jupiter struck Phaeton with a thunderbolt and hurled him into the river (*HL* 225–26). Lowry refers to the constellation on p. 123. Eridanus is also the name used in Lowry's fiction both for the Burrard Inlet and for Dollarton, British Columbia, the town on the north side of the Inlet where the Lowrys lived in a squatter's shack (see above, p. 63, *DG* 8–9, and *OF* 164). The reference here, however, is to a work that Lowry planned to write, entitled *Eridanus*, in which the Wildernesses spend

an evening in Mexico telling an acquaintance about their life in Eridanus. Lowry intended to insert this novel between *Dark as the Grave* and *La Mordida* in his sequence entitled *The Voyage That Never Ends*, but eventually he abandoned *Eridanus* and converted most of what he had written into material for *October Ferry to Gabriola*.

38. *In Ballast* [p. 108]: *In Ballast to the White Sea*, a novel Lowry wrote in the 1930s. See notes IV.20, XXVIII.11, and XLIII.1.

39. *Santayana in Fadiman* [p. 108]: Probably either George Santayana's statement of his personal philosophy in *I Believe: The Personal Philosophies of Certain Eminent Men and Women of Our Time*, ed. Clifton Fadiman (New York: Simon and Schuster, 1939), 231–52, or Santayana's essay "The Unknowable" in *Reading I've Liked: A Personal Selection*, ed. Clifton Fadiman (New York: Simon and Schuster, 1941), 213–32. The latter seems more likely because the volume also contains the "Snow" chapter from Thomas Mann's *The Magic Mountain* and Mann's "Mario and the Magician" (see notes I.38, II.27) as well as Conrad Aiken's story "Silent Snow, Secret Snow."

40. *what is above is like what is below from Hootnanny* [p. 108]: On the alchemical doctrine of correspondences, see note IV.4. "Hootnanny" is a nickname for Charles Stansfeld-Jones (see note I.45). See also pp. 111, 231 ff.

41. *"Light in the Sky" . . . My God why have you given this to me—* [p. 108]: I have not identified "Light in the Sky," "The Beagles," and "Salmon," although "Salmon" might be Lowry's poem "Salmon Drowns Eagle" (*CP* 146–47), whose central incident is also described in "The Forest Path to the Spring" (*HL* 244). "My God why have you given this to me" is a variation on the last line of Lowry's poem "Happiness": "My God, why have you given this to us?" (*CP* 136). The same line appears in "The Forest Path to the Spring" (*HL* 257).

42. *Monsignor Meglia* [p. 108]: The papal nuncio in Mexico who complicated matters for Maximilian. The phrase "truest picture of hell" is adapted from Roeder, 2:586 (see the annotation below); the remainder of the paragraph is taken almost verbatim from Roeder 2:585.

43. *the Virgin of Guadalupe* [p. 108]: In the typescript, Guadalupe is consistently spelled Guadeloupe, the right spelling for a pair of Caribbean islands rather than for a Mexican town, but I have assumed that Lowry would want to adopt the correct spelling, as in the published text of *Under the Volcano* and the edited version of *Dark as the Grave* (*UV* 200; *DG* 86, 101). The name is spelled correctly in Margerie's notes in Notebook III that Lowry used for the end of chapter XXXIX (see p. 280), but Lowry's spelling in the corresponding Draft A passage appears to be "Guadelupe" (UBC 13:14, ch. XXXIX, 4).

44. *Carlotta wrote to Eugenie (see Roeder)* [p. 108]: From a letter from Carlotta to Empress Eugénie, wife of Napoleon III; reported in Roeder 2:586.

45. *poor Maximilian even after having heard that Carlotta was dead* [p. 109]: See Roeder 2:668.

Chapter V

1. *Eddie* [p. 110]: Eduardo Ford (or Kent, in *Dark as the Grave*): see p. 12 above and *DG* 133 ff.

2. *Camiónes a Hartebeestepec y Anexas* [p. 110]: An abbreviated form of a playful note from Notebook I that begins "Oficina de Camiones a Har tebeestepec y Pronhorncuigo y Anexas" ("Office of Buses to Harte-beesteville and Pronghornburg and Environs"). In Lowry's love poems, the Hartebeeste is a figure for Margerie while the Pronghorn represents Lowry himself (see *CP*, Appendix A). The Hartebeeste reappears on p. 222. See also note XLI.1.

3. *Ally Sloper* [p. 110]: A grotesque comic character from a late Victorian humor magazine, *Ally Sloper's Half-Holiday*.

4. *the President of the United States* [p. 111]: Franklin Delano Roosevelt (president, 1933–45), whose affliction with polio made swimming "a sedate side-stroke" one of the few forms of exercise available to him.

5. *"We want to see Mr. Wilderness—who are you?"* [p. 112]: A left-margin note at this point in Draft A reads, "Broken dialogue."

6. *the degenerate Warner Baxter* [p. 113]: Warner Baxter (1892–1951), a film star who began his movie career in the silent era and continued almost up to his death, won an Oscar as Best Actor in 1929 for his role as the Cisco Kid in *In Old Arizona*; other memorable portrayals include the "harassed director" in *42nd Street* (1933) and Dr. Mudd in *The Prisoner of Shark Island* (1936). Although film biographies typically describe him as handsome, Lowry's description of him as "degenerate" may be related to the fact that in his films of the 1930s he seemed "a man under pressure, his character hardened by stress," while in the 1940s, "illness and public neglect added gravity to his face" (David Thomson, *A Biographical Dictionary of Film* [New York: William Morrow, 1976], 32). Baxter is also referred to on pp. 221, 223, 228, and 240–41.

Chapter VI

1. *and full* [p. 115]: The typescript reading, "awful," probably makes more sense, but it appears to derive from a misreading of Lowry's hand.

2. *particularly poignant* [p. 115]: Draft A has "peculiarly poignant."

3. *La Mordida is also involved etymologically with remorse* [p. 116]: In *Under the Volcano*, the Consul says, "Consider the word remorse. Remord. Mordeo, mordere. La Mordida! Agenbite too . . ." (*UV* 218–19). This passage was added to the text of *Under the Volcano* at a late stage, after the trip described in *La Mordida*.

4. *of not much importance to anyone, I should have thought* [p. 117]: In Draft A, this paragraph ends, "(of not much importance to anyone I shouldn't [*sic*] have thought. Whether you perish with noble thoughts or not you still can't get away.)"

5. *the lampalagua* [p. 117]: A reference to Hudson's *The Purple Land*; see p. 108 and note IV.35.

6. *rendering to Caesar* [p. 117]: See note I.7.

7. *Ah—they still had their holiday* [p. 119]: In Draft A there is a right-margin note, beginning here, that reads, "See also end to Chap XI—it might be better to end XI thus." On the next page, next to the paragraph that begins "Now the sea was silver grey," a note reads, "This is quite possible end to Chap XI, wholly or in part."

8. *the jail in Oaxaca . . . at Christmas Eve, the bells—dolente, dolore! . . . the policeman's shadow swinging against the wall* [p. 121]: On Lowry's imprisonment in the Oaxaca jail during Christmas 1937, see *SL* 29, Bowker 232–33, and Day 236–39. The bells that ring out "*dolente . . . dolore!*" in *Under the Volcano* (*UV* 42, 373) invoke the inscription over the gate to hell in Dante's *Inferno*: "Per me si va nella città dolente, / Per me si va nell' etterno dolore" (3.1–2: "Through me is the way to the mournful city, / Through me is the way to eternal pain"). On the policeman's lantern and shadow, see Lowry's poem "I have known a city of dreadful night" (*CP* 59–60), lines 9–10, as well as the version planned for inclusion in *Dark as the Grave* (*CP* 385). The pencil draft of this passage includes the parenthetical note "see poem."

Draft A of this chapter does not contain any of the Haitian dream sequence or the other materials from the rest of the Draft B version. Instead, after "swinging against the wall . . ." the chapter concludes:

Alternative Ending

'Death' suddenly said Martin Trumbaugh aloud, for no reason.

'What was that darling?'

'Nothing.' (UBC 13:4, ch. VI, 6)

This passage originated in a note in Malcolm's hand inserted in Notebook III, p. 33. In the typescript it was transferred to the end of chapter 11 (UBC 13:25, 253); see p. 186 and note X.2.

9. *The Dream—From Haitian Notes* [p. 121]: Most of the remainder of this chapter is based on the trip that the Lowrys made in late 1946 and early

1947, from Vancouver to Seattle by plane, then to New Orleans by bus—
with stops in such places as Salt Lake City, Kansas City, and St. Louis—and
on to Haiti aboard the *Donald S. Wright*. The return trip is not described
here. On the entire trip, see Day 369–84 and Bowker 382–405. There is no
extant manuscript for most of the remainder of the chapter, at least parts of
which might have been typed directly from the notebooks from which the
description of this trip is derived (V, VI, VIII).

10. *"We'll have a plate of beans in New Orleans."* [p. 121]: See *DG* 54.

11. *Tombeau de Rosémonde Bertonnière . . . 57 ans* [p. 121]: "Grave of
Rosémonde Bertonnière . . . died 12 November 1838, aged 57 years"; an
epitaph in French, from a cemetery in New Orleans. I have reproduced the
transcriptions of New Orleans tombstones from Notebook V even when
they involve errors such as *décedé* for *décedée*.

12. *St. Catherine's College, Cambridge* [p. 121]: Lowry typically misspelled the name of St. Catharine's College, so I have left this error uncorrected even though this might have been Margerie's. In Lowry's notebook
entry from which this was developed—the only extant pre-typescript draft
of the passage—the reading is "where a policeman (looking as if he'd been
at St Cats, Cambridge) is chatting under the magnolias" (Notebook V).
According to legend, when the Roman emperor Maxentius ordered that
St. Catharine be broken on a wheel, the wheel miraculously collapsed;
hence the wheel became her symbol and that of the college named after her.

13. *Ici repose . . . 1846* [p. 122]: "Here rests Antoine A. Piccaluga: here
lies Faustin Joe de Gruy, died 3 June 1846."

14. *Christ received them with his spreading arms* [p. 122]: On this
statue of Christ, see note VI.83.

15. *The stars of the Caribees. . . . No wonder Hart Crane committed
suicide here* [p. 122]: In a letter to me, Chris Ackerley calls this "a punning
allusion to [Eugene] O'Neill's *The Moon of the Caribees*, its relevance the
theme of approaching death (and hence linking with Hart Crane, who died
by jumping from the *Orizaba* into that sea)." On *The Moon of the Caribees*
see also *HL* 32.

16. *The sea rushing through your soul in great cold waves of anguish. . . .
vascular oceanic remorse* [p. 123]: See above, p. 42 and note I.39.

17. *Eridanus* [p. 123]: On the constellation Eridanus see note IV.37.

18. *Spanish moss upon my soul. (Mildew)* [p. 124]: Frederick Asals has
called my attention to the final line of Lowry's poem "On Reading Red-
burn," where the image of mildew on the soul also appears (*CP* 80).

19. *Julian Green's Dark Journey . . . Leviathan* [p. 124]: Julian Green's
novel was published in French as *Leviathan* (1925) and translated as *The
Dark Journey*. In *Dark as the Grave*, Sigbjørn poses a question related to

the one here: "why should books like *The Dark Journey* start up at you just when you are trying to make a journey into life, he asked himself" (*DG* 46). Later he opens the novel at random to a passage that seems to describe his own situation (*DG* 50–51).

20. *some sea animal (Conradian)* [p. 125]: I do not see a reference to a specific work by Joseph Conrad in this passage (which is repeated, p. 157).

21. *General Smedley Butler* [p. 125]: Major (and subsequently Lieutenant Colonel) Smedley Darlington Butler was a U.S. Marine officer who took part in the 1915 American invasion of Haiti and became the first Commandant of the American-organized Gendarmerie d'Haiti, in which he held the "equivalent" rank of Major General—a rank he attained in the Marine Corps only years later. He returned to the United States in March 1918. See also below, pp. 156, 158.

22. *O. Henry Memorial Prize Stories of 1919* [p. 125]: More precisely, *O. Henry Memorial Award Prize Stories: 1919*. Chosen by the Society of Arts and Sciences. Introduction by Blanche Colton Williams. Garden City: Doubleday, Page & Company, 1920.

23. *Guadalajara* [p. 126]: A popular Mexican song.

24. *Battement de tambours!* [p. 126]: French, "Beating of drums!" The phrase reappears below, pp. 128 and 135, and in "Through the Panama" (*HL* 32, 36, 97). Lowry's notes on *Hear Us O Lord* include preliminary plans for a story, "Battement de Tambours," based on the Lowrys' trip from Vancouver to New Orleans.

25. *Tipperary . . . death will take you there* [p. 126]: A British army song, circa World War I. Its concluding lyrics, "It's a long, long way to Tipperary / But my heart is there," are parodied here. "Guinea" may be an error for "Guiana" (or Guyana), which is twice spelled correctly and is once misspelled as Guina in the typescript of this chapter (UBC 13:23, 208, 210). This line does not appear in the notebook on which this section is based (Notebook VI).

26. *Sparks* [p. 126]: A common nickname for a radio operator, used also in the 1940 draft of *Under the Volcano* (*UV* [1940] 48).

27. *Bergson* [p. 126]: This might have been the third mate's name, but the fact that the name does not appear in the notebook reading of this passage (Notebook VI)—or in the later passage that is more directly dependent on the notebook reading (p. 160)—supports Chris Ackerley's suggestion that the name refers to Henri Bergson, whose description of human understanding of life processes in *Creative Evolution* (Bergson 273–74) is recalled by the rocket image here. Lowry referred specifically to the Bergsonian image of a rocket and its ashes in a 1951 letter to Albert Erskine (*SL* 229). On Lowry's adaptation of Bergson's images for his purposes in the screenplay for *Tender*

Is the Night, see Ackerley, "Notes Towards Lowry's Screenplay of *Tender Is the Night*," *Malcolm Lowry Review* no. 29/30 (Fall 1991–Spring 1992): 47–48. See also note I.4.

28. *"Coté route ça aller?"* ... *"No."* [p. 128]: The text of this dialogue in Creole is based on Lowry's transcription of a conversation in Notebook VI (in which the "senator" is named Kneer, after Anton Kneer, the agent for the Alcoa Steamship Company, on whose ship the Lowrys sailed to Haiti). A rough translation is "Where does this road lead to?" "This is the road that leads to Senator Erikson's house." "Is this the same road that leads to Senator Erikson's house?" "No." "Do you know the road that leads to Mr. Erikson's house?" "No."

29. *Morning I* [p. 128]: These lines are the only instance of marginalia in this chapter, but the entire chapter (and for that matter the entire type-script) has a very wide left margin, presumably so that marginalia could be added at a later stage.

30. *Milton ... threw his inkpot at the wall* [p. 128]: Chris Ackerley suggests that Lowry might be thinking of the story that Martin Luther threw his inkpot at the devil.

31. *arc du ciel* [p. 128]: An error for French *arc-en-ciel*, "rainbow."

32. *The sea rushing through your soul. ...* [p. 129]: See note I.39.

33. *Ma femme ... universelle* [p. 129]: French: literally, "My wife wants the costume. It's a universal complication." The first sentence is probably an error for "My wife wants to use the toilet" (*les toilettes*) or for "My wife wants to wash" (*faire sa toilette*).

34. *men of Harlech* [p. 130]: "Men of Harlech" is the English version of "Rhyfelgyrch gwyr Harlech," a Welsh patriotic song that celebrates Welsh resistance to a fifteenth-century English siege of Harlech Castle. For lyrics in Welsh and English, see John Philip Sousa, *National, Patriotic, and Typical Airs of All Lands* (1890; reprint, New York: Da Capo Press, 1977), 278–80.

35. *toy tin houses, with peaked roofs* [p. 130]: Many of the following details, through "being conclusive," are incorporated into Lowry's letter of 25 January 1947 to Albert Erskine, where Lowry calls them "various notes for another book" (*SL* 138–39). The details derive from Notebook VI.

36. *Paracelsus* [p. 130]: See note VIII.1.

37. *the real lost weekend* [p. 130]: The typescript reading is "Tragedy of real Last Week End—but the humour of it," an apparent reference to John Sommerfield's unpublished novel *The Last Week End*, in which Lowry claimed to have been portrayed as an alcoholic (see *SL* 46, 51, 63 and Day 153–55). I have adopted the reading in Notebook VI, which alludes to a scene from Charles Jackson's 1944 novel *The Lost Weekend*, also in the 1945 film version (on which see note XVIII.15), in which Don Birnam be-

lieves that he has lost money he needs to buy alcohol, later discovering it in a pocket where he forgot to look. In *Dark as the Grave*, *The Lost Weekend* is called *Drunkard's Rigadoon*. See also below, pp. 220, 228, 230, and my article "Lowry and *The Lost Weekend*," *Malcolm Lowry Review* no. 33 (Fall 1993): 38–47.

38. *"Fou" "Bouveur"* [p. 130]: French: "Madman," "Drunkard" (the latter an error for *buveur*).

39. *Baron S.* [p. 131]: Baron Samedi (see note II.33).

40. *Marcellin* [p. 131]: Philippe Thoby-Marcelin ("Phito"), 1904–75, a Haitian poet and novelist whom Lowry met during his trip to Haiti and stayed in touch with thereafter. On Thoby-Marcelin, see *Caribbean Writers: A Bio-Bibliographical-Critical Encyclopedia*, ed. Donald E. Herdeck (Washington, D.C.: Three Continents Press, 1979), 514–15.

41. *klang-maleri* [p. 131]: Cf. German *Klangmalerei*, "onomatopoeia."

42. *Avance ses montres* [p. 132]: French, "sets the hands of his watches forward."

43. *Rock of Ages. . . .* [p. 132]: From the first stanza of the Protestant hymn "Rock of Ages":

> Rock of Ages cleft for me
> Let me hide myself in Thee
> Let the water and the blood
> From Thy wounded side which flowed
> Be of sin the double cure
> Save from wrath and make me pure.

44. *the devil, with a tail, huge* [p. 132]: Cf. the devil dancer in Tecalpulco (note I.19).

45. *three small pictures* [p. 132]: (a) On Andrea del Sarto's "Caritas" ("Charity"; French translation, "La Charité"), which hangs in the Louvre, see S. J. Freedberg, *Andrea del Sarto: Catalogue Raisonné* (Cambridge: Harvard University Press, 1963), 85–87, and Freedberg, *Andrea del Sarto: Text and Illustrations* (Cambridge: Harvard University Press, 1963), 47–50, plates 88, 89, 90. (b) Margerie was unable to read "Albert Guillaume" in Notebook VIII; the typescript reads, "Albert Gui Hommes (can't read it)." Guillaume (1873–1942) was a painter and humorous illustrator of books. None of his pictures were in the 1929 Paris Salon, according to *The Salon 1929: An Illustrated Catalogue of the 1929 Exhibition with an Index of the Artists* (London: John Lane, The Bodley Head Limited, [1929]), nor do the exhibition catalogues for 1927 and 1928 include any of his work. I have not found a reproduction of "Une robe longue." (c) The English painter George Romney met Emma Hart (born Amy Lyon) in 1782. She later became Lady Hamilton, and Romney painted many pictures of her.

46. *moos with pain* [p. 133]: The typescript reading, "moans with pain," makes sense, but in Notebook VIII, from which this part of the Haitian sequence is taken, the reading is "*moos*" (the passage is underlined in the notebook).

47. *horrrible* [p. 133]: Spelled thus in the typescript; the notebook has "*horrible*" (Notebook VIII).

48. *monastic death surrogate (Huxley)* [p. 134]: The typescript has "Hurley," but the reading in Notebook VIII appears to be "Huxley." I have not identified the specific allusion, but I suspect that the passage refers to Aldous Huxley.

49. *a Will Rogers ropetrickster* [p. 134]: The American humorist Will Rogers (1879–1935) had a vaudeville act in which he did rope tricks during his monologue.

50. *Vous etes belle* [p. 135]: French: "vous êtes belle," "you are beautiful."

51. *Consul's whisky bottle* [p. 135]: Possibly the bottle of Johnny Walker in chapter 3 of *Under the Volcano*: see *UV* 68–69, 86, 87, 90–92.

52. *in the dark* [p. 135]: In Notebook VIII Lowry wrote, "surprised to find notebook in right place like Consul's whisky bottle: [illegible word] are full of hallucinations & the crickets are singing—I write this in the dark." In Draft B, "eyes?" is Margerie's first guess at the illegible word (which is *not* "eyes"; it looks more like "lamps"). After "dark" she typed three alternative guesses, arranged vertically on the page: "eyes?/ soup?/ things?"

53. *Like Philoctetes* [p. 135]: Wounded on the way to Troy, Philoctetes was left on the isle of Lemnos but later retrieved when the other Greeks heard that Troy could be conquered only by the bow and arrows of Heracles, which Philoctetes possessed. In some versions of the myth, Philoctetes was reluctant to leave Lemnos.

54. *Batterie de tambours* [p. 135]: French, "drum roll"—perhaps an error for "Battement de Tambours" (see note VI.24).

55. *Ultramarine . . . Lunar Caustic* [p. 135]: In Lowry's first novel, *Ultramarine* (1933), Dana Hilliot is reluctant to leave the security of the ship, partly because he fears catching a venereal disease in a brothel. In the posthumous novella *Lunar Caustic* (1963), based on Lowry's 1936 stay in a psychiatric ward, Bill Plantagenet is eventually expelled from the womblike environment of the hospital.

56. *Poe . . . House of Usher* [p. 135]: See Edgar Allan Poe's story "The Fall of the House of Usher" (1839).

57. *a contraption of Calder's, or a figure of Paul Valdes* [p. 136]: Alexander Calder (1898–1976), an American sculptor, is famous for his invention of mobiles. I have not identified Paul Valdes, and it is not certain that that is the correct reading in Lowry's note (Notebook V): Margerie typed "or a figure of Paul—Villers Valdes, what's his name?" indicating that she

could not read the last name. It is conceivable that "Paul" (an unlikely Spanish name) is a mistake for "Raúl," and that Lowry was thinking of the Mexican artist Raúl Anguiano Valdez (born 1915).

58. *to the negro . . . without rhythm* [p. 137]: This passage is not in the part of Notebook V from which this section is derived. Instead, the notebook has a bracketed memorandum, set off as a separate paragraph: "[mem, in notes to-night, truck full of cornstalks level with the setting sun, which was straight ahead of the bus]." The next paragraph begins, "—Going into New Orleans. . . ."

59. *(this is dubious . . . St. Malo, perhaps)* [p. 138]: This passage is not in Notebook V, the source of the surrounding material.

60. *Burma Shave . . . jumped for joy* [p. 138]: See note VI.73. The same sign is quoted accurately on p. 146.

61. *Alexander Nevsky* [p. 138]: Thirteenth-century Russian hero whose defeat of the knights of the Teutonic Order in 1242 helped to preserve Russia's independence from the West. Sigbjørn might be thinking of Sergei Eisenstein's 1938 film *Alexander Nevsky*.

62. *great plump boloneys* [p. 139]: The typescript originally followed the reading in Notebook V, "great plump poloneys," but "poloneys" is corrected in ink to "boloneys."

63. *When working in the square or on the apron, watch the hook, it can't watch you!* [p. 139]: A sign from a shipping dock that Lowry uses also in "Through the Panama" (*HL* 34) and in the screenplay for *Tender Is the Night* (*CML* 171).

64. *Rainier* [p. 140]: The name of this mountain is consistently misspelled "Ranier," both in Margerie's notes in Notebook V, from which this is derived, and in the typescript.

65. *E. M. Forster's Celestial Omnibus* [p. 141]: In Forster's "The Celestial Omnibus" (1908), a boy takes a bus to a literary heaven.

66. *Teeters* [p. 142]: I have adopted the apparent reading (in Malcolm's hand) from Notebook V rather than the typescript reading, "Tooters."

67. *Waac* [p. 142]: A female soldier in the British Army (acronym for "Women's Auxiliary Army Corps").

68. *The Killers* [p. 142]: A 1946 film, directed by Robert Siodmak and starring Edmond O'Brien, Ava Gardner, Albert Dekker, Sam Levine, and Burt Lancaster; based loosely on Ernest Hemingway's 1927 short story of the same title.

69. *nole me tangere* [p. 142]: Spelled thus in Notebook V and the typescript; more accurately, *noli me tangere*, "do not touch me," originally Christ's words to Mary Magdalene in the Latin Vulgate (John 20:17).

70. *moving story about the sea gulls . . . Moroni on the dome* [pp. 142–43]: A monument in Temple Square, Salt Lake City, commemo-

rates the unexpected arrival of sea gulls, hundreds of miles inland, that saved the early Mormon settlers in Utah from an infestation of crickets that threatened their crops. Joseph Smith, founder of the Church of Jesus Christ of the Latter-Day Saints (Mormons), claimed that he was led by the resurrected spirit of Moroni, an ancient prophet, to the tablets that he "translated" as *The Book of Mormon*.

71. *Byrd's Expedition* [p. 143]: Richard Evelyn Byrd's 1928–29 expedition to the South Pole; "Little America," mentioned above and below, was Byrd's base camp, and is also the name of a town in Wyoming.

72. *Farolito* [p. 144]: The sinister cantina where the Consul is murdered in chapter 12 of *Under the Volcano* is referred to also on pp. 280, 284, and 285. See also note III.16.

73. *Burma Shave: Big mistake, use your horn and not your brake* [p. 145]: See also pp. 138, 149 (notes VI.60, VI.79). From the 1920s until 1963, Burma-Shave, an American brand of brushless shaving cream, was promoted through sequences of five or six roadway signs, each sign containing one line of a humorous verse that ended with the words "Burma-Shave." The five sets of signs on p. 146 were used during the 1940s, but three are changed from the actual texts, which were: (1) "BIG MISTAKE / MANY MAKE / RELY ON HORN / INSTEAD OF / BRAKE / BURMA-SHAVE"; (2) "I USE IT TOO / THE BALD MAN SAID / IT KEEPS MY FACE / JUST LIKE / MY HEAD / BURMA-SHAVE"; AND (3) "THAT SHE / COULD COOK / HE HAD HIS DOUBTS / UNTIL SHE CREAMED / HIS BRISTLE SPROUTS / WITH / BURMA-SHAVE." (For the last sign, which is quoted more accurately in *CP* 365, the reading in Lowry's notebook is "That she could cook he had no doubt— until she creamed his bristle sprout with Burma Shave" [Notebook V]. The typescript reading probably derives from Margerie's attempt to emend the notebook reading.) See Frank Rowsome Jr., *The Verse by the Side of the Road: The Story of the Burma-Shave Signs and Jingles* (New York: E. P. Dutton, 1966), 99, 101–2.

74. *UBC 13:23, 195A* [p. 147]: Margerie typed page number 195 at the head of two successive pages and added the A in pencil to the second one, probably because she had already numbered successive pages before discovering her mistake.

75. *the strange warm spell which the Kansas City Morning Star claims is God's answer to Lewis' coal strike* [p. 147]: There is no *Kansas City Morning Star*, but the masthead of the *Kansas City Times* announces that it is the morning edition of the *Star*. The biggest news story in the United States during early December 1946 was a coal miners' strike called by John L. Lewis, head of the United Mine Workers, who on 4 December was fined ten thousand dollars for refusing to end the strike. The statement attributed to the newspaper (recorded in Margerie's notes and transferred to the type-

script) did not appear in the *Times*, as far as I can tell, but on 5 December a small front-page article entitled "Mild Days Are Forecast" began, "The mild weather, which the weather bureau contends is its answer to the growing coal shortage, probably will continue today and tomorrow beneath generally fair skies."

76. *road of glory* [p. 147]: The reading in Notebook V is "road of joy."

77. *just too fuerte* [p. 148]: Spanish *fuerte*, "strong."

78. *Melville* [p. 149]: I have not located the Melvillean allusion here.

79. *Join our Brushless happy throng . . .* [p. 149]: Another series of Burma-Shave signs (see note VI.73). The actual signs read "JOIN / OUR HAPPY / BRUSHLESS THRONG / SIX MILLION USERS / CAN'T BE WRONG / BURMA-SHAVE."

80. *Gorki's Lower Depths* [p. 150]: The room resembles the run-down basement apartment in which acts 1, 2, and 4 of Maxim Gorki's play *The Lower Depths* (1902) are set. Lowry also referred to the play in letters to Conrad Aiken and Downie Kirk (*SL* 19, 182).

81. *Delmar Blvd* [p. 150]: The typescript has "Delmar St.," but both Notebook V and the card from which this advertisement was copied into the typescript (UBC 32:15) have "Delmar Blvd."

82. *white Murnauesque façade* [p. 151]: Presumably this reminds Sigbjørn of a scene in one of F. W. Murnau's films, possibly *Sonnenaufgang* (*Sunrise*), which Lowry admired (see *SL* 239).

83. *The grotto, the peace: and Christ, with his spreading arms at the end of Dauphine (?) St.—or is it St. Peter?* [p. 153]: This is not a grotto but a large statue of Jesus on Royal Street, at the end of Orleans Avenue, behind St. Louis Cathedral in the French Quarter of New Orleans. The statue is lit up at night and may be seen from Dauphine. It is also referred to on p. 122.

84. *Boxing Day* [p. 153]: A Canadian holiday, 26 December.

85. *Adeline Cossé . . . 43 ans* [p. 154]: "Adeline Cossé, wife of Abraham Brown, died 11 September 1866, aged 43 years."

86. *{UBC 13:23, 205}* [p. 154]: In Draft C, this page is followed by a set of typed notes, numbered 206–19, that do not correspond to anything in Draft B; the notes in turn are followed by a carbon copy of the pages numbered 206–19 in Draft B. The first set of pages 206–19 (not reproduced here) are a transcription of Margerie's notes on New Orleans and Haiti, from Notebook VII; they are continuous with the typed notes in 7:8 that begin with a partial page headed "Margie Notes" and continue with pages numbered 220–30.

87. *The moon: lovely leewardings of Melville; her undinal vast belly moonward bends of Crane* [p. 154]: The Melville passage is from Ahab's monologue in chapter 135 of *Moby-Dick*: "'Forehead to forehead I meet thee, this third time, Moby Dick! . . . There's a soft shower to leeward. Such

lovely leewardings! They must lead somewhere—to something else than common land, more palmy than the palms. Leeward! the white whale goes that way; look to windward, then; the better if the bitterer quarter.'" The other passage comes from part 2 of Hart Crane's "Voyages":

> And yet this great wink of eternity,
> Of rimless floods, unfettered leewardings,
> Samite sheeted and processioned where
> Her undinal vast belly moonward bends,
> Laughing the wrapt inflections of our love[.]

88. *Mirebalais* ... [p. 155]: Apart from relocating a misplaced accent in Guantánamo, I have reproduced these names exactly as they are spelled in Notebook VI and transcribed into the typescript.

89. *General Smedley Butler's dead* [p. 156]: See note VI.21.

90. *Isn't that in San Domingo* [p. 158]: Santo Domingo is the capital of the Dominican Republic, ruled for three decades by the dictator Rafael Trujillo Molina until his assassination in 1961. From 1936 until 1961 the city was named Ciudad Trujillo (see pp. 156, 157).

91. *We boycotted them* [p. 158]: There was no official American boycott of Haiti during 1946, but it is possible that Alcoa (on whose ship the Lowrys sailed to Haiti) and some other American companies might have suspended trade with the island during a time of political turmoil.

92. *a man who likes the odious cover* [p. 161]: If this is an error for "a man who looks like the odious cover" (as one might suspect from the reading of a passage based on this one, pp. 127–28) it is Lowry's error rather than Margerie's, since this is the reading in his notebook (Notebook VI).

93. *Haiti Journal ... gloire au nom Haïtien* [pp. 161–62]: "*Haiti Journal*. Special Edition of Christmas 1943. Lago-Lago: Poems by Philippe Thoby-Marcelin. Prefaced by a letter from Valery Larbaud. . . . The Prince Distillery, Proprietor Alfred Vieux, sends to all its customers and friends who have known how to appreciate the quality of its products—particularly the Barbancourt Rum Distillery and the American firm of Krauss—its thanks and its wishes for a happy Christmas and a good New Year. . . . (For our subscribers and readers, etc.) / We are sure to please all our subscribers and readers in presenting a notebook of unpublished poems by Philippe Thoby-Marcelin, who has just added so much glory to the Haitian name." I have corrected these passages against a microfilm of Lowry's source, a special issue of *Haiti Journal* devoted to poems by Philippe Thoby-Marcelin. Lowry copied the passages into Notebook VIII.

94. *Is There a Hell?* [p. 162]: The following religious tract was apparently transcribed from a pamphlet that Lowry picked up during his trip across the United States. There is no copy of the pamphlet in the Malcolm

Lowry Archive, nor does one exist at the Gospel Missionary Union, according to Abe Reddekopp, director of publications for the G.M.U. The opening question about what to do when a house is on fire suggests one reason for Lowry's interest in this pamphlet, since the June 1944 fire that burned down his shack left Lowry obsessed with the subject of house fires.

95. *Lost Logger's Body . . . Trio Fight Off Sharks . . . Noted Empress Hotel . . . Lightning Reduces Home. . . .* [pp. 165–68]: All four of the following articles are derived from the *Vancouver Sun* for 27 November 1951: "Lost Logger's Body Found Upcoast" (30), "Trio Fight Off Sharks to Save Man" (3), "Noted Empress Hotel Lobby 'Fixture' Dies" (2), and "Lightning Reduces Home to Shambles" (1). I have corrected transcription errors in the typescript.

96. *UBC 14:11, 225* [p. 168]: I have used the carbon of this page, correcting it against a microfilm of the newspaper story, because this page has been lost from the original typescript.

CHAPTER VII

1. *Like Ahab, they were imprisoned in Paradise* [p. 168]: See note XI.1.

2. *one wakes on the floor in a cold prison cell, having dreamt one was comfortably in bed in one's childhood home* [p. 168]: This might be a sinister version of a phenomenon described in the opening pages of Marcel Proust's *Swann's Way*, where the narrator awakens at night, imagining himself in bed at his grandparents' home in the country, only to realize that it is years later and that he is visiting another home.

3. *the poor devil who is to be hanged next morning, in a disused elevator shaft . . . for lack of a decent scaffold* [p. 168]: See also p. 252 and note XXVII.1. In a 1951 letter to David Markson, Lowry wrote of his outrage over "a local injustice where a 16 year old boy was sentenced to hang (in a disused elevator shaft, painted yellow) for a rape he had not committed" (*SL* 269). For background on this incident, which is also mentioned in *October Ferry to Gabriola* (*OF* 7, 162, 264), see Victor Doyen, "From Innocent Story to Charon's Boat: Reading the 'October Ferry' Manuscripts," in *Swinging the Maelstrom: New Perspectives on Malcolm Lowry*, ed. Sherrill Grace (Montreal and Kingston: McGill-Queens University Press, 1992), 183, 198 n. 24.

4. *Lew Lehr* [p. 169]: "Fox Movietone's cockeyed comic narrator ('Monkies is the kwaziest people')." David Ragan, *Who's Who in Hollywood 1900–1976* (New Rochelle, N.Y.: Arlington House, 1976), 683.

5. *looking as though you'd swallowed Pat Murphy's goat and the horns were sticking out of your arse* [pp. 170–71]: See also below, p. 230. The

same joke appears in "Through the Panama" (*HL* 94) and in the revised edition of *Ultramarine* (*U* 71, 203).

6. *Primrose was asleep.... [p. 171]*: In Draft A (UBC 13:4, ch. VII, 3), next to this paragraph, a right-margin note reads: "Martin had another peculiar idea about death which was, as soon as he died, some sporting fiends, as if in compensation, would rush up to him with a delectable nymphomaniac woman. Martin, who did not like to think he could be disloyal to Primrose even with a succubus, [illegible] repressed this feeling with its perhaps all too excusable and [illegible] reason for dying." See below, p. 227.

7. *I never think of an immedicable grief—this poem* [p. 171]: See Lowry's poem "Jokes Aloft," which begins "I never picture an immedicable grief / Without some fifty bottles for relief" (*CP* 118). The typescript has "an immedicable gulf," but the reading in Draft A (UBC 13:4, ch. VII, 4) could be either "gulf" or "grief." I have chosen the latter reading because it fits the allusion to the poem.

8. *a manner which from time immemorial* [p. 172]: The typescript reading, "a manner from which time immemorial," apparently resulted from Margerie's emendation of the obviously wrong Draft A reading, "a manner from which from time immemorial" (UBC 13:4, ch. VII, 4).

CHAPTER VIII

1. *pitting, like Paracelsus, the effects of alcohol against the effects of increased physical exercise* [p. 174]: The sixteenth-century German physician Theophrastus Bombastus von Hohenheim, who adopted the epithet "Paracelsus," taught that diseases were caused by agents outside the body and advocated the use of minerals to protect the body. I do not know Lowry's source for this particular idea, but for other associations of Paracelsus and alcohol see p. 130 and *SL* 73, 139.

2. *the Tlaxcaltecans were even traitors to the Mexican tradition* [p. 175]: The idea that the Tlaxcalans were traitors because they helped Cortez defeat the Aztecs appears several times in *Under the Volcano*. See *SL* 82 and Ackerley and Clipper 347.

3. *Shades of the Prison House* [p. 175]: See Wordsworth's "Ode: Intimations of Immortality from Recollections of Early Childhood," lines 67–68: "Shades of the prison-house begin to close / Upon the growing Boy." On Wordsworth and the loss of inspired vision, see also note I.14.

4. *By name Haywood* [p. 176]: "'By name Haywood'" was added to Draft A to replace the next line, which read "'Mr & Mrs Haywood'"; then the next four lines were also added (UBC 13:5, ch. VIII, 4). "'Mr & Mrs Haywood'" was crossed out, but "'By name Haywood'" was not deleted, so Margerie copied it into the typescript even though it is made superfluous by the next few lines. See also note IV.26.

Chapter IX

1. *Cinco de Mayo* [p. 176]: The fifth of May, Mexican independence day (see below, p. 314).

2. *Keyserling (from whom take notes)* [p. 177]: The Malcolm Lowry Archive contains six pages of handwritten quotations from Hermann Keyserling's *The Recovery of Truth* (translated 1929)—whose title is erroneously given as *Rediscovery of Truth*—as well as a three-page typed transcription of the notes (UBC 14:17).

3. *"The Maker of Tragedies"* [p. 177]: See note III.20.

4. *hark back to the Carlins* [p. 177]: I have not identified these people, presumably tourists who were in Mexico at the same time as Lowry.

5. *he reads Rendon's Vanishing Enchantment* [p. 177]: On Eduardo Bolio Rendon's "Vanishing Enchantment?" see note IV.25.

6. *the general erloff* [p. 177]: This makes no sense to me, but I cannot improve on Margerie's transcription of this passage.

7. *under the sea—Illustrated London News* [p. 177]: This could be from "The World of Science," a weekly column in the *Illustrated London News*, but I have not found an article by this title in any issue that I believe would have been available to Lowry. See also the annotation on the *British Weekly* (note II.17).

8. *Soto* [p. 178]: This might be Lowry's error for "Tojo" (see note IX.8), but Drafts A and B both have "Soto" here.

9. *they run slap into Tojo* [p. 178]: Both Draft A and Draft B sometimes spell this name "Tojo" (presumably an allusion to Hideki Tojo, the infamous World War II Japanese military leader who was executed for war crimes in 1948) and at other times use the spelling "Togo" (see, e.g., p. 224). The problem is compounded by the fact that Lowry's handwritten "g" and "j" are sometimes virtually indistinguishable, but when the autograph reading is clear I have followed it; otherwise I have followed the typescript. See also the annotation on "To go or not Togo" (note XXI.2).

10. *(Mem: again Chambers and the gratitude he got)* [p. 178]: I have not identified Chambers.

11. *should be analysis of* [p. 178]: This is the reading in Draft A; the typescript has "should be analyzed."

12. *Janine* [p. 178]: Lowry's first wife, Janine Vanderheim, who took the name Jan Gabrial; referred to elsewhere in *La Mordida* as Ruth. See note I.61. In Draft A, a right-margin note at this point reads "whatever the name is," indicating that Lowry planned to change this name as he had others.

13. *a sort of good soldier Schweik scene* [p. 179]: See Jaroslav Hašek's satiric novel *The Good Soldier: Schweik*.

14. *Let there still be a niche . . . poetry disappears from the world* [p. 180]: Apart from the paragraph beginning "Point of this article," Sigbjørn's direct address to Primrose in the last paragraph, and the final sen-

tence, the remainder of the chapter is taken from Lowry's notes on Eduardo Bolio Rendon's "Vanishing Enchantment?" (UBC 7:4); the ultimate source of the quotes is pp. 14 and 16 of Bolio Rendon's article. See note IV.25.

CHAPTER X

1. *Hornos is "afternoon beach"* [p. 181]: This is the typescript reading. In Draft A, Lowry wrote "was then" above the line without crossing out "is."

2. *"When ye pray say 'our father'"* [p. 183]: See Luke 11:2.

CHAPTER XI

1. *Like Ahab, damnation in the midst of Paradise* [p. 184]: See also p. 168 above and *SL* 340. Lowry is probably referring to Ahab's monologue in chapter 37 of Melville's *Moby-Dick*: "Dry heat upon my brow? Oh! time was, when as the sunrise nobly spurred me, so the sunset soothed. No more. This lovely light, it lights not me; all loveliness is anguish to me, since I can ne'er enjoy. Gifted with the high perception, I lack the low, enjoying power; damned, most subtly and most malignantly! damned in the midst of Paradise! Good night—good night!"

2. *Margie's black notebook* [p. 186]: Here and below, Lowry is drawing on Notebook III. See notes XI.3 and XII.2.

3. *"Death," suddenly said Sigbjørn Wilderness . . . "Nothing."* [p. 186]: This ending derives ultimately from Notebook III, p. 33. See note VI.8.

CHAPTER XII

1. *Where has courtesy gone?* [p. 186]: Probably an allusion to Lowry's sonnet "Delirium in Vera Cruz," which begins "Where has tenderness gone" (*CP* 62).

2. *see p. 34, Margie's notebook* [p. 187]: The following passage is derived from Margerie's notes in pp. 34–35 of Notebook III.

3. *this ship is called the Narcissus* [p. 188]: There seems to be a glancing reference to Joseph Conrad's novel *The Nigger of the "Narcissus."*

4. *Henley, in which the captain crew etc, are various factions of his soul* [p. 188]: William Ernest Henley's famous poem "Invictus" (composed in 1873) does not make precisely the comparisons described here, but it proclaims that "In the fell clutch of circumstance / I have not winced nor cried aloud" and concludes "It matters not how strait the gate, / How charged with punishments the scroll, / I am the master of my fate; / I am the captain

of my soul." See p. 206 and note XII.6. In "Through the Panama," Sigbjørn thinks, "I am the chief steward of my fate, I am the fireman of my soul" (*HL* 41).

5. *like his grandfather, of going down with them* [p. 188]: In "Through the Panama" (*HL* 32), Sigbjørn claims that his "grandfather, captain of the windjammer *The Scottish Isles*, went down with his ship in the Indian Ocean." For different versions of the death of Lowry's own grandfather, John ("Captain Lyon") Boden, see Day 59 and Bowker 3–4.

6. *Mon âme est un trois mâts, cherchant son Icarie. That was where old Henley must have got it* [p. 188]: Lowry has slightly rephrased a line from part 2 of Charles Baudelaire's "Le Voyage" (from *Les Fleurs du mal*, 1857). The passage should read "Notre âme est un trois-mâts cherchant son Icarie" ("Our soul is a three-master searching for its Icaria"). I have found no evidence that Baudelaire's poem influenced Henley's "Invictus" (see note XII.4).

7. *the Saint Day of José* [p. 189]: March 19 is the feast day in honor of Saint Joseph (San José).

8. *the seat of judgment* [p. 190]: In Draft A, a left-margin note at this point reads "So much dust how could they have been so smart?"

9. *A qué hora . . . Quién sabe?* [p. 190]: "At what time will the gentleman return?" "Who knows?"

CHAPTER XIII

1. *The Mexican eagle tearing to pieces the Nazi flag, with a wild cloudy sky behind in colours of Mexican flag underneath the legend: México por la libertad* [p. 191]: This anti-Nazi poster with the slogan "Mexico for liberty" reappears on pp. 215, 241, 299, 301, 303, and 319, and is referred to on p. 288. The poster is probably the same as the one in *Dark as the Grave* (*DG* 78). The four paragraphs about posters on pp. 191–92 are taken verbatim from Margerie's notes headed "The posters in Migracion" in Notebook III.

2. *Ixta and Popo* [p. 192]: The two volcanoes, Ixtaccihuatl and Popocatepetl, that loom in the background of *Under the Volcano*.

3. *whom they had met again* [p. 192]: In Draft A Lowry wrote "whom they meet again" and inserted "had," apparently intending to change "meet" to "had met"; in the typescript, Margerie emended this to "whom they had to meet again."

4. *In the theatre* [p. 192]: At this point, the typescript inserts two marginal notes from Draft A (UBC 13:6, ch. XIII, 3): "(*should be an ending.* Although to apply the term Judas to such people—even if Jesus was waiting somewhere to redeem them—was to Sigbjorn's mind an insult to the mem-

ory of a relatively honest man.)" and "(Another ending: While the world rolled, or whatever it did, on into the Era of the Stool Pigeon.)" (UBC 13:26, 262, 264).

5. *next to this* [p. 192]: This ends page 3 of this chapter in Draft A. Page 4 begins with "Primrose and Martin are thus chewing the rag of frustration" (cf. p. 194). Between pages 3 and 4 is page 3A, a set of notes containing the material included here, and headed "Insert somewhere."

6. *Corazón . . . Verdad . . . Palpa—sí—palpa en su tinta. Muy sabroso* [p. 193]: *Corazón,* "heart." *Verdad,* "[That's] the truth," possibly an error for *en verdad,* "in fact." The last is an error for *pulpo en su tinta. Muy sabroso*—"octopus in its own ink. Very tasty"—which is in turn a play on the Spanish dish *calamares en su tinta,* "squid in their own ink."

7. *UBC 13:26, 264* [p. 193]: There is no page numbered 263 in the typescript.

8. *(This is flashback to home) . . . (A sudden vision or memory of home from which is deduced the following)* [p. 193]: In Draft A these are marginal notes next to the paragraph in which I have placed them. I have not followed Margerie's somewhat confusing placement of the notes.

9. *you could only have perceived* [p. 194]: Draft A has "you could have only have perceived," which the typescript emends to "you could have only perceived."

10. *Sí, el A.J.S. . . .* [p. 195]: A discussion of English automobiles and motorcycles that somehow includes Harley-Davidson, which as Sigbjørn notes is American, not British. *Muy bonito:* "very nice."

11. *Deportivos* [p. 195]: "Sportsmen" is *deportistas; deportivo* is an adjective meaning "sport." Sigbjørn is, however, correct in realizing that the word has nothing to do with deportation. See also p. 222 and note XVII.16.

12. *Estrella d'Oro . . . Flecha* [p. 197]: Two bus lines, the Gold Star (Estrella d'Oro) and the Red Arrow (Flecha Roja), both of which sell first- and second-class tickets.

13. *parcel of food* [p. 198]: Margerie inserted a slash after "food" and typed "describe this" above the line. In Draft A (UBC 13:6, ch. XIII, 10), the note "describe the food" is in the left margin.

14. *"Yo no estoy un Americano"* [p. 199]: An attempt at "Yo no soy un Americano," "I am not an American."

15. *the French film of Crime et Chatiment* [p. 199]: See also p. 252. *Crime et Châtiment* (1935), directed by Pierre Chenal, is based closely on Dostoevsky's *Crime and Punishment* (MPG 2:513). The scene is derived from part 3, chapter 6 of the novel, which—as Chris Ackerley has suggested to me—might also have provided the model for the scene in *Under*

the Volcano in which a man "threw, almost chanted, a laughing word at [the Consul] that sounded like: 'Mescalito!'" (*UV* 53; cf. *UV* 211).

16. *UBC 13:26, 273* [p. 199]: The remainder of this chapter is a set of notes copied from UBC 13:6, ch. XIII, 11; a note at the top right of that page reads "see page 4," referring to the statement, "for complete draft of the letter, which Sigbjorn might snatch, see end of this chapter" (UBC 13:26, 266).

17. *This document ran something as follows....* [pp. 199–201]: The English translations in the text are absurd. *Están muy Lejos . . . espiritualmente*: "Geographically our territories are far apart. Let's bring them together economically and spiritually." *Poder . . . México D.F.*: "The executive power of the federal government, United States of Mexico, Mexico City, Federal District." *Secretaría de Hacienda y Crédito Público*: "Department of Treasury and Public Credit." *Dependencia Número Expediente*: If this is an official form with blanks to fill in, there might be blanks after *Dependencia* ("Branch office") and *Número Expediente* ("Record [or proceedings] number"). *Direc. Gra de Población* : *Direccción General de Población*, the general address or main office for the Population department. *Dept. de Migración . . . inversionistas y rentistas*: "Immigration Department, [Department] of Studies and Promotional Activities, Investors, and Financiers." *Asunto . . . súbdito inglés*: "Subject: A fine in the amount of 350 [pesos] is levied against Mr. Sigbjørn Wilderness, English subject." *Hago de su conocimiento . . . de su documentación*: "I bring to your notice that this ministry in official communication #9781 last March 29th, sent to 621 Humboldt [Street], Cuernavaca, Morelos, imposed on you a fine of 50 pesos because your immigration documents expired the 17th of said month and you as well as your wife have not taken any action with regard to your documentation." *Se le concede . . . legalmente corresponda*: "You are granted a 15–day period beginning on the date that this letter leaves our office, in order to pay the fine in question in the internal revenue office at that location and at the same time remit bank documents confirming your status as a person of independent means, warning that in case you should not comply, appropriate legal action will be taken." *Atentamente . . . Andrés Landa y Pina (Rúbrica)*: The phrases *Sufragio Efectivo* ("duly elected") and *No Reelección* ("No re-election") seem to have been interpolated in this passage, which otherwise is just the end of a business letter signed by the departmental chief. *Un sello que dice . . . Acapulco. Gro.*: "A seal that says: Secretary of Interior, Department of Population, 12 May 1939, dispatched from Bureau of Correspondence and Control. Another seal that says the Federal Office of Treasury, 16 May 1939, Acapulco, Guerrero." *c.c.p. la Oficina de Población . . . Control de Vencimientos*: "Carbon copies on paper" to "the Office of Population in Acapulco, Guerrero, answering your telegram of

the seventh of the present month"; to "the Federal Office of Treasury, Acapulco, Guerrero, for your purposes and use"; and to "Control of Expira-
tions." *es copia del . . . 1941*: "is a copy of the original that was certified by
Acapulco, Guerrero, 21 August 1941."

18. *This around an eagle swallowing a snake* [p. 199]: In Draft A, this
design is drawn in the left margin.

CHAPTER XIV

1. *whether one is a writer or not* [p. 202]: At this point, in mid-
sentence, the typescript inserts a marginal note from Draft A: "(Sigbjørn
["Martin" in the pencil draft] should be pictured at least as a man of bravery and great compassion)."

2. *looking for peace she found a sword* [p. 203]: See Matthew 10:34:
"Do not think that I have come to bring peace on earth; I have not come to
bring peace, but a sword."

3. *disastar* [p. 203]: Draft A has "disastar" all three times here, but the
typescript follows Lowry's (mis)spelling only in the third instance. On "disastar" see note I.31.

4. *un otro ahí—dónde* [p. 204]: "Another there—where?"

5. *es muy sucio* [p. 204]: "It is very dirty."

6. *flash back to Blaine perhaps* [p. 204]: In September 1939, while trying to rejoin Margerie, who was in Los Angeles, Lowry was refused admission to the United States at Blaine, Washington. The event is recorded in
Lowry's poem "The Canadian Turned Back at the Border" (*CP* 147–49; see
Ackerley's annotation, *CP* 285).

7. *Iguala amor Americano* [p. 205]: The phrasing is unidiomatic and
confusing; Lowry probably intends something like "Iguala loves Americans."

8. *when I see the lights of Cuernavaca* [p. 205]: The text momentarily
shifts to Margerie's first-person narration, betraying its origins in her notebook description of the bus ride, beginning in Notebook II and continuing
in Notebook III. The next phrase, however ("the triple-barreled *meaning* of
Cuernavaca"), is not from the notebooks.

9. *Un poco crudo* [p. 205]: "A bit hung over."

10. *Todos es reglado con la goberno* [p. 206]: Bad Spanish for *Todo es
arreglado con el gobierno* ("Everything is being arranged with the government"). Perhaps this is what is rendered as "All is settled with the Gobierno" on p. 176.

11. *Communist Plot Sweeps Canada!* [p. 206]: See note IV.11.

12. *I am the Chief Steward of my soul* [p. 206]: See note XII.4.

13. *a scene in Simenon* [p. 206]: Georges Simenon is a well-known and prolific mystery writer. This sounds like a scene from a specific novel, but I have not identified it.

14. *the sound of the infernal machine* [p. 207]: The infernal machine (*máquina infernal*) is a loop-the-loop carnival machine on which the Consul takes a ride in chapter 7 of *Under the Volcano*.

15. *though my soul be not ready. For that final cross where all man's hands are steady* [p. 207]: If this is one of Lowry's poems, I have not located it. At this point in Draft A, the following note is written and crossed out:

> I've lost notes for this. He tries to write a poem. . . . But all he
> manages is:
> —whose hands are not yet ready
> for that final cross where all man's hands are steady . . .

Next to this passage is the following note (not crossed out): "Oh two condemned for theft of shakes, steal mine!" (UBC 13:7, ch. XIV, 10).

16. *horripilation* [p. 207]: The word recalls the Consul's "horripilating hangover" in *Under the Volcano* and Sigbjørn's "Horripilations" in *Dark as the Grave* (UV 126, DG 47). Ackerley and Clipper (187) trace "horripilation" to Conrad Aiken's *Blue Voyage*. It recurs on p. 254.

17. *But do I care!* [p. 208]: This is the end of this chapter in Draft A (UBC 13:7, ch. XIV, 11). The next paragraph is a note at the top of p. 10 in the pencil draft; to the right of this, Lowry wrote "This passage is v important," and to the left, he wrote "End." The final two paragraphs of the chapter in the typescript are notes from the top of p. 11 in Draft A.

CHAPTER XV

1. *He has even been down town* [p. 208]: I have adopted the reading of this passage from Draft A even though p. 209 makes it clear that Sigbjørn has *not* been down to meet the bus. The typescript reading, which reflects Margerie's attempt to reconcile the two passages, is very confusing.

2. *"It must have been dreadful."* [p. 208]: Immediately after this sentence, Margerie wrote, "P. has now had 2 nights *no* sleep."

3. *"Did you get the money from the bank?"* / *"The cheque was in the post then."* [p. 209]: I do not follow the alternation of voices here, and it is possible that Sigbjørn speaks both lines.

4. *Dostoievsky's Marmeladov . . . if only a carriage would come out of nowhere and drive over him* [pp. 209–10]: In Dostoevsky's *Crime and Punishment*, part 2, chapter 7, Raskolnikov recognizes a man who has been run over by a carriage as the drunkard Marmeladov.

5. *Chandler* [p. 210]: I have not identified this person, who is mentioned again on p. 213.

6. *Hotel Canada* [p. 211]: A Mexico City hotel, site of Lowry's 1938 break-up with his first wife, Jan Gabrial, where he took Margerie when he returned in 1945; mentioned again below and on pp. 219, 280. In *Dark as the Grave*, chapter 4, it is called the Hotel Cornada.

7. *anything that even looks like a M* [p. 212]: "M" is the first letter needed for Martin Trumbaugh (or for that matter Malcolm Lowry) to sign his name. This letter remains unchanged from Draft A.

8. *absolutely (?) quiet* [p. 212]: In Draft A, "absolutely" is followed by a word that I cannot read, then the comma, and then the remainder of the sentence as here ("making . . . side"). Apparently Margerie could not read the word either, but it is *not* "quiet"; it looks more like "nente." Perhaps even Malcolm could not read the word, because in the right margin of this page in Draft A are his notes "—a queer shining" and, immediately under that, "—can't see this word."

9. *Sorry. Yo—ich—bin—estoy . . . Yo avait un poco paludismo* [p. 212]: Mostly Spanish, but Sigbjørn lapses into German (*ich bin*) and then French (*avait*). The basic sense is "I am very sick. Let's go for a doctor and come back. . . . I had a little malaria." (The phrase *y redonde*, literally "and here over again," is apparently an error for *y regresar*, "and come back.")

10. *the shaking man* [p. 214]: See note I.68.

11. *When Dante speaks of the artist who "has the habit of art and a hand that trembles . . .* [p. 214]: See Gerald G. Walsh, S.J., *Dante Alighieri: Citizen of Christendom* (Milwaukee: Bruce Publishing Co., 1946), 141: "When Dante speaks of the artist who has 'the habit of art and a hand that trembles,' *C' ha l'abito dell' arte e man che trema*, he makes it clear that art is less in the hand than in the head, less in execution than in intuition." The passage Walsh refers to is from *Paradiso* 13.78.

12. *the Consul's That's the bit I like . . .* [p. 214]: The bit the Consul likes is a line about a shaking hand that he slightly misquotes from Shelley's *Alastor*. See UV 147, 202, and Ackerley and Clipper 211.

CHAPTER XVI

1. *—A timeless heaven—they call it Paradise, but its name is Acapulco* [p. 216]: From *Acapulco* 4 (see note I.13); quoted more fully and accurately on p. 221 below.

2. *We're writers (?)* [p. 216]: Draft A has "We're writer etc" (UBC 13:9, ch. XVI, 3); in the typescript, the question mark is probably Margerie's query about whether she is correct in making "writer" plural.

CHAPTER XVII

1. *Ouspensky's remarks 196–197 Tertium Organum* [p. 218]: The next three paragraphs are a quotation, with only incidental changes, from P. D. Ouspensky, *Tertium Organum: The Third Canon of Thought. A Key to the Enigmas of the World*, trans. Nicholas Bessaraboff and Claude Bragdon (New York: Alfred A. Knopf, 1923), 196–97. See also Ethan Llewelyn's concern with "the world of causes" in *October Ferry to Gabriola* (*OF* 121).

2. *the story of "Westward Ho!"* [p. 218]: The subsequent reference to a "fabulous [Spanish] name from Westward Ho" (below, p. 259) indicates that the reference is probably to Charles Kingsley's 1855 novel *Westward Ho!*, a blood-and-gore naval narrative involving romantic intrigue during the English battle against the Spanish Armada, rather than to *Westward Hoe*, a 1607 comedy by John Webster and Thomas Dekker.

3. *Tonio Kröger* [p. 218]: A 1903 novella by Thomas Mann, focusing on a writer's ambiguous relationship to ordinary bourgeois existence.

4. *(or Sigbjørn has)* [p. 218]: This parenthetical remark, which is not in Draft A, is probably Margerie's protest against Malcolm's version of events. A more obvious protest of this kind may be found in the next paragraph.

5. *disastar* [p. 219]: Spelled thus in Draft A, but spelled "disaster" in the previous sentence (UBC 13:9, ch. XVII, 2). The typescript has "disaster" in both places. On "disastar" see note I.31.

6. *I (she)* [p. 219]: This material originated in Margerie's notes in Notebook III. When Malcolm copied it into Draft A (UBC 13:9, ch. XVII, 4), he added "(she)" but otherwise left Margerie's (or Primrose's) first-person account unchanged.

7. *outside Mexico the bus falters on a hill—parallel with the Appointment in Samarra breakdown* [p. 219]: See also p. 276. The reference is to John O'Hara's 1934 novel *Appointment in Samarra*, which might have come to Lowry's attention because, even though it had been published thirteen years earlier, it was reviewed by D. S. Savage in 1947 along with *Under the Volcano* and two other novels (*Spectator* [10 October 1947]: 474–76). The reference here is mysterious: there are no mechanical breakdowns in *Appointment in Samarra*, although at one point Julian English has to repair his snow chains and at another his car starts sluggishly because of cold weather.

8. *decompuesto* [p. 219]: An error for *descompuesto*, "broken."

9. *media hora for commida* [p. 219]: "Half an hour for dinner," with *comida* misspelled as usual. Perhaps this is a variation on, or error for, the phrase *media hora para comer*, "half an hour to eat."

10. *The damas—muy oscuro* [p. 220]: "The ladies' room—very dark."
The conversation is translated below.

11. *The Lost Week End* [p. 220]: See note VI.37.

12. *Use of green guide book* [p. 221]: The paragraph contains several
references to the Acapulco guidebook (see note I.13): a section title, "Down
to the Sea in Ships: Galleons, Pirates and Buccaneers" (*Acapulco* 5); the beginning of the first sentence in the pamphlet, "Magic casements opening on
the foam of fairy seas" (*Acapulco* 3; this is in turn a variation on lines
69–70 of Keats's "Ode to a Nightingale"); and the final sentences of the
first section: "Here time stands still and beauty marches on, while the
traveller lingers reluctant to break the spell of so much happiness. It sounds
like heaven, but they call it Acapulco" (*Acapulco* 4). For a variation on that
last sentence, see p. 216 above.

13. *running commentary à la Ancient Mariner on the margin* [p. 221]:
See also "Through the Panama," which makes use of marginal notes, many
of them taken from Coleridge's marginal glosses in *The Rime of the Ancient
Mariner*, to provide a "running commentary" on the text.

14. *W. Baxter* [p. 221]: On Warner Baxter, see note V.6. The name will
be repeated several times.

15. *Hartebeeste* [p. 222]: See note V.2.

16. *terror at only too common word deportivos* [p. 222]: See p. 195 and
note XIII.11.

Chapter XVIII

1. *(Mem: Monday: terrific difficulty . . . Primrose* [p. 223]: In Draft A,
this is a right-margin note. In the typescript, its placement between the next
two paragraphs seems disruptive, so I have moved it.

2. *J'ai perdu . . . une significance sentimentale—* [pp. 223–24]: Mostly
French, but with a lapse into Spanish (*un cepillo para la cabeza*) as well as
numerous errors in the French. The basic sense is: "I lost . . . a hairbrush in
my room four days ago when I was in Mexico City—it is an irreplaceable
brush—and I spoke about it with the maids, and they said that they know
nothing: then, a day after my return I lost my dark glasses—it is possible
that I left them on the beach, but I think not. The dark glasses are good, and
hard to replace. After your generosity and the generosity of everyone in the
Quinta Eulalia we want to say nothing, but if it is possible for you to speak
with the maids discreetly I would be . . . very obliged, for possibly it was an
irresistible temptation. I only want their return. The objects are not very
valuable but are only quite useful and also had a sentimental significance."
The passage derives from Notebook I.

3. —*C'est difficile à dire en français . . . C'est la vie* [p. 224]: Poor French, apart from *Pero así es la vida*: "It is hard to say in French. So—But we would be very happy if you would have—if you want [to have] a cognac with us. Pardon me, the cognac is not cognac, it is habanero. I think too that it is possible that the habanero is not habanero. Unfortunately. But thus is life. That is life." The note derives from Notebook III.

4. *Togo* [p. 224]: See note IX.9 on "Tojo" and "Togo."

5. *and placate him* [p. 224]: In the left margin next to this paragraph in Draft A, written in large letters and underlined twice, is the note: "Mem: cashing that cheque" (UBC 13:10, ch. XVIII, 2).

6. *This phrasing is derived from Flaubert, Salammbô* [p. 225]: See chapter 5 of Gustave Flaubert's *Salammbô* (1862), in which Spendius tempts Mathô to steal the veil of Tanit at Corinth, asking "What punishment of the gods can you dread when once you possess, in your own person, their strength?": "A terrible longing consumed Mathô: he would have liked to abstain from the sacrilege, and yet desired to possess the veil. He thought to himself that perhaps he did not desire to take it[,] merely to monopolise its virtues. However, he did not probe to the foundation of his intentions, but paused at the limit where his thoughts frightened him" (*Salammbô* [New York: Modern Library, 1929], 78). On *Salammbô*, see also pp. 229, 250.

7. *rather formal manners* [p. 226]: Both Draft A and the typescript have "rather German manners," but in the typescript, "German" is crossed out and "formal" inserted in hand.

8. *Pobres* [p. 228]: "Poor things."

9. *Es Peligroso . . . Sí, es peligroso* [p. 229]: "It is dangerous—understand?—dangerous." "Yes, it is dangerous."

10. *also the telephone no. involved with the Consul's fate—Erikson* [p. 229]: Erikson, or Ericcson, is a Mexican telephone exchange. On its connection to the Consul and Lowry's fiction generally, see Ackerley and Clipper 118–19. See also notes II.20, VI.28, XX.11, and XXVI.10. In a draft of *Dark as the Grave*, a friend tells Sigbjørn, "Half the telephone numbers in Mexico are Erikson something or other. It's a Swedish company that owns the telephone exchange so there's nothing very mysterious about that" (UBC 9:5, 331).

11. *Use Warren's technique of replies not in inverted commas* [p. 229]: I assume that this refers to Robert Penn Warren, although I have not located this stylistic feature in his work. Lowry might be confusing him with another writer.

12. *the Lord Nelson England expects every man to do his duty voice* [p. 230]: A reference to Viscount Horatio Nelson's famous exhortation at the Battle of Trafalgar, October 1805. See also p. 241.

13. *Yvonne's* [p. 230]: Yvonne is the Consul's ex-wife, in *Under the Volcano*. Her name also appears at this point in Draft A (UBC 13:10, ch. XVIII, 6A).

14. *Pat Murphy's goat* [p. 230]: See note VII.5.

15. *The Hour of the Truth . . . The Lost Week End* [p. 230]: On *The Hour of the Truth*, see note I.80. *The Lost Weekend*, a 1945 film based on the novel by Charles Jackson (see note VI.37), won several Academy Awards, including Best Actor (Ray Milland), Best Director (Billy Wilder), and Best Picture.

CHAPTER XIX

1. *Sigbjørn suddenly shouts* [p. 231]: In the typescript, this sentence reads "On porch about 1 P.M. suddenly shouts." Both Draft A (UBC 13:10, ch. XIX, 1) and Margerie's note in Notebook III, from which the material here ultimately derives, have "M. suddenly shouts," with M. standing in one case for Martin and in the other for Malcolm.

2. *Raoul* [p. 231]: Spelled thus here and on p. 233, but spelled Raul on p. 217. The inconsistency derives from Draft A.

3. *uncle Hootnanny* [p. 231]: Probably a character based on Charles Stansfeld-Jones (see the annotation on "Stan's number," note I.45). On Hootnanny, see also note IV.40.

4. *I Ching Divination . . .* [p. 231 ff.]: The *I Ching* (*Book of Changes*) is an ancient Chinese text, consulted for the purposes of wisdom and divination. It includes 64 hexagrams and texts that explain each hexagram's significance. Through the manipulation of a set of fifty yarrow sticks or the dropping of three coins the individual is led to the hexagram which, properly interpreted, contains the answer to a question. The Fu hexagram, number 24, consists of one unbroken and five broken lines and signifies the principle of return or the turning point. I have not located the version of the *I Ching* from which Lowry quotes below, but similar renditions of the text and interpretations of the significance of the lines may be found in any of a number of translations.

5. *Yours with sincere affection, etc.* [p. 233]: Draft A includes a signature, "Uncle So & So" (UBC 13:10, ch. XIX, 3).

6. *marked O.H.M.S.* [p. 233]: "On His Majesty's Service," a sign that this is official British government business.

7. *Uncle Gwynn* [p. 234]: The change in the uncle's name, from Hootnanny to Gwynn, occurs in both Draft A and Draft B.

8. *happy days for them both* [p. 235]: In Draft A there is a line drawn from the end of the chapter to the following right-margin note: "As a conse-

quence they laughed, & also remembered that it was April's fool day [sic]. (For we might shift dates a little)" (UBC 13:10, ch. XIX, 5).

Chapter XX

1. *Dark things may happen to those in the Lion* [p. 236]: Bowker (322) says that Lowry "took seriously several mystical sayings from [Charles Stansfeld-Jones] such as 'Fear is the lion on the path.'" Here, the Lion refers to Lowry's astrological sign, Leo (his birthday was July 28). See, however, Lowry's poem "The Young Man from Oaxaca" (*CP* 226), where it is a pub.

2. *Swedenborg's dictum . . . When a man is in evils he is in the love of them* [p. 236]: Lowry was fascinated by the mystical writings of Emanuel Swedenborg (1688–1772). I have not identified the specific source of this reference.

3. *Goethe himself could have advised no better course [than] that they numb their minds to some extent, go on a prolonged debauch* [p. 236]: If this refers to a specific work by Goethe, I have not identified it. My colleague Frank Stringfellow suggests that, rather than referring to one of Goethe's works, the passage means that even Goethe, despite his intelligence and imagination, could not have improved on the suggestion that the Wildernesses get drunk.

4. *an extraJamesian turn of the screw* [p. 236]: See Henry James's story "The Turn of the Screw" (1898), which Lowry also refers to on p. 253.

5. *another system* [p. 236]: The apparent reading in Draft A is "any new system."

6. *Yeats' Vision . . . the phase of the hunchback* [p. 236]: See William Butler Yeats, *A Vision* (1925; revised, 1937; reprint, New York: Collier Books, 1967). In Yeats's cycle of the moon, "The Multiple Man, also called 'The Hunchback,'" is part of Phase 26, which Yeats calls "the most difficult of the phases" (see Yeats 176–79).

7. *God has deprived me . . . loves in me!* [p. 236]: I do not know what English king said this.

8. *Primrose began to cry* [p. 238]: Here and a few lines later, Draft A has "Yvonne" rather than "Primrose."

9. *they'll send you back to England* [p. 239]: Margerie's emendation of the Draft A reading, "Consequently they'll send you back to Mexico wherever they deport you from," etc., is obviously correct.

10. *they'll let us go home here at least* [p. 240]: I have adopted the apparent reading in Draft A in the belief that the typescript reading, "they'd let us go from *here* at least," resulted from Margerie's misreading of Malcolm's handwriting.

11. *Erikson is closed* [p. 240]: That is, the telephone exchange is closed, no operators being available at that time. See note XVIII.10.

CHAPTER XXI

1. *the diabolical coincidence of Clarence Hoover. Anatomise this: his own first name, Mary Hoover's last, best man, etc.* [p. 241]: See also p. 271. I have not identified Clarence Hoover. Lowry's full name was Clarence Malcolm Lowry, and Mary Hoover was Conrad Aiken's third wife, who was with Aiken in Cuernavaca during Lowry's stay there in 1937. Lowry attended Aiken's marriage to Mary Hoover, but I know of no evidence that he was Aiken's best man.

2. *To go or not Togo* [p. 242]: See Hamlet's "To be or not to be" speech (*Hamlet* 3.1.56 ff.) and the notes on Tojo (IX.9) and Togo (XVIII.4).

CHAPTER XXII

1. *his old 1938 swim* [p. 243]: In Draft A, the last number of this date is illegible, but the typescript reading, "1931," is clearly wrong since Lowry did not arrive in Mexico until 1936.

2. *not two quarts but nearly two litres* [p. 243]: Either Lowry or Sigbjørn is under the impression that a liter is substantially larger than a quart, but in fact an American quart is the equivalent of 0.946 liters while a British quart is 1.136 liters.

3. *the throne that looked, like King Stephen's, down on this rabbit warren of the past* [p. 244]: Stephen of Boulogne ruled as king of England, 1135–54; his throne was contested by the Empress Matilda, daughter of Henry I, and then by her son, who became Henry II. I do not follow the reference here.

4. *"But I've* been *to Cuernavaca—"* [p. 244]: Draft A has "'But I *have* to go to Cuernavaca.'" Over that is apparently a planned revision, "I have *been* to Cuernavaca!" and, to the right, a note: "The word Cuernavaca with its annotations [sic] of home broke their hearts for a moment."

5. *ley fuga* [p. 244]: See note S.10.

6. *UBC 14:3, 337* [p. 245]: The next three pages of Draft B, unnumbered in the typescript, consist of a Mexican train schedule. I have not included this material.

CHAPTER XXIII

1. *God gave his assent* [p. 246]: In Draft A, a right-margin note next to this paragraph says, "Point is Togo now lets them go: they go & have a beer

at the pub where they had their first beer in Acapulco & they ask 'What's wrong with us' & decide its [*sic*] the burned house, & continued failure" (UBC 13:11, ch. XXIII, 1). The typescript locates part of this paragraph a page and a half later; I have placed it next.

Chapter XXIV

1. *round the corner or somewhere* [p. 248]: In Draft A, Lowry wrote "round the corner or something," then wrote "where" above the second syllable of "something." The typescript has "something," but I have assumed that Lowry intended to substitute "somewhere" for "something."

2. *Oh god of battles! . . . compassing the crown . . .* [pp. 248–49]: See Shakespeare's *Henry V*, 4.1. 275 ff.

Chapter XXV

1. *Star of Gold* [p. 249]: Estrella d'Oro bus line; see note XIII.12.

2. *the shape of the cathedral where Hart Crane rang the sad church bells* [p. 249]: See Crane's poem "Purgatorio," which Lowry quotes in *Dark as the Grave* (DG 63).

3. *threats glimmered in the hills* [p. 250]: The typescript reading, "threats glimmered in the trees," is an erroneous transcription of Draft A.

4. *Like two little pilgrims, hand in hand* [p. 250]: Possibly echoing the end of Milton's *Paradise Lost*: "They hand in hand with wand'ring steps and slow, / Through Eden took thir solitary way."

Chapter XXVI

1. *like 3 pages of Salammbo read on an empty stomach* [p. 250]: For other references to Flaubert's novel, see pp. 225, 229.

2. *the room of Chapter VII* [p. 250]: See the description of Jacques Laruelle's home in chapter 7 of *Under the Volcano*. It is based on a building that Lowry had seen only from the outside during his original stay in Cuernavaca; when he and Margerie returned in late 1945, they found it for rent, and stayed there.

3. *the little postman of his chap VI* [p. 250]: Lowry later claimed that the news of *Under the Volcano*'s acceptance was brought to him by the postman on whom, years earlier, he had modeled the *cartero* who had brought Yvonne's long-delayed postcard to the Consul at the end of chapter 6 of *Under the Volcano* (UV 193); Margerie's notebook entry for 6 April

1946, however, does not mention any such coincidence (Notebook III). In *Dark as the Grave*, the same postman brings an unfavorable reader's report (*DG* 142; see also notes II.16, XXVI.8).

4. *Innes Rose* [p. 251]: Rose was for some time Lowry's literary agent in Britain.

5. *p. 1* [p. 251]: I.e., page 1 of this chapter in Draft A.

6. *the only thing light in the garden* [p. 251]: This is the Draft A reading; the typescript substitutes "bright" for "light."

7. *at the beginning of Dark as the Grave* [p. 251]: An early pencil draft of *Dark as the Grave* began with Martin Trumbaugh (as Sigbjørn was then called) in Cuernavaca, suffering from the noise made by birds. In the published text, which begins at an earlier stage in the trip, the passage is worked into chapter 6 (*DG* 115–16).

8. *Cape's virtual refusal* [p. 251]: On 29 November 1945 Jonathan Cape wrote Lowry a letter which reached him only on New Year's Eve. Along with the letter (most of which is printed in *SL* 424–25) Cape enclosed William Plomer's yet-unpublished reader's report, which advised that *Under the Volcano* not be published without substantial revision. In *Dark as the Grave*, where part of Plomer's report is incorporated into excerpts from a report for an American publisher, Lowry calls the report "something new in the language of rejection" (*DG* 143). Both the context of this passage and the reference in *Dark as the Grave* suggest that the typescript reading, "Cape's virtual refusal," makes a little more sense than the Draft A reading, "Cape's virtual acceptance." On Plomer's reader's report see also notes II.16 and XXVI.3.

9. *Maria Luisa* [p. 251]: Señora Maria Luisa Blanco de Arriola, the Lowrys' landlady in Cuernavaca (see p. 4).

10. *the dreadful coincidences surrounding Erikson* [p. 252]: About the ending of *Under the Volcano*, Lowry told Aiken that "there is a horrendous real coincidence in connection with this for the day after I'd written that scene for the first time in Mexico, a man was shot and pushed over a ravine in exactly the same way, by name, William Erickson. My character was at that time named William Erickson, the same name as the guy in *In Ballast*" (Sugars 126–27). In the far more elaborate version of this story recounted in a draft of *Dark as the Grave* (UBC 9:5, 331–41), Sigbjørn is warned that coincidences involving Erikson telephone exchanges are not remarkable (see note XVIII.10).

11. *"should you travel to the scene that has informed the work of some great artist you would be nearer truth (get this) and all it implies—"* [p. 252]: This appears to be a quotation, but I have not identified the source.

12. *a French film of Crime and Punishment* [p. 252]: See note XIII.15.

13. *shot, across the bed* [p. 252]: Draft A has "shot flat on to the bed."

Chapter XXVII

1. *disused elevator shaft . . . the deserter found in a refrigerator car in Empress* [p. 252]: On the elevator shaft, see note VII.3. On "the deserter found in a refrigerator car," see Lowry's poem "Deserter," several lines of which are echoed here, and Chris Ackerley's commentary (*CP* 139, 281–82).

2. *what shall it profit a man . . . lose his own soul?* [p. 253]: See Mark 8:36.

3. *Another point . . .* [p. 253]: This paragraph is continuous with the previous one in the typescript, but in Draft A it is a marginal note, and its subject does not follow directly from what precedes it.

4. *Notes: see The Insufficient Man artic. Times Lit Sup* [p. 254]: See "The Insufficient Man," *TLS* no. 2381 (20 September 1947): 478. On the recto of the page on which this anonymous essay on Dostoevsky appears is an unsigned review of new fiction, including a positive appraisal of *Under the Volcano*. The essay on Dostoevsky argues that he believed Christ did not seek to improve "social conditions" but regarded the world as "a testing-ground, a place of temptation, a place to which we are sent to learn humility and to eschew pride." Thus the worst idolater is the man "who worships at the altar of 'the bitch-goddess, success.'" Moreover, "Man's essential vice, as it was Lucifer's vice before him, is to claim self-sufficiency, to separate himself from his fellows." The reviewer fails to note that the phrase "the bitch-goddess, success" is not Dostoevsky's but is derived from a letter, dated 11 September 1906, from William James to H. G. Wells, and there is no evidence that Lowry knew the real source of the phrase.

In these notes, Lowry either quotes or refers to three passages from Dostoevsky's novels that are cited in the *TLS* review (in each case using the translations by Constance Garnett published by William Heinemann):

> Go, forthwith, go this very moment to the nearest public place, prostrate yourself, kiss the earth you have stained, bow down in every direction, and proclaim at the top of your voice to the passers-by, "I am a murderer" and God will give you peace again. (Sonya to Raskolnikov in *Crime and Punishment*, part 5, chapter 4)

> "You can love nothing but your shame" (Aglaia to Nastasya Filippovna in *The Idiot*, part 4, chapter 8)

> "It's your luxurious life," said Alyosha softly.
> "Is it better then to be poor?"
> "Yes, it is better." (from *The Brothers Karamazov*, part 4, book 11, chapter 3)

I have emended the typescript reading, "It is better than to be poor," which inadvertently reverses the point of both Dostoevsky's text and the *TLS* review (in which the line is printed correctly).

5. *Après la Guerre, etc. The Houngan* [p. 254]: "Après la guerre fini" is a slightly off-color British Army song from World War I, with variable lyrics; see Edward Arthur Dolph, *"Sound Off!": Soldier Songs from the Revolution to World War II* (New York: Farrar & Rinehart, 1942), 136–37, and Frank Lynn, *Songs for Singin'* (San Francisco: Chandler Publishing, 1961), 88. A *houngan* is a voodoo priest; I have not located a song entitled "The Houngan."

6. *"Undergraduate Suicide of Shame"* [p. 254]: The source of this is Lowry's recurrent sense of guilt over the November 1929 suicide of his friend Paul Leonard Charles Fitte at St. Catharine's College, Cambridge University ("Johns" refers to another Cambridge college, St. John's). The *Cambridge Daily News* for 15 and 16 November 1929 ran articles headed "Cambridge Tragedy / Student Found Dead" and "Suicide of Cambridge Freshman / Inquest Story of Money Troubles"; the latter includes Lowry's testimony at the inquest (copies in UBC 36:16). In *October Ferry to Gabriola*, Fitte is fictionalized as Peter Cordwainer; in the typescripts for *Dark as the Grave* and *The Ordeal of Sigbjørn Wilderness* (an unfinished novel), he is called Wensleydale. See Bradbrook 15, 113–16, 161–62, and Bowker 80, 97–100, 190, 523, 568. On Fitte see also notes II.25 and IV.20.

Chapter XXVIII

1. *Fair as herself is she* [p. 255]: From Lowry's poem "Song for My Wife"; see note IV.32. A barely legible pencil draft of the poem, not cited in the *Collected Poetry*, is written in the right margin of Draft A (UBC 13:12, ch. XXVIII, 1).

2. *this belies Tojo* [p. 255]: Both Notebook III and Draft A have "(this belies Baxter)."

3. *Important note* [p. 256]: Draft A reinforces the importance of this material with a left margin note in large letters: "V. important insert. FUNDAMENTAL."

4. *sentinel that Schopenhauer somewhere imagines* [p. 256]: I have not found where Arthur Schopenhauer uses this image. Apparently Lowry could not locate this passage either: see note XXVIII.10. See also note XLIII.3.

5. BOND *bookshop* [p. 256]: Sigbjørn has entered Bond's Book Shop, which in the 1940s was located at 523 Dunsmuir Street in downtown Vancouver.

6. *"You'll hate me for saying that! . . . poems."* [p. 256]: No book by this title is listed in the *National Union Catalogue: Pre-1956 Imprints*.

7. *"From here Black Majesty reigned over Haiti"* [p. 257]: This and the subsequent phrases "An Antiguan's Unique Memorial" and "the only place in the world where pigs have learned to swim" are taken from Frederich Simpich, "Skypaths through Latin America: Flying from Our Nation's Capital Southward over Jungles, Remote Islands, and Great Cities in an Aërial Survey of the East Coast of South America," *National Geographic Magazine* 59 (January 1931): 22, 30, 43.

8. *XII chap of Volcano* [p. 257]: Sigbjørn compares the runaway horse on the Antiguan's memorial to the one in chapters 11–12 of *Under the Volcano* that is released by the Consul and kills Yvonne.

9. *the end of Chap IX* [p. 257]: At the end of chapter 9 of *Under the Volcano* the Consul watches an old Indian carrying "another poor Indian, yet older and more decrepit than himself," on his back (*UV* 280).

10. *in bus read Schopenhauer passage . . . and Naples—etc—* [p. 257]: In Draft A there is a line drawn from "& Naples—etc—" to a marginal note reading, "Find passage in Schopenhauer." The passage is apparently the one referred to above (see note XXVIII.4).

11. *Cite also In Ballast. Have Sig. tell Prim. real story of In Ballast* [p. 258]: For Lowry's account of *In Ballast to the White Sea*, the manuscript novel that was destroyed in a fire in June 1944, see his August 1951 letter to David Markson (*SL* 255–57, 261–65). See also notes IV.20, IV.38, and XLIII.1.

CHAPTER XXIX

1. *UBC 14:5, 257* [p. 258]: This page should have been numbered 357, but Margerie either never caught or never corrected her error. As a result, all subsequent pages in the typescript are numbered 100 lower than they should be.

CHAPTER XXX

1. *Westward Ho* [p. 259]: See note XVII.2.

2. *this business of the bond re Vallejo* [p. 261]: Vallejo has not been identified.

3. *the Unitarian minister that had married them* [p. 261]: Malcolm and Margerie Lowry were married on 2 December 1940 by S. Theodore Page-smith, a Unitarian minister in Vancouver, according to the copy of the marriage certificate on file in the Malcolm Lowry Archive (Unitarian Church of Vancouver Papers).

4. *(also the apartment where we were married)* [p. 261]: In Draft A, this parenthetical memo is a left-margin note with a thin line drawn to "foreshadowed." In the typescript, the note is inserted immediately before "and

Sigbjørn thinks so too," but I have moved it to the end of the paragraph where it appears to make more sense.

5. *they think they have to go smack off to New York* [p. 261]: After accepting *Under the Volcano* for publication, Curtice Hitchcock originally wanted Lowry to come to New York so they could edit the book together; after rereading the manuscript, however, he changed his mind (*SL* 138).

6. *escribir en el escusado* [p. 261]: Spanish, "to write [while sitting] on the toilet." *Escusado* is a common error for *excusado*.

7. *half past tree by the cock* [p. 261]: The same phrase appears in *Under the Volcano* in the vicinity of "imposseebly" (*UV* 256).

8. *in the Calle Tierra del Fuego . . . a hearse was drawn up* [p. 263]: See *UV* 56–57 for the child's funeral with "the tiny lace-covered coffin followed by the band."

CHAPTER XXXI

1. *Hal* [p. 263]: Harold Matson, Lowry's American literary agent.

2. *where the Consul made his decision not to drink . . . long letter in defence of the Volcano itself* [p. 263]: "I have resisted temptation for two and a half minutes at least: my redemption is sure" (*UV* 69; cf. 85, 144). For the letter, see *SL* 57–89.

3. *Janice (the name like his wife's)* [p. 264]: Janice was an acquaintance of the Lowrys; her name resembles that of Lowry's first wife, Jan Gabrial, née Janine Vanderheim (see notes I.61 and IX.12).

4. *the lights fail as in book* [p. 264]: In *Under the Volcano*, the lights at the cinema fail with appalling regularity, the result of an overloaded and inadequately maintained electrical system. See also note XLIII.15.

CHAPTER XXXII

1. *XXXII . . .* [p. 264]: In Draft A, much of this chapter is a collection of marginal notes. The arrangement of those notes in the typescript has been followed here.

2. *Rhea Deverly* [p. 264]: Another of the Lowrys' acquaintances in Cuernavaca. This paragraph is derived from Notebook III.

3. *he felt himself drawn upwards, as by the singing of angels* [p. 265]: This image might have been suggested by Goethe's *Faust*, recalling the salvation of Faust at the end of part 2 (and, less directly, the salvation of Margaret at the end of part 1).

4. *if not Janice* [p. 265]: Both Draft A and the typescript have "if Janice."

5. *the ballet mécanique of the raindrops* [p. 265]: *Ballet mécanique*, a 1925 avant-garde musical composition by George Antheil (1900–59).

CHAPTER XXXIII

1. *the long long trip, that seems to get longer and longer, unlike the trip to the spring at the Martins* [p. 266]: I have not identified the Martins, but presumably they are based on some of the Lowrys' neighbors in Dollarton. In "The Forest Path to the Spring," the narrator says he "had the decided impression that the path *back* from the spring was growing shorter than the path *to* it, though the way there had seemed shorter too than on the previous day." He worries about "the path [becoming] shorter and shorter until I should disappear altogether one evening" (*HL* 268–69).

2. *Camacho* [p. 266]: Manuel Ávila Camacho, president of Mexico (1940–46).

3. *categorical imperative* [p. 268]: Immanuel Kant's precept, developed in *The Critique of Practical Reason* (1788), stated that the ultimate test of any action is whether or not everyone in similar circumstances should act the same way.

4. *Alemán—Moralización* [p. 268]: See note I.27. Political signs do in fact appear "everywhere, even on the volcanoes."

5. *Central de Fianzas . . . Cajero* [p. 269]: This receipt from Ramírez, a cashier (*cajero*) at the bonding agency, indicates Lowry's payment of 21 pesos, including one peso in interest, corresponding to the bond pledged by the company for the year beginning 15 April 1946. At the bottom of the page in Draft A, Lowry drew a line across the page under "Cajero"; under the line he wrote, "Etc. with a similar one for Margie."

CHAPTER XXXIV

1. *the scene of chapter VII, the tower* [p. 270]: During their 1945–46 trip the Lowrys stayed for a while at the tower described in chapter 7 of *Under the Volcano*, where it is occupied by Jacques Laruelle.

CHAPTER XXXV

1. *Mary Hoover . . . you are Clarence* [p. 271]: See note XXI.1.

2. *XXXVI* [p. 272]: Drafts A and B both read "XXVI," but this is obviously erroneous.

Chapter XXXVI

1. *Richard Knight. Fake Barrymore . . . Mrs. Gooch* [p. 273]: Richard Knight and Mrs. Gooch were acquaintances whose names appear in Notebook III; apparently they were staying at the Marik Hotel. One of Lowry's notes indicates that he considered working Knight into a scene in New Orleans (Notebook III). As a "fake Barrymore," perhaps he adopted a dashing pose that Lowry associated with John (1882–1942) and/or Lionel (1878–1954) Barrymore, leading men on stage and screen.

2. *Letter from Consul follows* [p. 273]: Immediately after "follows:" Draft A has an arrow drawn to a note that reads, "see 1a of this chapter." The next page, numbered 1a, is also numbered 280; in Draft B, however, the corresponding page is numbered 279 and there is no page 280.

3. *5th April, 1946* [p. 273]: In Draft A, "5th" is underlined twice and followed by an exclamation point, apparently to emphasize how long the letter has taken to arrive. At the left, on the same line (directly above "Sir:"), it reads: "AIRMAIL."

Chapter FXXVII

1. *S. is magnificent! . . .* [p. 274]: In Margerie's notes in Notebook III, from which this section is derived, the initial M. is used throughout the description of the day to refer to Malcolm; in Draft A, which retains the M., the initial refers to Martin. Margerie changed the first M. to S. (for Sigbjørn), but in the typescript all the following references are to "M." I have retained the inconsistent references here and later, as well as such uncorrected traces of the notebook reading as "Meantime I [Margerie] see Mr. Hughes."

2. *UBC 14:6, 281* [p. 274]: There is no page 280 in the typescript (see above, note XXXVI.2).

3. *build up this character of the sailor a little from Ultramarine* [p. 275]: This is probably not a reference to a specific character in *Ultramarine*, just an indication that details from that book might be reused here.

Chapter XXXVIII

1. *Appt in Samarra* [p. 276]: See note XVII.7.

2. *Farewell and adieu, my good Spanish ladies* [pp. 276–77]: For the "exact wording" of "Spanish Ladies," which begins "Farewell and adieu to you Spanish ladies," see Ruth Bauerle, *The James Joyce Songbook* (New York: Garland, 1982), 27–28.

3. *the Herr Doktor is busy etc. etc.* [p. 277]: Next to this paragraph in Draft A, a right-margin note reads, "Drama."

4. *abarrotes* [p. 278]: "Groceries"; here used in the sense of a grocery store. A left-margin note further down the page in Draft A reads "Mem of

Chap II—abarrotes," a reference to the shop in chapter 2 of *Under the Volcano* (*UV* 56).

5. *Morro Castle* [p. 278]: A fortress in Cuba, dating from Spanish colonial days: either the one overlooking Havana harbor or the one of the same name in Santiago de Cuba. A picture of the latter is on p. 12 of the *National Geographic* article that Sigbjørn reads on p. 257 (see note XXVIII.7). See also Lowry's poem "Prayer," line 7, and Chris Ackerley's annotation (*CP* 79, 256).

CHAPTER XXXIX

1. *no chance . . . pic is snapped* [p. 279]: This is probably Margerie's insertion, since the passage does not appear in Draft A.

2. *El Puente del Chavacano . . . Hay un Ford en su futuro* [p. 280]: The series includes signs for various bars, villages, and businesses, including Pemex, the Mexican national petroleum company. *Se vende esta casa*: "House for sale." *No se permite . . .*: "Putting up announcements is not permitted"—the equivalent of "Post no bills." *Gotas nasales*: "nose drops." *El Farolito*: "The Little Lighthouse," name of the seedy bar where the Consul is killed in *Under the Volcano. Supervulcanización*: See note I.69. *Llantas*: "tires." *Pulquería La Judía*: "The Jewess Pulqueria [bar where *pulque*, agave brandy, is served]." *Hay un Ford en su futuro*: "There's a Ford in your future."

3. *the Canada* [p. 280]: The Hotel Canada (see note XV.6).

4. *as we pray there* [p. 281]: In the left column, in Margerie's hand and placed within quotation marks, is written "—may as well pray—we've done everything else."

5. *in Oaxaca, before Soledad* [p. 281]: On the Iglesia de la Soledad (Church of the Solitary) in Oaxaca, see Ackerley and Clipper 13. At this point, the typescript has the following note, typed directly into the paragraph: "(1 theme of thing, Dark as the Grave, traces the impulse back to beginnings of Christianity in Western world—is working of faith)." This is a marginal note in Draft A, and it does not seem to fit where Margerie placed it.

CHAPTER XL

1. *I think . . . cursing Mexico* [p. 282]: This sentence appears in the upper right-hand corner of the page in Draft A and is typed above the chapter heading in Draft B.

2. *Charlie Pickard's . . . Sylvia Godwin* [p. 282]: These are more people the Lowrys knew in Cuernavaca.

3. *Orendain* [p. 282]: In Notebook IV, from which chapters XXXIX–XLII are elaborated, Margerie wrote "At Cuernavaca to Charlie Pickards—Orendain who says he can fix all, just sit & wait & he'll call us Thursday morning at 10, but all are drinking & we can't trust them." See also pp. 286, 287.

4. *(see telegram)* [p. 282]: At this point Draft A has, in the right margin, "see telegram etc quoted at end"; in the left margin is the note, "I've got the telegram here."

5. *La Sin Rival . . . La Reina (The Queen)* [p. 283]: The names of these shops are taken from Lowry's notes in Notebook I.

6. *worse, inevitably, would* [p. 284]: At this point, Draft A has the texts of two telegrams, only the second of which is included in the typescript. In the upper right corner of the page containing the first telegram, Lowry's note reads "This should be used on 1st page of XL"; the telegram is then introduced with the note, "This telegram looked & read as follows." The text of the first telegram in Draft A is as follows:

> Feliz Año   Cervecería Moctezuma S.A.
>
>   1946   Telegramas
>
>   Abr 30 1946
>
> Telegrama   Cuernavaca, Mor
>
> DTO. X-142 num 4316 . . . . 20/8 ord.-pd w MEXICO D.F. .30
> AB. D.17.10
>
> Jardin Morelos num 12 Duce
>
> Restaurant "Bahia," Cuernavaca, Mor.
>
> Hoy hizo efectivas secretarias gobernacion fianzas esposos Lowry / suplicamosle remitirnos inmediatamente un mil pesos importe garantias objeto no perjudicar intereses
>
>   Central de Fianzas S.A. (UBC 13:14, ch. XL, 5)

The body of this telegram is also reproduced in the prefatory statement, p. 20 (see note S.9 for translation).

7. *Secretaría de Gobernación . . . Angelica Machiavelo* [p. 284]: "Ministry of the Interior: I received the bonds #16090 and 16091—which in the amounts of $500 Canadian [were] issued by the company Central de Fianzas, in order to guarantee the repatriation of Mr. Clarence Malcolm Lowry and his wife Mrs. Margerie Lowry. Mexico, Federal District, 15 April 1946. The Head of Contracts and Bonds, Angelica Machiavelo."

CHAPTER XLI

1. *My own darling . . . Pray for help* [p. 284]: The first two paragraphs of this chapter are not included in Draft A but are taken directly from a note

(now in UBC 14:17) written by Margerie while they were in Cuernavaca. The only substantial differences between the note and this version are in the salutation and signature: addressed to "My own darling Lion" and signed "your hartebeeste," the note uses pet names that appear frequently in the Lowrys' love letters and in Malcolm's poems (see note V.2). The note also has a bracketed annotation in Malcolm's hand: "[attached to Chap. XLI La Mordida]."

2. *Sylvia says to Primrose* [p. 285]: I have adopted the typescript reading, which attributes the question to Sylvia, rather than the ambiguous Draft A reading, in which the question might be asked by Primrose.

3. *Farolito (El Universal) memories of chap XII and the end* [p. 285]: See notes III.16 and VI.72.

4. *Dr. Amann who gives us prescriptions for pheno* [p. 285]: In Notebook IV, Margerie recorded a visit to "Dr. A who gives us prescription." On Dr. Amann see note I.8.

5. *the agony in the garden* [p. 285]: One of the five "sorrowful mysteries" celebrated in the rosary, a Catholic devotion, in memory of Christ's prayers in the garden of Gethsemane shortly before his betrayal by Judas.

6. *Pantagruelian shots of rum* [p. 286]: Very large shots, after Gargantua's gigantic son in François Rabelais's *Gargantua and Pantagruel*.

7. *Sigbjørn feels better* [p. 286]: In Draft A, a left-margin note at this point reads "& the iron door still half down."

8. *equipajes . . . Pera dónde* [p. 286]: *Equipajes*: "bags" (luggage); however, the word is normally singular (*equipaje*). *Aquí*: "Here." *Pera dónde*: an error either for "*Pero dónde?*" ("But where?") or for "*Para dónde?*" ("Where to?").

CHAPTER XLII

1. *Recuerdo José Martinez* [p. 288]: Possibly, "souvenir [of] José Martinez."

2. *(Kilroy p-d here today . . . Kilroy was here today too)* [p. 288]: "El Pollo" means "The Chicken." On Kilroy and El Grafe see notes I.72 and I.73. That El Grafe was not Lowry's coinage is suggested by the fact that Notebook III includes the following graffiti recorded in Lowry's hand, apparently during the trip (with the obscene words partly obliterated but easily recognizable):

Kilroy pissed here to-day.

El Pollo was here too.

Kilroy was seen.

El Grafe did his cock-sucking here to-day.

Kilroy was looking.

El Pollo was here to-day too.

3. *muy limpio* [p. 289]: "Very clean."

CHAPTER XLIII

1. *the lost manuscripts (In Ballast, Men at Mazatlan)* [p. 290]: On *In Ballast to the White Sea*, see notes IV.38 and XXVIII.11. Lowry mentions the Pacific port of Mazatlán in his poem "Outside was the roar of the sea and the darkness" (*CP* 107), but I have seen no other reference to a lost manuscript entitled *Men at Mazatlan*.

2. *Alemán, Moralización* [p. 291]: See note I.27.

3. *Schopenhauer on the will* [p. 291]: In his best-known work, *The World as Will and Idea* (1819), Arthur Schopenhauer argued that the individual will is involved in everything experienced (even unconsciously) by the self; moreover, the entire range of existence, from human consciousness to inert matter, is part of a universal "will" that Schopenhauer viewed as "a nonrational force, a blind, striving power whose operations are without ultimate purpose or design" (Patrick Gardiner, "Schopenhauer, Arthur," in *The Encyclopedia of Philosophy*, ed. Paul Edwards [New York: Macmillan, 1967], 7:328). See also notes XXVIII.4 and XXVIII.10.

4. *Memories of other trains: Hotel Room in Chartres, Metal . . . dreams of trains are death dreams* [p. 291]: Lowry's stories "Hotel Room in Chartres" and "Metal" (an early title for a story that was posthumously published as "June the 30th, 1934") both involve train rides (*PS* 19–24, 36–48). On Lowry's knowledge of "Freudian death dreams" and their relevance in *Under the Volcano*, see *SL* 81 and Ackerley and Clipper 342.

5. *pigeon Spanish* [p. 292]: Lowry's error for "pidgin Spanish."

6. *punctum indifferens* [p. 292]: On Lowry's short story, "Punctum Indifferens Skibet Gaar Videre" (later expanded into chapter 4 of *Ultramarine*), see Ackerley and Clipper 230.

7. *!Salud! . . . R. F. Diaz Infante San Luis Potosi* [p. 293]: Advertisements: "Greetings! Eat in the Restaurant of the Railroads, San Luis Potosí." "Both Worlds Hotel. Visit it and you will be satisfied." "Hotel Progress. The best and the most central of the city. Manager: R. F. Diaz Infante. San Luis Potosí."

8. *Guerra a la Ignorancia. !Enseñe a leer!* [p. 293]: See the expanded version below and note XLIII.9.

9. *Guerra a la IGNORANCIA! . . . Disponible para Anuncio* [p. 294]: "War on ignorance! Illiteracy is the sorrow and the burden of the people. Teach [others] to read! Available by [posted] announcement."

10. *A corpse will be transported by express—deported* [p. 294]: See *UV* 43, 284, 301. The corpse in question is headed for the United States (*UV* 59–60), which might explain the reference to deportation.

11. *Monterrey es muy hermosa . . . Muchas fábricas* [p. 294]: An inane conversation between Sigbjørn and Fatty: "Monterrey is very beautiful." "Yes. Yes. Very beautiful." "But it is very industrial." "Yes. It is very industrial." "A lot of factories here." "Yes. A lot of factories." I have emended the Draft A reading by adding accents and correcting *Muchos fabricos* to *Muchas fábricas.* The sign Sigbjørn sees means "Hotel Papagayo, located on Hornos Beach [literally, 'beach of the ovens'] at the edge of the sea. Manager: Isauro Flores, Acapulco, Guerrero."

12. *Nosotros habemos . . . tres hermosa* [p. 294]: "We have arrived by airplane, etc. The mountains are very beautiful." Sigbjørn slips twice into French, substituting *par avion* ("by airplane," but usually meaning "by airmail") for *por avión,* and *très* for *muy.* Mistakes in Spanish include *habemos arriberado* for *hemos arribado, montanas* for *montañas,* and *hermosa* for *hermosas.*

13. *"Perhaps that has gone on a multa"* [p. 295]: The last three words are omitted in the typescript but are included on p. 300, when the passage is repeated. Spanish *multa,* "fine."

14. *the hastening and moaning train with its two engines that* [p. 296]: The reading here is basically an attempt to follow Lowry's revision of Draft A, but I have emended "with its two engines that late, seems now doing," since "late" makes no sense in this context. The typescript reading—"shattering and sliding along with the train, hastenint [sic] with its two engines, and moaning that late, seems now doing"—is clearly erroneous.

15. *Bustamente* [p. 296]: As the reference to "his cinema manager and the lights going out in the cinema" indicates, the town's name recalls that of Sr. Bustamente in *Under the Volcano* (*UV* 25). See also note XXXI.4.

16. HISTORICAL PLACES *(See Life, Mem American war)* [p. 296]: I have not yet found this article.

17. *Here Comes Everybody* [p. 296]: The universal hero of James Joyce's *Finnegans Wake* (1939) is known by various names with the initials HCE, including Here Comes Everybody.

18. *we shoota the espiders in Mexico* [p. 297]: See *SL* 29, *UV* 371, and *DG* 124. "Espider" is Lowry's rendition of a Mexican policeman's attempt to say "spy" (Spanish *espía*).

19. *Lista?* [p. 298]: "[Are you] ready?"

20. *Quauhnahuac . . . (cabrones!)* [p. 298]: Echoes of *Under the Volcano*: Quauhnahuac (the original Indian name for what the Spanish called Cuernavaca) is the town where the Consul lives, and a sign for *camarón* (shrimp) calls forth the insulting term *cabrón* (literally a billy goat or a

cuckold) which is hurled at Geoffrey Firmin in chapter 12 of *Under the Volcano*.

21. *Hotel Continental Albos Edificio Escamilla* [p. 298]: A left-margin note in Draft A (UBC 13:16, ch. XLIII, 10) reads "Hotel Ambos Mundos—with same appointments is better name." See note XLIV.5.

22. *Hotel Rendon . . . Se Marga Vd Cuando Pesca* [p. 298]: Various signs: "Hotel Rendon, every room with bath. Official hotel of the proprietress, Nuevo Laredo, Tamaulipas." "Hotel Continental Albos, Escamilla building, 25 rooms, 25 baths. . . ." "You will become dirty when you fish." The last makes no sense as a sign, so perhaps Sigbjørn caught a glimpse of the sign and misread it. Draft A has a question mark after this sign, possibly indicating Lowry's uncertainty as to the phrasing.

23. *UBC 14:8, 317* [p. 298]: The next page of the typescript, not reproduced here, is an unnumbered page with a transcription of a railroad timetable.

CHAPTER XLIV

1. *they are garish lights* [p. 299]: Possibly an error for "there are garish lights," but both Draft A and the typescript have "they."

2. *ley fuga* [p. 301]: See note S.10.

3. *the second narrows bridge at home* [p. 301]: The Second Narrows Bridge spans the Burrard Inlet, connecting Vancouver with North Vancouver.

4. *get away from Hemingway* [p. 301]: I have no idea what 165 pounds has to do with Hemingway.

5. *The Hotel Ambos Mundos . . . should be one of the names of the hotel seen from the train in XLIII* [p. 302]: See note XLIII.21. "Ambos mundos" means "both worlds."

CHAPTER XLV

1. *the fatal seven—the seven of the tower* [p. 304]: Lowry called seven "the fateful, the magic, the lucky good-bad number" of the chapter in *Under the Volcano* in which the Consul enters Jacques Laruelle's tower; he also noted, among other things, that "7 too is the number on the horse that will kill Yvonne and 7 the hour when the Consul will die" (*SL* 77).

2. *avoid chords of Kafka* [p. 305]: See the parable told to Joseph K. in chapter 9 of Franz Kafka's *The Trial* (sometimes published separately as "Before the Law").

3. *a visible Atlantis* [p. 305]: Many of Lowry's ideas about the mythical lost continent of Atlantis derive from his reading of *Atlantis: The Antedilu-*

vian World by Ignatius Donnelly, a book to which the Consul specifically refers in *Under the Volcano* (*UV* 86). On Donnelly, see Ackerley and Clipper 30, 132, 133, and Chris Ackerley, "The Consul's Book," *Malcolm Lowry Review* no. 23/24 (fall 1988–spring 1989): 78–92.

4. *the horns of elfland . . . magic Mexico* [p. 306]: Line 10 of Tennyson's "The Splendor Falls," a song from *The Princess* (1847), is "The horns of Elfland faintly blowing!" The adaptation of the line into an invitation to "magic Mexico" sounds like phrasing from a tourist brochure, but it does not come from *Acapulco: An Adventure in Living*.

5. *the Chateau d'If* [p. 306]: The prison where Edmond Dantes is held in Alexandre Dumas's *The Count of Monte Cristo* (see also *SL* 15, 29).

6. *(d) Sigbjørn's consciousness . . . ditto* [p. 308]: In Draft A, this passage concludes: "(d) Martin's consciousness of divine justice (e) the collective consciousness of injustice."

7. *Measure for Measure* [p. 309]: The only apparent connection between Shakespeare's problem play and *La Mordida* is their shared theme of official corruption and the abuse of power.

8. *it was 9:15* [p. 309]: A note in Draft A asks "where was the Mexican eagle."

9. *Temazunchale* [p. 310]: This is the apparent reading in Draft A; the typescript has "Temaznimilchno."

10. *Huerta, and General Goering* [p. 311]: Victoriano Huerta (1854–1916) was a Mexican general who overthrew President Francisco I. Madero in 1913 and named himself provisional president. He was forced to resign in 1914 and died in 1916 while being held in the United States on charges of conspiring against the Mexican government. His "equestrian statue" is glimpsed in *Under the Volcano* (*UV* 44). Hermann Wilhelm Goering (1893–1946), an early supporter of Adolf Hitler, was among the most prominent members of the Nazi regime. He pressed for German rearmament during the 1930s and was commander of the German air force during World War II. He poisoned himself on 15 October 1946, shortly before he was scheduled to hang for crimes against humanity.

11. *phenobarbital—Enobarbus* [p. 315]: In Shakespeare's *Antony and Cleopatra*, Enobarbus is Mark Antony's right-hand man who eventually deserts him and then commits suicide. Lowry is contemplating a pun like the one he uses in a 1950 letter to Downie Kirk: "My faithful enemy Phenobarbas—treacherous to the last" (*SL* 189). The pun also appears in "Through the Panama" (*HL* 48).

12. *the film Warning Shadows* [p. 316]: This 1922 German expressionist film, directed by Arthur Robison, concerned "a shadow-man who forces the inhabitants of an unhappy household to see themselves in a shadowy play" (Halliwell 667).

13. *stars don't go out* [p. 317]: This parenthetical insertion, which is not in Draft A, may be Margerie's correction of Malcolm's imprecise knowledge of astronomy.

14. *Lovers must notify clerk . . . guilty line* [p. 317]: This passage originated in Notebook II and was copied into Draft A in the following form: "Lovers must nattily look at clerk at 12 o'clock on the guilty line was Guests must notify clerk at Hotel office by 12 noon" (UBC 13:17, ch. XLV, 16). Lowry then tried to revise that by placing the correct sign first and the hallucination second, but forgot to reverse "Lovers" and "Guests." See also pp. 322 and 323 and note XLV.19.

15. *the Virgin for those who have nobody with* [p. 318]: Here and on p. 322 Lowry echoes the phrasing of Dr. Vigil in *Under the Volcano* (UV 6) and Juan Fernando in *Dark as the Grave* (DG 130).

16. *Parsifal* [p. 319]: Here and in *Dark as the Grave*, where Sigbjørn thinks of the flowers that sprang up during Parsifal's absence (DG 68, 245), the reference is to Richard Wagner's *Parsifal* (1882), act 3, in which the garden that was changed into a desert at the end of act 2 blooms again. On Wagner, see also note I.41.

17. *(Get dialogue from Margie . . . etc.)* [p. 320]: This insertion comes from Draft A; it is not in the typescript. I have added punctuation for the sake of clarity.

18. *more important* [p. 320]: This is my emendation; both Draft A and Draft B read "more importance."

19. *a soul* [p. 323]: In Draft A, a note here reads "and then follow with the vision of the Southern Cross."

20. *hallucinations . . . by 12 noon* [p. 323]: See note XLV.14. This passage, from Draft A, is omitted in the typescript, which reads "In hotel in Laredo Kilroy turns up here," etc., probably because Margerie realized that she had already typed two versions of the hallucinatory sign (pp. 317, 322).

21. *Mouris letters* [p. 323]: I have not identified this reference, which is not included in Draft A.

INDEX OF ANNOTATIONS

Index citations refer to the textual annotations and follow the system used in the notes themselves, including both chapter and note numbers (e.g., XVIII.15 for chapter XVIII, note 15). Literary works are generally listed under the authors' names; songs, films, and anonymous works are indexed under their titles.

Bible (Biblical references), I.7, I.46,
VI.6, VI.69, X.2, XIV.2,
XXVII.2
Blanco de Arriola, Maria Luisa,
XXVI.9
Boden, John ("Captain Lyon"),
XII.5
Bolio Rendon, Eduardo: "Vanishing
Enchantment?" IV.25, IX.5,
IX.14
Bond's Book Shop, XXVIII.5
Bonner, Margerie. *See* Lowry,
Margerie
Bonsfield, John. *See* Bousfield,
John
Book of Mormon, VI.70
Bousfield, John, I.3, I.36
Bowker, Gordon, S.3, I.3, I.9, I.25,
I.28, I.43, I.44, I.45, I.78, II.16,
III.8, IV.4, IV.30, VI.8, VI.9,
XII.5, XX.1, XXVII.6
Boy Scouts, II.24
Bradbrook, M. C., II.32, XXVII.6
British Weekly, II.17
Brooke, Rupert: "The Great Lover,"
IV.16
Burma-Shave, VI.60, VI.73, VI.79
Butler, Smedley D., VI.21, VI.89
Button, A. Ronald, S.1
Byrd, Richard Evelyn, VI.71

Calder, Alexander, VI.57
Camacho. *See* Ávila Camacho,
Manuel
Cambridge Daily News, XXVII.6
Canadian Price Control Board. *See*
Wartime Prices and Trade Board
Canadian spy scare, IV.11, XIV.11
Cape, Jonathan, I.24, XXVI.8
Cárdenas, Lázaro, I.6
Carey, A. B., III.8
Carlins, IX.4

Carlotta. *See* Maximilian and
Carlotta
Carnarvon, Lord, I.33
Carter, Howard, I.33
Catharine, St., VI.12
Chambers, IX.10
Chandler, XV.9
Churriguera, José, I.24
Clipper, Lawrence J., I.55, II.1,
IV.4, VIII.2, XIV.16, XV.12,
XVIII.10, XXXIX.5, XLIII.4,
XLIII.6, XLV.3
Coleridge, Samuel Taylor: *The
Rime of the Ancient Mariner*,
XVII.13
Conrad, Joseph, VI.20; *Heart of
Darkness*, III.13; *The Nigger of
the "Narcissus,"* XII.3
Correspondences, IV.4, IV.40
Cortez, Hernando, VIII.2
Craige, James, I.10
Crane, Hart, I.21, VI.15;
"Purgatorio," XXV.2;
"Voyages," VI.87
Crime et Châtiment (film), XIII.15,
XXVI.12. *See also* Dostoevsky,
Fyodor, *Crime and Punishment*
Crosby, Bing, III.17

Dante Alighieri: *Inferno*, VI.8;
Paradiso, XV.11
Day, Douglas, I.3, I.9, I.45, I.78,
II.33, IV.30, VI.8, VI.9, VI.37,
XII.5
Deverly, Rhea, XXXII.2
Dickens, Charles, III.10
"Disastar," I.31, XIV.3, XVII.5
Donnelly, Ignatius: *Atlantis: The
Antediluvian World*, XLV.3
Dos Passos, John, II.16
Dostoevsky, Fyodor, I.52, XXVII.4;
The Brothers Karamazov,